KILLING FLOOR

DIE TRYING

LEE CHILD

KILLING FLOOR
DIE TRYING

LEE CHILD

LONDON NEW YORK SYDNEY TORONTO

This edition published 1998
by BCA
by arrangement with Bantam Press
a division of Transworld Publishers Ltd

CN 9393

Printed and bound in Great Britain by
Mackays of Chatham PLC, Chatham, Kent

CONTENTS

KILLING FLOOR

My agent is Darley Anderson in London; my editors are David Highfill in New York and Marianne Velmans in London. They worked hard to get this writer his break. This book is dedicated to the three of them, in appreciation of all their efforts, which went way beyond the call of duty.

ONE

I WAS ARRESTED IN ENO'S DINER. AT TWELVE O'CLOCK. I WAS eating eggs and drinking coffee. A late breakfast, not lunch. I was wet and tired after a long walk in heavy rain. All the way from the highway to the edge of town.

The diner was small, but bright and clean. Brand-new, built to resemble a converted railroad car. Narrow, with a long lunch counter on one side and a kitchen bumped out back. Booths lining the opposite wall. A doorway where the centre booth would be.

I was in a booth, at a window, reading somebody's abandoned newspaper about the campaign for a President I didn't vote for last time and wasn't going to vote for this time. Outside, the rain had stopped but the glass was still pebbled with bright drops. I saw the police cruisers pull into the gravel lot. They were moving fast and crunched to a stop. Light bars flashing and popping. Red and blue light in the raindrops on my window. Doors burst open, policemen jumped out. Two from each car, weapons ready. Two revolvers, two shotguns. This was heavy stuff. One revolver and one shotgun ran to the back. One of each rushed the door.

I just sat and watched them. I knew who was in the diner. A cook in back. Two waitresses. Two old men. And me. This operation was for me. I had been in town less than a half-hour. The other five had probably been here all their lives. Any problem with any of them and an embarrassed sergeant would have shuffled in. He would be apologetic. He would mumble to them. He would ask them to come down to the station house. So the heavy weapons and the rush weren't for any of them. They were for me. I crammed egg into my mouth and trapped a five under the plate. Folded the abandoned newspaper into a square and shoved it into my coat pocket. Kept my hands above the table and drained my cup.

The guy with the revolver stayed at the door. He went into a crouch and pointed the weapon two-handed. At my head. The guy with the shotgun approached close. These were fit lean boys. Neat and tidy. Textbook moves. The revolver at the door could cover the room with a degree of accuracy. The shotgun up close could splatter me all over the window. The other way around would be a mistake. The revolver could miss in a close-quarters struggle and a long-range shotgun blast from the door would kill the arresting officer and the old guy in the rear booth as well as me. So far, they were doing it right. No doubt about that. They had the advantage. No doubt about that, either. The tight booth trapped me. I was too hemmed in to do much. I spread my hands on the table. The officer with the shotgun came near.

'Freeze! Police!' he screamed.

He was screaming as loud as he could. Blowing off his tension and trying to scare me. Textbook moves. Plenty of sound and fury to soften the target. I raised my hands. The guy with the revolver started in from the door. The guy with the shotgun came closer. Too close. Their first error. If I had to, I might have lunged for the shotgun barrel and forced it up. A blast into the ceiling perhaps and an elbow into the policeman's face and the shotgun could have been mine. The guy with the revolver had narrowed his angle and couldn't risk hitting his partner. It could have ended badly for them. But I just sat there, hands raised. The guy with the shotgun was still screaming and jumping.

'Out here on the floor!' he yelled.

I slid slowly out of the booth and extended my wrists to the officer with the revolver. I wasn't going to lie on the floor. Not for these country boys. Not if they brought along their whole police department with howitzers.

The guy with the revolver was a sergeant. He was pretty calm. The shotgun covered me as the sergeant holstered his revolver and unclipped the handcuffs from his belt and clicked them on my wrists. The backup team came in through the kitchen. They walked around the lunch counter. Took up position behind me. They patted me down. Very thorough. I saw the sergeant acknowledge the shakes of the heads. No weapon.

The backup guys each took an elbow. The shotgun still covered me. The sergeant stepped up in front. He was a compact, athletic white man. Lean and tanned. My age. The acetate nameplate above his shirt pocket said: Baker. He looked up at me.

'You are under arrest for murder,' he said. 'You have the right to remain silent. Anything you say may be used as evidence against you. You have the right to representation by an attorney. Should you be unable to afford an attorney, one will be appointed for you by the State of Georgia free of charge. Do you understand these rights?'

It was a fine rendition of Miranda. He spoke clearly. He didn't read it from a card. He spoke like he knew what it meant and why it was important. To him and to me. I didn't respond.

'Do you understand your rights?' he said again.

Again I didn't respond. Long experience had taught me that absolute silence is the best way. Say something, and it can be misheard. Misunderstood. Misinterpreted. It can get you convicted. It can get you killed. Silence upsets the arresting officer. He has to tell you silence is your right but he hates it if you exercise that right. I was being arrested for murder. But I said nothing.

'Do you understand your rights?' the guy called Baker asked me again. 'Do you speak English?'

He was calm. I said nothing. He remained calm. He had the calm of a man whose moment of danger had passed. He would just drive me to the station house and then I would become someone else's problem. He glanced round his three fellow officers.

'OK, make a note, he's said nothing,' he grunted. 'Let's go.'

I was walked towards the door. At the door we formed a single file. First Baker. Then the guy with the shotgun, walking backward, still with the big black barrel pointing at me. His nameplate said: Stevenson. He too was a medium white man in good shape. His weapon looked like a drainpipe. Pointing at my gut. Behind me were the backup guys. I was pushed through the door with a hand flat on my back.

Outside in the gravel lot the heat was up. It must have rained all night and most of the morning. Now the sun was blasting away and the ground was steaming. Normally this would be a dusty hot place. Today it was steaming with that wonderful heady aroma of drenched pavement under a hot noon sun. I stood face up to the sun and inhaled as the officers regrouped. One at each elbow for the short walk to the patrol cars. Stevenson still on the ball with the pump-action. At the first car he skipped backward a step as Baker opened the rear door. My head was pushed down. I was nudged into the car with a neat hip-to-hip contact from the left-hand backup. Good moves. In a town this far from anywhere, surely the result of a lot of training rather than a lot of experience.

I was alone in the back of the car. A thick glass partition divided the space. The front doors were still open. Baker and Stevenson got in. Baker drove. Stevenson was twisted around keeping me under observation. Nobody talked. The backup car followed. The cars were new. Quiet and smooth riding. Clean and cool inside. No ingrained traces of desperate and pathetic people riding where I was riding.

I looked out of the window. Georgia. I saw rich land. Heavy, damp red earth. Very long and straight rows of low bushes in the fields. Peanuts, maybe. Belly crops, but valuable to the grower. Or to the owner. Did people own their land here? Or did giant corporations? I didn't know.

The drive to town was short. The car hissed over the smooth soaked tarmac. After maybe a half-mile I saw two neat buildings, both new, both with tidy landscaping. The police station and the fire house. They stood alone together, behind a wide lawn with a statue, north edge of town. Attractive county architecture on a generous budget. Roads were smooth tarmac, sidewalks were red blocks. Three hundred yards south, I could see a blinding white church steeple behind a small huddle of buildings. I could see flagpoles, awnings, crisp paint, green lawns. Everything refreshed by the heavy rain. Now steaming and somehow intense in the heat. A prosperous community. Built, I guessed, on prosperous farm incomes and high taxes on the commuters who worked up in Atlanta.

Stevenson still stared at me as the car slowed to yaw into the approach to the station house. A wide semicircle of driveway. I read on a low masonry sign: Margrave Police Headquarters. I thought: should I be worried? I was under arrest. In a town where I'd never been before. Apparently for murder. But I knew two things. First, they couldn't prove something had happened if it hadn't happened. And second, I hadn't killed anybody.

Not in their town, and not for a long time, anyway.

TWO

WE PULLED UP AT THE DOORS OF THE LONG LOW BUILDING. Baker got out of the car and looked up and down along the frontage. The backup guys stood by. Stevenson walked around the back of our car. Took up a position opposite Baker. Pointed the shotgun at me. This was a good team. Baker opened my door.

'OK, let's go, let's go,' he said. Almost a whisper.

He was bouncing on the balls of his feet, scanning the area. I pivoted slowly and twisted out of the car. The handcuffs didn't help. Even hotter now. I stepped forward and waited. The backup fell in behind me. Ahead of me was the station house entrance. There was a long marble lintel crisply engraved: Town of Margrave Police Headquarters. Below it were plate-glass doors. Baker pulled one open. It sucked against rubber seals. The backup pushed me through. The door sucked shut behind me.

Inside it was cool again. Everything was white and chrome. Lights were fluorescent. It looked like a bank or an insurance office. There was carpet. A desk sergeant stood behind a long reception counter. The way the place looked, he should have said: how may I help you, sir? But he said nothing. He just looked at me. Behind him was a huge open-plan space. A dark-haired woman in uniform was sitting at a wide, low desk. She had been doing paperwork on a keyboard. Now she was looking at me. I stood there, an officer on each elbow. Stevenson was backed up

17

against the reception counter. His shotgun was pointed at me. Baker stood there, looking at me. The desk sergeant and the woman in uniform were looking at me. I looked back at them.

Then I was walked to the left. They stopped me in front of a door. Baker swung it open and I was pushed into a room. It was an interview facility. No windows. A white table and three chairs. Carpet. In the top corner of the room, a camera. The air in the room was set very cold. I was still wet from the rain.

I stood there and Baker ferreted into every pocket. My belongings made a small pile on the table. A roll of cash. Some coins. Receipts, tickets, scraps. Baker checked the newspaper and left it in my pocket. Glanced at my watch and left it on my wrist. He wasn't interested in those things. Everything else was swept into a large Ziplock bag. A bag made for people with more in their pockets than I carry. The bag had a white panel printed on it. Stevenson wrote some kind of a number on the panel.

Baker told me to sit down. Then they all left the room. Stevenson carried the bag with my stuff in it. They went out and closed the door and I heard the lock turning. It had a heavy, well-greased sound. The sound of precision. The sound of a big steel lock. Sounded like a lock that would keep me in.

I figured they would leave me isolated for a while. It usually happens that way. Isolation causes an urge to talk. An urge to talk can become an urge to confess. A brutal arrest followed by an hour's isolation is pretty good strategy.

But I figured wrong. They hadn't planned an hour's isolation. Maybe their second slight tactical mistake. Baker unlocked the door and stepped back in. He carried a plastic cup of coffee. Then he signalled the uniformed woman into the room. The one I'd seen at her desk in the open area. The heavy lock clicked behind her. She carried a metal flight case which she set on the table. She clicked it open and took out a long black number holder. In it were white plastic numbers.

She handed it to me with that brusque apologetic sympathy that dental nurses use. I took it in my cuffed hands. Squinted down to make sure it was the right way up and held it under my chin. The woman took an ugly camera out of the case and sat opposite me. She rested her elbows on the table to brace the camera. Sitting forward. Her breasts rested on the edge of the table. This was a good-looking woman. Dark hair, great eyes. I stared at her and smiled. The camera clicked and flashed. Before she could ask I turned sideways on the chair for the profile. Held the long number against my shoulder and stared at the wall. The camera clicked and flashed again. I turned back and held out the number. Two-handed, because of the cuffs. She took it from me with that pursed grin which says: yes, it's unpleasant, but it's necessary. Like the dental nurse.

Then she took out the fingerprint gear. A crisp ten-card, already labelled with a number. The thumb spaces are always too small. This one had a reverse side with two squares for palm prints. The handcuffs made the process difficult. Baker didn't offer to remove them. The woman inked my hands. Her fingers were smooth and cool. No wedding band. Afterwards she handed me a wad of tissues. The ink came off very easily. Some kind of new stuff I hadn't seen before.

The woman unloaded the camera and put the film with the prints card on the table. She repacked the camera into the flight case. Baker rapped on the door. The lock clicked again. The woman picked up her stuff. Nobody spoke. The woman left the room. Baker stayed in there with me. He shut the door and it locked with the same greased click. Then he leaned on the door and looked at me.

'My chief's coming on down,' he said. 'You're going to have to talk to him. We got a situation here. Got to be cleared up.'

I said nothing back to him. Talking to me wasn't going to clear any situation up for anybody. But the guy was acting civilized. Respectful. So I set him a test. Held out my hands toward him. An unspoken request to unlock the cuffs. He stood still for a moment then took out the key and unlocked them. Clipped them back on his belt. Looked at me. I looked back and dropped my arms to my sides. No grateful exhalation. No rueful rubbing of my wrists. I didn't want a relationship with this guy. But I did speak.

'OK,' I said. 'Let's go meet your chief.'

It was the first time I'd spoken since ordering breakfast. Now Baker was the one who looked grateful. He rapped twice on the door and it was unlocked from the outside. He opened it up and signalled me through. Stevenson was waiting with his back to the large open area. The shotgun was gone. The backup crew was gone. Things were calming down. They formed up, one on each side. Baker gripped my elbow, lightly. We walked down the side of the open area and came to a door at the back. Stevenson pushed it open and we walked through into a large office. Lots of rosewood all over it.

A fat guy sat at a big rosewood desk. Behind him were a couple of big flags. There was a Stars and Stripes with a gold fringe on the left and what I guessed was the Georgia state flag on the right. On the wall between the flags was a clock. It was a big old round thing framed in mahogany. Looked like it had decades of polish on it. I figured it must be the clock from whatever old station house they bulldozed to build this new place. I figured the architect had used it to give a sense of history to the new building. It was showing nearly twelve-thirty.

The fat guy at the big desk looked up at me as I was pushed in towards him. I saw him look blank, like he was trying to place me. He looked again, harder. Then he sneered at me and spoke in a wheezing gasp which would have been a shout if it hadn't been strangled by bad lungs.

'Get your ass in that chair and keep your filthy mouth shut,' he said.

This fat guy was a surprise. He looked like a real asshole. Opposite to what I'd seen so far. Baker and his arrest team were the business. Professional and efficient. The fingerprint woman had been decent. But this fat police chief was a waste of space. Thin dirty hair. Sweating, despite the chilly air. The blotchy red and grey complexion of an unfit, overweight mess. Blood pressure sky-high. Arteries hard as rocks. He didn't look halfway competent.

'My name is Morrison,' he wheezed. As if I cared. 'I am chief of the police department down here in Margrave. And you are a murdering outsider bastard. You've come down here to my town and you've messed up right there on Mr Kliner's private property. So now you're going to make a full confession to my chief of detectives.'

He stopped and looked up at me. Like he was still trying to place me. Or like he was waiting for a response. He didn't get one. So he jabbed his fat finger at me.

'And then you're going to jail,' he said. 'And then you're going to the chair. And then I'm going to take a dump on your shitty little pauper's grave.'

He hauled his bulk out of the chair and looked away from me.

'I'd deal with this myself,' he said. 'But I'm a busy man.'

He waddled out from behind his desk. I was standing there between his desk and the door. As he crabbed by, he stopped. His fat nose was about level with the middle button on my coat. He was still looking up at me like he was puzzled by something.

'I've seen you before,' he said. 'Where was it?'

He glanced at Baker and then at Stevenson. Like he was expecting them to note what he was saying and when he was saying it.

'I've seen this guy before,' he told them.

*

He slammed the office door and I was left waiting with the two cops until the chief of detectives swung in. A tall black guy, not old, but greying and balding. Just enough to give him a patrician air. Brisk and confident. Well-dressed, in an old-fashioned tweed suit. Moleskin vest. Shined shoes. This guy looked like a chief should look. He signalled Baker and Stevenson out of the office. Closed the door behind them. Sat down at the desk and waved me to the opposite chair.

He rattled open a drawer and pulled out a cassette recorder. Raised it high, arm's length, to pull out the tangle of cords. Plugged in the power and the microphone. Inserted a tape. Pressed record and flicked the microphone with his fingernail. Stopped the tape and wound it back. Pressed play. Heard the thunk of his nail. Nodded. Wound back again and pressed record. I sat and watched him.

For a moment there was silence. Just a faint hum, the air, the lights, or the computer. Or the recorder whirring slowly. I could hear the slow tick of the old clock. It made a patient sound, like it was prepared to tick on for ever, no matter what I chose to do. Then the guy sat right back in his chair and looked hard at me. Did the steepled fingers thing, like tall elegant people can.

'Right,' he said. 'We got a few questions, don't we?'

The voice was deep. Like a rumble. Not a southern accent. He looked and sounded like a Boston banker, except he was black.

'My name is Finlay,' he said. 'My rank is captain. I am chief of this department's detective bureau. I understand you have been apprised of your rights. You have not yet confirmed that you understood them. Before we go any further we must pursue that preliminary matter.'

Not a Boston banker. More like a Harvard guy.

'I understand my rights,' I said.

He nodded.

'Good,' he said. 'I'm glad about that. Where's your lawyer?'

'I don't need a lawyer,' I said.

'You're charged with murder,' he said. 'You need a lawyer. We'll provide one, you know. Free of charge. Do you want us to provide one, free of charge?'

'No, I don't need a lawyer,' I said.

21

The guy called Finlay stared at me over his fingers for a long moment.

'OK,' he said. 'But you're going to have to sign a release. You know, you've been advised you may have a lawyer, and we'll provide one, at no cost to yourself, but you absolutely don't want one.'

'OK,' I said.

He shuffled a form from another drawer and checked his watch to enter date and time. He slid the form across to me. A large printed cross marked the line where I was supposed to sign. He slid me a pen. I signed and slid the form back. He studied it. Placed it in a buff folder.

'I can't read that signature,' he said. 'So for the record we'll start with your name, your address and your date of birth.'

There was silence again. I looked at him. This was a stubborn guy. Probably forty-five. You don't get to be chief of detectives in a Georgia jurisdiction if you're forty-five and black except if you're a stubborn guy. No percentage in jerking him around. I drew a breath.

'My name is Jack Reacher,' I said. 'No middle name. No address.'

He wrote it down. Not much to write. I told him my date of birth.

'OK, Mr Reacher,' Finlay said. 'As I said, we have a lot of questions. I've glanced through your personal effects. You were carrying no ID at all. No driver's licence, no credit cards, no nothing. You have no address, you say. So I'm asking myself, who is this guy?'

He didn't wait for any kind of a comment on that from me.

'Who was the guy with the shaved head?' he asked me.

I didn't answer. I was watching the big clock, waiting for the minute hand to move.

'Tell me what happened,' he said.

I had no idea what had happened. No idea at all. Something had happened to somebody, but not to me. I sat there. Didn't answer.

'What is Pluribus?' Finlay asked.

I looked at him and shrugged.

'The United States motto?' I said. 'E Pluribus Unum? Adopted in 1776 by the second Continental Congress, right?'

He just grunted at me. I carried on looking straight at him. I figured this was the type of a guy who might answer a question.

'What is this about?' I asked him.

Silence again. His turn to look at me. I could see him thinking about whether to answer, and how.

'What is this about?' I asked him again.

He sat back and steepled his fingers.

'You know what this is about,' he said. 'Homicide. With some very disturbing features. Victim was found this morning up at the Kliner warehouse. North end of the county road, up at the highway cloverleaf. Witness has reported a man seen walking away from that location. Shortly after eight o'clock this morning. Description given was that of a white man, very tall, wearing a long black overcoat, fair hair, no hat, no baggage.'

Silence again. I am a white man. I am very tall. My hair is fair. I was sitting there wearing a long black overcoat. I didn't have a hat. Or a bag. I had been walking on the county road for the best part of four hours this morning. From eight until about eleven forty-five.

'How long is the county road?' I said. 'From the highway all the way down to here?'

Finlay thought about it.

'Maybe fourteen miles, I guess,' he said.

'Right,' I said. 'I walked all the way down from the highway into town. Fourteen miles, maybe. Plenty of people must have seen me. Doesn't mean I did anything to anybody.'

He didn't respond. I was getting curious about this situation.

'Is that your neighbourhood?' I asked him. 'All the way over at the highway?'

'Yes, it is,' he said. 'Jurisdiction issue is clear. No way out for you there, Mr Reacher. The town limit extends fourteen miles, right up to the highway. The warehousing out there is mine, no doubt about that.'

He waited. I nodded. He carried on.

'Kliner built the place, five years ago,' he said. 'You heard of him?'

I shook my head.

'How should I have heard of him?' I said. 'I've never been here before.'

'He's a big deal around here,' Finlay said. 'His operation out there pays us a lot of taxes, does us a lot of good. A lot of revenue and a lot of benefit for the town without a lot of mess, because it's so far away, right? So we try to take care of it for him. But now it's a homicide scene, and you've got explaining to do.'

The guy was doing his job, but he was wasting my time.

'OK, Finlay,' I said. 'I'll make a statement describing every little thing I did since I entered your lousy town limits until I got hauled in here in the middle of my damn breakfast. If you can make anything out of it, I'll give you a damn medal. Because all I did was to

23

place one foot in front of the other for nearly four hours in the pouring rain all the way through your precious fourteen damn miles.'

That was the longest speech I had made for six months. Finlay sat and gazed at me. I watched him struggling with any detective's basic dilemma. His gut told him I might not be his man. But I was sitting right there in front of him. So what should a detective do? I let him ponder. Tried to time it right with a nudge in the right direction. I was going to say something about the real guy still running around out there while he was wasting time in here with me. That would feed his insecurity. But he jumped first. In the wrong direction.

'No statements,' he said. 'I'll ask the questions and you'll answer them. You're Jack-none-Reacher. No address. No ID. What are you, a vagrant?'

I sighed. Today was Friday. The big clock showed it was already more than half over. This guy Finlay was going to go through all the hoops with this. I was going to spend the weekend in a cell. Probably get out Monday.

'I'm not a vagrant, Finlay,' I said. 'I'm a hobo. Big difference.'

He shook his head, slowly.

'Don't get smart with me, Reacher,' he said. 'You're in deep shit. Bad things happened up there. Our witness saw you leaving the scene. You're a stranger with no ID and no story. So don't get smart with me.'

He was still just doing his job, but he was still wasting my time.

'I wasn't leaving a homicide scene,' I said. 'I was walking down a damn road. There's a difference, right? People leaving homicide scenes run and hide. They don't walk straight down the road. What's wrong about walking down a road? People walk down roads all the damn time, don't they?'

Finlay leaned forward and shook his head.

'No,' he said. 'Nobody has walked the length of that road since the invention of the automobile. So why no address? Where are you from? Answer the questions. Let's get this done.'

'OK, Finlay, let's get it done,' I said. 'I don't have an address because I don't live anywhere. Maybe one day I'll live somewhere and then I'll have an address and I'll send you a picture postcard and you can put it in your damn address book, since you seem so damn concerned about it.'

Finlay gazed at me and reviewed his options. Elected to go the patient route. Patient, but stubborn. Like he couldn't be deflected.

24

'Where are you from?' he asked. 'What was your last address?'

'What exactly do you mean when you say where am I from?' I asked.

His lips were clamped. I was getting him bad-tempered, too. But he stayed patient. Laced the patience with an icy sarcasm.

'OK,' he said. 'You don't understand my question, so let me try to make it quite clear. What I mean is, where were you born, or where have you lived for that majority period of your life which you instinctively regard as predominant in a social or cultural context?'

I just looked at him.

'I'll give you an example,' he said. 'I myself was born in Boston, was educated in Boston and subsequently worked for twenty years in Boston, so I would say, and I think you would agree, that I come from Boston.'

I was right. A Harvard guy. A Harvard guy, running out of patience.

'OK,' I said. 'You've asked the questions. I'll answer them. But let me tell you something. I'm not your guy. By Monday you'll know I'm not your guy. So do yourself a favour. Don't stop looking.'

Finlay was fighting a smile. He nodded gravely.

'I appreciate your advice,' he said. 'And your concern for my career.'

'You're welcome,' I said.

'Go on,' he said.

'OK,' I said. 'According to your fancy definition, I don't come from anywhere. I come from a place called Military. I was born on a US Army base in West Berlin. My old man was Marine Corps and my mother was a French civilian he met in Holland. They got married in Korea.'

Finlay nodded. Made a note.

'I was a military kid,' I said. 'Show me a list of US bases all around the world and that's a list of where I lived. I did high school in two dozen different countries and I did four years up at West Point.'

'Go on,' Finlay said.

'I stayed in the army,' I said. 'Military Police. I served and lived in all those bases all over again. Then, Finlay, after thirty-six years of first being an officer's kid and then being an officer myself, suddenly there's no need for a great big army any more because the Soviets have gone belly up. So hooray, we get the peace dividend. Which for you means your taxes get spent on something else, but

25

for me means I'm a thirty-six year old unemployed ex-military policeman getting called a vagrant by smug civilian bastards who wouldn't last five minutes in the world I survived.'

He thought for a moment. Wasn't impressed.

'Continue,' he said.

I shrugged at him.

'So right now I'm just enjoying myself,' I said. 'Maybe eventually I'll find something to do, maybe I won't. Maybe I'll settle somewhere, maybe I won't. But right now, I'm not looking to.'

He nodded. Jotted some more notes.

'When did you leave the army?' he asked.

'Six months ago,' I said. 'April.'

'Have you worked at all since then?' he asked.

'You're joking,' I said. 'When was the last time you looked for work?'

'April,' he mimicked. 'Six months ago. I got this job.'

'Well, good for you, Finlay,' I said.

I couldn't think of anything else to say. Finlay gazed at me for a moment.

'What have you been living on?' he asked. 'What rank did you hold?'

'Major,' I said. 'They give you severance pay when they kick you out. Still got most of it. Trying to make it last, you know?'

A long silence. Finlay drummed a rhythm with the wrong end of his pen.

'So let's talk about the last twenty-four hours,' he said.

I sighed. Now I was heading for trouble.

'I came up on the Greyhound bus,' I said. 'Got off at the county road. Eight o'clock this morning. Walked down into town, reached that diner, ordered breakfast and I was eating it when your guys came by and hauled me in.'

'You got business here?' he asked.

I shook my head.

'I'm out of work,' I said. 'I haven't got any business anywhere.'

He wrote that down.

'Where did you get on the bus?' he asked me.

'In Tampa,' I said. 'Left at midnight last night.'

'Tampa in Florida?' he asked.

I nodded. He rattled open another drawer. Pulled out a Greyhound schedule. Riffed it open and ran a long brown finger down a page. This was a very thorough guy. He looked across at me.

'That's an express bus,' he said. 'Runs straight through north to Atlanta. Arrives there nine o'clock in the morning. Doesn't stop here at eight.'

I shook my head.

'I asked the driver to stop,' I said. 'He said he shouldn't, but he did. Stopped specially, let me off.'

'You been around here before?' he asked.

I shook my head again.

'Got family down here?' he asked.

'Not down here,' I said.

'You got family anywhere?' he asked.

'A brother up in DC,' I said. 'Works for the Treasury Department.'

'You got friends down here in Georgia?' he asked.

'No,' I said.

Finlay wrote it all down. Then there was a long silence. I knew for sure what the next question was going to be.

'So why?' he asked. 'Why get off the bus at an unscheduled stop and walk fourteen miles in the rain to a place you had absolutely no reason to go to?'

That was the killer question. Finlay had picked it out right away. So would a prosecutor. And I had no real answer.

'What can I tell you?' I said. 'It was an arbitrary decision. I was restless. I have to be somewhere, right?'

'But why here?' he said.

'I don't know,' I said. 'Guy next to me had a map, and I picked this place out. I wanted to get off the main drags. Thought I could loop back down toward the Gulf, further west, maybe.'

'You picked this place out?' Finlay said. 'Don't give me that shit. How could you pick this place out? It's just a name. It's just a dot on the map. You must have had a reason.'

I nodded.

'I thought I'd come and look for Blind Blake,' I said.

'Who the hell is Blind Blake?' he said.

I watched him evaluating scenarios like a chess computer evaluates moves. Was Blind Blake my friend, my enemy, my accomplice, conspirator, mentor, creditor, debtor, my next victim?

'Blind Blake was a guitar player,' I said. 'Died sixty years ago, maybe murdered. My brother bought a record, sleeve note said it happened in Margrave. He wrote me about it. Said he was through here a couple of times in the spring, some kind of business. I thought I'd come down and check the story out.'

Finlay looked blank. It must have sounded pretty thin to him. It would have sounded pretty thin to me too, in his position.

'You came here looking for a guitar player?' he said. 'A guitar player who died sixty years ago? Why? Are you a guitar player?'

'No,' I said.

'How did your brother write you?' he asked. 'When you got no address?'

'He wrote my old unit,' I said. 'They forward my mail to my bank, where I put my severance pay. They send it on when I wire them for cash.'

He shook his head. Made a note.

'The midnight Greyhound out of Tampa, right?' he said.

I nodded.

'Got your bus ticket?' he asked.

'In the property bag, I guess,' I said. I remembered Baker bagging up all my pocket junk. Stevenson tagging it.

'Would the bus driver remember?' Finlay said.

'Maybe,' I said. 'It was a special stop. I had to ask him.'

I became like a spectator. The situation became abstract. My job had been not that different from Finlay's. I had an odd feeling of conferring with him about somebody else's case. Like we were colleagues discussing a knotty problem.

'Why aren't you working?' Finlay asked.

I shrugged. Tried to explain.

'Because I don't want to work,' I said. 'I worked thirteen years, got me nowhere. I feel like I tried it their way, and to hell with them. Now I'm going to try it my way.'

Finlay sat and gazed at me.

'Did you have any trouble in the army?' he said.

'No more than you did in Boston,' I said.

He was surprised.

'What do you mean by that?' he said.

'You did twenty years in Boston,' I said. 'That's what you told me, Finlay. So why are you down here in this no-account little place? You should be taking your pension, going out fishing. Cape Cod or wherever. What's your story?'

'That's my business, Mr Reacher,' he said. 'Answer my question.'

I shrugged.

'Ask the army,' I said.

'I will,' he said. 'You can be damn sure of that. Did you get an honourable discharge?'

28

'Would they give me severance if I didn't?' I said.

'Why should I believe they gave you a dime?' he said. 'You live like a damn vagrant. Honourable discharge? Yes or no?'

'Yes,' I said. 'Of course.'

He made another note. Thought for a while.

'How did it make you feel, being let go?' he asked.

I thought about it. Shrugged at him.

'Didn't make me feel like anything,' I said. 'Made me feel like I was in the army, and now I'm not in the army.'

'Do you feel bitter?' he said. 'Let down?'

'No,' I said. 'Should I?'

'No problems at all?' he asked. Like there had to be something.

I felt like I had to give him some kind of an answer. But I couldn't think of anything. I had been in the service since the day I was born. Now I was out. Being out felt great. Felt like freedom. Like all my life I'd had a slight headache. Not noticing until it was gone. My only problem was making a living. How to make a living without giving up the freedom was not an easy trick. I hadn't earned a cent in six months. That was my only problem. But I wasn't about to tell Finlay that. He'd see it as a motive. He'd think I had decided to bankroll my vagrant lifestyle by robbing people. At warehouses. And then killing them.

'I guess the transition is hard to manage,' I said. 'Especially since I had the life as a kid, too.'

Finlay nodded. Considered my answer.

'Why you in particular?' he said. 'Did you volunteer to muster out?'

'I never volunteer for anything,' I said. 'Soldier's basic rule.'

Another silence.

'Did you specialize?' he asked. 'In the service?'

'General duties, initially,' I said. 'That's the system. Then I handled secrets security for five years. Then the last six years, I handled something else.'

Let him ask.

'What was that?' he asked.

'Homicide investigation,' I said.

Finlay leaned right back. Grunted. Did the steepled fingers thing again. He gazed at me and exhaled. Sat forward. Pointed a finger at me.

'Right,' he said. 'I'm going to check you out. We've got your prints. Those should be on file with the army. We'll get your service record. All of it. All the details. We'll check with the bus company.

Check your ticket. Find the driver, find the passengers. If what you say is right, we'll know soon enough. And if it's true, it may let you off the hook. Obviously, certain details of timing and methodology will determine the matter. Those details are as yet unclear.'

He paused and exhaled again. Looked right at me.

'In the meantime, I'm a cautious man,' he said. 'On the face of it, you look bad. A drifter. A vagrant. No address, no history. Your story may be bullshit. You may be a fugitive. You may have been murdering people left and right in a dozen states. I just don't know. I can't be expected to give you the benefit of the doubt. Right now, why should I even have any doubt? You stay locked up until we know for sure, OK?'

It was what I had expected. It was exactly what I would have said. But I just looked at him and shook my head.

'You're a cautious guy?' I said. 'That's for damn sure.'

He looked back at me.

'If I'm wrong, I'll buy you lunch on Monday,' he said. 'At Eno's place, to make up for today.'

I shook my head again.

'I'm not looking for a buddy down here,' I said.

Finlay just shrugged. Clicked off the tape recorder. Rewound. Took out the tape. Wrote on it. He buzzed the intercom on the big rosewood desk. Asked Baker to come back in. I waited. It was still cold. But I had finally dried out. The rain had fallen out of the Georgia sky and had soaked into me. Now it had been sucked out again by the dried office air. A dehumidifier had sucked it out and piped it away.

Baker knocked and entered. Finlay told him to escort me to the cells. Then he nodded to me. It was a nod which said: if you turn out not to be the guy, remember I was just doing my job. I nodded back. Mine was a nod which said: while you're covering your ass, there's a killer running about outside.

The cell block was really just a wide alcove off the main open-plan squad room. It was divided into three separate cells with vertical bars. The front wall was all bars. A gate section hinged into each cell. The metalwork had a fabulous dull glitter. Looked like titanium. Each cell was carpeted. But totally empty. No furniture or bed ledge. Just a high-budget version of the old-fashioned holding pens you used to see.

'No overnight accommodation here?' I asked Baker.

'No way,' he replied. 'You'll be moved to the state facility later.

Bus comes by at six. Bus brings you back Monday.'

He clanged the gate shut and turned his key. I heard bolts socket home all around the rim. Electric. I took the newspaper out of my pocket. Took off my coat and rolled it up. Lay flat on the floor and crammed the coat under my head.

Now I was truly pissed off. I was going to prison for the weekend. I wasn't staying in a station house cell. Not that I had any other plans. But I knew about civilian prisons. A lot of army deserters end up in civilian prisons. For one thing or another. The system notifies the army. Military policeman gets sent to bring them back. So I'd seen civilian prisons. They didn't make me wild with enthusiasm. I lay angrily listening to the hum of the squad room. Phones rang. Keyboards pattered. The tempo rose and fell. Officers moved about, talking low.

Then I tried to finish reading the borrowed newspaper. It was full of shit about the President and his campaign to get himself elected again for a second term. The old guy was down in Pensacola on the Gulf Coast. He was aiming to get the budget balanced before his grandchildren's hair turned white. He was cutting things like a guy with a machete blasting his way through the jungle. Down in Pensacola, he was sticking it to the Coast Guard. They'd been running an initiative for the last twelve months. They'd been out in force like a curved shield off Florida's coast every day for a year, boarding and searching all the marine traffic they didn't like the smell of. It had been announced with an enormous fanfare. And it had been successful beyond their wildest dreams. They'd seized all kinds of stuff. Drugs, mostly, but guns as well, illegal migrants from Haiti and Cuba. The interdiction was reducing crime all over the States months later and thousands of miles further down the line. A big success.

So it was being abandoned. It was very expensive to run. The Coast Guard's budget was into serious deficit. The President said he couldn't increase it. In fact, he'd have to cut it. The economy was in a mess. Nothing else he could do. So the interdiction initiative would be cancelled in seven days' time. The President was trying to come across like a statesman. Law enforcement big shots were angry, because they figured prevention was better than cure. Washington insiders were happy, because fifty cents spent on beat cops was much more visible than two bucks spent out on the ocean two thousand miles away from the voters. The arguments flew back and forth. And in the smudgy photographs, the President was just beaming away like a statesman saying

31

there was nothing he could do. I stopped reading, because it was just making me angrier.

To calm down, I ran music through my head. The chorus in 'Smokestack Lightning'. The Howling Wolf version puts a wonderful strangled cry on the end of the first line. They say you need to ride the rails for a while to understand the travelling blues. They're wrong. To understand the travelling blues you need to be locked down somewhere. In a cell. Or in the army. Someplace where you're caged. Someplace where smokestack lightning looks like a far-away beacon of impossible freedom. I lay there with my coat as a pillow and listened to the music in my head. At the end of the third chorus, I fell asleep.

I woke up again when Baker started kicking the bars. They made a dull ringing sound. Like a funeral bell. Baker stood there with Finlay. They looked down at me. I stayed on the floor. I was comfortable down there.

'Where did you say you were at midnight last night?' Finlay asked me.

'Getting on the bus in Tampa,' I said.

'We've got a new witness,' Finlay said. 'He saw you at the warehouse facility. Last night. Hanging around. At midnight.'

'Total crap, Finlay,' I said. 'Impossible. Who the hell is this new witness?'

'The witness is Chief Morrison,' Finlay said. 'The chief of police. He says he was sure he had seen you before. Now he has remembered where.'

THREE

THEY TOOK ME BACK TO THE ROSEWOOD OFFICE IN handcuffs. Finlay sat at the big desk, in front of the flags, under the old clock. Baker set a chair at the end of the desk. I sat opposite Finlay. He took out the tape machine. Dragged out the cords. Positioned the microphone between us. Tested it with his fingernail. Rolled the tape back. Ready.

'The last twenty-four hours, Reacher,' he said. 'In detail.'

The two policemen were crackling with repressed excitement. A weak case had suddenly grown strong. The thrill of winning was beginning to grip them. I recognized the signs.

'I was in Tampa last night,' I said. 'Got on the bus at midnight. Witnesses can confirm that. I got off the bus at eight this morning where the county road meets the highway. If Chief Morrison says he saw me at midnight, he's mistaken. At that time I was about four hundred miles away. I can't add anything more. Check it out.'

Finlay stared at me. Then he nodded to Baker who opened a buff file.

'Victim is unidentified,' Baker said. 'No ID. No wallet. No distinguishing marks. White male, maybe forty, very tall, shaved head. Body was found up there at eight this morning on the ground against the perimeter fence close to the main gate. It was partially covered with cardboard. We were able to fingerprint the body. Negative result. No match anywhere in the database.'

'Who was he, Reacher?' Finlay asked.

Baker waited for some sort of reaction from me. He didn't get one. I just sat there and listened to the quiet tick of the old clock. The hands crawled around to two-thirty. I didn't speak. Baker riffed through the file and selected another sheet. He glanced up again and continued.

'Victim received two shots to the head,' he said. 'Probably a small-calibre automatic with a silencer. First shot was close range, left temple, second was a contact shot behind the left ear. Obviously soft-nosed slugs, because the exit wounds removed the guy's face. Rain has washed away the powder deposits but the burn patterns suggest the silencer. Fatal shot must have been the first. No bullets remained in the skull. No shell cases were found.'

'Where's the gun, Reacher?' Finlay said.

I looked at him and made a face. Didn't speak.

'Victim died between eleven-thirty and one o'clock last night,' Baker said. 'Body wasn't there at eleven-thirty when the evening gateman went off duty. He confirms that. It was found when the day man came in to open the gate. About eight o'clock. He saw you leaving the scene and phoned it in.'

'Who was he, Reacher?' Finlay said again.

I ignored him and looked at Baker.

'Why before one o'clock?' I asked him.

'The heavy rain last night began at one o'clock,' he said. 'The pavement underneath the body was bone dry. So, the body was on the ground before one o'clock when the rain started. Medical opinion is he was shot at midnight.'

I nodded. Smiled at them. The time of death was going to let me out.

'Tell us what happened next,' Finlay said, quietly.

I shrugged at him.

'You tell me,' I said. 'I wasn't there. I was in Tampa at midnight.'

Baker leaned forward and pulled another sheet out of the file.

'What happened next is you got weird,' he said. 'You went crazy.'

I shook my head at him.

'I wasn't there at midnight,' I said again. 'I was getting on the bus in Tampa. Nothing too weird about that.'

The two cops didn't react. They looked pretty grim.

'Your first shot killed him,' Baker said. 'Then you shot him again, and then you went berserk and kicked the shit out of the body. There are massive postmortem injuries. You shot him and

34

then you tried to kick him apart. You kicked that corpse all over the damn place. You were in a frenzy. Then you calmed down and tried to hide the body under the cardboard.'

I was quiet for a long moment.

'Postmortem injuries?' I said.

Baker nodded.

'Like a frenzy,' he said. 'The guy looks like he was run over by a truck. Just about every bone is smashed. But the doctor says it happened after the guy was already dead. You're a weird guy, Reacher, that's for damn sure.'

'Who was he?' Finlay asked for the third time.

I just looked at him. Baker was right. It had got weird. Very weird. Homicidal frenzy is bad enough. But postmortem frenzy is worse. I'd come across it a few times. Didn't want to come across it any more. But the way they'd described it to me, it didn't make any sense.

'How did you meet the guy?' Finlay asked.

I carried on just looking at him. Didn't answer.

'What does Pluribus mean?' he asked.

I shrugged. Kept quiet.

'Who was he, Reacher?' Finlay asked again.

'I wasn't there,' I said. 'I don't know anything.'

Finlay was silent.

'What's your phone number?' he said. Suddenly.

I looked at him like he was crazy.

'Finlay, what the hell are you talking about?' I said. 'I haven't got a phone. Don't you listen? I don't live anywhere.'

'I mean your mobile phone,' he said.

'What mobile phone?' I said. 'I haven't got a mobile phone.'

A clang of fear hit me. They figured me for an assassin. A weird rootless mercenary with a mobile phone who went from place to place killing people. Kicking their dead bodies to pieces. Checking in with an underground organization for my next target. Always on the move.

Finlay leaned forward. He slid a piece of paper toward me. It was a torn-off section of computer paper. Not old. A greasy gloss of wear on it. The patina paper gets from a month in a pocket. On it was printed an underlined heading. It said: Pluribus. Under the heading was a telephone number. I looked at it. Didn't touch it. Didn't want any confusion over fingerprints.

'Is that your number?' Finlay asked.

'I don't have a telephone,' I said again. 'I wasn't here last night.

'The more you hassle me, the more time you're wasting, Finlay.'

'It's a mobile phone number,' he said. 'That we know. Operated by an Atlanta airtime supplier. But we can't trace the number until Monday. So we're asking you. You should co-operate, Reacher.'

I looked at the scrap of paper again.

'Where was this?' I asked him.

Finlay considered the question. Decided to answer it.

'It was in your victim's shoe,' he said. 'Folded up and hidden.'

I sat in silence for a long time. I was worried. I felt like somebody in a kid's book who falls down a hole. Finds himself in a strange world where everything is different and weird. Like Alice in Wonderland. Did she fall down a hole? Or did she get off a Greyhound in the wrong place?

I was in a plush and opulent office. I had seen worse offices in Swiss banks. I was in the company of two policemen. Intelligent and professional. Probably had more than thirty years' experience between them. A mature and competent department. Properly staffed and well funded. A weak point with the asshole Morrison at the top, but as good an organization as I had seen for a while. But they were all disappearing up a dead end as fast as they could run. They seemed convinced the earth was flat. That the huge Georgia sky was a bowl fitting snugly over the top. I was the only one who knew the earth was round.

'Two things,' I said. 'The guy is shot in the head close up with a silenced automatic weapon. First shot drops him. Second shot is insurance. The shell cases are missing. What does that say to you? Professionally?'

Finlay said nothing. His prime suspect was discussing the case with him like a colleague. As the investigator, he shouldn't allow that. He should cut me down. But he wanted to hear me out. I could see him arguing with himself. He was totally still, but his mind was struggling like kittens in a sack.

'Go on,' he said eventually. Gravely, like it was a big deal.

'That's an execution, Finlay,' I said. 'Not a robbery or a squabble. That's a cold and clinical hit. No evidence left behind. That's a smart guy with a flashlight scrabbling around afterward for two small-calibre shell cases.'

'Go on,' Finlay said again.

'Close range shot into the left temple,' I said. 'Could be the victim was in a car. Shooter is talking to him through the window and raises his gun. Bang. He leans in and fires the second shot.

Then he picks up his shell cases and he leaves.'

'He leaves?' Finlay said. 'What about the rest of the stuff that went down? You're suggesting a second man?'

I shook my head.

'There were three men,' I said. 'That's clear, right?'

'Why three?' he said.

'Practical minimum of two, right?' I said. 'How did the victim get out there to the warehouses? He drove, right? Too far from anywhere to walk. So where's his car now? The shooter didn't walk there, either. So the practical minimum would be a team of two. They drove up there together and they drove away separately, one of them in the victim's car.'

'But?' Finlay said.

'But the actual evidence points to a minimum of three,' I said. 'Think about it psychologically. That's the key to this thing. A guy who uses a silenced small-calibre automatic for a neat head shot and an insurance shot is not the type of guy who then suddenly goes berserk and kicks the shit out of a corpse, right? And the type of guy who does get in a frenzy like that doesn't then suddenly calm down and hide the body under some old cardboard. You're looking at three completely separate things there, Finlay. So there were three guys involved.'

Finlay shrugged at me.

'Two, maybe,' he said. 'Shooter could have tidied up afterward.'

'No way,' I said. 'He wouldn't have waited around. He wouldn't like that kind of frenzy. It would embarrass him. And it would worry him because it adds visibility and danger to the whole thing. And a guy like that, if he had tidied up afterward, he'd have done it right. He wouldn't have left the body where the first guy who came along was going to find it. So you're looking at three guys.'

Finlay thought hard.

'So?' he said.

'So which one am I supposed to be?' I said. 'The shooter, the maniac or the idiot who hid the body?'

Finlay and Baker looked at each other. Didn't answer me.

'So whichever one, what are you saying?' I asked them. 'I drive up there with my two buddies and we hit this guy at midnight, and then my two buddies drive away and I choose to stay there? Why would I do that? It's crap, Finlay.'

He didn't reply. He was thinking.

'I haven't got two buddies,' I said. 'Or a car. So the very best you

37

can do is to say the victim walked there, and I walked there. I met him, and I very carefully shot him, like a pro, then recovered my shell cases and took his wallet and emptied his pockets, but forgot to search his shoes. Then I stashed my weapon, silencer, flashlight, mobile phone, the shell cases, the wallet and all. Then I completely changed my whole personality and kicked the corpse to pieces like a maniac. Then I completely changed my whole personality again and made a useless attempt to hide the body. And then I waited eight hours in the rain and then I walked down into town. That's the very best you can do. And it's total crap, Finlay. Because why the hell would I wait eight hours, in the rain, until daylight, to walk away from a homicide?'

He looked at me for a long moment.

'I don't know why,' he said.

A guy like Finlay doesn't say a thing like that unless he's struggling. He looked deflated. His case was crap and he knew it. But he had a severe problem with the chief's new evidence. He couldn't walk up to his boss and say: you're full of shit, Morrison. He couldn't actively pursue an alternative when his boss had handed him a suspect on a plate. He could follow up my alibi. That he could do. Nobody would criticize him for being thorough. Then he could start again on Monday. So he was miserable because seventy-two hours were going to get wasted. And he could foresee a big problem. He had to tell his boss that actually I could not have been there at midnight. He would have to politely coax a retraction out of the guy. Difficult to do when you're a new subordinate who's been there six months. And when the person you're dealing with is a complete asshole. And your boss. Difficulties were all over him, and the guy was miserable as hell about it. He sat there, breathing hard. In trouble. Time to help him out.

'The phone number,' I said. 'You've identified it as a mobile?'

'By the code,' he said. 'Instead of an area code, they have a prefix which accesses the mobile network.'

'OK,' I said. 'But you can't identify who it belongs to because you have no reverse directories for mobiles and their office won't tell you, right?'

'They want a warrant,' he said.

'But you need to know whose number it is, right?' I said.

'You know some way of doing that without a warrant?' he asked.

'Maybe,' I said. 'Why don't you just call it up and see who answers?'

They hadn't thought of that. There was another silence. They were embarrassed. They didn't want to look at each other. Or me. Silence.

Baker bailed out of the situation. Left Finlay holding the ball. He collected up the files and mimed going outside to work on them. Finlay nodded and waved him away. Baker got up and went out. Closed the door very quietly indeed. Finlay opened his mouth. And closed it. He needed to save some face. Badly.

'It's a mobile,' he said. 'If I call it up I can't tell whose it is or where it is.'

'Listen, Finlay,' I said. 'I don't care whose it is. All I care is whose it isn't. Understand? It isn't my phone. So you call it up and John Doe in Atlanta or Jane Doe in Charleston answers it. Then you know it isn't mine.'

Finlay gazed at me. Drummed his fingers on the desk. Kept quiet.

'You know how to do this,' I said. 'Call the number, some bull-shit story about a technical fault or an unpaid bill, some computer thing, get the person to confirm name and address. Do it, Finlay, you're supposed to be a damn detective.'

He leaned forward to where he had left the number. Slid the paper back with his long brown fingers. Reversed it so he could read it and picked up the phone. Dialled the number. Hit the speakerphone button. The ring tone filled the air. Not a sonorous long tone like a home phone. A high, urgent electronic sound. It stopped. The phone was answered.

'Paul Hubble,' a voice said. 'How may I help you?'

A southern accent. A confident manner. Accustomed to telephones.

'Mr Hubble?' Finlay said. He was looking at the desk, writing down the name. 'Good afternoon. This is the phone company, mobile division. Engineering manager. We've had a fault reported on your number.'

'A fault?' the voice said. 'Seems OK to me. I didn't report a fault.'

'Calling out should be OK,' Finlay said. 'It's reaching you that may have been a problem, sir. I've got our signal-strength meter connected right now, and actually, sir, it's reading a bit low.'

'I can hear you OK,' the voice said.

'Hello?' Finlay said. 'You're fading a bit, Mr Hubble. Hello? It would help me to know the exact geographic location of your phone, sir, you know, right now, in relation to our transmitting stations.'

'I'm right here at home,' said the voice.

'OK,' Finlay said. He picked up his pen again. 'Could you just confirm that exact address for me?'

'Don't you have my address?' the voice said. Man-to-man jocular stuff. 'You seem to manage to send me a bill every month.'

Finlay glanced at me. I was smiling at him. He made a face.

'I'm here in engineering right now, sir,' he said. Also jocular. Just two regular guys battling technology. 'Customer details are in a different department. I could access that data, but it would take a minute, you know how it is. Also, sir, you've got to keep talking anyway while this meter is connected to give me an exact strength reading, you know? You may as well recite your address, unless you've got a favourite poem or anything.'

The tinny speakerphone relayed a laugh from the guy called Hubble.

'OK, here goes, testing, testing,' his voice said. 'This is Paul Hubble, right here at home, that's number twenty-five Beckman Drive, I say again, zero-two-five Beckman Drive, down here in little old Margrave, that's M-A-R-G-R-A-V-E, in the State of Georgia, USA. How am I doing on my signal strength?'

Finlay didn't respond. He was looking very worried.

'Hello?' the voice said. 'Are you still there?'

'Yes, Mr Hubble,' Finlay said. 'I'm right here. Can't find any problem at all, sir. Just a false alarm, I guess. Thank you for your help.'

'OK,' said the guy called Hubble. 'You're welcome.'

The connection broke and dial tone filled the room. Finlay replaced the phone. Leaned back and looked up at the ceiling. Spoke to himself.

'Shit,' he said. 'Right here in town. Who the hell is this Paul Hubble?'

'You don't know the guy?' I said.

He looked at me. A bit rueful. Like he'd forgotten I was there.

'I've only been here six months,' he said. 'I don't know everybody.'

He leaned forward and buzzed the intercom button on the rosewood desk. Called Baker back in.

'Ever heard of some guy called Hubble?' Finlay asked him. 'Paul Hubble, lives here in town, twenty-five Beckman Drive?'

'Paul Hubble?' Baker said. 'Sure. He lives here, like you say, always has. Family man. Stevenson knows him, some kind of an in-law or something. They're friendly, I think. Go bowling

40

together. Hubble's a banker. Some kind of a financial guy, you know, a big shot executive type, works up in Atlanta. Some big bank up there. I see him around, time to time.'

Finlay looked at him.

'He's the guy on the other end of this number,' he said.

'Hubble?' Baker said. 'Right here in Margrave? That's a hell of a thing.'

Finlay turned back to me.

'I suppose you're going to say you never heard of this guy?' he asked me.

'Never heard of him,' I said.

He glared at me briefly. Turned back to Baker.

'You better go on out and bring this Hubble guy in,' he said. 'Twenty-five Beckman Drive. God knows what he's got to do with anything, but we better talk to him. Go easy on him, you know, he's probably a respectable guy.'

He glared at me again and left the room. Banged the heavy door. Baker reached over and stopped the recording machine. Walked me out of the office. Back to the cell. I went in. He followed and removed the handcuffs. Put them back on his belt. Stepped back out and closed the gate. Operated the lock. The electric bolts snicked home. He walked away.

'Hey, Baker,' I called.

He turned and walked back. A level gaze. Not friendly.

'I want something to eat,' I said. 'And coffee.'

'You'll eat up at the state facility,' he said. 'Bus comes by at six.'

He walked away. He had to go and fetch the Hubble guy. He would shuffle up to him apologetically. Ask him to come down to the station house, where Finlay would be polite to him. While I stood in a cell, Finlay would politely ask Hubble why his phone number had been found in a dead man's shoe.

My coat was still balled up on the cell floor. I shook it out and put it on. I was cold again. Thrust my hands into the pockets. Leaned on the bars and tried to read through the newspaper again, just to pass the time. But I wasn't taking anything in. I was thinking about somebody who had watched his partner shoot a guy in the head. Who had seized the twitching body and kicked it around the floor. Who had used enough furious force to smash all the dead inert bones. I was standing there thinking about stuff I'd thought I was through with. Stuff I didn't want to think about anymore. So I dropped the paper on the carpet and tried to think about something else.

41

I found that if I leaned up in the front far corner of the cell I could see the whole of the open-plan area. I could see over the reception counter and out through the glass doors. Outside, the afternoon sun looked bright and hot. It looked like a dry and dusty place again. The heavy rain had moved on out. Inside was cool and fluorescent. The desk sergeant sat up on a stool. He worked on his keyboard. Probably filing. I could see behind his counter. Underneath were spaces designed not to be seen from the front. Neat compartments contained papers and hardback folders. There were sections with Mace sprays. A shotgun. Panic buttons. Behind the desk sergeant the uniformed woman who'd printed me was busy. Keyboard work. The large room was quiet but it hummed with the energy of investigation.

FOUR

PEOPLE SPEND THOUSANDS OF DOLLARS ON STEREOS. sometimes tens of thousands. There is a specialist industry right here in the States which builds stereo gear to a standard you wouldn't believe. Tubed amplifiers which cost more than a house. Speakers taller than me. Cables thicker than a garden hose. Some army guys had that stuff. I'd heard it on bases around the world. Wonderful. But they were wasting their money. Because the best stereo in the world is free. Inside your head. It sounds as good as you want it to. As loud as you want it to be.

I was leaning up in my corner running a Bobby Bland number through my head. An old favourite. It was cranked up real loud. 'Further On up the Road'. Bobby Bland sings it in G major. That key gives it a strange, sunny, cheerful cast. Takes out the spiteful sting from the lyric. Makes it a lament, a prediction, a consolation. Makes it do what the blues is supposed to do. The relaxed G major misting it almost into sweetness. Not vicious.

But then I saw the fat police chief walk by. Morrison, on his way past the cells, toward the big office in back. Just in time for the start of the third verse. I crunched the song down into E flat. A dark and menacing key. The real blues key. I deleted the amiable Bobby Bland. I needed a harder voice. Something much more vicious. Musical, but a real cigarettes-and-whisky rasp. Maybe Wild Child Butler. Someone you wouldn't want to mess with. I wound the level in my head up higher, for the part about reaping

43

what you sow, further on up the road.

Morrison was lying about last night. I hadn't been there at midnight. For a while I had been prepared to accept the possibility of a mistake. Maybe he had seen someone who looked like me. But that was giving him the benefit of the doubt. Right now I wanted to give him a forearm smash to the face. Burst his fat nose all over the place. I closed my eyes. Wild Child Butler and I promised ourselves it would happen. Further on up the road.

I opened my eyes and switched off the music in my head. Standing in front of me on the other side of the bars was the fingerprint officer. She was on her way back from the coffee hotplate.

'Can I get you a cup of coffee?' she asked me.

'Sure,' I said. 'Great. No cream, no sugar.'

She put her own cup down on the nearest desk and went back to the machine. Poured me a cup from the flask and walked back. This was a good-looking woman. About thirty, dark, not tall. But to call her medium would be unfair to her. She had a kind of vitality. It had come across as a sympathetic briskness in that first interview room. A professional bustle. Now she seemed unofficial. Probably was. Probably against the fat chief's rules to bring coffee to the condemned man. It made me like her.

She passed the cup in through the bars. Up close she looked good. Smelled good. I didn't recall that from earlier. I remembered thinking of her like a dentist's nurse. If dentist's nurses all looked that good, I'd have gone more often. I took the cup. I was glad of it. I was thirsty and I love coffee. Give me the chance and I drink coffee like an alcoholic drinks vodka. I took a sip. Good coffee. I raised the Styrofoam cup like a toast.

'Thank you,' I said.

'You're welcome,' she said, and she smiled, with her eyes too. I smiled back. Her eyes were like a welcome blast of sunshine on a rotten afternoon.

'So you think I didn't do it?' I asked her.

She picked up her own cup from where she'd put it down.

'You think I don't bring coffee to the guilty ones?' she said.

'Maybe you don't even talk to the guilty ones,' I said.

'I know you're not guilty of much,' she said.

'How can you tell?' I said. 'Because my eyes aren't too close together?'

'No, fool,' she laughed. 'Because we haven't heard from Washington yet.'

Her laugh was great. I wanted to look at her nameplate over her shirt pocket. But I didn't want her to think I was looking at her breasts. I remembered them resting on the edge of the table when she took my photograph. I looked. Nice breasts. Her name was Roscoe. She glanced around quickly and moved closer to the bars. I sipped coffee.

'I sent your prints to Washington over the computer link,' she said. 'That was at twelve-thirty-six. Big database there, you know, FBI? Millions of prints in their computer. Prints that get sent in are checked. There's a priority order. You get checked first of all against the top-ten wanted list, then the top hundred, then the top thousand, you understand? If you'd been near the top, you know, active and unsolved, we'd have heard almost right away. It's automatic. They don't want any big fugitive to slip away, so the system gets right back. But you've been in there almost three hours and we haven't heard. So I can tell you're not on record for anything very bad.'

The desk sergeant was looking over. Disapproving. She was going to have to go. I drained the coffee and handed her the cup back through the bars.

'I'm not on record for anything at all,' I said.

'No,' she said. 'You don't match the deviance profile.'

'I don't?' I said.

'I could tell right away,' she smiled. 'You got nice eyes.'

She winked and walked away. Trashed the cups and moved over to her work station. She sat down. All I could see was the back of her head. I moved into my corner and leaned up against the hard bars. I'd been a lonely wanderer for six months. I'd learned something. Like Blanche in that old movie, a wanderer depends on the kindness of strangers. Not for anything specific or material. For morale. I gazed at the back of Roscoe's head and smiled. I liked her.

Baker had been gone maybe twenty minutes. Long enough to get back from Hubble's place, wherever it was. I figured you could walk there and back in twenty minutes. This was a small town, right? A dot on the map. I figured you could walk anywhere and back in twenty minutes. On your hands. Although the town limits were pretty weird. Depended whether Hubble lived in town, or somewhere else within the outer boundaries. According to my experience, you were in town even when you were fourteen miles away. If that fourteen miles extended in all directions, then Margrave was about as big as New York City.

Baker had said Hubble was a family man. A banker who worked in Atlanta. That meant a family house somewhere near town. Near schools and friends for the kids. Near shops and the country club for the wife. An easy drive for him up the county road to the highway. Convenient commute up the highway to the office in the big city. The address sounded like a town address. Twenty-five Beckman Drive. Not too close to Main Street. Probably Beckman Drive ran from the centre of town out into the countryside. Hubble was a financial guy. Probably rich. Probably had a big white place on a big lot. Shade trees. Maybe a pool. Call it four acres. A square lot covering four acres was about a hundred and forty yards on a side. Homes on the left and the right of the street put number twenty-five about twelve lots out from town. About a mile, maybe.

Outside the big plate-glass doors the sun was falling away into afternoon. The light was redder. Shadows were longer. I saw Baker's patrol car yaw and bounce into the driveway. No flashing lights. It came slowly around the semicircle and eased to a stop. Bounced once on its springs. Its length filled the view through the plate glass. Baker got out on the far side and walked out of sight as he rounded the car. He reappeared as he approached his passenger's door. He opened it like a chauffeur. He looked all twisted up with conflicting body language. Part deferential, because this was an Atlanta banker. Part friendly, because this was his partner's bowling buddy. Part official, because this was a man whose phone number had been hidden in a corpse's shoe.

Paul Hubble got out of the car. Baker shut the door. Hubble waited. Baker skipped around him and pulled open the big plate-glass door of the station house. It sucked against the rubber seal. Hubble stepped inside.

He was a tall white man. He looked like a page from a magazine. An advertisement. The sort that uses a grainy photograph of money at play. He was in his early thirties. Trim but not strong. Sandy hair, tousled, receding just enough to show an intelligent brow. Just enough to say: yes, I was a preppie, but hey, I'm a man now. He wore gold-rimmed round eyeglasses. He had a square jaw. A decent tan. Very white teeth. Many of them were on show as he smiled at the desk sergeant.

46

He wore a faded polo shirt with a small logo and washed chino pants. The sort of clothes that look old when you buy them for five hundred bucks. He had a thick white sweater draped over his back. The arms were loosely tied in front. I couldn't see his feet because the reception desk was in the way. I was certain he would be wearing tan boat shoes. I made a substantial bet with myself he was wearing them without socks. This was a man who wallowed in the yuppie dream like a pig in shit.

He was in a state of some agitation. He placed his palms on the reception desk and then turned and dropped his hands to his sides. I saw sandy forearms and the flash of a heavy gold watch. I could see his natural approach would be to act like a friendly rich guy. Visiting the station house like our campaigning President would visit a factory. But he was distracted. Uptight. I didn't know what Baker had said to him. How much he had revealed. Probably nothing. A good sergeant like Baker would leave the bombshells to Finlay. So Hubble didn't know why he was here. But he knew something. I was a policeman of sorts for thirteen years and I can smell a worried man a mile away. Hubble was a worried man.

I stayed leaning up on the bars, motionless. Baker signalled Hubble to walk with him around the far side of the squad room. Towards the rosewood office in back. As Hubble rounded the end of the reception desk, I saw his feet. Tan boat shoes. No socks. The two men walked out of sight into the office. The door closed. The desk sergeant left his post and went outside to park Baker's cruiser.

He came back in with Finlay at his side. Finlay walked straight back toward the rosewood office where Hubble waited for him. Ignored me as he crossed the squad room. Opened the office door and went inside. I waited in my corner for Baker to come out. Baker couldn't stay in there. Not while his partner's bowling buddy entered the orbit of a homicide investigation. That would not be ethical. Not ethical at all. Finlay struck me as a guy who would go big on ethics. Any guy with a tweed suit like that and a moleskin vest and a Harvard education would go big on ethics. After a moment the door opened and Baker came out. He walked into the big open room and headed for his desk.

'Hey, Baker,' I called. He changed course and walked over to the cells. Stood in front of the bars. Where Roscoe had stood.

'I need to go to the bathroom,' I said. 'Unless I got to wait until I get up to the big house for that, too?'

He cracked a grin. Grudging, but a grin. He had a gold tooth way back. Gave him a rakish air. A bit more human. He shouted something to the desk guy. Probably a code for a procedure. He took out his keys and activated the electric lock. The bolts popped back. I wondered briefly how they did it if there was a power outage. Could they unlock these gates without electricity? I hoped so. Probably lots of thunderstorms down here. Lots of power lines crashing down.

He pushed the heavy gate inward. We walked to the back of the squad room. Opposite corner to the rosewood office. There was a lobby. Off the lobby were two bathrooms. He reached past me and pushed open the men's room door.

They knew I wasn't their guy. They weren't taking care. No care at all. Out there in the lobby I could have decked Baker and taken his revolver. No problem at all. I could have had his weapon off his belt before he hit the floor. I could have shot my way out of the station house and into a patrol car. They were all parked right out front. Keys in, for sure. I could have got out toward Atlanta before they organized effective opposition. Then I could have disappeared. No problem at all. But I just went into their bathroom.

'Don't lock it,' Baker said.

I didn't lock it. They were underestimating me in a big way. I had told them I had been a military policeman. Maybe they believed me, maybe they didn't. Maybe it didn't mean much to them either way. But it should. A military policeman deals with military lawbreakers. Those lawbreakers are service guys. Highly trained in weapons, sabotage, unarmed combat. Rangers, Green Berets, marines. Not just killers. Trained killers. Extremely well trained, at huge public expense. So the military policeman is trained even better. Better with weapons. Better unarmed. Baker had to be ignorant of all that. Hadn't thought about it. Otherwise he would have had a couple of shotguns aimed at me for the trip to the bathroom. If he thought I was their guy.

I zipped up and came back into the lobby. Baker was waiting. We walked back to the cell area. I stepped inside my cell. Leaned up in my corner. Baker pulled the heavy gate shut. Operated the electric lock with his key. The bolts snicked in. He walked away into the squad room.

There was silence for the next twenty minutes. Baker worked at a desk. So did Roscoe. The desk sergeant sat up on his stool. Finlay was in the big office with Hubble. There was a modern clock over the front doors. Not as elegant as the antique in the office, but it ticked around just as slowly. Silence. Four-thirty. I leaned up against the titanium bars and waited. Silence. Quarter of five.

Time restarted just before five o'clock. I heard a commotion coming out of the big rosewood office in back. Shouting, yelling, things banging. Somebody getting really stirred up. A buzzer sounded on Baker's desk and the intercom crackled. I heard Finlay's voice. Stressed. Asking Baker to get in there. Baker got up and walked over. Knocked and went in.

The big plate-glass door at the entrance sucked open and the fat guy came in. Chief Morrison. He headed straight back to the rosewood office. Baker came out as Morrison went in. Baker hurried over to the reception desk. Whispered a long excited sentence to the desk sergeant. Roscoe joined them. There was a huddle. Some big news. I couldn't hear what. Too far away.

The intercom on Baker's desk crackled again. He headed back to the office. The big front door opened again. The afternoon sun was blazing low in the sky. Stevenson walked into the station house. First time I'd seen him since my arrest. It was like the excitement was sucking people in.

Stevenson spoke to the desk sergeant. He became agitated. The desk sergeant put a hand on Stevenson's arm. Stevenson shook it off and ran toward the rosewood office. He dodged desks like a football player. As he got to the office door it opened. A crowd came out. Chief Morrison. Finlay. And Baker, holding Hubble by the elbow. A light but efficient grip, the same as he'd used on me. Stevenson stared blankly at Hubble and then grabbed Finlay by the arm. Pulled him back into the office. Morrison swivelled his sweating bulk and followed them in. The door slammed. Baker walked Hubble over toward me.

Hubble looked like a different guy. He was grey and sweating. The tan had gone. He looked smaller. He looked like someone had let the air out and deflated him. He was bent up like a man racked with pain. His eyes behind the gold rims were blank and staring with panic and fear. He stood shaking as Baker unlocked the cell next to mine. He didn't move. He was trembling. Baker caught his arm and levered him inside. He pulled the gate shut and locked it. The electric bolts snicked in. Baker walked back towards the rosewood office.

Hubble just stood where Baker had left him. Staring blankly into space. Then he slowly walked backward until he reached the rear wall of the cell. He pressed his back against it and slid to the floor. Dropped his head to his knees. Dropped his hands to the floor. I could hear the rattle of his thumb trembling on the stiff nylon carpet. Roscoe stared in at him from her desk. The sergeant at the reception counter gazed across. They were watching a man fall apart.

I heard raised voices in the rosewood office in back. The tenor of argument. The slap of a palm on a desk. The door opened and Stevenson walked out with Chief Morrison. Stevenson looked mad. He strode down the side of the open area. His neck was rigid with fury. His eyes were fixed on the front doors. He was ignoring the fat police chief. He walked straight past the reception counter and out through the heavy door into the bright afternoon. Morrison followed him.

Baker came out of the office and walked over to my cell. Didn't speak. Just unlocked the cage and gestured me out. I shrugged my coat tighter and left the newspaper with the big photographs of the President in Pensacola on the cell floor. Stepped out and followed Baker back into the rosewood office.

Finlay was at the desk. The tape recorder was there. The stiff cords trailed. The air was still and cool. Finlay looked harassed. His tie was pulled down. He blew out a big lungful of air in a rueful hiss. I sat down in the chair and Finlay waved Baker out of the room. The door closed softly behind him.

'We got us a situation here, Mr Reacher,' Finlay said. 'A real situation.'

He lapsed into a distracted silence. I had less than a half-hour before the prison bus came by. I wanted some conclusions pretty soon. Finlay looked up and focused again. Started talking, rapidly, the elegant Harvard syntax under pressure.

'We bring this Hubble guy in, right?' he said. 'You maybe saw him. Banker, from Atlanta, right? Thousand-dollar Calvin Klein outfit. Gold Rolex. Very uptight guy. At first I thought he was just annoyed. Soon as I started talking he recognized my voice. From the phone call on his mobile. Accuses me of deceitful behaviour. Says I shouldn't impersonate phone company people. He's right, of course.'

Another lapse into silence. He was struggling with his ethics problem.

'Come on, Finlay, move along,' I said. I had less than a half-hour.

'OK, so he's uptight and annoyed,' Finlay said. 'I ask him if he knows you. Jack Reacher, ex-army. He says no. Never heard of

50

you. I believe him. He starts to relax. Like all this is about some guy called Jack Reacher. He's never heard of any guy called Jack Reacher, so he's here for nothing. He's cool, right?'

'Go on,' I said.

'Then I ask him if he knows a tall guy with a shaved head,' he said. 'And I ask him about Pluribus. Well, my God! It's like I stuck a poker up his ass. He went rigid. Like with shock. Totally rigid. Won't answer. So I tell him we know the tall guy is dead. Shot to death. Well, that's like another poker up the ass. He practically fell off the chair.'

'Go on,' I said. Twenty-five minutes before the prison bus was due.

'He's shaking all over the place,' Finlay said. 'Then I tell him we know about the phone number in the shoe. His phone number printed on a piece of paper, with the word "Pluribus" printed above it. That's another poker up the ass.'

He stopped again. He was patting his pockets, each one in turn.

'He wouldn't say anything,' he went on. 'Not a word. He was rigid with shock. All grey in the face. I thought he was having a heart attack. His mouth was opening and closing like a fish. But he wasn't talking. So I told him we knew about the corpse getting beaten up. I asked him who else was involved. I told him we knew about hiding the body under the cardboard. He wouldn't say a damn word. He just kept looking around. After a while I realized he was thinking like crazy. Trying to decide what to tell me. He just kept silent, thinking like mad, must have been forty minutes. The tape was running the whole time. Recorded forty minutes of silence.'

Finlay stopped again. This time for effect. He looked at me.

'Then he confessed,' he said. 'I did it, he said. I shot him, he said. The guy is confessing, right? On the tape.'

'Go on,' I said.

'I ask him, do you want a lawyer?' he said. 'He says no, keeps repeating he killed the guy. So I Mirandize him, loud and clear, on the tape. Then I think to myself maybe he's crazy or something, you know? So I ask him, who did you kill? He says the tall guy with the shaved head. I ask him, how? He says, shot him in the head. I ask him, when? He says last night, about midnight. I ask him who kicked the body around? Who was the guy? What does Pluribus mean? He doesn't answer. Goes rigid with fright all over again. Refuses to say a damn word. I say to him, I'm not sure you did anything at all. He jumps up and grabs me. He's screaming I confess,

I confess, I shot him, I shot him. I shove him back. He goes quiet.'

Finlay sat back. Folded his hands behind his head. Looked a question at me. Hubble as the shooter? I didn't believe it. Because of his agitation. Guys who shoot somebody with an old pistol, in a fight or in a temper, a messy shot to the chest, they get agitated afterwards. Guys who put two bullets in the head, with a silencer, then collect up the shell cases, they're a different class of person. They don't get agitated afterwards. They just walk away and forget about it. Hubble was not the shooter. The way he had been dancing around in front of the reception counter disproved it. But I just shrugged and smiled.

'OK,' I said. 'You can let me go now, right?'

Finlay looked at me and shook his head.

'Wrong,' he said. 'I don't believe him. There were three guys involved here. You persuaded me of that yourself. So which one is Hubble claiming to be? I don't think he's the maniac. I can't see enough strength in him for that. I don't see him as the gofer. And he's definitely not the shooter, for God's sake. Guy like that couldn't shoot pool.'

I nodded. Like Finlay's partner. Worrying away at a problem.

'Got to throw his ass in the can for now,' he said. 'No option. He's confessed, couple of plausible details. But it definitely won't hold up.'

I nodded again. Sensed there was something more to come.

'Go on,' I said. With resignation.

Finlay looked at me. A level gaze.

'He wasn't even there at midnight,' he said. 'He was at some old couple's anniversary party. A family thing. Not far from where he lives. Got there around eight last night. He'd walked down with his wife. Didn't leave until after two o'clock in the morning. Two dozen people saw him arrive, two dozen people saw him leave. He got a ride home from his sister-in-law's brother-in-law. He got a ride because it was already pouring rain by then.'

'Go on, Finlay,' I said. 'Tell me.'

'His sister-in-law's brother-in-law?' he said. 'Drove him home, in the rain, two o'clock in the morning? Officer Stevenson.'

FIVE

FINLAY LEANED RIGHT BACK IN HIS CHAIR. HIS LONG ARMS were folded behind his head. He was a tall, elegant man. Educated in Boston. Civilized. Experienced. And he was sending me to jail for something I hadn't done. He levered himself upright. Spread his hands on the desk, palms up.

'I'm sorry, Reacher,' he said to me.

'You're sorry?' I said. 'You're sending two guys who couldn't have done it to jail and you're sorry?'

He shrugged. Looked unhappy about it.

'This is the way Chief Morrison wants it,' he said. 'He's calling it a done deal. Closing us down for the weekend. And he's the boss man, right?'

'You got to be joking,' I said. 'He's an asshole. He's calling Stevenson a liar. His own man.'

'Not exactly,' Finlay shrugged. 'He's saying it's maybe a conspiracy, you know, maybe Hubble wasn't literally there, but he recruited you to do it. A conspiracy, right? He reckons the confession is exaggerated because maybe Hubble's afraid of you and is scared to finger you right away. Morrison figures you were on your way down to Hubble's place to get paid when we hauled you in. He figures that's why you waited the eight hours. Figures that's why Hubble was at home today. Didn't go to work because he was waiting around to pay you off.'

I was silent. I was worried. Chief Morrison was dangerous. His

53

theory was plausible. Until Finlay did the checking. If Finlay did the checking.

'So, Reacher, I'm sorry,' he said. 'You and Hubble stay in the bag until Monday. You'll get through it. Over in Warburton. Bad place, but the holding pens are OK. Worse if you go there for a stretch. Much worse. Meantime, I'll work on it before Monday. I'll ask Officer Roscoe to come in Saturday and Sunday. She's the pretty one outside. She's good, the best we got. If what you say is right, you'll be free and clear on Monday. OK?'

I stared at him. I was getting mad.

'No, Finlay, not OK,' I said. 'You know I didn't do a damn thing. You know it wasn't me. You're just shit scared of that useless fat bastard Morrison. So I'm going to jail because you're just a spineless damn coward.'

He took it pretty well. His dark face flushed darker. He sat quietly for a long time. I took a deep breath and glared at him. My glare subsided to a gaze as my temper cooled. Back under control. His turn to glare at me.

'Two things, Reacher,' he said. Precise articulation. 'First, if necessary I'll take care of Chief Morrison on Monday. Second, I am not a coward. You don't know me at all. Nothing about me.'

I gazed back at him. Six o'clock. Bus time.

'I know more than you think,' I said. 'I know you're a Harvard postgrad, you're divorced and you quit smoking in April.'

Finlay looked blank. Baker knocked and entered to say the prison bus had arrived. Finlay got up and walked around the desk. Told Baker he would bring me out himself. Baker went back to fetch Hubble.

'How do you know that stuff?' Finlay asked me.

He was intrigued. He was losing the game.

'Easy,' I said. 'You're a smart guy, right? Educated in Boston, you told me. But when you were college age, Harvard wasn't taking too many black guys. You're smart, but you're no rocket scientist, so I figure Boston U for the first degree, right?'

'Right,' he conceded.

'And then Harvard for postgrad,' I said. 'You did well at Boston U, life moved on, you got into Harvard. You talk like a Harvard guy. I figured it straight away. PhD in criminology?'

'Right,' he said again. 'Criminology.'

'And then you got this job in April,' I said. 'You told me that. You've got a pension from Boston PD, because you did your twenty. So you've come down here with cash to spare. But you've come down here with no woman, because if you had, she'd have spent some of that spare cash on new clothes for you. She probably hated that wintry tweed thing you're wearing. She'd have junked it and put you in a Sunbelt outfit to start your new life on the right foot. But you're still wearing that terrible old suit, so the woman is gone. She either died or divorced you, so it was a fifty-fifty guess. Looks like I guessed right.'

He nodded blankly.

'And the smoking thing is easy,' I said. 'You were just stressed up and you were patting your pockets, looking for cigarettes. That means you quit fairly recently. Easy guess is you quit in April, you know, new life, new job, no more cigarettes. You figured quit now and you might beat the cancer thing.'

Finlay glared at me. A bit grudging.

'Very good, Reacher,' he said. 'Elementary deduction, right?'

I shrugged. Didn't say anything.

'So deduce who aced the guy up at the warehouse,' he said.

'I don't care who aced any guy anywhere,' I said. 'That's your problem, not mine. And it's the wrong question, Finlay. First you got to find out who the guy was, right?'

'So you got any way to do that, smart guy?' he asked me. 'No ID, no face left, nothing from the prints, Hubble won't say diddly?'

'Run the prints again,' I said. 'I'm serious, Finlay. Get Roscoe to do it.'

'Why?' he said.

'Something wrong there,' I said.

'What something?' he asked me.

'Run them again, OK?' I said. 'Will you do that?'

He just grunted. Didn't say yes or no. I opened the office door and stepped out. Roscoe had gone. Nobody was there except Baker and Hubble over at the cells. I could see the desk sergeant outside through the front doors. He was writing on a clipboard held by the prison bus driver. As a backdrop behind the two of them was the prison bus. It was stationary in the semicircular driveway. It filled the view through the big plate-glass entrance. It was a school bus painted light grey. On it was written: State of Georgia Department of Corrections. That inscription ran the full length of the bus, under the line of windows. Under the inscription was a crest. The windows had grilles welded over them.

Finlay came out of the office behind me. Touched my elbow and walked me over to Baker. Baker was holding three sets of handcuffs hooked over his thumb. They were painted bright orange. The paint was chipped. Dull steel showed through. Baker snapped a pair of handcuffs onto each of my wrists separately. He unlocked Hubble's cell and signalled the scared banker to come out. Hubble was blank and dazed, but he stepped out. Baker caught the dangling cuff on my left wrist and snapped it onto Hubble's right wrist. He put the third set of cuffs on Hubble's other wrist. Ready to go.

'Take his watch, Baker,' I said. 'He'll lose it in jail.'

He nodded. He knew what I meant. Guy like Hubble could lose a lot in jail. Baker unlatched the heavy Rolex from Hubble's wrist. The bracelet wouldn't slide over the handcuff, so Baker had to fiddle and fuss with taking the handcuff off and putting it back on again. The prison driver cracked the door and glared in. A man with a timetable. Baker dropped Hubble's watch on the nearest desk. Exactly where my friend Roscoe had put her coffee cup.

'OK, guys, let's hit the road,' Baker said.

He walked us to the doors. We went out into a dazzling hot bar of sunshine. Handcuffed together. Walking was awkward. Before crossing to the bus, Hubble stopped. He craned his neck and looked around carefully. He was being more vigilant than Baker or the prison driver. Maybe scared of a neighbour seeing him. But there was nobody around. We were three hundred yards north of the town. I could see the church steeple in the distance. We walked over to the bus through the evening warmth. My right cheek tingled in the low sun.

The driver pushed the bus door inward. Hubble shuffled sideways onto the step. I followed him. Made a clumsy turn into the aisle. The bus was empty. The driver directed Hubble into a seat. He slid over the vinyl to the window. I was pulled alongside. The driver knelt on the seat in front and clicked our outer wrists to the chromium hoop which ran across the top. He rattled each of our three cuffs in turn. Wanted to know they were secure. I didn't blame him. I've done that job. Nothing worse than driving with prisoners loose behind you.

The driver walked forward to his seat. He started the engine with a loud diesel clatter. The bus filled with vibration. The air was hot. Stifling. There was no air-conditioning. None of the windows opened. I could smell fuel fumes. The gears clashed and ground and the bus moved off. I glanced out to my right. Nobody waving goodbye.

We drove north out of the police lot, turning our backs on the town, heading up towards the highway. We passed Eno's diner after a half-mile. His lot was empty. Nobody looking for an early dinner. We carried on north for a spell. Then we turned a tight left off the county road and struck out west down a road between fields. The bus settled to a noisy cruise. Endless rows of bushes flicked past. Endless drills of red earth between. Ahead of me the sun was on the way down. It was a giant red ball heading for the fields. The driver had the large sun visor down. On it were printed manufacturer's instructions about how to operate the bus.

Hubble rocked and bounced beside me. He said nothing. He had slumped down with his face parallel to the floor. His left arm was raised because it was handcuffed to the chrome bar in front of us. His right arm rested inert between us. He still had his expensive sweater draped across his shoulders. Where the Rolex had been was a band of pale skin. The life force had just about drained out of him. He was in the grip of a paralyzing fear.

We rocked and bounced for the best part of another hour through the huge landscape. A small stand of trees flashed past on my right. Then way in the far distance I saw a structure. It sat alone in a thousand acres of flat farmland. Against the low red sun it looked like a protrusion from hell. Something forced up through the crust of the earth. It was a complex of buildings. Looked like a chemical factory or a nuclear place. Massive concrete bunkers and glittering metal walkways. Tubing running here and there with steam drifting. All surrounded with fencing punctuated by towers. As we drew closer I could see arc lights and razor wire. Searchlights and rifles in the towers. Layers of fences separated with ploughed red earth. Hubble didn't look up. I didn't nudge him. It wasn't the Magic Kingdom up ahead.

The bus slowed as we approached. The outermost fence was about a hundred yards out forming a giant perimeter. It was a substantial fence. Possibly fifteen feet tall, studded along its entire length with pairs of sodium floodlights. One of each pair was trained inward across the hundred-yard breadth of ploughed earth. One was trained out over the surrounding farmland. All the floodlights were lit. The whole complex blazed with yellow sodium light. Up close it was very bright. The yellow light turned the red earth to a ghastly tan.

The bus rattled to a halt. The idling engine set up a vibration. What little ventilation there had been ceased. It was stifling. Hubble finally looked up. He peered out through his gold rims. He looked around him and out the window. He groaned. It was a groan of hopeless dejection. He dropped his head.

The driver was waiting for a signal from the first gate guard. The guard was speaking into a radio. The driver blipped the engine and crunched into gear. The guard signalled to him, using his radio as a baton, waving us through. The bus ground forward into a cage. We passed a long low sign at the kerb: Warburton Correctional Facility, State of Georgia Department of Corrections. Behind us a gate swung closed. We were sealed in a wire cage. It was roofed with wire. At the far end a gate swung open. The bus ground through.

We drove the hundred yards to the next fence. There was another vehicle cage. The bus went in, waited, and drove on out. We drove right into the heart of the prison. We stopped opposite a concrete bunker. The reception area. The engine noise beat against the concrete surrounding us. Then it shut down and the vibration and clatter died away to silence. The driver swung out of his seat and walked up the aisle, stooping, pulling himself like a climber on the seatbacks. He pulled out his keys and unlocked the cuffs fixing us to the seat in front.

'OK, boys, let's go,' he grinned. 'Party time.'

We hauled ourselves out of our seat and shuffled down the bus. My left arm was pulled back by Hubble. The driver stopped us at the front. He removed all three sets of handcuffs and dropped them in a bin next to his cab. Hauled on a lever and sprang the door. We got out of the bus. A door opened opposite and a guard stepped out. Called us over. He was eating a doughnut and spoke with his mouth full. A sugar moustache frosted his lip. He was a pretty casual guy. We went through the door into a small concrete chamber. It was filthy. Deal chairs surrounded a painted table. Another guard sat on the table reading from a battered clipboard.

'Sit down, OK?' he said. We sat. He stood up. His partner with the doughnut locked the outer door and joined him.

'Here's the deal,' said the clipboard guy. 'You guys are Reacher and Hubble. In from Margrave. Not convicted of any crime. In custody pending investigation. No bail application for either of you. Hear what I say? Not convicted of any crime. That's the important thing. Excuses you from a lot of shit in here, OK? No uniform, no processing, no big deal, you understand? Nice accommodations on the top floor.'

'Right,' said the doughnut guy. 'Thing is, if you were convicts, we'd be poking and prodding and hitting on you, and you'd get the uniform, and we'd shove you on the convict floors with the other animals and we'd just set back and watch the fun, right?'

'Right,' his partner said. 'So what we're saying is this. We ain't here to give you a hard time, so don't you boys be giving us a hard time neither, you understand? This damn facility ain't got the manpower. Governor laid off about a half the staff, OK? Got to meet the budget, right? Got to cut the deficit, right? So we ain't got the men to do the job the way it ought to be done. Trying to do our job with half a crew on every shift, right? So what I'm saying is we shove you in there, and we don't want to see you again until we pull you out on Monday. No hassle, right? We ain't got the manpower for hassle. We ain't got the manpower for hassle on the convict floors, let alone hassle on the holding floor, you understand? Yo, Hubble, you understand?'

Hubble looked up at him and nodded blankly. Didn't speak.

'Reacher?' the clipboard guy said. 'You understand?'

'Sure,' I said. I understood. This guy was understaffed. Having problems because of a budget. While his friends collected unemployment. Tell me about it.

'Good,' he said. 'So the deal is this. The two of us are off duty at seven o'clock. Which is in about one minute's time. We ain't staying late for you boys. We don't want to and the union wouldn't let us anyway. So you get a meal, then you're locked down in here until they got manpower to take you upstairs. No manpower until lights out, maybe ten o'clock, OK? But then no guards will move prisoners around after lights out anyway, right? Union won't let 'em. So Spivey will come get you himself. Assistant warden. Top boy tonight. About ten o'clock, OK? You don't like it, you don't tell me, you tell the governor, OK?'

The doughnut eater went out into the corridor and came back a long moment later with a tray. On it were covered plates, paper cups and a thermos. He put the tray on the table and the two of them swung out through the corridor. Locked the door from the outside. It went quiet as a tomb in there.

We ate. Fish and rice. Friday food. Coffee in the thermos. Hubble didn't speak. He left most of the coffee for me. Score one for Hubble. I put the debris on the tray and the tray on the floor. Another three hours to waste. I tipped my chair back and put my feet up on the table. Not comfortable, but as good as I was going to get. A warm evening. September in Georgia.

I looked over at Hubble without curiosity. He was still silent. I had never heard him speak except on Finlay's speakerphone. He looked back at me. His face was full of dejection and fear. He looked at me like I was a creature from another world. He stared at me like I worried him. Then he looked away.

Maybe I wouldn't head back to the Gulf. But it was too late in the year to head north. Too cold up there. Maybe skip right down to the islands. Jamaica, maybe. Good music there. A hut on the beach. Live out the winter in a hut on a Jamaica beach. Smoke a pound of grass a week. Do whatever Jamaica people do. Maybe two pounds of grass a week with someone to share the hut. Roscoe kept drifting into the picture. Her uniform shirt was fabulously crisp. A crisp tight blue shirt. I had never seen a shirt look better. On a Jamaica beach in the sun she wouldn't need a shirt. I didn't think that would prove to be any kind of a major problem.

It was her wink that did it to me. She took my coffee cup. She said I had nice eyes. And she winked. Got to mean something, right? The eyes thing, I've heard that before. An English girl I'd had good times with for a while, she liked my eyes. Said it all the time. They're blue. Equally people have said they look like icebergs in an Arctic sea. If I concentrate I can stop them blinking. Gives a stare an intimidating effect. Useful. But Roscoe's wink had been the best part of the day. The only part of the day, really, except Eno's scrambled eggs, which weren't bad. Eggs you can get anywhere. But I'd miss Roscoe. I floated on through the empty evening.

Not long after ten the door from the corridor was unlocked. A uniformed man came in. He carried a clipboard. And a shotgun. I looked him over. A son of the South. A heavy, fleshy man. Reddened skin, a big hard belly and a wide neck. Small eyes. A tight greasy uniform straining to contain him. Probably born right there on the farm they commandeered to build the prison. Assistant Warden Spivey. This shift's top boy. Understaffed and harassed. Ushering the short-stay guests around by himself. With a shotgun in his big red farmer's hands.

He studied his clipboard.

'Which one of you is Hubble?' he asked.

He had a high-pitched voice. At odds with his bulk. Hubble raised his hand briefly, like a boy at grade school. Spivey's little eyes flicked over him. Up and down. Like a snake's eyes. He grunted and signalled with the clipboard. We formed up and moved out. Hubble was blank and acquiescent. Like an exhausted trooper.

60

'Turn left and follow the red line,' Spivey said.

He waved left with the shotgun. There was a red line painted on the wall at waist height. It was a fire lane guide. I guessed it must lead outside, but we were going in the wrong direction. Into the prison, not out of it. We followed the red line through corridors, up stairs and around corners. Hubble first, then me. Then Spivey with the shotgun. It was very dark. Just dim emergency lighting. Spivey called a halt on a landing. He overrode an electronic lock with his key. A lock which would spring the fire door when the alarm went.

'No talking,' he said. 'Rules here say absolute silence at all times after lights out. Cell at the end on the right.'

We stepped in through the out door. The foul odour of prison hit me. The night exhalation of countless dispirited men. It was nearly pitch black. A night-light glowed dimly. I sensed rather than saw rows of cells. I heard the babble of night sounds. Breathing and snoring. Muttering and whimpering. Spivey walked us to the end of the row. Pointed to an empty cell. We crowded in. Spivey swung the bars shut behind us. They locked automatically. He walked away.

The cell was very dark. I could just about see a bunk bed, a sink and a john. Not much floorspace. I took off my coat and lobbed it onto the top bunk. Reached up and remade the bed with the pillow away from the bars. I liked it better that way. Worn sheet and blanket, but they smelled clean enough.

Hubble sat quietly on the lower bed. I used the john and rinsed my face at the sink. Pulled myself up into bed. Took off my shoes. Left them on the foot of the bed. I wanted to know where they were. Shoes can get stolen, and these were good shoes. Bought many years ago in Oxford, England. A university town near the airbase where I was stationed. Big heavy shoes with hard soles and a thick welt.

The bed was too short for me, but most beds are. I lay there in the dark and listened to the restless prison. Then I closed my eyes and floated back to Jamaica with Roscoe. I must have fallen asleep there with her because the next thing I knew it was Saturday. I was still in prison. And an even worse day was beginning.

SIX

I WAS WOKEN UP BY BRIGHT LIGHTS COMING ON. THE PRISON HAD no windows. Day and night were created by electricity. At seven o'clock the building was suddenly flooded with light. No dawn or soft twilight. Just circuit-breakers thrown shut at seven.

The bright light did not make the cell look any better. The front wall was bars. Half would open outward on a hinge to form the door. The two stacked beds occupied just about half the width and most of the length. On the back wall were a steel sink and a steel toilet pan. The walls were masonry. Part poured concrete and part old bricks. All thickly covered with paint. The walls looked massively thick. Like a dungeon. Above my head was a low concrete ceiling. The cell didn't feel like a room bounded by walls, floor, ceiling. It felt like a solid block of masonry with a tiny living space grudgingly burrowed in.

Outside, the restless night mutter was replaced by the clatter of daytime. Everything was metal, brick, concrete. Noises were amplified and echoed around. It sounded like hell. Through the bars I could see nothing. Opposite our cell was a blank wall. Lying in bed I didn't have the angle to see down the row. I threw off the cover and found my shoes. Put them on and laced them up. Lay down again. Hubble was sitting on the bottom bunk. His tan boat shoes were planted on the concrete floor. I wondered if he'd sat like that all night or if he'd slept.

Next person I saw was a cleaner. He moved into view outside

our bars. This was a very old guy with a broom. An old black man with a fringe of snow-white hair. Bent up with age. Fragile like a wizened old bird. His orange prison uniform was washed almost white. He must have been eighty. Must have been inside for sixty years. Maybe stole a chicken in the Depression. Still paying his debt to society.

He stabbed the broom randomly over the corridor. His spine forced his face parallel to the floor. He rolled his head like a swimmer to see from side to side. He caught sight of Hubble and me and stopped. Rested on his broom and shook his head. Gave a kind of reflective chuckle. Shook his head again. He was chuckling away. An appreciative, delighted chuckle. Like at long last, after all these years, he'd been granted the sight of a fabled thing. Like a unicorn or a mermaid. He kept trying to speak, raising his hand as if his point was going to require emphasis. But every time, he'd start up with the chuckling again and need to clutch the broom. I didn't hurry him. I could wait. I had all weekend. He had the rest of his life.

'Well, yes indeed,' he grinned. He had no teeth. 'Well, yes indeed.'

I looked over at him.

'Well, yes what, Granddad?' I grinned back.

He was cackling away. This was going to take a while.

'Yes indeed,' he said. Now he had the chuckling under control. 'I've been in this joint since God's dog was a puppy, yes sir. Since Adam was a young boy. But here's something I ain't never seen. No sir, not in all those years.'

'What ain't you never seen, old man?' I asked him.

'Well,' he said, 'I been here all these years, and I ain't never seen anybody in that cell wearing clothes like yours, man.'

'You don't like my clothes?' I said. Surprised.

'I didn't say that, no sir, I didn't say I don't like your clothes,' he said. 'I like your clothes just fine. A very fine set of clothes, yes sir, yes indeed, very fine.'

'So what's the story?' I asked.

The old guy was cackling away to himself.

'The quality of the clothes ain't the issue,' he said. 'No sir, that ain't the issue at all. It's the fact you're wearing them, man, like not wearing the orange uniform. I never saw that before, and like I say, man, I been here since the earth cooled, since the dinosaurs said enough is enough. Now I seen everything, I really have, yes sir.'

'But guys on the holding floor don't wear the uniform,' I said.

'Yes indeed, that sure is true,' the old man said. 'That's a fact, for sure.'

'The guards said so,' I confirmed.

'They would say so,' he agreed. 'Because that's the rules, and the guards, they know the rules, yes sir, they know them because they make them.'

'So what's the issue, old man?' I said.

'Well, like I say, you're not wearing the orange suit,' he said.

We were going around in circles here.

'But I don't have to wear it,' I said.

He was amazed. The sharp bird eyes locked in on me.

'You don't?' he said. 'Why's that, man? Tell me.'

'Because we don't wear it on the holding floor,' I said. 'You just agreed with that, right?'

There was a silence. He and I got the message simultaneously.

'You think this is the holding floor?' he asked me.

'Isn't this the holding floor?' I asked him at the same time.

The old guy paused a beat. Lifted his broom and crabbed back out of sight. Quickly as he could. Shouting incredulously as he went.

'This ain't the holding floor, man,' he whooped. 'Holding floor is the top floor. Floor six. This here is floor three. You're on floor three, man. This is lifers, man. This is categorized dangerous people, man. This ain't even general population. This is the worst, man. Yes, indeed, you boys are in the wrong place. You boys are in trouble, yes indeed. You gonna get visitors. They gonna check you boys out. Oh man, I'm out of here.'

Evaluate. Long experience had taught me to evaluate and assess. When the unexpected gets dumped on you, don't waste time. Don't figure out how or why it happened. Don't recriminate. Don't figure out whose fault it is. Don't work out how to avoid the same mistake next time. All of that you do later. If you survive. First of all you evaluate. Analyze the situation. Identify the downside. Assess the upside. Plan accordingly. Do all that and you give yourself a better chance of getting through to the other stuff later.

We were not in the holding pens on the sixth floor. Not where unconvicted prisoners should be. We were among dangerous lifers on the third. There was no upside. The downside was extensive. We were new boys on a convict floor. We would not survive without status. We had no status. We would be challenged. We would be made to embrace our position at the absolute bottom of the pecking order. We faced an unpleasant weekend. Potentially a lethal one.

I remembered an army guy, a deserter. Young guy, not a bad recruit, went AWOL because he got some nut religion. Got into trouble in Washington, demonstrating. Ended up thrown in jail, among bad guys like on this floor. Died on his first night. Anally raped. An estimated fifty times. And at the autopsy they found a pint of semen in his stomach. A new boy with no status. Right at the bottom of the pecking order. Available to all those above him.

Assess. I could call on some heavy training. And experience. Not intended for prison life, but it would help. I had gone through a lot of unpleasant education. Not just in the army. Stretching right back into childhood. Between grade school and high school military kids like me get to go to twenty, maybe thirty new schools. Some on bases, most in local neighbourhoods. In some tough places. Philippines, Korea, Iceland, Germany, Scotland, Japan, Vietnam. All over the world. The first day at each new school, I was a new boy. With no status. Lots of first days. I quickly learned how to get status. In sandy hot schoolyards, in cold wet schoolyards, my brother and I had slugged it out together, back to back. We had got status.

Then in the service itself, that brutality was refined. I was trained by experts. Guys who traced their own training back to World War Two, Korea, Vietnam. People who had survived things I had only read about in books. They taught me methods, details, skills. Most of all they taught me attitude. They taught me that inhibitions would kill me. Hit early, hit hard. Kill with the first blow. Get your retaliation in first. Cheat. The gentlemen who behaved decently weren't there to train anybody. They were already dead.

At seven-thirty there was a ragged clunk along the row of cells. The time switch had unlocked the cages. Our bars sagged open an inch. Hubble sat motionless. Still silent. I had no plan. Best option would be to find a guard. Explain and get transferred. But I didn't expect to find a guard. On floors like this they wouldn't patrol singly. They would move in pairs, possibly in groups of three or four. The prison was understaffed. That had been made clear last night. Unlikely to be enough manpower to provide groups of guards on each floor. Probability was I wouldn't see a guard all day. They would wait in a crew room. Operate as a crash squad responding to emergencies. And if I did see a guard, what would I say? I shouldn't be here? They must hear that all day long. They would ask, who put you here? I would say Spivey, the top boy. They would say, well that's OK then, right? So the only plan was no plan. Wait and see. React accordingly. Objective, survival until Monday.

I could hear the grinding as the other inmates swung back their gates and latched them open. I could hear movement and shouted conversation as they strolled out to start another pointless day. I waited.

Not long to wait. From my tight angle on the bed, head away from the door, I saw our next-door neighbours stroll out. They merged with a small knot of men. They were all dressed the same. Orange prison uniform. Red bandannas tight over shaved heads. Huge black guys. Obviously bodybuilders. Several had torn the sleeves off their shirts. Suggesting that no available garment could contain their massive bulk. They may have been right. An impressive sight.

The nearest guy was wearing pale sunglasses. The sort which darken in the sun. Silver halide. The guy had probably last seen the sun in the seventies. May never see it again. So the shades were redundant, but they looked good. Like the muscles. Like the bandannas and the torn shirts. All image. I waited.

The guy with the sunglasses spotted us. His look of surprise quickly changed to excitement. He alerted the group's biggest guy by hitting his arm. The big man looked round. He looked blank. Then he grinned. I waited. The knot of men assembled outside our cell. They gazed in. The big guy pulled open our gate. The others passed it from hand to hand through its arc. They latched it open.

'Look what they sent us,' the big guy said. 'You know what they sent us?'

'What they sent us?' the sunglasses guy said.

'They sent us fresh meat,' the big guy answered.

'They sure did, man,' the sunglasses guy said. 'Fresh meat.'

'Fresh meat for everybody,' the big guy said.

He grinned. He looked around his gang and they all grinned back. Exchanged low fives. I waited. The big guy stepped half a pace into our cell. He was enormous. Maybe an inch or two shorter than me but probably twice as heavy. He filled the doorway. His dull eyes flicked over me, then Hubble.

'Yo, white boy, come here,' he said. To Hubble.

I could sense Hubble's panic. He didn't move.

'Come here, white boy,' the big guy repeated. Quietly.

Hubble stood up. Took half a pace toward the man at the door. The big guy was glaring with that rage glare that is supposed to chill you with its ferocity.

'This is Red Boy territory, man,' the big guy said. Explaining the bandannas. 'What's whitey doing in Red Boy territory?'

Hubble said nothing in reply.

'Residency tax, man,' the big guy said. 'Like they got in Florida hotels, man. You got to pay the tax. Give me your sweater, white boy.'

Hubble was rigid with fear.

'Give me your sweater, white boy,' he said again. Quietly.

Hubble unwrapped his expensive white sweater and held it out. The big man took it and threw it behind him without looking.

'Give me the eyeglasses, white boy,' he said.

Hubble flicked a despairing glance up at me. Took off his gold glasses. Held them out. The big man took them and dropped them to the floor. Crunched them under his shoe. Screwed his foot around. The glasses smashed and splintered. The big man scraped his foot back and flicked the wreckage backwards into the corridor. The other guys all took turns stamping on them.

'Good boy,' the big guy said. 'You paid the tax.'

Hubble was trembling.

'Now come here, white boy,' said his tormentor.

Hubble shuffled nearer.

'Closer, white boy,' the big man said.

Hubble shuffled nearer. Until he was a foot away. He was shaking.

'On your knees, white boy,' said the big guy.

Hubble knelt.

'Unzip me, whitey,' he said.

Hubble did nothing. Filled with panic.

'Unzip me, white boy,' the big guy said again. 'With your teeth.'

Hubble gave a gasp of fear and revulsion and jumped back. He scuttled backwards to the rear of the cell. Tried to hide behind the john. He was practically hugging the pan.

Time to intervene. Not for Hubble. I felt nothing for him. But I had to intervene for myself. Hubble's abject performance would taint me. We would be seen as a pair. Hubble's surrender would disqualify us both. In the status game.

'Come back, white boy, don't you like me?' the big guy called to Hubble.

I took a long silent breath. Swung my feet over the side of the bunk and landed lightly in front of the big man. He stared at me. I stared back, calmly.

'You're in my house, fat boy,' I said. 'But I'm going to give you a choice.'

'Choice of what?' said the big guy. Blankly. Surprised.

'A choice of exit strategies, fat boy,' I said.

'Say what?' he said.

'What I mean is this,' I said. 'You're going to leave. That's for sure. Your choice is about how you leave. Either you can walk out of here by yourself, or these other fat boys behind you are going to carry you out in a bucket.'

'Oh yeah?' he said.

'For sure,' I said. 'I'm going to count to three, OK, so you better choose real quick, right?'

He glared at me.

'One,' I counted. No response.

'Two,' I counted. No response.

Then I cheated. Instead of counting three I headbutted him full in the face. Came off the back foot with a thrust up the legs and whipped my head forward and smashed it into his nose. It was beautifully done. The forehead is a perfect arch in all planes and very strong. The skull at the front is very thick. I have a ridge up there like concrete. The human head is very heavy. All kinds of neck muscles and back muscles balance it. It's like getting hit in the face with a bowling ball. It's always a surprise. People expect punching or kicking. A headbutt is always unexpected. It comes out of the blue.

It must have caved his whole face in. I guess I pulped his nose and smashed both his cheekbones. Jarred his little brain around real good. His legs crumpled and he hit the floor like a puppet with the strings cut. Like an ox in the slaughter house. His skull cracked on the concrete floor.

I stared around the knot of men. They were busy reassessing my status.

'Who's next?' I said. 'But this is like Vegas now, it's double or quits. This guy is going to the hospital, maybe six weeks in a metal mask. So the next guy gets twelve weeks in the hospital, you understand that? Couple of smashed elbows, right? So who's next?'

There was no reply. I pointed at the guy in sunglasses.

'Give me the sweater, fat boy,' I said.

He bent and picked up the sweater. Passed it to me. Leaned over and held it out. Didn't want to get too close. I took the sweater and tossed it onto Hubble's bunk.

'Give me the eyeglasses,' I said.

He bent and swept up the twisted gold wreckage. Handed it to me. I tossed it back at him.

'They're broken, fat boy,' I said. 'Give me yours.'

There was a long pause. He looked at me. I looked at him. Without blinking. He took off his sunglasses and handed them to me. I put them in my pocket.

'Now get this carcass out of here,' I said.

The bunch of men in their orange uniforms and their red bandannas straightened out the slack limbs and dragged the big man away. I crawled back up into my bunk. I was shaking with adrenalin rush. My stomach was churning and I was panting. My circulation had just about shut down. I felt terrible. But not as bad as I would have felt if I hadn't done it. They'd have finished with Hubble by then and started in on me.

I didn't eat any breakfast. No appetite. I just lay on the bunk until I felt better. Hubble sat on his bed. He was rocking back and forward. He still hadn't spoken. After a while I slid to the floor. Washed at the sink. People were strolling up to the doorway and gazing in. Strolling away. The word had gotten around fast. The new guy in the cell at the end had sent a Red Boy to the hospital. Check it out. I was a celebrity.

Hubble stopped his rocking and looked at me. Opened his mouth and closed it again. Opened it for a second time.

'I can't take this,' he said.

They were the first words I had heard him say since his assured banter on Finlay's speakerphone. His voice was low, but his statement was definite. Not a whine or a complaint, but a statement of fact. He couldn't take this. I looked over at him. Considered his statement for a long moment.

'So why are you here?' I asked him. 'What are you doing?'

'I'm not doing anything,' he said. Blankly.

'You confessed to something you didn't do,' I said. 'You asked for this.'

'No,' said Hubble. 'I did what I said. I did it and I told the detective.'

'Bullshit, Hubble,' I said. 'You weren't even there. You were at a party. The guy who drove you home is a policeman, for God's sake. You didn't do it, you know that, everybody knows that. Don't give me that shit.'

Hubble looked down at the floor. Thought for a moment.

'I can't explain it,' he said. 'I can't say anything about it. I just need to know what happens next.'

I looked at him again.

'What happens next?' I said. 'You stay here until Monday morning, and then you go back to Margrave. Then I guess they'll let you go.'

'Will they?' he said. Like he was debating with himself.

'You weren't even there,' I said again. 'They know that. They might want to know why you confessed, when you didn't do anything. And they'll want to know why the guy had your phone number.'

'What if I can't tell them?' he said.

'Can't or won't?' I asked him.

'I can't tell them,' he said. 'I can't tell anybody anything.'

He looked away and shuddered. Very frightened.

'But I can't stay in here,' he said. 'I can't stand it.'

Hubble was a financial guy. They give out their phone numbers like confetti. Talking to anybody they meet about hedge funds or tax havens. Anything to transfer some guy's hard-earned dollars their way. But this phone number was printed on a scrap of torn computer paper. Not engraved on a business card. And hidden in a shoe, not stuffed in a wallet. And playing in the background like a rhythm section was the fear coming out of the guy.

'Why can't you tell anybody?' I asked him.

'Because I can't,' he said. Wouldn't say anything more.

I was suddenly weary. Twenty-four hours ago I had jumped off a Greyhound at a cloverleaf and walked down a new road. Striding out happily through the warm morning rain. Avoiding people, avoiding involvement. No baggage, no hassle. Freedom. I didn't want it interrupted by Hubble, or by Finlay, or by some tall guy who got himself shot in his shaved head. I didn't want any part of it. I just wanted some peace and quiet and to go looking for Blind Blake. I wanted to find some eighty-year-old who might remember him from some bar. I should be talking to that old guy who swept up around the prison, not Hubble. Yuppie asshole.

He was thinking hard. I could see what Finlay had meant. I had never seen anybody think so visibly. His mouth was working soundlessly and he was fiddling with his fingers. Like he was checking off positives and negatives. Weighing things up. I

70

watched him. I saw him make his decision. He turned and looked over at me.

'I need some advice,' he said. 'I've got a problem.'

I laughed at him.

'Well, what a surprise,' I said. 'I'd never have guessed. I thought you were here because you were bored with playing golf on the weekend.'

'I need help,' he said.

'You've had all the help you're going to get,' I said. 'Without me, you'd be bent forward over your bed right now, with a line of big horny guys forming at the door. And so far you haven't exactly overwhelmed me with gratitude for that.'

He looked down for a moment. Nodded.

'I'm sorry,' he said. 'I'm very grateful. Believe me, I am. You saved my life. You took care of it. That's why you've got to tell me what to do. I'm being threatened.'

I let the revelation hang in the air for a moment.

'I know that,' I said. 'That's pretty obvious.'

'Well, not just me,' he said. 'My family as well.'

He was getting me involved. I looked at him. He started thinking again. His mouth was working. He was pulling on his fingers. Eyes flicking left and right. Like over here was a big pile of reasons, and over there was another big pile of reasons. Which pile was bigger?

'Have you got family?' he asked me.

'No,' I said. What else could I say? My parents were both dead. I had a brother somewhere who I never saw. So I had no family. No idea whether I wanted one, either. Maybe, maybe not.

'I've been married ten years,' Hubble said. 'Ten years last month. Had a big party. I've got two children. Boy, age nine, girl, age seven. Great wife, great kids. I love them like crazy.'

He meant it. I could see that. He lapsed into silence. Misting over as he thought about his family. Wondering how the hell he came to be in here without them. He wasn't the first guy to sit in this cell wondering that. And he wouldn't be the last.

'We've got a nice place,' he said. 'Out on Beckman Drive. Bought there five years ago. A lot of money, but it was worth it. You know Beckman?'

'No,' I said again. He was afraid to get to the point. Pretty soon he'd be telling me about the wallpaper in the downstairs half bath. And how he planned to pay for his daughter's orthodonture. I let him talk. Prison conversation.

'Anyway,' he said eventually. 'It's all falling apart now.'

He sat there in his chinos and his polo shirt. He had picked up his white sweater and wrapped it around his shoulders again. Without his glasses he looked older, more vacant. People who wear glasses, without them they always look unfocused, vulnerable. Out in the open. A layer removed. He looked like a tired old man. One leg was thrust forward. I could see the patterned sole of his shoe.

What did he call a threat? Some kind of exposure or embarrassment? Something that might blow away the perfect life he'd described on Beckman Drive? Maybe it was his wife who was involved in something. Maybe he was covering for her. Maybe she'd been having an affair with the tall dead guy. Maybe lots of things. Maybe anything. Maybe his family was threatened by disgrace, bankruptcy, stigma, cancellation of country club membership. I went around in circles. I didn't live in Hubble's world. I didn't share his frame of reference. I had seen him trembling and shaking with fear. But I had no idea how much it took to make a guy like that afraid. Or how little. When I first saw him at the station house yesterday he had looked upset and agitated. Since then he had been from time to time trembling, paralyzed, staring with fear. Sometimes resigned and apathetic. Clearly very afraid of something. I leaned on the cell wall and waited for him to tell me what.

'They're threatening us,' he said again. 'If I ever tell anybody what's going on, they said they'll break into our house. Round us all up. In my bedroom. They said they'll nail me to the wall and cut my balls off. Then they'll make my wife eat them. Then they'll cut our throats. They said they'll make our children watch and then they'll do things to them after we're dead that we'll never know about.'

SEVEN

'SO WHAT SHOULD I DO?' HUBBLE ASKED ME. 'WHAT WOULD you do?'

He was staring over at me. Waiting for a reply. What would I do? If somebody threatened me like that, they would die. I'd rip them apart. Either as they spoke, or days or months or years later. I would hunt them down and rip them apart. But Hubble couldn't do that. He had a family. Three hostages waiting to be taken. Three hostages already taken. Taken as soon as the threat was made.

'What should I do?' he asked me again.

I felt pressure. I had to say something. And my forehead hurt. It was bruising up after the massive impact with the Red Boy's face. I stepped to the bars and glanced down the row of cells. Leaned against the end of the bunk. Thought for a moment. Came up with the only possible answer. But not the answer Hubble wanted to hear.

'Nothing you can do,' I said. 'You've been told to keep your mouth shut, so you keep it shut. Don't tell anybody what's going on. Ever.'

He looked down at his feet. Dropped his head into his hands. Gave a moan of abject misery. Like he was crushed with disappointment.

'I've got to talk to somebody,' he said. 'I've got to get out of this. I mean it, I've got to get out. I've got to talk to somebody.'

I shook my head at him.

'You can't do that,' I said. 'They've told you to say nothing, so you say nothing. That way you stay alive. You and your family.'

He looked up. Shuddered.

'Something very big is going on,' he said. 'I've got to stop it if I can.'

I shook my head again. If something very big was going on around people who used threats like that, then he was never going to stop it. He was on board, and he was going to stay on board. I smiled a bleak smile at him and shook my head for the third time. He nodded like he understood. Like he finally accepted the situation. He went back to rocking and staring at the wall. His eyes were open. Red and naked without the gold rims. He sat silently for a long time.

I couldn't understand the confession. He should have kept his mouth shut. He should have denied any involvement with the dead guy. Should have said he had no idea why his phone number was written down in the guy's shoe. Should have said he had no idea what Pluribus was. Then he could have just gone home.

'Hubble?' I said. 'Why did you confess?'

He looked up. Waited a long moment before replying.

'I can't answer that,' he said. 'I'd be telling you more than I should.'

'I already know more than I should,' I said. 'Finlay asked about the dead guy and Pluribus and you flipped. So I know there's a link between you and the dead guy and whatever Pluribus is.'

He gazed at me. Looking vague.

'Is Finlay that black detective?' he said.

'Yes,' I said. 'Finlay. Chief of detectives.'

'He's new,' Hubble said. 'Never seen him before. It was always Gray. He was there years, since I was a kid. There's only one detective, you know, don't know why they say chief of detectives when there's only one. There's only eight people in the whole police department. Chief Morrison, he's been there years, then the desk man, four uniformed men, a woman, and the detective, Gray. Only now it's Finlay. The new man. Black guy, the first we've ever had. Gray killed himself, you know. Hung himself from a rafter in his garage. February, I think.'

I let him ramble on. Prison conversation. It passes the time. That's what it's for. Hubble was good at it. But I still wanted him to answer my question. My forehead hurt and I wanted to bathe it with cold water. I wanted to walk around for a while. I wanted to eat. I wanted coffee. I waited without listening as Hubble rambled through the municipal history of Margrave. Suddenly he stopped.

'What were you asking me?' he said.

'Why did you confess to killing the guy?' I repeated.

He looked around. Then he looked straight at me.

'There's a link,' he said. 'That's all it's safe to say right now. The detective mentioned the guy, and used the word "Pluribus", which made me jump. I was startled. I couldn't believe he knew the connection. Then I realized he hadn't known there was a connection, but I'd just told him by being startled. You see? I'd given it away. I felt I'd blown it. Given away the secret. And I mustn't do that, because of the threat.'

He tailed off and went quiet. An echo of the fright and panic he had felt in Finlay's office was back. He looked up again. Took a deep breath.

'I was terrified,' he said. 'But then the detective told me the guy was dead. He'd been shot. I got scared because if they had killed him, they might kill me, too. I can't really tell you why. But there's a link, like you worked out. If they got that particular guy, does that mean they are going to get me too? Or doesn't it? I had to think it out. I didn't even know for sure who had killed the guy. But then the detective told me about the violence. Did he tell you about that?'

I nodded.

'The injuries?' I said. 'Sounded pretty unpleasant.'

'Right,' Hubble said. 'And it proves it was who I thought it was. So I was really scared. I was thinking, are they looking for me too? Or aren't they? I just didn't know. I was terrified. I thought for ages. It was going around and around in my head. The detective was going crazy. I didn't say anything because I was thinking. Seemed like hours. I was terrified, you know?'

He fell back into silence. He was running it through his head again. Probably for the thousandth time. Trying to figure out if his decision had been the right one.

'I suddenly figured out what to do,' he said. 'I had three problems. If they were after me too, I had to avoid them. Hide, you know? To protect myself. But if they weren't after me, then I had to stay silent, right? To protect my wife and kids. And from their point of view that particular guy needed shooting. Three problems. So I confessed.'

I didn't follow his reasoning. Didn't make much sense, the way he was explaining it to me. I looked blankly at him.

'Three separate problems, right?' he said. 'I decided to get arrested. Then I was safe if they were after me. Because they can't get at me in here, right? They're out there and I'm in here. That's problem number one solved. But I also figured, this is the complicated bit, if they actually were not after me at all, then why don't I get arrested but don't say anything about them? They would think I had got arrested by mistake or whatever, and they see that I'm not talking. They see, OK? It proves I'm safe. It's like a demonstration that I'm dependable. A sort of proof. Trial by ordeal sort of a thing. That's problem number two solved. And by saying it was me actually killed the guy, it sort of definitely puts me on their side. It's like a statement of loyalty, right? And I thought they might be grateful I'd pointed the heat in the wrong direction for a while. So that was problem number three solved.'

I stared at him. No wonder he had clammed up and thought like crazy for forty minutes when he was in with Finlay. Three birds with one stone. That's what he had been aiming for.

The part about proving he could be trusted not to spill his guts was OK. Whoever they were, they would notice that. A spell in jail without talking was a rite of passage. A badge of honour. Counted for a lot. Good thinking, Hubble.

Unfortunately the other part was pretty shaky. They couldn't get to him in here? He had to be joking. No better place in the world to ace a guy than prison. You know where he is, you've got all the time you need. Lots of people who'll do it for you. Lots of opportunity. Cheap, too. On the street, a hit would cost you what? A grand, two grand? Plus a risk. Inside, it costs you a carton of cigarettes. Plus no risk. Because nobody would notice. No, prison was not a safe hiding place. Bad thinking, Hubble. And there was another flaw, too.

'What are you going to do on Monday?' I asked him. 'You'll be back home, doing whatever you do. You'll be walking around Margrave or Atlanta or wherever it is you walk around. If they're after you, won't they get you then?'

He started up with the thinking again. Going at it like crazy. He hadn't thought very far ahead before. Yesterday afternoon it had been blind panic. Deal with the present. Not a bad principle. Except pretty soon the future rolls in and that needs dealing with, too.

'I'm just hoping for the best,' Hubble said. 'I sort of felt if they wanted to get me, they might cool off after a while. I'm very useful to them. I hope they'll think about that. Right now it's a very tense situation. But it's all going to calm back down very soon. I might just make it through. If they get me, they get me. I don't care any more. It's my family I'm worried about.'

He stopped and shrugged. Blew a sigh. Not a bad guy. He hadn't set out to be some big criminal. It had crept up on the blind side. Sucked him in so gently he hadn't noticed. Until he wanted out. If he was very lucky they wouldn't break all his bones until after he was dead.

'How much does your wife know?' I asked him.

He glanced over. An expression of horror on his face.

'Nothing,' he said. 'Nothing at all. I haven't told her anything. Not a thing. I couldn't. It's all my secret. Nobody else knows a thing.'

'You'll have to tell her something,' I said. 'She's sure to have noticed you're not at home, vacuuming the pool or whatever you do on the weekend.'

I was just trying to lighten it up, but it didn't work out. Hubble went quiet. Misting over again at the thought of his backyard in the early fall sunlight. His wife maybe fussing over rose bushes or whatever. His kids darting about shrieking. Maybe they had a dog. And a three-car garage with European sedans waiting to be hosed off. A basketball hoop over the middle door waiting for the nine-year-old to grow strong enough to dunk the heavy ball. A flag over the porch. Early leaves waiting to be swept. Family life on a Saturday. But not this Saturday. Not for this guy.

'Maybe she'll think it's all a mistake,' he said. 'Maybe they've told her, I don't know. We know one of the policemen, Dwight Stevenson. My brother married his wife's sister. I don't know what he'll have said to her. I guess I'll deal with that on Monday. I'll say it was some kind of terrible mistake. She'll believe it. Everybody knows mistakes are made.'

He was thinking out loud.

'Hubble?' I said. 'What did the tall guy do to them that was liable to get himself shot in the head?'

He stood up and leaned on the wall. Rested his foot on the edge of the steel toilet pan. Looked at me. Wouldn't answer. Now for the big question.

'What about you?' I asked him. 'What have you done to them liable to get yourself shot in the head?'

He wouldn't answer. The silence in our cell was terrible. I let it crash around for a while. Couldn't think of anything more to say.

Hubble clunked his shoe against the metal toilet pan. A rattly little rhythm. Sounded like a Bo Diddley riff.

'You ever heard of Blind Blake?' I asked him.

He stopped clunking and looked up.

'Who?' he said blankly.

'Doesn't matter,' I said. 'I'm going to find a bathroom. I need to put a wet towel on my head. It hurts.'

'I'm not surprised,' he said. 'I'll come with you.'

He was anxious not to be left alone. Understandable. I was going to be his minder for the weekend. Not that I had any other plans.

We walked down the cell row to a kind of open area at the end. I saw the fire door Spivey had used the night before. Beyond it was a tiled opening. Over the opening was a clock. Nearly twelve noon. Clocks in prisons are bizarre. Why measure hours and minutes when people think in years and decades?

The tiled entrance was clogged with men. I pushed through and Hubble followed. It was a large tiled room, square. A strong disinfectant stink. One wall had the doorway. On the left was a row of shower stalls. Open. The back wall was a row of toilet cubicles. Open at the front, divided by waist-high partitions. The right wall was a row of washbasins. Very communal. Not a big deal if you'd been in the army all your life, but Hubble wasn't happy. Not what he was used to at all.

All the fittings were steel. Everything that would normally be porcelain was stainless steel. For safety. A smashed-up porcelain washbasin yields some pretty good shards. A decent-sized sharp piece would make a good weapon. For the same reason the mirrors over the basins were sheets of polished steel. A bit dull, but fit for the purpose. You could see yourself in them, but you couldn't smash them up and stab somebody with a fragment.

I stepped over to a basin and ran cold water. Took a wad of paper towels from the dispenser and soaked them. Held them to my bruised forehead. Hubble stood around doing nothing. I kept the cold towels on for a while and then took some more. Water ran down my face. Felt good. There was no real injury. No flesh there, just skin over solid bone. Not much to injure, and impossible to break. A perfect arch, nature's strongest structure. That's why I avoid hitting anything with my hands. Hands are pretty fragile. All kinds of small bones and tendons in there. A punch big enough to deck that Red Boy would have smashed my hand up pretty good.

I'd have joined him in the hospital. Not much point in that.

I patted my face dry and leaned up close to the steel mirror to check out the damage. Not bad. I combed my hair with my fingers. As I leaned against the sink I could feel the sunglasses in my pocket. The Red Boy's shades. The spoils of victory. I took them out and put them on. Gazed at my dull reflection.

As I messed about in front of the steel mirror I saw the start of some kind of a commotion happening behind me. I heard a brief warning from Hubble and I turned around. The sunglasses dimmed the bright light. Five white guys were trawling across the room. Biker types. Orange suits, of course, more torn-off sleeves, but with black leather additions. Caps, belts, fingerless gloves. Big beards. All five were big, heavy men, with that hard, slabby fat which is almost muscle but not quite. All five had crude tattoos on their arms and their faces. Swastikas. On their cheeks under their eyes and on their foreheads. The Aryan Brotherhood. White trash prison gang.

As the five swept the room, the other occupants melted away. Any who didn't get the message were seized and hustled to the door. Thrown out into the corridor. Even the soapy naked guys from the shower stalls. Within seconds the big bathroom was empty. Except for the five bikers and Hubble and me. The five big men fanned out in a loose arc around us. These were big ugly guys. The swastika tattoos on their faces were scratched in. Roughly inked.

My assumption was they'd come to recruit me. Somehow hijack the fact that I'd knocked over a Red Boy. Claim my bizarre celebrity for their cause. Turn it into a race triumph for the Brotherhood. But I was wrong. My assumption was way out. So I was left unprepared. The guy in the middle of the five was looking back and forth between Hubble and me. His eyes flicked across. They stopped on me.

'OK, he's the one,' he said. Looking straight at me.

Two things happened. The end two bikers grabbed Hubble and ran him to the door. And the boss man swung a big fist at my face. I saw it late. Dodged left and it caught me on the shoulder. I was spun around by the blow. Grabbed from behind by the neck. Two huge hands at my throat. Strangling me. The boss man lined up for another shot at my gut. If it landed, I was a dead man. I knew that much. So I leaned back and kicked out. Smashed the boss man's balls like I was trying to punt a football right out of the stadium. The big Oxford shoe crunched him real good. The welt hit him like a blunt axe.

My shoulders were hunched and I was pumping up my neck to resist the strangler. He was wrenching hard. I was losing it. I reached up and broke his little fingers. I heard the knuckles splinter over the roaring in my ears. Then I broke his ring fingers. More splintering. Like pulling a chicken apart. He let go.

The third guy waded in. He was a solid mountain of lard. Sheathed with heavy slabs of meat. Like armour. Nowhere to hit him. He was pounding me with short jabs to the arm and chest. I was jammed back between two sinks. The mountain of lard pressing up. Nowhere to hit him. Except his eyes. I jammed my thumb into his eye. Hooked the tips of my fingers in his ear and squeezed. My thumbnail popped his eyeball sideways. I pushed my thumb in. His eyeball was nearly out. He was screaming and pulling on my wrist. I held on.

The boss man was up on one knee. I kicked hard at his face. Missed. Caught him in the throat instead. Smashed his voicebox. He went back down. I went for the big guy's other eye. Missed. I held on with my thumb. Like pushing it through a bloody steak. He went down. I spun away from the wall. The guy with the broken fingers ran for the door. The guy with the eye out was flopping about on the floor. Screaming. The boss man was choking on his smashed voicebox.

I was grabbed from behind again. I twisted away. A Red Boy. Two of them. I was dizzy. I was going to lose it now. But they just grabbed me and ran me to the door. Sirens were going off.

'Get out of here, man,' screamed the Red Boys over the sirens. 'This is ours. We did this. Understand? Red Boys did this. We'll take the fall, man.'

They hurled me into the crowd outside. I understood. They were going to say they did it. Not because they wanted to protect me from the blame. Because they wanted to claim the credit. A race victory.

I saw Hubble bouncing around in the crowd. I saw guards. I saw hundreds of men. I saw Spivey. I grabbed Hubble and we hustled back to the cell. Sirens were blasting. Guards were tumbling out of a door. I could see shotguns and clubs. Boots clattered. Shouting and screaming. Sirens. We raced to the cell. Fell inside. I was dizzy and panting. I had taken a battering. The sirens were deafening. Couldn't talk. I splashed water on my face. The sunglasses were gone. Must have fallen off.

I heard screaming at the door. I turned and saw Spivey. He was screaming at us to get out. He rushed into the cell. I grabbed my coat from the bunk. Spivey seized Hubble by the elbow. Then he grabbed me and straight-armed both of us out of there. He was screaming at us to run. Sirens were blasting. He ran us to the emergency door where the guards had rushed out. Shoved us through and ran us up stairs. Up and up. My lungs were giving out. There was a door at the top of the last flight painted with a big figure six. We crashed through. He hustled us down a row of cells. Shoved us into an empty cell and flung the iron gate shut. It crashed and locked. He ran off. I collapsed on the bed, eyes tight shut.

When I opened them again Hubble was sitting on a bed looking over at me. We were in a big cell. Probably twice as wide as the last one. Two separate beds, one on each side. A sink, a john. A wall of bars. Everything was brighter and cleaner. It was very quiet. The air smelled better. This was the holding floor. This was floor six. This was where we should have been all the time.

'What the hell happened to you in there?' Hubble asked.

I just shrugged at him. A meal cart appeared outside our cell. It was dragged by an old white guy. Not a guard, some kind of an orderly. Looked more like an old steward on an ocean liner. He passed a tray through an oblong slot in the bars. Covered plates, paper cups, thermos. We ate the food sitting on our beds. I drank all the coffee. Then I paced the cell. Shook the gate. It was locked. The sixth floor was calm and quiet. A big clean cell. Separate beds. A mirror. Towels. I felt much better up here.

Hubble piled the meal debris on the tray and shoved it out under the gate into the corridor. He lay down on his bed. Put his hands behind his head. Stared at the ceiling. Doing time. I did the same. But I was thinking hard. Because they had definitely gone through a selection process. They had looked us both over very carefully and chosen me. Quite definitely chosen me. Then they had tried to strangle me.

They would have killed me. Except for one thing. The guy with his hands around my throat had made a mistake. He had me from behind, which was in his favour, and he was big enough and strong enough. But he hadn't balled up his fingers. The best way is to use the thumbs on the back of the neck but fold up the fingers. Do it with knuckle pressure, not finger pressure. The guy had left his fingers out straight. So I had been able to reach up and snap them off. His mistake had saved my life. No doubt about that.

Soon as he was neutralized, it was two against one. And I'd never had a problem with those kind of odds.

But it was still a straightforward attempt to kill me. They came in, chose me, tried to kill me. And Spivey had just happened to be outside the bathroom. He had set it up. He had employed the Aryan Brotherhood to kill me. He had ordered the attack and waited ready to burst in and find me dead.

And he had planned it yesterday before ten in the evening. That was clear. That's why he had left us on the wrong floor. On the third, not the sixth. On a convict floor, not the holding floor. Everybody had known we should have been on the holding floor. The two guards last night in the reception bunker, they had been totally clear about it. It had said so on their battered clipboard. But at ten o'clock, Spivey had left us on the third floor where he knew he could have me killed. He'd told the Aryans to attack me at twelve o'clock the next day. He had been waiting outside that bathroom at twelve o'clock ready to burst in. Ready to see my body lying on the tiles.

But then his plan had fouled up. I wasn't killed. The Aryans were beaten off. The Red Boys had piled in to seize the moment. Mayhem had broken out. A riot was starting. Spivey was panicking. He hit the alarms and called the crash squads. Rushed us off the floor, up to the sixth, and left us up here. According to all the paperwork, the sixth floor is where we'd been all the time.

A neat fallback. It made me fireproof as far as investigation went. Spivey had chosen the fallback option which said we were never there. He had a couple of serious injuries on his hands, probably even a dead guy. I figured the boss man must have choked to death. Spivey must know I had done it. But he could never say so now. Because according to him, I was never there.

I lay on the bed and stared at the concrete ceiling. I exhaled gently. The plan was clear. No doubt about Spivey's plan at all. The fallback was coherent. An aborted plan with a neat fallback position. But why? I didn't understand it. Let's say the strangler had balled up his fingers. They would have got me then. I would have been dead. Dumped on the bathroom floor with my big swollen tongue sticking out. Spivey would have rushed in and found me. Why? What was Spivey's angle? What did he have against me? I'd never seen him before. Never been anywhere near him or his damn prison. Why the hell should he operate an elaborate plan to get me dead? I couldn't begin to figure it out.

EIGHT

HUBBLE SLEPT FOR A WHILE ON THE COT ACROSS FROM MINE. Then he stirred and woke up. Writhed around. Looked disoriented for a moment, until he remembered where he was. Tried to check the time on his watch but saw only a band of pale skin where the heavy Rolex had been. Pushed against the bridge of his nose and remembered he'd lost his eyeglasses. Sighed and flopped his head back onto the striped prison pillow. One very miserable guy.

I could understand his fear. But he also looked defeated. Like he'd just rolled the dice and lost. Like he'd been counting on something to happen, and it hadn't happened, so now he was back in despair.

Then I began to understand that, too.

'The dead guy was trying to help you, wasn't he?' I said.

The question scared him.

'I can't tell you that, can I?' he answered.

'I need to know,' I said. 'Maybe you approached the guy for help. Maybe you talked to him. Maybe that's why he got killed. Maybe it looks like now you'll start talking to me. Which could get me killed, too.'

Hubble nodded and rocked back and forth on his bed. Took a deep breath. Looked straight at me.

'He was an investigator,' he said. 'I brought him down here because I want this whole thing stopped. I don't want to be involved any more. I'm not a criminal. I'm scared to death and I want out. He was going to get me out and take down the scam. But he slipped up somehow and now he's dead and I'm never going to get out. And if they find out it was me brought him down here, they'll kill me. And if they don't kill me, I'll probably go to jail for a thousand years anyway, because right now the whole damn thing is very exposed and very dangerous.'

'Who was the guy?' I asked him.

'He didn't have a name,' Hubble said. 'Just a contact code. He said it was safer that way. I can't believe they got him. He seemed like a capable guy to me. Tell the truth, you remind me of him. You seem like a capable guy to me, too.'

'What was he doing up there at the warehouse?' I asked him.

He shrugged and shook his head.

'I don't understand that situation,' he said. 'I put him together with another guy, and he was meeting with him up there, but wouldn't they have shot the other guy as well? I don't understand why they only got one of them.'

'Who was the other guy he was meeting with?' I said.

He stopped and shook his head.

'I've told you way too much already,' he said. 'I must be crazy. They'll kill me.'

'Who's on the inside of this thing?' I asked him.

'Don't you listen?' he said. 'I'm not saying another word.'

'I don't want names,' I said. 'Is it a big deal?'

'It's huge,' he said. 'Biggest thing you ever heard of.'

'How many people?' I said.

He shrugged and thought about it. Counted up in his head.

'Ten people,' he said. 'Not counting me.'

I looked at him and shrugged.

'Ten people doesn't sound like a big deal,' I said.

'Well, there's hired help,' he said. 'They're around when they're needed. I mean a core of ten people around here. Ten people in the know, not counting me. It's a very tight situation, but believe me, it's a big deal.'

'What about the guy you sent to meet with the investigator?' I said. 'Is he one of the ten people?'

Hubble shook his head.

'I'm not counting him either,' he said.

'So there's you and him and ten others?' I said. 'Some kind of a big deal?'

He nodded glumly.

'Biggest thing you ever heard of,' he said again.

'And right now it's very exposed?' I asked him. 'Why? Because of this investigator poking about?'

Hubble shook his head again. He was writhing around like my questions were tearing him up.

'No,' he said. 'For another reason altogether. It's like a window of vulnerability is wide open right now. An exposure. It's been very risky, getting worse all the time. But now it could go either way. If we get through it, nobody will ever know anything. But if we don't get through it, it'll be the biggest sensation you ever heard of, believe me. Either way, it's going to be a close call.'

I looked at him. He didn't look to me much like the sort of a guy who could cause the biggest sensation I ever heard of.

'So how long is this exposure going to last?' I asked him.

'It's nearly over,' he said. 'Maybe a week. A week tomorrow is my guess. Next Sunday. Maybe I'll live to see it.'

'So after next Sunday you're not vulnerable any more?' I said. 'Why not? What's going to happen next Sunday?'

He shook his head and turned his face away. It was like if he couldn't see me, I wasn't there, asking him questions.

'What does Pluribus mean?' I asked him.

He wouldn't answer. Just kept on shaking his head. His eyes were screwed shut with terror.

'Is it a code for something?' I said.

He wasn't hearing me. The conversation was over. I gave it up and we lapsed back into silence. That suited me well enough. I didn't want to know anything more. I didn't want to know anything at all. Being an outsider and knowing Hubble's business didn't seem to be a very smart combination. It hadn't done the tall guy with the shaved head a whole lot of good. I wasn't interested in sharing the same fate as him, dead at a warehouse gate, partially hidden under some old cardboard, two holes in my head, all my bones smashed. I just wanted to pass the time until Monday, and then get the hell out. By next Sunday, I planned to be a very long way away indeed.

'OK, Hubble,' I said. 'No more questions.'

He shrugged and nodded. Sat silent for a long time. Then he spoke, quietly, with a lot of resignation in his voice.

'Thanks,' he said. 'It's better that way.'

I was rolled over on the narrow cot trying to float away into some kind of limbo. But Hubble was restless. He was tossing and turning and blowing tight sighs. He was coming close to irritating me again. I turned to face him.

'I'm sorry,' he said. 'I'm very uptight. It was doing me good just to talk to somebody. I'd go crazy in here on my own. Can't we talk about something else? What about you? Tell me about yourself. Who are you, Reacher?'

I shrugged at him.

'I'm nobody,' I said. 'Just a guy passing through. I'll be gone on Monday.'

'Nobody's nobody,' he said. 'We've all got a story. Tell me.'

So I talked for a while, lying on my bed, running through the last six months. He lay on his bed, looking at the concrete ceiling, listening, keeping his mind off his problems. I told him about leaving from the Pentagon. Washington, Baltimore, Philadelphia, New York, Boston, Pittsburgh, Detroit, Chicago. Museums, music, cheap hotels, bars, buses and trains. Solitude. Travelling through the land of my citizenship like a cheap tourist. Seeing most things for the first time. Looking at the history I'd learned in dusty schoolrooms half a world away. Looking at the big things that had shaped the nation. Battlefields, factories, declarations, revolutions. Looking for the small things. Birthplaces, clubs, roads, legends. The big things and the small things which were supposed to represent home. I'd found some of them.

I told Hubble about the long hop through the endless plains and deltas all the way down from Chicago to New Orleans. Sliding around the Gulf Coast as far as Tampa. Then the Greyhound blasting north toward Atlanta. The crazy decision to bail out near Margrave. The long walk in the rain yesterday morning. Following a whim. Following some half-remembered note from my brother saying he'd been through some little place where Blind Blake might have died over sixty years ago. As I told him about it, I felt pretty stupid. Hubble was scuffling with a nightmare and I was following a meaningless pilgrimage. But he understood the urge.

'I did that once,' he said. 'On our honeymoon. We went to Europe. We stopped off in New York and I spent half a day looking for the Dakota building, you know, where John Lennon was shot. Then we spent three days in England walking around Liverpool, looking for the Cavern Club. Where the Beatles started out. Couldn't find it, I guess they knocked it down.'

He talked on for a while. Mostly about travelling. He'd taken plenty of trips with his wife. They'd enjoyed it. Been all over,

Europe, Mexico, the Caribbean. All over the States and Canada. Had a great time together.

'Don't you get lonely?' he asked me. 'Travelling on your own all the time?'

I told him no, I enjoyed it. I told him I appreciated the solitude, the anonymity. Like I was invisible.

'How do you mean, invisible?' he said. He seemed interested.

'I travel by road,' I said. 'Always by road. Walk a bit, and ride the buses. Sometimes trains. Always pay cash. That way there's never a paper trail. No credit card transactions, no passenger manifests, nothing. Nobody could trace me. I never tell anybody my name. If I stay in a hotel, I pay cash and give them a made-up name.'

'Why?' he said. 'Who the hell's after you?'

'Nobody,' I said. 'It's just a bit of fun. I like anonymity. I feel like I'm beating the system. And right now, I'm truly pissed at the system.'

I saw him fall back to thinking. He thought a long time. I could see him deflate as he struggled with the problems that wouldn't go away. I could see his panic come and go like a tide.

'So give me your advice about Finlay,' he said. 'When he asks me about the confession, I'll say I was stressed out because of some business situation. I'll say there was some kind of rivalry, threats against my family. I'll say I don't know anything about the dead guy or anything about the phone number. I'll deny everything. Then I'll just try to settle everything down. What do you think?'

I thought it sounded like a pretty thin plan.

'Tell me one thing,' I said. 'Without giving me any more details, do you perform a useful function for them? Or are you just some kind of onlooker?'

He pulled on his fingers and thought for a moment.

'Yes, I perform a useful function for them,' he said. 'Crucial, even.'

'And if you weren't there to do it?' I asked him. 'Would they have to recruit someone else?'

'Yes, they would,' he said. 'And it would be moderately difficult to do that, given the parameters of the function.'

He was rating his chances of staying alive like he would rate a credit application up at his office.

'OK,' I said. 'Your plan is as good as you're going to get. Go for it.'

I didn't see what else he could do. He was a small cog in some kind of a big operation. But a crucial cog. And nobody wrecks a big operation for no reason. So his future was actually clear-cut. If they ever figured it was him who had brought in the outside investigator, then he was definitely dead. But if they never found that out, then he was definitely safe. Simple as that. I figured he had a good enough chance, because of one very persuasive fact.

He had confessed because he had thought prison was some kind of a safe sanctuary where they couldn't get him. That had been part of his thinking behind it. It was bad thinking. He'd been wrong. He wasn't safe from attack, quite the reverse. They could have got him if they had wanted to. But the other side of that particular coin was that he hadn't been attacked. As it happened, I had been. Not Hubble. So I figured there was some kind of a proof there that he was OK. They weren't out to get him, because if they had wanted to kill him, they could have killed him by now, and they would have killed him by now. But they hadn't. Even though they were apparently very uptight right now because of some kind of a temporary risk. So it seemed like proof. I began to think he would be OK.

'Yes, Hubble,' I said again. 'Go for it, it's the best you can do.'

The cell stayed locked all day. The floor was silent. We lay on our beds and drifted through the rest of the afternoon. No more talking. We were all talked out. I was bored and wished I had brought that newspaper with me from the Margrave station house. I could have read it all over again. All about the President cutting crime prevention so he could get re-elected. Saving a buck on the Coast Guard today so he could spend ten bucks on prisons like this one tomorrow.

At about seven the old orderly came by with dinner. We ate. He came back and picked up the tray. We drifted through the empty evening. At ten the power banged off and we were in darkness. Nightfall. I kept my shoes on and slept lightly. Just in case Spivey had any more plans for me.

At seven in the morning the lights came back on. Sunday. I woke up tired, but I forced myself to get up. Forced myself to do a bit of stretching to ease off my sore body. Hubble was awake, but silent. He was vaguely watching me exercise. Still drifting. Breakfast arrived before eight. The same old guy dragging the meal cart. I ate the breakfast and drank the coffee. As I finished up the flask, the gate lock clunked and sprang the door. I pushed it open and stepped out and bumped into a guard aiming to come in.

'It's your lucky day,' the guard said. 'You're getting out.'

'I am?' I said.

'You both are,' he said. 'Reacher and Hubble, released by order of the Margrave PD. Be ready in five minutes, OK?'

I stepped back into the cell. Hubble had hauled himself up onto his elbows. He hadn't eaten his breakfast. He looked more worried than ever.

'I'm scared,' he said.

'You'll be OK,' I said.

'Will I?' he said. 'Once I'm out of here, they can get to me.'

I shook my head.

'It would have been easier for them to get you in here,' I said. 'Believe me, if they were looking to kill you, you'd be dead by now. You're in the clear, Hubble.'

He nodded to himself and sat up. I picked up my coat and we stood together outside the cell, waiting. The guard was back within five minutes. He walked us along a corridor and through two sets of locked gates. Put us in a back elevator. Stepped in and used his key to send it down. Stepped out again as the doors began to close.

'So long,' he said. 'Don't come back.'

The elevator took us down to a lobby and then we stepped outside into a hot concrete yard. The prison door sucked shut and clicked behind us. I stood face up to the sun and breathed in the outside air. I must have looked like some guy in a corny old movie who gets released from a year in solitary.

There were two cars parked in the yard. One was a big dark sedan, an English Bentley, maybe twenty years old, but it looked brand-new. There was a blonde woman in it, who I guessed was Hubble's wife, because he was on his way over to her like she was the sweetest sight he ever saw. The other car had Officer Roscoe in it.

She got out and walked straight over to me. Looked wonderful. Out of uniform. Dressed in jeans and a soft cotton shirt. Leather jacket. Calm intelligent face. Soft dark hair. Huge eyes. I'd thought she was nice on Friday. I'd been right.

'Hello, Roscoe,' I said.

'Hello, Reacher,' she said, and smiled.

Her voice was wonderful. Her smile was great. I watched it for as long as it lasted, which was a good long time. Ahead of us, the Hubbles drove off in the Bentley, waving. I waved back and wondered how things would turn out for them. Probably I would never know, unless they got unlucky and I happened to read about it in a newspaper somewhere.

Roscoe and I got into her car. Not really hers, she explained, just a department unmarked she was using. A brand-new Chevrolet something, big, smooth and quiet. She'd kept the motor running and the air on and inside it was cool. We wafted out of the concrete yard and shunted through the wire vehicle cages. Outside the last cage Roscoe spun the wheel and we blasted away down the road. The nose of the car rose up and the back end squatted down on the soft suspension. I didn't look back. I just sat there, feeling good. Getting out of prison is one of life's good feelings. So is not knowing what tomorrow holds. So is cruising silently down a sunny road with a pretty woman at the wheel.

'So what happened?' I said after a mile. 'Tell me.'

She told me a pretty straightforward story. They'd started work on my alibi late Friday evening. She and Finlay. A dark squad room. A couple of desk lights on. Pads of paper. Cups of coffee. Telephone books. The two of them cradling phones and chewing pencils. Low voices. Patient enquiries. A scene I'd been in myself a thousand times.

They'd called Tampa and Atlanta and by midnight they'd gotten hold of a passenger from my bus and the ticket clerk at the Tampa depot. Both of them remembered me. Then they got the bus driver as well. He confirmed he'd stopped at the Margrave cloverleaf to let me out, eight o'clock Friday morning. By midnight my alibi was looking rock-solid, just like I'd said it would be.

Saturday morning, a long fax was in from the Pentagon about my service record. Thirteen years of my life, reduced to a few curling fax pages. It felt like somebody else's life now, but it backed my story. Finlay had been impressed by it. Then my prints came back from the FBI database. They'd been matched by the tireless computer at two-thirty in the morning. US Army, printed on induction, thirteen years ago. My alibi was solid, and my background checked out.

'Finlay was satisfied,' Roscoe told me. 'You are who you say you are, and midnight Thursday you were over four hundred miles away. That was nailed down. He called the medical examiner again just in case he had a new opinion on the time of death, but no, midnight was still about right.'

I shook my head. Finlay was one very cautious guy.

'What about the dead guy?' I said. 'Did you run his prints again?'

She concentrated on passing a farm truck. The first vehicle we'd seen in a quarter-hour. Then she looked across and nodded.

'Finlay told me you wanted me to,' she said. 'But why?'

'They came back too quickly for a negative result,' I said.

'Too quickly?' she said.

'You told me there was a pyramid system, right?' I said. 'The top ten, then the top hundred, then the top thousand, all the way down, right?'

She nodded again.

'So take me as an example,' I said. 'I'm in the database, but I'm pretty low down the pyramid. You just said it took fourteen hours to get down to me, right?'

'Right,' she said. 'I sent your prints in about twelve-thirty at lunchtime and they were matched at two-thirty in the morning.'

'OK,' I said. 'Fourteen hours. So if it takes fourteen hours to reach nearly to the bottom of the pyramid, it's got to take more than fourteen hours to get all the way down to the bottom. That's logical, right?'

'Right,' she said.

'But what happened with this dead guy?' I said. 'The body was found at eight o'clock, so the prints went in when? Eight-thirty, earliest. But Baker was already telling me there was no match on file when they were talking to me at two-thirty. I remember the time, because I was looking at the clock. That's only six hours. If it took fourteen hours to find out that I'm in there, how could it take just six hours to say the dead guy's not in there?'

'God,' she said. 'You're right. Baker must have screwed up. Finlay took the prints and Baker sent them. He must have screwed up the scan. You got to be careful, or it doesn't transmit clearly. If the scan's not clear, the database tries to decipher it, then it comes back as unreadable. Baker must have thought that meant a null result. The codes are similar. Anyway, I sent them again, first thing. We'll know soon enough.'

We drove on east and Roscoe told me she'd pushed Finlay to get me out of Warburton right away yesterday afternoon. Finlay had grunted and agreed, but there was a problem. They'd had to wait until today, because yesterday afternoon Warburton had been just about shut down. They had told Finlay there had been some trouble in a bathroom. One convict was dead, one had lost an eye, and a full-scale riot had started, black and white gangs at war.

I just sat there next to Roscoe and watched the horizon reeling in. I'd killed one guy and blinded another. Now I'd have to confront my feelings. But I didn't feel much at all. Nothing, in fact. No guilt, no remorse. None at all. I felt like I'd chased two roaches around that bathroom and stomped on them. But at least a roach is a rational, reasonable, evolved sort of a creature. Those Aryans in that bathroom had been worse than vermin. I'd kicked one of them in the throat and he had suffocated on his smashed larynx. Well, tough shit. He started it, right? Attacking me was like pushing open a forbidden door. What waited on the other side was his problem. His risk. If he didn't like it, he shouldn't have pushed open the damn door. I shrugged and forgot about it. Looked over at Roscoe.

'Thank you,' I said. 'I mean it. You worked hard to help me out.'

She waved away my thanks with a blush and a small gesture and just drove on. I was starting to like her a lot. But probably not enough to stop me getting the hell out of Georgia as soon as I could. Maybe I might just stay an hour or two and then get her to drive me to a bus depot somewhere.

'I want to take you to lunch,' I said. 'Kind of a thank-you thing.'

She thought about it for a quarter-mile and then smiled across at me.

'OK,' she said.

She jinked the right turn onto the county road and accelerated south towards Margrave. Drove past Eno's shiny new place and headed down to town.

NINE

I GOT HER TO DUCK IN AT THE STATION HOUSE AND BRING ME OUT the property bag with my money in it. Then we drove on and she dropped me in the centre of Margrave and I arranged to meet her up at the station house in a couple of hours. I stood on the sidewalk in the fierce Sunday morning heat and waved her off. I felt a whole lot better. I was back in motion. I was going to check out the Blind Blake story, then take Roscoe to lunch, then get the hell out of Georgia and never come back.

So I spent a while wandering around looking at the town, doing the things I should have been doing on Friday afternoon. There wasn't really much to the place. The old county road ran straight through, north to south, and for about four blocks it was labelled Main Street. Those four blocks had small stores and offices facing each other across the width of the road, separated by little service alleys which ran round to the back of the buildings. I saw a small grocery, a barbershop, an outfitters, a doctor's office, a lawyer's office and a dentist's office. In back of the commercial buildings was parkland with white picket fences and ornamental trees. On the street, the stores and offices had awnings over wide sidewalks. There were benches set on the sidewalks, but they were empty. The whole place was deserted. Sunday morning, miles from anywhere.

Main Street ran north, straight as a die, past a few hundred yards of more parkland up to the station house and the fire house, and a half-mile farther on than that was Eno's diner. A few miles beyond Eno's was the turn west out to Warburton where the prison was. North of that junction there was nothing on the county road until you reached the warehouses and the highway cloverleaf, fourteen empty miles from where I stood.

On the south edge of town I could see a little village green with a bronze statue and a residential street running away to the west. I strolled down there and saw a discreet green sign which read: Beckman Drive. Hubble's street. I couldn't see any real distance down it because pretty much straight away it looped left and right around a wide grass square with a big white wooden church set on it. The church was ringed by cherry trees and the lawn was circled by cars with clean quiet paint parked in neat lines. I could just about make out the growl of the organ and the sound of the people singing.

The statue on the village green was of a guy called Caspar Teale who'd done something or other about a hundred years ago. More or less opposite Beckman Drive on the other side of the green was another residential street, running east, with a convenience store standing alone on the corner. And that was it. Not much of a town. Not much going on. Took me less than thirty minutes to look over everything the place had to offer.

But it was the most immaculate town I had ever seen. It was amazing. Every single building was either brand-new or recently refurbished. The roads were smooth as glass, and the sidewalks were flat and clean. No potholes, no cracks, no heave. The little offices and stores looked like they got repainted every week. The lawns and the plantings and the trees were clipped to perfection. The bronze statue of old Caspar Teale looked like somebody licked it clean every morning. The paint on the church was so bright it hurt my eyes. Flags flew everywhere, sparkling white and glowing red and blue in the sun. The whole place was so tidy it could make you nervous to walk around in case you left a dirty footprint somewhere.

The convenience store on the southeastern corner was selling the sort of stuff which gave it a good enough excuse to be open on a Sunday morning. Open, but not busy. There was nobody in there except the guy behind the register. But he had coffee. I sat up at the little counter and ordered a big mug and bought a Sunday newspaper.

The President was still on the front page. Now he was in

California. He was explaining to defence contractors why their gravy train was grinding to a halt after fifty glorious years. The aftershock from his Pensacola announcement about the Coast Guard was still rumbling on. Their boats were returning to their harbours on Saturday night. They wouldn't go out again without new funding. The paper's editorial guys were all stirred up about it.

I stopped reading and glanced up when I heard the door open. A woman came in. She took a stool at the opposite end of the counter. She was older than me, maybe forty. Dark hair, very slender, expensively dressed in black. She had very pale skin. So pale, it was almost luminous. She moved with a kind of nervous tension. I could see tendons like slim ropes in her wrists. I could see some kind of an appalling strain in her face. The counter guy slid over to her and she ordered coffee in a voice so quiet I could barely hear it, even though she was pretty close by and it was a silent room.

She didn't stay long. She got through half her coffee, watching the window all the time. Then a big black pickup truck pulled up outside and she shivered. It was a brand-new truck and obviously it had never hauled anything worth hauling. I caught a glimpse of the driver as he leaned over inside to spring the door. He was a tough-looking guy. Pretty tall. Broad shoulders and a thick neck. Black hair. Black hair all over long knotted arms. Maybe thirty years old. The pale woman slid off her stool like a ghost and stood up. Swallowed once. As she opened the shop door I heard the burble of a big motor idling. The woman got into the truck, but it didn't move away. Just sat there at the kerb. I swivelled on my stool to face the counter guy.

'Who is that?' I asked him.

The guy looked at me like I was from another planet.

'That's Mrs Kliner,' he said. 'You don't know the Kliners?'

'I heard about them,' I said. 'I'm a stranger in town. Kliner owns the warehouses up near the highway, right?'

'Right,' he said. 'And a whole lot more besides. Big deal round here, Mr Kliner.'

'He is?' I said.

'Sure,' the guy said. 'You heard about the Foundation?'

I shook my head. Finished my coffee and pushed the mug over for a refill.

'Kliner set up the Kliner Foundation,' the guy said. 'Benefits the town in a lot of ways. Came here five years ago, been like Christmas ever since.'

I nodded.

'Is Mrs Kliner OK?' I asked him.

He shook his head as he filled my mug.

'She's a sick woman,' he said. 'Very sick. Very pale, right? Sort of wan? A very sick woman. Could be tuberculosis. I seen tuberculosis do that to folks. She used to be a fine-looking woman, but now she looks like something grown in a closet, right? A very sick woman, that's for damn sure.'

'Who's the guy in the truck?' I said.

'Stepson,' he said. 'Kliner's kid by his first wife. Mrs Kliner's his second. I've heard she don't get along so good with the kid.'

He gave me the sort of nod that terminates casual conversations. Moved away to wipe off some kind of a chromium machine behind the other end of the counter. The black pickup was still waiting outside. I agreed with the guy that the woman looked like something grown in a closet. She looked like some kind of a rare orchid starved of light and sustenance. But I didn't agree with him that she looked sick. I didn't think she had tuberculosis. I thought she was suffering from something else. Something I'd seen once or twice before. I thought she was suffering from sheer terror. Terror of what, I didn't know. Terror of what, I didn't want to know. Not my problem. I stood up and dropped a five on the counter. The guy made change all in coins. He had no dollar bills. The pickup was still there, stationary at the kerb. The driver was leaning up, chest against the wheel, looking sideways across his stepmother, staring in straight at me.

There was a mirror opposite me behind the counter. I looked exactly like a guy who'd been on an all-night bus and then spent two days in jail. I figured I needed to get cleaned up before I took Roscoe to lunch. The counter guy saw me figuring.

'Try the barbershop,' he said.

'On a Sunday?' I said.

The guy shrugged.

'They're always in there,' he said. 'Never exactly closed. Never exactly open, either.'

I nodded and pushed out through the door. I saw a small crowd of people coming out of the church and chatting on the lawns and getting into their cars. The rest of the town was still deserted. But the black pickup was still at the kerb, right outside the convenience store. The driver was still staring at me.

I walked north in the sun and the pickup moved slowly alongside, keeping pace. The guy was still hunched forward, staring sideways. I stretched out a couple of steps and the truck sped up to keep station. Then I stopped dead and he overshot. I stood there. The guy evidently decided backing up wasn't on his agenda. He floored it and took off with a roar. I shrugged and carried on. Reached the barbershop. Ducked under the striped awning and tried the door. Unlocked. I went in.

Like everything else in Margrave, the barbershop looked wonderful. It gleamed with ancient chairs and fittings lovingly polished and maintained. It had the kind of barbershop gear everybody tore out thirty years ago. Now everybody wants it back. They pay a fortune for it because it recreates the way people want America to look. The way they think it used to look. It's certainly the way I thought it used to look. I would sit in some schoolyard in Manila or Munich and imagine green lawns and trees and flags and a gleaming chrome barbershop like this one.

It was run by two old black guys. They were just hanging out there. Not really open for business, not really closed. But they indicated they would serve me. Like they were there, and I was there, so why not? And I guess I looked like an urgent case. I asked them for the works. A shave, a haircut, a hot towel and a shoeshine. There were framed newspaper front pages here and there on the walls. Big headlines. Roosevelt dies, VJ Day, JFK assassinated, Martin Luther King murdered. There was an old mahogany table radio thumping warmly away. The new Sunday paper was crisply folded on a bench in the window.

The old guys mixed up soapy lather in a bowl, stropped a straight razor, rinsed a shaving brush. They shrouded me with towels and got to work. One guy shaved me with the old straight razor. The other guy stood around doing not much of anything. I figured maybe he came into play later. The busy guy started chatting away, like barbers do. Told me the history of his business. The two of them had been buddies since childhood. Always lived here in Margrave since way back. Started out as barbers way before World War Two. Apprenticed in Atlanta. Opened a shop together as young men. Moved it to this location when the old neighbourhood was razed. He told me the history of the county from a barber's perspective. Listed the personalities who'd been in and out of these old chairs. Told me about all kinds of people.

'So tell me about the Kliners,' I said.

He was a chatty guy, but that question shut him up. He stopped work and thought about it.

97

'Can't help you with that enquiry, that's for sure,' he said. 'That's a subject we prefer not to discuss in here. Best if you ask me about somebody else altogether.'

I shrugged under the shroud of towels.

'OK,' I said. 'You ever heard of Blind Blake?'

'Him I heard of, that's for sure,' the old man said. 'That's a guy we can discuss, no problem at all.'

'Great,' I said. 'So what can you tell me?'

'He was here, time to time, way back,' he said. 'Born in Jacksonville, Florida, they say, just over the state line. Used to kind of trek on up from there, you know, through here, through Atlanta, all the way up north to Chicago, and then trek all the way back down again. Back through Atlanta, back through here, back home. Very different then, you know. No highway, no automobiles, at least not for a poor black man and his friends. All walking or riding on the freight cars.'

'You ever hear him play?' I asked him.

He stopped work again and looked at me.

'Man, I'm seventy-four years old,' he said. 'This was back when I was just a little boy. We're talking about Blind Blake here. Guys like that played in bars. Never was in no bars when I was a little boy, you understand. I would have got my behind whupped real good if I had been. You should talk to my partner here. He's a whole lot older than I am. He may have heard him play, only he may not remember it because he don't remember much. Not even what he ate for breakfast. Am I right? Hey, my old friend, what you eat for breakfast?'

The other old guy creaked over and leaned up on the next sink to mine. He was a gnarled old fellow the colour of the mahogany radio.

'I don't know what I ate for breakfast,' he said. 'Don't even know if I ate any breakfast at all. But listen up. I may be an old guy, but the truth is old guys remember stuff real well. Not recent things, you understand, but old things. You got to imagine your memory is like an old bucket, you know? Once it's filled up with old stuff there ain't no way to get new stuff in. No way at all, you understand? So I don't remember any new stuff because my old bucket is all filled up with old stuff that happened way back. You understand what I'm saying here?'

'Sure I understand,' I said. 'So way back, did you ever hear him play?'

'Who?' he said.

I looked at both of them in turn. I wasn't sure whether this was some kind of a rehearsed routine.

'Blind Blake,' I said. 'Did you ever hear him play?'

'No, I never heard him play,' the old guy said. 'But my sister did. Got me a sister more than about ninety years old or thereabouts, may she be spared. Still alive. She did a little singing way back and she sang with old Blind Blake many a time.'

'She did?' I said. 'She sang with him?'

'She sure did,' said the gnarled old guy. 'She sang with just about anybody passing through. You got to remember this old town lay right on the big road to Atlanta. That old county road out there used to come on down through here straight on south into Florida. It was the only route through Georgia north to south. Of course now you got the highway runs right by without stopping off, and you got airplanes and all. No importance to Margrave now, nobody coming on through any more.'

'So Blind Blake stopped off here?' I prompted him. 'And your sister sang with him?'

'Everybody used to stop off here,' he said. 'North side of town was just pretty much a mess of bars and rooming houses to cater to the folks passing through. All these fancy gardens between here and the fire house is where the bars and rooming houses used to be. All tore down now, or else all fell down. Been no passing trade at all for a real long time. But back then, it was a different kind of a town altogether. Streams of people in and out, the whole time. Workers, crop pickers, drummers, fighters, hoboes, truckers, musicians. All kinds of those guys used to stop off and play and my old sister would be right in there singing with them all.'

'And she remembers Blind Blake?' I asked him.

'She sure does,' the old man said. 'Used to think he was the greatest thing alive. Says he used to play real sporty. Real sporty indeed.'

'What happened to him?' I said. 'Do you know?'

The old guy thought hard. Trawled back through his fading memories. He shook his grizzled head a couple of times. Then he took a wet towel from a hot box and put it over my face. Started cutting my hair. Ended up shaking his head with some kind of finality.

'Can't rightly say,' he said. 'He came back and forth on the road, time to time. I remember that pretty well. Three, four years later he was gone. I was up in Atlanta for a spell, wasn't here to know.

Heard tell somebody killed him, maybe right here in Margrave, maybe not. Some kind of big trouble, got him killed stone dead.'

I sat listening to their old radio for a while. Then I gave them a twenty off my roll of bills and hurried out onto Main Street. Strode out north. It was nearly noon and the sun was baking. Hot for September. Nobody else was out walking. The black road blasted heat at me. Blind Blake had walked this road, maybe in the noon heat. Back when those old barbers had been boys this had been the artery reaching north to Atlanta, Chicago, jobs, hope, money. Noon heat wouldn't have stopped anybody getting where they were going. But now the road was just a smooth blacktop byway going nowhere at all.

It took me a few minutes in the heat to get up to the station house. I walked across its springy lawn past another bronze statue and pulled open the heavy glass entrance door. Stepped into the chill inside. Roscoe was waiting for me, leaning on the reception counter. Behind her in the squad room, I could see Stevenson talking urgently into a telephone. Roscoe was pale and looking very worried.

'We found another body,' she said.

'Where?' I asked her.

'Up at the warehouse again,' she said. 'The other side of the road this time, underneath the cloverleaf, where it's raised up.'

'Who found it?' I said.

'Finlay,' she said. 'He was up there this morning, poking around, looking for something to help us with the first one. Some help, right? All he finds is another one.'

'Do you know who this one is?' I asked her.

She shook her head.

'Unidentified,' she said. 'Same as the first one.'

'Where's Finlay now?' I asked her.

'Gone to get Hubble,' she said. 'He thinks Hubble may know something about it.'

I nodded.

'How long was this one up there?' I said.

'Two or three days, maybe,' she said. 'Finlay says it could have been a double homicide on Thursday night.'

I nodded again. Hubble did know something about it. This was the guy he had sent to meet with the tall investigator with the shaved head. He couldn't figure out how the guy had gotten away with it. But the guy hadn't gotten away with it.

100

I heard a car in the lot outside and then the big glass door sucked open. Finlay stuck his head in.

'Morgue, Roscoe,' he said. 'You too, Reacher.'

We followed him back outside into the heat. We all got into Roscoe's unmarked sedan. Left Finlay's car where he'd parked it. Roscoe drove. I sat in the back. Finlay sat in the front passenger seat, twisted around so he could talk to the both of us at once. Roscoe nosed out of the police lot and headed south.

'I can't find Hubble,' Finlay said. Looking at me. 'There's nobody up at his place. Did he say anything to you about going anywhere?'

'No,' I said. 'Not a word. We hardly spoke all weekend.'

Finlay grunted at me.

'I need to find out what he knows about all this,' he said. 'This is serious shit and he knows something about it, that's for damn sure. What did he tell you about it, Reacher?'

I didn't answer. I wasn't entirely sure whose side I was on yet. Finlay's, probably, but if Finlay started blundering around in whatever Hubble was mixed up in, Hubble and his family were going to end up dead. No doubt about that. So I figured I should just stay impartial and then get the hell out of there as fast as possible. I didn't want to get involved.

'You try his mobile number?' I asked him.

Finlay grunted and shook his head.

'Switched off,' he said. 'Some automatic voice came on and told me.'

'Did he come by and pick up his watch?' I asked him.

'His what?' he said.

'His watch,' I said. 'He left a ten-thousand-dollar Rolex with Baker on Friday. When Baker was cuffing us for the ride out to Warburton. Did he come pick it up?'

'No,' Finlay said. 'Nobody said so.'

'OK,' I said. 'So he's got some urgent business somewhere. Not even an asshole like Hubble's going to forget about a ten-thousand-dollar watch, right?'

'What urgent business?' Finlay said. 'What did he tell you about it?'

'He didn't tell me diddly,' I said. 'Like I told you, we hardly spoke.'

Finlay glared at me from the front seat.

'Don't mess with me, Reacher,' he said. 'Until I get hold of Hubble, I'm going to keep hold of you and sweat your ass for what he told you. And don't make out he kept his mouth shut all weekend, because guys like that never do. I know that and you know that, so don't mess with me, OK?'

I just shrugged at him. He wasn't about to arrest me again. Maybe I could get a bus from wherever the morgue was. I'd have to pass on lunch with Roscoe. Pity.

'So what's the story on this one?' I asked him.

'Pretty much the same as the last one,' Finlay said. 'Looks like it happened at the same time. Shot to death, probably the same weapon. This one didn't get kicked around afterwards, but it was probably part of the same incident.'

'You don't know who it is?' I said.

'His name is Sherman,' he said. 'Apart from that, no idea.'

'Tell me about it,' I said. I was asking out of habit. Finlay thought for a moment. I saw him decide to answer. Like we were partners.

'Unidentified white male,' he said. 'Same deal as the first one, no ID, no wallet, no distinguishing marks. But this one had a gold wristwatch, engraved on the back: to Sherman, love Judy. He was maybe thirty or thirty-five. Hard to tell, because he'd been lying there for three nights and he was well gnawed by the small animals, you know? His lips are gone, and his eyes, but his right hand was OK because it was folded up under his body, so I got some decent prints. We ran them an hour ago and something may come of that, if we're lucky.'

'Gunshot wounds?' I asked him.

Finlay nodded.

'Looks like the same gun,' he said. 'Small-calibre, soft-nose shells. Looks like maybe the first shot only wounded him and he was able to run. He got hit a couple more times but made it to cover under the highway. He fell down and bled to death. He didn't get kicked around because they couldn't find him. That's how it looks to me.'

I thought about it. I'd walked right by there at eight o'clock on Friday morning. Right between the two bodies.

'And you figure he was called Sherman?' I said.

'His name was on his watch,' Finlay said.

'Might not have been his watch,' I said. 'The guy could have stolen it. Could have inherited it, bought it from a pawnshop, found it in the street.'

Finlay just grunted again. We must have been more than ten miles south of Margrave. Roscoe was keeping up a fast pace down the old county road. Then she slowed and slid down a left fork which led straight to the distant horizon.

'Where the hell are we going?' I said.

'County hospital,' Finlay said. 'Down in Yellow Springs. Next-but-one town to the south. Not long now.'

We drove on. Yellow Springs became a smudge in the heat haze on the horizon. Just inside the town limit was the county hospital, standing more or less on its own. Put there back when diseases were infectious and sick people were isolated. It was a big hospital, a warren of wide low buildings sprawled over a couple of acres. Roscoe slowed and swung into the entrance lane. We wallowed over speed bumps and threaded our way around to a spread of buildings clustered on their own in back. The mortuary was a long shed with a big roll-up door standing open. We stopped well clear of the door and left the car in the yard. We looked at each other and went in.

A medical guy met us and led us into an office. He sat behind a metal desk and waved Finlay and Roscoe to some stools. I leaned on a counter, between a computer terminal and a fax machine. This was not a big-budget facility. It had been cheaply equipped some years ago. Everything was worn and chipped and untidy. Very different from the station house up at Margrave. The guy at the desk looked tired. Not old, not young, maybe Finlay's sort of age. White coat. He looked like the type of guy whose judgement you wouldn't worry about too much. He didn't introduce himself. Just took it for granted we all knew who he was and what he was for.

'What can I tell you folks?' he said.

He looked at all three of us in turn. Waited. We looked back.

'Was it the same incident?' Finlay asked. His deep Harvard tones sounded out of place in the shabby office. The medical guy shrugged at him.

'I've only had the second corpse for an hour,' he said. 'But, yes, I would say it's the same incident. It's almost certainly the same weapon. Looks like small-calibre soft-nose bullets in both cases. The bullets were slow, looks like the gun had a silencer.'

'Small calibre?' I said. 'How small?'

The doctor swivelled his tired gaze my way.

'I'm not a firearms expert,' he said. 'But I'd vote for a twenty-two. Looks that small to me. I'd say we're looking at soft-nose twenty-two-gauge shells. Take the first guy's head, for example.

103

Two small splintery entry wounds and two big messy exit wounds, characteristic of a small soft-nose bullet.'

I nodded. That's what a soft-nose bullet does. It goes in and flattens out as it does so. Becomes a blob of lead about the size of a quarter tumbling through whatever tissue it meets. Rips a great big exit hole for itself. And a nice slow soft-nose .22 makes sense with a silencer. No point using a silencer except with a subsonic muzzle velocity. Otherwise the bullet is making its own sonic boom all the way to the target, like a tiny fighter plane.

'OK,' I said. 'Were they killed up there where they were found?'

'No doubt about it,' the guy said. 'Hypostasis is clear in both corpses.'

He looked at me. Wanted me to ask him what hypostasis was. I knew what it was, but I felt polite. So I looked puzzled for him.

'Postmortem hypostasis,' he said. 'Lividity. When you die, your circulation stops, right? Heart isn't beating anymore. Your blood obeys the law of gravity. It settles to the bottom of your body, into the lowest available vessels, usually into the tiny capillaries in the skin next to the floor or whatever you've fallen down onto. The red cells settle first. They stain the skin red. Then they clot, so the stain is fixed, like a photograph. After a few hours, the stains are permanent. The stains on the first guy are entirely consistent with his position on the warehouse forecourt. He was shot, he fell down dead, he was kicked around in some sort of mad frenzy for a few minutes, then he lay there for around eight hours. No doubt about it.'

'What do you make of the kicking?' Finlay asked him.

The doctor shook his head and shrugged.

'Never seen anything like it,' he said. 'I've read about it in the journals, time to time. Some kind of a psychopathic thing, obviously. No way to explain it. It didn't make any difference to the dead guy. Didn't hurt him, because he was dead. So it must have gratified the kicker somehow. Unbelievable fury, tremendous strength. The injuries are grievous.'

'What about the second guy?' Finlay asked.

'He ran for it,' the doctor said. 'He was hit close up in the back with the first shot, but it didn't drop him, and he ran. He took two more on the way. One in the neck, and the fatal shot in the thigh. Blew away his femoral artery. He made it as far as the raised-up section of highway, then lay down and bled to death. No doubt about that. If it hadn't rained all night Thursday, I'm sure you'd have seen the trail of blood on the road. There must have been

104

about a gallon and a half lying about somewhere, because it sure as hell isn't inside the guy any more.'

We all fell quiet. I was thinking about the second guy's desperate sprint across the road. Trying to reach cover while the bullets smashed into his flesh. Hurling himself under the highway ramp and dying amid the quiet scuffling of the small night animals.

'OK,' Finlay said. 'So we're safe to assume the two victims were together. The shooter is in a group of three, he surprises them, shoots the first guy in the head twice, meanwhile the second guy takes off and gets hit by three shots as he runs, right?'

'You're assuming there were three assailants?' the doctor said.

Finlay nodded across to me. It was my theory, so I got to explain it.

'Three separate personality characteristics,' I said. 'A competent shooter, a frenzied maniac, and an incompetent concealer.'

The doctor nodded slowly.

'I'll buy that,' he said. 'The first guy was hit at point-blank range, so maybe we should assume he knew the assailants and allowed them to get next to him?'

Finlay nodded.

'Had to be that way,' he said. 'Five guys meeting together. Three of them attack the other two. This is some kind of a big deal, right?'

'Do we know who the assailants were?' the doctor asked.

'We don't even know who the victims were,' Roscoe said.

'Got any theories on the victims?' Finlay asked the doctor.

'Not on the second guy, apart from the name on his watch,' the doctor said. 'I only just got him on the table an hour ago.'

'So you got theories on the first guy?' Finlay said.

The doctor started shuffling some notes on his desk, but his telephone rang. He answered it and then held it out to Finlay.

'For you,' he said. Finlay crouched forward on his stool and took the call. Listened for a moment.

'OK,' he said into the phone. 'Just print it out and fax it to us here, will you?'

Then he passed the phone back to the doctor and rocked back on his stool. He had the beginnings of a smile on his face.

'That was Stevenson, up at the station house,' he said. 'We finally got a match on the first guy's prints. Seems like we did the right thing to run them again. Stevenson's faxing it through to us here in a minute, so tell us what you got, doc, and we'll put it all together.'

The tired guy in the white coat shrugged and picked up a sheet of paper.

'The first guy?' he said. 'I haven't got much at all. The body was in a hell of a mess. He was tall, he was fit, he had a shaved head. The main thing is the dental work. Looks like the guy got his teeth fixed all over the place. Some of it is American, some of it looks American, some of it is foreign.'

Next to my hip, the fax machine started beeping and whirring. A sheet of thin paper fed itself in.

'So what do we make of that?' Finlay said. 'The guy was foreign? Or an American who lived abroad or what?'

The thin sheet of paper fed itself out, covered in writing. Then the machine stopped and went quiet. I picked up the paper and glanced at it. Then I read it through twice. I went cold. I was gripped by an icy paralysis and I couldn't move. I just couldn't believe what I was seeing on that piece of fax paper. The sky crashed in on me. I stared at the doctor and spoke.

'He grew up abroad,' I said. 'He had his teeth fixed wherever he was living. He broke his right arm when he was eight and had it set in Germany. He had his tonsils out in the hospital in Seoul.'

The doctor looked up at me.

'They can tell all that from his fingerprints?' he said.

I shook my head.

'The guy was my brother,' I said.

TEN

ONCE I SAW A NAVY FILM ABOUT EXPEDITIONS IN THE FROZEN Arctic. You could be walking over a solid glacier. Suddenly the ice would heave and shatter. Some kind of unimaginable stresses in the floes. A whole new geography would be forced up. Massive escarpments where it had been flat. Huge ravines behind you. A new lake in front of you. The world all changed in a second. That's how I felt. I sat there rigid with shock on the counter between the fax machine and the computer terminal and felt like an Arctic guy whose whole world changes in a single step.

They walked me through to the cold store in back to make a formal identification of his body. His face had been blown away by the gunshots and all his bones were broken but I recognized the star-shaped scar on his neck. He'd got it when we were messing with a broken bottle, twenty-nine years ago. Then they took me back up to the station house in Margrave. Finlay drove. Roscoe sat with me in the back of the car and held my hand all the way. It was only a twenty-minute ride, but in that time I lived through two whole lifetimes. His and mine.

My brother Joe. Two years older than me. He was born on a base in the Far East right at the end of the Eisenhower era. Then I had been born on a base in Europe, right at the start of the Kennedy era. Then we'd grown up together all over the world inside that tight isolated transience that service families create for themselves. Life was all about moving on at random and unpredictable intervals. It got so that it felt weird to do more than a semester and a half in any one place. Several times we went years without seeing a winter. We'd get moved out of Europe at the start of the fall and go down to the Pacific somewhere and summer would begin all over again.

Our friends kept just disappearing. Some unit would get shipped out somewhere and a bunch of kids would be gone. Sometimes we saw them again months later in a different place. Plenty of them we never saw again. Nobody ever said hello or goodbye. You were just either there or not there.

Then as Joe and I got older, we got moved around more. The Vietnam thing meant the military started shuffling people around the world faster and faster. Life became just a blur of bases. We never owned anything. We were only allowed one bag each on the transport planes.

We were together in that blur for sixteen years. Joe was the only constant thing in my life. And I loved him like a brother. But that phrase has a very precise meaning. A lot of those stock sayings do. Like when people say they slept like a baby. Do they mean they slept well? Or do they mean they woke up every ten minutes, screaming? I loved Joe like a brother, which meant a lot of things in our family.

The truth was I never knew for sure if I loved him or not. And he never knew for sure if he loved me or not, either. We were only two years apart, but he was born in the fifties and I was born in the sixties. That seemed to make a lot more than two years' worth of a difference to us. And like any pair of brothers two years apart, we irritated the hell out of each other. We fought and bickered and sullenly waited to grow up and get out from under. Most of those sixteen years, we didn't know if we loved each other or hated each other.

But we had the thing that army families have. Your family was your unit. The men on the bases were taught total loyalty to their units. It was the most fundamental thing in their lives. The boys copied them. They translated that same intense loyalty onto their families. So time to time you might hate your brother, but you didn't let anybody mess with him. That was what we had, Joe and I. We had that unconditional loyalty. We stood back to back in every new schoolyard and punched our way out of trouble together. I watched out for him, and he watched out for me, like brothers did. For sixteen years. Not much of a normal childhood, but it was the only childhood I was ever going to get. And Joe was just about the beginning and end of it. And now somebody had killed him. I sat there in the back of the police Chevrolet listening to a tiny voice in my head asking me what the hell I was going to do about that.

Finlay drove straight through Margrave and parked up outside the station house. Right at the kerb opposite the big plate-glass entrance doors. He and Roscoe got out of the car and stood there waiting for me, just like Baker and Stevenson had forty-eight hours before. I got out and joined them in the noontime heat. We stood there for a moment and then Finlay pulled open the heavy door and we went inside. Walked back through the empty squad room to the big rosewood office.

Finlay sat at the desk. I sat in the same chair I'd used on Friday. Roscoe pulled a chair up and put it next to mine. Finlay rattled open the desk drawer. Took out the tape recorder. Went through his routine of testing the microphone with his fingernail. Then he sat still and looked at me.

'I'm very sorry about your brother,' he said.

I nodded. Didn't say anything.

'I'm going to have to ask you a lot of questions, I'm afraid,' he said.

I just nodded again. I understood his position. I'd been in his position plenty of times myself.

'Who would be his next of kin?' he asked.

'I am,' I said. 'Unless he got married without telling me.'

'Do you think he might have done that?' Finlay asked me.

'We weren't close,' I said. 'But I doubt it.'

'Your parents dead?'

I nodded. Finlay nodded. Wrote me down as next of kin.

'What was his full name?'

'Joe Reacher,' I said. 'No middle name.'

'Is that short for Joseph?'

'No,' I said. 'It was just Joe. Like my name is just Jack. We had a father who liked simple names.'

'OK,' Finlay said. 'Older or younger?'

'Older,' I said. I gave him Joe's date of birth. 'Two years older than me.'

'So he was thirty-eight?'

I nodded. Baker had said the victim had been maybe forty. Maybe Joe hadn't worn well.

'Do you have a current address for him?'

I shook my head.

'No,' I said. 'Washington DC, somewhere. Like I said, we weren't close.'

'OK,' he said again. 'When did you last see him?'

'About twenty minutes ago,' I said. 'In the morgue.'

Finlay nodded gently. 'Before that?'

'Seven years ago,' I said. 'Our mother's funeral.'

'Have you got a photograph of him?'

'You saw the stuff in the property bag,' I said. 'I haven't got a photograph of anything.'

He nodded again. Went quiet. He was finding this difficult.

'Can you give me a description of him?'

'Before he got his face shot off?'

'It might help, you know,' Finlay said. 'We need to find out who saw him around, when and where.'

I nodded.

'He looked like me, I guess,' I said. 'Maybe an inch taller, maybe ten pounds lighter.'

'That would make him what, about six-six?' he asked.

'Right,' I said. 'About two hundred pounds, maybe.'

Finlay wrote it all down.

'And he shaved his head?' he said.

'Not the last time I saw him,' I said. 'He had hair like anybody else.'

'Seven years ago, right?' Finlay said.

I shrugged.

'Maybe he started going bald,' I said. 'Maybe he was vain about it.'

Finlay nodded.

'What was his job?' he asked.

'Last I heard, he worked for the Treasury Department,' I said. 'Doing what, I'm not sure.'

'What was his background?' he asked. 'Was he in the service too?'

I nodded.

'Military Intelligence,' I said. 'Quit after a while, then he worked for the government.'

'He wrote you that he had been here, right?' he asked.

'He mentioned the Blind Blake thing,' I said. 'Didn't say what brought him down here. But it shouldn't be difficult to find out.'

Finlay nodded.

'We'll make some calls first thing in the morning,' he said. 'Until

110

then, you're sure you got no idea why he should be down here?'

I shook my head. I had no idea at all why he had come down here. But I knew Hubble did. Joe had been the tall investigator with the shaved head and the code name. Hubble had brought him down here and Hubble knew exactly why. First thing to do was to find Hubble and ask him about it.

'Did you say you couldn't find Hubble?' I asked Finlay.

'Can't find him anywhere,' he said. 'He's not up at his place on Beckman Drive and nobody's seen him around town. Hubble knows all about this, right?'

I just shrugged. I felt like I wanted to keep some of the cards pretty close to my chest. If I was going to have to squeeze Hubble for something he wasn't very happy to talk about, then I wanted to do it in private. I didn't particularly want Finlay watching over my shoulder while I was doing it. He might think I was squeezing too hard. And I definitely didn't want to have to watch anything over Finlay's shoulder. I didn't want to leave the squeezing to him. I might think he wasn't squeezing hard enough. And anyway, Hubble would talk to me faster than he would talk to a policeman. He was already halfway there with me. So exactly how much Hubble knew was going to stay my secret. Just for now.

'No idea what Hubble knows,' I said. 'You're the one claims he fell apart.'

Finlay just grunted again and looked across the desk at me. I could see him settling into a new train of thought. I was pretty sure what it was. I'd been waiting for it to surface. There's a rule of thumb about homicide. It comes from a lot of statistics and a lot of experience. The rule of thumb says: when you get a dead guy, first you take a good look at his family. Because a hell of a lot of homicide gets done by relatives. Husbands, wives, sons. And brothers. That was the theory. Finlay would have seen it in action a hundred times in his twenty years up in Boston. Now I could see him trying it out in his head down in Margrave. I needed to run interference on it. I didn't want him thinking about it. I didn't want to waste any more of my time in a cell. I figured I might need that time for something else.

'You're happy with my alibi, right?' I said.

He saw where I was going. Like we were colleagues on a knotty case. He flashed me a brief grin.

'It held up,' he said. 'You were in Tampa when this was going down.'

'OK,' I said. 'And is Chief Morrison comfortable with that?'

'He doesn't know about it,' Finlay said. 'He's not answering his phone.'

'I don't want any more convenient mistakes,' I said. 'The fat moron said he saw me up there. I want him to know that won't fly any more.'

Finlay nodded. Picked up the phone on the desk and dialled a number. I heard the faint purr of the ring tone from the earpiece. It rang for a long time and cut off when Finlay put the phone back down.

'Not at home,' he said. 'Sunday, right?'

Then he pulled the phone book out of a drawer. Opened it to H. Looked up Hubble's number on Beckman Drive. Dialled it and got the same result. A lot of ring tone and nobody home. Then he tried the mobile number. An electronic voice started to tell him the phone was switched off. He hung up before it finished.

'I'm going to bring Hubble in, when I find him,' Finlay said. 'He knows stuff he should be telling us. Until then, not a lot I can do, right?'

I shrugged. He was right. It was a pretty cold trail. The only spark that Finlay knew about was the panic Hubble had shown on Friday.

'What are you going to do, Reacher?' he asked me.

'I'm going to think about that,' I said.

Finlay looked straight at me. Not unfriendly, but very serious, like he was trying to communicate an order and an appeal with a single stern eye-to-eye gaze.

'Let me deal with this, OK?' he said. 'You're going to feel pretty bad, and you're going to want to see justice done, but I don't want any independent action going on here, OK? This is police business. You're a civilian. Let me deal with it, OK?'

I shrugged and nodded. Stood up and looked at them both.

'I'm going for a walk,' I said.

I left the two of them there and strolled through the squad room. Pushed out through the glass doors into the hot afternoon. Wandered through the parking lot and crossed the wide lawn in front, over as far as the bronze statue. It was another tribute to Caspar Teale, whoever the hell he had been. Same guy as on the village green on the southern edge of town. I leaned up against his warm metal flank and thought.

The United States is a giant country. Millions of square miles. Best part of three hundred million people. I hadn't seen Joe for

112

seven years, and he hadn't seen me, but we'd ended up in exactly the same tiny spot, eight hours apart. I'd walked within fifty yards of where his body had been lying. That was one hell of a big coincidence. It was almost unbelievable. So Finlay was doing me a big favour by treating it like a coincidence. He should be trying to tear my alibi apart. Maybe he already was. Maybe he was already on the phone to Tampa, checking again.

But he wouldn't find anything, because it was a coincidence. No point going over and over it. I was only in Margrave because of a crazy last-minute whim. If I'd taken a minute longer looking at the guy's map, the bus would have been past the cloverleaf and I'd have forgotten all about Margrave. I'd have gone on up to Atlanta and never known anything about Joe. It might have taken another seven years before the news caught up with me. So there was no point getting all stirred up about the coincidence. The only thing I had to do was to decide what the hell I was going to do about it.

I was about four years old before I caught on to the loyalty thing. I suddenly figured I was supposed to watch out for Joe the way he was watching out for me. After a while, it became second nature, like an automatic thing. It was always in my head to scout around and check he was OK. Plenty of times I would run out into some new schoolyard and see a bunch of kids trying it on with the tall skinny newcomer. I'd trot over there and haul them off and bust a few heads. Then I'd go back to my own buddies and play ball or whatever we were doing. Duty done, like a routine. It was a routine which lasted twelve years, from when I was four right up to the time Joe finally left home. Twelve years of that routine must have left faint tracks in my mind, because for ever afterwards I always carried a faint echo of the question: where's Joe? Once he was grown up and away, it didn't much matter where he was. But I was always aware of the faint echo of that old routine. Deep down, I was always aware I was supposed to stand up for him, if I was needed.

But now he was dead. He wasn't anywhere. I leaned up against the statue in front of the station house and listened to the tiny voice inside my head saying: you're supposed to do something about that.

The station house door sucked open. I squinted through the heat and saw Roscoe step out. The sun was behind her and it lit her hair like a halo. She scanned around and saw me leaning on the statue in the middle of the lawn. Started over toward me. I pushed off the warm bronze.

'You OK?' she asked me.

'I'm fine,' I said.

'You sure?' she said.

'I'm not falling apart,' I said. 'Maybe I should be, but I'm not. I just feel numb, to be honest.'

It was true. I wasn't feeling much of anything. Maybe it was some kind of a weird reaction, but that was how I felt. No point in denying it.

'OK,' Roscoe said. 'Can I give you a ride somewhere?'

Maybe Finlay had sent her out to keep track of me, but I wasn't about to put up a whole lot of objections to that. She was standing there in the sun looking great. I realized I liked her more every time I looked at her.

'Want to show me where Hubble lives?' I asked her.

I could see her thinking about it.

'Shouldn't we leave that to Finlay?' she said.

'I just want to see if he's back home yet,' I said. 'I'm not going to eat him. If he's there, we'll call Finlay right away, OK?'

'OK,' she said. She shrugged and smiled. 'Let's go.'

We walked together back over the lawn and got into her police Chevy. She started it up and pulled out of the lot. Turned left and rolled south through the perfect little town. It was a gorgeous September day. The bright sun turned it into a fantasy. The brick sidewalks were glowing and the white paint was blinding. The whole place was quiet and basking in the Sunday heat. Deserted.

Roscoe hung a right at the little village green and made the turn into Beckman Drive. Skirted around the square with the church on it. The cars were gone and the place was quiet. Worship was over. Beckman opened out into a wide tree-lined residential street, set on a slight rise. It had a rich feel. Cool and shady and prosperous. It was what real-estate people mean when they talk about location. I couldn't see the houses. They were set far back behind wide grassy shoulders, big trees, high hedges. Their driveways wound out of sight. Occasionally I glimpsed a white portico or a red roof. The further out we got, the bigger the lots became. Hundreds of yards between mailboxes. Enormous mature trees. A solid sort of a place. But a place with stories hiding behind the leafy facades. In Hubble's case, some sort of a desperate story which had caused him to reach out to my brother. Some sort of a story which had got my brother killed.

Roscoe slowed at a white mailbox and turned left into the drive of number twenty-five. About a mile from town, on the left, its back to the afternoon sun. It was the last house on the road. Up ahead, peach groves stretched into the haze. We nosed slowly up a winding driveway around massed banks of garden. The house was not what I had imagined. I had pictured a big white place, like a normal house, but bigger. This was more splendid. A palace. It was huge. Every detail was expensive. Expanses of gravel drive, expanses of velvet lawn, huge exquisite trees, everything shining and dappled in the blazing sun. But there was no sign of the dark Bentley I'd seen up at the prison. It looked like there was nobody home.

Roscoe pulled up near the front door and we got out. It was silent. I could hear nothing except the heavy buzz of afternoon heat. We rang on the bell and knocked on the door. No response from inside. We shrugged at each other and walked across a lawn around the side of the house. There were acres of grass and a blaze of some kind of flowers surrounding a garden room. Then a wide patio and a long lawn sloping down to a giant swimming pool. The water was bright blue in the sun. I could smell the chlorine hanging in the hot air.

'Some place,' Roscoe said.

I nodded. I was wondering if my brother had been there.

'I hear a car,' she said.

We got back to the front of the house in time to see the big Bentley easing to a stop. The blonde woman I'd seen driving away from the prison got out. She had two children with her. A boy and a girl. This was Hubble's family. He loved them like crazy. But he wasn't there with them.

The blonde woman seemed to know Roscoe. They greeted each other and Roscoe introduced me to her. She shook my hand and said her name was Charlene, but I could call her Charlie. She was an expensive-looking woman, tall, slim, good bones, carefully dressed, carefully looked after. But she had a seam of spirit running through her face like a flaw. Enough spirit there to make me like her. She held on to my hand and smiled, but it was a smile with a whole lot of strain behind it.

'This hasn't been the best weekend of my life, I'm afraid,' she said. 'But it seems that I owe you a great deal of thanks, Mr Reacher. My husband tells me you saved his life in prison.'

She said it with a lot of ice in her voice. Not aimed at me. Aimed at whatever circumstance it was forcing her to use the words

115

'husband' and 'prison' in the same sentence.

'No problem,' I said. 'Where is he?'

'Taking care of some business,' Charlie said. 'I expect him back later.'

I nodded. That had been Hubble's plan. He'd said he would spin her some kind of a yarn and then try to settle things down. I wondered if Charlie wanted to talk about it, but the children were standing silently next to her, and I could see she wouldn't talk in front of them. So I grinned at them. I hoped they would get all shy and run off somewhere, like children usually do with me, but they just grinned back.

'This is Ben,' Charlie said. 'And this is Lucy.'

They were nice-looking kids. The girl still had that little-girl chubbiness. No front teeth. Fine sandy hair in pigtails. The boy wasn't much bigger than his little sister. He had a slight frame and a serious face. Not a rowdy hooligan like some boys are. They were a nice pair of kids. Polite and quiet. They both shook hands with me and then stepped back to their mother's side. I looked at the three of them and I could just about see the terrible cloud hanging there over them. If Hubble didn't take care, he could get them all as dead as he'd gotten my brother.

'Will you come in for some iced tea?' Charlie asked us.

She stood there, her head cocked like she was waiting for an answer. She was maybe thirty, similar age to Roscoe. But she had a rich woman's ways. A hundred and fifty years ago, she'd have been the mistress of a big plantation.

'OK,' I said. 'Thanks.'

The kids ran off to play somewhere and Charlie ushered us in through the front door. I didn't really want to drink any iced tea, but I did want to stick around in case Hubble got back. I wanted to catch him on my own for five minutes. I wanted to ask him some pretty urgent questions before Finlay started in with the Miranda warnings.

It was a fabulous house. Huge. Beautifully furnished. Light and fresh. Cool creams and sunny yellows. Flowers. Charlie led us through to the garden room we'd seen from the outside. It was like something from a magazine. Roscoe went off with her to help fix the tea. Left me alone in the room. It made me uneasy. I wasn't accustomed to houses. Thirty-six years old and I'd never lived in a house. Lots of service accommodations and a terrible bare dormitory on the Hudson when I was up at the Point. That's where I'd lived. I sat down like an ugly alien on a flowered cushion on a cane sofa and waited. Uneasy, numb, in that dead zone between action and reaction.

The two women came back with the tea. Charlie was carrying a silver tray. She was a handsome woman, but she was nothing next to Roscoe. Roscoe had a spark in her eyes so electric it made Charlie just about invisible.

Then something happened. Roscoe sat down next to me on the cane sofa. As she sat, she pushed my leg to one side. It was a casual thing but it was very intimate and familiar. A numbed nerve end suddenly clicked in and screamed at me: she likes you too. She likes you too. It was the way she touched my leg.

I went back and looked at things in that new light. Her manner as she took the fingerprints and the photographs. Bringing me the coffee. Her smile and her wink. Her laugh. Working Friday night and Saturday so she could get me out of Warburton. Driving all the way over there to pick me up. Holding my hand after I'd seen my brother's broken body. Giving me a ride over here. She liked me too.

All of a sudden I was glad I had jumped off that damn bus. Glad I made that crazy last-minute decision. I suddenly relaxed. Felt better. The tiny voice in my head quieted down. Right then there was nothing for me to do. I'd speak to Hubble when I saw him. Until then I would sit on a sofa with a good-looking friendly dark-haired woman in a soft cotton shirt. The trouble would start soon enough. It always does.

Charlie Hubble sat down opposite us and started pouring the iced tea from the pitcher. The smell of lemon and spices drifted over. She caught my eye and smiled the same strained smile she'd used before.

'Normally, at this point, I'd ask you how you were enjoying your visit with us here in Margrave,' she said, looking at me, strained, smiling.

I couldn't think of a reply to that. I just shrugged. It was clear Charlie didn't know anything. She thought her husband had been arrested because of some kind of a mistake. Not because he was grabbed up in some kind of trouble which had just got two people murdered. One of which was the brother of the stranger she was busy smiling at. Roscoe rescued the conversation and the two of them started passing the time of day. I just sat there and drank the tea and waited for Hubble. He didn't show up. Then the conversation died and we had to get out of there. Charlie was fidgeting

117

like she had things to do. Roscoe put her hand on my arm. Her touch burned me like electricity.

'Let's go,' she said. 'I'll give you a ride back to town.'

I felt bad I wasn't staying to wait for Hubble. It made me feel disloyal to Joe. But I just wanted to be on my own with Roscoe. I was burning up with it. Maybe some kind of repressed grief was intensifying it. I wanted to leave Joe's problems until tomorrow. I told myself I had no choice anyway. Hubble hadn't shown up. Nothing else I could do. So we got back in the Chevy together and nosed down the winding driveway. Cruised down Beckman. The buildings thickened up at the bottom of the mile. We jinked around the church. The little village green with the statue of old Caspar Teale was ahead.

'Reacher?' Roscoe said. 'You'll be around for a while, right? Until we get this thing about your brother straightened out?'

'I guess I will,' I said.

'Where are you going to stay?' she asked.

'I don't know,' I said.

She pulled over to the kerb near the lawn. Nudged the selector into Park. She had a tender look on her face.

'I want you to come home with me,' she said.

I felt like I was out of my mind, but I was burning up with it so I pulled her to me and we kissed. That fabulous first kiss. The new and unfamiliar mouth and hair and taste and smell. She kissed hard and long and held on tight. We came up for air a couple of times before she took off again for her place.

She blasted a quarter-mile down the street which opened up opposite Beckman Drive. I saw a blur of greenery in the sun as she swooped into her driveway. The tyres chirped as she stopped. We more or less tumbled out and ran to the door. She used her key and we went in. The door swung shut and before it clicked she was back in my arms. We kissed and stumbled through to her living room. She was a foot shorter than me and her feet were off the ground.

We tore each other's clothes off like they were on fire. She was gorgeous. Firm and strong and a shape like a dream. Skin like silk. She pulled me to the floor through bars of hot sunlight from the window. It was frantic. We were rolling and nothing could have stopped us. It was like the end of the world. We shuddered to a stop and lay gasping. We were bathed in sweat. Totally spent.

We lay there clasped and caressing. Then she got off me and pulled me up. We kissed again as we staggered through to her bedroom. She pulled back the covers on the bed and we collapsed in. Held each other and fell into a deep afterglow stupor. I was wrecked. I felt like all my bones and sinews were rubber. I lay in the unfamiliar bed and drifted away to a place far beyond relaxation. I was floating. Roscoe's warm heft was snuggled beside me. I was breathing through her hair. Our hands were lazily caressing unfamiliar contours.

She asked me if I wanted to go find a motel. Or to stay there with her. I laughed and told her the only way to get rid of me now would be to go fetch a shotgun from the station house and chase me away. I told her even that might not work. She giggled and pressed even closer.

'I wouldn't fetch a shotgun,' she whispered. 'I'd fetch some handcuffs. I'd chain you to the bed and keep you here for ever.'

We dozed through the afternoon. I called the Hubble place at seven in the evening. He still wasn't back. I left Roscoe's number with Charlie and told her to have Hubble call me as soon as he got in. Then we drifted on through the rest of the evening. Fell fast asleep at midnight. Hubble never called.

Monday morning I was vaguely aware of Roscoe getting up for work. I heard the shower and I know she kissed me tenderly and then the house was hot and quiet and still. I slept on until after nine. The phone didn't ring. That was OK. I needed some quiet thinking time. I had decisions to make. I stretched out in Roscoe's warm bed and started answering the question the tiny voice in my head was asking me again.

What was I going to do about Joe? My answer came very easily. I knew it would. I knew it had been waiting there since I first stood next to Joe's broken body in the morgue. It was a very simple answer. I was going to stand up for him. I was going to finish his business. Whatever it was. Whatever it took.

I didn't foresee any major difficulties. Hubble was the only link I had, but Hubble was the only link I needed. He would cooperate. He'd depended on Joe to help him out. Now he'd depend on me. He'd give me what I needed. His masters were vulnerable for a week. What had he said? A window of exposure wide open until Sunday? I'd use it to tear them apart. My mind was made up. I couldn't do it any other way. I couldn't leave it to Finlay. Finlay wouldn't understand all those years of history. Finlay wouldn't sanction the sort of punishments that were going to be necessary. Finlay couldn't understand the simple truth I'd learned at the age

119

of four: you don't mess with my brother. So this was my business. It was between me and Joe. It was duty.

I lay there in Roscoe's warm bed and scoped it out. It was going to be a simple process. About as simple as you could get. Getting hold of Hubble wasn't going to be difficult. I knew where he lived. I knew his phone number. I stretched and smiled and filled with restless energy. Got out of bed and found coffee. There was a note propped against the pot. The note said: *Early lunch at Eno's? Eleven o'clock? Leave Hubble to Finlay, OK?* The note was signed with lots of kisses and a little drawing of a pair of handcuffs. I read it and smiled at the drawing, but I wasn't going to leave Hubble to Finlay. No way. Hubble was my business. So I looked up the number again and called Beckman Drive. There was nobody home.

I poured a big mug of coffee and wandered through to the living room. The sun was blinding outside. It was another hot day. I walked through the house. It was a small place. A living room, an eat-in kitchen, two bedrooms, one and a half baths. Very new, very clean. Decorated in a cool, simple way. What I would expect from Roscoe. A cool simple style. Some nice Navajo art, some bold rugs, white walls. She must have been to New Mexico and liked it.

It was still and quiet. She had a stereo, a few records and tapes, more sweet and melodic than the howl and buzz that I call music. I got more coffee from her kitchen. Went out back. There was a small yard out there, a neat coarse lawn and some recent evergreen planting. Shredded bark to smother weeds and rough timber edging against the planted areas. I stood in the sun and sipped the coffee.

Then I ducked back inside and tried Hubble's number again. No reply. I showered and dressed. Roscoe had a small shower stall, the head set low, feminine soaps in the dish. I found a towel in a closet and a comb on a vanity. No razor. I put my clothes on and rinsed out the coffee mug. Tried Hubble's number again from the kitchen phone. I let it ring for a long time. Nobody home. I figured I'd get a ride up there from Roscoe after lunch. This thing wasn't going to wait for ever. I relocked the back door and went out the front.

It was about ten-thirty. A mile and a quarter up to Eno's place. A gentle half-hour stroll in the sun. It was already very hot. Well into the eighties. Glorious fall weather in the South. I walked the quarter-mile to Main Street up a gently winding rise. Everything was beautifully manicured. There were towering magnolia trees everywhere and late blossom in the shrubs.

I turned at the convenience store and strolled up Main Street. The sidewalks had been swept. I could see crews of gardeners in the little park areas. They were setting up sprinklers and barrowing stuff out of smart green trucks marked 'Kliner Foundation' in gold. A couple of guys were painting the picket fence. I waved in at the two old barbers in their shop. They were leaning up inside their doorway, like they were waiting for custom. They waved back and I strolled on.

Eno's came into sight. The polished aluminium siding gleamed in the sun. Roscoe's Chevrolet was in the lot. Standing next to it on the gravel was the black pickup I'd seen the day before outside the coffee shop. I reached the diner and pushed in through the door. I had been prodded out through it on Friday with Stevenson's shotgun pointed at my gut. I had been in handcuffs. I wondered if the diner people would remember me. I figured they probably would. Margrave was a very quiet place. Not a whole lot of strangers passing through.

Roscoe was in a booth, the same one I'd used on Friday. She was back in uniform and she looked like the sexiest thing on earth. I stepped over to her. She smiled a tender smile up at me and I bent to kiss her mouth. She slid over the vinyl to the window. There were two cups of coffee on the table. I passed hers across.

The driver from the black pickup was sitting at the lunch counter. The Kliner boy, the pale woman's stepson. He'd spun the stool and his back was against the counter. He was sitting legs apart, elbows back, head up, eyes blazing, staring at me again. I turned my back on him and kissed Roscoe again.

'Is this going to ruin your authority?' I asked her. 'To be seen kissing a vagrant who got arrested in here on Friday?'

'Probably,' she said. 'But who cares?'

So I kissed her again. The Kliner kid was watching. I could feel it on the back of my neck. I turned to look back at him. He held my gaze for a second, then he slid off his stool and left. Stopped in the doorway and glared at me one last time. Then he hustled over to his pickup and took off. I heard the roar of the motor and then the diner was quiet. It was more or less empty, just like on Friday. A couple of old guys and a couple of waitresses. They were the same women as on Friday. Both blonde, one taller and heavier than the other. Waitress uniforms. The shorter one wore eyeglasses. Not really alike, but similar. Like sisters or cousins. The same genes in there somewhere. Small town, miles from anywhere.

'I made a decision,' I said. 'I have to find out what happened with Joe. So I just want to apologize in advance in case that gets in the way, OK?'

Roscoe shrugged and smiled a tender smile. Looked concerned for me.

'It won't get in the way,' she said. 'No reason why it should.'

I sipped my coffee. It was good coffee. I remembered that from Friday.

'We got an ID on the second body,' she said. 'His prints matched with an arrest two years ago in Florida. His name was Sherman Stoller. That name mean anything at all to you?'

I shook my head.

'Never heard of him,' I said.

Then her beeper started going. It was a little black pager thing clipped to her belt. I hadn't seen it before. Maybe she was only required to use it during working hours. It was beeping away. She reached around and clicked it off.

'Damn,' she said. 'I've got to call in. Sorry. I'll use the phone in the car.'

I slid out of the booth and stepped back to let her by.

'Order me some food, OK?' she said. 'I'll have whatever you have.'

'OK,' I said. 'Which one is our waitress?'

'The one with the glasses,' she said.

She walked out of the diner. I was aware of her leaning into her car, using the phone. Then she was gesturing to me from the parking lot. Miming urgency. Miming that she had to get back. Miming that I should stay put. She jumped into the car and took off, south. I waved vaguely after her, not really looking, because I was staring at the waitresses instead. I had almost stopped breathing. I needed Hubble. And Roscoe had just told me Hubble was dead.

ELEVEN

I STARED BLANKLY OVER AT THE TWO BLONDE WAITRESSES. ONE was perhaps three inches taller than the other. Perhaps fifteen pounds heavier. A couple of years older. The smaller woman looked petite in comparison. Better looking. She had longer, lighter hair. Nicer eyes behind the glasses. As a pair, the waitresses were similar in a superficial kind of a way. But not alike. There were a million differences between them. No way were they hard to distinguish one from the other.

I'd asked Roscoe which was our waitress. And how had she answered? She hadn't said the smaller one, or the one with the long hair, or the blonder one, or the slimmer one, or the prettier one or the younger one. She'd said the one with glasses. One was wearing glasses, the other wasn't. Ours was the one with glasses. Wearing glasses was the major difference between them. It overrode all the other differences. The other differences were matters of degree. Taller, heavier, longer, shorter, smaller, prettier, darker, younger. The glasses were not a matter of degree. One woman wore them, the other didn't. An absolute difference. No confusion. Our waitress was the one with glasses.

That's what Spivey had seen on Friday night. Spivey had come into the reception bunker a little after ten o'clock. With a shotgun and a clipboard in his big red farmer's hands. He had asked which one of us was Hubble. I remembered his high voice in the stillness of the bunker. There was no reason for his question. Why the hell

123

should Spivey care which one of us was which? He didn't need to know. But he'd asked. Hubble had raised his hand. Spivey had looked him over with his little snake eyes. He had seen that Hubble was smaller, shorter, lighter, sandier, balder, younger than me. But what was the major difference he had hung on to? Hubble wore glasses. I didn't. The little gold rims. An absolute difference. Spivey had said to himself that night: Hubble's the one with glasses.

But by the next morning I was the one with glasses, not Hubble. Because Hubble's gold rims had been smashed up by the Red Boys outside our cell. First thing in the morning. The little gold rims were gone. I had taken some shades from one of them as a trophy. Taken them and forgotten about them. I'd leaned up against the sink in that bathroom inspecting my tender forehead in the steel mirror. I'd felt those shades in my pocket. I'd pulled them out and put them on. They weren't dark because they were supposed to react to sunlight. They looked like ordinary glasses. I'd been standing there with them on when the Aryans came trawling into the bathroom. Spivey had just told them: find the new boys and kill the one with glasses. They'd tried hard. They'd tried very hard to kill Paul Hubble.

They had attacked me because the description they'd been given was suddenly the wrong description. Spivey had reported that back long ago. Whoever had set him on Hubble hadn't given up. They'd made a second attempt. And the second attempt had succeeded. The whole police department had been summoned up to Beckman Drive. Up to number twenty-five. Because somebody had discovered an appalling scene there. Carnage. He was dead. All four of them were dead. Tortured and butchered. My fault. I hadn't thought hard enough.

I ran over to the counter. Spoke to our waitress. The one with glasses.

'Can you call me a taxi?' I asked her.

The cook was watching from the kitchen hatch. Maybe he was Eno himself. Short, stocky, dark, balding. Older than me.

'No, we can't,' he called through. 'What do you think this place is? A hotel? This ain't the Waldorf-Astoria, pal. You want a taxi, you find it yourself. You ain't particularly welcome here, pal. You're trouble.'

I gazed back at him bleakly. Too drained for any reaction. But the waitress just laughed at him. Put her hand on my arm.

'Don't pay no mind to Eno,' she said. 'He's just a grumpy old thing. I'll call you the taxi. Just wait out in the parking lot, OK?'

I waited out on the road. Five minutes. The taxi drove up. Brand-new and immaculate, like everything else in Margrave.

'Where to, sir?' the driver asked.

I gave him Hubble's address and he made a wide, slow turn, shoulder to shoulder across the county road. Headed back to town. We passed the fire house and the police headquarters. The lot was empty. Roscoe's Chevy wasn't there. No cruisers. They were all out. Up at Hubble's. We made the right at the village green and swung past the silent church. Headed up Beckman. In a mile I would see a cluster of vehicles outside number twenty-five. The cruisers with their light bars flashing and popping. Unmarked cars for Finlay and Roscoe. An ambulance or two. The coroner would be there, up from his shabby office in Yellow Springs.

But the street was empty. I walked into Hubble's driveway. The taxi turned and drove back to town. Then it was silent. That heavy silence you get in a quiet street on a hot, quiet day. I rounded the big banks of garden. There was nobody there. No police cars, no ambulances, no shouting. No clattering gurneys, no gasps of horror. No police photographers, no tape sealing off the access.

The big dark Bentley was parked up on the gravel. I walked past it on my way to the house. The front door crashed open. Charlie Hubble ran out. She was screaming. She was hysterical. But she was alive.

'Hub's disappeared,' she screamed.

She ran over the gravel. Stood right in front of me.

'Hub's gone,' she screamed. 'He's disappeared. I can't find him.'

It was just Hubble on his own. They'd taken him and dumped him somewhere. Someone had found the body and called the police. A screaming, gagging phone call. The cluster of cars and ambulances was there. Not here on Beckman. Somewhere else. But it was just Hubble on his own.

'Something's wrong,' Charlie wailed. 'This prison thing. Something's gone wrong at the bank. It must be that. Hub's been so uptight. Now he's gone. He's disappeared. Something's happened, I know it.'

She screwed her eyes tight shut. Started screaming. She was losing it. Getting more and more hysterical. I didn't know how to handle her.

'He got back late last night,' she screamed. 'He was still here this morning. I took Ben and Lucy to school. Now he's gone. He hasn't gone to work. He got a call from his office telling him to stay home, and his briefcase is still here, his phone is still here, his jacket is still here, his wallet is still here, his credit cards are in it, his driver's licence is in it, his keys are in the kitchen. The front door was standing wide open. He hasn't gone to work. He's just disappeared.'

I stood still. Paralyzed. He'd been dragged out of there by force and killed. Charlie sagged in front of me. Then she started whispering to me. The whispering was worse than the screaming.

'His car is still here,' she whispered. 'He can't have walked anywhere. He never walks anywhere. He always takes his Bentley.'

She waved vaguely toward the back of the house.

'Hub's Bentley is green,' she said. 'It's still in the garage. I checked. You've got to help us. You've got to find him. Mr Reacher, please. I'm asking you to help us. Hub's in trouble, I know it. He's vanished. He said you might help. You saved his life. He said you knew how to do things.'

She was hysterical. She was pleading. But I couldn't help her. She would know that soon enough. Baker or Finlay would come up to the house very soon. They would tell her the shattering news. Probably Finlay would handle it. Probably he was very good at it. Probably he had done it a thousand times in Boston. He had dignity and gravity. He would break the news, gloss over the details, drive her down to the morgue to identify the body. The morgue people would shroud the corpse with heavy gauze to hide the appalling wounds.

'Will you help us?' Charlie asked me.

I decided not to wait with her. I decided to go down to the station house. Find out details like where and when and how. But I'd come back with Finlay. This was my fault, so I should come back.

'You stay here,' I said. 'You'll have to lend me your car, OK?'

She rooted in her bag and pulled out a big bunch of keys. Handed them to me. The car key had a big letter 'B' embossed on it. She nodded vaguely and stayed where she was. I stepped over to the Bentley and slid into the driver's seat. Backed it up and swung it down the curving driveway. Glided down Beckman in silence. Made the left onto Main Street up toward the station house.

There were cruisers and unmarked units sprawled right across the police parking lot. I left Charlie's Bentley at the kerb and stepped inside. They were all milling around the open area. I saw Baker, Stevenson, Finlay. I saw Roscoe. I recognized the backup team from Friday. Morrison wasn't there. Nor was the desk guy. The long counter was unattended. Everybody was stunned. They were all vague and staring. Horrified. Distracted. Nobody would talk to me. They looked over bleakly. Didn't really look away, it was like they didn't see me at all. There was total silence. Finally Roscoe came over. She'd been crying. She walked up to me. Pressed her face against my chest. She was burning up. She put her arms around me and held on.

'It was horrible,' she said. Wouldn't say any more.

I walked her around to her desk and sat her down. Squeezed her shoulder and stepped over towards Finlay. He was sitting on a desk, looking blank. I nodded him over to the big office in back. I needed to know, and Finlay was the guy who would tell me. He followed me into the office. Sat down in the chair in front of the desk. Where I had sat in handcuffs on Friday. I sat behind the desk. Roles reversed.

I watched him for a while. He was really shaken up. I went cold inside all over again. Hubble must have been left in a hell of a mess to be getting a reaction like that from Finlay. He was a twenty-year man from a big city. He must have seen all there is to see. But now he was really shaken up. I sat there and burned with shame. Sure, Hubble, I'd said, you look safe enough to me.

'So what's the story?' I said.

He lifted his head up with an effort and looked at me.

'Why should you care?' he said. 'What was he to you?'

A good question. One I couldn't answer. Finlay didn't know what I knew about Hubble. I'd kept quiet about it. So Finlay didn't see why Hubble was so important to me.

'Just tell me what happened,' I said.

'It was pretty bad,' he said. Wouldn't go on.

He was worrying me. My brother had been shot in the head. Two big messy exit wounds had removed his face. Then somebody had turned his corpse into a bag of pulp. But Finlay hadn't fallen apart over that. The other guy had been all gnawed up by rats. There wasn't a drop of blood left in him. But Finlay hadn't fallen apart over that, either. Hubble was a local guy, which made it a bit worse, I could see that. But on Friday, Finlay hadn't even known who Hubble was. And now Finlay was acting like he'd seen a ghost. So it must have been some pretty spectacular work.

Which meant that there was some kind of a big deal going down in Margrave. Because there's no point in spectacular work unless it serves a purpose. The threat of it beforehand works on the guy himself. It had certainly worked on Hubble. He had taken a lot of notice of it. That's the point of a threat. But to actually carry out something like that has a different point. A different purpose. Carrying it out is not about the guy himself. It's about backing up the threat against the next guy in line. It says, see what we did to that other guy? That's what we could do to you. So by doing some spectacular work on Hubble, somebody had just revealed there was a high-stakes game going down, with other guys waiting next in line, right there in the locality.

'Tell me what happened, Finlay,' I said again.

He leaned forward. Cupped his mouth and nose with his hands and sighed heavily into them.

'OK,' he said. 'It was pretty horrible. One of the worst I've ever seen. And I've seen a few, let me tell you. I've seen some pretty bad ones, but this was something else. He was naked. They nailed him to the wall. Six or seven big carpentry nails through his hands and up his arms. Through the fleshy parts. They nailed his feet to the floor. Then they sliced his balls off. Just hacked them off. Blood everywhere. Pretty bad, let me tell you. Then they slit his throat. Ear to ear. Bad people, Reacher. These are bad people. As bad as they come.'

I was numb. Finlay was waiting for a comment. I couldn't think of anything. I was thinking about Charlie. She would ask if I'd found anything out. Finlay should go up there. He should go up there right now and break the news. It was his job, not mine. I could see why he was reluctant. Difficult news to break. Difficult details to gloss over. But it was his job. I'd go with him. Because it was my fault. No point running away from that.

'Yes,' I said to him. 'It sounds pretty bad.'

He leaned his head back and looked around. Blew another sigh up at the ceiling. A sombre man.

'That's not the worst of it,' he said. 'You should have seen what they did to his wife.'

'His wife?' I said. 'What the hell do you mean?'

'I mean his wife,' he said. 'It was like a butcher's shop.'

For a moment I couldn't speak. The world was spinning backwards.

'But I just saw her,' I said. 'Twenty minutes ago. She's OK. Nothing happened to her.'

'You saw who?' Finlay said.

'Charlie,' I said.

'Who the hell is Charlie?' he asked.

'Charlie,' I said blankly. 'Charlie Hubble. His wife. She's OK. They didn't get her.'

'What's Hubble got to do with this?' he said.

I just stared at him.

'Who are we talking about?' I said. 'Who got killed?'

Finlay looked at me like I was crazy.

'I thought you knew,' he said. 'Chief Morrison. The chief of police. Morrison. And his wife.'

TWELVE

I WAS WATCHING FINLAY VERY CAREFULLY, TRYING TO DECIDE how far I should trust him. It was going to be a life or death decision. In the end I figured his answer to one simple question would make up my mind for me.

'Are they going to make you chief now?' I asked him.

He shook his head.

'No,' he said. 'They're not going to make me chief.'

'You sure about that?' I said.

'I'm sure,' he said.

'Whose decision is it?' I asked him.

'The mayor's,' Finlay said. 'Town mayor appoints the chief of police. He's coming over. Guy named Teale. Some kind of an old Georgia family. Some ancestor was a railroad baron who owned everything in sight around here.'

'Is that the guy you've got statues of?' I said.

Finlay nodded.

'Caspar Teale,' he said. 'He was the first. They've had Teales here ever since. This mayor must be the great-grandson or something.'

I was in a minefield. I needed to find a clear lane through.

'What's the story with this guy Teale?' I asked him.

Finlay shrugged. Tried to find a way to explain it.

'He's just a southern asshole,' he said. 'Old Georgia family, probably a long line of southern assholes. They've been the

130

mayors around here since the beginning. I dare say this one's no worse than the others.'

'Was he upset?' I said. 'When you called him about Morrison?'

'Worried, I think,' Finlay said. 'He hates mess.'

'Why won't he make you chief?' I said. 'You're the senior guy, right?'

'He just won't,' Finlay said. 'Why not is my business.'

I watched him for a moment longer. Life or death.

'Somewhere we can go to talk?' I said.

He looked over the desk at me.

'You thought it was Hubble got killed, right?' he said. 'Why?'

'Hubble did get killed,' I said. 'Fact that Morrison got killed as well doesn't change it.'

We walked down to the convenience store. Sat side by side at the empty counter, near the window. I sat at the same place the pale Mrs Kliner had used when I was in there the day before. That seemed like a long time ago. The world had changed since then. We got tall mugs of coffee and a big plate of doughnuts. Didn't look at each other directly. We looked at each other in the mirror behind the counter.

'Why won't you get the promotion?' I asked him.

His reflection shrugged in the mirror. He was looking puzzled. He couldn't see the connection. But he'd see it soon enough.

'I should get it,' he said. 'I'm better qualified than all the others put together. I've done twenty years in a big city. A real police department. What the hell have they done? Look at Baker, for instance. He figures himself for a smart boy. But what has he done? Fifteen years in the sticks? In this backwater? What the hell does he know?'

'So why won't you get it?' I said.

'It's a personal matter,' he said.

'You think I'm going to sell it to the newspaper?' I asked him.

'It's a long story,' he said.

'So tell it to me,' I said. 'I need to know.'

He looked at me in the mirror. Took a deep breath.

'I finished in Boston in March,' he said. 'Done my twenty years. Unblemished record. Eight commendations. I was one hell of a detective, Reacher. I had retirement on full pension to look forward to. But my wife was going crazy. Since last fall, she was getting agitated. It was so ironic. We were married all through those twenty years. I was working my ass off. Boston PD was a

131

madhouse. We were working seven days a week. All day and all night. All around me guys were seeing their marriages fall apart. They were all getting divorced. One after the other.'

He stopped for a long pull on his coffee. Took a bite of doughnut.

'But not me,' he said. 'My wife could take it. Never complained, never once. She was a miracle. Never gave me a hard time.'

He lapsed back into silence. I thought about twenty years in Boston. Working around the clock in that busy old city. Grimy nineteenth-century precincts. Overloaded facilities. Constant pressure. An endless parade of freaks, villains, politicians, problems. Finlay had done well to survive.

'It started last fall,' he said again. 'We were within six months of the end. It was all going to be over. We were thinking of a cabin somewhere, maybe. Vacations. Plenty of time together. But she started panicking. She didn't want plenty of time together. She didn't want me to retire. She didn't want me at home. She said she woke up to the fact that she didn't like me. Didn't love me. Didn't want me around. She'd loved the twenty years. Didn't want it to change. I couldn't believe it. It had been my dream. Twenty years and then retire at forty-five. Then maybe another twenty years enjoying ourselves together before we got too old, you know? It was my dream and I'd worked towards it for twenty years. But she didn't want it. She ended up saying the thought of twenty more years with me in a cabin in the woods was making her flesh crawl. It got really bitter. We fell apart. I was a total basket case.'

He tailed off again. We got more coffee. It was a sad story. Stories about wrecked dreams always are.

'So obviously, we got divorced,' he said. 'Nothing else to do. She demanded it. It was terrible. I was totally out of it. Then in my last month in the department I started reading the union vacancy lists again. Saw this job down here. I called an old buddy in Atlanta FBI and asked him about it. He warned me off. He said forget it. He said it was a Mickey Mouse department in a town that wasn't even on the map. The job was called the chief of detectives, but there was only one detective. The previous guy was a weirdo who hung himself. The department was run by a fat moron. The town was run by some old Georgia type who couldn't remember slavery had been abolished. My friend up in Atlanta said forget it. But I was so screwed up I wanted it. I thought I could bury myself down here as a punishment, you know? A kind of penance. Also, I needed the money. They were offering top dollar and I was looking at alimony and lawyer bills, you know? So I applied for it and came down. It was Mayor Teale and Morrison who saw me. I was a basket case, Reacher. I was a wreck. I couldn't string two words together. It had to be the worst job application in the history of the world. I must have come across as an idiot. But they gave me the job. I guess they needed a black guy to look good. I'm the first black cop in Margrave's history.'

I turned on the stool and looked straight at him.

'So you figure you're just a token?' I said. 'That's why Teale won't make you chief?'

'It's obvious, I guess,' he said. 'He's got me marked down as a token and an idiot. Not to be promoted further. Makes sense in a way. Can't believe they gave me the job in the first place, token or not.'

I waved to the counter guy for the check. I was happy with Finlay's story. He wasn't going to be chief. So I trusted him. And I trusted Roscoe. It was going to be the three of us, against whoever. I shook my head at him in the mirror.

'You're wrong,' I said. 'That's not the real reason. You're not going to be chief because you're not a criminal.'

I paid the check with a ten and got all quarters for change. The guy still had no dollar bills. Then I told Finlay I needed to see the Morrison place. Told him I needed all the details. He just shrugged and led me outside. We turned and walked south. Passed by the village green and put the town behind us.

'I was the first one there,' he said. 'About ten this morning. I hadn't seen Morrison since Friday and I needed to update the guy, but I couldn't get him on the phone. It was middle of the morning on a Monday and we hadn't done anything worth a damn about a double homicide from last Thursday night. We needed to get our asses in gear. So I went up to his house to start looking for him.'

He went quiet and walked on. Revisiting in his mind the scene he'd found.

'Front door was standing open,' he said. 'Maybe a half-inch. It had a bad feel. I went in, found them upstairs in the master bedroom. It was like a butcher's shop. Blood everywhere. He was nailed to the wall, sort of hanging off. Both of them sliced up, him and his wife. It was terrible. About twenty-four hours of decomposition. Warm weather. Very unpleasant. So I called in the whole crew and we went over every inch and pieced it all together. Literally, I'm afraid.'

He tailed off again. Just went quiet.

'So it happened Sunday morning?' I said.

He nodded.

'Sunday papers on the kitchen table,' he said. 'Couple of sections opened out and the rest untouched. Breakfast things on the table. Medical examiner says about ten o'clock Sunday morning.'

'Any physical evidence left behind?' I asked him.

He nodded again. Grimly.

'Footprints in the blood,' he said. 'The place was a lake of blood. Gallons of it. Partly dried up now, of course. They left footprints all over. But they were wearing rubber overshoes, you know? Like you get for the winter up north? No chance of tracing them. They must sell millions every year.'

They had come prepared. They'd known there was going to be a lot of blood. They'd brought overshoes. They must have brought overalls. Like the nylon bodysuits they wear in the slaughterhouse. On the killing floor. Big white nylon suits, hooded, the white nylon splashed and smeared with bright red blood.

'They wore gloves, too,' he said. 'There are rubbery smears in the blood on the walls.'

'How many people?' I asked him. I was trying to build up a picture.

'Four,' he said. 'The footprints are confused, but I think I can see four.'

I nodded. Four sounded right. About the minimum, I reckoned. Morrison and his wife would have been fighting for their lives. It would take four of them, at least. Four out of the ten Hubble had mentioned.

'Transport?' I said.

'Can't really tell,' Finlay said. 'Gravel driveway, washed into ruts here and there. I saw some wide ruts which look new, maybe. Could have been wide tyres. Maybe a big four-wheel-drive or a small truck.'

We were a couple of hundred yards south of where Main Street had petered out. We turned west up a gravel driveway which must have been just about parallel with Beckman Drive. At the end of the driveway was Morrison's house. It was a big formal place, white columns at the front, symmetrical evergreen trees dotted about. There was a new Lincoln parked near the door and a lot of police tape strung at waist height between the columns.

'We going in?' Finlay asked.

'May as well,' I said.

We ducked under the tape and pushed in through Morrison's front door. The house was a wreck. Grey metallic fingerprint powder everywhere. Everything tossed and searched and photographed.

'You won't find anything,' Finlay said. 'We went over the whole place.'

I nodded and headed for the staircase. Went up and found the master bedroom. Stopped at the door and peered in. There was nothing to see except the ragged outline of the nail holes in the wall and the massive bloodstains. The blood was turning black. It looked like somebody had flung buckets of tar around. The carpet was crusty with it. On the parquet in the doorway I could see the footprints from the overshoes. I could make out the intricate pattern of the treads. I headed back downstairs and found Finlay leaning on a porch column out front.

'OK?' he asked me.

'Terrific,' I said. 'You search the car?'

He shook his head.

'That's Morrison's,' he said. 'We just looked for stuff the intruders might have left behind.'

I stepped over to the Lincoln and tried the door. Unlocked. Inside, there was a strong new-car smell and not much else. This was a chief's car. It wasn't going to be full of cheeseburger wrappings and soda cans like a patrolman's would be. But I checked it out. Poked around in the door pockets and under the seats. Found nothing at all. Then I opened the glovebox and found something. There was a switchblade in there. It was a handsome thing. Ebony handle with Morrison's name in gold-filled engraving. I popped the blade. Double edged, seven inches, Japanese surgical steel. Looked good. Brand new, never been used. I closed it up and slipped it into my pocket. I was unarmed and facing big trouble. Morrison's switchblade might make a difference. I slid out of the Lincoln and rejoined Finlay on the gravel.

'Find anything?' he asked.

'No,' I said. 'Let's go.'

We crunched back down the driveway together and turned north on the county road. Headed back to town. I could see the church steeple and the bronze statue in the distance, waiting for us.

THIRTEEN

'SOMETHING I NEED TO CHECK WITH YOU,' I SAID.

Finlay's patience was running thin. He looked at his watch.

'You better not be wasting my time, Reacher,' he said.

We walked on north. The sun was dropping away from overhead, but the heat was still fierce. I didn't know how Finlay could wear a tweed jacket. And a moleskin vest. I led him over to the village green. We crossed the grass and leaned up on the statue of old Caspar Teale, side by side.

'They cut his balls off, right?' I said.

He nodded. Looked at me, waiting.

'OK,' I said. 'So the question is this: did you find his balls?'

He shook his head.

'No,' he said. 'We went over the whole place. Ourselves and the medical examiner. They weren't there. His testicles are missing.'

He smiled as he said it. He was recovering his cop's sense of humour.

'OK,' I said. 'That's what I needed to know.'

His smile widened. Reached his eyes.

'Why?' he said. 'Do you know where they are?'

'When's the autopsy?' I asked him.

He was still smiling.

'His autopsy won't help,' he said. 'They were cut off. They're not connected to him any more. They weren't there. They're missing.

So how can they find them at his autopsy?'

'Not his autopsy,' I said. 'Her autopsy. His wife's. When they check what she ate.'

Finlay stopped smiling. Went quiet. Just looked at me.

'Talk, Reacher,' he said.

'OK,' I said. 'That's why we came out here, remember? So answer another question for me. How many homicides have they had in Margrave?'

He thought about it. Shrugged.

'None,' he said. 'At least, not for maybe thirty years or so. Not since voter registration days, I guess.'

'And now you've had four in four days,' I said. 'And pretty soon you'll find the fifth.'

'Fifth?' he said. 'Who's the fifth?'

'Hubble,' I said. 'My brother, this Sherman Stoller guy, the two Morrisons and Hubble makes five. No homicides in thirty years and now you've got five all at once. That can't be any kind of a co-incidence, right?'

'No way,' he said. 'Of course not. They're linked.'

'Right,' I said. 'Now I'll tell you some more links. But first of all, you got to understand something, right? I was just passing through here. On Friday and Saturday and Sunday right up to the time those prints came through on my brother, I wasn't paying the slightest bit of attention to anything at all. I was just figuring I'd wait around and get the hell out of here as soon as possible.'

'So?' he said.

'So I was told stuff,' I said. 'Hubble told me things in Warburton, but I didn't pay a lot of attention. I wasn't interested in him, OK? He told me things, and I didn't follow them up with him and I probably don't recall some of them.'

'Like what things?' Finlay said.

So I told him the things I remembered. I started the same way Hubble had started. Trapped inside some kind of a racket, terror-ized by a threat against himself and his wife. A threat consisting of the same things, word for word, that Finlay had just seen for him-self that morning.

'You sure about that?' he said. 'Exactly the same?'

'Word for word,' I said. 'Totally identical. Nailed to the wall, balls cut off, the wife forced to eat the balls, then they get their throats cut. Word-for-word identical, Finlay. So unless we got two threateners at the same time in the same place making the exact same threat, that's another link.'

'So Morrison was inside the same scam as Hubble?' he said.

'Owned and operated by the same people,' I said.

Then I told him Hubble had been talking to an investigator. And I told him the investigator had been talking to Sherman Stoller, whoever he had been.

'Who was the investigator?' he asked. 'And where does Joe fit in?'

'Joe was the investigator,' I said. 'Hubble told me the tall guy with the shaved head was an investigator, trying to get him free.'

'What sort of an investigator was your brother?' Finlay said. 'Who the hell was he working for?'

'Don't know,' I said. 'Last I heard he was working for the Treasury Department.'

Finlay pushed off the statue and started walking back north.

'I got to make some calls,' he said. 'Time to go to work on this thing.'

'Walk slow,' I said. 'I haven't finished yet.'

Finlay was on the sidewalk. I was in the road, staying clear of the low awnings in front of every store. There was no traffic on the street to worry about. Monday, two o'clock in the afternoon, and the town was deserted.

'How do you know Hubble's dead?' Finlay asked me.

So I told him how I knew. He thought about it. He agreed with me.

'Because he was talking to an investigator?' he said.

I shook my head. Stopped outside the barbershop.

'No,' I said. 'They didn't know about that. If they had, they'd have got to him much earlier. Thursday at the latest. I figure they took the decision to waste him Friday, about five o'clock. Because you pulled him in with the phone number in Joe's shoe. They figured he couldn't be allowed to talk to cops or prison guards. So they set it up with Spivey. But Spivey's boys blew it, so they tried over again. His wife said he got a call to wait at home today. They were setting him up for a second attempt. Looks like it worked.'

Finlay nodded slowly.

'Shit,' he said. 'He was the only link we had to exactly what the hell is going on here. You should have hit on him while you had the chance, Reacher.'

'Thanks, Finlay,' I said. 'If I'd known the dead guy was Joe, I'd have hit on him so hard, you'd have heard him yelling all the way over here.'

He just grunted. We moved over and sat together on the bench under the barbershop window.

'I asked him what Pluribus was,' I said. 'He wouldn't answer. He said there were ten local people involved in the scam, plus hired help in from the outside when necessary. And he said the scam is vulnerable until something happens on Sunday. Exposed, somehow.'

'What happens on Sunday?' Finlay asked.

'He didn't tell me,' I said.

'And you didn't press him?' he asked.

'I wasn't very interested,' I said. 'I told you that.'

'And he gave you no idea what the scam is all about?' he asked.

'No idea,' I said.

'Did he say who these ten people are?' he asked.

'No,' I said.

'Christ, Reacher, you're a big help, you know that?' he said.

'I'm sorry, Finlay,' I said. 'I thought Hubble was just some asshole. If I could go back and do it again, I'd do it a lot different, believe me.'

'Ten people?' he said again.

'Not counting himself,' I said. 'Not counting Sherman Stoller, either. But I assume he was counting Chief Morrison.'

'Great,' Finlay said. 'That only leaves me another nine to find.'

'You'll find one of them today,' I said.

The black pickup I'd last seen leaving Eno's parking lot pulled up short at the opposite kerb. It waited there, motor running. The Kliner kid leaned his head on his forearm and stared out of the window at me from across the street. Finlay didn't see him. He was looking down at the sidewalk.

'You should be thinking about Morrison,' I said to him.

'What about him?' he said. 'He's dead, right?'

'But dead how?' I said. 'What should that be saying to you?'

He shrugged.

'Somebody making an example of him?' he said. 'A message?'

'Correct, Finlay,' I said. 'But what had he done wrong?'

'Screwed something up, I guess,' he said.

'Correct, Finlay,' I said again. 'He was told to cover up what went down at the warehouse Thursday night. That was his task for the day. He was up there at midnight, you know.'

'He was?' Finlay said. 'You said that was a bullshit story.'

'No,' I said. 'He didn't see me up there. That part was the bullshit story. But he was up there himself. He saw Joe.'

'He did?' Finlay said. 'How do you know that?'

'First time he saw me was Friday, right?' I said. 'In the office? He was staring at me like he'd seen me before, but he couldn't place where. That was because he'd seen Joe. He noticed a resemblance. Hubble said the same thing. He said I reminded him of his investigator.'

'So Morrison was there?' Finlay said. 'Was he the shooter?'

'Can't figure it that way,' I said. 'Joe was a reasonably smart guy. He wouldn't let a fat idiot like Morrison shoot him. The shooter must have been somebody else. I can't figure Morrison for the maniac, either. That much physical exertion would have dropped him with a heart attack. I think he was the third guy. The clean-up guy. But he didn't search Joe's shoes. And because of that, Hubble got hauled in. That got somebody mad. It meant they had to waste Hubble, so Morrison was wasted as a punishment.'

'Some punishment,' Finlay said.

'Also a message,' I said. 'So think about it.'

'Think about what?' he said. 'Wasn't a message for me.'

'So who was it a message for?' I said.

'Who is any such message for?' he said. 'The next guy in line, right?'

I nodded.

'See why I was worried who was going to be the next chief?' I said.

Finlay dropped his head again and stared at the sidewalk.

'Christ,' he said. 'You think the next chief will be in the scam?'

'Got to be,' I said. 'Why would they have Morrison inside? Not for his wonderful personality, right? They had him inside because they need the chief on board. Because that's useful to them in some particular way. So they wouldn't waste Morrison unless they had a replacement ready. And whoever it is, we're looking at a very dangerous guy. He'll be going in there with Morrison's example staring him in the face. Somebody will have just whispered to him: see what we did to Morrison? That's what we'll do to you if you screw up the way he did.'

'So who is it?' Finlay said. 'Who's going to be the new chief?'

'That's what I was asking you,' I said.

We sat quiet on the bench outside the barbershop for a moment. Enjoyed the sun creeping in under the edge of the striped awning.

'It's you, me and Roscoe,' I said. 'Right now, the only safe thing is to assume everybody else is involved.'

'Why Roscoe?' he said.

'Lots of reasons,' I said. 'But mainly because she worked hard to get me out of Warburton. Morrison wanted me in there as a fall guy for Thursday night, right? So if Roscoe was inside the scam, she'd have left me in there. But she got me out. She pulled in the exact opposite direction from Morrison. So if he was bent, she isn't.'

He looked at me. Grunted.

'Only three of us?' he said. 'You're a cautious guy, Reacher.'

'You bet your ass I'm a cautious guy, Finlay,' I said. 'People are getting killed here. One of them was my only brother.'

We stood up from the bench on the sidewalk. Across the street, the Kliner kid killed his motor and got out of the pickup. Started walking slowly over. Finlay rubbed his face with his hands, like he was washing without water.

'So what now?' he said.

'You got things to do,' I said. 'You need to get Roscoe on one side and fill her in with the details, OK? Tell her to take a lot of care. Then you need to make some calls and find out from Washington what Joe was doing down here.'

'OK,' Finlay said. 'What about you?'

I nodded across at the Kliner kid.

'I'm going to have a talk with this guy,' I said. 'He keeps looking at me.'

Two things happened as the Kliner kid came near. First, Finlay left in a hurry. He just strode off north without another word. Second, I heard the barbershop blinds coming down in the window behind me. I glanced around. There could have been nobody else on the planet except for me and the Kliner kid.

Up close, the kid was an interesting study. He was no lightweight. Probably six-two, maybe one ninety, shot through with some kind of a restless energy. There was a lot of intelligence in his eyes, but there was also some kind of an eerie light burning in there. His eyes told me this probably wasn't the most rational character I was ever going to meet in my whole life. He came close and stood in front of me. Just stared at me.

'You're trespassing,' he said.

'This is your sidewalk?' I said.

'It sure is,' the kid said. 'My daddy's Foundation paid for every inch of it. Every brick. But I'm not talking about the sidewalk. I'm talking about Miss Roscoe. She's mine. She's mine, right from when I first saw her. She's waiting for me. Five years, she's been

141

waiting for me, until the time is right.'

I gazed back at him.

'You understand English?' I said.

The kid tensed up. He was just about hopping from foot to foot.

'I'm a reasonable guy,' I said. 'First time Miss Roscoe tells me she wants you instead of me, I'm out of here. Until then, you back off. Understand that?'

The kid was boiling. But then he changed. It was like he was operated by a remote control and somebody had just hit a button and switched the channel. He relaxed and shrugged and smiled a wide, boyish smile.

'OK,' he said. 'No hard feelings, right?'

He stuck out his hand to shake on it and he nearly fooled me. Right at the last split second I pulled my own hand back a fraction and closed around his knuckles, not his palm. It's an old army trick. They go to shake your hand, but they're aiming to crush it. Some big macho ritual. The way out is to be ready. You pull back a fraction and you squeeze back. You're squeezing their knuckles, not the meat of their palm. Their grip is neutralized. If you catch it right, you can't lose.

He started crushing, but he never stood a chance. He was going for the steady squeeze, so he could stare into my eyes while I sweated it out. But he never got near. I crunched his knuckles once, then twice, a little harder, and then I dropped his hand and turned away. I was a good sixty yards north before I heard the truck start up. It rumbled south and its noise was lost in the buzz of the heat.

FOURTEEN

BACK AT THE STATION HOUSE THERE WAS A BIG WHITE CADILLAC parked right across the entrance. Brand-new, fully loaded. Full of puffy black leather and fake wood. It looked like a Vegas whorehouse after the stern walnut and old hide in Charlie Hubble's Bentley. Took me five strides to get around its hood to the door.

Inside in the chill everybody was milling around a tall old guy with silver hair. He was in an old-fashioned suit. Bootlace tie with a silver clasp. Looked like a real asshole. Some kind of a politician. The Cadillac driver. He must have been about seventy-five years old and he was limping around, leaning on a thick cane with a huge silver knob at the top. I guessed this was Mayor Teale.

Roscoe was coming out of the big office in back. She had been pretty shaken up after being at the Morrison place. Wasn't looking too good now, but she waved and tried a smile. Gestured me over. Wanted me to go into the office with her. I took another quick glance at Mayor Teale and walked over to her.

'You OK?' I said.

'I've had better days,' she said.

'You up to speed?' I asked her. 'Finlay give you the spread?'

She nodded.

'Finlay told me everything,' she said.

We ducked into the big rosewood office. Finlay was sitting at the desk under the old clock. It showed a quarter of four. Roscoe closed the door and I looked back and forth between the two of them.

'So who's getting it?' I said. 'Who's the new chief?'

Finlay looked up at me from where he was sitting. Shook his head.

'Nobody,' he said. 'Mayor Teale is going to run the department himself.'

I went back to the door and cracked it open an inch. Peered out and looked at Teale across the squad room. He had Baker pinned up against the wall. Looked like he was giving him a hard time about something. I watched him for a moment.

'So what do you make of that?' I asked them.

'Everybody else in the department is clean,' Roscoe said.

'Looks that way, I guess,' I said. 'But it proves Teale himself is on board. Teale's their replacement, so Teale's their boy.'

'How do we know he's just their boy?' she said. 'Maybe he's the big boss. Maybe he's running the whole thing.'

'No,' I said. 'The big boss had Morrison carved up as a message. If Teale was the big boss, why would he send a message to himself? He belongs to somebody. He's been put in here to run interference.'

'That's for sure,' Finlay said. 'Started already. Told us Joe and Stoller are going on the back burner. We're throwing everything at the Morrison thing. Doing it ourselves, no outside help, no FBI, no nothing. He says the pride of the department is at stake. And he's already driving us up a blind alley. Says it's obvious Morrison was killed by somebody just out of prison. Somebody Morrison himself put away a long time ago, out for revenge.'

'And it's a hell of a blind alley,' Roscoe said. 'We've got to trawl through twenty years of old files and cross-check every name in every file against parole records from across the entire country. It could take us months. He's pulled Stevenson in off the road for it. Until this is over, he drives a desk. So do I.'

'It's worse than a blind alley,' Finlay said. 'It's a coded warning. Nobody in our files looks good for violent revenge. Never had that sort of crime here. We know that. And Teale knows we know that. But we can't call his bluff, right?'

'Can't you just ignore him?' I said. 'Just do what needs doing?'

He leaned back in his chair. Blew a sigh at the ceiling and shook his head.

'No,' he said. 'We're working right under the enemy's nose. Right now, Teale's got no reason to think we know anything about any of this. And we've got to keep it that way. We've got to play dumb and act innocent, right? That's going to limit our scope. But the big problem is authorization. If I need a warrant or something, I'm going to need his signature. And I'm not going to get it, am I?'

I shrugged at him.

'I'm not planning on using warrants,' I said. 'Did you call Washington?'

'They're getting back to me,' he said. 'Just hope Teale doesn't grab the phone before I can.'

I nodded.

'What you need is somewhere else to work,' I said. 'What about that buddy of yours up in Atlanta FBI? The one you told me about? Could you use his office as a kind of private facility?'

Finlay thought about it. Nodded.

'Not a bad idea,' he said. 'I'll have to go off the record. I can't ask Teale to make a formal request, right? I'll call from home, tonight. Guy called Picard. Nice guy, you'll like him. He's from the Quarter, down in New Orleans. He did a spell in Boston about a million years ago. Great big guy, very smart, very tough.'

'Tell him we need it kept very quiet,' I said. 'We don't want his agents down here until we're ready.'

'What are you going to do about Teale?' Roscoe asked me. 'He works for the guys who killed your brother.'

I shrugged again.

'Depends how involved he was,' I said. 'He wasn't the shooter.'

'He wasn't?' Roscoe said. 'How do you know that?'

'Not fast enough,' I said. 'Limps around with a cane in his hand. Too slow to pull a gun. Too slow to get Joe, anyway. He wasn't the kicker, either. Too old, not vigorous enough. And he wasn't the gofer. That was Morrison. But if he starts messing with me, then he's in deep shit. Otherwise, to hell with him.'

'So what now?' she said.

I shrugged at her. Didn't reply.

'I think Sunday is the thing,' Finlay said. 'Sunday is going to solve some kind of a problem for them. Teale being put in here feels so temporary, you know? The guy's seventy-five years old. He's got no police experience. It's a temporary fix, to get them through until Sunday.'

The buzzer on the desk went off. Stevenson's voice came over the intercom asking for Roscoe. They had files to check. I opened the door for her. But she stopped. She'd just thought of something.

'What about Spivey?' she said. 'Over at Warburton? He was ordered to arrange the attack on Hubble, right? So he must know who gave him the order. You should go ask him. Might lead somewhere.'

'Maybe,' I said. Closed the door behind her.

'Waste of time,' Finlay said to me. 'You think Spivey's just going to tell you a thing like that?'

I smiled at him.

'If he knows, he'll tell me,' I said to him. 'A question like that, it's how you ask it, right?'

'Take care, Reacher,' he said. 'They see you getting close to what Hubble knew, they'll waste you like they wasted him.'

Charlie and her kids flashed into my mind and I shivered. They would figure Charlie was close to what Hubble had known. That was inevitable. Maybe even his kids as well. A cautious person would assume kids could have overheard something. It was four o'clock. The kids would be out of school. There were people out there who had loaded up with rubber overshoes, nylon bodysuits and surgical gloves. And sharp knives. And a bag of nails. And a hammer.

'Finlay, call your buddy Picard right now,' I said. 'We need his help. We've got to put Charlie Hubble somewhere safe. And her kids. Right now.'

Finlay nodded gravely. He saw it. He understood.

'For sure,' he said. 'Get your ass up to Beckman. Right now. Stay there. I'll organize Picard. You don't leave until he shows up, OK?'

He picked up the phone. Dialled an Atlanta number from memory.

Roscoe was back at her desk. Mayor Teale was handing her a thick wad of file folders. I stepped over to her and pulled up a spare chair. Sat down next to her.

'What time do you finish?' I said.

'About six, I guess,' she said.

'Bring some handcuffs home, OK?' I said.

'You're a fool, Jack Reacher,' she said.

Teale was watching so I got up and kissed her hair. Went out into the afternoon and headed for the Bentley. The sun was dropping away and the heat was gone. Shadows were lengthening up. Felt like the fall was on its way. Behind me I heard a shout. Mayor Teale had followed me out of the building. He called me back. I stayed where I was. Made him come to me. He limped over, tapping his cane, smiling. Stuck out his hand and introduced himself. Said his name was Grover Teale. He had that politician's knack of fixing you with a look and a smile like a searchlight. Like he was thrilled to bits just to be talking to me.

'Glad I caught you,' he said. 'Sergeant Baker has brought me up to date on the warehouse homicides. It all seems pretty clear to me. We made a clumsy mistake in apprehending you, and we're all very sorry indeed about your brother, and we'll certainly let you know just as soon as we get to any conclusions. So before you get on your way, I'd be grateful if you'd kindly accept my apology on behalf of this department. I wouldn't want you to take away a bad impression of us. May we just call it a mistake?'

'OK, Teale,' I said. 'But why do you assume I'm leaving?'

He came back smoothly. Not more than a tiny hesitation.

'I understood you were just passing through,' he said. 'We have no hotel here in Margrave and I imagined you would find no opportunity to stay.'

'I'm staying,' I said. 'I received a generous offer of hospitality. I understand that's what the South is famous for, right? Hospitality?'

He beamed at me and grasped his embroidered lapel.

'Oh, undoubtedly that's true, sir,' he said. 'The South as a whole, and Georgia in particular, is indeed famous for the warmth of its welcome. However, as you know, just at the present time, we find ourselves in a most awkward predicament. In the circumstances, a motel in Atlanta or Macon would really suit you much better. Naturally, we would keep in close touch, and we would extend you every assistance in arranging your brother's funeral, when that sad time comes. Here in Margrave, I'm afraid, we're all going to be very busy. It'll be boring for you. Officer Roscoe's going to have a lot of work to do. She shouldn't be distracted just at the moment, don't you think?'

'I won't distract her,' I said evenly. 'I know she's doing vital work.'

He looked at me. An expressionless gaze. Eye to eye, but he wasn't really tall enough. He'd get a crick in his scrawny old neck. And if he kept on staring at me like that, he'd get his scrawny old neck broken. I gave him a wintry smile and stepped away to the Bentley. Unlocked it and got in. Gunned the big motor and whirred the window down.

'See you later, Teale,' I called as I drove away.

147

The end of the school day was the busiest I'd ever seen the town. I passed two people on Main Street and saw another four in a knot near the church. Some kind of an afternoon club, maybe. Reading the Bible or bottling peaches for the winter. I drove past them and hustled the big car up the sumptuous mile of Beckman Drive. Turned in at the Hubbles' white mailbox and spun the old Bakelite steering wheel through the driveway curves.

The problem with trying to warn Charlie was I didn't know how much I wanted to tell her. Certainly I wasn't about to give her the details. Didn't even feel right to tell her Hubble was dead at all. We were stuck in some kind of a limbo. But I couldn't keep her in the dark for ever. She needed to know some context. Or else she wouldn't listen to the warning.

I parked her car at her door and rang her bell. The children dashed around from somewhere as Charlie opened up and let me in. She was looking pretty tired and strained. The children looked happy enough. They hadn't picked up on their mother's worries. She chased them off and I followed her back to the kitchen. It was a big, modern room. I got her to make me some coffee. I could see she was anxious to talk, but she was having trouble getting started. I watched her fiddling with the filter machine.

'Don't you have a maid?' I asked her.

She shook her head.

'I don't want one,' she said. 'I like to do things myself.'

'It's a big house,' I said.

'I like to keep busy, I guess,' she said.

Then we were silent. Charlie switched on the coffee machine and it started with a faint hiss. I sat at a table in a window nook. It overlooked an acre of velvet lawn. She came and sat opposite me. Folded her hands in front of her.

'I heard about the Morrisons,' she said at last. 'Is my husband involved in all of this?'

I tried to think exactly what I could say to her. She waited for an answer. The coffee machine burbled away in the big silent kitchen.

'Yes, Charlie,' I said. 'I'm afraid he was. But he didn't want to be involved, OK? Some kind of blackmail was going on.'

She took it well. She must have figured it out for herself, anyway. Must have run every possible speculation through her head. This explanation was the one which fit. That was why she didn't look surprised or outraged. She just nodded. Then she relaxed. She looked like it had done her good to hear someone else say it.

Now it was out in the open. It was acknowledged. It could be dealt with.

'I'm afraid that makes sense,' she said.

She got up to pour the coffee. Kept talking as she went.

'That's the only way I can explain his behaviour,' she said. 'Is he in danger?'

'Charlie, I'm afraid I have no idea where he is,' I said.

She handed me a mug of coffee. Sat down again on the kitchen counter.

'Is he in danger?' she asked again.

I couldn't answer. Couldn't get any words out. She moved off the counter and came to sit opposite me again at the table in the window. She cradled her cup in front of her. She was a fine-looking woman. Blonde and pretty. Perfect teeth, good bones, slim, athletic. A lot of spirit. I had seen her as a plantation type. What they call a belle. I had said to myself that a hundred and fifty years ago she would have been a slaveowner. I began to change that opinion. I felt a crackle of toughness coming from her. She enjoyed being rich and idle, sure. Beauty parlours and lunch with the girls in Atlanta. The Bentley and the gold cards. The big kitchen which cost more than I ever made in a year. But if it came to it, here was a woman who might get down in the dirt and fight. Maybe a hundred and fifty years ago she would have been on a wagon train heading west. She had enough spirit. She looked hard at me across the table.

'I panicked this morning,' she said. 'That's not really like me at all. I must have given you a very bad impression, I'm afraid. After you left, I calmed down and thought things out. I came to the same conclusion you've just described. Hub's blundered into something and he's got all tangled up in it. So what am I going to do about it? Well, I'm going to stop panicking and start thinking. I've been a mess since Friday and I'm ashamed of it. That's not the real me at all. So I did something, and I hope you'll forgive me for it?'

'Go on,' I said.

'I called Dwight Stevenson,' she said. 'He had mentioned he had seen a fax from the Pentagon about your service as a military policeman. I asked him to find it and read it to me. I thought it was an excellent record.'

She smiled at me. Hitched her chair in closer.

'So what I want to do is to hire you,' she said. 'I want to hire you in a private capacity to solve my husband's problem. Would you consider doing that for me?'

'No,' I said. 'I can't do that, Charlie.'

'Can't or won't?' she said.

'There would be a sort of a conflict of interest,' I said. 'It might mean I couldn't do a proper job for you.'

'A conflict?' she said. 'In what way?'

I paused for a long moment. Tried to figure out how to explain it.

'Your husband felt bad, OK?' I said. 'He got hold of some kind of an investigator, a government guy, and they were trying to fix the situation. But the government guy got killed. And I'm afraid my interest is in the government guy, more than your husband.'

She followed what I was saying and nodded.

'But why?' she asked. 'You don't work for the government.'

'The government guy was my brother,' I told her. 'Just a crazy coincidence, I know, but I'm stuck with it.'

She went quiet. She saw where the conflict could lie.

'I'm very sorry,' she said. 'You're not saying Hub betrayed your brother?'

'No,' I said. 'That's the very last thing he would have done. He was depending on him to get him out from under. Something went wrong, is all.'

'May I ask you a question?' she said. 'Why do you refer to my husband in the past tense?'

I looked straight at her.

'Because he's dead,' I said. 'I'm very sorry.'

Charlie hung in there. She went pale and clenched her hands until her knuckles shone waxy white. But she didn't fall apart.

'I don't think he's dead,' she whispered. 'I would know. I would be able to feel it. I think he's just hiding out somewhere. I want you to find him. I'll pay you whatever you want.'

I just slowly shook my head at her.

'Please,' she said.

'I won't do it, Charlie,' I said. 'I won't take your money for that. I would be exploiting you. I can't take your money because I know he's already dead. I'm very sorry, but there it is.'

There was a long silence in the kitchen. I sat there at the table, nursing the coffee she'd made for me.

'Would you do it if I didn't pay you?' she said. 'Maybe you could just look around for him while you find out about your brother?'

I thought about it. Couldn't see how I could say no to that.

'OK,' I said. 'I'll do that, Charlie. But like I say, don't expect miracles. I think we're looking at something very bad here.'

'I think he's alive,' she said. 'I would know if he wasn't.'

I started worrying about what would happen when his body was found. She was going to come face to face with reality the same way a runaway truck comes face to face with the side of a building.

'You'll need expense money,' Charlie said.

I wasn't sure about taking it, but she passed me a thick envelope.

'Will that do?' she asked.

I looked in the envelope. There was a thick wad of hundred dollar bills in there. I nodded. That would do.

'And please keep the car,' she said. 'Use it as long as you need it.'

I nodded again. Thought about what else I needed to say and forced myself to use the present tense.

'Where does he work?' I asked her.

'Sunrise International,' she said. 'It's a bank.'

She reeled off an Atlanta address.

'OK, Charlie,' I said. 'Now let me ask you something else. It's very important. Did your husband ever use the word "Pluribus"?'

She thought about it and shrugged.

'Pluribus?' she said. 'Isn't that something to do with politics? Like on the podium when the President gives a speech? I never heard Hub talking about it. He graduated in banking studies.'

'You never heard him use that word?' I asked her again. 'Not on the phone, not in his sleep or anything?'

'Never,' she said.

'What about next Sunday?' I asked her. 'Did he mention next Sunday? Anything about what's going to happen?'

'Next Sunday?' she repeated. 'I don't think he mentioned it. Why? What's going to happen next Sunday?'

'I don't know,' I said. 'That's what I'm trying to find out.'

She pondered it again for a long moment, but just shook her head and shrugged, palms upward, like it meant nothing to her.

'I'm sorry,' she said.

'Don't worry about it,' I said. 'Now you've got to do something.'

'What do I have to do?' she said.

'You've got to get out of here,' I said.

Her knuckles were still white, but she was staying in control.

'I've got to run and hide?' she said. 'But where to?'

'An FBI agent is coming here to pick you up,' I said.

She stared at me in panic.

'FBI?' she said. She went paler still. 'This is really serious, isn't it?'

'It's deadly serious,' I said. 'You need to get ready to leave right now.'

'OK,' she said, slowly. 'I can't believe this is happening.'

I walked out of her kitchen and into the garden room where we had drunk iced tea the day before. Stepped through the French doors and strolled a slow circuit outside the house. Down the driveway, through the banks of greenery, out onto Beckman Drive. Leaned up on the white mailbox on the shoulder. It was silent. I could hear nothing at all except the dry rustle of the grass cooling under my feet.

Then I could hear a car coming west out of town. It slowed just before the crest of the rise and I heard the automatic box slur a change down as the speed dropped. The car rose up over the crest into view. It was a brown Buick, very plain, two guys in it. They were small dark guys, Hispanic, loud shirts. They were slowing, drifting to the left of the road, looking for the Hubble mailbox. I was leaning on the Hubble mailbox, looking at them. Their eyes met mine. The car accelerated again and swerved away. Blasted on into the empty peach country. I stepped out and watched them go. I saw a dust plume rising as they drove off Margrave's immaculate blacktop onto the dusty rural roadway. Then I sprinted back up to the house. I wanted Charlie to hurry.

She was inside, flustered, chattering away like a kid going on vacation. Making lists out loud. Some kind of a mechanism to burn off the panic she was feeling. On Friday she'd been a rich idle woman married to a banker. Now on Monday a stranger who said the banker was dead was telling her to hurry up and run for her life.

'Take the mobile phone with you,' I called to her.

She didn't reply. I just heard a worried silence. Footsteps and closet doors banging. I sat in her kitchen with the rest of the coffee for most of an hour. Then I heard a car horn blow and the crunch of heavy steps on the gravel. A loud knock on the front door. I put my hand in my pocket and closed it around the ebony handle of Morrison's switchblade. Walked out into the hallway and opened up.

There was a neat blue sedan next to the Bentley and a gigantic black guy standing back from the doorstep. He was as tall as me, maybe even taller, but he must have outweighed me by at least a hundred pounds. Must have been three-ten, three-twenty. Next to him, I was a featherweight. He stepped forward with the easy elastic grace of an athlete.

'Reacher?' the giant said. 'Pleased to meet you. I'm Picard, FBI.'

He shook hands with me. He was enormous. He had a casual competence about him which made me glad he was on my side. He looked like my type of a guy. Like he could be very useful in a tight corner. I suddenly felt a flood of encouragement. I stood aside to let him into Charlie's house.

'OK,' Picard said to me. 'I got all the details from Finlay. Real sorry about your brother, my friend. Real sorry. Somewhere we can talk?'

I led him through to the kitchen. He loped beside me and covered the distance in a couple of strides. Glanced around and poured himself the dregs of the stewed coffee. Then he stepped over next to me and dropped his hand on my shoulder. Felt like somebody had hit me with a bag of cement.

'Ground rules,' he said. 'This whole thing is off the record, right?'

I nodded. His voice matched his bulk. It was a low rumble. It was what a brown bear would sound like if it learned to talk. I couldn't tell how old the guy was. He was one of those big fit men whose peak years stretch on for decades. He nodded and moved away. Rested his giant frame against the counter.

'This is a huge problem for me,' he said. 'Bureau can't act without a call from the responsible official in the local jurisdiction. That would be this guy Teale, right? And from what Finlay tells me, I assume old Teale's not going to be making that call. So I could end up with my big ass in a sling for this. But I'll bend the rules for Finlay. We go back quite a ways. But you got to remember, this is all unofficial, OK?'

I nodded again. I was happy with that. Very happy. Unofficial help suited me fine. It would get the job done without hanging me up on procedure. I had five clear days before Sunday. This morning, five days had seemed more than generous. But now, with Hubble gone, I felt like I was very short of time. Much too short of time to waste any of it on procedure.

'Where are you going to put them?' I asked him.

'Safe house up in Atlanta,' Picard said. 'Bureau place, we've had it for years. They'll be secure there, but I'm not going to say exactly where it is, and I'm going to have to ask you not to press Mrs Hubble about it afterwards, OK? I got to watch my back on this thing. I blow a safe house, I'm in really deep shit.'

'OK, Picard,' I said. 'I won't cause you a problem. And I appreciate it.'

He nodded, gravely, like he was way out on a limb. Then Charlie and the kids burst in. They were burdened down with badly packed bags. Picard introduced himself. I could see that Charlie's daughter was terrified by the size of the guy. The little boy's eyes grew round as he gazed at the FBI Special Agent's shield Picard was holding out. Then the five of us carried the bags outside and piled them in the blue sedan's trunk. I shook hands with Picard and Charlie. Then they all got in the car. Picard drove them away. I waved after them.

FIFTEEN

I HEADED OVER TO WARBURTON A DAMN SIGHT FASTER THAN THE prison driver had and I was there in less than fifty minutes. It was a hell of a sight. There was a storm coming in quickly from the west and shafts of low afternoon sun were escaping the clouds and hitting the place. The glittering metal towers and turrets were catching the orange rays. I slowed up and pulled into the prison approach. Stopped outside the first vehicle cage. I wasn't going in there. I'd had enough of that. Spivey was going to have to come out to me. I got out of the Bentley and walked over to the guard. He seemed friendly enough.

'Spivey on duty?' I asked him.

'You want him?' the guard said.

'Tell him Mr Reacher's here,' I said.

The guy ducked under a Perspex hood and made a call. Ducked back out again and shouted over to me.

'He doesn't know any Mr Reacher,' he said.

'Tell him Chief Morrison sent me,' I said. 'Over from Margrave.'

The guy went under the Perspex thing again and started talking. After a minute he was back out.

'OK, drive on through,' he said. 'Spivey will meet you at reception.'

'Tell him he's got to come out here,' I said. 'Meet me on the road.'

I walked away and stood in the dust on the edge of the black-top. It was a battle of nerves. I was betting Spivey would come on out. I'd know in five minutes. I waited. I could smell rain coming out of the west. In an hour, it was going to roll right over us. I stood and waited.

Spivey came out. I heard the grilles on the vehicle cage grinding across. I turned and saw a dirty Ford driving through. It came out and stopped next to the Bentley. Spivey heaved himself out. He walked over. Big guy, sweating, red face and hands. His uniform was dirty.

'Remember me?' I asked him.

His small snake eyes flicked around. He was adrift and worried. 'You're Reacher,' he said. 'So what?'

'Right,' I said. 'I'm Reacher. From Friday. What was the deal?'

He shifted from foot to foot. He was going to play hard to get. But he'd already showed his hand. He'd come out to meet me. He'd already lost the game. But he didn't speak.

'What was the deal on Friday?' I said again.

'Morrison is dead,' he said. Then he shrugged and clamped his thin lips. Wouldn't say any more.

I stepped casually to my left. Just a foot or so, to put Spivey's bulk between me and the gate guard. So the gate guard couldn't see. Morrison's switchblade appeared in my hand. I held it up at Spivey's eye level for a second. Just long enough for him to read the gold-filled engraving in the ebony. Then the blade popped out with a loud click. Spivey's small eyes were fixed on it.

'You think I used this on Morrison?' I said.

He was staring at the blade. It shone blue in the stormy sun.

'It wasn't you,' he said. 'But maybe you had good reason.'

I smiled at him. He knew it wasn't me who killed Morrison. Therefore he knew who had. Therefore he knew who Morrison's bosses were. Simple as that. Three little words, and I was getting somewhere. I moved the blade a fraction closer to his big red face.

'Want me to use this on you?' I said.

Spivey looked around wildly. Saw the gate guard thirty yards away.

'He's not going to help you,' I said. 'He hates your useless fat guts. He's just a guard. You sucked ass and got promotion. He wouldn't piss on you if you were on fire. Why should he?'

'So what do you want?' Spivey said.

'Friday,' I said. 'What was the deal?'

'And if I tell you?' he said.

I shrugged at him.

'Depends what you tell me,' I said. 'You tell me the truth, I'll let you go back inside. Want to tell me the truth?'

He didn't reply. We were just standing there by the road. A battle of nerves. His nerves were shot to hell. So he was losing. His little eyes were darting about. They always came back to the blade.

'OK, I'll tell you,' he said. 'Time to time, I helped Morrison out. He called me Friday. Said he was sending two guys over. Names meant nothing to me. Never heard of you or the other guy. I was supposed to get the Hubble guy killed. That's all. Nothing was supposed to happen to you, I swear it.'

'So what went wrong?' I asked him.

'My guys screwed up,' he said. 'That's all, I swear it. It was the other guy we were after. Nothing was supposed to happen to you. You got out of there, right? No damage done, right? So why give me a hard time?'

I flashed the blade up real quick and nicked his chin. He froze in shock. A moment later a fat worm of dark blood welled out of the cut.

'What was the reason?' I asked him.

'There's never a reason,' he said. 'I just do what I'm told.'

'You do what you're told?' I said.

'I do what I'm told,' he said again. 'I don't want to know any reasons.'

'So who told you what to do?' I said.

'Morrison,' he said. 'Morrison told me what to do.'

'And who told Morrison what to do?' I asked him.

I held the blade an inch from his cheek. He was just about whimpering with fear. I stared into his small snake eyes. He knew the answer. I could see that, far back in those eyes. He knew who told Morrison what to do.

'Who told him what to do?' I asked him again.

'I don't know,' he said. 'I swear it, grave of my mother.'

I stared at him for a long moment. Shook my head.

'Wrong, Spivey,' I said. 'You do know. You're going to tell me.'

Now Spivey shook his head. His big red face jerked from side to side. The blood was running down his chin onto his slabby jowls.

'They'll kill me if I do,' he said.

I flicked the knife at his belly. Slit his greasy shirt.

'I'll kill you if you don't,' I said.

Guy like Spivey, he thinks short term. If he told me, he'd die tomorrow. If he didn't tell me, he'd die today. That's how he thought. Short term. So he set about telling me. His throat started working up and down, like it was too dry to speak. I stared into his eyes. He couldn't get any words out. He was like a guy in a movie who crawls up a desert dune and tries to call for water. But he was going to tell me.

Then he wasn't. Over his shoulder, I saw a dust plume far in the east. Then I heard the faint roar of a diesel engine. Then I made out the grey shape of the prison bus rolling in. Spivey snapped his head around to look at his salvation. The gate guard wandered out to meet the bus. Spivey snapped his head back to look at me. There was a mean gleam of triumph in his eyes. The bus was getting closer.

'Who was it, Spivey?' I said. 'Tell me now, or I'll come back for you.'

But he just backed off and turned and hustled over to his dirty Ford. The bus roared in and blew dust all over me. I closed up the switchblade and put it back in my pocket. Jogged over to the Bentley and took off.

The coming storm chased me all the way back east. I felt I had more than a storm after me. I was sick with frustration. This morning I had been just one conversation away from knowing everything. Now I knew nothing. The situation had suddenly turned sour.

I had no backup, no facilities, no help. I couldn't rely on Roscoe or Finlay. I couldn't expect either of them to agree with my agenda. And they had troubles of their own up at the station house. What had Finlay said? Working under the enemy's nose? And I couldn't expect too much from Picard. He was already way out on a limb. I couldn't count on anybody but myself.

On the other hand, I had no laws to worry about, no inhibitions, no distractions. I wouldn't have to think about Miranda, probable cause, constitutional rights. I wouldn't have to think about reasonable doubt or rules of evidence. No appeal to any higher authority for these guys. Was that fair? You bet your ass. These were bad people. They'd stepped over the line a long time ago. Bad people. What had Finlay said? As bad as they come. And they had killed Joe Reacher.

I rolled the Bentley down the slight hill to Roscoe's house. Parked on the road outside her place. She wasn't home. The

Chevrolet wasn't there. The big chrome clock on the Bentley's dash showed ten of six. Ten minutes to wait. I got out of the front seat and got into the back. Stretched out on the big old car's leather bench.

I wanted to get away from Margrave for the evening. I wanted to get out of Georgia altogether. I found a map in a pocket on the back of the driver's seat. I peered at it and figured if we went west for an hour, hour and a half, back past Warburton again, we'd cross the state line into Alabama. That's what I wanted to do. Blast west with Roscoe into Alabama and pull into the first live music bar we came to. Put my troubles on hold until tomorrow. Eat some cheap food, drink some cold beer, hear some dirty music. With Roscoe. My idea of a hell of an evening. I settled back to wait for her. The dark was gathering in. I felt a faint chill in the evening air. About six o'clock huge drops started hammering on the roof of the Bentley. It felt like a big evening thunderstorm was moving in, but it never really arrived. It never really let loose. Just the big early drops spattering down like the sky was straining to unload but wouldn't let go. It went very dark and the heavy car rocked gently in the damp wind.

Roscoe was late. The storm had been threatening for about twenty minutes before I saw her Chevy winding down the rise. Her headlights swept and arced left and right. They washed over me as she swung into her driveway. They blazed against her garage door, then died as she cut the power. I got out of the Bentley and stepped over to her. We held each other and kissed. Then we went inside.

'You OK?' I asked her.

'I guess,' she said. 'Hell of a day.'

I nodded. It had been.

'Upset?' I asked her.

She was moving around switching lamps on. Pulling drapes.

'This morning was the worst thing I've ever seen,' she said. 'By far the worst thing. But I'm going to tell you something I would never tell anyone else. I wasn't upset. Not about Morrison. You can't get upset about a guy like that. But I'm upset about his wife. Bad enough living with a guy like Morrison without dying because of him too, right?'

'What about the rest of it?' I asked her. 'Teale?'

'I'm not surprised,' she said. 'That whole family has been scumbags for two hundred years. I know all about them. His family and my family go way back together. Why should he be any different? But, God, I'm glad everybody else in the department turned out clean. I was dreading finding out one of those guys had been in it, too. I don't know if I could have faced that.'

She went into the kitchen and I followed. She went quiet. She wasn't falling apart, but she wasn't happy. She pulled open the refrigerator door. It was a gesture which said: the cupboard is bare. She smiled a tired smile at me.

'You want to buy me dinner?' she said.

'Sure,' I said. 'But not here. In Alabama.'

I told her what I wanted to do. She liked the plan. She brightened up and went to take a shower. I figured I could use a shower too, so I went with her. But we hit a delay because as soon as she started to unbutton her crisp uniform shirt, my priorities shifted. The lure of an Alabama bar receded. And the shower could wait, too. She was wearing black underwear beneath the uniform. Not very substantial items. We ended up in a frenzy on the bedroom floor. The thunderstorm was finally breaking outside. The rain was lashing the little house. Lightning was blazing and the thunder was crashing about.

We finally made it to the shower. By then, we really needed it. Afterwards I lay on the bed while Roscoe dressed. She put on faded denims and a silky shirt. We turned off the lamps again and locked up and took off in the Bentley. It was seven-thirty and the storm was drifting off to the east, heading for Charleston before boiling out over the Atlantic. Might hit Bermuda tomorrow. We headed west toward a pinker sky. I found the road back out to Warburton. Cruised down the farm roads between the endless dark fields and blasted past the prison. It squatted glowering in its ghastly yellow light.

A half-hour after Warburton we stopped to fill the old car's gigantic tank. Threaded through some tobacco country and crossed the Chattahoochee by an old river bridge in Franklin. Then a sprint down to the state line. We were in Alabama before nine o'clock. We agreed to take a chance and stop at the first bar.

We saw an old roadhouse maybe a mile later. Pulled into the parking lot and got out. Looked OK. Big enough place, wide and low, built from tarred boards. Plenty of neon, plenty of cars in the lot, and I could hear music. The sign at the door said The Pond, live music seven nights a week at nine-thirty. Roscoe and I held hands and walked in.

We were hit by bar noise and jukebox music and a blast of

beery air. We pushed through to the back and found a wide ring
of booths around a dance floor with a stage beyond. The stage was
really just a low concrete platform. It might once have been some
kind of a loading bay. The ceiling was low and the light was dim.
We found an empty booth and slid in. Watched the band setting up
while we waited for service. The waitresses were rushing around
like basketball centres. One dived over and we ordered beers,
cheeseburgers, fries, onion rings. Pretty much right away she ran
back with a tin tray with our stuff on it. We ate and drank and
ordered more.

'So what are you going to do about Joe?' Roscoe asked me.

I was going to finish his business. Whatever it was. Whatever it
took. That was the decision I had taken in her warm bed that
morning. But she was a police officer. She was sworn to uphold all
kinds of laws. Laws that were designed to get in my way. I didn't
know what to say. But she didn't wait for me to say anything.

'I think you should find out who it was killed him,' she said.

'And then what?' I asked her.

But that was as far as we got. The band started up. We couldn't
talk any more. Roscoe gave an apologetic smile and shook her
head. The band was loud. She shrugged, saying sorry for the fact
that I couldn't hear her talking. She sketched me a tell-you-later
gesture across the table and we turned to face the stage. I wished
I could have heard her reply to my question.

The bar was called The Pond and the band was called Pond Life.
They started pretty well. A classic trio. Guitar, bass, drums.
Firmly into the Stevie Ray Vaughan thing. Since Stevie Ray died in
his helicopter up near Chicago it seemed like you could count up
all the white men under forty in the southern states, divide by
three, and that was the number of Stevie Ray Vaughan tribute
bands. Everybody was doing it. Because it didn't require much.
Didn't matter what you looked like, didn't matter what gear you
had. All you needed was to get your head down and play. The best
of them could match Stevie Ray's on-a-dime changes from loose
bar rock to the old Texas blues.

This lot was pretty good. Pond Life. They lived up to their ironic
name. The bass and the drums were big messy guys, lots of hair
all over, fat and dirty. The guitar player was a small dark guy, not
unlike old Stevie Ray himself. The same gappy grin. He could play,
too. He had a black Les Paul copy and a big Marshall stack. Good
old-fashioned sound. The loose heavy strings and the big pickups

overloading the ancient Marshall tubes, giving that glorious fat buzzy scream you couldn't get any other way.

We were having a good time. We drank a lot of beer, sat tight together in the booth. Then we danced for a while. Couldn't resist it. The band played on and on. The room got hot and crowded. The music got louder and faster. The waitresses sprinted back and forth with long-neck bottles.

Roscoe looked great. Her silky shirt was damp. She wasn't wearing anything underneath it. I could see that because of the way the damp silk stuck to her skin. I was in heaven. I was in a plain old bar with a stunning woman and a decent band. Joe was on hold until tomorrow. Margrave was a million miles away. I had no problems. I didn't want the evening to end.

The band played on until pretty late. Must have been way past midnight. We were juiced up and sloppy. Couldn't face the drive back. It was raining again, lightly. Didn't want to drive an hour and a half in the rain. Not so full of beer. Might end up in a ditch. Or in jail. There was a sign to a motel a mile further on. Roscoe said we should go there. She was giggly about it. Like we were eloping or something. Like I'd transported her across the state line for that exact purpose. I hadn't, specifically. But I wasn't about to put up a whole lot of objections.

So we stumbled out of the bar with ringing ears and got into the Bentley. We rolled the big old car cautiously and slowly down the streaming road for a mile. Saw the motel up ahead. A long, low old place, like something out of a movie. I pulled into the lot and went into the office. Roused the night guy at the desk. Gave him the money and arranged an early morning call. Got the key and went back out to the car. I pulled it around to our cabin and we went in. It was a decent, anonymous place. Could have been anywhere in America. But it felt warm and snug with the rain pattering on the roof. And it had a big bed.

I didn't want Roscoe to catch a chill. She ought to get out of that damp shirt. That's what I told her. She giggled at me. Said she hadn't realized I had medical qualifications. I told her we'd been taught enough for basic emergencies.

'Is this a basic emergency?' she giggled.

'It will be soon,' I laughed. 'If you don't take that shirt off.'

So she did take it off. Then I was all over her. She was so beautiful, so provocative. She was ready for anything.

Afterwards we lay in an exhausted tangle and talked. About who we were, about what we'd done. About who we wanted to be and what we wanted to do. She told me about her family. It was a bad luck story stretching back generations. They sounded like decent people, farmers, people who had nearly made it but never did. People who had struggled through the hard times before chemicals, before machinery, hostages to the power of nature. Some old ancestor had nearly made it big, but he lost his best land when Mayor Teale's great-grandfather built the railroad. Then some mortgages were called in and the grudge rolled on down the years so that now she loved Margrave but hated to see Teale walking around like he owned it, which he did, and which Teales always had.

I talked to her about Joe. I told her things I'd never told anybody else. All the stuff I'd kept to myself. All about my feelings for him and why I felt driven to do something about his death. And how I was happy to do it. We went through a lot of personal stuff. Talked for a long time and fell asleep in each other's arms.

Seemed like more or less straight away the guy was banging on the door with the early morning call. Tuesday. We got up and staggered around. The early sun was struggling against a damp dawn. Within five minutes we were back in the Bentley rolling east. The rising sun was blinding in the dewy screen.

Slowly we woke up. We crossed the state line back into Georgia. Crossed the river in Franklin. Settled into a fast cruise through the empty farming country. The fields were hidden under a floating quilt of morning mist. It hung over the red earth like steam. The sun climbed up and set about burning it off.

Neither of us spoke. We wanted to preserve the quiet intimate cocoon as long as possible. Arriving back in Margrave was going to burst the bubble soon enough. So I guided the big stately car down the country roads and hoped. Hoped there'd be plenty more nights like that one. And quiet mornings like this one. Roscoe was curled up on the big hide chair beside me. Lost in thought. She looked very content. I hoped she was.

We blasted past Warburton again. The prison floated like an alien city on the carpet of low mist. We passed the little copse I'd seen from the prison bus. Passed the rows of bushes invisible in the fields. Reached the junction and turned south onto the county road. Past Eno's diner and the station house and the fire house. Down onto Main Street. We turned left at the statue of the man who took good land for the railroad. Down the slope to Roscoe's place. I parked at the kerb and we got out, yawning and

163

stretching. We grinned briefly at each other. We'd had fun. We walked hand in hand down the driveway.

Her door was open. Not wide open, but an inch or two ajar. It was ajar because the lock was smashed. Someone had used a crowbar on it. The tangle of broken lock and splinters wouldn't allow the door to close all the way. Roscoe put her hand to her mouth and gave a silent gasp. Her eyes were wide. They slid from the door to me.

I grabbed her elbow and pulled her away. We stood flat against the garage door. Crouched down. Stuck close to the walls and circled right around the house. Listened hard at every window and risked ducking our heads up for a quick glance into every room. We arrived back at the smashed front door. We were wet from kneeling on the soaked ground and from brushing against the dripping evergreens. We stood up. Looked at each other and shrugged. Pushed the door open and went inside.

We checked everywhere. There was nobody in the house. No damage. No disturbance. Nothing was stolen. The stereo was still there, the TV was still there. Roscoe checked her closet. The police revolver was still on her belt. She checked her drawers and her bureau. Nothing had been touched. Nothing had been searched. Nothing was missing. We stood back in the hallway and looked at each other. Then I noticed something that had been left behind.

The low morning sun was coming in through the open door and playing a shallow beam over the floor. I could see a line of footprints on the parquet. A lot of footprints. Several people had tracked through from the front door into the living room. The line of prints disappeared on the bold living room rug. Reappeared on the wood floor leading into the bedroom. Came back out, through the living room, back to the front door. They had been made by people coming in from the rainy night. A slight film of muddy rainwater had dried on the wood leaving faint prints. Faint, but perfect. I could see at least four people. In and out. I could see the tread patterns they had left behind. They had been wearing rubber overshoes. Like you get for the winter up north.

SIXTEEN

THEY HAD COME FOR US IN THE NIGHT. THEY HAD COME expecting a lot of blood. They had come with all their gear. Their rubber overshoes and their nylon bodysuits. Their knives, their hammer, their bag of nails. They had come to do a job on us, like they'd done on Morrison and his wife.

They had pushed open the forbidden door. They had made a second fatal mistake. Now they were dead men. I was going to hunt them down and smile at them as they died. Because to attack me was a second attack on Joe. He was no longer here to stand up for me. It was a second challenge. A second humiliation. This wasn't about self-defence. This was about honouring Joe's memory.

Roscoe was following the trail of footprints. Showing a classic reaction. Denial. Four men had come to butcher her in the night. She knew that, but she was ignoring it. Closing it out of her mind. Dealing with it by not dealing with it. Not a bad approach, but she'd fall off the high wire before long. Until then, she was making herself busy tracing the faint footprints on her floors.

They had searched the house for us. They had split up in the bedroom and looked around. Then they had regrouped in the bedroom and left. We looked for tracks outside on the road, but there was nothing. The smooth tarmac was wet and steaming. We went back inside. No evidence at all except the wrenched lock and the faint footprints throughout the house.

Neither of us spoke. I was burning with anger. Still watching Roscoe. Waiting for the dam to break. She'd seen the Morrison corpses. I hadn't. Finlay had sketched in the details for me. That was bad enough. He'd been there. He'd been shaken by the whole thing. Roscoe had been there too. She'd seen exactly what somebody wanted to do to the two of us.

'So who were they after?' she said at last. 'Me, you, both of us?'

'They were after both of us,' I said. 'They figure Hubble talked to me in prison. They figure I've told you all about it. So they think you and I know whatever it was Hubble knew.'

She nodded, vaguely. Then she moved away and leaned up near her back door. Looking out at her neat evergreen garden. I saw her go pale. She shuddered. The defences crashed down. She pressed herself into the corner by the door. Tried to flatten herself onto the wall. Stared into space like she was seeing all the nameless horrors. Started crying like her heart was broken. I stepped over and held her tight. Pressed her against me and held her as she cried out the fear and the tension. She cried for a long time. She felt hot and weak. My shirt was soaked with her tears.

'Thank God we weren't here last night,' she whispered.

I knew I had to sound confident. Fear wouldn't get her anywhere. Fear would just sap her energy. She had to face it down. And she had to face down the dark and the quiet again tonight, and every other night of her life.

'I wish we had been here,' I said. 'We could have gotten a few answers.'

She looked at me like I was crazy. Shook her head.

'What would you have done?' she said. 'Killed four men?'

'Only three,' I said. 'The fourth would have given us the answers.'

I said it with total certainty. Total conviction. Like absolutely no other possibility existed. She looked at me. I wanted her to see this huge guy. A soldier for thirteen long years. A bare-knuckle killer. Icy blue eyes. I was giving it everything I had. I was willing myself to project all the invincibility, all the implacability, all the protection I felt. I was doing the hard, no-blink stare that used to shrivel up drunken marines two at a time. I wanted Roscoe to feel safe. After what she was giving me, I wanted to give her that. I didn't want her to feel afraid.

'It's going to take more than four little country boys to get me,' I said. 'Who are they kidding? I've shit better opponents than that. They come in here again, they'll go out in a bucket. And I'll tell you what, Roscoe, someone even thinks about hurting you, they die before they finish thinking.'

It was working. I was convincing her. I needed her to be bright, tough, self-confident. I was willing her to pick it up. It was working. Her amazing eyes were filling with spirit.

'I mean it, Roscoe,' I said. 'Stick with me and you'll be OK.'

She looked at me again. Pushed her hair back.

'Promise?' she said.

'You got it, babe,' I said. Held my breath.

She sighed a ragged sigh. Pushed off the wall and stepped over. Tried a brave smile. The crisis was gone. She was up and running.

'Now we get the hell out of here,' I said. 'We can't stay around like sitting targets. So throw what you need into a bag.'

'OK,' she said. 'Are we going to fix my door first?'

I thought about her question. It was an important tactical issue.

'No,' I said. 'If we fix it, it means we've seen it. If we've seen it, it means we know we're under attack. Better if they figure we don't know we're under attack. Because then they'll figure they don't need to be too careful next time. So we don't react at all. We make out we haven't been back here. We make out we haven't seen the door. We carry on acting dumb and innocent. If they think we're dumb and innocent, they'll get careless. Easier to spot them coming next time.'

'OK,' she said.

She didn't sound convinced, but she was agreeing.

'So throw what you need into a bag,' I said again.

She wasn't happy, but she went off to gather up some stuff. The game was starting. I didn't know exactly who the other players were. I didn't even know exactly what the game was. But I knew how to play. Opening move was I wanted them to feel like we were always one step behind.

'Should I go to work today?' Roscoe asked.

'Got to,' I said. 'Can't do anything different from normal. And we need to speak with Finlay. He's expecting the call from Washington. And we need what we can get on Sherman Stoller. But don't worry, they're not going to gun us down in the middle of the squad room. They'll go for somewhere quiet and isolated, probably at night. Teale's the only bad guy up there, so just don't be on your own with him. Stick around Finlay or Baker or Stevenson, OK?'

She nodded. Went to get showered and dressed for work. Within twenty minutes, she came out of the bedroom in her uniform. Patted herself down. Ready for the day. She looked at me.

'Promise?' she said.

The way she said it was like a question, an apology, a reassurance all in one word. I looked back at her.

'You bet your ass,' I said, and winked.

She nodded. Winked back. We were OK. We went out the front door and left it slightly open, just like we'd found it.

I hid the Bentley in her garage to maintain the illusion that we hadn't been back to her house. Then we got in her Chevy and decided to start with breakfast up at Eno's. She took off and gunned the car up the hill. It felt loose and low after the upright old Bentley. Coming down the hill toward us was a panel van. Smart dark green, very clean, brand-new. It looked like a utility van, but on the side was sign in fancy gold script. It said: Kliner Foundation. Same as I'd seen the gardeners using.

'What's that truck?' I said to Roscoe.

She wafted through the right at the coffee shop. Up onto Main Street.

'Foundation's got a lot of trucks,' she said.

'What is it they do?' I asked her.

'Big deal round here,' she said. 'Old man Kliner. The town sold him the land for his warehouses and part of the deal was he set up a community programme. Teale runs it out of the mayor's office.'

'Teale runs it?' I said. 'Teale's the enemy.'

'He runs it because he's the mayor,' she said. 'Not because he's Teale. The programme assigns a lot of money, spends it on public things, roads, gardens, the library, local business grants. Gives the police department a hell of a lot. Gives me a mortgage subsidy, just because I'm with the department.'

'Gives Teale a lot of power,' I said. 'And what's the story with the Kliner boy? He tried to warn me off you. Made out he had a prior claim.'

She shuddered.

'He's a jerk,' she said. 'I avoid him when I can. You should do the same.'

She drove on, looking edgy. Kept glancing around, startled. Like she felt under threat. Like someone was going to jump out in front of the car and gun us down. Her quiet life in the Georgia countryside was over. Four men in the night up at her house had shattered that.

We pulled into Eno's gravel lot and the big Chevy rocked gently on its soft springs. I slid out of the low seat and we crunched across the gravel together to Eno's door. It was a grey day. The night rain had chilled the air and left rags of cloud all over the sky. The siding on the diner reflected the dullness. It was cold. It felt like a new season.

We went in. The place was empty. We took a booth and the woman with glasses brought us coffee. We ordered eggs and bacon with all kinds of extras on the side. A black pickup was pulling into the lot outside. Same black pickup as I'd seen three times before. Different driver. Not the Kliner kid. This was an older guy. Maybe approaching sixty, but bone-hard and lean. Iron-grey hair shaved close to his scalp. He was dressed like a rancher in denim. Looked like he lived outdoors in the sun. Even through Eno's window I could sense his power and feel the glare in his eyes. Roscoe nudged me and nodded at the guy.

'That's Kliner,' she said. 'The old man himself.'

He pushed in through the door and stood for a moment. Looked left, looked right, and moved in to the lunch counter. Eno came around from the kitchen. The two of them talked quietly. Heads bent together. Then Kliner stood up again. Turned to the door. Stopped and looked left, looked right. Rested his gaze on Roscoe for a second. His face was lean and flat and hard. His mouth was a line carved into it. Then he moved his eyes onto me. I felt like I was being illuminated by a searchlight. His lips parted in a curious smile. He had amazing teeth. Long canines, canted inward, and flat square incisors. Yellow, like an old wolf. His lips closed again and he snapped his gaze away. Pulled the door and crunched over the gravel to his truck. Took off with the roar of a big motor and a spray of small stones.

I watched him go and turned to Roscoe.

'So tell me more about these Kliner people,' I said.

She still looked edgy.

'Why?' she said. 'We're fighting for our lives here and you want to talk about the Kliners?'

'I'm looking for information,' I said. 'Kliner's name crops up everywhere. He looks like an interesting guy. His son is a piece of work. And I saw his wife. She looked unhappy. I'm wondering if all that's got anything to do with anything.'

She shrugged and shook her head.

'I don't see how,' she said. 'They're newcomers, only been here five years. The family made a fortune in cotton processing, generations back, over in Mississippi. Invented some kind of a new chemical thing, some kind of a new formula. Chlorine or sodium something, I don't know for sure. Made a huge fortune, but they ran into trouble with the EPA over there, you know, about five years ago, pollution or something. There were fish dying all the way down to New Orleans because of dumping into the river.'

'So what happened?' I asked her.

'Kliner moved the whole plant,' she said. 'The company was his by then. He shut down the whole Mississippi operation and set it up again in Venezuela or somewhere. Then he tried to diversify. He turned up here in Georgia five years ago with this warehouse thing, consumer goods, electronics or something.'

'So they're not local?' I said.

'Never saw them before five years ago,' she said. 'Don't know much about them. But I never heard anything bad. Kliner's probably a tough guy, maybe even ruthless, but he's OK as long as you're not a fish, I guess.'

'So why is his wife so scared?' I said.

Roscoe made a face.

'She's not scared,' she said. 'She's sick. Maybe she's scared because she's sick. She's going to die, right? That's not Kliner's fault.'

The waitress arrived with the food. We ate in silence. The portions were huge. The fried stuff was great. The eggs were delicious. This guy Eno had a way with eggs. I washed it all down with pints of coffee. I had the waitress running back and forth with the refill jug.

'Pluribus means nothing at all to you?' Roscoe asked. 'You guys never knew anything about some Pluribus thing? When you were kids?'

I thought hard and shook my head.

'Is it Latin?' she asked.

'It's part of the United States' motto, right?' I said. 'E Pluribus Unum. It means out of many, one. One nation built out of many former colonies.'

'So Pluribus means many?' she said. 'Did Joe know Latin?'

I shrugged.

'I've got no idea,' I said. 'Probably. He was a smart guy. He probably knew bits and pieces of Latin. I'm not sure.'

'OK,' she said. 'You got no other ideas at all why Joe was down here?'

'Money, maybe,' I said. 'That's all I can think of. Joe worked for the Treasury Department, as far as I know. Hubble worked for a bank. Their only thing in common would be money. Maybe we'll find out from Washington. If we don't, we're going to have to start from the beginning.'

'OK,' she said. 'You need anything?'

'I'll need that arrest report from Florida,' I said.

'For Sherman Stoller?' she said. 'That's two years old.'

'Got to start somewhere,' I said.

'OK, I'll ask for it,' she shrugged. 'I'll call Florida. Anything else?'

'I need a gun,' I said.

She didn't reply. I dropped a twenty on the laminate table top and we slid out and stood up. Walked out to the unmarked car.

'I need a gun,' I said again. 'This is a big deal, right? So I'll need a weapon. I can't just go to the store and buy one. No ID, no address.'

'OK,' she said. 'I'll get you one.'

'I've got no permit,' I said. 'You'll have to do it on the quiet, OK?' She nodded.

'That's OK,' she said. 'There's one nobody else knows about.'

We kissed a long hard kiss in the station house lot. Then we got out of the car and went in through the heavy glass door. More or less bumped into Finlay rounding the reception counter on his way out.

'Got to go back to the morgue,' he said. 'You guys come with me, OK? We need to talk. Lot to talk about.'

So we went back out into the dull morning. Got back into Roscoe's Chevy. Same system as before. She drove. I sat across the back. Finlay sat in the front passenger seat, twisted around so he could look at the both of us at once. Roscoe started up and headed south.

'Long call from the Treasury Department,' Finlay said. 'Must have been twenty minutes, maybe a half-hour. I was nervous about Teale.'

'What did they say?' I asked him.

'Nothing,' he said. 'They took a half-hour to tell me nothing.'

'Nothing?' I said. 'What the hell does that mean?'

'They wouldn't tell me anything,' he said. 'They want a shitload of formal authorization from Teale before they say word one.'

'They confirmed Joe worked there, right?' I said.

'Sure, they went that far,' he said. 'He came from Military

Intelligence ten years ago. They headhunted him. Recruited him specially.'

'What for?' I asked him.

Finlay just shrugged.

'They wouldn't tell me,' he said. 'He started some new project exactly a year ago, but the whole thing is a total secret. He was some kind of a very big deal up there, Reacher, that's for sure. You should have heard the way they were all talking about him. Like talking about God.'

I went quiet for a while. I had known nothing about Joe. Nothing at all.

'So that's it?' I said. 'Is that all you got?'

'No,' he said. 'I kept pushing until I got a woman called Molly Beth Gordon. You ever heard that name?'

'No,' I said. 'Should I have?'

'Sounds like she was very close to Joe,' Finlay said. 'Sounds like they may have had a thing going. She was very upset. Floods of tears.'

'So what did she tell you?' I asked him.

'Nothing,' Finlay said. 'Not authorized. But she promised to tell you what she can. She said she'll step out of line for you, because you're Joe's little brother.'

I nodded.

'OK,' I said. 'That's better. When do I speak to her?'

'Call her about one-thirty,' he said. 'Lunch break, when her office will be empty. She's taking a big risk, but she'll talk to you. That's what she said.'

'OK,' I said again. 'She say anything else?'

'She let one little thing slip,' Finlay said. 'Joe had a big debrief meeting scheduled. For next Monday morning.'

'Monday?' I said. 'As in the day after Sunday?'

'Correct,' he said. 'Looks like Hubble was right. Something is due to happen on or before Sunday. Whatever the hell he was doing, it looks like Joe knew he would have won or lost by then. But she wouldn't say anything more. She was out of line talking to me at all and she sounded like she was being overheard. So call her, but don't pin your hopes on her, Reacher. She may not know anything. Left hand doesn't know what the right hand is doing up there. Big-time secrecy, right?'

'Bureaucracy,' I said. 'Who the hell needs it? OK, we have to assume we're on our own here. At least for a while. We're going to need Picard again.'

Finlay nodded.

'He'll do what he can,' he said. 'He called me last night. The Hubbles are secure. Right now, he's sitting on it, but he'll stand up for us if we need him.'

'He should start tracing Joe,' I said. 'Joe must have used a car. Probably flew down from Washington, into Atlanta, got a hotel room, rented a car, right? We should look for the car. He must have driven it down here Thursday night. It must have been dumped somewhere in the area. It might lead us back to the hotel. Maybe there would be something in Joe's hotel room. Files, maybe.'

'Picard can't do that,' Finlay said. 'FBI isn't equipped to go looking for abandoned rental cars. And we can't do it ourselves, not with Teale around.'

I shrugged.

'We'll have to,' I said. 'No other way. You can sell Teale some story. You can double bluff him. Tell him you figure the escaped con who he says did the Morrison thing must have been in a rental car. Tell him you need to check it out. He can't say no to that, or else he's undermining his own cover story, right?'

'OK,' Finlay said. 'I'll try it. Might work, I guess.'

'Joe must have had phone numbers,' I said. 'The number you found in his shoe was torn off a computer printout, right? So where's the rest of the printout? I bet it's in his hotel room, just sitting there, covered with phone numbers, with Hubble's number torn off the top. So you find the car, then you twist Picard's arm to trace the hotel through the rental company, OK?'

'OK,' he said. 'I'll do my best.'

In Yellow Springs we slipped into the hospital entrance lane and slowed over the speed bumps. Nosed around to the lot in back. Parked near the morgue door. I didn't want to go inside. Joe was still in there. I started to think vaguely about funeral arrangements. I'd never had to do it before. The Marine Corps handled my father's. Joe arranged my mother's.

But I got out of the car with the two of them and we walked through the chill air to the door. Found our way back to the shabby office. The same doctor was at the desk. Still in a white coat. Still looking tired. He waved us in and we sat down. I took one of the stools. I didn't want to sit next to the fax machine again. The doctor looked at all of us in turn. We looked back at him.

'What have you got for us?' Finlay said.

The tired man at the desk prepared to answer. Like preparing for a lecture. He picked up three files from his left and dropped them on his blotter. Opened the top one. Pulled out the second one and opened that, too.

'Morrison,' he said. 'Mr and Mrs.'

He glanced around the three of us again. Finlay nodded to him.

'Tortured and killed,' the pathologist said. 'The sequence is pretty clear. The woman was restrained. Two men, I'd say, one on each arm, gripping and twisting. Heavy bruising on the forearms and the upper arms, some ligament damage from twisting the arms up her back. Obviously the bruising continued to develop from the time she was first seized until the time she died. The bruising stops developing when the circulation stops, you understand?'

We nodded. We understood.

'I'd put it at about ten minutes,' he said. 'Ten minutes, beginning to end. So the woman was being held. The man was being nailed to the wall. I'd guess both were naked by then. They were in nightwear before the attack, right?'

'Robes,' Finlay said. 'They were having breakfast.'

'OK, the robes came off early on,' the doctor said. 'The man was nailed to the wall, technically to the floor also, through the feet. His genital area was attacked. The scrotum was severed. Postmortem evidence suggests that the woman was persuaded to swallow the amputated testicles.'

The office was silent. Silent as a tomb. Roscoe looked at me. Stared at me for a while. Then she looked back at the doctor.

'I found them in her stomach,' the doctor said.

Roscoe was as white as the guy's coat. I thought she was going to pitch forward off her stool. She closed her eyes and hung on. She was hearing about what somebody had planned for us last night.

'And?' Finlay said.

'The woman was mutilated,' the doctor said. 'Breasts severed, genital area attacked, throat cut. Then the man's throat was cut. That was the last wound inflicted. You could see the arterial spray from his neck overlaying all the other bloodstains in the room.'

There was dead silence in the room. Lasted quite a while.

'Weapons?' I asked.

The guy at the desk swivelled his tired gaze towards me.

'Something sharp, obviously,' he said. A slight grin. 'Straight, maybe five inches long.'

'A razor?' I said.

'No,' he said. 'Certainly something as sharp as a razor, but rigid, not folding, and double-edged.'

'Why?' I said.

'There's evidence it was used back and forth,' the guy said. He swished his hand back and forth in a tiny arc. 'Like this. On the woman's breasts. Cutting both ways. Like filleting a salmon.'

I nodded. Roscoe and Finlay were silent.

'What about the other guy?' I said. 'Stoller?'

The pathologist pushed the two Morrison files to one side and opened up the third. Glanced through it and looked across at me. The third file was thicker than the first two.

'His name was Stoller?' he said. 'We've got him down as John Doe.'

Roscoe looked up.

'We sent you a fax,' she said. 'Yesterday morning. We traced his prints.'

The pathologist rooted around on the messy desk. Found a curled-up fax. Read it and nodded. Crossed out 'John Doe' on the folder and wrote in 'Sherman Stoller'. Gave us his little grin again.

'I've had him since Sunday,' he said. 'Been able to do a more thorough job, you know? A bit chewed up by the rats, but not pulped like the first guy, and altogether a lot less mess than the Morrisons.'

'So what can you tell us?' I said.

'We've talked about the bullets, right?' he said. 'Nothing more to add about the exact cause of death.'

'So what else do you know?' I asked him.

The file was too thick for just the shooting and running and bleeding to death bits. This guy clearly had more to tell us. I saw him put his fingers on the pages and press lightly. Like he was trying to get vibrations or read the file in Braille.

'He was a truck driver,' he said.

'He was?' I said.

'I think so,' the guy said. Sounded confident.

Finlay looked up. He was interested. He loved the process of deduction. It fascinated him. Like when I'd scored with those long shots about Harvard, his divorce, quitting smoking.

'Go on,' he said.

'OK, briefly,' the pathologist said. 'I found certain persuasive factors. A sedentary job, because his musculature was slack, his posture poor, flabby buttocks. Slightly rough hands, a fair bit of old diesel fuel ingrained in the skin. Also traces of old diesel fuel on the soles of his shoes. Internally, a poor diet, high in fat, plus a bit too much hydrogen sulphide in the blood gases and the tissues. This guy spent his life on the road, sniffing other people's catalytic converters. I make him a truck driver, because of the diesel fuel.'

Finlay nodded. I nodded. Stoller had come in with no ID, no history, nothing but his watch. This guy was pretty good. He watched us nod our approval. Looked pleased. Looked like he had more to say.

'But he's been out of work for a while,' he said.

'Why?' Finlay asked him.

'Because all that evidence is old,' the doctor said. 'Looks to me like he was driving a lot for a long period, but then he stopped. I think he's done very little driving for nine months, maybe a year. So I make him a truck driver, but an unemployed truck driver.'

'OK, doc, good work,' Finlay said. 'You got copies of all that for us?'

The doctor slid a large envelope across the desk. Finlay stepped over and picked it up. Then we all stood up. I wanted to get out. I didn't want to go back to the cold store again. I didn't want to see any more damage. Roscoe and Finlay sensed it and nodded. We hustled out like we were ten minutes late for something. The guy at the desk let us go. He'd seen lots of people rushing out of his office like they were ten minutes late for something.

We got into Roscoe's car. Finlay opened the big envelope and pulled out the stuff on Sherman Stoller. Folded it into his pocket.

'That's ours, for the time being,' he said. 'It might get us somewhere.'

'I'll get the arrest report from Florida,' Roscoe said. 'And we'll find an address for him somewhere. Got to be a lot of paperwork on a trucker, right? Union, medical, licences. Should be easy enough to do.'

We rode the rest of the way back to Margrave in silence. The station house was deserted, apart from the desk guy. Lunch break in Margrave, lunch break in Washington DC. Same time zone. Finlay handed me a scrap of paper from his pocket and stood guard on the door to the rosewood office. I went inside to call the woman who may have been my brother's lover.

The number Finlay had handed me reached Molly Beth Gordon's private line. She answered on the first ring. I gave her my name. It made her cry.

'You sound so much like Joe,' she said.

I didn't reply. I didn't want to get into a whole lot of reminiscing. Neither should she, not if she was stepping out of line and was in danger of being overheard. She should just tell me what she had to tell me and get off the line.

'So what was Joe doing down here?' I asked her.

I heard her sniffing, and then her voice came back clear.

'He was running an investigation,' she said. 'Into what, I don't know specifically.'

'But what sort of a thing?' I asked her. 'What was his job?'

'Don't you know?' she said.

'No,' I said. 'We found it very hard to keep in touch, I'm afraid. You'll have to start from the beginning for me.'

There was a long pause on the line.

'OK,' she said. 'I shouldn't tell you this. Not without clearance. But I will. It was counterfeiting. He ran the Treasury's anti-counterfeiting operation.'

'Counterfeiting?' I said. 'Counterfeit money?'

'Yes,' she said. 'He was head of the department. Ran the whole show. He was an amazing guy, Jack.'

'But why was he down here in Georgia?' I asked her.

'I don't know,' she said. 'I really don't. What I aim to do is find out for you. I can copy his files. I know his computer password.'

There was another pause. Now I knew something about Molly Beth Gordon. I'd spent a lot of time on computer passwords. Any military cop does. I'd studied the pyschology. Most users make bad choices. A lot of them write the damn word on a Post-It note and stick it on the monitor case. The ones who are too smart to do that use their spouse's name, or their dog's name, or their favourite car or ball player, or the name of the island where they took their honeymoon or balled their secretary. The ones who think they're really smart use figures, not words, but they choose their birthday or their wedding anniversary or something pretty obvious. If you can find something out about the user, you've normally got a better than even chance of figuring their password.

But that would never work with Joe. He was a professional. He'd spent important years in Military Intelligence. His password would be a random mixture of numbers, letters, punctuation marks, upper and lower case. His password would be unbreakable. If Molly Beth Gordon knew what it was, Joe must have told her. No other way. He had really trusted her. He had been really close to her. So I put some tenderness into my voice.

177

'Molly, that would be great,' I said. 'I really need that information.'

'I know you do,' she said. 'I hope to get it tomorrow. I'll call you again, soon as I can. Soon as I know something.'

'Is there counterfeiting going on down here?' I asked her. 'Is that what this could be all about?'

'No,' she said. 'It doesn't happen like that. Not inside the States. All that stuff about little guys with green eyeshades down in secret cellars printing dollar bills is all nonsense. Just doesn't happen. Joe stopped it. Your brother was a genius, Jack. He set up procedures years ago for the special paper sales and the inks, so if somebody starts up, he gets nailed within days. One hundred per cent foolproof. Printing money in the States just doesn't happen any more. Joe made sure of that. It all happens abroad. Any fakes we get here are shipped in. That's what Joe spent his time chasing. International stuff. Why he was in Georgia, I don't know. I really don't. But I'll find out tomorrow, I promise you that.'

I gave her the station house number and told her to speak to nobody except me or Roscoe or Finlay. Then she hung up in a hurry like somebody had just walked in on her. I sat for a moment and tried to imagine what she looked like.

Teale was back in the station house. And old man Kliner was inside with him. They were over by the reception counter, heads together. Kliner was talking to Teale like I'd seen him talking to Eno at the diner. Foundation business, maybe. Roscoe and Finlay were standing together by the cells. I walked over to them. Stood between them and talked low.

'Counterfeiting,' I said. 'This is about counterfeit money. Joe was running the Treasury Department's defence for them. You know anything about that sort of a thing down here? Either of you?'

They both shrugged and shook their heads. I heard the glass door suck open. Looked up. Kliner was on his way out. Teale was starting in toward us.

'I'm out of here,' I said.

I brushed past Teale and headed for the door. Kliner was standing in the lot, next to the black pickup. Waiting for me. He smiled. Wolf's teeth showing.

'Sorry for your loss,' he said.

His voice had a quiet, cultured tone. Educated. A slight hiss on the sibilants. Not the voice to go with his sunbaked appearance.

'You upset my son,' he said.

He looked at me. Something burning in his eyes. I shrugged.

'The kid upset me first,' I said.

'How?' Kliner asked. Sharply.

'He lived and breathed?' I said.

I moved on across the lot. Kliner slid into the black pickup. Fired it up and nosed out. He turned north. I turned south. Started the walk down to Roscoe's place. It was a half-mile through the new fall chill. Ten minutes at a brisk pace. I got the Bentley out of the garage. Drove it back up the slope to town. Made the right onto Main Street and cruised along. I was peering left and right in under the smart striped awnings, looking for the clothes store. Found it three doors north of the barbershop. Left the Bentley on the street and went in. Paid out some of Charlie Hubble's expenses cash to a sullen middle-aged guy for a pair of pants, a shirt and a jacket. A light fawn colour, pressed cotton, as near to formal as I was prepared to go. No tie. I put it all on in the changing cubicle in the back of the store. Bagged up the old stuff and threw it in the Bentley's trunk as I passed.

I walked the three doors south to the barbershop. The younger of the two old guys was on his way out of the door. He stopped and put his hand on my arm.

'What's your name, son?' he asked me.

No reason not to tell him. Not that I could see.

'Jack Reacher,' I said.

'You got any Hispanic friends in town?'

'No,' I said.

'Well, you got some now,' he said. 'Two guys, looking all over for you.'

I looked at him. He scanned the street.

'Who were they?' I asked him.

'Never saw them before,' the old guy said. 'Little guys, brown car, fancy shirts. Been all over, asking for Jack Reacher. We told them we never heard of no Jack Reacher.'

'When was this?' I said.

'This morning,' he said. 'After breakfast.'

I nodded.

'OK,' I said. 'Thanks.'

The guy held the door open for me.

'Go right in,' he said. 'My partner will take care of you. But he's a bit skittish this morning. Getting old.'

'Thanks,' I said again. 'See you around.'

179

'Sure hope so, son,' he said.

He strolled off down Main Street and I went inside his shop. The older guy was in there. The gnarled old man whose sister had sung with Blind Blake. No other customers. I nodded to the old guy and sat down in his chair.

'Good morning, my friend,' he said.

'You remember me?' I said.

'Sure do,' he said. 'You were our last customer. Nobody in between to muddle me up.'

I asked him for a shave and he set about whipping up the lather.

'I was your last customer?' I said. 'That was Sunday. Today is Tuesday. Business always that bad?'

The old guy paused and gestured with the razor.

'Been that bad for years,' he said. 'Old Mayor Teale won't come in here, and what the old mayor won't do, nobody else white will do neither. Except old Mr Gray from the station house, came in here regular as clockwork three, four times a week, until he went and hung himself, God rest his soul. You're the first white face in here since last February, yes sir, that's for sure.'

'Why won't Teale come in here?' I asked him.

'Man's got a problem,' the old guy said. 'I figure he don't like to sit all swathed up in the towel while there's a black man standing next him with a razor. Maybe worried something bad might happen to him.'

'Might something bad happen to him?' I said.

He laughed a short laugh.

'I figure there's a serious risk,' he said. 'Asshole.'

'So you got enough black customers to make a living?' I asked him.

He put the towel around my shoulders and started brushing on the lather.

'Man, we don't need customers to make a living,' he said.

'You don't?' I said. 'Why not?'

'We got the community money,' he said.

'You do?' I said. 'What's that?'

'Thousand dollars,' he said.

'Who gives you that?' I asked him.

He started scraping my chin. His hand was shaking like old people do.

'Kliner Foundation,' he whispered. 'The community programme. It's a business grant. All the merchants get it. Been getting it five years.'

180

I nodded.

'That's good,' I said. 'But a thousand bucks a year won't keep you. It's better than a poke in the eye, but you need customers too, right?'

I was just making conversation, like you do with barbers. But it set the old guy off. He was shaking and cackling. Had a whole lot of trouble finishing the shave. I was staring into the mirror. After last night, it would be a hell of a thing to get my throat cut by accident.

'Man, I shouldn't tell you about it,' he whispered. 'But seeing as you're a friend of my sister's, I'm going to tell you a big secret.'

He was getting confused. I wasn't a friend of his sister's. Didn't even know her. He'd told me about her, was all. He was standing there with the razor. We were looking at each other in the mirror. Like with Finlay in the coffee shop.

'It's not a thousand dollars a year,' he whispered. Then he bent close to my ear. 'It's a thousand dollars a week.'

He started stomping around, chuckling like a demon. He filled the sink and dabbed off the spare lather. Patted my face down with a hot wet cloth. Then he whipped the towel off my shoulders like a conjurer doing a trick.

'That's why we don't need no customers,' he cackled.

I paid him and got out. The guy was crazy.

'Say hello to my sister,' he called after me.

SEVENTEEN

THE TRIP TO ATLANTA WAS THE BEST PART OF FIFTY MILES. took nearly an hour. The highway swept me right into the city. I headed for the tallest buildings. Soon as I started to see marble foyers I dumped the car and walked to the nearest corner and asked a cop for the commercial district.

He gave me a half-mile walk after which I found one bank after another. Sunrise International had its own building. It was a big glass tower set back behind a piazza with a fountain. That part looked like Milan, but the entranceway at the base of the tower was clad in heavy stone, trying to look like Frankfurt or London. Trying to look like a big heavy-duty bank. Foyer full of dark carpet and leather. Receptionist behind a mahogany counter. Could have been a quiet hotel.

I asked for Paul Hubble's office and the receptionist flipped through a directory. She said she was sorry, but she was new in the job and she didn't recognize me, so would I wait while she got clearance for my visit? She dialled a number and started a low conversation. Then she covered the phone with her hand.

'May I say what it's in connection with?'

'I'm a friend,' I said.

She resumed the phone call and then directed me to an elevator. I had to go to reception on the seventeenth floor. I got in the elevator and tapped the button. Stood there while it carried me up.

The seventeenth floor looked even more like a gentleman's club than the entrance foyer had. It was carpeted and panelled and dim. Full of glowing antiques and old pictures. As I waded across the thick pile a door opened and a suit stepped out to meet me. Shook my hand and fussed me back into a little anteroom. He introduced himself as some sort of a manager and we sat down.

'So how may I help you?' he asked.

'I'm looking for Paul Hubble,' I said.

'May I know why?'

'He's an old friend,' I said. 'I remembered him saying he works here, so I thought I'd look him up while I'm passing through.'

The guy in the suit nodded. Dropped his gaze.

'Thing is, you see,' he said, 'Mr Hubble doesn't work here any more. We had to let him go, I'm afraid, about eighteen months ago.'

I just nodded blankly. Then I sat there in the clubby little office and looked at the guy in the suit and waited. A bit of silence might set him talking. If I asked him questions straight out, he might clam up. He might go all confidential, like lawyers do. But I could see he was a chatty type of a guy. A lot of those managers are. They love to impress the hell out of you, given the chance. So I sat tight and waited. Then the guy started apologizing to me because I was Hubble's friend.

'No fault of his own, you understand,' he said. 'He did an excellent job, but it was in a field we moved out of. A strategic business decision, very unfortunate for the people concerned, but there you are.'

I nodded at him like I understood.

'I haven't been in touch for a long time,' I said. 'I didn't know. I didn't even really know what he did here.'

I smiled at him. Tried to look amiable and ignorant. Didn't take much effort, in a bank. I gave him my best receptive look. Guaranteed to set a chatty guy talking. It had worked for me plenty of times before.

'He was part of our retail operation,' the guy said. 'We closed it down.'

I looked enquiringly at him.

'Retail?' I said.

'Over-the-counter banking,' he said. 'You know, cash, cheques, loans, personal customers.'

'And you closed that down?' I said. 'Why?'

'Too expensive,' he said. 'Big overhead, small margin. It had to go.'

'And Hubble was a part of that?' I asked him.

He nodded.

'Mr Hubble was our currency manager,' he said. 'It was an important position. He was very good.'

'So what was his exact role?' I asked him.

The guy didn't know how to explain it. Didn't know where to start. He made a couple of attempts and gave them up.

'Do you understand cash?' he said.

'I've got some,' I said. 'I don't know if I understand it, exactly.'

He got to his feet and gave me a fussy gesture. Wanted me to join him at the window. We peered out together at the people on the street, seventeen floors down. He pointed at a guy in a suit, hurrying along the sidewalk.

'Take that gentleman,' he said. 'Let's make a few guesses, shall we? Probably lives in the outer suburbs, maybe has a vacation cabin somewhere, two big mortgages, two cars, half a dozen mutual funds, pension provision, some blue chip stock, college plans, five or six credit cards, store cards, charge cards. Net worth about a half-million, shall we say?'

'OK,' I said.

'But how much cash does he have?' the guy asked me.

'No idea,' I said.

'Probably about fifty dollars,' he said. 'About fifty dollars in a leather billfold which cost him a hundred and fifty dollars.'

I looked at him. I wasn't following his drift. The guy changed gear. Became very patient with me.

'The US economy is huge,' he said. 'Net assets and net liabilities are incalculably large. Trillions of dollars. But almost none of it is actually represented by cash. That gentleman had a net worth of a half-million dollars, but only fifty of it was in actual cash. All the rest of it is on paper or in computers. The fact is, there isn't much actual cash around. There's only about a hundred and thirty billion actual cash dollars inside the whole US.'

I shrugged at him again.

'Sounds like enough to me,' I said.

The guy looked at me severely.

'But how many people are there?' he asked me. 'Nearly three hundred million. That's only about four hundred and fifty actual cash dollars per head of population. That's the problem a retail bank has to deal with, day by day. Four hundred and fifty dollars is a very modest cash withdrawal, but if everybody chose to make such a withdrawal, the nation's banks would run out of cash in the blink of an eye.'

He stopped and looked at me. I nodded.

'OK,' I said. 'I see that.'

'And most of that cash isn't in banks,' he said. 'It's in Vegas or at the racetrack. It's concentrated in what we call cash-intensive areas of the economy. So a good currency manager, and Mr Hubble was one of the very best, has a constant battle just to keep enough paper dollars on hand in our part of the system. He has to reach out and find them. He has to know where to locate them. He has to sniff them out. It's not easy. In the end, it was one of the factors which made retail so expensive for us. One of the reasons why we pulled out. We kept it going as long as we could, but we had to close the operation eventually. We had to let Mr Hubble go. We were very sorry about it.'

'Any idea where he's working now?' I said.

He shook his head.

'I'm afraid not,' he said.

'Must be working somewhere, right?' I said.

The guy shook his head again.

'Professionally, he's dropped out of sight,' he said. 'He's not working in banking, I'm sure of that. His institute membership lapsed immediately, and we've never had an enquiry for a recommendation. I'm sorry, but I can't help you. If he was working anywhere in banking, I'd know it, I can assure you of that. He must be in something else now.'

I shrugged. Hubble's trail was stone cold. And the discussion with this guy was over. His body language indicated it. He was shifting forward, ready to get up and get on. I stood up with him. Thanked him for his time. Shook his hand. Stepped through the antique gloom to the elevator. Hit the button for the street and walked out into the dull grey weather.

My assumptions had been all wrong. I had seen Hubble as a banker, doing a straight job. Maybe turning a blind eye to some peripheral con, maybe with half a finger in some dirty pie. Maybe signing off on a few bogus figures. With his arm twisted way up his back. Involved, useful, tainted, but somehow not central. But he hadn't been a banker. Not for a year and a half. He had been a criminal. Full time. Right inside the scam. Right at the centre. Not peripheral at all.

I drove straight back to the Margrave station house. Parked up and went looking for Roscoe. Teale was stalking around in the

185

open area, but the desk guy winked and nodded me back to a file room. Roscoe was in there. She looked weary. She had an armful of old files. She smiled.

'Hello, Reacher,' she said. 'Come to take me away from all this?'

'What's new?' I said.

She dumped the stack of paper onto a cabinet top. Dusted herself off and flicked her hair back. Glanced at the door.

'Couple of things,' she said. 'Teale's got a Foundation board meeting in ten minutes. I'm getting the fax from Florida soon as he's out of here. And we're due a call from the state police about abandoned cars.'

'Where's the gun you've got for me?' I asked her.

She paused. Bit her lip. She was remembering why I needed one.

'It's in a box,' she said. 'In my desk. We'll have to wait until Teale is gone. And don't open it here, OK? Nobody knows about it.'

We stepped out of the file room and walked over toward the rosewood office. The squad room was quiet. The two backup guys from Friday were paging through computer records. Neat stacks of files were everywhere. The bogus hunt was on for the chief's killer. I saw a big new bulletin board on the wall. It was marked: Morrison. It was empty. Not much progress was being made.

We waited in the rosewood office with Finlay. Five minutes. Ten. Then we heard a knock and Baker ducked his head around the door. He grinned in at us. I saw his gold tooth again.

'Teale's gone,' he said.

We went out into the open area. Roscoe turned on the fax machine and picked up the phone to call Florida. Finlay dialled the state police for news on abandoned rental cars. I sat down at the desk next to Roscoe's and called Charlie Hubble. I dialled the mobile number that Joe had printed out and hidden in his shoe. I got no answer. Just an electronic sound and a recorded voice telling me the phone I was calling was switched off.

I looked across at Roscoe.

'She's got the damn mobile switched off,' I said.

Roscoe shrugged and moved over to the fax machine. Finlay was still talking to the state police. I saw Baker hanging around on the fringe of the triangle the three of us were making. I got up and went to join Roscoe.

'Does Baker want in on this?' I asked her.

'He seems to,' she said. 'Finlay's got him acting as a kind of a

186

lookout. Should we get him involved?'

I thought about it for a second, but shook my head.

'No,' I said. 'Smaller the better, a thing like this, right?'

I sat down again at the desk I was borrowing and tried the mobile number again. Same result. Same patient electronic voice telling me it was switched off.

'Damn,' I said to myself. 'Can you believe that?'

I needed to know where Hubble had spent his time for the last year and a half. Charlie might have given me some idea. The time he left home in the morning, the time he got home at night, toll receipts, restaurant bills, things like that. And she might have remembered something about Sunday or something about Pluribus. It was possible she might have come up with something useful. And I needed something useful. I needed it very badly. And she'd switched the damn phone off.

'Reacher?' Roscoe said. 'I got the stuff on Sherman Stoller.'

She was holding a couple of fax pages. Densely typed.

'Great,' I said. 'Let's take a look.'

Finlay got off the phone and stepped over.

'State guys are calling back,' he said. 'They may have something for us.'

'Great,' I said again. 'Maybe we're getting somewhere.'

We all went back into the rosewood office. Spread the Sherman Stoller stuff out on the desk and bent over it together. It was an arrest report from the police department in Jacksonville, Florida.

'Blind Blake was born in Jacksonville,' I said. 'Did you know that?'

'Who's Blind Blake?' Roscoe asked.

'Singer,' Finlay said.

'Guitar player, Finlay,' I said.

Sherman Stoller had been flagged down by a sector car for exceeding the speed limit on the river bridge between Jacksonville and Jacksonville Beach at a quarter to midnight on a September night, two years ago. He had been driving a small panel truck eleven miles an hour too fast. He had become extremely agitated and abusive toward the sector car crew. This had caused them to arrest him for suspected DUI. He had been printed and photographed at Jacksonville Central and both he and his vehicle had been searched. He had given an Atlanta address and stated his occupation as truck driver.

The search of his person produced a negative result. His truck was searched by hand and with dogs and produced a negative result. The truck contained nothing but a cargo of twenty new air conditioners boxed for export from Jacksonville Beach. The boxes were sealed and marked with the manufacturer's logo, and each box was marked with a serial number.

After being Mirandized, Stoller had made one phone call. Within twenty minutes of the call, a lawyer named Perez from the respected Jacksonville firm of Zacarias Perez was in attendance, and within a further ten minutes Stoller had been released. From being flagged down to walking out with the lawyer, fifty-five minutes had elapsed.

'Interesting,' Finlay said. 'The guy's three hundred miles from home, it's midnight, and he gets lawyered up within twenty minutes? With a partner from a respected firm? Stoller was some kind of a truck driver, that's for sure.'

'You recognize his address?' I asked Roscoe.

She shook her head.

'Not really,' she said. 'But I could find it.'

The door cracked open and Baker stuck his head in again.

'State police on the line,' he said. 'Sounds like they got a car for you.'

Finlay checked his watch. Decided there was time before Teale got back.

'OK,' he said. 'Punch it through here, Baker.'

Finlay picked up the phone on the big desk and listened. Scribbled some notes and grunted a thank-you. Hung the phone up and got out of his chair.

'OK,' he said. 'Let's go take a look.'

We all three filed out quickly. We needed to be well clear before Teale got back and started asking questions. Baker watched us go. Called out after us.

'What should I tell Teale?' he said.

'Tell him we traced the car,' Finlay said. 'The one the crazy ex-con used to get down to Morrison's place. Tell him we're making some real progress, OK?'

This time Finlay drove. He was using an unmarked Chevy, identical to Roscoe's issue. He bounced it out of the lot and turned south. Accelerated through the little town. The first few miles I recognized as the route down toward Yellow Springs, but then we swung off onto a track which struck out due east. It led out toward the highway and ended up in a kind of maintenance area, right below the roadway. There were piles of asphalt and tar barrels

188

lying around. And a car. It had been rolled off the highway and it was lying on its roof. And it was burned out.

'They noticed it Friday morning,' Finlay said. 'Wasn't here Thursday, they're sure about that. It could have been Joe's.'

We looked it over very carefully. Wasn't much left to see. It was totally burned out. Everything that wasn't steel had gone. We couldn't even tell what make it had been. By the shape, Finlay thought it had been a General Motors product, but we couldn't tell which division. It had been a midsize sedan, and once the plastic trim has gone, you can't tell a Buick from a Chevy from a Pontiac.

I got Finlay to support the front fender and I crawled under the upside-down hood. Looked for the number they stamp on the scuttle. I had to scrape off some scorched flakes, but I found the little aluminium strip and got most of the number. Crawled out again and recited it to Roscoe. She wrote it down.

'So what do you think?' Finlay asked.

'Could be the one,' I said. 'Say he rented it Thursday evening up at the airport in Atlanta, full tank of gas. Drove it to the warehouses at the Margrave cloverleaf, then somebody drove it on down here afterward. Couple of gallons gone, maybe two and a half. Plenty left to burn.'

Finlay nodded.

'Makes sense,' he said. 'But they'd have to be local guys. This is a great spot to dump a car, right? Pull onto the shoulder up there, wheels in the dirt, push the car off the edge, scramble down and torch it, then jump in with your buddy who's already down here in his own car waiting for you, and you're away. But only if you knew about this little maintenance track. And only a local guy would know about this little maintenance track, right?'

We left the wreck there. Drove back up to the station house. The desk sergeant was waiting for Finlay.

'Teale wants you in the office,' he said.

Finlay grunted and was heading back there, but I caught his arm.

'Keep him talking a while,' I said. 'Give Roscoe a chance to phone in that number from the car.'

He nodded and carried on to the back. Roscoe and I headed over to her desk. She picked up the phone, but I stopped her.

'Give me the gun,' I whispered. 'Before Teale is through with Finlay.'

She nodded and glanced around the room. Sat down and unclipped the keys from her belt. Unlocked her desk and rolled open a deep drawer. Nodded down to a shallow cardboard box. I picked it out. It was an office storage box, about two inches deep, for holding papers. The cardboard was printed with elaborate woodgrain. Someone had written a name across the top. Gray. I tucked it under my arm and nodded to Roscoe. She rolled the drawer shut and locked it again.

'Thanks,' I said. 'Now make those calls, OK?'

I walked down to the entrance and levered the heavy glass door open with my back. Carried the box over to the Bentley. I set the box on the roof of the car and unlocked the door. Dumped the box on the passenger seat and got in. Pulled the box over onto my lap. Saw a brown sedan slowing up on the road about a hundred yards to the north.

Two Hispanic men in it. The same car I'd seen outside Charlie Hubble's place the day before. The same guys. No doubt about that. Their car came to a stop about seventy-five yards from the station house. I saw it settle, like the engine had been turned off. Neither of the guys got out. They just sat there, seventy-five yards away, watching the station house parking lot. Seemed to me they were looking straight at the Bentley. Seemed to me my new friends had found me. They'd looked all morning. Now they didn't have to look any more. They didn't move. Just sat there, watching. I watched them back for more than five minutes. They weren't going to get out. I could see that. They were settled there. So I turned my attention back to the box.

It was empty apart from a box of bullets and a gun. A hell of a weapon. It was a Desert Eagle automatic. I'd used one before. They come from Israel. We used to get them in exchange for all kinds of stuff we sent over there. I picked it up. Very heavy, four-teen inch barrel, more than a foot and a half long, front to back. I clicked out the magazine. This was the eight-shot .44 version. Takes eight .44-Magnum shells. Not what you would call a subtle weapon. The bullet weighs about twice as much as the .38 in a police revolver. It leaves the barrel going way faster than the speed of sound. It hits the target with more force than anything this side of a train wreck. Not subtle at all. Ammunition is a problem. You've got a choice. If you load up with a hard-nose bullet, it goes right through the guy you're shooting and probably right on through some other guy a hundred yards away. So you use a soft-nose bullet and it blows a hole out of your guy about the size of a garbage can. Your choice.

The bullets in the box were all soft-nose. OK with me. I checked the weapon over. Brutal, but in fine condition. Everything worked. The grip was engraved with a name. Gray. Same as the file box. The dead detective, the guy before Finlay. Hanged himself last February. Must have been a gun collector. This wasn't his service piece. No police department in the world would authorize the use of a cannon like this on the job. Altogether too heavy.

I loaded the dead detective's big handgun with eight of his shells. Put the spares back in the box and left the box on the floor of the car. Cocked the gun and clicked the safety catch on. Cocked and locked, we used to call it. Saves you a split-second before your first shot. Saves your life, maybe. I put the gun in the Bentley's walnut glove compartment. It was a tight fit.

Then I sat for a moment and watched the two guys in their car. They were still watching me. We looked at each other from seventy-five yards away. They were relaxed and comfortable. But they were watching me. I got out of the Bentley and locked it up again. Stepped back to the entrance and pulled the door. Glanced back toward the brown sedan. Still there. Still watching.

Roscoe was at her desk, talking on the phone. She waved. Looked excited. Held her hand up to tell me to wait. I watched the door to the rosewood office. Hoped Teale wouldn't come out before she finished her call.

He came out just as she hung up. He was all red in the face. Looked mad. Started stamping around the squad room, banging his heavy stick on the floor. Glaring up at the big empty bulletin board. Finlay stuck his head out of the office and nodded me in. I shrugged at Roscoe and went to see what Finlay had to say.

'What was that all about?' I asked him.

He laughed.

'I was winding him up,' he said. 'He asked what we'd been doing, looking at a car. I said we weren't. Said we'd told Baker we weren't going far, but he'd misheard it as we're looking at a car.'

'Take care, Finlay,' I said. 'They're killing people. This is a big deal.'

He shrugged.

'It's driving me crazy,' he said. 'Got to have some fun, right?'

He'd survived twenty years in Boston. He might survive this.

'What's happening with Picard?' I asked him. 'You heard from him?'

'Nothing,' he said. 'Just standing by.'

191

'No possibility he might have put a couple of guys on surveillance?' I said.

Finlay shook his head. Looked definite about it.

'No way,' he said. 'Not without telling me first. Why?'

'There's a couple of guys watching this place,' I said. 'Got here about ten minutes ago. Plain brown sedan. They were at Hubble's yesterday and around town this morning, asking after me.'

He shook his head again.

'They're not Picard's,' he said. 'He'd have told me.'

Roscoe came in and shut the door. Held it shut with her hand like Teale might try to burst in after her.

'I called Detroit,' she said. 'It was a Pontiac. Delivered four months ago. Big fleet order for a rental company. DMV is tracing the registration. I told them to get back to Picard up in Atlanta. The rental people might be able to give him the story about where it was rented. We might be getting somewhere.'

I felt I was getting closer to Joe. Like I was hearing a faint echo.

'Great,' I said to her. 'Good work, Roscoe. I'm out of here. Meet you back here at six. You two stick close together, OK? Watch your backs.'

'Where are you going?' Finlay said.

'I'm going for a drive in the country,' I said.

I left them there in the office and walked back to the entrance. Pushed the door open and stepped outside. Scanned north up the road. The plain sedan was still there, seventy-five yards away. The two guys were still in it. Still watching. I walked over to the Bentley. Unlocked the door and got in. Nosed out of the parking lot and pulled out onto the county road. Wide and slow. Drove slowly past the two guys and carried on north. In the mirror I saw the plain sedan start up. Saw it pull out and turn in the road. It accelerated north and fell in behind me. Like I was towing it on a long invisible rope. I slowed, it slowed. I sped up, it sped up. Like a game.

EIGHTEEN

I DROVE PAST ENO'S DINER AND ROLLED ON NORTH AWAY FROM town. The plain sedan followed. Forty yards back. No attempt to hide. The two guys just cruised behind me. Gazing forward. I swung west on the road to Warburton. Slowed to a cruise. The plain sedan followed. Still forty yards back. We cruised west. We were the only things moving in that vast landscape. I could see the two guys in the mirror. Gazing at me. They were spotlit by the low afternoon sun. The low, brassy light made them vivid. Young guys, Hispanic, loud shirts, black hair, very neat, very similar. Their car sat steadily in my wake.

I cruised seven or eight miles. I was looking for a place. There were bumpy earth tracks off to the left and right, every half-mile or so. They led into the fields. Looped around aimlessly. I didn't know what they were for. Maybe they led to gathering points where farmers parked machinery for the harvest. Whenever that was. I was looking for a particular track I'd seen before. It led around behind a small stand of trees on the right-hand side of the road. The only cover for miles. I'd seen it from the prison bus on Friday. Seen it again driving back in from Alabama. A sturdy stand of trees. This morning it had been floating on the mist. A little oval copse, next to the road, on the right, an earth track looping behind it, then joining up with the road again.

I saw it a couple of miles ahead. The trees were a smudge on the horizon. I drove on towards it. Snapped the glove compartment open and lifted the big automatic out. Wedged it between the squabs on the seat next to me. The two guys followed. Still forty yards back. A quarter-mile from the woods I slammed the selector into second and floored the pedal. The old car gulped and shot forwards. At the track I hauled the wheel around and bounced and slewed the Bentley off the road. Hurled it around to the back of the copse. Jammed it to a stop. Grabbed the gun and jumped. Left the driver's door swinging open like I'd tumbled out and dived straight left into the trees.

But I went the other way. I went to the right. I danced around the hood and hurled myself fifteen feet into the peanut field and flattened into the ground. Crawled through the bushes and put myself on a level with where their car would have to stop on the track behind the Bentley. Pressed myself up against the brawny stalks, low down under the leaves, on the damp red earth. Then I waited. I figured they'd dropped off maybe sixty or seventy yards. They hadn't tracked my sudden acceleration. I snicked the safety catch off. Then I heard their brown Buick. I caught the noise of the motor and the groan of the suspension. It bounced into view on the track in front of me. It stopped behind the Bentley, framed against the trees. It was about twenty feet away from me.

They were reasonably smart guys. Not at all the worst I'd ever seen. The passenger had gotten out on the road before they turned in. He thought I was in the woods. He thought he was going to come at me from behind. The driver scrambled across inside the car and rolled out of the passenger door on the far side from the trees. Right in front of me. He was holding a gun and he knelt down in the dirt, his back turned to me, hidden from where he thought I was by the Buick, looking through the car at the woods. I'd have to make him move. I didn't want him to stay next to the car. The car had to stay driveable. I didn't want it damaged.

They were wary of the copse. That had been the idea. Why would I drive all the way to the only woods for miles, and then hide in a field? A classic diversion. They'd fallen for it without even thinking. The guy by the car was staring through at the woods. I was staring at his back. I had the Desert Eagle lined up on him, breathing low. His partner was creeping slowly through the trees, looking for me. Pretty soon he'd come right out into view.

He arrived after about five minutes. He was holding a gun out in front of him. He dodged around the back of the Buick. Kept distance between himself and the Bentley. He crouched down next to his partner and they exchanged shrugs. Then they started peering at the Bentley. Worried that I was lying on the floor or crouching behind the stately chrome radiator. The guy who'd just come out of the woods crawled along in the dirt, keeping the Buick between himself and the trees, right in front of me, staring under the Bentley, looking for my feet.

He crawled the whole length of the Bentley. I could hear him grunting and gasping as he hauled himself along on his elbows. Then he crawled all the way back and knelt up again beside his partner. They both shuffled sideways and slowly stood up next to the Buick's hood. They stepped over and checked inside the Bentley. They walked together to the edge of the copse and peered into the darkness. They couldn't find me. Then they came back and stood together on the rough track, away from the cars, framed against the orange sky, staring at the trees, their backs to the field, their backs to me.

They didn't know what to do. They were city boys. Maybe from Miami. They wore Florida clothes. They were used to neon alleys and construction sites. They were used to action under raised highways, in the trash-filled lots the tourists never saw. They didn't know what to do about a small copse standing alone in a million acres of peanuts.

I shot them both in the back as they stood there. Two quick shots. Aimed high up between their shoulder blades. The big automatic made a sound like hand grenades going off. Birds wheeled into the air from all around. The twin crashes rolled over the countryside like thunder. The recoils pounded my hand. The two guys were hurled forward off their feet. Landed on their faces sprawled against the trees on the far side of the earth track. I raised my head and peered over. They had that slack, empty look that is left behind when life has departed.

I held onto the gun and stepped over to them. They were dead. I had seen a lot of dead people, and these two were as dead as any of them. The big Magnum shells had caught them high up on their backs. Where the big arteries and veins are, going on up into the head. The bullets had made quite a mess. I looked down at the two guys in the silence and thought about Joe.

Then I had things to do. I stepped back to the Bentley. Clicked the safety on and tossed the Desert Eagle back on the seat. Stepped over to their Buick and yanked the keys out. Popped the trunk. I guess I was hoping to find something in there. I didn't feel bad about the two boys. But I was going to feel better still if I found something in there. Like a silenced .22 automatic. Or like four pairs of rubber overshoes and four nylon bodysuits. A few five-inch blades. Things like that. But I didn't find things like that. I found Spivey.

He'd been dead a few hours. He'd been shot through the forehead with a .38. From close range. The revolver barrel must have been about six inches from his head. I rubbed my thumb across the skin around the bullet hole. Looked at it. There was no soot, but there were tiny gunpowder particles blasted into the skin. They wouldn't rub off. That kind of tattooing means a fairly close range. Six inches will do it, maybe eight. Somebody had suddenly raised a gun and the slow heavy assistant warden hadn't been quick enough to duck.

There was a scab on his chin where I'd cut him with Morrison's blade. His small snake eyes were open. He was still in his greasy uniform. His white hairy belly showed through where I'd slashed at his shirt. He had been a big guy. To fit him in the trunk, they'd broken his legs. Probably with a shovel. They'd broken them and folded them sideways at the knee to get his body in. I gazed at him and felt angry. He'd known, and he hadn't told me. But they'd killed him anyway. The fact that he hadn't told me hadn't counted for anything. They were panicking. They were silencing everybody, while the clock ticked slowly around to Sunday. I gazed into Spivey's dead eyes, like there was information still in there.

Then I ran back to the bodies on the edge of the copse and searched them. Two wallets and a car rental agreement. A mobile phone. That was all. The rental agreement was for the Buick. Rented at the Atlanta airport, Monday morning at eight. An early flight in from somewhere. I went through the wallets. No airline tickets. Florida driver's licences, both with Jacksonville addresses. Bland photographs, meaningless names. Credit cards to match. Lots of cash in the wallets. I stole it all. They weren't going to spend it.

I took the battery out of the mobile phone and put the phone in one guy's pocket and the battery in the other's. Then I dragged the bodies over to the Buick and heaved them into the trunk with Spivey. Not easy. They weren't tall guys, but they were floppy and awkward. Made me sweat, despite the chill. I had to shove them around to get them both in the space Spivey was leaving. I scouted around and found their revolvers. Both .38 calibre. One had a full load. The other had fired once. Smelled recent. I pitched the guns into the trunk. Found the passenger's shoes. The Desert Eagle had blown him right out of them. I threw them in the trunk and slammed the lid. Walked back into the field and found my hiding place in the bushes. Where I'd shot them from. Scrabbled around and picked up the two shell cases. Put them in my pocket.

Then I locked up the Buick and left it. Popped the Bentley's trunk. Pulled out the bag with my old clothes in. My new gear was covered in red mud and streaked with the dead guys' blood. I put the old things back on. Balled up the muddy bloodstained stuff and shoved it in the bag. Threw the bag in the Bentley's trunk and closed the lid on it. Last thing I did was use a tree branch to sweep away all the footprints I could see.

I drove the Bentley slowly back east to Margrave and used the time to calm down. A straightforward ambush, no technical difficulty, no real danger. I had thirteen years of hard time behind me. I should be able to walk through a one-on-two against amateurs in my sleep. But my heart was thumping harder than it should have been and a cold blast of adrenalin was shaking me up. It was the sight of Spivey lying there with his legs folded sideways that had done it. I breathed hard and got myself under control. My right arm was sore. Like somebody had hit my palm with a hammer. It jarred all the way up to the shoulder. That Desert Eagle had a hell of a recoil. And it made a hell of a noise. My ears were still ringing from the twin explosions. But I felt good. It had been a job well done. Two tough guys had followed me out there. They weren't following me back.

I parked up in the station house lot, furthest slot from the door. Put my gun back in the glove compartment and got out of the car. It was getting late. The evening gloom was gathering. The huge Georgia sky was darkening. Turning a deep inky shade. The moon was coming up.

Roscoe was at her desk. She got up when she saw me and walked over. We went back out through the door. Walked a few paces. Kissed.

'Anything from the car rental people?' I asked her.

She shook her head.

'Tomorrow,' she said. 'Picard's dealing with it. He's doing his best.'

'OK,' I said. 'What hotels you got up at the airport?'

She reeled off a list of hotels. Pretty much the same list you got at any airport. I picked the first name she'd listed. Then I told her what had happened with the two Florida boys. Last week, she'd have arrested me for it. Sent me to the chair. Now, her reaction was different. Those four men who had padded through her place in their rubber shoes had changed her mind about a lot of things. So she just nodded and smiled a tight grim smile of satisfaction.

'Two down,' she said. 'Good work, Reacher. Were they the ones?'

'From last night?' I said. 'No. They weren't local. We can't count them in Hubble's ten. They were hired help from outside.'

'Were they any good?' she asked.

I shrugged at her. Rocked my hand from side to side, equivocally.

'Not really,' I said. 'Not good enough, anyway.'

Then I told her what I had found in the Buick's trunk. She shivered again.

'So is he one of the ten?' she asked. 'Spivey?'

I shook my head.

'No,' I said. 'I can't see it. He was outside help, too. Nobody would have a slug like that on the inside.'

She nodded. I opened up the Bentley and got the gun out of the glove box. It was too big to go in my pocket. I put it back in the old file box with the bullets. Roscoe put the whole thing in the trunk of her Chevy. I got the carrier bag of stained clothes out. Locked the Bentley up and left it there in the police lot.

'I'm going to call Molly again,' I said. 'I'm getting in pretty deep. I need some background. There are things I don't understand.'

The place was quiet so I used the rosewood office. I dialled the Washington number and got Molly on the second ring.

'Can you talk?' I asked her.

She told me to wait, and I heard her get up and close her office door.

'It's too soon, Jack,' she said. 'I can't get the stuff until tomorrow.'

'I need background,' I said. 'I need to understand this international stuff Joe was doing. I need to know why things are happening here, if the action is supposed to be overseas.'

I heard her figuring out where to start.

'OK, background,' she said. 'I guess Joe's assumption was it's maybe controlled from this country. And it's a very difficult problem to explain, but I'll try. The forging happens abroad, and the trick is most of it stays abroad. Only a few of the fake bills ever come back here, which is not a huge deal domestically, but obviously it's something we want to stop. But abroad, it presents a completely different type of problem. You know how much cash is inside the US, Jack?'

I thought back to what the bank guy had told me.

'A hundred and thirty billion dollars,' I said.

'Right,' she said. 'But exactly twice that much is held offshore. That's a fact. People all over the world are holding onto two hundred and sixty billion dollars' worth of American cash. It's in safety deposits in London, Rome, Berlin, Moscow, stuffed into mattresses all over South America, Eastern Europe, hidden under floorboards, false walls, in banks, travel agencies, everywhere. And why is that?'

'Don't know,' I said.

'Because the dollar is the world's most trusted currency,' she said. 'People believe in it. They want it. And naturally, the government is very, very happy about that.'

'Good for the ego, right?' I said.

I heard her change the phone to the other hand.

'It's not an emotional thing,' she said. 'It's business. Think about it, Jack. If there's a hundred-dollar bill in somebody's bureau in Bucharest, that means somebody somewhere once exchanged a hundred dollars' worth of foreign assets for it. It means our government sold them a piece of paper with green and black ink on it for a hundred bucks. Good business. And because it's a trusted currency, chances are that hundred-dollar bill will probably stay in that bureau in Bucharest for many years. The US will never have to deliver the foreign assets back again. As long as the dollar stays trusted, we can't lose.'

'So what's the problem?' I asked her.

'Difficult to describe,' Molly said. 'It's all about trust and faith. It's almost metaphysical. If foreign markets are getting flooded with fake dollars, that doesn't really matter in itself. But if the people in those foreign markets find out, then it does matter. Because they panic. They lose their faith. They lose their trust. They don't want dollars anymore. They'll turn to Japanese yen or German marks to stuff their mattresses with. They'll get rid of their dollars. In effect, overnight, the government would have to repay a two-hundred-sixty-billion dollar foreign loan. Overnight. And we couldn't do that, Jack.'

'Big problem,' I said.

'That's the truth,' she said. 'And a remote problem. The fakes are all made abroad, and they're mostly distributed abroad. It makes sense that way. The factories are hidden away in some remote foreign region, where we don't know about them, and the

199

fakes are distributed to foreigners who are happy as long as the stuff looks vaguely like real dollars are supposed to look. That's why not very many are imported. Only the very best fakes come back to the States.'

'How many come back?' I asked her.

I heard her shrug. A little breath sound, like she had pursed her lips.

'Not many,' she said. 'A few billion, now and then, I guess.'

'A few billion?' I said. 'That's not many?'

'A drop in the ocean,' she said. 'From a macroeconomic point of view. Compared to the size of the economy, I mean.'

'And what exactly are we doing about it?' I asked her.

'Two things,' she said. 'First thing is Joe was trying like mad to stop it from happening. The reason behind that is obvious. Second thing is we're pretending like mad it isn't happening at all. So as to keep the faith.'

I nodded. Started to see some shape behind the big-time secrecy going on up there in Washington.

'OK,' I said. 'So if I were to call the Treasury and ask them about it?'

'We'd deny everything,' she said. 'We'd say, what counterfeiting?'

I walked through the silent squad room and joined Roscoe in her car. Told her to drive out toward Warburton. It was dark when we reached the little stand of trees. Just enough moonlight to pick it out. Roscoe pulled up where I showed her. I kissed her and got out. Told her I'd see her up at the hotel. Slapped lightly on the Chevy's roof and waved her off. She turned in the road. Drove slowly away.

I pushed directly through the copse. Didn't want to leave footprints on the track. The fat carrier bag made it awkward. It kept snagging in the brush. I came out right by the Buick. Still there. All quiet. I unlocked the driver's door with the key and got in. Started up and bounced down the track. The rear suspension kept bottoming out on the ruts. I wasn't too surprised about that. Must have been about five hundred pounds weight in the trunk.

I jounced out onto the road and drove east toward Margrave. But I turned left at the county road and headed north. Cruised the rest of the fourteen miles up to the highway. Passed by the warehouses and joined the stream north to Atlanta. I didn't drive fast, didn't drive slow. Didn't want to get noticed. The plain Buick was very anonymous. Very inconspicuous. That was how I wanted to keep it.

After an hour I followed the airport signs. Found my way round to the long-term parking. Took a ticket at the little automated barrier and nosed in. It was a huge lot. Couldn't be better. I found a slot near the middle, about a hundred yards from the nearest fence. Wiped off the wheel and the transmission. Got out with the carrier bag. Locked the Buick and walked away.

After a minute, I looked back. Couldn't pick out the car I'd just dumped. What's the best place to hide a car? In an airport long-term lot. Like where's the best place to hide a grain of sand? On the beach. The Buick could sit there for a month. Nobody would think twice.

I walked back toward the entrance barrier. At the first trash can I dumped the carrier bag. At the second I got rid of the parking ticket. At the barrier I caught the little courtesy bus and rode to the departure terminal. Walked in and found a bathroom. Wrapped the Buick keys in a paper towel and dropped them in the garbage. Then I slipped down to the arrivals hall and stepped out into the damp night again. Caught the hotel courtesy bus and rode off to meet Roscoe.

I found her in the neon glare of a hotel lobby. I paid cash for a room. Used a bill I'd taken from the Florida boys. We went up in the elevator. The room was a dingy, dark place. Big enough. Looked out over the airport sprawl. The window had three layers of glass against the jet noise. The place was airless.

'First, we eat,' I said.

'First, we shower,' Roscoe said.

So we showered. Put us in a better frame of mind. We soaped up and started fooling around. Ended up making love in the stall with the water beating down on us. Afterwards, I just wanted to curl up in the glow. But we were hungry. And we had things to do. Roscoe put on the clothes she'd brought from her place in the morning. Jeans, shirt, jacket. Looked wonderful. Very feminine, but very tough. She had a lot of spirit.

We rode up to a restaurant on the top floor. It was OK. A big panoramic view of the airport district. We sat in candlelight by a window. A cheerful foreign guy brought us food. I crammed it all down. I was starving. I had a beer and a pint of coffee. Started to feel halfway human again. Paid for the meal with more of the dead guys' money. Then we rode down to the lobby and picked up an

Atlanta street map at the desk. Walked out to Roscoe's car.

The night air was cold and damp and stank of kerosene. Airport smell. We got in the Chevy and pored over the street map. Headed out northwest. Roscoe drove and I tried to direct her. We battled traffic and ended up roughly in the right place. It was a sprawl of low-rise housing. The sort of place you see from planes coming in to land. Small houses on small lots, hurricane fencing, above ground pools. Some nice yards, some dumps. Old cars up on blocks. Everything bathed in yellow sodium glare.

We found the right street. Found the right house. Decent place. Well looked after. Neat and clean. A tiny one-storey. Small yard, small single-car garage. Narrow gate in the wire fence. We went through. Rang the bell. An old woman cracked the door against the chain.

'Good evening,' Roscoe said. 'We're looking for Sherman Stoller.'

Roscoe looked at me after she said it. She should have said we were looking for his house. We knew where Sherman Stoller was. Sherman Stoller was in the Yellow Springs morgue, seventy miles away.

'Who are you?' the old woman asked, politely.

'Ma'am, we're police officers,' Roscoe said. Half true.

The old lady eased the door and took the chain off.

'You better come in,' she said. 'He's in the kitchen. Eating, I'm afraid.'

'Who is?' said Roscoe.

The old lady stopped and looked at her. Puzzled.

'Sherman,' she said. 'That's who you want, isn't it?'

We followed her into the kitchen. There was an old guy eating supper at the table. When he saw us, he stopped and dabbed at his lips with a napkin.

'Police officers, Sherman,' the old lady said.

The old guy looked up at us blankly.

'Is there another Sherman Stoller?' I asked him.

The old guy nodded. Looked worried.

'Our son,' he said.

'About thirty?' I asked him. 'Thirty-five?'

The old guy nodded again. The old lady moved behind him and put her hand on his arm. Parents.

'He don't live here,' the old man said.

'Is he in trouble?' the old lady asked.

'Could you give us his address?' Roscoe said.

They fussed around like old people do. Very deferential to authority. Very respectful. Wanted to ask us a lot of questions, but just gave us the address.

'He hasn't lived here for two years,' the old man said.

He was afraid. He was trying to distance himself from the trouble his son was in. We nodded to them and backed out. As we were shutting their front door, the old man called out after us.

'He moved out there two years ago,' he said.

We trooped out through the gate and got back in the car. Looked on the street map again. The new address wasn't on it.

'What did you make of those two?' Roscoe asked me.

'The parents?' I said. 'They know their boy was up to no good. They know he was doing something bad. Probably don't know exactly what it was.'

'That's what I thought,' she said. 'Let's go find this new place.'

We drove off. Roscoe got gas and directions at the first place we saw.

'About five miles the other way,' she said. Pulled the car around and headed away from the city. 'New condominiums on a golf course.'

She was peering into the gloom, looking for the landmarks the gas station attendant had given her. After five miles she swung off the main drag. Nosed along a new road and pulled up by a developer's sign. It advertised condominiums, top quality, built right on the fairway. It boasted that only a few remained unsold. Beyond the billboard were rows of new buildings. Very pleasant, not huge, but nicely done. Balconies, garages, good details. Ambitious landscaping loomed up in the dark. Lighted pathways led over to a health club. On the other side was nothing. Must have been the golf course.

Roscoe killed the motor. We sat in the car. I stretched my arm along the back of her seat. Cupped her shoulder. I was tired. I'd been busy all day. I wanted to sit like this for a while. It was a quiet, dull night. Warm in the car. I wanted music. Something with an ache to it. But we had things to do. We had to find Judy. The woman who had bought Sherman Stoller's watch and had it engraved. To Sherman, love Judy. We had to find Judy and tell her the man she'd loved had bled to death under a highway.

'What do you make of this?' Roscoe said. She was bright and awake.

'Don't know,' I said. 'They're for sale, not rental. They look expensive. Could a truck driver afford this?'

203

'Doubt it,' she said. 'These probably cost as much as my place, and I couldn't make my payments without the subsidy I get. And I make more than any truck driver, that's for sure.'

'OK,' I said. 'So our guess is old Sherman was getting some kind of a subsidy, too, right? Otherwise he couldn't afford to live here.'

'Sure,' she said. 'But what kind of a subsidy?'

'The kind that gets people killed,' I said.

Stoller's building was way in back. Probably the first phase to have been built. The old man in the poor part of town had said his son had moved out two years ago. That could be about right. This first block could be about two years old. We threaded through walkways and around raised up flowerbeds. Walked up a path to Sherman Stoller's door. The path was stepping stones set in the wiry lawn. Forced an unnatural gait on you. I had to step short. Roscoe had to stretch her stride from one flagstone to the next. We reached the door. It was blue. No shine on it. Old-fashioned paint.

'Are we going to tell her?' I said.

'We can't not tell her, can we?' Roscoe said. 'She's got to know.'

I knocked on the door. Waited. Knocked again. I heard the floor creaking inside. Someone was coming. The door opened. A woman stood there. Maybe thirty, but she looked older. Short, nervous, tired. Blonde from a bottle. She looked out at us.

'We're police officers, ma'am,' Roscoe said. 'We're looking for the Sherman Stoller residence.'

There was silence for a moment.

'Well, you found it, I guess,' the woman said.

'May we come in?' Roscoe asked. Gently.

Again there was silence. No movement. Then the blonde woman turned and walked back down the hallway. Roscoe and I looked at each other. Roscoe followed the woman. I followed Roscoe. I shut the door behind us.

The woman led us into a living room. A decent-sized space. Expensive furniture and rugs. A big TV. No stereo, no books. It all looked a bit half-hearted. Like somebody had spent twenty minutes with a catalogue and ten thousand dollars. One of these, one of those, two of that. All delivered one morning and just kind of dumped in there.

'Are you Mrs Stoller?' Roscoe asked the woman. Still gentle.

'More or less,' the woman said. 'Not exactly Mrs, but as near as makes no difference anyhow.'

'Is your name Judy?' I asked her.

She nodded. Kept on nodding for a while. Thinking.

'He's dead, isn't he?' Judy said.

I didn't answer. This was the part I wasn't good at. This was Roscoe's part. She didn't say anything, either.

'He's dead, right?' Judy said again, louder.

'Yes, he is,' Roscoe said. 'I'm very sorry.'

Judy nodded to herself and looked around the hideous room. Nobody spoke. We just stood there. Judy sat down. She waved us to sit as well. We sat, in separate chairs. We were all sitting in a neat triangle.

'We need to ask you some questions,' Roscoe said. She was sitting forward, leaning towards the blonde woman. 'May we do that?'

Judy nodded. Looked pretty blank.

'How long did you know Sherman?' Roscoe asked.

'About four years, I guess,' Judy said. 'Met him in Florida, where I lived. Came up here to be with him four years ago. Lived up here ever since.'

'What was Sherman's job?' Roscoe asked.

Judy shrugged miserably.

'He was a truck driver,' she said. 'He got some kind of a big driving contract up here. Supposed to be long term, you know? So we bought a little place. His folks moved in too. Lived with us for a while. Then we moved out here. Left his folks in the old house. He made good money for three years. Busy all the time. Then it stopped, a year ago. He hardly worked at all since. Just an odd day, now and then.'

'You own both the houses?' Roscoe said.

'I don't own a damn thing,' Judy said. 'Sherman owned the houses. Yes, both of them.'

'So he was doing well for the first three years?' Roscoe asked her.

Judy gave her a look.

'Doing well?' she said. 'Grow up, for God's sake. He was a thief. He was ripping somebody off.'

'You sure?' I said.

Judy swung her gaze my way. Like an artillery piece traversing.

'It don't need much brains to figure it out,' she said. 'In three years he paid cash for two houses, two lots of furniture, cars, God knows what. And this place wasn't cheap, either. We got lawyers and doctors and all sorts living here. And he had enough saved so he didn't have to work at all since last September. If he did all that on the level, then I'm the First Lady, right?'

She was giving us a defiant stare. She'd known about it all along. She'd known what would happen when he was found out. She was challenging us to deny her the right to blame him.

'Who was his big contract with?' Roscoe asked her.

'Some outfit called Island Air-conditioning,' she said. 'He spent three years hauling air conditioners. Taking them down to Florida. Maybe they went on to the islands, I don't know. He used to steal them. There's two old boxes in the garage right now. Want to see?'

She didn't wait for a reply. Just jumped up and stalked out. We followed. We all went down some back stairs and through a basement door. Into a garage. It was empty except for a couple of old cartons dumped against a wall. Cardboard cartons, could have been a year or two old. Marked with a manufacturer's logo. Island Air-conditioning, Inc. This End Up. The sealing tape was torn and hanging off. Each box had a long serial number written on by hand. Each box must have held a single unit. The sort you jam in your window frame, makes a hell of a noise. Judy glared at the boxes and glared at us. It was a glare which said: I gave him a gold watch and he gave me a shitload of worry.

I walked over and looked at the cartons. They were empty. I smelled a faint, sour odour in them. Then we went back upstairs. Judy got an album out of a cupboard. Sat and looked at a photograph of Sherman.

'What happened to him?' she asked.

It was a simple question. Deserved a simple answer.

'He was shot in the head,' I lied. 'Died instantly.'

Judy nodded. Like she wasn't surprised.

'When?' she asked.

'On Thursday night,' Roscoe told her. 'At midnight. Did he say where he was going on Thursday night?'

Judy shook her head.

'He never told me much,' she said.

'Did he ever mention meeting an investigator?' Roscoe asked.

Judy shook her head again.

'What about Pluribus?' I asked her. 'Did he ever use that word?'

She looked blank.

'Is that a disease?' she said. 'Lungs or something?'

'What about Sunday?' I said. 'This Sunday coming? Did he ever say anything about that?'

'No,' Judy said. 'He never said much about anything.'

She sat and stared at the photographs in the album. The room was quiet.

'Did he know any lawyers in Florida?' Roscoe asked her.

'Lawyers?' Judy said. 'In Florida? Why should he?'

'He was arrested in Jacksonville,' Roscoe said. 'Two years ago. It was a traffic violation in his truck. A lawyer came to help him out.'

Judy shrugged, like two years ago was ancient history to her.

'There are lawyers sniffing everywhere, right?' she said. 'No big deal.'

'This guy wasn't an ambulance-chaser,' Roscoe said. 'He was a partner in a big firm down there. Any idea how Sherman could have gotten hold of him?'

Judy shrugged again.

'Maybe his employer did it,' she said. 'Island Air-conditioning. They gave us good medical insurance. Sherman let me go to the doctor, any old time I needed to.'

We all went quiet. Nothing more to say. Judy sat and gazed at the photographs in the album.

'Want to see his picture?' she said.

I walked around behind her chair and bent to look at the photograph. It showed a sandy, rat-faced man. Small, slight, with a grin. He was standing in front of a yellow panel van. Grinning and squinting at the camera. The grin gave it poignancy.

'That's the truck he drove,' Judy said.

But I wasn't looking at the truck or Sherman Stoller's poignant grin. I was looking at a figure in the background of the picture. It was out of focus and turned half away from the camera, but I could make out who it was. It was Paul Hubble.

I waved Roscoe over and she bent beside me and looked at the photograph. I saw a wave of surprise pass over her face as she recognized Hubble. Then she bent closer. Looked harder. I saw a second wave of surprise. She had recognized something else.

'When was this picture taken?' she asked.

Judy shrugged.

'Summer last year, I guess,' she said.

Roscoe touched the blurred image of Hubble with her finger-nail.

'Did Sherman say who this guy was?'

'The new boss,' Judy said. 'He was there six months, then he fired Sherman's ass.'

'Island Air-conditioning's new boss?' Roscoe said. 'Was there a reason he laid Sherman off?'

'Sherman said they didn't need him no more,' Judy said. 'He never said much.'

'Is this where Island Air-conditioning is based?' Roscoe asked. 'Where this picture was taken?'

Judy shrugged and nodded her head, tentatively.

'I guess so,' she said. 'Sherman never told me much about it.'

'We need to keep this photograph,' Roscoe told her. 'We'll let you have it back later.'

Judy fished it out of the plastic. Handed it to her.

'Keep it,' she said. 'I don't want it.'

Roscoe took the picture and put it in her inside jacket pocket. She and I moved back to the middle of the room and stood there.

'Shot in the head,' Judy said. 'That's what happens when you mess around. I told him they'd catch up with him, sooner or later.'

Roscoe nodded sympathetically.

'We'll keep in touch,' she said to her. 'You know, the funeral arrangements, and we might want a statement.'

Judy glared at us again.

'Don't bother,' she said. 'I'm not going to his funeral. I wasn't his wife, so I'm not his widow. I'm going to forget I ever knew him. That man was trouble from beginning to end.'

She stood there glaring at us. We shuffled out, down the hall, out through the door. Across the awkward path. We held hands as we walked back to the car.

'What?' I asked her. 'What's in the photograph?'

She was walking fast.

'Wait,' she said. 'I'll show you in the car.'

NINETEEN

WE GOT IN THE CHEVY AND SHE SNAPPED ON THE DOME light. Pulled the photograph out of her pocket. Leaned over and tilted the picture so the light caught the shiny surface. Checked it carefully. Handed it to me.

'Look at the edge,' she said. 'On the left.'

The picture was of Sherman Stoller standing in front of a yellow truck. Paul Hubble was turned away, in the background. The two figures and the truck filled the whole frame apart from a wedge of blacktop at the bottom. And a thin margin of background to the left. The background slice was even more out of focus than Hubble was, but I could see the edge of a modern metal building, with silver siding. A tall tree beyond. The frame of a door. It was a big industrial door, rolled up. The frame was a dark red colour. Some kind of baked-on industrial coating. Partly decorative, partly preservative. Some kind of a shed door. There was gloom inside the shed.

'That's Kliner's warehouse,' she said. 'At the top of the county road.'

'Are you sure?' I said.

'I recognize the tree,' she said.

I looked again. It was a very distinctive tree. Dead on one side. Maybe split by lightning.

'That's Kliner's warehouse,' she said again. 'No doubt about that.'

Then she clicked her car phone on and took the photograph back. Dialled DMV in Atlanta and called in the number from the front of Stoller's truck. Waited a long moment, tapping her index finger on the steering wheel. I heard the crackle of the response in the earpiece. Then she clicked the phone off and turned to me.

'The truck is registered to Kliner Industries,' she said. 'And the registered address is Zacarias Perez, Attorneys-at-Law, Jacksonville, Florida.'

I nodded. She nodded back. Sherman Stoller's buddies. The ones who had got him out of Jacksonville Central in fifty-five minutes flat, two years ago.

'OK,' she said. 'Put it all together. Hubble, Stoller, Joe's investigation. They're printing counterfeit money down in Kliner's warehouse, right?'

I shook my head.

'Wrong,' I said. 'There's no printing going on inside the States. It all happens abroad. Molly Beth Gordon told me that, and she ought to know what she's talking about. She said Joe had made it impossible. And whatever Stoller was doing, Judy said he stopped doing it a year ago. And Finlay said Joe only started this whole thing a year ago. Around the same time Hubble fired Stoller.'

Roscoe nodded. Shrugged.

'We need Molly's help,' she said. 'We need a copy of Joe's file.'

'Or Picard's help,' I said. 'We might find Joe's hotel room and get hold of the original. It's a race to see who's going to call us first, Molly or Picard.'

Roscoe clicked off the dome light. Started the car for the ride back to the airport hotel. I just sprawled out beside her, yawning. I could sense she was getting uptight. She had run out of things to do. Run out of distractions. Now she had to face the quiet vulnerable hours of the night. The first night after last night. The prospect was making her agitated.

'You got that gun, Reacher?' she asked.

I squirmed around in the seat to face her.

'It's in the trunk,' I said. 'In that box. You put it in there, remember?'

'Bring it inside, OK?' she said. 'Makes me feel better.'

I grinned sleepily in the dark. Yawned.

'Makes me feel better too,' I said. 'It's a hell of a gun.'

Then we lapsed back into silence. Roscoe found the hotel lot. We got out of the car and stood stretching in the dark. I opened the trunk. Lifted the box out and slammed the lid. Went in through our lobby and up in the elevator.

In the room we just crashed out. Roscoe laid her shiny .38 on the carpet on her side of the bed. I reloaded my giant .44 and laid it on my side. Cocked and locked. We wedged a chair under the doorhandle. Roscoe felt safer that way.

I woke early and lay in bed, thinking about Joe. Wednesday morning. He'd been dead five days. Roscoe was already up. She was standing in the middle of the floor, stretching. Some kind of a yoga thing. She'd taken a shower and she was only half dressed. She had no trousers on. Just a shirt. She had her back to me. As she stretched, the shirt was riding way up. Suddenly I wasn't thinking about Joe any more.

'Roscoe?' I said.

'What?' she said.

'You've got the most wonderful ass on the planet,' I said.

She giggled. I jumped on her. Couldn't help it. Couldn't do anything else. She drove me crazy. It was the giggle that did it to me. It made me crazy. I hauled her back into the big hotel bed. The building could have fallen down and we wouldn't have noticed it. We finished in an exhausted tangle. Lay there for a while. Then Roscoe got up again and showered for the second time that morning. Got dressed again. Trousers and everything. Grinned at me as if to say she was sparing me from any further temptation.

'So did you mean it?' she said.

'Mean what?' I said, with a smile.

'You know what,' she smiled back. 'When you told me I had a cute ass.'

'I didn't say you had a cute ass,' I said. 'I've seen plenty of cute asses. I said yours was the most wonderful ass on the whole damn planet.'

'But did you mean it?' she said.

'You bet I meant it,' I said. 'Don't underestimate the attraction of your ass, Roscoe, whatever you do.'

I called room service for breakfast. Removed the chair from under the door handle ready for the little cart. Pulled the heavy drapes. It was a glorious morning. A bright blue sky, no clouds at all, brilliant fall sunshine. The room was flooded with light. We cracked the window and let in the air and the smells and the sounds of the day. The view was spectacular. Right over the airport and to the city beyond. The cars in the lots caught the sun and looked like jewels on beige velvet. The planes clawed their

211

way into the air and wheeled slowly away like fat, important birds. The buildings downtown grew tall and straight in the sun. A glorious morning. But it was the sixth straight morning my brother wasn't alive to see.

Roscoe used the phone to call Finlay down in Margrave. She told him about the photograph of Hubble and Stoller standing in the sun on the warehouse forecourt. Then she gave him our room number and told him to call us if Molly got back to us from Washington. Or if Picard got back to us with information from the car rental people about the burned Pontiac. I figured we should stay in Atlanta in case Picard beat Molly and we got a hotel trace on Joe. Chances were he stayed in the city, maybe near the airport. No point in us driving all the way back down to Margrave and then having to drive all the way back up to Atlanta again. So we waited. I fiddled with the radio built into the nightstand thing. Came up with a station playing something halfway decent. Sounded like they were playing through an early Canned Heat album. Bouncy and sunny and just right for a bright empty morning.

Breakfast came and we ate it. The whole bit. Pancakes, syrup, bacon. Lots of coffee in a thick china jug. Afterward, I lay back on the bed. Pretty soon started feeling restless. Started feeling like it had been a mistake to wait around. It felt like we weren't doing anything. I could see Roscoe was feeling the same way. She propped the photograph of Hubble and Stoller and the yellow van on the nightstand and glared at it. I glared at the telephone. It wasn't ringing. We wandered around the room, waiting. Then I stooped to pick up the Desert Eagle off the floor by the bed. Hefted it in my hand. Traced the engraved name on the grip with my finger. Looked across at Roscoe. I was curious about the guy who'd bought that massive automatic.

'What was Gray like?' I asked.

'Gray?' she said. 'He was so thorough. You want to get Joe's files? You should see Gray's paperwork. There are twenty-five years of his files in the station house. All meticulous, all comprehensive. Gray was a good detective.'

'Why did he hang himself?' I asked her.

'I don't know,' she said. 'I never understood it.'

'Was he depressed?' I said.

'Not really,' she said. 'I mean, he was always sort of depressed. Lugubrious, you know? A very dour sort of guy. And bored. He was a good detective, and he was wasted in Margrave. But no worse in February than any other time. It was a total surprise to me. I was very upset.'

'Were you close?' I asked her.

She shrugged.

'Yes, we were,' she said. 'In a way, we were pretty close. He was a dour guy, you know, not really that close to anybody. Never married, always lived alone, no relatives. He was a teetotaller, so he would never come out for a beer or anything. He was quiet, messy, a little overweight. No hair and a big straggly beard. A very self-contained, comfortable type of a guy. A loner, really. But he was as close to me as he was ever going to get to anybody. We liked each other, in a quiet sort of a way.'

'And he never said anything?' I asked her. 'Just hanged himself one day?'

'That's how it was,' she said. 'A total shock. I'll never understand it.'

'Why did you have his gun in your desk?' I said.

'He asked if he could keep it in there,' she said. 'He had no space in his own desk. He generated a lot of paperwork. He just asked if I could keep a box for him with the gun hidden in it. It was his private weapon. He said he couldn't get it approved by the department because the calibre was too big. He made it feel like some kind of a big secret.'

I put the dead man's secret gun down on the carpet again and the silence was shattered by the phone ringing. I sprinted for the nightstand and answered it. Heard Finlay's voice. I gripped the phone and held my breath.

'Reacher?' Finlay said. 'Picard got what we need. He traced the car.'

I breathed out and nodded to Roscoe.

'Great, Finlay,' I said. 'So what's the story?'

'Go to his office,' he said. 'He'll give you the spread, face to face. I didn't want too much conversation on the phones down here.'

I closed my eyes for a second and felt a surge of energy.

'Thanks, Finlay,' I said. 'Speak to you later.'

'OK,' he said. 'Take care, right?'

Then he hung up and left me sitting there holding the phone, smiling.

'I thought he'd never call,' Roscoe laughed. 'But I guess eighteen hours isn't too bad, even for the Bureau, right?'

*

The Atlanta FBI was housed in a new federal building downtown. Roscoe parked at the kerb outside. The Bureau reception called upstairs and told us Special Agent Picard would come right down to meet with us. We waited for him in the lobby. It was a big hall, with a brave stab at decoration, but it still had the glum atmosphere government buildings have. Picard came out of an elevator within three minutes. He loped over. He seemed to fill the whole hall. He nodded to me and took Roscoe's hand.

'Heard a lot about you from Finlay,' he said to her.

His bear's voice rumbled. Roscoe nodded and smiled.

'The car Finlay found?' he said. 'Rental Pontiac. Booked out to Joe Reacher, Atlanta airport, Thursday night at eight.'

'Great, Picard,' I said. 'Any guess about where he was holed up?'

'Better than a guess, my friend,' Picard said. 'They had the exact location. It was a prebooked car. They delivered it right to his hotel.'

He mentioned a place a mile the other way from the hotel we were using.

'Thanks, Picard,' I said. 'I owe you.'

'No problem, my friend,' he said. 'You take care now, OK?'

He loped off back to the elevator and we raced back south to the airport. Roscoe swung onto the perimeter road and accelerated into the flow. Across the divider, a black pickup flashed by. Brand-new. I spun around and caught a glimpse of it disappearing behind a raft of trucks. Black. Brand-new. Probably nothing. They sell more pickups down here than anything else.

Roscoe pulled her badge at the desk where Picard said Joe had checked in on Thursday. The clerk did some keyboard work and told us he had been in 621, sixth floor, far end of the corridor. She said a manager would meet us up there. So we went up in the elevator and walked the length of a dark corridor. Stood waiting outside the door to Joe's room.

The manager came by more or less straight away and opened the room up with his pass key. We stepped in. The room was empty. It had been cleaned and tidied. It looked like it was ready for new occupants.

'What about his stuff?' I said. 'Where is it all?'

'We cleared it out Saturday,' the manager said. 'The guy was booked in Thursday night, supposed to vacate by eleven Friday morning. What we do is we give them an extra day, then if they don't show, we clear them out, down to housekeeping.'

'So his stuff is in a closet somewhere?' I asked.

'Downstairs,' the manager said. 'You should see the stuff we got down there. People leave things all the time.'

'So can we go take a look?' I said.

'Basement,' he said. 'Use the stairs from the lobby. You'll find it.'

The manager strolled off. Roscoe and I walked the length of the corridor again and rode back down in the elevator. We found the service staircase and went down to the basement. Housekeeping was a giant hall stacked with linens and towels. There were hampers and baskets full of soap and those free sachets you find in the showers. Maids were pulling in and out with the trolleys they use for servicing the rooms. There was a glassed-in office cubicle in the near corner with a woman at a small desk. We walked over and rapped on the glass. She looked up. Roscoe held out her badge.

'Help you?' the woman said.

'Room six-two-one,' Roscoe said. 'You cleared out some belongings, Saturday morning. You got them down here?'

I was holding my breath again.

'Six-two-one?' the woman said. 'He came by for them already. They're gone.'

I breathed out. We were too late. I went numb with disappointment.

'Who came by?' I asked. 'When?'

'The guest,' the woman said. 'This morning, maybe nine, nine-thirty.'

'Who was he?' I asked her.

She pulled a small book off a shelf and thumbed it open. Licked a stubby finger and pointed to a line.

'Joe Reacher,' she said. 'He signed the book and took the stuff.'

She reversed the book and slid it toward us. There was a scrawled signature on the line.

'What did this Reacher guy look like?' I asked her.

She shrugged.

'Foreign,' she said. 'Some kind of a Latino. Maybe from Cuba? Little dark guy, slender, nice smile. Very polite sort of a guy, as I recall.'

'You got a list of the stuff?' I said.

She slid the stubby finger further along the line. There was a small column filled with tight handwriting. It listed a garment bag, eight articles of clothing, a toilet bag, four shoes. The last item

215

listed was: one briefcase.

We just walked away from her and found the stairs back to the lobby. Walked out into the morning sun. It didn't feel like such a great day any more.

We reached the car. Leaned side by side on the front fender. I was weighing up in my mind whether Joe would have been smart enough and careful enough to do what I would have done. I figured maybe he would have been. He'd spent a long time around smart and careful people.

'Roscoe?' I said. 'If you were the guy walking out of here with Joe's stuff, what would you do?'

She stopped with the car door half open. Thought about it.

'I'd keep the briefcase,' she said. 'Take it wherever I was supposed to take it. The rest of the stuff, I'd get rid of it.'

'That's what I would do as well,' I said. 'Where would you get rid of it?'

'First place I saw, I guess,' she said.

There was a service road running between the hotel and the next one in line. It looped behind the hotels and then out onto the perimeter road. There was a line of dumpsters along a twenty-yard stretch of it. I pointed.

'Suppose he drove out that way?' I said. 'Suppose he stopped and lobbed the garment bag straight into one of those dumpsters?'

'But he'd have kept the briefcase, right?' Roscoe said.

'Maybe we aren't looking for the briefcase,' I said. 'Yesterday, I drove miles and miles out to that stand of trees, but I hid in the field. A diversion, right? It's a habit. Maybe Joe had the same habit. Maybe he carried a briefcase but kept his important stuff in the garment bag.'

Roscoe shrugged. Wasn't convinced. We started walking down the service road. Up close, the dumpsters were huge. I had to lever myself up on the edge of each one and peer in. The first one was empty. Nothing in it at all, except the baked-on kitchen dirt from years of use. The second one was full. I found a length of studding from some demolished drywall and poked around with it. Couldn't see anything. I heaved myself down and walked to the next one.

There was a garment bag in it. Lying right on top of some old cartons. I fished for it with the length of wood. Hauled it out. Tossed it onto the ground at Roscoe's feet. Jumped down next to it. It was a battered, well-travelled bag. Scuffed and scratched.

Lots of airline tags all over it. There was a little nameplate in the shape of a miniature gold credit card fastened to the handle. It said: Reacher.

'OK, Joe,' I said to myself. 'Let's see if you were a smart guy.'

I was looking for the shoes. They were in the outside pocket of the bag. Two pairs. Four shoes, just like it said on the housekeeper's list. I pulled the inner soles out of each one in turn. Under the third one, I found a tiny Ziplock bag. With a sheet of computer paper folded up inside it.

'Smart as a whip, Joe,' I said to myself, and laughed.

TWENTY

ROSCOE AND I DANCED AROUND THE SERVICE ALLEY TOGETHER like players in the dugout watching the winning run soar out of sight. Then we hustled over to the Chevy and raced the mile back to our hotel. Ran into the lobby, into the elevator. Unlocked our room and fell in. The telephone was ringing. It was Finlay, on the line from Margrave again. He sounded as excited as we were.

'Molly Beth Gordon just called,' he said. 'She did it. She's got the files we need. She's flying down here, right now. She told me it was amazing stuff. Sounded high as a kite. Atlanta arrivals, two o'clock. I'll meet you there. Delta, from Washington. Picard give you anything?'

'Sure did,' I said. 'He's quite a guy. I got the rest of the printout, I think.'

'You think?' Finlay said. 'You don't know?'

'Only just got back,' I said. 'Haven't looked at it yet.'

'So look at it, for Christ's sake,' he said. 'It's important, right?'

'See you later, Harvard guy,' I said.

We sat down at the table over by the window. Unzipped the little plastic bag and pulled out the paper. Unfolded it carefully. It was a sheet of computer paper. The top inch had been torn off the right-hand corner. Half the heading had been left behind. It said: Operation E Unum.

'Operation E Unum Pluribus,' Roscoe said.

Underneath was a triple-spaced list of initials with telephone numbers opposite. The first set of initials was P.H. The phone number was torn off.

'Paul Hubble,' Roscoe said. 'His number and the other half of the heading was what Finlay found.'

I nodded. Then there were four more sets of initials. The first two were W.B. and K.K. They had phone numbers alongside. I recognized a New York area code against K.K. The W.B. area code I figured I'd have to look up. The third set of initials was J.S. The code was 504. New Orleans area. I'd been there less than a month ago. The fourth set of initials was M.B.G. There was a phone number with a 202 area code. I pointed to it, so Roscoe could see it.

'Molly Beth Gordon,' she said. 'Washington DC.'

I nodded again. It wasn't the number I had called from the rosewood office. Maybe her home number. The final two items on the torn paper were not initials, and there were no corresponding phone numbers. The second-to-last item was just two words: Stollers' Garage. The last item was three words: Gray's Kliner File. I looked at the careful capital letters and I could just about feel my dead brother's neat, pedantic personality bursting off the page.

Paul Hubble we knew about. He was dead. Molly Beth Gordon we knew about. She'd be here at two o'clock. We'd seen the garage up at Sherman Stoller's place on the golf course. It held nothing but two empty cartons. That left the underlined heading, three sets of initials with three phone numbers, and the three words: Gray's Kliner File. I checked the time. Just past noon. Too early to sit back and wait for Molly Beth to arrive. I figured we should make a start.

'First we think about the heading,' I said. 'E Unum Pluribus.'

Roscoe shrugged.

'That's the US motto, right?' she said. 'The Latin thing?'

'No,' I said. 'It's the motto backwards. This more or less means out of one comes many. Not out of many comes one.'

'Could Joe have written it down wrong?' she said.

I shook my head.

'I doubt it,' I said. 'I don't think Joe would make that kind of a mistake. It must mean something.'

Roscoe shrugged again.

'Doesn't mean anything to me,' she said. 'What else?'

'Gray's Kliner File,' I said. 'Did Gray have a file on Kliner?'

'Probably,' Roscoe said. 'He had a file on just about everything.

Somebody spat on the sidewalk, he'd put it in a file.'

I nodded. Stepped back to the bed and picked up the phone. Called Finlay down in Margrave. Baker told me he'd already left. So I dialled the other numbers on Joe's printout. The W.B. number was in New Jersey. Princeton University. Faculty of modern history. I hung up straight away. Couldn't see the connection. The K.K. number was in New York City. Columbia University. Faculty of modern history. I hung up again. Then I dialled J.S. in New Orleans. I heard one ring tone and a busy voice.

'Fifteenth squad, detectives,' the voice said.

'Detectives?' I said. 'Is that the NOPD?'

'Fifteenth squad,' the voice said again. 'Can I help you?'

'You got somebody there with the initials J.S.?' I asked.

'J.S.?' the voice said. 'I got three of them. Which one do you want?'

'Don't know,' I said. 'Does the name Joe Reacher mean anything to you?'

'What the hell is this?' the voice said. 'Twenty Questions or something?'

'Ask them, will you?' I said. 'Ask each J.S. if they know Joe Reacher. Will you do that? I'll call back later, OK?'

Down in New Orleans, the fifteenth squad desk guy grunted and hung up. I shrugged at Roscoe and put the phone back on the nightstand.

'We wait for Molly?' she said.

I nodded. I was a little nervous about meeting Molly. It was going to be like meeting a ghost connected to another ghost.

We waited at the cramped table in the window. Watched the sun fall away from its noontime peak. Wasted time passing Joe's torn printout back and forth between us. I stared at the heading. E Unum Pluribus. Out of one comes many. That was Joe Reacher, in three words. Something important, all bound up in a wry little pun.

'Let's go,' Roscoe said.

We were early, but we were anxious. We gathered up our things. Rode the elevator to the lobby and let the dead guys settle up for our phone calls. Then we walked over to Roscoe's Chevy. Started threading our way around to arrivals. It wasn't easy. The airport hotels were planned for people heading out of arrivals or heading into departures. Nobody had thought of people going our way.

220

'We don't know what Molly looks like,' Roscoe said.

'But she knows what I look like,' I said. 'I look like Joe.'

The airport was vast. We saw most of it as we crabbed over to the right quarter. It was bigger than some cities I'd been in. We drove for miles. Found the right terminal. Missed a lane change and passed the short-term parking. Came around again and lined up at the barrier. Roscoe snatched the ticket and eased into the lot.

'Go left,' I said.

The lot was packed. I was craning over, looking for spaces. Then I saw a vague black shape slide by in the line on my right. I caught it out of the corner of my eye.

'Go right, go right,' I said.

I thought it was the rear end of a black pickup. Brand-new. Sliding by on my right. Roscoe hauled the wheel over and we swung into the next aisle. Caught a flash of red brake lights in black sheet metal. A pickup swung out of sight. Roscoe howled down the aisle and cornered hard.

The next aisle was empty. Nothing moving. Just ranks of automobiles standing quiet in the sun. Same thing in the next aisle. Nothing on the move. No black pickup. We drove all over the lot. Took us a long time. We were held up by the cars moving in and out. But we covered the whole area. Couldn't find a black pickup anywhere.

But we did find Finlay. We parked up in an empty space and started the long walk to the terminal. Finlay had parked in a different quarter and was walking in on a different diagonal. He walked the rest of the way with us.

The terminal was very busy. And it was huge. Built low, but it spread horizontally over acres. The whole place was crowded. Flickering screens high up announced the arrivals. The two o'clock Delta from Washington was in and taxiing. We walked down toward the gate. Felt like a half-mile walk. We were in a long corridor with a ribbed rubber floor. A pair of moving walkways ran down the centre of the corridor. On the right was an endless row of bright gaudy advertisements about the attractions of the Sunbelt. Business or pleasure, it was all down here, that's for sure. On the left was a glass partition, floor to ceiling, with a white etched stripe at eye level to stop people trying to walk through the glass.

Behind the glass were the gates. There was an endless sequence of them. The passengers came out of the planes and

221

walked along on their side of the glass. Half of them disappeared sideways into the baggage claim areas. Then they came out again and found exit doors in the glass partition which let them out into the main corridor. The other half were the short-haul fliers with no checked baggage. They went straight to the doors. Each set of doors was mobbed by big knots of meeters and greeters. We pushed our way through them as we headed down.

Passengers were spilling out of the doors, every thirty yards. Friends and relatives were moving in close and the two streams of people were colliding. We fought through eight separate crowds before we got to the right gate. I just pushed my way through. I felt anxious. The glimpse of the black pickup in the lot had unsettled me.

We reached the gate. We walked on our side of the glass right past the doors. Right down to level with the end of the jetway. People were already coming off the plane. I watched them spilling out of the jetway and turning to walk up toward the baggage area and the exit doors. On our side of the glass, people were walking down to the gates farther on. They were pushing at us as they passed. We were being dragged down the corridor. Like swimming in a heavy sea. We were stepping backward all the time just to stay standing still.

There was a stream of people behind the glass. I saw a woman coming in who could have been Molly. She was about thirty-five, dressed well in a business suit, carrying a briefcase and a garment bag. I was standing there, trying to get recognized, but she suddenly saw somebody else and pointed and gave a silent shriek behind the glass and blew a kiss to a guy ten yards from me. He shouldered backwards towards the doors to wait for her.

Then it seemed like just about any of the women could be Molly. There must have been a couple of dozen candidates. There were blondes and brunettes, tall ones, short ones, pretty ones, homely ones. All dressed for business, all carrying efficient luggage, all striding in with the weary purposeful manner of tired executives in the middle of a busy day. I watched them all. They flowed with the tide behind the glass, some of them peering out for husbands, lovers, drivers, business contacts, some of them looking straight ahead. All of them carried along in the swarming crowd.

One of them had matching burgundy leather luggage, a heavy briefcase in one hand and a carry-on which she was wheeling on a long handle with the other. She was small, blonde, excited. She

222

slowed as she turned out of the jetway and scanned the crowd through the glass. Her eyes flashed past me. Then they snapped back. She looked straight at me. Stopped. People piled up behind her. She was pushed forward. She fought her way over to the glass. I moved in close on my side. She stared at me. Smiled. Greeted her dead lover's brother with her eyes.

'Molly?' I mouthed through the glass at her.

She held up the heavy briefcase like a trophy. Nodded towards it. Smiled a big wide smile of excited triumph. She was pushed in the back. Borne along by the crowd towards the exit. She looked back to see if I was following. Roscoe and Finlay and I struggled after her.

On Molly's side of the glass, the flow was with her. Our side, it was against us. We were being separated at double speed. There was a solid mob of college kids bearing down on us. Aiming to fly out of a gate further down. Big, well-fed kids, clumsy luggage, rowdy. The three of us were shoved backwards five yards. Through the glass, Molly was way ahead. I saw her blonde head disappear. I fought sideways and vaulted over onto the moving walkway. It was going the wrong way. I was carried another five yards before I made it over the moving handgrip onto the other side.

Now I was going in the right direction, but the walkway was a solid mass of people just standing still on it. Content with the snail's pace the rubber floor was carrying them. They were standing three abreast. No way through at all. I climbed up onto the narrow handrail and tried to walk along it like a tightrope. I had to crouch because I couldn't balance. I fell heavily to my right. Got carried five yards the wrong way before I could struggle up. I looked around in panic. Through the glass, I could see Molly was being crowded into the baggage claim. I could see Roscoe and Finlay were way behind me. I was moving slowly the wrong way.

I didn't want Molly to go into the baggage claim. She'd flown down here in a hurry. She had urgent news. No way would she have packed a big valise. No way would she have checked any luggage. She shouldn't be going into the baggage claim. I put my head down and ran. Barged people out of the way. I was travelling against the pace of the walkway. The rubber floor was grabbing at my shoes. Each impact was costing me time. People were yelling in outrage. I didn't care. I tore through them and left them sprawling. Vaulted off the walkway and clawed through the crowd at the exit doors.

The baggage claim was a wide low hall, lit with dull yellow

lights. I fought my way in through the exit lane. Looking everywhere for Molly. Couldn't find her. The hall was jammed with people. There must have been a hundred passengers standing around the carousel, three deep. The belt was grinding around under a heavy load of bags. There were ragged lines of luggage carts on the side wall. People were lining up to put quarters in a slot and pull them free. They were wheeling them away through the crowd. Carts were clashing and tangling. People were pushing and shoving.

I waded into the mass. Shouldered my way through and spun people around, searching for Molly. I'd seen her go in. I hadn't seen her come out. But she wasn't in there. I checked every face. I trawled through the whole hall. I let myself be carried outside on the relentless tide. Fought ahead to the exit door. Roscoe was holding tight to the doorframe, battling the flow.

'She come out?' I said.

'No,' she said. 'Finlay's gone to the end of the corridor. He's waiting there. I'm waiting here.'

We stood there with people pouring past us. Then the crowd coming towards us from the gate was suddenly thinning. The whole planeload was just about through. The last stragglers were strolling down. An old woman in a wheelchair was bringing up the rear. She was being pushed along by an airline employee. The guy had to pause and manoeuvre his way around something lying in the entrance to the baggage hall. It was a burgundy leather carry-on. It was lying on its side. Its extending handle was still pulled out. From fifteen feet away, I could read the fancy gold monogram on the front. It read: M.B.G.

Roscoe and I dived back into the baggage claim. In the few minutes I'd been out of there, the place had just about emptied. Not more than a dozen people still in there. Most of them were already hauling their bags off the belt and heading out as we headed in. Within a minute, the hall was deserted. The luggage belt was grinding round, empty. Then it stopped. The hall fell silent. Roscoe and I stood in the sudden quiet and looked at each other.

The hall had four walls and a floor and a ceiling. There was an entrance door and an exit door. The carousel snaked in through a hole a yard square and snaked out again through a hole a yard square. Both holes were draped with black rubber curtains cut into slats a few inches wide. Next to the carousel was a cargo door. On our side, it was blank. No handle. Locked.

Roscoe darted back and grabbed Molly Beth's carry-on. Opened it up. It held a change of clothes and a toilet bag. And a photograph. Eight by ten, in a brassed frame. It was Joe. He looked like me, but a little thinner. A shaved, tanned scalp. A wry, amused smile.

The hall was filled with the shriek of a warning siren. It sounded for a moment and then the luggage belt graunched back into motion. We stared at it. Stared at the shrouded hole it was coming through. The rubber curtains bellied. A briefcase came out. Burgundy leather. The straps were slashed through. The case was open. It was empty.

It wobbled mechanically around toward us. We stared at it. Stared at the cut straps. They had been severed with a sharp blade. Severed by somebody in too much of a hurry to click open the catches.

I leapt onto the moving carousel. Ran back against the belt's lurching motion and dived like a swimmer head first through the rubber slats shrouding the yard-square hole. I landed hard and the belt started to drag me back out. I scrambled and crawled like a kid on my hands and knees. Rolled off and jumped up. I was in a loading bay. Deserted. The afternoon blazed outside. There was a stink of kerosene and diesel fuel from the baggage trains hauling in from the planes on the tarmac.

All around me were tall piles of forlorn cargo and forgotten suitcases. They were all stacked in three-sided storage bays. The rubber floor was littered with old labels and long barcodes. The place was like a filthy maze. I dodged and skidded about, hopelessly looking for Molly. I ran behind one tall pile after another. Into one bay and then the next. I grabbed at the metal racking and heaved myself around the tight corners. Glancing around desperately. Nobody there. Nobody anywhere. I ran on, sliding and skidding on the litter.

I found her left shoe. It was lying on its side at the entrance to a dark bay. I plunged in. Nothing there. I tried the next bay. Nothing there. I held onto the shelving, breathing hard. I had to organize. I ran to the far end of the corridor. Started ducking into each bay in turn. Left and right, left and right, working my way back as fast as I could, in a desperate breathless zigzag.

I found her right shoe three bays from the end. Then I found her blood. At the entry to the next bay, it was pooled on the floor, sticky, spreading. She was slumped at the back of the bay, on her back in the gloom, jammed between two towers of crates. Just sprawled there on the rubber floor. Blood was pouring out of her. Her gut was torn open. Somebody had jammed a knife in her and ripped it savagely upward under her ribs.

But she was alive. One pale hand was fluttering. Her lips were flecked with bright bubbles of blood. Her head was still, but her eyes were roving. I ran to her. Cradled her head. She gazed at me. Forced her mouth to work.

'Got to get in before Sunday,' she whispered.

Then she died in my arms.

TWENTY-ONE

I STUDIED CHEMISTRY IN MAYBE SEVEN DIFFERENT HIGH SCHOOLS. Didn't learn much of it. Just came away with general impressions. One thing I remember is how you can throw some little extra thing into a glass tube and make everything blow up with a bang. Just some little powder, produces a result way bigger than it should.

That was how I felt about Molly. I'd never met her before. Never even heard of her. But I felt angry, way out of all proportion. I felt worse about her than I felt about Joe. What happened to Joe was in the line of his duty. Joe knew that. He would have accepted that. Joe and I knew about risk and duty right from the moment we first knew about anything at all. But Molly was different.

The other thing I remember from the chemistry lab is stuff about pressure. Pressure turns coal into diamonds. Pressure does things. It was doing things to me. I was angry and I was short of time. In my mind I was seeing Molly coming out of that jetway. Striding out, determined to find Joe's brother and help him. Smiling a wide smile of triumph. Holding up a briefcase of files she shouldn't have copied. Risking a lot. For me. For Joe. That image in my mind was building up like massive pressure on some old geological seam. I had to decide how to use that pressure. I had to decide whether it was going to crush me or turn me into a diamond.

We were leaning on the front fender of Roscoe's car in the

227

airport short-term lot. Stunned and silent. Wednesday afternoon, nearly three o'clock. I had hold of Finlay's arm. He had wanted to stay inside and get involved. He had said it was his duty. I had screamed at him that we didn't have time. I had dragged him out of the terminal by force. I had marched him straight to the car, because I knew what we did in the next few moments was going to make the difference between winning and losing.

'We've got to go get Gray's file,' I said. 'It's the next best thing.'

Finlay shrugged. Gave up the struggle.

'It's all we got,' he said.

Roscoe nodded.

'Let's go,' she said.

She and I drove down together in her car. Finlay was in front of us all the way. She and I didn't speak a single word. But Finlay was talking to himself through the whole trip. He was shouting and cursing. I could see his head jerking back and forth in his car. Cursing and shouting and yelling at his windshield.

Teale was waiting just inside the station house doors. Back against the reception counter. Stick clutched in his spotty old hand. He saw the three of us coming in and limped away into the big open squad room. Sat down at a desk. The desk nearest to the file room door.

We walked past him into the rosewood office. Sat down to wait it out. I pulled Joe's torn printout from my pocket and passed it across the desk. Finlay scanned it through.

'Not much, is it?' he said. 'What does the heading mean? E Unum Pluribus? That's backwards, right?'

I nodded.

'Out of one comes many,' I said. 'I don't get the significance.'

He shrugged. Started reading it through again. I watched him study it. Then there was a loud knock on the office door and Baker came in.

'Teale's on his way out of the building,' he said. 'Talking to Stevenson in the parking lot. You guys need anything?'

Finlay handed him the torn printout.

'Get me a xerox of this, will you?' he said.

Baker stepped out to do it and Finlay drummed his fingers on the desk.

'Who are all those initials?' he said.

'We only know the dead ones,' I said. 'Hubble and Molly Beth.

Two are college numbers. Princeton and Columbia. Last one is a detective down in New Orleans.'

'What about Stoller's garage?' he said. 'You get a look at that?'

'Nothing,' I said. 'Just a couple of empty air conditioner cartons from last year when he was hauling them to Florida and stealing them.'

Finlay grunted and Baker came back in. Handed me Joe's paper with a copy of it. I kept the original and gave the copy to Finlay.

'Teale's gone,' Baker said.

We hustled out of the office. Caught a glimpse of the white Cadillac easing out of the lot. Pushed open the file room door.

Margrave was a tiny town in the middle of nowhere but Gray had spent twenty-five years filling that file room with paper. There was more paper in there than I'd seen in a long time. All four walls had floor-to-ceiling cabinets with doors in crisp white enamel. We pulled open all the doors. Each cabinet was full of rows of files. There must have been a thousand letter-size boxes in there. Fibreboard boxes, labels on the spines, little plastic loops under the labels so you could pull the boxes out when you needed them. Left of the door, top shelf, was the A section. Right of the door, low down, the last Z. The K section was on the wall facing the door, left of centre, eye level.

We found a box labelled 'Kliner'. Right between three boxes labelled 'Klan' and one labelled 'Klipspringer v State of Georgia'. I put my finger in the little loop. Pulled the box out. It was heavy. I handed it to Finlay. We ran back to the rosewood office. Laid the box on the rosewood desk. Opened it up. It was full of old yellowing paper.

But it was the wrong paper. It had nothing to do with Kliner. Nothing at all. It was a three-inch pile of ancient police department memos. Operational stuff. Stuff that should have been junked decades ago. A slice of history. Procedures to be followed if the Soviet Union aimed a missile at Atlanta. Procedures to be followed if a black man wanted to ride in the front of the bus. A mass of stuff. But none of the headings began with the letter K. Not one word concerned Kliner. I gazed at the three-inch pile and felt the pressure build up.

'Somebody beat us to it,' Roscoe said. 'They took out the Kliner stuff and substituted this junk instead.'

Finlay nodded. But I shook my head.

'No,' I said. 'Doesn't make any sense. They'd have pulled the whole box and just thrown it in the trash. Gray did this himself. He needed to hide the stuff, but he couldn't bring himself to spoil his sequence in the file room. So he took the contents out of the box and put in this old stuff instead. Kept everything neat and tidy. You said he was a meticulous guy, right?'

Roscoe shrugged.

'Gray hid it?' she said. 'He could have done. He hid his gun in my desk. He didn't mind hiding things.'

I looked at her. Something she had said was ringing a warning bell.

'When did he give you the gun?' I asked her.

'After Christmas,' she said. 'Not long before he died.'

'There's something wrong with that,' I said. 'The guy was a detective with twenty-five years in the job, right? A good detective. A senior, respected guy. Why would a guy like that feel his choice of off-duty weapon should have to be a secret? That wasn't his problem. He gave you the box because it held something needed hiding.'

'He was hiding the gun,' Roscoe said. 'I told you that.'

'No,' I said. 'I don't believe that. The gun was a decoy, to make sure you kept the box in a locked drawer. He didn't need to hide the gun. Guy like that could have a nuclear warhead for an off-duty weapon if he wanted to. The gun wasn't the big secret. The big secret was something else in the box.'

'But there isn't anything else in the box,' Roscoe said. 'Certainly no files, right?'

We stood still for a second. Then we ran for the doors. Crashed through and ran over to Roscoe's Chevy in the lot. Pulled Gray's file box out of the trunk. Opened it up. I handed the Desert Eagle to Finlay. Examined the box of bullets. Nothing there. There was nothing else in the file box. I shook it out. Examined the lid. Nothing there. I tore the box apart. Forced the glued seams and flattened the cardboard out. Nothing there. Then I tore the lid apart. Hidden under the corner flap there was a key. Taped to the inside face. Where it could never be seen. Where it had been carefully hidden by a dead man.

We didn't know what the key fit. We discounted anything in the station house. Discounted anything in Gray's home. Felt those places were too obvious for a cautious man to choose. I stared at the key and felt the pressure building. Closed my eyes and built a picture of Gray easing back the corner of that lid and taping his key under it. Handing the box to his friend Roscoe. Watching her put it in her drawer. Watching the drawer roll shut. Watching her lock it. Relaxing. I built that picture into a movie and ran it in my head twice before it told me what the key fitted.

'Something in the barbershop,' I said.

I snatched the Desert Eagle back from Finlay and hustled him and Roscoe into the car. Roscoe drove. She fired it up and slewed out of the lot. Turned south toward town.

'Why?' she said.

'He used to go in there,' I said. 'Three, four times a week. The old guy told me that. He was the only white guy ever went in there. It felt like safe territory. Away from Teale and Kliner and everybody else. And he didn't need to go in there, did he? You said he had a big messy beard and no hair. He wasn't going in there to get barbered. He was going in there because he liked the old guys. He turned to them. Gave them the stuff to hide.'

Roscoe jammed the Chevy to a stop on the street outside the barbershop and we jumped out and ran in. There were no customers in there. Just the two old guys sitting in their own chairs, doing nothing. I held up the key.

'We've come for Gray's stuff,' I said.

The younger guy shook his head.

'Can't give it to you, my friend,' he said.

He walked over and took the key from me. Stepped over and pressed it into Roscoe's palm.

'Now we can,' he said. 'Old Mr Gray told us, give it up to nobody except his friend Miss Roscoe.'

He took the key back from her. Stepped back to the sink and stooped down to unlock a narrow mahogany drawer built in underneath. Pulled out three files. They were thick files, each in an old furred buff paper cover. He handed one to me, one to Finlay and one to Roscoe. Then he signalled his partner and they walked through to the back. Left us alone. Roscoe sat on the upholstered bench in the window. Finlay and I hitched ourselves into the barber chairs. Put our feet up on the chrome rests. Started reading.

My file was a thick stack of police reports. They had all been xeroxed and faxed. Doubly blurred. But I could read them. They formed a dossier put together by Detective James Spirenza, Fifteenth Squad, New Orleans Police Department, Homicide Bureau. Spirenza had been assigned a homicide, eight years ago. Then he had been assigned seven more. He had ended up with a case involving eight homicides. He hadn't cleared any of them. Not one. A total failure.

But he'd tried hard. His investigation had been meticulous. Painstaking. The first victim had been the owner of a textile plant. A specialist, involved in some new chemical process for cotton. The second victim was the first guy's foreman. He'd left the first guy's operation and was trying to raise seed money to start up on his own.

The next six victims were government people. EPA employees. They had been running a case out of their New Orleans office. The case concerned pollution in the Mississippi Delta. Fish were dying. The cause was traced two hundred and fifty miles upriver. A textile processing plant in Mississippi State was pumping chemicals into the river, sodium hydroxide and sodium hypochlorite and chlorine, all mixing with the river water and forming a deadly acidic cocktail.

All eight victims had died the same way. Two shots to the head with a silenced automatic pistol. A .22 calibre. Neat and clinical. Spirenza had assumed they were professional hits. He went after the shooter two ways. He called in every favour he could and shook all the trees. Professional hit men are thin on the ground. Spirenza and his buddies talked to them all. None of them knew a thing.

Spirenza's second approach was the classic approach. Figure out who is benefiting. Didn't take him long to piece it together. The textile processor up in Mississippi State looked good. He was under attack from the eight who died. Two of them were attacking him commercially. The other six were threatening to close him down. Spirenza pulled him apart. Turned him inside out. He was on his back for a year. The paperwork in my hand was a testimony to that. Spirenza had pulled in the FBI and the IRS. They'd searched every cent in every account for unexplained cash payments to the elusive shooter.

They'd searched for a year and found nothing. On the way, they turned up a lot of unsavoury stuff. Spirenza was convinced the guy had killed his wife. Plain beat her to death was his verdict. The guy had married again and Spirenza had faxed the local police department with a warning. The guy's only son was a psychopath. Worse than his father, in Spirenza's view. A stone-cold psychopath. The textile processor had protected his son every step of the way. Covered for him. Paid his way out of trouble. The boy had records from a dozen different institutions.

But nothing would stick. New Orleans FBI had lost interest. Spirenza had closed the case. Forgotten all about it, until an old detective from an obscure Georgia jurisdiction had faxed him, asking for information on the Kliner family.

Finlay closed his file. Spun his barber chair to face mine.

'The Kliner Foundation is bogus,' he said. 'Totally bogus. It's a cover for something else. It's all here. Gray bust it wide open. Audited it from top to bottom. The Foundation is spending millions every year, but its audited income is zero. Precisely zero.'

He selected a sheet from the file. Leaned over. Passed it over to me. It was a sort of balance sheet, showing the Foundation's expenditures.

'See that?' he said. 'It's incredible. That's what they're spending.'

I looked at it. The sheet contained a huge figure. I nodded.

'Maybe a lot more than that,' I said. 'I've been down here five days, right? Prior to that I was all over the States for six months. Prior to that I was all over the world. Margrave is by far the cleanest, best maintained, most manicured place I've ever seen. It's better looked after than the Pentagon or the White House. Believe me, I've been there. Everything in Margrave is either brand-new or else perfectly renovated. It's completely perfect. It's so perfect it's frightening. That must cost an absolute fortune.'

He nodded.

'And Margrave is a very weird place,' I said. 'It's deserted most of the time. There's no life. There's practically no commercial activity in the whole town. Nothing ever goes on. Nobody is earning any money.'

He looked blank. Didn't follow.

'Think about it,' I said. 'Look at Eno's, for example. Brand-new place. Gleaming, state-of-the-art diner. But he never has any customers. I've been in there a couple of times. There were never more than a couple of people in the place. The waitresses outnumber the customers. So how is Eno paying the bills? The overhead? The mortgage? Same goes for everywhere in town. Have you ever seen lines of customers rushing in and out of any of the stores?'

Finlay thought about it. Shook his head.

'Same goes for this barbershop,' I said. 'I was in here Sunday morning and Tuesday morning. The old guy said they'd had no customers in between. No customers in forty-eight hours.'

I stopped talking then. I thought about what else the old guy had said. That gnarled old barber. I suddenly thought about it in a new light.

'The old barber,' I said. 'He told me something. It was pretty weird. I thought he was crazy. I asked him how they make a living with no customers. He said they don't need customers to make a living because of the money they get from the Kliner Foundation. So I said, what money? He said a thousand bucks. He said all the merchants get it. So I figured he meant some kind of a business grant, a thousand bucks a year, right?'

Finlay nodded. Seemed about right to him.

'I was just chatting,' I said. 'Like you do in the barber's chair. So I said a thousand bucks a year is OK, but it's not going to keep the wolf from the door, something like that, right? You know what he said then?'

He shook his head and waited. I concentrated on remembering the old guy's exact words. I wanted to see if he would dismiss it as easily as I had done.

'He made it sound like a big secret,' I said. 'Like he was way out on a limb even to mention it. He was whispering to me. He said he shouldn't tell me, but he would, because I knew his sister.'

'You know his sister?' Finlay asked. Surprised.

'No, I don't,' I said. 'He was acting very confused. On Sunday, I'd been asking him about Blind Blake, you know, the old guitar player, and he said his sister had known the guy, sixty years ago. From that, he'd got mixed up, must have thought I'd said I knew his sister.'

'So what was the big secret?' he said.

'He said it wasn't a thousand dollars a year,' I said. 'He said it was a thousand dollars a week.'

'A thousand dollars a week?' Finlay said. 'A week? Is that possible?'

'I don't know,' I said. 'At the time, I assumed the old guy was crazy. But now, I think he was just telling the truth.'

'A thousand a week?' he said again. 'That's a hell of a business grant. That's fifty-two thousand bucks a year. That's a hell of a lot of money, Reacher.'

I thought about it. Pointed at the total on Gray's audit.

'They'd need figures like that,' I said. 'If this is how much they're spending, they'd need figures like that just to get rid of it all.'

Finlay was pensive. Thinking it through.

'They've bought the whole town,' he said. 'Very slowly, very quietly. They've bought the whole town for a grand a week, here and there.'

'Right,' I said. 'The Kliner Foundation has become the golden goose. Nobody will run the risk of killing it. They all keep their mouths shut and look away from whatever needs looking away from.'

'Right,' he said. 'The Kliners could get away with murder.'

I looked at him.

'They have got away with murder,' I said.

'So what do we do about it?' Finlay said.

'First we figure out exactly what the hell they're doing,' I said.

He looked at me like I was crazy.

'We know what they're doing, right?' he said. 'They're printing a shitload of funny money up in that warehouse.'

I shook my head at him.

'No, they're not,' I said. 'There's no serious manufacture of counterfeit money in the US. Joe put a stop to all that. The only place it happens is abroad.'

'So what's going on?' Finlay asked. 'I thought this was all about counterfeit money. Why else would Joe be involved?'

Roscoe looked over at us from the bench in the window.

'It is all about counterfeit money,' she said. 'I know exactly what it's all about. Every last little detail.'

She held up Gray's file in one hand.

'Part of the answer is in here,' she said.

Then she picked up the barbers' daily newspaper with the other hand.

'And the rest of the answer is in here,' she said.

Finlay and I joined her on the bench. Studied the file she'd been reading. It was a surveillance report. Gray had hidden out under the highway cloverleaf and watched the truck traffic in and out of the warehouses. Thirty-two separate days. The results were carefully listed, in three parts. On the first eleven occasions, he'd seen one truck a day incoming from the south, arriving early in the morning. He'd seen outgoing trucks all day long, heading north and west. He'd listed the outgoing trucks by destination, according to their licence plates. He must have been using field glasses. The list of destinations was all over the place. A complete spread, from California all the way up and over to Massachusetts. Those first eleven days, he'd logged eleven incoming trucks and sixty-seven outgoing. An average of one truck a day coming in, six going out, small trucks, maybe a ton of cargo in a week.

The first section of Gray's log covered the first calendar year. The second section covered the second calendar year. He'd hid out on nine separate occasions. He'd seen fifty-three outgoing trucks, the same six a day as before, with a similar list of destinations. But the log of incoming trucks was different. In the first half of the year, one truck a day was coming in, like normal. But in the second half of the year, the deliveries picked up. They built up to two trucks a day incoming.

The final twelve days of his surveillance were different again. They were all from the final five months of his life. Between last fall and February, he was still logging about six trucks a day going out to the same wide spread of destinations. But there were no incoming trucks listed at all. None at all. From last fall, stuff was being moved out, but it wasn't coming in.

'So?' Finlay asked Roscoe.

She sat back and smiled. She had it all figured.

'It's obvious, right?' she said. 'They're bringing counterfeit money into the country. It's printed in Venezuela, some place Kliner set up alongside his new chemical place there. It comes in by boat and they're hauling it up from Florida to the warehouse in Margrave. Then they're trucking it north and west, up to the big cities, LA, Chicago, Detroit, New York, Boston. They're feeding it into the cash flows in the big cities. It's an international counterfeit money distribution network. It's obvious, Finlay.'

'Is it?' he said.

'Of course it is,' she said again. 'Think of Sherman Stoller. He drove up and down to Florida to meet the boat coming in from the sea, at Jacksonville Beach. He was on his way out there to meet the boat when he got picked up for speeding on the bridge, right? That's why he was so agitated. That's why he got the fancy lawyer out so fast, right?'

Finlay nodded.

'It all fits,' she said. 'Think of a map of the States. The money is printed in South America, comes here by sea. Lands in Florida. Flows up the southeast, and then sort of branches out from Margrave. Flows on out to LA in the west, up to Chicago in the middle, New York and Boston in the east. Separate branches, right? It looks like a candelabra or a menorah. You know what a menorah is?'

'Sure,' Finlay said. 'It's that candlestick Jewish people use.'

'Right,' she said. 'That's how it looks on a map. Florida to Margrave is the stem. Then the individual arms lead out and up to the big cities, LA across to Chicago across to Boston. It's an import network, Finlay.'

She was giving him plenty of help. Her hands were tracing menorah shapes in the air. The geography sounded OK to me. It made sense. An import flow, rolling north in trucks, up from Florida. It would need to use that knot of highways around Atlanta to branch itself out and head for the big cities in the north and west. The menorah idea was good. The left-hand arm of the candlestick would have to be bent out horizontally, to reach LA. Like somebody had dropped the thing and somebody else had accidentally stepped on it. But the idea made sense. Almost certainly Margrave itself was the pivot. Almost certainly that warehouse was the actual distribution centre. The geography was right. Using a sleepy nowhere place like Margrave as the distribution centre would be smart. And they would have a huge amount of available cash. That was for sure. Forged cash, but it would spend just the same. And there was a lot of it. They were shipping a ton a week. It was an industrial-scale operation. Huge. It would explain the Kliner Foundation's massive spending. If they ever ran short, they could just print some more. But Finlay still wasn't convinced.

'What about the last twelve months?' he said. 'There's been no import flow at all. Look at Gray's list. The incoming deliveries didn't happen. They stopped exactly a year ago. Sherman Stoller got laid off, right? There's been nothing coming up for a year. But they're still distributing something. There were still six trucks a day going out. Nothing coming in, but six trucks a day going out? What does that mean? What kind of an import flow is that?'

Roscoe just grinned at him and picked up the newspaper.

'The answer's in here,' she said. 'It's been in the papers since Friday. The Coast Guard. Last September, they started their big operation against smuggling, right? There was a lot of advance publicity. Kliner must have known it was coming. So he built up a stockpile ahead of time. See Gray's list? For the six months before last September, he doubled the incoming deliveries. He was building up a stockpile in the warehouse. He's kept on distributing it all year. That's why they've been panicking about exposure. They've been sitting there on top of a massive stockpile of counterfeit money for a year. Now the Coast Guard is going to abandon its operation, right? So they can start importing again as usual. That's what's going to happen on Sunday. That's what poor Molly meant when she said we have to get in before Sunday. We have to get in the warehouse while the last of the stockpile is still in there.'

TWENTY-TWO

FINLAY NODDED. HE WAS CONVINCED. THEN HE SMILED. HE stood up from the bench in the barbershop window and took Roscoe's hand. Shook it very formally.

'Good work,' he said to her. 'A perfect analysis. I always said you were smart, Roscoe. Right, Reacher? Didn't I tell you she's the best we got?'

I nodded and smiled and Roscoe blushed. Finlay held on to her hand and kept on smiling. But I could see him combing backward and forward through her theory, looking for loose ends. He only found two.

'What about Hubble?' he asked. 'Where did he fit in? They wouldn't recruit a bank executive just to load trucks, would they?'

I shook my head.

'Hubble used to be a currency manager,' I said. 'He was there to get rid of the fake money. He was feeding it into the system. He knew where it could be slipped in. Where it was needed. Like his old job, but in reverse.'

He nodded.

'What about the air conditioners?' he asked. 'Sherman Stoller was hauling them to Florida. That woman told you. We know that's for real because you saw two old cartons in her garage. And his truck was full of them when the Jacksonville PD searched it. What was that all about?'

'Legitimate business, I guess,' I said. 'Like a decoy. It concealed

239

the illegal part. Like camouflage. It explained the truck movements up and down to Florida. They would have had to run south
empty otherwise.'

Finlay nodded.

'Smart move, I guess,' he said. 'No empty run. Makes sense.
Sell a few air conditioners, it makes money both ways, right?'

He nodded again and let go of Roscoe's hand.

'We need samples of the money,' he said.

I smiled at him. I had suddenly realized something.

'I've got samples,' I said. I put my hand in my pocket and pulled
out my thick roll of hundreds. Pulled one off the back of the roll
and one off the front. Gave the two banknotes to Finlay.

'These are their counterfeits?' he said.

'Got to be,' I said. 'Charlie Hubble gave me a wad of hundreds
for expense money. She probably got them from Hubble. Then I
took another wad from those guys who were out looking for me
Tuesday.'

'And that means they're counterfeit?' Finlay said. 'Why?'

'Think about it,' I said. 'Kliner needs operating cash, why
should he use real money? I bet he paid Hubble in counterfeit
money. And I bet he gave those Jacksonville boys counterfeit
money for their operating expenses, too.'

Finlay held the two hundreds right up to the bright light in the
window. Roscoe and I crowded him for a look.

'Are you sure?' Roscoe said. 'They look real to me.'

'They're fakes,' I said. 'Got to be. Stands to reason, right?
Hundreds are what fakers like to print. Anything bigger is hard to
pass, anything smaller isn't worth the effort. And why should they
spend real bucks when they've got truckloads of forgeries available?'

We took a good look at them. Peered at them, felt them,
smelled them, rubbed them between our fingers. Finlay opened
up his billfold and pulled out a hundred of his own. We compared
the three notes. Passed them back and forth. Couldn't see any
difference at all.

'If these are fakes, they're damn good,' Finlay said. 'But what
you said makes sense. Probably the whole of the Kliner
Foundation is funded with fakes. Millions every year.'

He put his own hundred back in his billfold. Slid the fakes into
his pocket.

'I'm going back to the station house,' he said. 'You two come in
tomorrow, about noon. Teale will be gone for lunch. We'll take it
from there.'

240

Roscoe and I drove fifty miles south, to Macon. I wanted to keep on the move. It's a basic rule for safety. Keep moving around. We chose an anonymous motel on the southeastern fringe. As far from Margrave as you can get in Macon, with the city sprawl between us and our enemies. Old Mayor Teale had said a motel in Macon would suit me. Tonight, he was right.

We showered in cold water and fell into bed. Fell into a restless sleep. The room was warm. We tossed around fitfully most of the night. Gave it up and got up again with the dawn. Stood there yawning in the half-light. Thursday morning. Felt like we hadn't slept at all. We groped around and got dressed in the dark. Roscoe put her uniform on. I put my old things on. I figured I'd need to buy some new stuff soon. I'd do it with Kliner's forgeries.

'What are we going to do?' Roscoe said.

I didn't answer. I was thinking about something else.

'Reacher?' she said. 'What are we going to do about all this?'

'What did Gray do about it?' I said.

'He hung himself,' she said.

I thought some more.

'Did he?' I asked her.

There was a silence.

'Oh God,' Roscoe said. 'You think there's some doubt about that?'

'Maybe,' I said. 'Think about it. Suppose he confronted one of them? Suppose he was found poking around somewhere he shouldn't have been?'

'You think they killed him?' she asked. There was panic in her voice.

'Maybe,' I said again. 'I think they killed Joe and Stoller and the Morrisons and Hubble and Molly Beth Gordon. I think they tried to kill you and me. If somebody is a threat, they kill him. That's how Kliner operates.'

Roscoe was quiet for a while. Thinking about her old colleague. Gray, the dour and patient detective. Twenty-five years of meticulous work. A guy like that was a threat. A guy who took thirty-two patient days to cross-check a suspicion was a threat. Roscoe looked up and nodded.

'He must have made a wrong move,' she said.

I nodded gently at her.

'They lynched him,' I said. 'Made it look like suicide.'

'I can't believe it,' she said.

'Was there an autopsy?' I asked her.

'Guess so,' she said.

'Then we'll check it out,' I said. 'We'll have to speak to that doctor again. Down in Yellow Springs.'

'But he'd have said, right?' she asked me. 'If he'd had doubts, wouldn't he have raised them at the time?'

'He'd have raised them with Morrison,' I said. 'Morrison would have ignored them. Because his people had caused them in the first place. We'll have to check it out for ourselves.'

Roscoe shuddered.

'I was at his funeral,' she said. 'We were all there. Chief Morrison made a speech on the lawn outside the church. So did Mayor Teale. They said he was a fine officer. They said he was Margrave's finest. But they killed him.'

She said it with a lot of feeling. She'd liked Margrave. Her family had toiled there for generations. She was rooted. She'd liked her job. Enjoyed the sense of contribution. But the community she'd served was rotten. It was dirty and corrupted. It wasn't a community. It was a swamp, wallowing in dirty money and blood. I sat and watched her world crumble.

We drove north on the road between Macon and Margrave. Halfway home Roscoe hung a right and we headed for Yellow Springs down a back road. Over toward the hospital. I was hungry. We hadn't eaten breakfast. Not the best state for revisiting the morgue. We swung into the hospital lot. Took the speed bumps slowly and nosed around to the back. Parked up a little way from the big metal roller door.

We got out of the car. Stretched our legs on a roundabout route to the office door. The sun was warming the day up. It would have been pleasant to stay outside. But we ducked in and went looking for the doctor. We found him in his shabby office. He was at his chipped desk. Still looking tired. Still in a white coat. He looked up and nodded us in.

'Morning, folks,' he said. 'What can I do for you?'

We sat down on the same stools as Tuesday. I stayed away from the fax machine. I let Roscoe do the talking. Better that way. I had no official standing.

'February this year,' she said. 'My chief of detectives up at the Margrave PD killed himself. Do you remember?'

'Was that some guy called Gray?' the doctor said.

Roscoe nodded and the doctor got up and walked around to a

file cabinet. Pulled open a drawer. It was tight and made a screech-ing sound. The doctor ran his fingers backwards over the files.

'February,' he said. 'Gray.'

He pulled a file and carried it back to his desk. Dropped it on his blotter. Sat back down heavily and opened it up. It was a thin file. Not much in it.

'Gray,' he said again. 'Yes, I remember this guy. Hung himself, right? First time we had a Margrave case in thirty years. I was called up to his house. In the garage, wasn't it? From a rafter?'

'That's right,' Roscoe said. She went quiet.

'So how can I help you?' the doctor said.

'Anything wrong with it?' she asked.

The doctor looked at the file. Turned a page.

'Guy hangs himself, there's always something wrong with it,' he said.

'Anything specially wrong with it?' I said.

The doctor swung his tired gaze over from Roscoe to me.

'Suspicious?' he said.

He was nearly smiling the same little smile he'd used on Tuesday.

'Was there anything suspicious about it?' I asked him.

He shook his head.

'No,' he said. 'Suicide by hanging. Open and shut. He was on a kitchen stool in his garage. Made himself a noose, jumped off the stool. Everything was consistent. We got the background story from the local people up there. I couldn't see a problem.'

'What was the background story?' Roscoe asked him.

He swung his gaze back to her. Glanced through the file.

'He was depressed,' he said. 'Had been for a while. The night it happened he was out drinking with his chief, who was the Morrison guy we just had in here, and the town mayor up there, some guy called Teale. The three of them were drowning their sorrows over some case Gray had screwed up on. He got falling down drunk and they had to help him home. They got him in to his house and left him there. He must have felt bad. He made it to the garage and hung himself.'

'That was the story?' Roscoe said.

'Morrison signed a statement,' the doctor said. 'He was real upset. Felt he should have done more, you know, stayed with him or something.'

'Did it sound right to you?' she asked him.

'I didn't know Gray at all,' he said. 'This facility deals with a dozen police departments. I'd never seen anybody from Margrave before then. Quiet sort of a place, right? At least, it used to be. But what happened with this guy is consistent with what usually happens. Drinking sets people off.'

'Any physical evidence?' I asked him.

The doctor looked back in the file. Looked over at me.

'Corpse stank of whisky,' he said. 'Some fresh bruising on the upper and lower arms. Consistent with him being walked home by two men while inebriated. I couldn't see a problem.'

'Did you do a postmortem?' Roscoe asked him.

The doctor shook his head.

'No need,' he said. 'It was open and shut, we were very busy. Like I say, we have more to worry about down here than suicides over in Margrave. February, we had cases all over the place. Up to our eyes. Your Chief Morrison asked for minimum fuss. I think he sent us a note. Said it was kind of sensitive. Didn't want Gray's family to know that the old guy had been blind drunk. Wanted to preserve some kind of dignity. It was OK with me. I couldn't see a problem and we were very busy, so I released the body for cremation right away.'

Roscoe and I sat looking at each other. The doctor stepped back to the cabinet and put the file away. Closed the drawer with a screech.

'OK, folks?' he said. 'If you'll excuse me, I've got things to do.'

We nodded and thanked him for his time. Then we shuffled out of the cramped office. Got back out into the warm fall sunshine. Stood around blinking. We didn't speak. Roscoe was too upset. She'd just heard about her old friend getting murdered.

'I'm sorry,' I said.

'A bullshit story from beginning to end,' she said. 'He hadn't just screwed up on a case. He never screwed up on any case. He wasn't especially depressed. And he didn't drink. Never touched a drop. So he certainly wasn't falling down drunk. And he would never socialize with Morrison. Or the damn mayor. He just wouldn't. He didn't like them. Never in a million years would he spend a social evening with them. And he had no family. So all that stuff about his family and sensitivity and dignity is total bullshit. They killed him and bullshitted the coroner so he wouldn't look too closely.'

I sat there in the car and let the rage pour out of her. Then she was quiet and still. She was figuring out how they'd done it.

'Do you think it was Morrison and Teale?' she asked me.

244

'And somebody else,' I said. 'There were three guys involved. I figure the three of them went around to his place and knocked on the door. Gray opened up and Teale pulled a gun. Morrison and the third guy grabbed him and held him by the arms. That explains the bruising. Teale maybe poured a bottle of whisky down his throat, or at least splashed it all over his clothes. They hustled him off to the garage and strung him up.'

Roscoe started the car and eased it out of the hospital lot. She drove slowly over the speed bumps. Then she swung the wheel and blasted up the road through the countryside toward Margrave.

'They killed him,' she said. Just a simple statement. 'Like they killed Joe. I think I know how you must be feeling.'

I nodded.

'They'll pay for it,' I said. 'For both of them.'

'You bet your ass,' she said.

We fell silent. Sped north for a while, then merged with the county road. A straight twelve miles up to Margrave.

'Poor old Gray,' she said. 'I can't believe it. He was so smart, so cautious.'

'Not smart enough,' I said. 'Or cautious enough. We've got to remember that. You know the rules, right? Don't be on your own. If you see somebody coming, run like hell. Or shoot the bastard. Stick with Finlay if you can, OK?'

She was concentrating on driving. She was doing a hell of a speed up the straight road. Thinking about Finlay.

'Finlay,' she repeated. 'You know what I can't figure?'

'What?' I said.

'There's the two of them, right?' she said. 'Teale and Morrison. They run the town for Kliner. They run the police department. Between them, they run everything. Their chief of detectives is Gray. An old guy, a wise head, smart and stubborn. He's been there for twenty-five years, since well before any of this shit started up. They inherited him and they can't get rid of him. So sure enough, one day their smart and stubborn detective sniffs them out. He's found out that something is going on. And they find out that he's found out. So they put him out of the way. They murder him to keep it all safe. Then what do they do next?'

'Go on,' I said.

'They hire in a replacement,' she said. 'Finlay, down from Boston. A guy who is even smarter and even more stubborn than Gray was. Why the hell would they do that? If Gray was a danger

245

to them, then Finlay would be twice as dangerous. So why did they do that? Why did they hire somebody even smarter than the last guy?'

'That's easy,' I said. 'They thought Finlay was really dumb.'

'Dumb?' she said. 'How the hell could they think that?'

So I told her the story Finlay had told me on Monday over doughnuts at the convenience store counter. About his divorce. About his mental state at the time. What had he said? He was a basket case. An idiot. Couldn't string two words together.

'Chief Morrison and Mayor Teale interviewed him,' I told her. 'He thought it was the worst job application in history. He thought he had come across as an idiot. He was totally amazed they gave him the job. Now I understand why they did. They really were looking for an idiot.'

Roscoe laughed. That made me feel better.

'God,' she said. 'That's ironic. They must have sat down and planned it out. Gray was a problem, they said. Better replace him with a fool, they said. Better pick the worst candidate who applies, they said.'

'Right,' I said. 'And they did. They picked a shell-shocked idiot from Boston. But by the time he turns up to start work, he's calmed down and turned back into the cool and intelligent guy he always was.'

She smiled about that for two miles. Then we crested a slight rise and began the long sweep down into Margrave. We were tensed up. It was like entering the battle zone. We'd been out of it for a while. Sweeping back into it didn't feel good. I had expected to feel better when I had identified the opposing players. But it wasn't what I had expected. It wasn't me against them, played out against a neutral background. The background wasn't neutral. The background was the opposition. The whole town was in it. The whole place was bought and paid for. Nobody would be neutral. We were barrelling down the rise at seventy miles an hour toward a dangerous mess. More dangerous than I had expected.

Roscoe slowed up at the town limit. The big Chevy glided onto Margrave's glassy blacktop. The magnolia and dogwood scrub to the left and right was replaced by velvet lawns and ornamental cherries. Those trees with smooth shiny trunks. Like the bark was buffed by hand. In Margrave, it probably was. The Kliner Foundation was probably paying somebody a handsome salary to do it.

We passed the neat blocks of stores, all of them empty and complacent, floating on an unearned thousand a week. We jinked around the village green with the statue of Caspar Teale. Wafted past the turn down to Roscoe's house with its smashed front door. Past the coffee shop. Past the benches under the smart awnings. Past the parkland where the bars and rooming houses had been, back when Margrave was honest. Then up to the station house. We pulled off into the lot and parked up. Charlie Hubble's Bentley was still there where I'd left it.

Roscoe killed the motor and we sat for a minute. Didn't want to get out. We squeezed hands, her right, my left. A brief good luck gesture. We got out of the car. Into battle.

The station house was cool and deserted except for Baker at his desk and Finlay on his way out of the rosewood office in back. He saw us and hurried over.

'Teale's back in ten minutes,' he said. 'And we got a slight problem.'

He hustled us back to the office. We went in and he shut the door.

'Picard called,' he said.

'So what's the problem?' I said.

'It's the safe house,' he said. 'Where Charlie and the kids are hiding out? That situation has to stay unofficial, right?'

'He told me that,' I said. 'He's out on a limb up there.'

'Exactly,' he said. 'That's the problem. He can't staff it. He needs somebody to be up there with Charlie. He's been doing duty himself. But he can't do any more. Can't take any more time out. And he feels it's not appropriate, you know, Charlie being a woman, and the little girl and all. Kid's terrified of him.'

He looked over at Roscoe. She saw where the conversation was going.

'He wants me up there?' she asked.

'Just for twenty-four hours,' Finlay said. 'That's what he's asking for. Will you do it for him?'

Roscoe shrugged. Smiled.

'Of course I will,' she said. 'No problem. I can spare a day. As long as you promise to get me back when the fun starts, OK?'

'That's automatic,' Finlay said. 'Fun can't start until we've got the detail, and as soon as we've got the detail, Picard goes official and he puts his own agents into the safe house. You come back here.'

'OK,' Roscoe said. 'When do I go?'

'Right now,' Finlay said. 'He'll be here any minute.'

She grinned at him.

'So you already figured I'd agree to it?' she said.

He grinned back at her.

'Like I told Reacher,' he said, 'you're the best we got.'

She and I went back through the squad room and out through the glass doors. Roscoe took her valise out of the Chevy and set it on the kerb.

'See you tomorrow, I guess,' she said.

'You going to be OK?' I asked her.

'Sure,' she said. 'I'm going to be fine. Can't get much safer than an FBI safe house, right? But I'm going to miss you, Reacher. I didn't figure to spend time apart just yet.'

I squeezed her hand. She kissed me on the cheek. Just stretched up for a quick peck. Finlay pushed the station house door open. I heard the suck of the rubber seal. He stuck his head out and called over to Roscoe.

'You better give Picard an update, OK?' he said.

Roscoe nodded to him. Then we stood waiting in the sun. Didn't have to wait long. Picard's blue sedan squealed into the lot within a couple of minutes. Bounced to a stop right next to us. The big guy folded himself out of the seat and stood up. Just about blotted out the sun.

'I appreciate this, Roscoe,' he said to her. 'You're really helping me out.'

'No problem,' she said. 'You're helping us out, right? Where is this place I'm going?'

Picard grinned a harassed grin. Nodded toward me.

'I can't say where it is,' he told her. 'Not in front of civilians, right? I'm way out of line already. And I'm going to have to ask you not to tell him afterward, OK? And Reacher, don't you press her about it, or Charlie, OK?'

'OK,' I said. I wouldn't press her about it. She'd tell me anyway.

'Good,' Picard said.

He nodded a busy goodbye and picked up Roscoe's bag. Threw it onto his rear seat. Then the two of them got into the blue sedan and drove off. Nosed out of the lot and headed north. I waved after them. Then the car was lost to sight.

TWENTY-THREE

DETAILS. EVIDENCE GATHERING. SURVEILLANCE. IT'S THE basis of everything. You've got to settle down and watch long enough and hard enough to get what you need. While Roscoe made cups of coffee for Charlie Hubble and Finlay sat in the rosewood office, I was going to have to watch the warehouse operation. Long enough and hard enough until I got a feel for exactly how they did it. It could take me a full twenty-four hours. Could be Roscoe would get back before I did.

I got in the Bentley and cruised up the fourteen miles to the cloverleaf. Slowed down as I passed the warehouses. I needed to scout out a vantage point. The northbound on-ramp dived under the southbound off-ramp. There was a kind of low overpass. Short, wide concrete pillars hoisted the road overhead. I figured the thing to do would be to hole up behind one of those pillars. I would be well hidden in the gloom and the slight elevation would give me a good view of the whole warehouse area. That was my spot.

I accelerated the Bentley up the ramp and carried on north to Atlanta. Took an hour. I was picking up a rough idea of the geography. I wanted the low-rent shopping area and I found it easily enough. Saw the sort of street I wanted. Automobile customizers, pool table wholesalers, repossessed office furniture. I parked on the street in front of a storefront mission. Opposite me were two survival shops. I picked the left-hand one and went in.

The door worked a bell. The guy at the counter looked up. He was the usual type of guy. White man, black beard, camouflage fatigues, boots. He had a huge gold hoop in one ear. Looked like some kind of a pirate. He might have been a veteran. Might just have wanted to be one. He nodded to me.

He had the stuff I needed. I picked up olive fatigue pants and a shirt. Found a camouflage jacket big enough to fit. Looked at the pockets carefully. I had to get the Desert Eagle in there. Then I found a water canteen and some decent field glasses. Humped the whole lot over to the cash desk and piled it up. Pulled out my wad of hundreds. The guy with the beard looked at me.

'I could use a blackjack,' I said.

He looked at me and looked at my wad of hundreds. Then he ducked down and hoisted a box up. Looked heavy. I chose a fat sap about nine inches long. It was a leather tube. Taped at one end for a grip. Built around a plumber's spring. The thing they put inside pipes before they bend them. It was packed around with lead shot. An efficient weapon. I nodded. Paid for everything and left. The bell rang again as I pushed open the door.

I moved the Bentley along a hundred yards and parked up in front of the first automobile shop I saw advertising window tinting. Leaned on the horn and got out to meet the guy coming out of the door.

'Can you put tints on this for me?' I asked him.

'On this thing?' he said. 'Sure I can. I can put tints on anything.'

'How long?' I said.

The guy stepped up to the car and ran his finger down the silky coachwork.

'Thing like this, you want a first-rate job,' he said. 'Take me a couple of days, maybe three.'

'How much?' I said.

He carried on feeling the paint and sucked air in through his teeth, like all car guys do when you ask them how much.

'Couple of hundred,' he said. 'That's for a first-rate job, and you don't want anything less on a thing like this.'

'I'll give you two fifty,' I said. 'That's for a better than first-rate job, and you loan me a car the two or three days it's going to take you to do it, OK?'

The guy sucked in some more air and then slapped lightly on the Bentley's hood.

'It's a done deal, my friend,' he said.

I took the Bentley key off Charlie's ring and exchanged it for an eight-year-old Cadillac the colour of an old avocado pear. It seemed to drive pretty well and it was about as anonymous as you could hope to get. The Bentley was a lovely automobile, but it was not what I needed if the surveillance went mobile. It was about as distinctive as the most distinctive thing you could ever think of.

I cleared the southern rim of the city and stopped at a gas station. Brimmed the old Cadillac's big tank and bought candy bars and nuts and bottles of water. Then I used their toilet cubicle to get changed. I put on the military surplus gear and threw my old stuff into the towel bin. Went back out to the car. Put the Desert Eagle in the long inside pocket of my new jacket. Cocked and locked. Poured the spare bullets into the outside top pocket. Morrison's switchblade was in the left side pocket and I put the blackjack in the right.

I shared the nuts and the candy bars around the other pockets. Poured a bottle of water into the canteen and went to work. Took me another hour to get back to Margrave. I drove the old Cadillac right around the cloverleaf. Up the on-ramp again, heading north. Backed up about a hundred yards along the shoulder and stopped right in the no-man's-land between the off-ramp and the on-ramp. Where nobody would pass either leaving or joining the highway. Nobody would see the car except people shooting right past Margrave. And they wouldn't care.

I popped the hood and propped it open. Locked up the car and left it like that. It made it invisible. Just a broken-down old sedan on the shoulder. A sight so ordinary, you don't see it. Then I climbed over the low concrete wall at the edge of the shoulder. Scrambled down the high bank. Ran south and sprinted across the on-ramp. Carried on running for the shelter of the low overpass. I ran under the width of the highway to the other side and holed up behind a broad pillar. Over my head, the trucks coming off the highway rumbled around to the old county road. Then they ground their gears and branched right for the warehouses.

I settled back and got comfortable behind the pillar. I had a pretty good vantage point. Maybe two hundred yards distant, maybe thirty feet of elevation. The whole place was laid out below me like a diagram. The field glasses I'd bought were clear and powerful. There were actually four separate warehouses. All identical, built in a tight line, running away from me at an oblique angle. The whole area was ringed by a serious fence. Plenty of razor wire at the top. Each of the four compounds had its own inner fence. Each inner fence had its own gate. The outer fence held the main gate, fronting onto the road. The whole place was swarming with activity.

The first compound was totally innocent. The big roller door stood open. I could see local farm trucks rattling in and out. People were loading and unloading in plain view. Sturdy burlap sacks bulging with something or other. Maybe produce, maybe seed or fertilizer. Whatever farmers use. I had no idea. But there was nothing secret. Nothing hidden. All the trucks were local. Georgia plates on all of them. No out-of-state vehicles. Nothing big enough to roll south to north along the height of the nation. The first compound was clean, no doubt about that.

Same went for the second and third. Their gates stood open, their doors were up. All their activity was a cheerful swarm on their forecourts. Nothing secret. All in plain view. Different type of trucks, but all local. Couldn't see what they were hauling. Wholesale stuff for the little country stores, maybe. Possibly manufactured goods going somewhere. Some kind of oil drums in the third shed. But nothing to get excited about.

The fourth warehouse was the one I was looking for. The one at the end of the row. No doubt about it. It was a smart location. Made a lot of sense. It was screened by the chaos on the first three forecourts. But because it was the last in line, none of the local farmers or merchants would ever need to pass it by. Nobody would get a look at it. A smart location. It was definitely the one. Beyond it, maybe seventy-five yards away in a field, was the blasted tree. The one Roscoe had picked out of the photograph of Stoller and Hubble and the yellow truck. A camera on the forecourt would pick up the tree just beyond the far corner of the structure. I could see that. This was the place, no doubt about it.

The big roller door across the front was closed. The gate was closed. There were two gatemen hanging around on the forecourt. Even from two hundred yards, the field glasses picked up their alert glances and the wary tension in their walks. Some kind of a security role. I watched them for a while. They strode around, but nothing was happening. So I shifted around to watch the road. Waited for a truck bound for the fourth compound.

It was a good long wait. I was uptight about the time ticking away, so I sang to myself. I went through every version of 'Rambling on My Mind' that I knew. Everybody has a version. It's always listed as a traditional song. Nobody knows whose it was. Nobody knows where it came from. Probably from way back in the Delta. It's a song for people who can't stay around. Even though maybe there's a good reason to. People like me. I'd been around Margrave practically a week. Longest I'd ever stayed anywhere voluntarily. I should stay for ever. With Roscoe, because she was good for me. I was beginning to imagine a future with her. It felt good.

But there were going to be problems. When Kliner's dirty money was taken out, the whole town was going to fall apart. There wouldn't be anyplace left to stay around in. And I had to wander. Like the song I was singing in my head. I had to ramble. A traditional song. A song that could have been written for me. In my heart, I believed Blind Blake had made it up. He had wandered. He had walked right by this place, when the concrete pillars were old shade trees. Sixty years ago, he had walked down the road I was watching, maybe singing the song I was singing.

Joe and I used to sing that old song. We'd sing it as an ironic comment on army family life. We'd stumble off a plane somewhere and ride to an airless empty base house. Twenty minutes after moving in, we'd start up singing that song. Like we'd been there long enough and we were ready to move on again. So I leaned back on the concrete pillar and sang it for him, as well as for me.

Took me thirty-five minutes to run through every version of that old song, once for me and once for Joe. During that time I saw maybe a half-dozen trucks pull into the warehouse approach. All local guys. All little dusty Georgia trucks. Nothing with long-haul grime blasted all over it. Nothing headed for the end building. I sang softly for thirty-five minutes and picked up no information at all.

But I did get some applause. I finished the last song and heard a slow ironic handclap coming out of the darkness behind me. I whipped around the broad concrete pillar and stared into the gloom. The clapping stopped and I heard a shuffling sound. Picked up the vague shape of a man crawling towards me. The shape firmed up. Some kind of a hobo. Long grey matted hair and layers of heavy clothing. Bright eyes burning in a seamed and dirty face. The guy stopped out of reach.

'Who the hell are you?' I asked him.

He swiped his curtain of hair aside and grinned at me.

'Who the hell are you?' he said. 'Coming to my place and bawling like that?'

'This is your place?' I said. 'You live under here?'

He settled on his haunches and shrugged at me.

'Temporarily,' he said. 'Been here a month. You got a problem with that?'

I shook my head. I had no problem with that. The guy had to live somewhere.

'Sorry to disturb you,' I said. 'I'll be out of here by tonight.'

His smell was drifting over to me. Wasn't pleasant. This guy smelled like he'd been on the road all his life.

'Stay as long as you like,' he said. 'We just decided to move on. We're vacating the premises.'

'We?' I said. 'There's somebody else here?'

The guy looked at me oddly. Turned and pointed to the air beside him. There was nobody there. My eyes had adjusted to the gloom. I could see all the way back to the concrete cantilever under the elevated road. Just empty space.

'My family,' he said. 'We're pleased to meet you. But we got to go. Time to move on.'

He reached behind him and dragged a canvas kit bag out of the gloom. Army issue. There was a faint stencil on it. Pfc something, with a serial number and a unit designation. He pulled it up close and shuffled away.

'Wait up,' I said. 'Were you here last week? Thursday?'

The guy stopped and half-turned back.

'Been here a month,' he said. 'Didn't see anything last Thursday.'

I looked at him and his kit bag. A soldier. Soldiers don't volunteer anything. Their basic rule. So I eased off the concrete and pulled a candy bar out of my pocket. Wrapped it in a hundred dollar bill. Tossed it over to him. He caught it and put it in his coat. Nodded to me, silently.

'So what didn't you see last Thursday?' I asked him.

He shrugged.

'I didn't see anything,' he said. 'That's the honest truth. But my wife did. She saw plenty of things.'

'OK,' I said, slowly. 'Will you ask her what things she saw?'

He nodded. Turned and had a whispered conversation with the air beside him. Turned back to me.

'She saw aliens,' he said. 'An enemy starship, disguised like a shiny black truck. Two aliens disguised like regular earth guys in it. She saw lights in the sky. Smoke. Spaceship comes down, turns into a big car, starfleet commander comes out dressed as a cop, short fat guy. Then a white car comes off the highway, but it's really a starfighter landing, two guys in it, earth guys, pilot and co-pilot. They all do a dance, right there by the gate, because they come from another galaxy. She said it was exciting. She loves that stuff. Sees it everywhere she goes.'

He nodded at me. He meant it.

'I missed the whole thing,' he said. Gestured to the air beside him. 'The baby needed her bath. But that's what my wife saw. She loves that stuff.'

'She hear anything?' I asked him.

He asked her. Got her reply and shook his head like I was crazy.

'Space beings don't make sound,' he said. 'But the starfighter co-pilot got all shot up with stun phasers, crawled in here later. Bled to death right where you're sitting. We tried to help him, but there's really nothing you can do about stun phasers, right? The medics got him out Sunday.'

I nodded. He crawled off, dragging his kit bag. I watched him go and then slid back around the pillar. Watched the road. Picked through his wife's story. An eyewitness report. The guy wouldn't have convinced the Supreme Court, but he sure as hell convinced me. It wasn't the Supreme Court's brother who had flown down in a starfighter and done a dance at the warehouse gate.

It was another hour before anything showed up. I'd eaten a candy bar and sipped most of a pint of water. I was just sitting and waiting. A decent-sized panel truck rolled in, coming south. It slowed up at the warehouse approach. I saw New York commercial plates through the field glasses. Dirty white rectangles. The truck nosed along the tarmac and waited at the fourth gate. The guys in the compound swung open the gate and signalled the truck through. It stopped again and the two guys swung the gate shut behind it. Then the driver backed up to the roller door and stopped. Got out of the truck. One of the gatemen climbed into the truck and the other ducked into a side door and cranked the roller open. The truck backed into the dark and the roller came down again. The New York driver was left on the forecourt, stretching in the sun. That was it. About thirty seconds, beginning to end. Nothing on show.

I watched and waited. The truck was in there eighteen minutes. Then the roller door winched open again and the gateman drove the truck back out. As soon as it was clear, the roller came down again and the gateman jumped down from the cab. The New York guy hoisted himself back into the seat while the gateman ran ahead to swing the gates. The truck passed through and rattled out and back onto the county road. It turned north and passed by twenty yards from where I was leaning up on the concrete overpass pillar. It swung onto the on-ramp and roared up to join the northbound traffic stream.

Pretty much straight away another truck was rumbling down the off-ramp, leaving the traffic stream coming down from the north. It was a similar truck. Same make, same size, same highway grime. It lumbered and bounced into the warehouse approach. I squinted through the field glasses. Illinois plates. It went through the same ritual. Paused at the gates. Backed up to the roller door. The driver was replaced by the gateman. The roller came up just long enough to swallow the truck into the gloom inside. Quick and efficient. About thirty seconds again, beginning to end. And secret. The long-haul drivers weren't allowed into the warehouse. They had to wait outside.

The Illinois truck was out quicker. Sixteen minutes. The driver reclaimed his place at the wheel and headed out, back to the highway. I watched him pass by, twenty yards away.

Our theory said both trucks had been loaded up with some of the stockpile and were grinding their way north. Thundering their way back to the big cities up there, ready to unload. So far, our theory looked good. I couldn't fault it.

The next hour, nothing happened. The fourth compound stayed closed up tight. I started to get bored. I started to wish the hobo hadn't left. We could have chatted awhile. Then I saw the third truck of the day come heading in. I raised the field glasses and saw California plates. Same type of truck, dirty red colour, rumbling in off the highway, heading for the end compound. It went through a different routine from the first two. It went in through the gates, but there was no change of driver. The truck just reversed straight in through the roller door. This guy was obviously authorized to see inside the shed. Then a wait. I timed it at twenty-two minutes. Then the roller door winched up and the truck came back out. Drove straight back out through the gates and headed for the highway.

I took a fast decision. Time to go. I wanted to see inside one of those trucks. So I scrambled to my feet and grabbed the field glasses and the water canteen. Ran under the overpass to the northbound side. Clawed my way up the steep bank and leapt the concrete wall. Back to the old Cadillac. I slammed the hood shut

256

and got in. Started up and rolled along the shoulder. Waited for a gap and gunned the big motor. Nudged the wheel and accelerated north.

I figured the red truck might be three or four minutes ahead. Not much more than that. I hopped past bunches of vehicles and pushed the big old car on. Then settled back to a fast cruise. I figured I was gaining all the time. After a few miles I spotted the truck. Eased off and sat well back, maybe three hundred yards behind him. Kept a half-dozen vehicles between him and me. I settled back and relaxed. We were going to LA, according to Roscoe's menorah theory.

We cruised slowly north. Not much more than fifty miles an hour. The Cadillac's tank was near enough full. Might get me three hundred miles, maybe three-fifty. At this slow cruise, maybe more. Acceleration was the killer. Gunning the worn eight-year-old V-8 would use gas faster than coffee comes out of a pot. But a steady cruise would give me reasonable mileage. Might get me up to four hundred miles. Enough to get as far west as Memphis, maybe.

We rolled on. The dirty red truck sat up big and obvious, three hundred yards ahead. It bore left around the southern fringe of Atlanta. Setting itself to strike out west, across the country. The distribution theory was looking good. I slowed down and hung back through the interchange. Didn't want the driver to get suspicious about being followed. But I could see by the way he was handling his lane changes this was not a guy who made much use of his rear-view mirrors. I closed up a little tighter.

The red truck rolled on. I stayed eight cars behind it. Time rolled by. It got late in the afternoon. It got to be early evening. I ate candy and sipped water for dinner as I drove. I couldn't work the radio. It was some kind of a fancy Japanese make. The guy at the auto shop must have transplanted it. Maybe it was busted. I wondered how he was doing with tinting the Bentley's windows. I wondered what Charlie was going to say about getting her car back with black glass. I figured maybe that was going to be the least of her worries. We rolled on.

We rolled on for almost four hundred miles. Eight hours. We drove out of Georgia, right through Alabama, into the northeast corner of Mississippi. It got pitch-dark. The fall sun had dropped away up ahead. People had switched their lights on. We drove on through the dark for hours. It felt like I had been following the guy all my life. Then, approaching midnight, the red truck slowed down. A half-mile ahead, I saw it pull off into a truck stop in the middle of nowhere. Near a place called Myrtle. Maybe sixty miles short of the Tennessee state line. Maybe seventy miles shy of Memphis. I followed the truck into the lot. Parked up well away from it.

I saw the driver get out. A tall, thickset type of a guy. Thick neck and wide, powerful shoulders. Dark, in his thirties. Long arms, like an ape. I knew who he was. He was Kliner's son. A stone-cold psychopath. I watched him. He did some stretching and yawning in the dark standing by his truck. I stared at him and pictured him Thursday night, at the warehouse gate, dancing.

The Kliner kid locked up the truck and ambled off toward the buildings. I waited a spell and followed him. I figured he would have gone straight for the bathroom, so I hung around the newsstand in the bright neon and watched the door. I saw him come out and watched him amble into the diner area. He settled at a table and stretched again. Picked up the menu with the expansive air of a guy who was taking his time. He was there for a late dinner. I figured he'd take twenty-five minutes. Maybe a half-hour.

I headed back out to the parking lot. I wanted to break into the red truck and get a look inside. But I saw there was no chance of doing it out there in the lot. No chance at all. People were walking around and a couple of police cruisers were loafing about. The whole place was lit up with bright lights. Breaking into that truck was going to have to wait.

I walked back to the buildings. Crammed myself into a phone booth and dialled the station house in Margrave. Finlay answered right away. I heard his deep Harvard tones. He'd been sitting by the phone, waiting for me to check in.

'Where are you?' he said.

'Not far from Memphis,' I said. 'I watched a truck load up and I'm sticking with it until I get a chance to look inside. The driver's the Kliner kid.'

'OK,' he said. 'I heard from Picard. Roscoe's safely installed. Fast asleep now, if she's got any sense. He said she sends her love.'

'Send mine back if you get the chance,' I said. 'Take care, Harvard guy.'

'Take care yourself,' he said. Hung up.

I strolled back to the Cadillac. Got in and waited. It was a half-hour before the Kliner kid came out again. I saw him walk back toward the red truck. He was wiping his mouth with the back of his hand. Looked like he'd had a good dinner. Certainly taken him long enough. He walked out of sight. A minute later the truck rattled by and lurched onto the exit road. But the kid didn't head back to the highway. He ducked a left onto a service road. He was going around to the motel. He was going to stay overnight.

He drove right up to the row of motel cabins. Parked the red truck up against the second cabin from the end. Right in the glow of a big amp on a pole. He got out and locked up. Took a key from his pocket and opened up the cabin. Went in and shut the door. I saw the light go on and the blind come down. He'd had the key in his pocket. He hadn't gone into the office. He must have booked the room when he was inside for dinner. He must have paid for it and picked up the key. That's what had taken him so damn long in there.

It gave me a problem. I needed to see inside the truck. I needed the evidence. I needed to know I was in the right. And I needed to know soon. Sunday was forty-eight hours away. I had things to do before Sunday. A lot of things. I was going to have to break into the truck, right there in the glare of the light on the pole. While the psychopathic Kliner kid was ten feet away in his motel room. Not the safest thing in the world to do. I was going to have to wait to do it. Until the kid was sound asleep and wouldn't hear the boom and scrape as I went to work.

I waited a half-hour. Couldn't wait any more. I started the old Cadillac and moved it through the stillness. The tappets were out and the pistons were slapping. The motor was making a hell of a noise in the silence. I parked the car tight up to the red truck. Nose in, facing the kid's motel room door. I climbed out across the passenger seat. Stood still and listened. Nothing.

I took Morrison's switchblade from my jacket pocket and stepped up onto the Cadillac's front fender. Stepped onto the hood and up over the windshield. Up onto the Cadillac's roof. Stood still, up high. Listened hard. Nothing. I leaned over to the truck and hauled myself upward onto its roof.

A panel truck like that has a translucent roof. It's some kind of a fibreglass sheet. They make the roof out of it, or at least a sort of skylight set into the sheet metal. It's there to let a dim light down into the cargo area. Helps with loading and unloading. Maybe it's lighter in weight. Maybe cheaper. Manufacturer will do anything to save a buck. The roof is the best way into a truck like that.

My upper body was flat on the fibreglass panel and my feet were scrabbling for the Cadillac's gutter. I reached out as far as I could and sprang the switchblade. Stabbed it down through the plastic panel, right in the centre of the roof. Used the blade to saw a flap about ten inches deep, eighteen inches wide. I could push it down and peer in. Like looking down through a shallow slot.

The light in the motel room snapped on. The window blind threw a yellow square of light out over the Cadillac. Over the side of the red truck. Over my legs. I grunted and pushed off. Swam out onto the truck's roof. Lay flat and silent. Held my breath.

The motel room door opened. The Kliner kid came out. Stared at the Cadillac. Stooped and looked inside. Walked around and checked the truck. Checked the cab doors. Tugged the handles. The vehicle shook and rocked under me. He walked around to the back and tried the rear doors. Tugged the handles. I heard the doors rattle against their locks.

He walked a circuit of the truck. I lay there and listened to the crack of his footsteps below. He checked the Cadillac again. Then he went back inside. The room door slammed. The light snapped off. The yellow square of light died.

I waited five minutes. Just lay there up on the roof and waited. Then I hauled myself up onto my elbows. Reached for the slot in the fibreglass that I'd just cut. Forced the flap down and hooked my fingers in. Dragged myself over and peered through.

The truck was empty. Totally empty. Nothing in it at all.

TWENTY-FOUR

IT WAS OVER FOUR HUNDRED MILES BACK TO THE MARGRAVE station house. I drove all of them as fast as I dared. I needed to see Finlay. Needed to lay out a brand-new theory for him. I slotted the old Cadillac into a space right next to Teale's brand-new model. Went inside and nodded to the desk guy. He nodded back.

'Finlay here?' I asked him.

'In back,' he told me. 'The mayor's with him.'

I skirted the reception counter and ran through the squad room to the rosewood office. Finlay was in there with Teale. Finlay had bad news for me. I could see it in the slope of his shoulders. Teale looked at me, surprised.

'You back in the army, Mr Reacher?' he said.

Took me a second to catch on. He was talking about my fatigues and the camouflage jacket. I looked him up and down. He was in a shiny grey suit with embroidered patterns all over it. Bootlace tie with a silver clasp.

'Don't you be talking to me about clothes, asshole,' I said.

He looked down at himself in surprise. Brushed off a speck that hadn't been there. Glared up at me.

'I could have you arrested for language like that,' he said.

'And I could tear your head off,' I said to him. 'And then I could stick it up your ratty old ass.'

We stood and glared at each other for what seemed like a long time. Teale gripped his heavy cane like he wanted to raise it up

261

and hit me with it. I could see his hand tightening around it and his glance darting towards my head. But in the end he just stalked out of the office and slammed the door. I reopened it a crack and peered out after him. He was picking up a phone at one of the squad room desks. He was going to call Kliner. He was going to ask him when the hell he was going to do something about me. I shut the door again and turned to Finlay.

'What's the problem?' I asked him.

'Serious shit,' he said. 'But did you get a look in the truck?'

'I'll get to that in a minute,' I said. 'What's the problem here?'

'You want the small problem first?' he said. 'Or the big problem?'

'Small first,' I said.

'Picard's keeping Roscoe another day,' he said. 'No option.'

'Shit,' I said. 'I wanted to see her. She happy with that?'

'According to Picard she is,' he said.

'Shit,' I said again. 'So what's the big problem?'

'Somebody's ahead of us,' he whispered.

'Ahead of us?' I asked him. 'What do you mean?'

'Your brother's list?' he said. 'The initials and the note about Sherman Stoller's garage? First thing is there's a telex in from the Atlanta PD this morning. Stoller's house burned down in the night. Out by the golf course, where you went with Roscoe? Totally destroyed, garage and all. Torched. Somebody threw gasoline all over the place.'

'Christ,' I said. 'What about Judy?'

'Neighbour says she bailed out Tuesday night,' he said. 'Right after you spoke to her. Hasn't been back. The house was empty.'

I nodded.

'Judy's a smart woman,' I said. 'But that doesn't put them ahead of us. We already saw the inside of the garage. If they were trying to hide something, they were too late. Nothing to hide anyway, right?'

'The initials?' he said. 'The colleges? I identified the Princeton guy this morning. W.B. was Walter Bartholomew. Professor. He was killed last night, outside his house.'

'Shit,' I said. 'Killed how?'

'Stabbed,' he said. 'Jersey police are calling it a mugging. But we know better than that, right?'

'Any more good news?' I asked him.

He shook his head.

'Gets worse,' he said. 'Bartholomew knew something. They got to him before he could talk to us. They're ahead of us, Reacher.'

'He knew something?' I said. 'What?'

'Don't know,' Finlay said. 'When I called the number, I got some research assistant guy, works for Bartholomew. Seems Bartholomew was excited about something, stayed at his office late last night, working. This assistant guy was ferrying him all kinds of old material. Bartholomew was checking it through. Late on, he packed up, e-mailed Joe's computer and went home. He ran into the mugger, and that was that.'

'What did the e-mail say?' I asked him.

'It said stand by for a call in the morning,' he told me. 'The assistant guy said it felt like Bartholomew had hit on something important.'

'Shit,' I said again. 'What about the New York initials? K.K.?'

'Don't know yet,' he said. 'I'm guessing it's another professor. If they haven't gotten to him yet.'

'OK,' I said. 'I'm going to New York to find him.'

'Why the panic?' Finlay asked. 'Was there a problem with the truck?'

'There was one major problem,' I said. 'The truck was empty.'

There was silence in the office for a long moment.

'It was going back empty?' Finlay said.

'I got a look inside just after I called you,' I said. 'It was empty. Nothing in it at all. Just fresh air.'

'Christ,' he said.

He looked upset. He couldn't believe it. He'd admired Roscoe's distribution theory. He'd congratulated her. Shook her hand. The menorah shape. It was a good theory. It was so good, he couldn't believe it was wrong.

'We've got to be right,' he said. 'It makes so much sense. Think of what Roscoe said. Think of the map. Think of Gray's figures. It all fits together. It's so obvious, I can just about feel it. I can just about see it. It's a traffic flow. It can't be anything else. I've been over it so many times.'

'Roscoe was right,' I agreed. 'And everything you just said is right. The menorah shape is right. Margrave is the centre. It's a traffic flow. We only got one little detail wrong.'

'What detail?' he said.

'We got the direction wrong,' I said. 'We got it ass-backward. The flow goes exactly the opposite direction. Same shape, but it's flowing down here, not out of here.'

He nodded. He saw it.

'So they're not loading up here,' he said. 'They're unloading here. They're not dispersing a stockpile. They're building up a stockpile. Right here in Margrave. But a stockpile of what? You're certain they're not printing money somewhere and bringing it down here?'

I shook my head.

'Doesn't make any sense,' I said. 'Molly said there's no printing going on in the States. Joe stopped it.'

'So what are they bringing down here?' he said.

'We need to figure that out,' I said. 'But we know it adds up to about a ton a week. And we know it fits into air conditioner boxes.'

'We do?' Finlay said.

'That's what changed last year,' I said. 'Before last September, they were smuggling it out of the country. That's what Sherman Stoller was doing. The air conditioner runs weren't a decoy operation. They were the actual operation itself. They were exporting something boxed up in air conditioner cartons. Sherman Stoller was driving them down to Florida every day to meet a boat. That's why he got so uptight when he was flagged down for speeding. That's why the fancy lawyer came running over. Not because he was on his way to load up. Because he was on his way to unload. He had the Jacksonville police sniffing around a full load for fifty-five minutes.'

'But a full load of what?' Finlay said.

'I don't know,' I said. 'The cops didn't think to look. They saw a load of sealed-up air conditioner cartons, brand-new, serial numbers and everything, and they just assumed it was kosher. The air conditioner cartons were damn good cover. Very plausible product to be hauling south. Nobody would be suspicious of brand-new air conditioners heading south, right?'

'But they stopped a year ago?' he said.

'Correct,' I said. 'They knew the Coast Guard thing was coming, so they got as much out as they could ahead of time. Remember the double runs in Gray's notes? Then they stopped altogether, a year ago. Because they felt just as vulnerable smuggling outward past the Coast Guard as we figured they'd feel smuggling inward.'

Finlay nodded. Looked displeased with himself.

'We missed that,' he said.

'We missed a lot of things,' I said. 'They fired Sherman Stoller because they didn't need him any more. They decided just to sit on the stuff and wait for the Coast Guard thing to stop. That's why they're vulnerable right now. That's why they're panicking, Finlay.

It's not the last remains of a stockpile they've got in there until Sunday. It's the whole damn thing.'

Finlay stood guard at the office door. I sat at the rosewood desk and called Columbia University in New York. The number reached the modern history department. The early part of the call was very easy. I got a helpful woman in their administrative office. I asked if they had a professor with the initials K.K. Straight away she identified a guy called Kelvin Kelstein. Been there many years. Sounded like he was a very eminent type of a guy. Then the call got very difficult. I asked if he would come to the phone. The woman said no he wouldn't. He was very busy and could not be disturbed again.

'Again?' I said. 'Who's been disturbing him already?'

'Two detectives from Atlanta, Georgia,' she said.

'When was this?' I asked her.

'This morning,' she said. 'They came in here asking for him and they wouldn't take no for an answer.'

'Can you describe these two men to me?' I asked her.

There was a pause as she tried to remember.

'They were Hispanic,' she said. 'I don't recall any details. The one who did the talking was very neat, very polite. Unremarkable, really, I'm afraid.'

'Have they met with him yet?' I asked her.

'They made a one o'clock appointment,' she said. 'They're taking him to lunch somewhere, I believe.'

I held the phone tighter.

'OK,' I said. 'This is very important. Did they ask for him by name? Or by the initials K.K.? Like I just did?'

'They asked exactly the same question you did,' she said. 'They asked if we had any faculty with those initials.'

'Listen to me,' I said. 'Listen very carefully. I want you to go see Professor Kelstein. Right now. Interrupt him, whatever he's doing. Tell him this is life or death. Tell him those Atlanta detectives are bogus. They were at Princeton last night and they murdered Professor Walter Bartholomew.'

'Are you kidding?' the woman said. Almost a scream.

'This is for real,' I said. 'My name is Jack Reacher. I believe Kelstein had been in touch with my brother, Joe Reacher, from the Treasury Department. Tell him my brother was murdered also.'

The woman paused again. Swallowed. Then she came back, calm.

'What should I tell Professor Kelstein to do?' she said.

'Two things,' I said. 'First, he must not, repeat, must not meet with the two Hispanic men from Atlanta. At any time. Got that?'

'Yes,' she said.

'Good,' I said. 'Second, he must go right now to the campus security office. Right now, OK? He must wait there for me. I'll be there in about three hours. Kelstein must sit in the security office and wait for me with a guard right next to him until I get there. Can you make absolutely sure he does that?'

'Yes,' she said again.

'Tell him to call Princeton from the security office,' I said. 'Tell him to ask after Bartholomew. That should convince him.'

'Yes,' the woman said again. 'I'll make sure he does what you say.'

'And give my name to your security desk,' I said. 'I don't want any problem getting in when I arrive. Professor Kelstein can ID me. Tell him I look like my brother.'

I hung up. Shouted across the room to Finlay.

'They've got Joe's list,' I said. 'They've got two guys up in New York. One of them is the same guy who got Joe's briefcase. Neat, polite guy. They've got the list.'

'But how?' he said. 'The list wasn't in the briefcase.'

A clang of fear hit me. I knew how. It was staring me in the face.

'Baker,' I said. 'Baker's inside the scam. He made an extra xerox copy. You sent him to copy Joe's list. He made two copies and gave one to Teale.'

'Christ,' Finlay said. 'Are you sure?'

I nodded.

'There were other indications,' I said. 'Teale's pulled a bluff. We figured everybody in the department was clean. But he was just keeping them hidden. So now we don't know who the hell is involved and who the hell isn't. We've got to get out of here, right now. Let's go.'

We ran out of the office. Through the squad room. Out through the big plate-glass doors and into Finlay's car.

'Where to?' he said.

'Atlanta,' I told him. 'The airport. I've got to get to New York.'

He started up and headed out north along the county road.

'Baker was in it from the start,' I said. 'It was staring me in the face.'

I went through it with him as he drove. Step by step. Last Friday

I had been alone in the small white interview room at the station house with Baker. I had held out my wrists to him. He'd removed my handcuffs. He'd taken the cuffs off a guy he was supposed to believe was a murderer. A murderer who had pulped his victim's body. He was willing to put himself alone in a room with such a guy. Then later I had called him over and made him escort me to the bathroom. He had been sloppy and careless. I'd had opportunities to disarm him and escape. I'd taken it as a sign he'd listened to me answering Finlay's questions and slowly become convinced I was innocent.

But he'd always known I was innocent. He knew exactly who was innocent and exactly who wasn't. That's why he had been so casual. He knew I was just a convenient fall guy. He knew I was just an innocent passerby. Who worries about taking the cuffs off an innocent passerby? Who takes a whole lot of precautions escorting an innocent passerby to the bathroom?

And he had brought Hubble in for questioning. I'd noticed his body language. He was all twisted up with conflict. I had figured he was feeling awkward because Hubble was Stevenson's buddy and his relative by marriage. But it wasn't that. He was all twisted up because he was caught in a trap. He knew bringing Hubble in was a disaster. But he couldn't disobey Finlay without alerting him. He was trapped. Damned if he did, damned if he didn't.

And there had been a deliberate attempt to conceal Joe's identity. Baker had deliberately screwed up the prints thing with the computer so that Joe would remain unidentified. He knew Joe was a government investigator. He knew Joe's prints would be in the Washington database. So he tried to make damn sure they didn't get matched. But he had blown his cover by announcing the null result far too early. It was inexperience. He'd always left the technical work to Roscoe. So he didn't know the system. But I hadn't put two and two together. I had been too overwhelmed when the second attempt with the prints had brought back my brother's name.

Since then, he had been poking and prying, hovering around on the edge of our hidden investigation. He had wanted in and he had been a willing helper. Finlay had used him on lookout duty. And all the time he was running to Teale with the snippets he was getting from us.

Finlay was blasting north at a hell of a speed. He flung the Chevy around the cloverleaf and mashed the pedal. The big car hurtled forward up the highway.

'Could we try the Coast Guard?' he said. 'Get them to stand by Sunday for when they start shipping out? Some kind of an extra patrol?'

'You're joking,' I said. 'The political flak the President's taken over that, he's not going to reverse himself the very first day, just because you ask him to.'

'So what do we do?' he said.

'Call Princeton back,' I told him. 'Get hold of that research assistant again. He may be able to piece together what Bartholomew figured out last night. Hole up somewhere safe and get busy.'

He laughed.

'Where the hell's safe now?' he said.

I told him to use the Alabama motel we'd used Monday. It was in the middle of nowhere and it was as safe as he needed to get. I told him I'd find him there when I got back. Asked him to bring the Bentley to the airport and to leave the key and the parking claim at the arrivals information desk. He repeated all the arrangements back to me to confirm he was solid. He was doing more than ninety miles an hour, but he was turning his head to look at me every time he spoke.

'Watch the road, Finlay,' I said. 'No good to anybody if you kill us in a damn car.'

He grinned and faced forward. Jammed his foot down harder. The big police Chevy eased up over a hundred. Then he turned again and looked straight into my eyes for about three hundred yards.

'Coward,' he said.

TWENTY-FIVE

NO EASY WAY TO GET THROUGH THE AIRPORT SECURITY hoops with a sap and a knife and a big metal gun, so I left my camouflage jacket in Finlay's car and told him to transfer it to the Bentley. He ducked into Departures with me and put the best part of seven hundred bucks on his credit card for my round trip ticket on Delta to New York. Then he took off to find the Alabama motel and I went through to the gate for the plane to La Guardia.

I was airborne for a shade over two hours and in a cab for thirty-five minutes. Arrived in Manhattan just after four-thirty. I'd been there in May and it looked pretty much the same in September. The summer heat was over and the city was back to work. The cab took me over the Triborough Bridge and headed west on 116th. Slid around Morningside Park and dropped me at Columbia University's main entrance. I went in and found my way to the campus security office. Knocked on the glass.

A campus policeman checked a clipboard and let me in. Led me through to a room in back and pointed to Professor Kelvin Kelstein. I saw a very old guy, tiny, wizened with age, sporting a huge shock of white hair. He looked exactly like that cleaner I'd seen on the third floor at Warburton, except he was white.

'The two Hispanic guys been back?' I asked the college cop.

He shook his head.

'Haven't seen them,' he said. 'The old guy's office told them that

269

the lunch date was cancelled. Maybe they went away.'

'I hope so,' I said. 'Meanwhile, you're going to have to watch over this guy for a spell. Give it until Sunday.'

'Why?' he said. 'What's going on?'

'Not sure, exactly,' I said. 'I'm hoping the old guy can tell me.'

The guard walked us back to Kelstein's own office and left us there. It was a small and untidy room crammed full to the ceiling with books and thick journals. Kelstein sat in an old armchair and gestured me to sit opposite him in another.

'What exactly happened to Bartholomew?' he asked.

'I don't know exactly,' I said. 'Jersey police say he got stabbed during a mugging outside his home.'

'But you remain sceptical?' Kelstein asked.

'My brother made a list of contacts,' I said. 'You're the only one of them still alive.'

'Your brother was Mr Joe Reacher?' he said.

I nodded.

'He was murdered last Thursday,' I said. 'I'm trying to find out why.'

Kelstein inclined his head and peered out of a grimy window.

'I'm sure you know why,' he said. 'He was an investigator. Clearly he was killed in the course of an investigation. What you need to know is what he was investigating.'

'Can you tell me what that was?' I said.

The old professor shook his head.

'Only in the most general terms,' he said. 'I can't help you with specifics.'

'Didn't he discuss specifics with you?' I said.

'He used me as a sounding board,' he said. 'We were speculating together. I enjoyed it tremendously. Your brother Joe was a stimulating companion. He had a keen mind and a very attractive precision about the manner in which he expressed himself. It was a pleasure to work with him.'

'But you didn't discuss specifics?' I said again.

Kelstein cupped his hands like a man holding an empty vessel.

'We discussed everything,' he said. 'But we came to no conclusions.'

'OK,' I said. 'Can we start at the beginning? The discussion was about counterfeit currency, right?'

Kelstein tilted his great head to one side. Looked amused.

'Obviously,' he said. 'What else would Mr Joe Reacher and I find to discuss?'

'Why you?' I asked him bluntly.

The old professor smiled a modest smile which faded into a frown. Then he came up with an ironic grin.

'Because I am the biggest counterfeiter in history,' he said. 'I was going to say I was one of the two biggest in history, but after the events of last night at Princeton, sadly now I alone remain.'

'You and Bartholomew?' I said. 'You were counterfeiters?'

The old guy smiled again.

'Not by choice,' he said. 'During the Second World War, young men like Walter and me ended up with strange occupations. He and I were considered more useful in an intelligence role than in combat. We were drafted into the SIS, which as you know was the very earliest incarnation of the CIA. Other people were responsible for attacking the enemy with guns and bombs. We were handed the job of attacking the enemy with economics. We derived a scheme for shattering the Nazi economy with an assault on the value of its paper currency. Our project manufactured hundreds of billions of counterfeit reichsmarks. Spare bombers littered Germany with them. They came down out of the sky like confetti.'

'Did it work?' I asked him.

'Yes and no,' he said. 'Certainly, their economy was shattered. Their currency was worthless very quickly. But of course, much of their production used slave labour. Slaves aren't interested one way or the other whether the content of somebody else's wage packet is worth anything. And of course, alternative currencies were found. Chocolate, cigarettes, anything. Altogether, it was only a partial success. But it left Walter and me two of history's greatest forgers. That is, if you use sheer volume as a measure. I can't claim any great talent for the inky end of the process.'

'So Joe was picking your brains?' I asked him.

'Walter and I became obsessed,' Kelstein said. 'We studied the history of money forging. It started the day after paper money was first introduced. It's never gone away. We became experts. We carried on the interest after the war. We developed a loose relationship with the government. Finally, some years ago, a Senate subcommittee commissioned a report from us. With all due modesty, I can claim that it became the Treasury's anti-counterfeiting bible. Your brother was familiar with it, of course. That's why he was talking to Walter and me.'

'But what was he talking to you about?' I said.

'Joe was a new broom,' Kelstein said. 'He was brought in to solve problems. He was a very talented man indeed. His job was to eradicate counterfeiting. Now, that's an impossible job. Walter and I told him that. But he nearly succeeded. He thought hard, and he applied strokes of appealing simplicity. He just about halted all illicit printing within the United States.'

I sat in his crowded office and listened to the old guy. Kelstein had known Joe better than I had. He had shared Joe's hopes and plans. Celebrated his successes. Sympathized over his setbacks. They had talked at length, animatedly, sparking off each other. The last time I had spoken to Joe face to face was very briefly after our mother's funeral. I hadn't asked him what he was doing. I'd just seen him as my older brother. Just seen him as Joe. I hadn't seen the reality of his life as a senior agent, with hundreds of people under him, trusted by the White House to solve big problems, capable of impressing a smart old bird like Kelstein. I sat there in the armchair and felt bad. I'd lost something I never knew I'd had.

'His systems were brilliant,' Kelstein said. 'His analysis was acute. He targeted ink and paper. In the end, it all boils down to ink and paper, doesn't it? If anybody bought the sort of ink or paper that could be used to forge a banknote, Joe's people knew within hours. He swept people up within days. Inside the States, he reduced counterfeiting activity by ninety per cent. And he tracked the remaining ten per cent so vigorously he got almost all of them before they'd even distributed the fakes. He impressed me greatly.'

'So what was the problem?' I asked him.

Kelstein made a couple of precise little motions with his small white hands, like he was moving one scenario aside and introducing another.

'The problem lay abroad,' he said. 'Outside the United States. The situation there is very different. Did you know there are twice as many dollars outside the US as inside?'

I nodded. I summarized what Molly had told me about foreign holdings. The trust and the faith. The fear of a sudden collapse in the desirability of the dollar. Kelstein was nodding away like I was his student and he liked my thesis.

'Quite so,' he said. 'It's more about politics than crime. In the end, a government's primary duty is to defend the value of its currency. We have two hundred and sixty billion dollars abroad. The dollar is the unofficial currency of dozens of nations. In the new Russia, for instance, there are more dollars than rubles. In effect, it's like Washington has raised a massive foreign loan. Raised any other way, that loan would cost us twenty-six billion dollars a year in interest payments alone. But this way, it costs us nothing at all except what we spend on printing pictures of dead politicians on little pieces of paper. That's what it's all about, Mr Reacher. Printing currency for foreigners to buy is the best racket a government can get into. So Joe's job in reality was worth twenty-six billion dollars a year to this country. And he pursued it with an energy appropriate to those high stakes.'

'So where was the problem?' I said. 'Geographically?'

'Two main places,' Kelstein said. 'First, the Middle East. Joe believed there was a plant in the Bekaa Valley that turned out fake hundreds which were practically perfect. But there was very little he could do about it. Have you been there?'

I shook my head. I'd been stationed in Beirut for a while. I had known a few people who had gone out to the Bekaa Valley for one reason or another. Not too many of them had come back.

'Syrian-controlled Lebanon,' Kelstein said. 'Joe called it the badlands. They do everything there. Training camps for the world's terrorists, drug processing laboratories, you name it, they've got it. Including a pretty good replica of our own Bureau of Printing and Engraving.'

I thought about it. Thought about my time there.

'Protected by who?' I asked him.

Kelstein smiled at me again. Nodded.

'A perceptive question,' he said. 'You instinctively grasp that an operation of that size is so visible, so complex, that it must be in some way sponsored. Joe believed it was protected by, or maybe even owned by, the Syrian government. Therefore his involvement was marginal. His conclusion was that the only solution was diplomatic. Failing that, he was in favour of air strikes against it. We may live to see such a solution one day.'

'And the second place?' I asked him.

He pointed his finger at his grimy office window. Aiming south down Amsterdam Avenue.

'South America,' he said. 'The second source is Venezuela. Joe had located it. That is what he was working on. Absolutely outstanding counterfeit hundred dollar bills are coming out of Venezuela. But strictly private enterprise. No suggestion of government involvement.'

I nodded.

'We got that far,' I said. 'A guy called Kliner, based down in Georgia where Joe was killed.'

'Quite so,' Kelstein said. 'The ingenious Mr Kliner. It's his operation. He's running the whole thing. We knew that for certain. How is he?'

'He's panicking,' I said. 'He's killing people.'

Kelstein nodded sadly.

'We thought Kliner might panic,' he said. 'He's protecting an outstanding operation. The very best we've ever seen.'

'The best?' I said.

Kelstein nodded enthusiastically.

'Outstanding,' he said again. 'How much do you know about counterfeiting?'

I shrugged at him.

'More than I did last week,' I said. 'But not enough, I guess.'

Kelstein nodded and shifted his frail weight forward in his chair. His eyes lit up. He was about to start a lecture on his favourite subject.

'There are two sorts of counterfeiters,' he said. 'The bad ones and the good ones. The good ones do it properly. Do you know the difference between intaglio and lithography?'

I shrugged and shook my head. Kelstein scooped up a magazine from a pile and handed it to me. It was a quarterly bulletin from a history society.

'Open it,' he said. 'Any page will do. Run your fingers over the paper. It's smooth, isn't it? That's lithographic printing. That's how virtually everything is printed. Books, magazines, newspapers, everything. An inked roller passes over the blank paper. But intaglio is different.'

He suddenly clapped his hands together. I jumped. The sound was very loud in his quiet office.

'That's intaglio,' he said. 'A metal plate is smashed into the paper with considerable force. It leaves a definite embossed feel to the product. The printed image looks three dimensional. It feels three dimensional. It's unmistakable.'

He eased himself up and took his wallet out of his hip pocket. Pulled out a ten dollar bill. Passed it over to me.

'Can you feel it?' he asked. 'The metal plates are nickel, coated with chromium. Fine lines are engraved into the chromium and the lines are filled with ink. The plate hits the paper and the ink is printed onto its topmost surface. Understand? The ink is in the valleys of the plate, so it's transferred to the ridges on the paper. Intaglio printing is the only way to get that raised image. The only way to make the forgery feel right. It's how the real thing is done.'

'What about the ink?' I said.

'There are three colours,' he said. 'Black, and two greens. The back of the bill is printed first, with the darker green. Then the paper is left to dry, and the next day, the front is printed with the black ink. That dries, and the front is printed again, with the lighter green. That's the other stuff you see there on the front, including the serial number. But the lighter green is printed by a different process, called letterpress. It's a stamping action, the same as intaglio, but the ink is stamped into the valleys on the paper, not onto the peaks.'

I nodded and looked at the ten dollar bill, front and back. Ran my fingers over it carefully. I'd never really studied one before.

'So, four problems,' Kelstein said. 'The press, the plates, the inks, and the paper. The press can be bought, new or used, anywhere in the world. There are hundreds of sources. Most countries print money and securities and bonds on them. So the presses are obtainable abroad. They can even be improvised. Joe found one intaglio operation in Thailand which was using a converted squid-processing machine. Their hundreds were absolutely immaculate.'

'What about the plates?' I asked him.

'Plates are problem number two,' he said. 'But it's a matter of talent. There are people in the world who can forge Old Master paintings and there are people who can play a Mozart piano concerto after hearing it once. And certainly there are engravers who can reproduce banknotes. It's a perfectly logical proposition, isn't it? If a human being in Washington can engrave the original, certainly there's a human being somewhere else who can copy it. But they're rare. Really good copyists, rarer still. There are a few in Armenia. The Thai operation using the squid-processor got a Malaysian to make the plates.'

'OK,' I said. 'So Kliner has bought a press, and he's found an engraver. What about the inks?'

'The inks are problem number three,' he said. 'You can't buy anything vaguely like them in the US. Joe saw to that. But abroad, they're available. As I said, virtually every country in the world has its own banknote printing industry. And obviously, Joe couldn't enforce his systems in every country in the world. So the inks are easy enough to find. The greens are only a question of colour. They mix them and experiment until they get them right. The black ink is magnetic, did you know that?'

I shook my head again. Looked at the sawbuck closely. Kelstein smiled.

'You can't see it,' he said. 'A liquid ferrous chemical is mixed with the black ink. That's how electronic money counters work. They scan the engraving down the centre of the portrait, and the machine reads the signal it gives off, like a tape head reads the sounds on a music cassette.'

'And they can get that ink?' I said.

'Anywhere in the world,' he said. 'Everybody uses it. We lag behind other countries. We don't like to admit we worry about counterfeiting.'

I remembered what Molly had said. Faith and trust. I nodded.

'The currency must look stable,' Kelstein said. 'That's why we're so reluctant to change it. It's got to look reliable, solid, unchanging. Turn that ten over and take a look.'

I looked at the green picture on the back of the ten. The Treasury Building was standing in a deserted street. Only one car was driving past. It looked like a Model-T Ford.

'Hardly changed since 1929,' Kelstein said. 'Psychologically, it's very important. We choose to put the appearance of dependability before security. It made Joe's job very difficult.'

I nodded again.

'Right,' I said. 'So we've covered the press, the plates, and the inks. What about the paper?'

Kelstein brightened up and clasped his small hands like we'd reached the really interesting part.

'Paper is problem number four,' he said. 'Actually, we should really say it's problem number one. It's by far the biggest problem. It's the thing Joe and I couldn't understand about Kliner's operation.'

'Why not?' I asked him.

'Because their paper is perfect,' he said. 'It's one hundred per cent perfect. Their paper is better than their printing. And that is absolutely unheard of.'

He started shaking his great white head in wonderment. Like he was lost in admiration for Kliner's achievement. We sat there, knee to knee in the old armchairs in silence.

'Perfect?' I prompted him.

He nodded and started up with the lecture again.

'It's unheard of,' he said again. 'The paper is the hardest part of the whole process. Don't forget, we're not talking about some amateur thing here. We're talking about an industrial-scale

276

operation. In a year, they're printing four billion dollars' worth of hundreds.'

'That many?' I said, surprised.

'Four billion,' he said again. 'About the same as the Lebanon operation. Those were Joe's figures. He was in a position to know. And that makes it inexplicable. Four billion in hundreds is forty million banknotes. That's a lot of paper. That's a completely inexplicable amount of paper, Mr Reacher. And their paper is perfect.'

'What sort of paper would they need?' I asked him.

He reached over and took the ten dollar bill back from me. Crumpled it and pulled it and snapped it.

'It's a blend of fibres,' he said. 'Very clever and entirely unique. About eighty per cent cotton, about twenty per cent linen. No wood pulp in it at all. It's got more in common with the shirt on your back than with a newspaper, for instance. It's got a very clever chemical colourant in it, to give it a unique cream tint. And it's got random red and blue polymer threads pulped in, as fine as silk. Currency stock is wonderful paper. Durable, lasts for years, won't come apart in water, hot or cold. Absolutely precise absorbency, capable of accepting the finest engraving the platemakers can achieve.'

'So the paper would be difficult to copy?' I said.

'Virtually impossible,' he said. 'In a way, it's so difficult to copy that even the official government supplier can't copy it. They have tremendous difficulty just keeping it consistent, batch to batch, and they're by far the most sophisticated papermaker in the entire world.'

I ran it all through in my head. Press, plates, ink and paper.

'So the paper supply is really the key to all this?' I said.

Kelstein nodded ruefully.

'That was our conclusion,' he said. 'We agreed the paper supply was crucial, and we agreed we had no idea how they were managing it. That's why I can't really help you. I couldn't help Joe, and I can't help you. I'm terribly sorry.'

I looked at him.

'They've got a warehouse full of something,' I said. 'Could that be paper?'

He snorted in derision. Snapped his great head around towards me.

'Don't you listen?' he said. 'Currency stock is unobtainable. Completely unobtainable. You couldn't get forty sheets of currency stock, never mind forty million sheets. The whole thing

277

is a total mystery. Joe and Walter and I racked our brains for a year and we came up with nothing.'

'I think Bartholomew came up with something,' I said.

Kelstein nodded sadly. He levered himself slowly out of his chair and stepped to his desk. Pressed the replay button on his telephone answering machine. The room was filled with an electronic beep, then with the sound of a dead man's voice.

'Kelstein?' the voice said. 'Bartholomew here. It's Thursday night, late. I'm going to call you in the morning and I'm going to tell you the answer. I knew I'd beat you to it. Goodnight, old man.'

The voice had excitement in it. Kelstein stood there and gazed into space as if Bartholomew's spirit was hanging there in the still air. He looked upset. I couldn't tell if that was because his old colleague was dead, or because his old colleague had beaten him to the answer.

'Poor Walter,' he said. 'I knew him fifty-six years.'

I sat quietly for a spell. Then I stood up as well.

'I'll figure it out,' I said.

Kelstein put his head on one side and looked at me sharply.

'Do you really think you will?' he said. 'When Joe couldn't?'

I shrugged at the old guy.

'Maybe Joe did,' I said. 'We don't know what he'd figured out before they got him. Anyway, right now I'm going back to Georgia. Carry on the search.'

Kelstein nodded and sighed. He looked stressed.

'Good luck, Mr Reacher,' he said. 'I hope you finish your brother's business. Perhaps you will. He spoke of you often. He liked you, you know.'

'He spoke of me?' I said.

'Often,' the old guy said again. 'He was very fond of you. He was sorry your job kept you so far away.'

For a moment I couldn't speak. I felt unbearably guilty. Years would pass, I wouldn't think about him. But he was thinking about me?

'He was older, but you looked after him,' he said. 'That's what Joe told me. He said you were very fierce. Very tough. I guess if Joe wanted anybody to take care of the Kliners, he'd have nominated you.'

I nodded.

'I'm out of here,' I said.

I shook his frail hand and left him with the cops in the security office.

I was trying to figure where Kliner was getting his perfect paper, and I was trying to figure if I could get the six o'clock flight back to Atlanta if I hurried, and I was trying to ignore what Kelstein had told me about Joe speaking fondly of me. The streets were clogged and I was busy thinking about it all and scanning for an empty cab, which was why I didn't notice two Hispanic guys strolling up to me. But what I did notice was the gun the leading guy showed me. It was a small automatic held in a small hand, concealed under one of those khaki raincoats city people carry on their arms in September.

He showed me the weapon and his partner signalled to a car waiting twenty yards away at the kerb. The car lurched forward and the partner stood ready to open a door like the top-hatted guys do outside the expensive apartment houses up there. I was looking at the gun and looking at the car, making choices.

'Get into the car,' the guy with the gun said softly. 'Or I'll shoot you.'

I stood there and all that was passing through my mind was that I might miss my flight. I was trying to remember when the next non-stop left. Seven o'clock, I thought.

'In the car,' the guy said again.

I was pretty sure he wouldn't fire the gun on the street. It was a small gun, but there was no silencer on it. It would make a hell of a noise, and it was a crowded street. The other guy's hands were empty. He maybe had a gun in his pocket. There was just the driver in the car. Probably a gun on the seat beside him. I was unarmed. My jacket with the blackjack and the knife and the Desert Eagle was eight hundred miles away in Atlanta. Choices.

I chose not to get into the car. I just stood there in the street, gambling with my life that the guy wouldn't shoot in public. He stood there, holding the raincoat out towards me. The car stopped next to us. His partner stood on the other side of me. They were small guys. The both of them wouldn't have made one of me. The car waited, idling at the kerb. Nobody moved. We were just frozen there like some kind of a display in a store window. Like new fashions for the fall, old army fatigues put with Burberry raincoats.

It gave the two guys a big problem. In a situation like that, there's a split-second opportunity to carry out your threat. If you say you're going to shoot, you've got to shoot. If you don't, you're a spent force. Your bluff is called. If you don't shoot, you're nothing. And the guy didn't shoot. He just stood there, twisted up with indecision. People swirled around us on the busy sidewalk. Cars were blasting their horns at the guy stopped at the kerb.

They were smart guys. Smart enough not to shoot me on a busy New York street. Smart enough to know I'd called their bluff. Smart enough to never again make a threat they weren't going to keep. But not smart enough to walk away. They just stood there.

So I swayed backwards, as if I was going to take a step away. The gun under the raincoat prodded forwards at me. I tracked the movement and grabbed the little guy's wrist with my left hand. Pulled the gun around behind me and hugged the guy close with my right arm around his shoulders. We looked like we were dancing the waltz together or we were lovers at a train station. Then I fell forward and crushed him against the car. All the time I was squeezing his wrist as hard as I could, with my nails dug in. Left-handed, but it was hurting him. My weight leaning up on him was giving him a struggle to breathe.

His partner still had his hand on the car door. His glance was darting back and forth. Then his other hand was going for his pocket. So I jackknifed my weight back and rolled around my guy's gun hand and threw him against the car. And then I ran like hell. In five strides I was lost in the crowd. I dodged and barged my way through the mass of people. Ducked in and out of doorways and ran through shrieking and honking traffic across the streets. The two guys stayed with me for a spell, but the traffic eventually stopped them. They weren't taking the risks I was taking.

I got a cab eight blocks away from where I had started and made the six o'clock non-stop, La Guardia to Atlanta. Going back it took longer, for some reason. I was sitting there for two and a half hours. I thought about Joe all the way through the airspace above Jersey, Maryland and Virginia. Above the Carolinas and into Georgia, I thought about Roscoe. I wanted her back. I missed her like crazy.

We came down through storm clouds ten miles thick. The Atlanta evening gloom was turned to pitch-black by the clouds. Looked like an enormous weather system was rolling in from somewhere. When we got off the plane, the air in the little tunnel was thick and heavy, and smelled of storm as well as kerosene.

I picked up the Bentley key from the information counter in the arrivals hall. It was in an envelope with a parking claim. I walked out to find the car. Felt a warm wind blowing out of the north. The storm was going to be a big one. I could feel the voltage building up for the lightning. I found the car in the short-term lot. The rear windows were all tinted black. The guy hadn't gotten around to doing the front side glass or the windshield. It made the car look like something royalty might use, with a chauffeur driving them. My jacket was laid out in the trunk. I put it on and felt the reassuring weight of the weaponry in the pockets again. I got in the driver's seat and nosed out of the lot and headed south down the highway in the dark. It was nine o'clock, Friday evening. Maybe thirty-six hours before they could start shipping the stockpile out on Sunday.

It was ten o'clock when I got back to Margrave. Thirty-five hours to go. I had spent the hour thinking about some stuff we had learned back in Staff College. We'd studied military philosophies, mostly written by those old Krauts who loved all that stuff. I hadn't paid much attention, but I remember some big thing which said sooner or later, you've got to engage the enemy's main force. You don't win the war unless you do that. Sooner or later, you seek out their main force, and you take it on, and you destroy it.

I knew their main force had started with ten people. Hubble had told me that. Then there were nine, after they ditched Morrison. I knew about the two Kliners, Teale, and Baker. That left me five more names to find. I smiled to myself. Pulled off the county road into Eno's gravel lot. Parked up on the far end of the row and got out. Stretched and yawned in the night air. The storm was holding off, but it was going to break. The air was still thick and heavy. I could still feel the voltage in the clouds. I could still feel the warm wind on my back. I got into the back of the car. Stretched out on the leather bench and went to sleep. I wanted to get an hour, hour and a half.

I started dreaming about John Lee Hooker. In the old days, before he got famous again. He had an old steel-strung guitar, played it sitting on a little stool. The stool was placed on a square of wooden board. He used to press old beer bottle caps into the soles of his shoes to make them noisy. Like homemade tap shoes. He'd sit on his stool and play that guitar with his bold, choppy style. All the while pounding on the wooden board with his noisy shoes. I was dreaming of him pounding out the rhythm with his shoes on that old board.

But it wasn't John Lee's shoes making the noise. It was

somebody knocking on the Bentley's windshield. I snapped awake and struggled up. Sergeant Baker was looking in at me. The big chrome clock on the dash showed ten-thirty. I'd slept a half-hour. That was all I was going to get.

First thing I did was to change my plan. A much better one had fallen right into my lap. The old Krauts would have approved. Tactical flexibility was big with them. Second thing I did was to put my hand in my pocket and snick the safety off the Desert Eagle. Then I got out of the opposite door and looked along the car roof at Baker. He was using his friendly grin, gold tooth and all.

'How you doing?' he said. 'Sleeping in a public place, around here you could get arrested for vagrancy.'

I grinned a friendly grin right back at him.

'Highway safety,' I said. 'They tell you don't drive if you're tired. Pull off and take a nap, right?'

'Come on in and I'll buy you a cup of coffee,' he said. 'You want to wake up, Eno's coffee should do it for you.'

I locked the car. Kept my hand in my pocket. We crunched over the gravel and into the diner. Slid into the end booth. The woman with the glasses brought us coffee. We hadn't asked. She just seemed to know.

'So how you doing?' Baker said. 'Feeling bad about your brother?'

I shrugged at him. Drank my coffee left-handed. My right hand was wrapped around the Desert Eagle in my pocket.

'We weren't close,' I said.

Baker nodded.

'Roscoe still helping the Bureau out?' he said.

'Guess so,' I said.

'And where's old Finlay tonight?' he asked.

'Jacksonville,' I said. 'He had to go to Florida, check something out.'

'Jacksonville?' he said. 'What does he need to check out in Jacksonville?'

I shrugged again. Sipped my coffee.

'Search me,' I said. 'He doesn't tell me anything. I'm not on the payroll. I'm just an errand boy. Now he's got me running up to Hubble's place to fetch him something.'

'Hubble's place?' Baker said. 'What you got to fetch from there?'

'Some old papers,' I said. 'Anything I can find, I guess.'

'Then what?' he said. 'You going to Florida too?'

I shook my head. Sipped more coffee.

'Finlay told me to stick them in the mail,' I said. 'Some Washington address. I'm going to sleep up at Hubble's place and mail them in the morning.'

Baker nodded slowly. Then he flashed his friendly grin again. But it was forced. We finished up our coffee. Baker dropped a couple of bucks on the table and we slid out and left. He got into his patrol car. Waved at me as he drove off. I let him go ahead and strolled over the gravel to the Bentley. I rolled south to the end of the dark little town and made the right turn up Beckman Drive.

TWENTY-SIX

I HAD TO BE VERY CAREFUL ABOUT WHERE I PUT THE BENTLEY. I wanted it to look like it was just casually dumped. But it had to be left so nobody could get past it. I inched it back and forth for a while. Left it at the top of Hubble's driveway with the wheels turned away. It looked like I'd driven up in a hurry and just slewed to a stop.

I wanted the house to look like I was in there. Nothing is more obvious than an empty building. That quiet, abandoned look is a giveaway. There's a stillness. No human vibrations. So I opened the front door with the key from the big bunch Charlie had given me. Walked through and turned on some random lights. In the den, I switched the television set on and left it at a low murmur. Same thing with the radio in the kitchen. Pulled a few drapes. Went back outside. It looked pretty good. Looked like there might be someone in there.

Then the first stop was the coat closet off the main hallway. I was looking for gloves. Not easy to find in the Sunbelt. Not much call for them. But Hubble had some. Two pairs, lying neatly on a shelf. One was a pair of ski gloves. Lime green and lilac. Not much good to me. I wanted something dark. The other pair was what I wanted. Dressy things in thin black leather. Banker's gloves. Very soft. Like a second skin.

The ski gloves made me look for a hat. If the Hubbles had taken trips up to Colorado, they'd have had all the gear. I found a box of hats. There was a kind of watch cap in there, some sort of a synthetic fibre. The bottom part rolled down to make earflaps. The hat was printed up in a dark green pattern. It would do.

Next stop was the master bedroom. I found Charlie's vanity table. It was bigger than some of the rooms I'd lived in. She had a mass of cosmetics. All kinds of things. I took a tube of waterproof mascara into the bathroom. Smeared it all over my face. Then I fastened the jacket, put on the hat, put on the gloves. I walked back into the bedroom and checked the result in the full-length mirrors on the closet doors. Not bad. Just about right for night work.

I went back outside. Locked up the front door again. I could feel the huge storm clouds clamping down overhead. It was very dark. I stood by the front door and checked myself over. Put the pistol in the inside jacket pocket. Moved the zip down and checked the draw. Came out OK. Loaded, cocked. Safety on. Spare shells in the outside top right pocket. Switchblade in the left side pocket. Blackjack in the right side pocket. Shoes tightly laced.

I walked down the driveway, away from the house, past the parked Bentley, twelve or fifteen yards. Pushed through the greenery and settled in a spot where I could just about see up and down the drive. I sat on the cold earth and got ready to wait. In an ambush situation, waiting is what wins the battle. If the other guy is wary, he'll come early or late. When he figures you won't be expecting him. So however early he might make it, you've got to be ready earlier. However late he might leave it, you've got to wait it out. You wait in a kind of trance. You need infinite patience. No use fretting or worrying. You just wait. Doing nothing, thinking nothing, burning no energy. Then you burst into action. After an hour, five hours, a day, a week. Waiting is a skill like anything else.

It was a quarter to midnight when I settled in for the wait. I could feel the storm boiling up overhead. The air was like soup. It was pitch-dark. About midnight, the storm broke. Heavy drops the size of quarters spattered the leaves around me. They built into a deluge within seconds. It was like sitting in a shower stall. Awesome thunderclaps crashed about. They ripped and banged and the lightning blazed in sheets. The garden around me was lit up like day for seconds at a time. I sat under the lashing rain and waited. Ten minutes. Fifteen.

They came for me at twenty minutes past midnight. The rain was still bad and the thunder was still crashing and rolling. I didn't hear their truck until it was well up the driveway. I heard it crunching over the gravel about forty feet away. It was a dark green panel truck. Gold lettering. Kliner Foundation. Like the one I'd seen near Roscoe's place on Tuesday morning. It crunched past me, about six feet away. Wide tyres on the gravel. That's what Finlay had seen up at the Morrison place. Marks in the gravel made by wide tyres.

The truck stopped a few yards beyond me. It pulled up sharp just behind the Bentley. Couldn't get past. Just where I wanted it. I heard the engine stop and the parking brake ratchet on.

First guy out was the driver. He was wearing a white nylon bodysuit. It had a hood pulled tight around his face. Over his face was a surgical mask. He was wearing thin rubber gloves. On his feet, rubber overshoes. He vaulted out of the driver's seat and walked around to the rear doors. I knew that walk. I knew that tall, heavy build. I knew those long powerful arms. It was the Kliner kid. The Kliner kid himself had come to kill me.

He slapped his palm on the rear door. It made a hollow boom. Then he turned the handle and opened up. Four men came out. All dressed the same. White nylon bodysuits, hoods pulled tight, masks, gloves, rubber overshoes. Two were carrying bags. Two had long fat shotguns. A total of five men. I'd expected four. Five was going to be harder. But more productive.

The rain was lashing down on them. I could hear the brittle spatter as it hit their stiff nylon suits. I could hear the metallic clang as the heavy drops bounced off the roof of their truck. I saw them caught by a lightning flash. They looked like banshees. Like something escaped from hell. They were a terrifying sight. For the first time, I doubted if I would have beaten them on Monday night. But I was going to beat them tonight. Tonight, I would have the advantage of surprise. I would be an invisible nightmare figure let loose among them.

The Kliner kid was organizing them. He reached into the back of the truck and pulled out a crowbar. Pointed to three of his soldiers and walked off with them through the downpour to the house. The fifth guy was going to wait with the truck. Because of the rain, he was going to get back in the cab. I saw him glance up at the black sky and glance forward at the driver's seat. I pulled out the sap. Forced my way through the bushes. The guy couldn't hear me. The rain was roaring in his ears.

He turned his back and took a step toward the driver's door. I shut my eyes for a second and pictured Joe lying on the slab at the morgue with no face. Pictured Roscoe shaking with horror as she stared at the footprints on her hallway floor. Then I crashed out of the bushes. Skipped up behind the guy. Smashed the sap across the back of his skull. It was a big sap and I gave it all I had. I felt the bone explode under it. The guy went down on the gravel like a tree. He lay face down and the rain hammered on his nylon suit. I broke his neck with a single mighty kick. One down.

I dragged the body across the gravel and left it at the back of the truck. Walked around and pulled the keys out of the ignition. Crept on up to the house. I put the sap back in my pocket. Popped the switchblade and carried it in my right hand. I didn't want to use the gun in the house. Too noisy, even with the thunder crashing outside. I stopped inside the front door. The lock was forced and the wood was splintered. I saw the crowbar on the hallway floor.

It was a big house. It was going to take them some time to search it. My guess was they'd stick together as a group of four. They'd search together. Then they'd split up. I could hear them tramping through the upper floor. I stepped back outside to wait for one of them to come down into the hallway. I waited, pressed against the wall, next to the broken door. I was sheltered by the overhang of the roof. The rain was still torrential. It was as bad as a tropical storm.

I waited nearly five minutes before the first one came downstairs. I heard the creak of his tread in the hallway. Heard him open the coat closet door. I stepped inside the house. His back was to me. He was one of the shotgun carriers, tall, lighter than me. I fell in behind him. Reached over the top of his head with my left hand. Stuck my fingers in his eyes. He dropped the shotgun. It thudded onto the carpet. I pulled him backward and turned him and ran him out through the door. Into the downpour. Dug my fingers deeper into his eyes. Hauled his head back. Cut his throat. You don't do it with one elegant swipe. Not like in the movies. No knife is sharp enough for that. There's all kinds of tough gristle in the human throat. You have to saw back and forth with a lot of strength. Takes a while. But it works. It works well. By the time you've sawed back to the bone, the guy is dead. This guy was no exception. His blood hosed out and mixed with the rain. He sagged against my grip. Two down.

I dragged the body over to the lawn by the top of his hood. No good picking him up under the knees and shoulders. His head would have lolled back and fallen off. I left him on the grass. Ran back inside. Picked up the shotgun and grimaced. It was a serious weapon. An Ithaca Mag-10. I'd seen them in the army. They fire an enormous cartridge. People call them the Roadblocker. There's enough power in them to kill people through the side of a soft-skinned vehicle. Face to face, they're devastating. They only hold three cartridges, but like we used to say, by the time you've fired three rounds, the battle is definitely over.

I kept the blade out as my weapon of choice. Silent. But the shotgun would be better than the Desert Eagle as backup. Thing is with a shotgun, aiming is a luxury. A shotgun sprays a wide cone of lead. With a Mag-10, as long as it's pointed vaguely in the right direction, you're going to score.

I stepped back out through the splintered door and pressed against the wall, out of the deluge. I waited. Now my guess was they'd start coming out of the house. They wouldn't find me in there and they'd miss the guy I'd just dropped. So they'd start coming out. It was inevitable. They couldn't stay in there for ever. I waited. Ten minutes. I could hear creaking from the floor inside. Ignored it. Sooner or later, they'd come out.

They came out. Two guys together. They came as a pair. That made me hesitate a fraction. They stepped out into the downpour and I heard the rain start roaring against their nylon hoods. I pulled out the sap again. Swapped it into my right hand. The first guy went down easily enough. I caught him square on the back of his neck with the heavy sap and his head nearly came off. But the second guy reacted and twisted away so that I missed with the next swing. The sap just smashed his collar bone and dropped him to his knees. I stabbed him left-handed in the face. Lined up for another shot with the sap. Took me two more blows to break his neck. He was a wiry guy. But not wiry enough. Four down.

I dragged the two bodies through the lashing rain to the lawn at the edge of the gravel drive. Piled them with the other guy. I had four down and one shotgun captured. The truck keys in my pocket. The Kliner kid with a shotgun still on the loose.

I couldn't find him. I didn't know where he was. I stepped into the house, out of the rain, and listened. Couldn't hear a thing. The roar of the rain on the roof and on the gravel outside was too much. It was putting up a mask of white noise over everything else. If the kid was alerted and creeping around, I wouldn't hear him. It was going to be a problem.

I crept into the garden room. The rain was hammering on the roof. I stood still and listened hard. Heard the kid in the hallway.

He was on his way out. He was going out the front door. If he turned right, he was going to trip over his three dead grunts piled on the lawn. But he turned left. He walked past the garden room windows. He was headed across the soaking lawn to the patio area. I watched him walk by, through the deluge, maybe eight feet away. Looked like a ghost from hell. A ghost from hell holding a long black shotgun out in front of him.

I had the garden room key in my pocket, on the Bentley ring. I unlocked the door and stepped out. The rain hit me like a drenching from a fire hose. I crept around to the patio. The Kliner kid was standing there, looking down towards the big swimming pool. I crouched in the rain, and watched him. From twenty feet, I could hear the downpour thrashing against his white nylon bodysuit. Lightning was searing the sky and the thunder was a continuous crashing.

I didn't want to shoot him with the Mag-10 I was holding. I had to dispose of the bodies. I had to leave old man Kliner unsettled. I had to keep him guessing about what had happened. About where his boy had disappeared to. It would unbalance him. And it was crucial to my own safety. I couldn't afford to leave the slightest shred of evidence behind. Using the big Ithaca against the kid would make a hell of a mess. Disposing of his body would be a severe problem. Finding all of it would be difficult. I waited.

The kid set off down the long sloping lawn to the pool. I looped around, staying on the wet grass. The kid walked slowly. He was worried. He was on his own. His vision wasn't good. The tight hood around his face was limiting his field of view. He kept turning his head from side to side, stiff-necked, like a mechanical thing. He stopped at the edge of the pool. I was a yard behind him. I was swaying left and right, left and right, staying out of the edge of his vision as he swung his gaze from side to side. His massive shotgun was traversing left and right over the teeming pool.

The books I used to read, the movies people see, I should have fought him nobly. I was here to stand up for my brother. And right in front of me was the guy who'd kicked his body around like a bundle of rags. We should have duked it out, face to face. He should have been made aware of who his opponent was. He should have been made aware of why he had to die. All that noble, man-to-man stuff. But real life wasn't like that. Joe would have laughed at all that.

I swung the sap with all my strength at his head. Just as he turned to walk back to the house. The sap glanced off the slick nylon and the momentum of the heavy lead-filled tube pulled me hopelessly off balance. I was falling like a man on ice. The kid spun and raised the shotgun. Pumped a shell into the chamber. I flung my arm up and knocked the barrel aside. Rolled right under his field of fire. He squeezed the trigger and there was an enormous explosion, louder than the worst of the thunder. I heard leaves tearing and ripping as the shot smashed into the trees beyond us.

The ferocious recoil rocked him back, but he pumped the second shell. I heard the menacing double crunch-crunch of the mechanism. I was on my back on the poolside tiles, but I lunged up and grabbed the gun with both hands. Forced the barrel up and the stock down and he fired into the air again. Another terrifying explosion. This time I pulled with the recoil and tore the gun out of his hands. Thrust up and jabbed the stock at his face. It was a poor blow. The Ithaca has a big rubber pad on the stock. It protects the shooter's shoulder from the savage recoil. Now it protected the kid's head from my jab. He just rocked back. I dived at his legs and slammed him backward. Swiped at his feet and tripped him into the pool. He splashed in on his back. I jumped in on top of him.

We were in the deep end of the pool, thrashing about for the winning hold. The rain was hammering. Chlorine was burning my eyes and nose. I fought on until I got his throat. Tore the nylon hood back and got my hands right on his neck. Locked my arms and thrust the kid's head far under the water. I was crushing his throat with all my strength. That biker in Warburton had thought he was doing a job on me, but that had been like a lover's caress compared to what I was doing to the Kliner kid. I was tearing his head off. I squeezed and wrenched and held him a yard underwater until he died. Didn't take long. Never does, in that situation. The first guy under stays under. It could have been me.

I was treading water and gasping through the chlorine stink. The rain was chopping up the surface. It was impossible to tell where the water ended and the air began. I let his body float off and swam to the side. Clung on and got my breath. The weather was a nightmare. The thunder was now a continuous roar and the lightning blazed in sheets. The rain was a relentless downpour. It would have kept me drier to stay in the pool. But I had things to do.

I swam back to fetch the kid's body. It was floating a yard down. I towed it back to the side. Hauled myself out. Grabbed a bunch of

290

nylon in each hand and dragged the body out after me. It weighed a ton. It lay on the poolside with water gushing out of the suit at the wrists and ankles. I left it there and staggered back up toward the garage.

Walking was not easy. My clothes were soaking wet and cold. It was like walking in chain-mail. But I made it to the garage and found the key. Unlocked the door and hit the light. It was a three-car garage. Just the other Bentley in there. Hubble's own car, same vintage as Charlie's. Gorgeous dark green, lovingly polished to a deep gloss. I could see my reflection in the paint as I moved about. I was looking for a wheelbarrow or a garden truck. Whatever gardeners use. The garage was full of garden gear. A big ride-on mower, hoses, tools. In the far corner, a sort of a barrow thing with big spoke wheels like a bicycle.

I wheeled it out into the storm and down to the pool. Scrabbled around and found the two shotguns and the wet sap. Dropped the shotguns in the barrow and put the sap back in my pocket. Checked the kid's corpse still had its shoes on and heaved it into the barrow. Wheeled it up to the house and down the driveway. Squeezed it past the Bentley and rolled it around to the back of the truck. I opened the rear doors and heaved the corpse inside. Scrambled up and dragged it well in. The rain was clattering on the roof. Then I lifted the first guy's body in and dragged it up next to the Kliner kid. Threw the shotguns in on top of them. Two stowed.

Then I took the barrow up to where I'd piled the other three. They were sprawled on the soaking lawn with the rain roaring on their hideous suits. I wheeled them back to the truck they'd come in. Got all five laid out inside.

Then I ran the barrow back through the deluge to the garage. Put it back in the corner where I'd found it. Took a flashlight from the workbench. I wanted to get a look at the four boys young Kliner had brought with him. I ran back through the rain to the truck and stepped up inside. Switched on the flashlight and crouched over the forlorn row of corpses.

The Kliner kid, I knew. The other four, I pulled back their hoods and tore away their masks. Played the flashlight beam over their faces. Two of them were the gatemen from the warehouse. I'd watched them through the field glasses on Thursday and I was sure of it. Maybe I wouldn't have sworn to it in a court-martial, but I wasn't interested in that kind of a judicial procedure tonight.

The other two, I did know for sure. No doubt about it. They

291

were police. They were the backup crew from Friday. They'd come with Baker and Stevenson to the diner to arrest me. I'd seen them around the station house a few times since. They had been inside the scam. More of Mayor Teale's concealed troops.

I scrambled out of the truck again and took the flashlight back to the garage. Locked up the doors and ran through the rain to the front of the house. Scooped up the two bags they'd brought. Dumped them inside Hubble's hallway and hit the light. Looked through the bags. Spare gloves and masks. A box of 10-gauge shotgun shells. A hammer. A bag of six-inch nails. And four knives. Medical type of thing. They could cut you just looking at them.

I picked up the crowbar from where they'd dropped it after breaking the lock. Put it in one of the bags. Carried the bags down to the truck and hurled them in on top of the five bodies. Then I shut and locked the rear doors and ran through the lashing rain up to the house again.

I ran through and locked up the garden room. Ran back to the kitchen. I opened the oven door and emptied my pockets. Laid everything out on the floor. Found a couple of baking sheets in the next cupboard. I stripped down the Desert Eagle and laid the parts carefully on one of the trays. Piled the spare bullets next to them. Put the knife, the sap, the Bentley keys and my money and papers on the other tray. I put the trays in the oven and turned the heat on very low.

I went out the front and pulled the splintered door as far shut as it would go. Ran past the Bentley and got into the Kliner Foundation truck. Fiddled with the unfamiliar key and started it up. Reversed carefully down the driveway and swung backward out onto Beckman Drive. Rolled down the slope to town. The windshield wipers beat furiously against the rain. I skirted the big square with the church. Made the right turn at the bottom and headed south. The place was deserted. Nobody else on the road.

Three hundred yards south of the village green, I turned into Morrison's driveway. Drove the truck up to the house and parked it next to his abandoned Lincoln. Locked the door. Ran over to Morrison's boundary fence and hurled the keys far into the field beyond. Shrugged my jacket tight around me and started walking back through the rain. Started thinking hard.

Saturday was already more than an hour old. Therefore Sunday was less than a day away. The shape of the thing was clear. I had three facts, for sure. Fact one, Kliner needed special paper. Fact two, it wasn't obtainable in the States. But fact three, the warehouse was jammed with something.

And the writing on those air conditioner boxes was bothering me. Not the Island Air-conditioning, Inc. Not the printed bit. The other writing. The serial numbers. The boxes I'd seen had handwritten serial numbers in printed rectangles. I'd seen them quite clearly. The Jacksonville cops had described the same thing on the boxes in Stoller's speeding truck. Long handwritten serial numbers. But why? The boxes themselves were good cover. Good camouflage. Hauling something secret to Florida and beyond in air conditioner boxes was a smart move. No product was more plausible for the markets down there. The boxes had fooled the Jacksonville cops. They hadn't thought twice about it. But the serial numbers bothered me. If there were no electrical appliances in the boxes, why write serial numbers on them? That was taking camouflage to absurd lengths. So what the hell did the serial numbers mean? What the hell had been in those damn boxes?

That was the question I was asking myself. In the end, it was Joe who answered it for me. I was walking along in the rain thinking about what Kelstein had said about precision. He had said Joe had a very attractive precision about the manner in which he expressed himself. I knew that. I was thinking about the neat little list he'd printed out for himself. The proud capital letters. The rows of initials. The column of telephone numbers. The two notes at the bottom. Stollers' Garage. Gray's Kliner File. I needed to check the list again. But I was suddenly sure Joe was telling me if I wanted to know what Kliner had been putting into those boxes, it might be worth going up to the Stollers' garage and taking a look.

TWENTY-SEVEN

F IRST THING I DID BACK AT THE HOUSE WAS ROOT AROUND IN Charlie Hubble's expensive kitchen for coffee. Started the machine burbling away. Then I opened up the oven. Got all my things out. They had been warmed for the best part of an hour and they were bone dry. The leather on the sap and the key ring had stiffened up some. Other than that, no damage. I put the gun back together and loaded it. Left it on the kitchen table. Cocked and locked.

Then I checked Joe's computer printout for the confirmation I thought was there. But there was a problem. A major problem. The paper was bone dry and crisp, but the writing had gone. The paper was completely blank. The swimming pool water had washed all the ink off. There were very faint blurred smudges, but I couldn't make out the words. I shrugged to myself. I'd read it through a hundred times. I'd rely on my memory of what it had said.

Next stop was the basement. I fiddled around with the furnace until it kicked in. Then I stripped off and shoved all my clothes in Charlie's electric dryer. Set it on low for an hour. I had no idea what I was doing. In the army, some corporal had done my laundry. Took it away, brought it back clean and folded. Since then, I always bought cheap stuff and just junked it.

I walked upstairs naked and went into Hubble's bathroom. Took a long hot shower and scrubbed the mascara off my face.

Stood for a long time in the hot water. Wrapped myself up in a towel and went down for the coffee.

I couldn't go up to Atlanta that night. I couldn't get there before maybe three-thirty in the morning. That was the wrong time to be sure of talking my way inside. I had no ID to show and no proper status. A night visit could turn into a problem. I would have to leave it until tomorrow, first thing. No choice.

So I thought about sleeping. I turned the kitchen radio off and wandered through to Hubble's den. Turned the television off. Looked around. It was a dark, snug room. Lots of wood panelling and big leather chairs. Next to the television was a stereo. Some kind of a Japanese thing. Rows of compact discs and cassette tapes. Big emphasis on the Beatles. Hubble had said he'd been interested in John Lennon. He'd been to the Dakota in New York City and to Liverpool in England. He had just about everything. All the albums, a few bootlegs, that singles collection on CD they sold in a wooden box.

Over the desk was a bookshelf. Stacks of professional periodicals and a row of heavy books. Technical banking journals and reports. The professional periodicals took up a couple of feet of shelf space. They looked pretty deadly. Random copies of something calling itself the *Banking Journal*. A couple of issues of a solid magazine called *Bank Management*. One called *Banker. Banker's Magazine, Banker's Monthly, Business Journal, Business Week, Cash Management Bulletin, The Economist, the Financial Post*. All filed in line with the alphabet, all in neat date order. Just random copies, ranging back over the last few years. No complete sets. At the end of the row were some US Treasury Department dispatches and a couple of issues of something calling itself *World of Banking*. A curious collection. Seemed very selective. Maybe they were especially heavy issues. Maybe Hubble had read them through when he couldn't sleep.

I wasn't going to have any trouble sleeping. I was on my way out of the den, off to find a bed to borrow, when something occurred to me. I stepped back to the desk and peered at the bookshelf again. Ran my finger along the row of magazines and journals. Checked the dates printed on the spines, under the pompous titles. Some of them were recent issues. The random sequence continued right up to the latest issue of a couple of them. More than a dozen were from this year. Fully a third of them were published after Hubble had left his job at the bank. After he had been let go. They were published for bankers, but by then Hubble hadn't been a banker any more. But he had still been ordering up these heavy professional journals. He had still been getting them. Still reading all this complicated stuff. Why?

I pulled out a couple of the periodicals. Looked at the covers. They were thick, glossy magazines. I held them in my fingers at the top and bottom of the spines. They fell open at the pages Hubble had consulted. I looked at those pages. Pulled out some more issues. Let them fall open. I sat down in Hubble's leather chair. I sat there wrapped in his towel, reading. I read right through the shelf. From left to right, from beginning to end. All the periodicals. It took me an hour.

Then I started in on the books. I ran my finger along the dusty row. Stopped with a little shock when I spotted a couple of names I knew. Kelstein and Bartholomew. A big old volume. Bound in red leather. Their Senate subcommittee report. I pulled it out and started flicking through. It was an amazing publication. Kelstein had modestly described it as the anticounterfeiter's bible. And it was. He'd been too modest. It was totally exhaustive. It was a painstaking history of every known forging technique. Copious examples and instances were taken from every racket ever discovered. I hefted the heavy volume onto my lap. Read for another solid hour.

At first I concentrated on paper problems. Kelstein had said that paper was the key. He and Bartholomew had provided a long appendix about paper. It expanded on what he'd told me face to face. The cotton and linen fibres, the chemical colourant, the introduction of the red and blue polymer threads. The paper was produced in Dalton, Massachusetts, by an outfit called Crane and Company. I nodded to myself. I'd heard of them. Seemed to me I'd bought some Christmas cards made by them. I remembered the thick heavy card and the creamy rag envelopes. I'd liked them. The company had been making currency stock for the Treasury since 1879. For over a century, it had been trucked down to Washington under heavy guard in armoured cars. None had ever been stolen. Not a single sheet.

Then I flipped backward from the appendix and started looking at the main text. I piled Hubble's little library on his desk. Trawled through it all again. Some things I read twice, three times. I kept diving back into the untidy sprawl of dense articles and reports. Checking, cross-referencing, trying to understand the arcane language. I kept going back to the big red Senate report. There were three paragraphs I read over and over again. The first was about an old counterfeiting ring in Bogotá, Colombia. The second was about a much earlier Lebanese operation. The Christian Phalangists had teamed up with some Armenian engravers during an old civil war. The third was some basic stuff about chemistry. Lots of complicated formulas, but there were a few words I recognized. I read the three paragraphs time and time again. I wandered through to the kitchen. Picked up Joe's blank list. Stared at it for a long time. Wandered back to the dark quiet den and sat in a pool of light and thought and read halfway through the night.

It didn't put me to sleep. It had exactly the opposite effect. It woke me up. It gave me a hell of a buzz. It left me shaking with shock and excitement. Because by the time I had finished, I knew exactly how they were getting their paper. I knew exactly where they were getting it from. I knew what had been in those air conditioner boxes last year. I didn't need to go up to Atlanta and look. I knew. I knew what Kliner was stockpiling at his warehouse. I knew what all those trucks were bringing in every day. I knew what Joe's heading had meant. E Unum Pluribus. I knew why he'd chosen that reversed motto. I knew everything, with twenty-four hours still to go. The whole thing, from beginning to end. From top to bottom. From the inside out. And it was one hell of a clever operation. Old Professor Kelstein had said the paper was unobtainable. But Kliner had proved him wrong. Kliner had found a way of obtaining it. A very simple way.

I jumped up from the desk and ran down to the basement. Wrenched open the dryer door and pulled my clothes out. Dressed hopping from foot to foot on the concrete floor. Left the towel where it fell. Ran back up to the kitchen. Loaded up my jacket with the things I was going to need. Ran outside, leaving the splintered door swinging. Ran over the gravel to the Bentley. Started it up and threaded it backward down the drive. Roared off down Beckman and squealed a left onto Main Street. Gunned it through the silent town and out beyond the diner. Howled another left onto the Warburton road and pushed the stately old car along as fast as I dared.

The Bentley's headlights were dim. Twenty-year-old design. The night was patchy. Dawn was hours away and the last of the trailing storm clouds were scudding across the moon. The road was never quite straight. The camber was off and the surface was lumpy. And slick with storm water. The old car was sliding and wallowing. So I cut the speed back to a cruise. Figured it was smarter to take an extra ten minutes than to go ploughing off into a field. I didn't want to join Joe. I didn't want to be another Reacher brother who knew, but who was dead.

I passed the copse of trees. It was just a darker patch against the dark sky. Miles away, I could see the perimeter lights of the prison. They were blazing out over the night landscape. I cruised past. Then for miles I could see their glow in the mirror, behind me. Then I was over the bridge, through Franklin, out of Georgia, into Alabama. I rushed past the old roadhouse Roscoe and I had been in. The Pond. It was closed up and dark. Another mile, I was at the motel. I left the motor running and ducked into the office to rouse the night guy.

'You got a guest called Finlay here?' I asked him.

He rubbed his eyes and looked at the register.

'Eleven,' he said.

The whole place had that night look on it. Slowed down and silent and asleep. I found Finlay's cabin. Number eleven. His police Chevy was parked up outside. I made a lot of noise banging on his door. Had to keep banging for a while. Then I heard an irritated groan. Couldn't make out any words. I banged some more.

'Come on, Finlay,' I called.

'Who's there?' I heard him shout.

'It's Reacher,' I said. 'Open the damn door.'

There was a pause. Then the door opened. Finlay was standing there. I'd woken him up. He was wearing a grey sweatshirt and boxer shorts. I was amazed. I realized I had expected him to be sleeping in his tweed suit. With the moleskin vest.

'What the hell do you want?' he said.

'Something to show you,' I told him.

He stood yawning and blinking.

'What the hell time is it?' he said.

'I don't know,' I said. 'Five o'clock, six, maybe. Get dressed. We're going somewhere.'

'Going where?' he said.

'Atlanta,' I said. 'Something to show you.'

'What something?' he said. 'Just tell me, can't you?'

'Get dressed, Finlay,' I said again. 'Got to go.'

He grunted, but he went to get dressed. Took him a while. Fifteen minutes, maybe. He disappeared into the bathroom. Went in there looking like a normal sort of a guy, just woken up. Came out looking like Finlay. Tweed suit and all.

'OK,' he said. 'This better be damn good, Reacher.'

We went out into the night. I walked over to the car while he locked his cabin door. Then he joined me.

'You driving?' he said.

'Why?' I said. 'You got a problem with that?'

He looked irritable as hell. Glared at the gleaming Bentley.

'Don't like people driving me,' he said. 'You want to let me drive?'

'I don't care who drives,' I said. 'Just get in the damn car, will you?'

He got in the driver's side and I handed him the keys. I was happy enough to do that. I was very tired. He started the Bentley up and backed it out of the lot. Swung east. Settled in for the drive. He went fast. Faster than I had. He was a hell of a good driver.

'So what's going on?' he said to me.

I looked across at him. I could see his eyes in the glow from the dash.

'I figured it out,' I said. 'I know what it's all about.'

He glanced back again.

'So are you going to tell me?' he said.

'Did you call Princeton?' I asked him.

He grunted and slapped the Bentley's wheel in irritation.

'I was on the phone for an hour,' he said. 'The guy knew a hell of a lot, but in the end he knew nothing at all.'

'What did he tell you?' I asked him.

'He gave me the whole thing,' he said. 'He was a smart guy. History postgrad, working for Bartholomew. Turns out Bartholomew and the other guy, Kelstein, were the big noises in counterfeiting research. Joe had been using them for background.'

I nodded across at him.

'I got all that from Kelstein,' I said.

He glanced over again. Still irritable.

'So why are you asking me about it?' he said.

'I want your conclusions,' I told him. 'I want to see where you got to.'

'We didn't get to anywhere,' he said. 'They all talked for a year and decided there was no way Kliner could be getting so much good paper.'

'That's exactly what Kelstein said,' I told him. 'But I figured it out.'

He glanced over at me again. Surprise on his face. In the far distance I could see the glow of the prison lights at Warburton.

'So tell me about it,' he said.

'Wake up and figure it out for yourself, Harvard guy,' I said.

He grunted again. Still irritable. We drove on. We hurtled into the pool of light spilling from the prison fence. Passed by the prison approach. Then the fierce yellow glare was behind us.

'So start me off with a clue, will you?' he said.

'I'll give you two clues,' I said. 'The heading Joe used on his list. E Unum Pluribus. And then think about what's unique about American currency.'

He nodded. Thought about it. Drummed his long fingers on the wheel.

'E Unum Pluribus,' he said. 'It's a reversal of the US motto. So we can assume it means out of one comes many, right?'

'Correct,' I said. 'And what's unique about American banknotes, compared to any other country in the world?'

He thought about it. He was thinking about something so familiar he wasn't spotting it. We drove on. Shot past the stand of trees on the left. Up ahead, a faint glimmer of dawn in the east.

'What?' he said.

'I've lived all over the world,' I said. 'Six continents, if you count a brief spell in an air force weather hut in Antarctica. Dozens of countries. I've had lots of different sorts of paper money in my pocket. Yen, deutschmarks, pounds, lire, pesos, wons, francs, shekels, rupees. Now I've got dollars. What do I notice?'

Finlay shrugged.

'What?' he said.

'Dollars are all the same size,' I said. 'Fifties, hundreds, tens, twenties, fives and ones. All the same size. No other country I've seen does that. Anywhere else, the high-value notes are bigger than the small-value notes. There's a progression, right? Anywhere else, the one is a small bill, the five is bigger, the ten is bigger and so on. The biggest value bills are usually great big sheets of paper. But American dollars are all the same size. The hundred-dollar bill is the same size as the one-dollar bill.'

'So?' he asked.

'So where are they getting their paper from?' I asked him.

I waited. He glanced out of his window. Away from me. He wasn't getting it and that was irritating him.

'They're buying it,' I said. 'They're buying the paper for a buck a sheet.'

He sighed and gave me a look.

'They're not buying it, for God's sake,' he said. 'Bartholomew's guy made that clear. It's manufactured up in Dalton and the whole operation is as tight as a fish's asshole. They haven't lost a single sheet in a hundred and twenty years. Nobody's selling it off on the side, Reacher.'

'Wrong, Finlay,' I said. 'It's for sale on the open market.'

He grunted again. We drove on. Came to the turn onto the county road. Finlay slowed and swung left. Headed north toward the highway. Now the glimmer of dawn was on our right. It was getting stronger.

'They're scouring the country for one-dollar bills,' I said. 'That was the role Hubble took over a year and a half ago. That used to be his job at the bank, cash management. He knew how to get hold of cash. So he arranged to obtain one-dollar bills from banks, malls, retail chains, supermarkets, racetracks, casinos, anywhere he could. It was a big job. They needed a lot of them. They're using bank cheques and wire transfers and bogus hundreds and they're buying in genuine one-dollar bills from all over the US. About a ton a week.'

Finlay stared across at me. Nodded. He was beginning to understand.

'A ton a week?' he said. 'How many is that?'

'A ton in singles is a million dollars,' I said. 'They need forty tons a year. Forty million dollars in singles.'

'Go on,' he said.

'The trucks bring them down to Margrave,' I said. 'From wherever Hubble sourced them. They come in to the warehouse.'

Finlay nodded. He was catching on. He could see it.

'Then they got shipped out again in the air conditioner cartons,' he said.

'Correct,' I said. 'Until a year ago. Until the Coast Guard stopped them. Nice new fresh boxes, probably ordered from some cardboard box factory two thousand miles away. They packed them up, sealed them with tape, shipped them out. But they used to count them first, before shipping them.'

He nodded again.

'To keep the books straight,' he said. 'But how the hell do you count a ton of dollar bills a week?'

'They weighed them,' I said. 'Every time they filled a box, they stuck it on a scale and weighed it. With singles, an ounce is worth thirty bucks. A pound is worth four hundred and eighty. I read about all that last night. They weighed it, they calculated the value, then they wrote the amount on the side of the box.'

'How do you know?' he said.

'The serial numbers,' I said. 'Showed how much money was in the box.'

Finlay smiled a rueful smile.

'OK,' he said. 'Then the boxes went to Jacksonville Beach, right?'

I nodded.

'Got put on a boat,' I said. 'Got taken down to Venezuela.'

Then we fell silent. We were approaching the warehouse complex up at the top of the old county road. It loomed up on our left like the centre of our universe. The metal siding reflected the pale dawn. Finlay slowed. We looked over at the place. Our heads swivelled around as we drove past. Then we swung up the ramp onto the highway. Headed north for Atlanta. Finlay mashed the pedal and the stately old car hummed along faster.

'What's in Venezuela?' I asked him.

He shrugged across at me.

'Lots of things, right?' he said.

'Kliner's chemical works,' I said. 'It relocated there after the EPA problem.'

'So?' he said.

'So what does it do?' I asked him. 'What's that chemical plant for?'

'Something to do with cotton,' he said.

'Right,' I said. 'Involving sodium hydroxide, sodium hypochlorite, chlorine and water. What do you get when you mix all those chemicals together?'

He shrugged. The guy was a cop, not a chemist.

'Bleach,' I said. 'Bleach, pretty strong, specially for cotton fibre.'

'So?' he said again.

'What did Bartholomew's guy tell you about currency paper?' I asked him.

Finlay inhaled sharply. It was practically a gasp.

'Christ,' he said. 'Currency paper is mostly cotton fibre. With a bit of linen. They're bleaching the dollar bills. My God, Reacher, they're bleaching the ink off. I don't believe it. They're bleaching the ink off the singles and giving themselves forty million sheets of genuine blank paper to play with.'

I grinned at him and he held out his right hand. We smacked a high five and whooped at each other, alone in the speeding car.

'You got it, Harvard guy,' I said. 'That's how they're doing it. No doubt about that. They've figured out the chemistry and they're reprinting the blank bills as hundreds. That's what Joe meant. E Unum Pluribus. Out of one comes many. Out of one dollar comes a hundred dollars.'

'Christ,' Finlay said again. 'They're bleaching the ink off. This is something else, Reacher. And you know what this all means? Right now, that warehouse is stuffed full to the ceiling with forty tons of genuine dollar bills. There's forty million dollars in there. Forty tons, all piled up, waiting for the Coast Guard to pull back. We've caught them with their pants down, right?'

I laughed, happily.

'Right,' I said. 'Their pants are down around their ankles. Their asses are hanging out in the breeze. That's what they were so worried about. That's why they're panicking.'

Finlay shook his head. Grinned at the windshield.

'How the hell did you figure this out?' he asked.

I didn't answer right away. We drove on. The highway was hoisting us through the gathering sprawl of Atlanta's southern edge. Blocks were filling up. Construction and commerce were busy confirming the Sunbelt's growing strength. Cranes stood ready to shore up the city's southern wall against the rural emptiness outside.

'We're going to take this one step at a time,' I said. 'First of all, I'm going to prove it to you. I'm going to show you an air conditioner box stuffed with genuine one dollar bills.'

'You are?' he said. 'Where?'

I glanced across at him.

'In the Stollers' garage,' I said.

'Christ's sake, Reacher,' he said. 'It got burned down. And there was nothing in it, right? Even if there was, now it's got the Atlanta PD and fire chiefs swarming all over it.'

'I've got no information says it got burned down,' I said.

'What the hell are you talking about?' he said. 'I told you, it was on the telex.'

'Where did you go to school?' I asked him.

'What's that got to do with anything?' he said.

'Precision,' I said. 'It's a habit of mind. It can get reinforced by good schooling. You saw Joe's computer printout, right?'

Finlay nodded.

'You recall the second-to-last item?' I asked him.

'Stollers' garage,' he said.

'Right,' I said. 'But think about the punctuation. If the

303

apostrophe was before the final letter, it would mean the garage belonging to one person called Stoller. The singular possessive, they call it in school, right?'

'But?' he said.

'It wasn't written like that,' I said. 'The apostrophe came after the final letter. It meant the garage belonging to the Stollers. The plural possessive. The garage belonging to two people called Stoller. And there weren't two people called Stoller living at the house out by the golf course. Judy and Sherman weren't married. The only place we're going to find two people called Stoller is the little old house where Sherman's parents live. And they've got a garage.'

Finlay drove on in silence. Trawled back to his grade-school grammar.

'You think he stashed a box with his folks?' he said.

'It's logical,' I said. 'The boxes we saw in his own place were empty. But Sherman didn't know he was going to die last Thursday. So it's reasonable to assume he had more savings stashed away somewhere else. He thought he was going to live for years without working.'

We were just about into Atlanta. The big interchange was coming up.

'Loop around past the airport,' I told him.

We skirted the city on a raised ribbon of concrete. We passed near the airport. I found my way back to the poor part of town. It was nearly seven-thirty in the morning. The place looked pretty good in the soft morning light. The low sun gave it a spurious glow. I found the right street, and the right house, crouching inoffensively behind its hurricane fencing.

We got out of the car and I led Finlay through the gate in the wire fence. Along the straight path to the door. I nodded to him. He pulled his badge and pounded on the door. We heard the hallway floor creak. We heard bolts and chains snapping and clinking. Then the door opened. Sherman Stoller's mother stood there. She looked awake. Didn't look like we'd got her out of bed. She didn't speak. Just stared out at us.

'Morning, Mrs Stoller,' I said. 'Remember me?'

'You're a police officer,' she said.

Finlay held his badge out toward her. She nodded.

'Better come in,' she said.

We followed her down the hall into the cramped kitchen.

'What can I do for you?' the old lady asked.

'We'd like to see the inside of your garage, ma'am,' Finlay said. 'We have reason to believe your son may have placed some stolen property there.'

The woman stood silently in her kitchen for a moment. Then she turned and took a key off a nail on the wall. Handed it to us without a word. Walked off down the narrow hallway and disappeared into another room. Finlay shrugged at me and we went back out the front door and walked around to the garage.

It was a small tumble-down structure, barely big enough for a single car. Finlay used the key on the lock and swung the door open. The garage was empty except for two tall cartons. They were stacked side by side against the end wall. Identical to the empty boxes I'd seen at Sherman Stoller's new house. Island Air-conditioning, Inc. But these were still sealed with tape. They had long handwritten serial numbers. I took a good look at them. According to those numbers, there was a hundred thousand dollars in each box.

Finlay and I stood there looking at the boxes. Just staring at them. Then I walked over and rocked one out from the wall. Took out Morrison's knife and popped the blade. Pushed the point under the sealing tape and slit the top open. Pulled up the flaps on the top and pushed the box over.

It landed with a dusty thump on the concrete floor. An avalanche of paper money poured out. Cash fluttered over the floor. A mass of paper money. Thousands and thousands of dollar bills. A river of singles, some new, some crumpled, some in thick rolls, some in wide bricks, some loose and fluttering. The carton spilled its contents and the flood tide of cash reached Finlay's polished shoes. He crouched down and plunged his hands into the lake of money. He grabbed two random fistfuls of cash and held them up. The tiny garage was dim. Just a small dirty window-pane letting in the pale morning light. Finlay stayed down on the floor with his big hands full of dollar bills. We looked at the money and we looked at each other.

'How much was in there?' Finlay asked.

I kicked the box over to find the handwritten number. More cash spilled out and fluttered over the floor.

'Nearly a hundred thousand,' I told him.

'What about the other one?' he said.

I looked over at the other box. Read the long handwritten number.

'A hundred grand plus change,' I said. 'Must be packed tighter.'

He shook his head. Dropped the dollar bills and started swishing his hands through the pile. Then he got up and started kicking it around. Like a kid does with fall leaves. I joined him. We were laughing and kicking great sprays of cash all over the place. The air was thick with it. We were whooping and slapping each other on the back. We were smacking high tens and dancing around in a hundred thousand dollars on a garage floor.

Finlay reversed the Bentley up to the garage door. I kicked the cash into piles and started stuffing it back into the air conditioner box. It wouldn't all go in. Problem was the tight rolls and bricks had sprung apart. It was just a mess of loose dollar bills. I stood the box upright and crushed the money down as far as I could, but it was hopeless. I must have left about thirty grand on the garage floor.

'We'll take the sealed box,' Finlay said. 'Come back for the rest later.'

'It's a drop in the bucket,' I said. 'We should leave it for the old folks. Like a pension fund. An inheritance from their boy.'

He thought about it. Shrugged, like it didn't matter. The cash was just lying around like litter. There was so much of it, it didn't seem like anything at all.

'OK,' he said.

We dragged the sealed box out into the morning light. Heaved it into the Bentley's trunk. It wasn't easy. The box was very heavy. A hundred thousand dollars weighs about two hundred pounds. We rested up for a moment, panting. Then we shut the garage door. Left the other hundred grand in there.

'I'm going to call Picard,' Finlay said.

He went back into the old couple's house to borrow their phone. I leaned against the Bentley's warm hood and enjoyed the morning sun. Two minutes, he was back out again.

'Got to go to his office,' he said. 'Strategy conference.'

He drove. He threaded his way out of the untidy maze of little streets toward the centre. Spun the big Bakelite wheel and headed for the towers.

'OK,' he said. 'You proved it to me. Tell me how you figured it.'

I squirmed around in the big leather seat to face him.

'I wanted to check Joe's list,' I said. 'That punctuation thing with the Stollers' garage. But the list had gotten soaked in chlorinated water. All the writing had bleached off.'

He glanced across.

'You put it together from that?' he said.

I shook my head.

'I got it from the Senate report,' I said. 'There were a couple of little paragraphs. One was about an old scam in Bogotá. There was another about an operation in the Lebanon years ago. They were doing the same thing, bleaching real dollar bills so they could reprint the blank paper.'

Finlay ran a red light. Glanced over at me.

'So Kliner's idea isn't original?' he asked.

'Not original at all,' I said. 'But those other guys were very small scale. Very low-level stuff. Kliner built it up to a huge scale. Sort of industrial. He's the Henry Ford of counterfeiting. Henry Ford didn't invent the automobile, right? But he invented mass production.'

He stopped at the next red light. There was traffic on the cross street.

'The bleaching thing was in the Senate report?' he said. 'So how come Bartholomew or Kelstein didn't get it? They wrote the damn thing, right?'

'I think Bartholomew did get it,' I said. 'I think that's what he finally figured out. That's what the e-mail was about. He'd just remembered it. It was a very long report. Thousands of pages, written a long time ago. The bleaching thing was just one tiny footnote in a mass of other stuff. And it referred to very small-scale operations. No comparison at all with the volume Kliner's into. Can't blame Bartholomew or Kelstein. They're old guys. No imagination.'

Finlay shrugged. Parked up next to a hydrant in a tow zone.

TWENTY-EIGHT

PICARD MET US IN HIS DOUR LOBBY AND TOOK US OFF INTO A side room. We ran through what we knew. He nodded and his eyes gleamed. He was looking at a big case.

'Excellent work, my friends,' he said. 'But who are we dealing with now? I think we got to say all these little Hispanic guys are outsiders. They're the hired help. They're not concealed. But locally, we still got five out of the original ten hidden away. We haven't identified them. That could make things very tricky for us. We know about Morrison, Teale, Baker and the two Kliners, right? But who are the other five? Could be anybody down there, right?'

I shook my head at him.

'We only need to ID one more,' I said. 'I sniffed out four more last night. There's only the tenth guy we don't know.'

Picard and Finlay both sat up.

'Who are they?' Picard said.

'The two gatemen from the warehouse,' I said. 'And two more cops. The backup crew from last Friday.'

'More cops?' Finlay said. 'Shit.'

Picard nodded. Laid his giant hands palm down on the table.

'OK,' he said. 'You guys head back to Margrave right now. Try to stay out of trouble, but if you can't, then make the arrests. But be very careful of this tenth guy. Could be anybody at all. I'll be right behind you. Give me twenty minutes to go get Roscoe back, and I'll see you down there.'

We all stood up. Shook hands all round. Picard headed upstairs and Finlay and I headed back out to the Bentley.

'How?' he asked me.

'Baker,' I said. 'He bumped into me last night. I spun him a yarn about going up to Hubble's place looking for some document-ation, then I went up there and waited to see what would happen. Along came the Kliner kid and four of his pals. They came to nail me to Hubble's bedroom wall.'

'Christ,' he said. 'So what happened?'

'I took them out,' I said.

He did his thing of staring sideways at me at ninety miles an hour.

'You took them out?' he said. 'You took the Kliner kid out?'

I nodded. He was quiet for a while. Slowed to eighty-five.

'How did it go down?' he asked.

'I ambushed them,' I said. 'Three of them, I hit on the head. One of them, I cut his throat. The Kliner kid, I drowned in the swimming pool. That's how Joe's list got soaked. Washed all the writing off.'

'Christ,' he said again. 'You killed five men. That's a hell of a thing, Reacher. How do you feel about that?'

I shrugged. Thought about my brother Joe. Thought about him as a tall gawky eighteen-year-old, just off to West Point. Thought about Molly Beth Gordon, holding up her heavy burgundy leather briefcase, smiling at me. I glanced across at Finlay and answered his question with one of my own.

'How do you feel when you put roach powder down?' I asked him.

He shook his head in a spasm like a dog clearing its coat of cold water.

'Only four left,' he said.

He started kneading the old car's steering wheel like he was a baker making a pastry twist. He looked through the windshield and blew a huge sigh.

'Any feeling for this tenth guy?' he said.

'Doesn't really matter who it is,' I said. 'Right now he's up at the warehouse with the other three. They're short of staff now, right? They'll all be on guard duty overnight. Loading duty tomorrow. All four of them.'

I flicked on the Bentley's radio. Some big chrome thing. Some kind of a twenty-year-old English make. But it worked. It pulled in a decent station. I sat listening to the music, trying not to fall asleep.

'Unbelievable,' Finlay said. 'How the hell did a place like Margrave start up with a thing like this?'

'How did it start?' I said. 'It started with Eisenhower. It's his fault.'

'Eisenhower?' he said. 'What's he got to do with it?'

'He built the interstates,' I said. 'He killed Margrave. Way back, that old county road was the only road. Everybody and everything had to pass through Margrave. The place was full of rooming houses and bars, people were passing through, spending money. Then the highways got built, and air travel got cheap, and suddenly the town died. It withered away to a dot on the map because the highway missed it by fourteen miles.'

'So it's the highway's fault?' he said.

'It's Mayor Teale's fault,' I said. 'The town sold the land for the warehouses to earn itself some new money, right? Old Teale brokered the deal. But he didn't have the courage to say no when the new money turned out to be bad money. Kliner was fixing to use it for the scam he was setting up, and old Teale jumped straight into bed with him.'

'He's a politician,' Finlay said. 'They never say no to money. And it was a hell of a lot of money. Teale rebuilt the whole town with it.'

'He drowned the whole town with it,' I said. 'The place is a cesspool. They're all floating around in it. From the mayor right down to the guy who polishes the cherry trees.'

We stopped talking again. I fiddled with the radio dial and heard Albert King tell me if it wasn't for bad luck, he wouldn't have no luck at all.

'But why Margrave?' Finlay said again.

Old Albert told me bad luck and trouble's been his only friend.

'Geography and opportunity,' I said. 'It's in the right place. All kinds of highways meet down here and it's a straight run on down to the boatyards in Florida. It's a quiet place and the people who run the town were greedy scumbags who'd do what they were told.'

He went quiet. Thinking about the torrent of dollar bills rushing south and east. Like a storm drain after a flood. A little tidal wave. A small and harassed workforce in Margrave keeping it rolling on. The slightest hitch and tens of thousands of dollars would back up and jam. Like a sewer. Enough money to drown a whole town in. He drummed his long fingers on the wheel. Drove the rest of the way in silence.

We parked up in the slot nearest the station house door. The car was reflected in the plate glass. An antique black Bentley, worth a hundred grand on its own. With another hundred grand in the trunk. The most valuable vehicle in the State of Georgia. I popped the trunk lid. Laid my jacket on top of the air conditioner box. Waited for Finlay and walked up to the door.

The place was deserted apart from the desk sergeant. He nodded to us. We skirted the reception counter. Walked through the big quiet squad room to the rosewood office in back. Stepped in and closed the door. Finlay looked uneasy.

'I want to know who the tenth guy is,' he said. 'It could be anybody. Could be the desk sergeant. There's been four cops in this already.'

'It's not him,' I said. 'He never does anything. Just parks his fat ass on that stool. Could be Stevenson, though. He was connected to Hubble.'

He shook his head.

'No,' he said. 'Teale pulled him in off the road when he took over. He wanted him where he could see him. So it's not Stevenson. I guess it could be anybody. Could be Eno. Up at the diner? He's a bad-tempered type of a guy.'

I looked at him.

'You're a bad-tempered type of a guy, Finlay,' I said. 'Bad temper never made anybody a criminal.'

He shrugged. Ignored the jibe.

'So what do we do?' he said.

'We wait for Roscoe and Picard,' I said. 'We take it from there.'

I sat on the edge of the big rosewood desk, swinging my leg. Finlay paced up and down on the expensive carpet. We waited like that for about twenty minutes and then the door opened. Picard stood there. He was so big, he filled the whole doorway. I saw Finlay staring at him, like there was something wrong with him. I followed his gaze.

There were two things wrong with Picard. First, he didn't have Roscoe with him. Second, he was holding a government-issue .38 in his giant hand. He was holding it rock steady, and he was pointing it straight at Finlay.

TWENTY-NINE

'**Y**OU?' FINLAY GASPED.

Picard smiled a cold smile at him.

'None other,' he said. 'The pleasure's all mine, believe me. You've been very helpful, both of you. Very considerate. You've kept me in touch every step of the way. You've given me the Hubbles, and you've given me Officer Roscoe. I really couldn't have asked for anything more.'

Finlay was rooted to the spot. Shaking.

'You?' he said again.

'Should have spotted it Wednesday, asshole,' Picard said. 'I sent the little guy to Joe's hotel two hours before I told you about it. You disappointed me. I expected to be doing this scene way before now.'

He looked at us and smiled. Finlay turned away. Looked at me. I couldn't think of anything to say to him. I couldn't think about anything at all. I just looked at Picard's huge bulk in the doorway and had a strong feeling that this was going to be the last day of my life. Today, it would end.

'Get over there,' Picard said to me. 'Next to Finlay.'

He had taken two giant strides into the room and he was pointing the gun straight at me. I noticed mechanically that it was a new .38 with a short barrel. I calculated automatically that it would be accurate over such a short distance. But that a .38 couldn't be relied on to put a target down. And there were two of us and one

312

of him. And that Finlay had a weapon in a shoulder holster under the tweed jacket. I spent a fraction of a second weighing up the odds. Then I abandoned the calculation because Mayor Teale stepped through the open door behind Picard. He had his heavy cane in his left hand. But in his right hand he was carrying a police-issue shotgun. It was an Ithaca Mag-10. Didn't really matter where he was pointing it.

'Get over there,' Picard said to me again.

'Where's Roscoe?' I said to him.

He laughed at me. Just laughed and gestured with the gun barrel that I should stand up and move over next to Finlay. I heaved myself off the desk and stepped over. I felt like I was weighted down with lead. I clamped my lips and moved with the grim determination of a cripple trying to walk.

I stood next to Finlay. Teale covered us with the giant scatter gun. Picard darted his hand up under Finlay's jacket. Took the revolver out of his holster. Slipped it into the pocket of his own enormous jacket. The jacket flapped open under the weight. It was the size of a tent. He stepped sideways and patted me down. I was unarmed. My jacket was outside in the Bentley's trunk. Then he stepped back and stood side by side with Teale. Finlay stared at Picard like his heart was breaking.

'What's this all about?' Finlay said. 'We go back a long way, right?'

Picard just shrugged at him.

'I told you to stay away,' he said. 'Back in March, I tried to stop you coming down here. I warned you off. That's true, right? But you wouldn't listen, would you, you stubborn asshole? So you get what you get, my friend.'

I listened to Picard's growl and felt worse for Finlay than I did for myself. But then Kliner stepped in through the door. His bone-hard face was cracked into a grin. His feral teeth glittered. His eyes bored into me. He was carrying another Ithaca Mag-10 in his left hand. In his right hand, he was carrying the gun that had killed Joe. It was pointed straight at me.

It was a Ruger Mark II. A sneaky little .22-calibre automatic. Fitted with a fat silencer. It was a gun for a killer who enjoys getting close. I stared at it. Nine days ago, the end of that silencer had touched my brother's temple. There was no doubt about that. I could feel it.

Picard and Teale moved around behind the desk. Teale sat in the chair. Picard towered over his shoulder. Kliner was gesturing

Finlay and me to sit. He was using his shotgun barrel as a baton. Short jerky movements to move us around. We sat. We were side by side in front of the big rosewood desk. We stared straight at Teale. Kliner closed the office door and leaned on it. He held the shotgun one-handed, at his hip. Pointed at the side of my head. The silenced .22 was pointing at the floor.

I looked hard at the three of them in turn. Old Teale was staring at me with all kinds of hate showing in his leathery old face. He was shaken up. He looked like a man under terrible stress. He looked desperate. Like he was near collapse. He looked twenty years older than the smooth old guy I'd met on Monday. Picard looked better. He had the calm of a great athlete. Like a football star or an Olympic champion on a visit to his old high school. But there was a tightening around his eyes. And he was rattling his thumb against his thigh. There was some strain there.

I stared sideways at Kliner. Looked hard at him. But there was nothing on show. He was lean and hard and dried out. He didn't move. He was absolutely still. His face and body betrayed nothing. He was like a statue hewn from teak. But his eyes burned with a kind of cruel energy. They sneered at me out of his blank, bone-hard face.

Teale rattled open a drawer in the rosewood desk. Pulled out the cassette recorder Finlay had used on me. Handed it to Picard, behind him. Picard put his revolver down on the desk and fiddled with the stiff cords. He plugged in the power. Didn't bother with the microphone. They weren't going to record anything. They were going to play us something. Teale leaned forward and thumbed the intercom button on the desk. In the stillness, I heard the buzzer sound faintly outside in the squad room.

'Baker?' Teale said. 'In here, please.'

Kliner moved off the door and Baker came in. He was in his uniform. A .38 in his holster. He looked at me. Didn't grin. He was carrying two cassettes. Teale took them from him. Selected the second one.

'A tape,' he said. 'Listen up. You're going to find this interesting.'

He fiddled the cassette in and clicked the little door shut. Pressed play. The motor whirred and the speaker hissed. Underneath the hiss, I could hear a boomy acoustic. Then we heard Roscoe's voice. It was loud with panic. It filled the silent office.

'Reacher?' Roscoe's voice said. 'This is a message for you, OK?

314

The message is you better do what they tell you, or I'm in trouble. The message is if you're in any doubt about what kind of trouble, you should go back down to the morgue and pull Mrs Morrison's autopsy report. That's the kind of trouble I'm going to be in. So help me out, OK? End of message, Reacher.'

Her voice tailed off into the boomy hiss. I heard a faint gasp of pain as if she'd been roughly dragged away from the microphone. Then Teale snapped the recorder off. I stared at him. My temperature had dropped away to nothing. I didn't feel human any more.

Picard and Baker were looking at me. Beaming in satisfaction. Like they were holding the winning hole card. Teale clicked the little door open and took the tape out. Laid it on one side on the desk. Held up the other tape for me to see and then put it in the machine. Closed the little door again and pressed play.

'Another one,' he said. 'Listen up.'

We heard the same hiss. The same boomy acoustic. Then we heard Charlie Hubble's voice. She sounded hysterical. Like she had on Monday morning, standing out on her bright gravel driveway.

'Hub?' Charlie's voice said. 'This is Charlie. I've got the children with me. I'm not at home, you understand what that means? I've got to give you a message. If you don't come back, something will happen to the children. They tell me you know what that something is. It's the same thing they said would happen to you and me, but it'll be the children instead. So you have to come back straight away, OK?'

The voice ended on a rising note of panic and then died away in the boomy hiss. Teale stabbed the stop button. Took the tape out and placed it carefully on the edge of the desk. Right in front of me. Then Kliner walked around into my field of vision and spoke.

'You're going to take that with you,' he said to me. 'You're going to take it to wherever you've hidden Hubble and you're going to play it to him.'

Finlay and I looked at each other. Just stared at each other in blank astonishment. Then I snapped back and stared at Kliner.

'You killed Hubble already,' I said.

Kliner hesitated for a second.

'Don't try that shit,' he said. 'We were going to, but you got him out of the way. You're hiding him. Charlie told us.'

'Charlie told you?' I said.

'We asked her where he was,' he said. 'She promised us you'd be able to find him. She was most insistent about it. We had a knife

315

between her little girl's legs at the time. She became very anxious to convince us that her husband was not beyond our reach. She said you'd given him all sorts of advice and guidance. She said you'd given him all sorts of help. She said you'd be able to find him. I hope for everybody's sake she wasn't lying.'

'You killed him,' I said again. 'I don't know anything about it.'

Kliner nodded and sighed. His voice was low.

'Let's cut the crap,' he said. 'You're hiding him, and we need him back. We need him back right away. It's a matter of urgency to us. We've got a business to run. So we've got a number of options. We could beat it out of you. We discussed that. It's a tactical problem, right? But we figured you might send us off in the wrong direction, because time is tight right now. You might figure that was your best option, right?'

He waited for some kind of a comment from me. He didn't get one.

'So what we're going to do is this,' he said. 'Picard is going to go with you to pick him up. When you get wherever he is, Picard is going to call me. On my mobile. He knows the number. Then you all three come on back here. OK?'

I didn't respond.

'Where is he?' Kliner asked suddenly.

I started to speak, but he held up his hand and stopped me.

'Like I told you, let's cut the crap,' he said. 'For instance, you've been sitting there thinking as hard as you can. No doubt you were trying to figure some way you might be able to take Picard out. But you won't be able to do that.'

I shrugged. Said nothing.

'Two problems,' Kliner said. 'I doubt if you could take Picard out. I doubt if anybody could. Nobody ever has. And my mobile number isn't written down. It's in Picard's head.'

I shrugged again. Kliner was a smart guy. The worst sort.

'Let me add a couple of factors,' he said. 'We don't know exactly how far away Hubble is. And you're not going to tell us the truth about that. So I'll tell you what we're going to do. We're going to give you a time limit.'

He stopped talking and walked around to where Finlay was sitting. He raised the .22 and put the tip of the silencer in Finlay's ear. Pushed it in hard until Finlay was tilting over in his chair.

'The detective here is going in a cell,' he said. 'He's going to be handcuffed to the bars. If Picard hasn't called me by one hour before dawn tomorrow, I'm going to aim my shotgun into the

316

detective's cell and blow him apart. Then I'm going to make the delightful Officer Roscoe clean his guts off the back wall with a sponge. Then I'm going to give you another hour. If Picard hasn't called me by the time the sun comes up, I'm going to start in on the delightful Officer Roscoe herself. She'll end up in a lot of pain, Reacher. But first there will be a great deal of sexual interference. A great deal. You have my word on that, Reacher. It'll be very messy. Very messy indeed. Mayor Teale and I have spent a pleasant hour discussing just exactly what we're going to do to her.'

Kliner was forcing Finlay practically out of the chair with the pressure of the automatic in his ear. Finlay's lips were clamped. Kliner was sneering at me. I smiled at him. Kliner was a dead man. He was as dead as a man who has just jumped off a high building. He hadn't hit the ground yet. But he'd jumped.

'Understand?' Kliner said to me. 'Call it six o'clock tomorrow morning to save Mr Finlay's life, seven o'clock to save Miss Roscoe's life. And don't go messing with Picard. Nobody else knows my phone number.'

I shrugged at him again.

'Do you understand?' he repeated.

'I think so,' I said. 'Hubble's run away and you don't know how to find him, right? Is that what you're telling me?'

Nobody spoke.

'You can't find him, can you?' I said. 'You're useless, Kliner. You're a useless piece of shit. You think you're some kind of a smart guy, but you can't find Hubble. You couldn't find your asshole if I gave you a mirror on a stick.'

I could hear that Finlay wasn't breathing. He thought I was playing with his life. But old man Kliner left him alone. Moved across into my field of vision again. He had gone pale. I could smell his stress. I was just about getting used to the idea that Hubble was still alive. He'd been dead all week, and now he was alive again. He was alive, and hiding out somewhere. He'd been hiding out somewhere all week, while they looked for him. He was on the run. He hadn't been dragged out of his house on Monday morning. He'd walked out by himself. He'd taken that stay-at-home call and smelled a rat and run for his life. And they couldn't find him. Paul Hubble had given me the tiny edge I was going to need.

'What's Hubble got that you want so much?' I said.

Kliner shrugged at me.

'He's the only loose end left,' he said. 'I've taken care of every-thing else. And I'm not going out of business just because an ass-hole like Hubble is running around somewhere shooting his stupid mouth off. So I need him at home. Where he belongs. So you're going to get him for me.'

I leaned forward and stared right into his eyes.

'Can't your son get him for you?' I said, quietly.

Nobody spoke. I leaned forward some more.

'Tell your boy to go pick him up,' I said.

Kliner was silent.

'Where's your son, Kliner?' I asked him.

He didn't say anything.

'What happened to him?' I said. 'Do you know?'

He knew, but he didn't know. I could see that. He hadn't accepted it. He'd sent his boy after me, and his boy hadn't come back. So he knew, but he hadn't admitted it to himself. His hard face went slack. He wanted to know. But he couldn't ask me. He wanted to hate me for killing his boy. But he couldn't do that either. Because to do that would be to admit it was true.

I stared at him. He wanted to raise that big shotgun and blow me into a red dew. But he couldn't. Because he needed me to get Hubble back. He was churning away inside. He wanted to shoot me right then. But forty tons of money was more important to him than his son's life.

I stared into his dead eyes. Unblinking. Spoke softly.

'Where's your son, Kliner?' I said.

There was silence in the office for a long time.

'Get him out of here,' Kliner said. 'If you're not out of here in one minute, Reacher, I'll shoot the detective right now.'

I stood up. Looked around the five of them. Nodded to Finlay. Headed out. Picard followed me and closed the door quietly.

THIRTY

PICARD AND I WALKED OUT TOGETHER THROUGH THE SQUAD room. It was deserted. Quiet. The desk sergeant was gone. Teale must have sent him away. The coffee machine was on. I could smell it. I saw Roscoe's desk. I saw the big bulletin board. The Morrison investigation. It was still empty. No progress. I dodged around the reception counter. Pushed open the heavy glass door against its stiff rubber seal. Stepped out into the bright afternoon.

Picard signalled with the stubby gun barrel that I should get in the Bentley and drive. I didn't argue with the guy. Just headed across the lot to the car. I was closer to panic than I'd ever been in my whole life. My heart was thumping and I was taking little short breaths. I was putting one foot in front of the other and using every ounce of everything I had just to stay in control. I was telling myself that when I arrived at that driver's door, I better have some damn good idea about what the hell I was going to do next.

I got into the Bentley and drove up to Eno's diner. Reached around to the seat pocket and found the map. Walked over through the bright afternoon sun and pushed in through Eno's door. Slid into an empty booth. Ordered coffee and eggs.

I was screaming at myself to listen to what I'd learned through thirteen hard years. The shorter the time, the cooler you've got to be. If you've only got one shot, you've got to make it count. You

319

can't afford to miss because you screwed up the planning. Or because you ran out of blood sugar and got sick and dizzy in the small hours of the morning. So I forced the eggs down and drank the coffee. Then I pushed the empty mug and the plate aside and spread the map on the table. Started looking for Hubble. He could be anywhere. But I had to find him. I had one shot at it. I couldn't rush around from place to place. I had to find him inside my head. It had to be a thought process. I had to find him inside my head first and then go straight to him. So I bent over Eno's table. Stared at the map. Stared at it for a long time.

I spent the best part of an hour with the map. Then I folded it up and squared it on the table. Picked up the knife and the fork from the egg plate. Palmed them into my trouser pocket. Looked around me. The waitress walked over. The one with glasses.

'Planning a trip, honey?' she asked me.

I looked up at her. I could see myself reflected in her glasses. I could see Picard's huge bulk glowering in the booth behind me. I could just about feel his hand wrapping tight around the butt of his .38. I nodded at the woman.

'That's the idea,' I said. 'A hell of a trip. The trip of a lifetime.'

She didn't know what to say to that.

'Well, you take care, OK?' she said.

I got up and left one of Charlie's hundreds on the table for her. Maybe it was real, maybe it wasn't. It would spend just the same. And I wanted to leave her a big tip. Eno was getting a dirty grand a week, but I didn't know if he was passing much of it on. Probably not, looking at the guy.

'See you again, mister,' the one with glasses said.

'Maybe,' I said.

Picard pushed me out through the door. It was four o'clock. I hustled over the gravel to the Bentley. Picard followed me with his hand in his pocket. I slid in and fired it up. Eased out of the lot and scooted north up the old county road. Blasted the fourteen miles away in about twelve minutes.

Picard had made me use the Bentley. Not his own car. Had to be a reason for that. Not just because he wanted the extra leg-room. Because it was a very distinctive car. Which meant there was going to be extra insurance. I looked in the mirror and picked up a plain sedan. About a hundred yards behind. Two guys in it. I shrugged to myself. Slowed and glanced left at the warehouses at the top of the county road. Swooped up the ramp and round the cloverleaf. Hit the highway going as fast as I dared. Time was crucial.

The road skirted us around the southeast corner of the Atlanta sprawl. I threaded through the interchanges. Headed due east on I-20. Cruised on, with the two guys in their plain sedan a hundred yards back, mile after mile.

'So where is he?' Picard asked me.

It was the first time he'd spoken since leaving the station house. I glanced across at him and shrugged.

'No idea,' I said. 'Best I can do is go find a friend of his in Augusta.'

'Who's this friend?' he said.

'Guy called Lennon,' I said.

'In Augusta?' he said.

'Augusta,' I said. 'That's where we're going.'

Picard grunted. We cruised on. The two guys stayed behind us.

'So who is this guy in Augusta?' Picard said. 'Lennon?'

'Friend of Hubble's,' I said. 'Like I told you.'

'He doesn't have a friend in Augusta,' he said. 'Don't you think we check things like that?'

I shrugged. Didn't reply.

'You better not be bullshitting, my friend,' Picard said. 'Kliner wouldn't like that. It'll make it worse for the woman. He's got a cruel streak in him a mile wide. Believe me, I've seen him in action.'

'Like when?' I said.

'Lots of times,' he said. 'Like Wednesday, at the airport. That woman, Molly Beth. Screamer, he enjoys that. Like Sunday. Up at the Morrison place.'

'Kliner was there Sunday?' I said.

'He loved it,' Picard said. 'Him and his damn son. You did the world a favour, taking that kid out. You should have seen him on Sunday. We gave those two cops the day off. Didn't seem right they should off their own chief. The Kliners and I stood in for them. The old man loved every minute of it. Cruel streak, a mile wide, like I said. You better make sure I get to make that call on time, or your woman friend's in a lot of trouble.'

I went quiet for a moment. I'd seen the Kliner kid on Sunday. He'd picked his stepmother up from the coffee shop. About ten thirty. He'd been staring at me. He'd been on his way back from dismembering the Morrisons.

'Did old man Kliner shoot my brother?' I asked Picard.

321

'Thursday night?' he said. 'Sure. That's his weapon, the .22 with the suppressor.'

'And then the kid kicked him around?' I said.

Picard shrugged.

'The kid was berserk,' he said. 'Wrong in the head.'

'And then Morrison was supposed to clean up?' I said.

'Supposed to,' Picard grunted. 'Asshole was supposed to burn the bodies in the car. But he couldn't find Stoller's body. So he just left both of them there.'

'And Kliner killed eight guys in Louisiana, right?' I said.

Picard laughed.

'Eight they know about,' he said. 'That asshole Spirenza was on his back for a year. Looking for payments to a shooter. But there never was a shooter. Kliner did it all himself. Like a hobby, right?'

'You knew Kliner back then?' I said.

'I've always known Kliner,' he said. 'Got myself assigned as Spirenza's Bureau liaison. Kept everything neat and tidy.'

We drove on in silence for a mile or two. The two guys in the plain sedan kept station a hundred yards behind the Bentley. Then Picard looked at me.

'This guy Lennon?' he said. 'He's not another damn Treasury spook working for your brother, right?'

'Friend of Hubble's,' I said.

'Like hell,' he said. 'We checked, he's got no friends in Augusta. Hell, he's got no friends anywhere. He thought Kliner was his damn friend, giving him a job and all.'

Picard started chuckling to himself in the passenger seat. His giant frame was shaking with mirth.

'Like Finlay thought you were his friend, right?' I said.

He shrugged.

'I tried to keep him away,' he said. 'I tried to warn him off. So what should I do? Get myself killed on his behalf?'

I didn't answer that. We cruised on in silence. The plain sedan sat steady, a hundred yards back.

'We need gas,' I said.

Picard craned over and peered at the needle. It was nudging the red.

'Pull over at the next place,' he said.

I saw a sign for gas near a place called Madison. I pulled off and drove the Bentley over to the pumps. Chose the furthest island and eased to a stop.

'Are you going to do this for me?' I asked Picard.

322

He looked at me in surprise.

'No,' he said. 'What the hell do you think I am? A damn pump jockey? Do it yourself.'

That was the answer I wanted to hear. I got out of the car. Picard got out on the other side. The plain sedan pulled up close by and the two guys got out. I looked them over. They were the same two I'd scuffled with in New York, on that crowded sidewalk outside Kelstein's college. The smaller guy had his khaki raincoat on. I nodded amiably to the two of them. I figured they had less than an hour to live. They strolled over and stood with Picard in a knot of three. I unhooked the nozzle and shoved it in the Bentley's tank.

It was a big tank. Well over twenty gallons. I trapped my finger under the trigger on the nozzle so that it wouldn't pump at full speed. I held it in a casual backhand grip and leaned against the car as the gas trickled in. I wondered whether I should start whistling. Picard and the two Hispanics lost interest. There was a breeze coming up and they shuffled about in the slight evening chill.

I slipped Eno's flatware out of my pocket and pressed the tip of the knife into the tyre tread next to my right knee. From where Picard was standing, it looked like I was maybe rubbing my leg. Then I took the fork and bent one of the tines outward. Pressed it into the cut I'd made and snapped it off. Left a half inch sticking into the tyre. Then I finished up pumping the gas and latched the nozzle back into the pump.

'You paying for this?' I called to Picard.

He looked around and shrugged. Peeled a bill off his roll and sent the guy in the raincoat off to pay. Then we got back into the car.

'Wait,' Picard said.

I waited until the plain sedan had started up behind me and flashed its headlights twice. Then I moved out and accelerated gently back onto the highway and settled into the same steady cruise. Kept on going and the signs started flashing past. Augusta, seventy miles. Augusta, sixty miles. Augusta, forty miles. The old Bentley hummed along. Rock steady. The two guys followed. The setting sun behind me was red in the mirror. The horizon up ahead was black. It was already night far out over the Atlantic Ocean. We drove on.

The rear tyre went flat about twenty miles out from Augusta. It was past seven thirty and it was getting dark. We both felt the rumbling from the wheel and the car wouldn't track straight.

'Shit,' I said. 'Flat tyre.'

'Pull over,' Picard said.

I slewed to a stop well over on the shoulder. The plain sedan pulled over and stopped behind us. We all four got out. The breeze had freshened up to a cold wind blowing in from the east. I shivered and popped the trunk. Picked up my jacket and put it on, like I was grateful for the warmth.

'Spare wheel's under the trunk floor,' I said to Picard. 'Want to help me get this box out?'

Picard stepped over and looked at the box of dollar bills.

'We burned the wrong house,' he said, and laughed.

He and I heaved the heavy box out and set it on its end on the highway shoulder. Then he pulled his gun out and showed it to me. His huge jacket was flapping in the wind.

'We'll let the little guys change the wheel,' he said. 'You stand still, right there, next to the box.'

He waved the two Hispanics over and told them to do the work. They found the jack and the wrench for the bolts. Jacked up the car and took the wheel off. Then they lined up the spare and lifted it into place. Bolted it carefully on. I was standing there next to the carton of money, shivering in the wind, wrapping my coat tight around me. Thrusting my hands deep in the pockets and stamping from foot to foot, trying to look like a guy who was getting cold standing around doing nothing.

I waited until Picard stepped around to check the bolts were tight. He put his weight on the lever and I could hear the metal graunching. I came out with Morrison's switchblade already open and sliced up one side of the air conditioner box. Then across the top. Then down the other side. Before Picard could line up his gun, the box fell open like a steamer trunk and the wind caught a hundred thousand dollar bills and blew them all over the highway like a blizzard.

Then I dived over the concrete wall at the edge of the shoulder and rolled down the shallow bank. Pulled out the Desert Eagle. Shot at the guy with the raincoat as he came over the wall after me, but I missed my aim and just blew his leg away. Beyond him I saw a truck with dollar bills plastered all over its windshield run off the road and smash into the plain sedan behind the Bentley. Picard was batting away the snowstorm of cash and dancing over to the wall. I could hear tyres shrieking as cars on the highway braked and swerved to avoid the wreckage of the truck. I rolled

over and aimed up the bank and shot the second Hispanic guy.
Caught him through the chest and he came crashing down toward
me. The guy with the raincoat was rolling around at the top of the
slope, screaming, clutching his shattered leg, trying to free the
small automatic he'd shown me in New York. I fired a third time
and shot him through the head. I could see Picard aiming his .38
down at me. All the time the wind was howling and cars were
sliding to a stop on the highway. I could see drivers getting out
and jumping around, snatching at the money swirling in the air. It
was chaos.

'Don't shoot me, Picard,' I yelled. 'You won't get Hubble if you
do.'

He knew that. And he knew he was a dead man if he didn't get
Hubble. Kliner wouldn't tolerate failure. He stood there with his
.38 aimed at my head. But he didn't shoot. I ran up the bank and
circled the car, forcing him out toward the traffic with the Desert
Eagle.

'You don't shoot me, either,' Picard screamed. 'My phone call is
the only way you're going to save that woman. That's for sure. You
better believe it.'

'I know that, Picard,' I yelled back. 'I believe it. I'm not going to
shoot you. Are you going to shoot me?'

He shook his head over the .38.

'I'm not going to shoot you, Reacher,' he said.

It looked like a stalemate. We circled the Bentley with our
fingers white on the triggers, telling each other we weren't going
to shoot.

He was telling the truth. But I was lying. I waited until he was
lined up with the wreckage of the truck and I was next to the
Bentley. Then I pulled the trigger. The .44 shell caught him and
smashed his huge bulk backwards into the tangled metal. I didn't
wait around for a second shot. I slammed the trunk lid and jumped
for the driver's seat. Fired the car up and burned rubber. I peeled
away from the shoulder and dodged the people running around
after the dollar bills. Jammed my foot down and hurtled east.

Twenty miles to go. Took me twenty minutes. I was gasping
and shaky with adrenalin. I forced my heartbeat down and took
big gulps of air. Then I yelled to myself in triumph. Screamed and
yelled out loud. Picard was gone.

THIRTY-ONE

I T WAS DARK WHEN I HIT THE OUTLYING AUGUSTA SUBURBS. I
pulled off the highway as soon as the taller buildings started
to thicken up. Drove down the city streets and stopped at the
first motel I saw. Locked the Bentley up and dodged into the
office. Stepped over to the desk. The clerk looked up.

'Got a room?' I asked him.

'Thirty-six bucks,' the guy said.

'Phone in the room?' I asked him.

'Sure,' he said. 'Air conditioning and cable TV.'

'Yellow Pages in the room?' I asked him.

He nodded.

'Got a map of Augusta?' I said.

He jerked his thumb over to a rack next to a cigarette machine.
It was stuffed with maps and brochures. I peeled off thirty-six
bucks from the roll in my trouser pocket. Dropped the cash on the
desk. Filled in the register. I put my name down as Roscoe Finlay.

'Room twelve,' the guy said. Slid me the key.

I stopped to grab a map and hustled out. Ran down the row to
room twelve. Let myself in and locked the door. I didn't look at the
room. Just looked for the phone and the Yellow Pages. I lay on the
bed and unfolded the map. Opened up the Yellow Pages to H for
hotels.

There was a huge list. In Augusta, there were hundreds of
places where you could pay for a bed for the night. Literally

326

hundreds. Pages and pages of them. So I looked at the map. Concentrated on a wedge a half-mile long and four blocks deep, either side of the main drag in from the west. That was my target area. I downgraded the places right on the main drag. I upgraded the places a block or two off. Prioritized the places between a quarter-mile and a half-mile out. I was looking at a rough square, a quarter-mile long and a quarter-mile deep. I put the map and the phone book side by side and made a hit list.

Eighteen hotels. One of them was the place I was lying there in. So I picked up the phone and dialled zero for the desk. The clerk answered.

'You got a guy called Paul Lennon registered?' I asked him.

There was a pause. He was checking the book.

'Lennon?' he said. 'No, sir.'

'OK,' I said. Put the phone down.

I took a deep breath and started at the top of my list. Dialled the first place.

'You got a guy called Paul Lennon registered?' I asked the guy who answered.

There was a pause.

'No, sir,' the guy said.

I worked down the list. Dialled one place after another.

'You got a guy called Paul Lennon registered?' I asked each clerk.

There was always a pause while they checked their registers. Sometimes I could hear the pages turning. Some of them had computers. I could hear keyboards pattering.

'No, sir,' they all said. One after the other.

I lay there on the bed with the phone balanced on my chest. I was down to number thirteen out of the eighteen on my list.

'You got a guy called Paul Lennon registered?' I asked.

There was a pause. I could hear pages turning.

'No, sir,' the thirteenth clerk said.

'OK,' I said. Put the phone down.

I picked it up again and stabbed out the fourteenth number. Got a busy signal. So I dabbed the cradle and stabbed out the fifteenth number.

'You got a guy called Paul Lennon registered?' I asked.

There was a pause.

'Room one twenty,' the fifteenth clerk said.

'Thank you,' I said. Put the phone down.

I lay there. Closed my eyes. Breathed out. I put the phone back on the nightstand thing and checked the map. The fifteenth hotel was three blocks away. North of the main drag. I left the room key on the bed and went back out to the car. The engine was still warm. I'd been in there about twenty-five minutes.

I had to drive three blocks east before I could make a left. Then three blocks north before I could make another. I went around a kind of jagged spiral. I found the fifteenth hotel and parked at the door. Went into the lobby. It was a dingy sort of a place. Not clean, not well lit. It looked like a cave.

'Can I help you?' the desk guy asked.

'No,' I said.

I followed an arrow down a warren of corridors. Found room one twenty. Rapped on the door. I heard the rattle of the chain going on. I stood there. The door cracked open.

'Hello, Reacher,' he said.

'Hello, Hubble,' I said.

He was spilling over with questions for me, but I just hustled him out to the car. We had four hours on the road for all that stuff. We had to get going. I was over two hours ahead of schedule. I wanted to keep it that way. I wanted to put those two hours in the bank. I figured I might need them later.

He looked OK. He wasn't a wreck. He'd been running for six days and it had done him good. It had burned off that complacent gloss he'd had. Left him looking a little more tight and rangy. A bit tougher. More like my type of a guy. He was dressed up in cheap chainstore clothes and he was wearing socks. He was using an old pair of spectacles made from stainless steel. A seven-dollar digital watch covered the band of pale skin where the Rolex had been. He looked like a plumber or the guy who runs your local muffler franchise.

He had no bags. He was travelling light. He just glanced around his room and walked out with me. Like he couldn't believe his life on the road was over. Like he might be going to miss it to a degree. We stepped through the dark lobby and out into the night. He stopped when he saw the car parked at the door.

'You came in Charlie's car?' he said.

'She was worried about you,' I told him. 'She asked me to find you.'

He nodded. Looked blank.

'What's with the tinted glass?' he said.

I grinned at him and shrugged.

328

'Don't ask,' I said. 'Long story.'

I started up and eased away from the hotel. He should have asked me right away how Charlie was, but something was bothering him. I had seen when he cracked the hotel room door that a tidal wave of relief had hit him. But he had a tiny reservation. It was a pride thing. He'd been running and hiding. He'd thought he'd been doing it well. But he hadn't been, because I had found him. He was thinking about that. He was relieved and disappointed all at the same time.

'How the hell did you find me?' he asked.

I shrugged at him again.

'Easy,' I said. 'I've had a lot of practice. I've found a lot of guys. Spent years picking up deserters for the army.'

I was threading through the grids, working my way back to the highway. I could see the line of lights streaming west, but the on-ramp was like the prize at the centre of a maze. I was unwinding the same jagged spiral I'd been forced around on the way in.

'But how did you do it?' he said. 'I could have been anywhere.'

'No, you couldn't,' I said. 'That was the exact point. That's what made it easy. You had no credit cards, no driver's licence, no ID. All you had was cash. So you weren't using planes or rental cars. You were stuck with the bus.'

I found the on-ramp. Concentrated on the lane-change and nudged the wheel. Accelerated up the ramp and merged with the flow back toward Atlanta.

'That gave me a start,' I said to him. 'Then I put myself in your shoes, psychologically. You were terrified for your family. So I figured you'd circle around Margrave at a distance. You'd want to feel you were still connected, consciously or subconsciously. You took the taxi up to the Atlanta bus depot, right?'

'Right,' he said. 'First bus out of there was to Memphis, but I waited for the next one. Memphis was too far. I didn't want to go that far away.'

'That's what made it easy,' I said. 'You were circling Margrave. Not too close, not too far. And counterclockwise. Give people a free choice, they always go counterclockwise. It's a universal truth, Hubble. All I had to do was to count the days and study the map and predict the hop you'd take each time. I figure Monday you were in Birmingham, Alabama. Tuesday was Montgomery, Wednesday was Columbus. I had a problem with Thursday. I gambled on Macon, but I thought it was maybe too close to Margrave.'

329

He nodded.

'Thursday was a nightmare,' he said. 'I was in Macon, some terrible dive, didn't sleep a wink.'

'So Friday morning you came out here to Augusta,' I said. 'My other big gamble was you stayed here two nights. I figured you were shaken up after Macon, maybe running out of energy. I really wasn't sure. I nearly went up to Greenville tonight, up in South Carolina. But I guessed right.'

Hubble went quiet. He'd thought he'd been invisible, but he'd been circling Margrave like a beacon flashing away in the night sky.

'But I used a false name,' he said. Defiantly.

'You used five false names,' I said. 'Five nights, five hotels, five names. The fifth name was the same as the first name, right?'

He was amazed. He thought back and nodded.

'How the hell did you know that?' he said again.

'I've hunted a lot of guys,' I said. 'And I knew a little about you.'

'Knew what?' he said.

'You're a Beatles guy,' I said. 'You told me about visiting the Dakota building and going to Liverpool in England. You've got just about every Beatles CD ever made in your den. So the first night, you were at some hotel desk and you signed Paul Lennon, right?'

'Right,' he said.

'Not John Lennon,' I said. 'People usually stick with their own first name. I don't know why, but they usually do. So you were Paul Lennon. Tuesday, you were Paul McCartney. Wednesday, you were Paul Harrison. Thursday, you were Paul Starr. Friday in Augusta, you started over again with Paul Lennon, right?'

'Right,' he said. 'But there's a million hotels in Augusta. Conventions, golf. How the hell did you know where to look?'

'I thought about it,' I said. 'You got in Friday, late morning, coming in from the west. Guy like you walks back the way he's already seen. Feels safer that way. You'd been on the bus four hours, you were cramped up, you wanted the air, so you walked a spell, maybe a quarter-mile. Then you got panicky and dived off the main drag a block or two. So I had a pretty small target area. Eighteen places. You were in number fifteen.'

He shook his head. Mixed feelings. We barrelled on down the road in the dark. The big old Bentley loped along, a hair over the legal limit.

'How are things in Margrave now?' he asked me.

That was the big question. He asked it tentatively, like he was

330

nervous about it. I was nervous about answering it. I backed off the gas a little and slowed down. Just in case he got so upset that he grabbed at me. I didn't want to wreck the car. Didn't have time for that.

'We're in deep shit,' I told him. 'We've got about seven hours to fix it.'

I saved the worst part for last. I told him Charlie and the kids had gone with an FBI agent back on Monday. Because of the danger. And then I told him the FBI agent had been Picard.

There was silence in the car. I drove on three, four miles in the silence. It was more than a silence. It was a crushing vacuum of stillness. Like all the atmosphere had been sucked off the planet. It was a silence that roared and buzzed in my ears.

He started clenching and unclenching his hands. Started rocking back and forth on the big leather chair beside me. But then he went quiet. His reaction never really got going. Never really took hold. His brain just shut down and refused to react any more. Like a circuit-breaker clicking open. It was too big and too awful to react to. He just looked at me.

'OK,' he said. 'Then you'll have to get them back, won't you?'

I sped up again. Charged on toward Atlanta.

'I'll get them back,' I said. 'But I'll need your help. That's why I picked you up first.'

He nodded again. He had crashed through the barrier. He had stopped worrying and started relaxing. He was up on that plateau where you just did whatever needed doing. I knew that place. I lived there.

Twenty miles out from Augusta we saw flashing lights up ahead and guys waving danger flares. There was an accident on the other side of the divider. A truck had ploughed into a parked sedan. A gaggle of other vehicles were slewed all over the place. There were drifts of what looked like litter lying around. A big crowd of people was milling about, collecting it up. We crawled past in a slow line of traffic. Hubble watched out the window.

'I'm very sorry about your brother,' he said. 'I had no idea. I guess I got him killed, didn't I?'

He slumped down in the seat. But I wanted to keep him talking. He had to stay on the ball. So I asked him the question I'd been waiting a week to ask.

'How the hell did you get into all this?' I said.

He shrugged. Blew a big sigh at the windshield. Like it was

331

impossible to imagine any way of getting into it. Like it was impossible to imagine any way of staying out of it.

'I lost my job,' he said. A simple statement. 'I was devastated. I felt angry and upset. And scared, Reacher. We'd been living a dream, you know? A golden dream. It was a perfect, idyllic life. I was earning a fortune and I was spending a fortune. It was totally fabulous. But then I started hearing things. The retail operation was under threat. My department was under review. I suddenly realized I was just one pay cheque away from disaster. Then the department got shut down. I got canned. And the pay cheques stopped.'

'And?' I said.

'I was out of my head,' he said. 'I was so angry. I had worked my butt off for those bastards. I was good at my job. I had made them a fortune. And they just slung me out like suddenly I was shit on their shoe. And I was scared. I was going to lose it all, right? And I was tired. I couldn't start again at the bottom of something else. I was too old and I had no energy. I just didn't know what to do.'

'And then Kliner turned up?' I said.

He nodded. Looked pale.

'He had heard about it,' he said. 'I guess Teale told him. Teale knows everything about everybody. Kliner called me within a couple of days. I hadn't even told Charlie at that point. I couldn't face it. He called me and asked me to meet him up at the airport. He was in a private jet, on his way back from Venezuela. He flew me out to the Bahamas for lunch, and we talked. I was flattered, to be honest.'

'And?' I said.

'He gave me a lot of crap,' Hubble said. 'He was telling me to look at it as an opportunity to get out. He was saying I should dump the corporate thing, I should come and do a real job, make some real money, with him. I didn't know much about him. I knew about the family fortune and the Foundation, obviously, but I'd never met him face to face. But he was clearly a very rich and successful guy. And very, very smart. And there he was, sitting in a private jet, asking me to work with him. Not for him, with him. I was flattered and I was desperate and I was worried and I said yes.'

'And then?' I said.

'He called me again the next day,' Hubble said. 'He was sending the plane for me. I had to fly down to the Kliner plant in Venezuela to meet with him. So I did. I was only there one day. Didn't get to see anything. Then he flew me to Jacksonville. I was in the lawyer's office for a week. After that, it was too late. I couldn't get out.'

'Why not?' I asked him.

'It was a hell of a week,' he said. 'It sounds like a short time, right? Just a week. But he did a real job on me. First day, it was all flattery. All temptation. He signed me up to a huge salary, bonuses, whatever I wanted. We went to clubs and hotels and he was spending money like it was out of a faucet. Tuesday, I started work. The actual job was a challenge. It was very difficult after what I'd been doing at the bank. It was so specialized. He wanted cash, of course, but he wanted dollars only. Nothing but singles. I had no idea why. And he wanted records. Very tight books. But I could handle it. And he was a relaxed boss. No pressures, no problems. The problems started Wednesday.'

'How?' I said.

'Wednesday, I asked him what was going on,' he said. 'And he told me. He just told me exactly what he was doing. But he said now I was doing it too. I was involved. I had to stay quiet. Thursday, I was getting really unhappy. I couldn't believe it. I told him I wanted out. So he drove me down to some awful place. His son was there. He had two Hispanic guys there with him. There was this other guy chained up in a back room. Kliner said this was a guy who had stepped out of line. He told me to watch carefully. His son just kicked the guy to a pulp. All over the room, right in front of me. Then the Hispanic guys got their knives out and just hacked the poor guy apart. There was blood everywhere. It was horrible. I couldn't believe it. I threw up all over the place.'

'Go on,' I said.

'It was a nightmare,' Hubble said. 'I couldn't sleep that night. I thought I'd never sleep again, any night. Friday morning, we flew home. We sat together on the little jet and he told me what would happen. He said it wouldn't be just me who got cut up. It would be Charlie too. He was discussing it with me. Which of her nipples would he slice off first? Left or right? Then after we were dead, which of the children would he start with? Lucy or Ben? It was a nightmare. He said they'd nail me to the wall. I was shitting myself. Then we landed and he called Charlie and insisted we go to dinner with him. He told her we were doing business together. Charlie was delighted because Kliner is such a big deal in the county. It was a total nightmare because I had to pretend there was nothing wrong. I hadn't even told Charlie I'd lost my job. I had

333

to pretend I was still at the bank. And the whole evening that bastard was asking politely after Charlie and the children and smiling at me.'

We went quiet. I skirted around the southeast corner of Atlanta again, looking for the highway south. The big city glowed and glittered on the right. To the left was the dark empty mass of the rural southeast. I found the highway and accelerated south. Down toward one little dot in that dark empty mass.

'Then what?' I asked him.

'I started work at the warehouse,' he said. 'That's where he wanted me.'

'Doing what?' I said.

'Managing the supply,' he said. 'I had a little office in there, and I had to arrange to get the dollars, and then I'd supervise the loading and shipping.'

'Sherman Stoller was the driver?' I asked him.

'Right,' he said. 'He was trusted to do the Florida run. I'd send him out with a million dollar bills a week. Sometimes the gatemen did it if Sherman had a day off. But it was usually him. He helped me with the boxes and the loading. We had to work like crazy. A million dollars in singles is a hell of a sight. You've got no idea. It was like trying to empty a swimming pool with a shovel.'

'But Sherman was stealing, right?' I said.

He nodded. I saw the flash of his steel glasses in the glow from the dash.

'The money got counted properly in Venezuela,' he said. 'I used to get accurate totals back after about a month or so. I used them to cross-check my weighing formula. Many times, we were about a hundred grand down. No way had I made that kind of mistake. It was a trivial amount, because we were generating four billion in excellent fakes at the other end, so who cared? But it was about a boxful every time. That would be a large margin of error, so I figured Sherman was stealing the occasional box.'

'And?' I said.

'I warned him off,' Hubble said. 'I mean, I wasn't going to tell anybody about it. I just told him to take care, because Kliner would kill him if he found out. Might get me into trouble as well. I was already worried enough about what I was doing. The whole thing was insane. Kliner was importing a lot of the fakes. He couldn't resist it. I thought it made the whole thing way too visible. Teale was spending the fakes like confetti, prettying up the town.'

334

'And what about the last twelve months?' I asked him.

He shrugged and shook his head.

'We had to stop the shipping,' he said. 'The Coast Guard thing made it impossible. Kliner decided to stockpile instead. He figured the interdiction couldn't last. He knew the Coast Guard budget wouldn't stand it for long. But it just lasted and lasted. It was a hell of a year. The tension was awful. And now the Coast Guard's finally pulling back, it's caught us by surprise. Kliner figured it's lasted this long, it would last until after the election in November. We're not ready to ship. Not ready at all. It's all just piled up in there. It's not boxed yet.'

'When did you contact Joe?' I asked him.

'Joe?' he said. 'Was that your brother's name? I knew him as Polo.'

I nodded.

'Palo,' I said. 'It's where he was born. It's a town on Leyte. Philippine Islands. The hospital was converted from an old cathedral. I had malaria shots there when I was seven.'

He went quiet for a mile, like he was paying his respects.

'I called Treasury a year ago,' he said. 'I didn't know who else to call. Couldn't call the police because of Morrison, couldn't call the FBI because of Picard. So I called Washington and tipped off this guy who called himself Polo. He was a smart guy. I thought he'd get away with it. I knew his best chance was to strike while they were stockpiling. While there was evidence in there.'

I saw a sign for gas and took a last-minute decision to pull off. Hubble filled the tank. I found a plastic bottle in a trash can and got him to fill that, too.

'What's that for?' he asked me.

I shrugged at him.

'Emergencies?' I said.

He didn't come back on that. We just paid at the window and pulled back onto the highway. Carried on driving south. We were a half-hour from Margrave. It was approaching midnight.

'So what made you take off on Monday?' I asked him.

'Kliner called me,' he said. 'He told me to stay home. He said two guys would be coming by. I asked him why, and he said there was a problem at the Florida end and I had to go sort it out.'

'But?' I said.

'I didn't believe him,' he said. 'Soon as he mentioned two guys, it flashed into my mind what had happened down in Jacksonville that first week. I panicked. I called the taxi and ran.'

335

'You did good, Hubble,' I said. 'You saved your life.'

'You know what?' he said.

I glanced a question at him.

'If he'd said one guy, I wouldn't have noticed,' he said. 'You know, if he'd said stay home, a guy is coming by, I'd have fallen for it. But he said two guys.'

'He made a mistake,' I said.

'I know,' Hubble said. 'I can't believe it. He never makes mistakes.'

I shook my head. Smiled in the dark.

'He made a mistake last Thursday.'

The big chrome clock on the Bentley's dash said midnight. I needed this whole deal over and done by five in the morning. So I had five hours. If all went well, that was way more than I needed. If I screwed up, it didn't matter if I had five hours or five days or five years. This was a once-only thing. In and out. In the service we used to say: do it once and do it right. Tonight I was going to add: and do it quickly.

'Hubble?' I said. 'I need your help.'

He roused himself and looked over at me.

'How?' he asked.

I spent the last ten minutes of the highway cruise going over it. Over and over it, until he was totally solid. I swung off the highway where it met the county road. Blasted past the warehouses and on down the fourteen miles to town. Slowed as I passed the station house. It was quiet, lights off. No cars in the lot. The fire house next door looked OK. The town was silent and deserted. The only light showing in the whole place was in the barbershop.

I made the right onto Beckman and drove up the rise to Hubble's place. Turned in at the familiar white mailbox and spun the wheel through the curves up the driveway. Pulled up at the door.

'My car keys are in the house,' Hubble said.

'It's open,' I said.

He went to check it out. Pushed at the splintered door gingerly, with one finger, like it might be booby-trapped. I saw him go in. A minute later, he was back out. He had his keys, but he didn't walk round to the garage. He came back over to me and leaned into the car.

'It's a hell of a mess in there,' he said. 'What's been going on?'

'I used this place for an ambush,' I said. 'Four guys were tramping all over the place looking for me. It was raining at the time.'

He leaned down and looked in at me.

'Were they the ones?' he said. 'You know, the ones Kliner would have sent if I'd talked?'

I nodded.

'They had all their gear with them,' I said.

I could see his face in the dim glow from the old dials on the dash. His eyes were wide open, but he wasn't seeing me. He was seeing what he'd seen in his nightmares. He nodded slowly. Then he reached in and put his hand on my arm. Squeezed it. Didn't speak. Then he ducked back out and was gone. I was left sitting there, wondering how the hell I'd ever hated the guy a week ago.

I used the time to reload the Desert Eagle. I replaced the four shells I'd used out there on the highway near Augusta. Then I saw Hubble drive his old green Bentley around from the garage. The engine was cold and he was trailing a cloud of white vapour. He gave me a thumbs-up as he passed and I followed the white cloud down the driveway and down Beckman. We passed by the church and turned left onto Main Street in stately procession. Two fine old cars, nose to tail through the sleeping town, ready to do battle.

Hubble pulled up forty yards shy of the station house. Pulled in to the kerb just where I'd told him to. Killed his lights and waited, motor running. I wafted past him and nosed into the police department lot. Parked up in the end slot and got out. Left all four doors unlocked. Pulled the big automatic out of my pocket. The night air was cold and the silence was crushing. I could hear Hubble's motor idling from forty yards away. I unlatched the Desert Eagle's safety and the click sounded deafening in the stillness.

I ran to the station house wall and dropped to the ground. Slid forward until I could see in through the bottom of the heavy glass door. Watched and listened. Held my breath. I watched and listened long enough to be sure.

I stood up and clicked the safety back on. Put the gun back in my pocket. Stood there and made a calculation. The fire house and the station house stood together three hundred yards from the north end of Main Street. Further on up the road, Eno's was eight hundred yards away. I figured the earliest anybody could get to us would be maybe three minutes. Two minutes to react, and a minute for a fast jog up from Main Street. So we had three minutes. Halve that for a margin of safety, call it ninety seconds, beginning to end.

I ran out to the middle of the county road and waved a signal to

Hubble. I saw his car pull away from the kerb and I ran over to the fire house entrance. Stood to the side of the big red door and waited.

Hubble drove up and slewed his old Bentley in a tight turn across the road. Ended up at a right angle, just about lined up with the fire house entrance, facing away from me. I saw the car lurch as he slammed the shift into reverse. Then he hit the gas and the big old sedan shot backward toward me.

It accelerated all the way and smashed backwards into the fire house door. That old Bentley must have weighed two tons and it tore the metal door right off its mountings with no trouble at all. There was a tremendous crashing and tearing of metal and I heard the rear lights smash and the clang of the fender as it fell off and bounced on the concrete. I was through the gap between the door and the frame before Hubble slammed into drive and dragged clear of the wreckage. It was dark in there, but I found what I was looking for. It was clipped to the side of the fire truck, horizontally, at head height. A bolt cutter, a huge thing, must have been four feet long. I wrenched it out of its mountings and ran for the door.

Soon as Hubble saw me come out, he pulled a wide circle across the road. The back end of his Bentley was wrecked. The trunk lid was flapping and the sheet metal was crunched and screeching. But he did his job. He made the wide turn and lined up with the station house entrance. Paused for a second and floored the gas. Accelerated straight towards the heavy glass doors. This time head on.

The old Bentley smashed through the doors in a shower of glass and demolished the reception desk. Ploughed on into the squad room and stopped. I ran in right behind it. Finlay was standing in the middle cell. Frozen in shock. He was handcuffed by his left wrist to the bars separating him from the end cell. Well to the back. Couldn't have been better.

I tore and shoved at the wreckage of the reception counter and cleared a path behind Hubble. Waved him back. He spun the wheel and reversed into the space I'd cleared. I hauled and shoved the squad room desks out of the way to give him a clear run in front. Turned and gave him the signal.

The front end of his car was as bad as the back. The hood was buckled and the radiator was smashed. Green water was pouring out of the bottom and steam was hissing out of the top. The head-lights were smashed and the fender was rubbing the tyre. But

Hubble was doing his job. He was holding the car on the brake and speeding the motor. Just like I'd told him to.

I could see the car shuddering against the brake. Then it shot forward and hurtled toward Finlay in the middle cell. Smashed into the titanium bars at an angle and ripped them open like a swung axe on a picket fence. The Bentley's hood flew up and the windshield exploded. Torn metal clanged and screeched. Hubble came to a stop a yard short of where Finlay was standing. The wrecked car settled in a loud hiss of steam. The air was thick with dust.

I dived through the gap into the cell and clamped the bolt cutter on the link fixing Finlay's wrist to the bars. Leaned on the four-foot levers until the handcuffs sheared through. I gave Finlay the bolt cutter and hauled him through the gap and out of the cell. Hubble was climbing out of the Bentley's window. The impact had distorted the door and it wouldn't open. I pulled him out and leaned in and yanked the keys. Then we all three ran through the shattered squad room and crunched over the shards of plate glass where the big doors had been. Ran over to the car and dived in. I started it up and howled backward out of the lot. Slammed into drive and took off down the road towards town.

Finlay was out. Ninety seconds, beginning to end.

THIRTY-TWO

I SLOWED DOWN AT THE NORTH END OF MAIN STREET AND ROLLED gently south through the sleeping town. Nobody spoke. Hubble was lying on the rear bench, shaken up. Finlay was beside me in the front passenger seat. Just sitting there, rigid, staring out through the windshield. We were all breathing heavily. We were all in that quiet zone which follows an intense blast of danger.

The clock on the dash showed one in the morning. I wanted to hole up until four. I had a superstitious thing about four o'clock in the morning. We used to call it KGB time. Story was it was the time they chose to go knocking on doors. Four o'clock in the morning. Story was it had always worked well for them. Their victims were at a low ebb at that hour. Progress was easy. We had tried it ourselves, time to time. It had always worked well for me. So I wanted to wait until four, one last time.

I jinked the car left and right, down the service alleys behind the last block of stores. Switched the running lights off and pulled up in the dark behind the barbershop. Killed the motor. Finlay glanced around and shrugged. Going to the barber at one in the morning was no more crazy than driving a hundred-thousand-dollar Bentley into a building. No more crazy than getting locked in a cell for ten hours by a madman. After twenty years in Boston and six months in Margrave, there wasn't a whole lot left that Finlay was ever going to raise an eyebrow at.

340

Hubble leaned forward from the back seat. He was pretty shaken up. He'd deliberately driven into three separate crashes. The three impacts had left him battered and jarred. And drained. It had taken a lot to keep his foot jammed down on the gas, heading for one solid object after another. But he'd done it. Not everybody would have. But he was suffering for it now. I slid out of the seat and stood in the alley. Gestured Hubble out of the car. He joined me in the dark. Stood there, a bit unsteady.

'You OK?' I asked him.

He shrugged.

'I guess,' he said. 'I banged my knee and my neck hurts like hell.'

'Walk up and down,' I said. 'Don't stiffen up.'

I walked him up and down the dark alley. Ten paces up and back, a couple of times. He was pecking his stride on the left. Maybe the door had caved in and hit his left knee. He was rolling his head around, loosening the jarred muscles in his neck.

'OK?' I said.

He smiled. Changed it to a grimace as a tendon graunched.

'I'll live,' he said.

Finlay got out and joined us in the alley. He was coming round. He was stretching like he was waking up. Getting excited. He smiled at me in the dark.

'Good job, Reacher,' he said. 'I was wondering how the hell you were going to get me out. What happened to Picard?'

I made a gun with my fingers, like a child's mime. He nodded a sort of partner's nod to me. Too reserved to go any further. I shook his hand. Seemed like the right thing to do. Then I turned and rapped softly on the service door at the back of the barbershop. It opened up straight away. The older guy was standing there like he'd been waiting for us to knock. He held the door like some kind of an old butler. Gestured us in. We trooped single file down a passage into a storeroom. Waited next to shelves piled high with barber stuff. The gnarled old man caught up to us.

'We need your help,' I said.

The old guy shrugged. Held up his mahogany palm in a wait gesture. Shuffled through to the front and came back with his partner. The younger old guy. They discussed my request in loud rasping whispers.

'Upstairs,' the younger guy said.

We filed up a narrow staircase. Came out in an apartment above the shop. The two old barbers showed us through to the living

341

room. They pulled the blinds and switched on a couple of dim lamps. Waved us to sit. The room was small and threadbare, but clean. It had a cosy feel. I figured if I had a room, I'd want it to look like that. We sat down. The younger guy sat with us and the older guy shuffled out again. Closed the door. The four of us sat there looking at each other. Then the barber leaned forward.

'You boys ain't the first to hide out with us,' he said.

Finlay glanced around. Appointed himself spokesman.

'We're not?' he said.

'No sir, you're not,' the barber said. 'We've had lots of boys hiding out with us. And girls too, tell the truth.'

'Like who?' Finlay asked.

'You name it, we had it,' the old guy said. 'We've had farmworkers' union boys from the peanut farms. We've had farmworkers' union boys from the peach growers. We've had civil rights girls from the voter registration. We've had boys who didn't want their ass sent to Vietnam. You name it, we had it.'

Finlay nodded.

'And now you've got us,' he said.

'Local trouble?' the barber asked.

Finlay nodded again.

'Big trouble,' he said. 'Big changes coming.'

'Been expecting it,' the old guy said. 'Been expecting it for years.'

'You have?' Finlay said.

The barber nodded and stood up. Stepped over to a large closet. Opened the door and waved us over to take a look. It was a big closet, fitted with deep shelves. The shelves were stacked with money. Bricks and bricks of cash held together with rubber bands. It filled the closet from floor to ceiling. Must have been a couple of hundred thousand dollars in there.

'Kliner Foundation's money,' the old guy said. 'They just keep on throwing it at us. Something wrong with it. I'm seventy-four years old. Seventy years, people are pissing all over me. Now people are throwing money all over me. Something wrong with that, right?'

He closed the door on the cash.

'We don't spend it,' he said. 'We don't spend a cent we don't earn. We just put it in the closet. You boys going after the Kliner Foundation?'

'Tomorrow there won't be any Kliner Foundation,' I said.

The old guy just nodded. Glanced at the closet door as he

342

passed by and shook his head. Closed the door on us and left us alone in the small cosy room.

'Not going to be easy,' Finlay said. 'Three of us and three of them. They hold four hostages. Two of the hostages are children. We're not even certain where they're holding them.'

'They're at the warehouse,' I said. 'That's for sure. Where else would they be? No manpower available to hold them anyplace else. And you heard that tape. That boomy echo? That was the warehouse, for sure.'

'What tape?' Hubble asked.

Finlay looked at him.

'They had Roscoe make a tape for Reacher,' he said. 'A message. To prove they were holding her.'

'Roscoe?' Hubble said. 'What about Charlie?'

Finlay shook his head.

'Just Roscoe,' he lied. 'Nothing from Charlie.'

Hubble nodded. Smart move, Harvard guy, I thought. The image of Charlie being held down at a microphone with a sharp knife at her throat would have tipped Hubble right over the edge. Right off the plateau, back down to where panic would make him useless.

'The warehouse is where they are,' I said again. 'No doubt about it.'

Hubble knew the warehouse well. He'd been working up there most days for a year and a half. So we got him to go over and over it, describing the layout. We found paper and pencil and got him to draw plans. We went over and over the plans, putting in all the doors, the stairs, the distances, the details. We ended up with the sort of drawing an architect would have been proud of.

The warehouse stood in its own compound at the end of the row of four. It was very close in line with the third shed, which was a farmers' operation. There was a fence running between the two with just a path's width between it and the metal siding. The other three sides were ringed by the main fence running around the whole complex. That fence ran close to the warehouse across the back and down the far end, but there was plenty of space in front for trucks to turn.

The big roller door covered just about the whole of the front wall. There was a small staff door just around the far corner which gave on to the main floor. There was a cage just inside the staff door where the roller door winch was sited. Go in the staff door

343

and turn left, there was an open metal staircase running up to an office. The office was cantilevered way up into the top back corner of the huge shed, hanging there about forty feet above the main floor. The office had big windows and a railed balcony looking down into the shed for supervision. In back, the office had a door leading out to an external fire escape which was another open metal staircase bolted to the outside back wall.

'OK,' I said. 'Clear enough, right?'

Finlay shrugged.

'I'm worried about reinforcements,' he said. 'Guards on the exterior.'

I shrugged back.

'There won't be reinforcements,' I said. 'I'm more worried about the shotguns. It's a big space. And there are two kids in there.'

Finlay nodded. Looked grim. He knew what I was saying. Shotguns spray a cone of lead over a big wide angle. Shotguns and children don't mix. We went quiet. It was nearly two in the morning. An hour and a half to wait. We would leave at three-thirty. Get up there at four. My favourite attack time.

The waiting period. Like soldiers in a dugout. Like pilots before a raid. It was silent. Finlay dozed. He had done this before. Probably many times. He sprawled in his chair. His left arm hung over the side. Half of the shattered handcuff dangled from his wrist. Like a silver bracelet.

Hubble sat upright. He hadn't done this before. He just fidgeted around, burning energy. Couldn't blame him. He kept looking over at me. Questions in his eyes. I just kept on shrugging back at him.

Two-thirty, there was a knock on the door. Just a soft tap. The door opened a foot. The older of the two old barbers was there. He pointed a gnarled and trembling finger into the room. Aimed straight at me.

'Someone to see you, son,' he said.

Finlay sat up and Hubble looked scared. I signalled them both to stay put. Stood up and pulled the big automatic out of my pocket. Clicked the safety off. The old guy flapped his hand at me and fussed.

'You don't need that, son,' he said. 'Don't need that at all.'

He was impatient, beckoning me out to join him. I put the gun away again. Shrugged at the other two and went with the old guy.

344

He led me into a tiny kitchen. There was a very old woman in there, sitting on a stool. Same mahogany colour as the old guy, stick thin. She looked like an old tree in winter.

'This is my sister,' the old barber said. 'You boys woke her up, chattering.'

Then he stepped over to her. Bent down and spoke right in her ear.

'This is the boy I told you about,' he said.

She looked up and smiled at me. It was like the sun coming out. I caught a flash of the beauty she must have had, long ago. She held out her hand and I took it. Felt like thin wires in a soft dry glove. The old barber left us alone together in the kitchen. Stopped as he passed me.

'Ask her about him,' he said.

The old guy shuffled out. I still had the old lady's hand in mine. I squatted down next to her. She didn't try to pull her hand away. Just left it nestled there, like a brown twig in my huge paw.

'I don't hear so good,' she said. 'You got to lean close.'

I spoke in her ear. She smelled like an old flower. Like a faded bloom.

'How's this?' I said.

'That's good, son,' she said. 'I can hear that OK.'

'I was asking your brother about Blind Blake,' I said.

'I know that, son,' she said. 'He told me all about it.'

'He told me you knew him,' I said, in her ear.

'I sure did,' she said. 'I knew him real well.'

'Will you tell me about him?' I asked her.

She turned her head and gazed at me sadly.

'What's to tell?' she said. 'He's been gone a real long time.'

'What was he like?' I said.

She was still gazing at me. Her eyes were misting over as she trawled backwards sixty, seventy years.

'He was blind,' she said.

She didn't say anything more for a while. Her lips fluttered soundlessly and I could feel a strong pulse hammering in her bony wrist. She moved her head as if she was trying to hear something from far away.

'He was blind,' she said again. 'And he was a sweet boy.'

She was more than ninety years old. She was as old as the twentieth century. So she was remembering back to her twenties and thirties. Not to her childhood or her teens. She was remembering back to her womanhood. And she was calling Blake a sweet boy.

'I was a singer,' she said. 'And he played the guitar. You know that old expression, he could play the guitar just like ringing a bell? That's what I used to say about Blake. He would pick up that old instrument of his and the notes would just come tumbling out, faster than you could sing them. But each note was just a perfect little silver bell, floating off into the air. We'd sing and play all night long, then in the morning I'd lead him out into a meadow, and we'd sit under some old shade tree, and we'd sing and play some more. Just for the joy of it. Just because I could sing and he could play.'

She hummed a couple of bars of something under her breath. Her voice was about a fifth lower pitched than it ought to have been. She was so thin and fragile, you'd have expected a high, faltering soprano. But she was singing with a low, breathy contralto. I thought back with her and put the two of them in an old Georgia meadow. The heavy smell of wildflower blossom, the buzz of lazy noontime insects, the two of them backs against a tree, singing and playing for the joy of it. Belting out the wry, defiant songs that Blake had made up and that I loved so much.

'What happened to him?' I asked her. 'Do you know?'

She nodded.

'Two people on this earth know that,' she whispered. 'I'm one of them.'

'Will you tell me?' I said. 'I sort of came down here to find out.'

'Sixty-two years,' she said. 'I never told a soul in sixty-two years.'

'Will you tell me?' I asked her again.

She nodded. Sadly. Tears in her misty old eyes.

'Sixty-two years,' she said. 'You're the first person ever asked me.'

I held my breath. Her lips fluttered and her hand scrabbled in my palm.

'He was blind,' she said. 'But he was sporty. You know that word? Sporty? It means kind of uppity. Uppity with a smile and a grin is sporty. Blake was sporty. Had a lot of spirit and energy. Walked fast and talked fast, always moving, always smiling his sweet fool head off. But one time, we came out of a place in town here, walking down the sidewalk, laughing. Nobody else around but for two white folks coming towards us on the sidewalk. A man and a boy. I saw them and ducked off the sidewalk, like we were supposed to. Stood in the dirt to let them pass. But poor Blake was blind. Didn't see them. Just crashed into the white boy. A white boy, maybe ten years old, maybe twelve. Blake sent him flying into the dirt. White boy cut his head on a stone, set up such a hollering like you never heard. The white boy's daddy was there with him. I knew him. He was a big important man in this town. His boy was screaming fit to burst. Screaming at his daddy to punish the nigger. So the daddy lost his temper and set about Blake with his cane. Big silver knob on the top. He beat poor Blake with that cane until his head was just split open like a burst watermelon. Killed him stone dead. Picked up the boy and turned to me. Sent me over to the horse trough to wash poor Blake's hair and blood and brains off from the end of his cane. Told me never to say a word about it, or he'd kill me too. So I just hid out and waited until somebody else found poor Blake there on the sidewalk. Then I ran out screaming and hollering with the rest of them all. Never said a word about it to another living soul, that day to this.'

Big wet tears were welling out of her eyes and rolling slowly down her thin cheeks. I reached over and smudged them dry with the back of my finger. Took her other hand in mine.

'Who was the boy?' I asked her.

'Somebody I seen around ever since,' she said. 'Somebody I seen sneering around just about every day since, reminding me of my poor Blake lying there with his head split open.'

'Who was he?' I said.

'It was an accident,' she said. 'Anybody could have seen that. Poor Blake was a blind man. Boy didn't have to set up such a hollering. He wasn't hurt so bad. He was old enough to know better. It was his fault for hollering and screaming like he did.'

'Who was the boy?' I asked her again.

She turned to me and stared into my eyes. Told me the sixty-two-year-old secret.

'Grover Teale,' she said. 'Grew up to be mayor, just like his old daddy. Thinks he's king of the damn world, but he's just a screaming brat who got my poor Blake killed for no reason at all except he was blind and he was black.'

THIRTY-THREE

WE PILED BACK INTO CHARLIE'S BLACK BENTLEY IN THE alley behind the barbershop. Nobody spoke. I fired it up. Swung out and rolled north. Kept the lights off and drove slow. The big dark sedan rolled north through the night like a stealthy animal leaving its lair. Like a big black submarine slipping its mooring and gliding out into icy water. I drove through the town and pulled up shy of the station house. Quiet as a tomb.

'I want to get a weapon,' Finlay said.

We picked our way through the shattered wreckage of the entrance. Hubble's own Bentley was sitting in the squad room, inert in the gloom. The front tyres had blown and it had settled nose-down, buried in the wreckage of the cells. There was a stink of gasoline. The tank must have split. The trunk lid was up because of the way the rear end was smashed in. Hubble didn't even glance at it.

Finlay picked his way past the wrecked car to the big office in back. Disappeared inside. I waited with Hubble in the heap of shards that had been the entrance doors. Finlay came back out of the dark with a stainless-steel revolver and a book of matches. And a grin. He waved the two of us out to the car and struck a match. Threw it under the rear of the wrecked green Bentley and crunched on out to join us.

'Diversion, right?' he said.

We saw the fire start as we nosed out of the lot. Bright blue

348

flames were rolling across the carpet like a wave on the beach. The fire took hold of the splintered wood and rolled outward, feeding itself on the huge gasoline stain. The flames changed to yellow and orange and the air started sucking in through the hole where the entrance had been. Within a minute, the whole place was burning. I smiled and took off up the county road.

I used headlights for most of the fourteen miles. Drove fast. Took maybe twelve minutes. Doused the lights and pulled up a quarter-mile short of the target. Turned around in the road and backed up a little way. Left the car facing south. Down towards town. Doors unlocked. Keys in.

Hubble carried the big bolt cutter. Finlay checked the revolver he'd taken from the office. I reached under the seat and pulled out the plastic bottle we'd filled with gas. Slipped it into my pocket with the blackjack. It was heavy. Pulled my jacket down on the right and brought the Desert Eagle up high on my chest. Finlay gave me the matches. I put them in the other pocket.

We stood together in the dark in the dirt on the side of the road. Exchanged tight nods. Struck out over the field to the blasted tree. It was silhouetted against the moon. Took us a couple of minutes to get there. We slogged over the soft earth. Paused against the distorted tree trunk. I took the bolt cutter from Hubble and we nodded again and headed for the fence where it ran close to the back of the warehouse. It was ten to four in the morning. Nobody had spoken since leaving the burning police building.

It was seventy-five yards from the tree to the fence. Took us a minute. We kept on going until we were opposite the bottom of the fire escape. Right where it was bolted down to the concrete path which ran around the whole building. Finlay and Hubble grabbed the chain link to put some tension on it and I bit through each strand in turn with the bolt cutter. Went through it like it was liquorice. I cut a big piece out, seven feet high, right up to where the razor wire started, maybe eight feet wide.

We stepped through the gap. Walked over to the bottom of the stairs. Waited. I could hear sounds inside. Movement and scraping, muffled to a dull boom by the huge space. I took a deep breath. Motioned the others to flatten themselves against the metal siding. I still wasn't sure about exterior guards. My gut said there wouldn't be any reinforcements. But Finlay was worried about it. And I'd learned a long time ago to take account of what people like Finlay worried about.

So I motioned the others to stay put and I crept around to the corner of the massive building. Crouched down and dropped the bolt cutter onto the concrete path from a height of about a foot. It made just about the right amount of noise. It sounded like somebody trying to break into the compound. I flattened myself against the wall and waited with the blackjack in my right hand.

Finlay was right. There was an exterior guard. And I was right. There were no reinforcements. The exterior guard was Sergeant Baker. He was on duty patrolling outside the shed. I heard him before I saw him. I heard his tense breathing and his feet on the concrete. He came around the corner of the building and stopped a yard away from me. He stood and stared at the bolt cutter. He had his .38 in his hand. He looked at the bolt cutter and then swung his gaze along the fence as far as the missing panel. Then he started to run towards it.

Then he died. I swung the sap and hit him. But he didn't go down. He dropped his revolver. Danced a circle on rubber legs. Finlay came up behind me. Caught him by the throat. Looked like a country boy wringing a chicken's neck. Made a fine job of it. Baker was still wearing his acetate nameplate above his uniform pocket. First thing I'd noticed, nine days ago. We left his body on the path. Waited five minutes. Listened hard. Nobody else came.

We went back to where Hubble was waiting. I took another deep breath. Stepped onto the fire escape. Went up. Planted each foot carefully and silently on each step. Eased my way up. The staircase was cast from some kind of iron or steel. Open treads. The whole thing would ring like a damn bell if we were clumsy. Finlay was behind me, gripping the handrail with his right hand, gun in his left. Behind him came Hubble, too scared to breathe.

We crept up. Took us minutes to do the forty feet. We were very cautious. We stood on the little platform at the top. I pressed my ear to the door. Quiet. No sound. Hubble pulled out his office keys. Clenched in his hand to stop them jingling. He selected the right one, slowly, carefully. Inched it into the lock. We held our breath. He turned the key. The lock clicked back. The door sagged open. We held our breath. No sound. No reaction. Quiet. Hubble eased the door back, slowly, carefully. Finlay took it from him and eased it further. Passed it to me. I eased it back flat against the wall. Propped it all the way open with the bottle of gasoline from my pocket.

Light was flooding out of the office, spilling over the fire escape and laying a bright bar down on the fence and the field forty feet below. Arc lamps were lit inside the body of the warehouse and they were flooding in through the big office windows. I could see everything in the office. And what I saw made my heart stop.

I'd never believed in luck. Never had any cause to. Never relied on it, because I never could. But now I was lucky in a big way. Thirty-six years of bad luck and trouble were wiped away in one single bright glance. The gods were sitting on my shoulder, whooping and driving me on. In that one single bright glance, I knew that I had won.

Because the children were asleep on the office floor. Hubble's kids. Ben and Lucy. Sprawled out on a pile of empty burlap sacks. Fast asleep, wide open and innocent like only sleeping children can be. They were filthy and ragged. Still dressed in their school clothes from Monday. They looked like ragamuffins in a sepia picture of old New York. Sprawled out, fast asleep. Four o'clock in the morning. My lucky time.

The children had been worrying the hell out of me. They were what made this whole damn thing just about impossible. I'd thought it through a thousand times. I'd run war-games through my head, trying to find one that would work. I hadn't found one. I'd always come up with some kind of a bad outcome. What the staff colleges call unsatisfactory results. I'd always come up with the children splattered all over the place by the big shotguns. Children and shotguns don't mix. And I'd always visualized the four hostages and the two shotguns in the same place at the same time. I'd visualized panicking children and Charlie screaming and the big Ithacas booming. All in the same place. I hadn't come up with any kind of a solution. If I could have given anything I ever had or ever would have, I'd have given it to have the children fast asleep somewhere else on their own. And it had happened. It had happened. The elation roared in my ears like a hysterical crowd in a huge stadium.

I turned to the other two. Cupped a hand behind each of their heads and pulled them close to mine. Spoke in the faintest of whispers.

'Hubble, take the girl,' I whispered. 'Finlay, take the boy. Put a hand over their mouths. No sound at all. Carry them back to the tree. Hubble, take them on back to the car. Stay there with them and wait. Finlay, come back here. Do it now. Do it quietly.'

I pulled out the Desert Eagle and clicked the safety off. Clamped my wrist against the door frame and aimed across the office at the inner door. Finlay and Hubble crept into the office.

They did it right. They kept low. They kept quiet. They clamped their palms over the little mouths. Scooped the children up. Crept back out. Straightened up and looped past the barrel of my big .44. The children woke up and struggled. Their wide eyes stared at me. Hubble and Finlay carried them to the top of the long staircase. Eased their way quietly down. I backed out of the doorway to the far corner of the metal platform. Found an angle to cover them all the way. Watched them pick their way slowly down the fire escape, to the ground, to the fence, through the gap and away. They stepped through the bright bar of light spilling over the field, forty feet below me, and vanished into the night.

I relaxed. Lowered the gun. Listened hard. Heard nothing but the faint noises scraping up from inside the huge metal shed. I crept into the office. Crawled over the floor to the windows. Slowly raised my head up and looked out and down. Saw a sight I would never ever forget.

There were a hundred arc lights bolted up inside the roof of the warehouse. They lit the place up brighter than day. It was a big space. Must have been a hundred feet long, maybe eighty deep. Maybe sixty feet high. And it was full of dollar bills. A gigantic dune of money filled the whole shed. It was piled maybe fifty feet high into the back far corner. It sloped down to the floor like a mountainside. It was a mountain of cash. It reared up like a gigantic green iceberg. It was huge.

I saw Teale at the far end of the shed. He was sitting on the lower slope of the mountain, maybe ten feet up. Shotgun across his knees. He was dwarfed by the huge green pile rearing above him. Fifty feet closer to me, I saw old man Kliner. Sitting higher up on the slope. Sitting on forty tons of money. Shotgun across his knees.

The two shotguns were triangulated on Roscoe and Charlie Hubble. They were tiny figures forty feet below me. They were being made to work. Roscoe had a snow shovel. One of those curved things they use in the snow states to clear their driveways. She was pushing drifts of dollars toward Charlie. Charlie was scooping them into air conditioner cartons and tamping them in firmly with a garden rake. There was a line of sealed boxes behind the two women. In front of them was the huge stockpile. They toiled away far below me, dwarfed like two ants below the mountain of dollar bills.

I held my breath. I was transfixed. It was an utterly unbelievable sight. I could see Kliner's black pickup truck. It was backed in, just inside the roller door. Next to it was Teale's white Cadillac. Both were big automobiles. But they were nothing next to the mountain of cash. They were just like toys on the beach. It was awesome. It was a fantastic scene from a fairy tale. Like a huge underground cavern in an emerald mine from some glittering fable. All brightly lit by the hundred arc lights. Tiny figures far below. I couldn't believe it. Hubble had said a million dollars in singles was a hell of a sight. I was looking at forty million. It was the height of the drift that did it to me. It towered way up. Ten times higher than the two tiny figures working at floor level. Higher than a house. Higher than two houses. It was incredible. It was a huge warehouse. And it was full of a solid mass of money. Full of forty million genuine one-dollar bills.

The two women were moving with the dullness of extreme fatigue, like exhausted troopers at the end of some cruel manoeuvre. Asleep on their feet, moving about automatically while their minds screamed for rest. They were packing armful after armful of dollars from the gigantic stockpile into the boxes. It was a hopeless task. The Coast Guard retreat had caught Kliner by surprise. He wasn't ready. The warehouse was hopelessly jammed. Roscoe and Charlie were being worked like exhausted slaves. Teale and Kliner were watching them like overseers, list-lessly, like they knew they were at the end of the road. The enormous drift of cash was going to bury them. It was going to engulf them and choke them to death.

I heard the faint clang of Finlay's feet on the fire escape. I crawled back out of the office and met him on the metal platform outside.

'They're back at the car,' he whispered to me. 'How we doing here?'

'Two shotguns out and ready,' I whispered. 'Roscoe and Charlie look OK.'

He glanced in towards the bright light and the faint noises.

'What are they all doing in there?' he asked me in a whisper.

'Come take a look,' I said softly. 'But hold your breath.'

We crawled in together. Crawled over the floor to the windows. Slowly popped our heads up. Finlay looked down at the fantastic scene below. He stared down for a long time. His eyes flicked all over the place. Ended up staring at me. Holding his breath.

'Christ,' he whispered.

I nodded him back out. We crawled to the fire escape platform.

'Christ,' he whispered again. 'Can you believe that?'

I shook my head.

'No,' I whispered back to him. 'I can't believe it.'

'What are we going to do?' he asked me.

I held my hand up to make Finlay wait on the platform. Crawled back inside and peered down through the window. I looked all over the place. Looked at where Teale was sitting, looked at the office inner door, checked Kliner's field of fire, guessed where Roscoe and Charlie might end up. I calculated angles and estimated distances. I came up with one definite conclusion. It was a hell of a problem.

Old man Kliner was the nearest person to us. Roscoe and Charlie were working between him and Teale. Teale was the dangerous one because he was at the far end of the warehouse. When I came out at the top of the inside stairs, they were all four going to look up at me. Kliner was going to raise his shotgun. Teale was going to raise his shotgun. They were both going to shoot at me.

Kliner had a straight shot, sixty degrees upward, like a duck hunter. But Roscoe and Charlie were down there between Teale and me. Teale was going to be shooting on a fairly shallow angle. He was already perched ten feet up the slope. He would be looking for another thirty feet of elevation from a distance of a hundred feet. A shallow angle. Maybe fifteen or twenty degrees. His big Ithaca was designed to cover a much wider spread than fifteen or twenty degrees. His shot was going to catch the women in a murderous spray. His shot was going to kill them. When Teale looked up at me and fired, Roscoe and Charlie were going to die.

I crawled back out of the office and joined Finlay on the fire escape. Bent down and picked up the plastic bottle of gasoline. Handed it to him with the matchbook. Leaned close and told him what to do. We whispered together and he set off slowly back down the long flight of metal steps. I crawled through the office and laid the Desert Eagle carefully on the floor by the inner door. Safety off. Crawled back under the window. Eased my head up and waited.

Three minutes went by. I was staring at the far end of the roller door. Staring and waiting. Watching the crack between the bottom of the door and the concrete, right at the far end, diagonally opposite me across the whole huge space. I stared and waited.

Four minutes had gone by. The tiny figures below toiled on. Roscoe and Charlie stuffing boxes, under Teale's careful gaze. Kliner clambering his way over the mountainside to kick a new river of dollars down the slope toward the women. Five minutes had gone by. Kliner had put his shotgun down. He was thirty feet away from it, scrabbling in the pile, starting a small avalanche which rolled down to Roscoe's feet. Six minutes had gone by. Seven.

Then I saw the dark wet stain of gasoline seeping under the roller door. It flowed into a semicircular pool. It kept coming. It reached the bottom of the enormous dune of dollars, ten feet below where Teale was sprawled on the lower slopes. It kept growing outward. A dark stain on the concrete. Kliner was still working, forty feet across the mountain from Teale. Still thirty feet away from his weapon.

I crawled back to the inner door. Eased the handle down. The door came free of the catch. I picked up my gun. Eased the door halfway open. Crawled back to the window. Watched the growing pool of gasoline.

I had been afraid Teale would smell it straight away. That was the weak part of the plan. But he couldn't smell it. Because the whole shed was full of a powerful, appalling stink. It had hit me like a hammer as soon as I opened the door. A heavy, sour, greasy smell. The smell of money. Millions and millions of crumpled and greasy dollar bills were seeping out the stink of sweaty hands and sour pockets. The smell hung in the air. It was the same smell I had noticed in the empty boxes in Sherman Stoller's garage. The sour smell of used money.

Then I saw the flame bloom under the door. Finlay had dropped the match. It was a low blue flame. It raced in under the door and bloomed out over the wide stain like a flower opening. It reached the bottom of the huge green mountain. I saw Teale snap his head around and stare at it, frozen in horror.

I stepped to the door and squeezed out. Aimed the gun. Braced my wrist against the balcony railing. Pulled the trigger and blew Teale's head off, a hundred feet away. The big bullet caught him in the temple and exploded his skull all over the metal siding behind him.

Then everything went wrong. I saw it happen in that terrible slow motion you get when your mind is racing faster than you can move. My gun hand was drifting left to track Kliner on his way back to his own weapon. But Kliner dived to the right. He launched himself in a desperate leap down the mountainside to the spot where Teale had dropped his shotgun. He wasn't going back for his own gun. He was going to use Teale's weapon. He was going to use the same lethal geometry that Teale would have used. I saw my hand reverse its direction. It was cutting a graceful smooth arc through the air just behind Kliner tumbling and sliding down in a great spray of dollars. Then I heard the crash of the staff door bursting open below. The crash of the door fought with the echo of the roar of the shot which had killed Teale and I saw Picard stagger onto the warehouse floor.

His jacket was gone and I saw blood soaking his enormous white shirt. I saw him taking giant lurching strides towards the women. His head was turning and his right arm was windmilling upward to point at me. I saw his .38 dwarfed in his hand. A hundred feet from him I saw Kliner reach Teale's shotgun where it had fallen and buried itself in the cash pile.

I saw the blue flames bursting upward at the bottom of the huge dune of dollars. I saw Roscoe spinning slowly to look up at me. I saw Charlie Hubble spinning slowly the other way to look at Teale. I saw her start to scream. Her hands were slowly moving up to her face and her mouth was opening and her eyes were closing. The sound of her screaming drifted gently up to me and fought the dying echo of the Desert Eagle's bullet and the crash of the door.

I grasped the balcony railing in front of me and hauled myself one-handed toward it. Swung my gun hand vertically down and fired and hit Picard through the right shoulder a tiny fraction before his .38 came to rest on me. I saw him hit the floor in an explosion of blood as I hauled my aim back over to Kliner.

My mind was detached. Just treating it like a purely mechanical problem. I had locked my shoulder so that the big automatic's recoil would kick it upwards. That won me a tiny fraction as I hauled the sights over to the other end of the warehouse. I felt the smack in my palm as the burnt gases hurled the spent shell case out and crashed the next bullet in. Kliner had the Ithaca barrel on the way up in a slow motion flurry of dollar bills and he was pumping the shell. I heard the double crunch-crunch of the mechanism over the roar of the shot that had stopped Picard.

My detached mind computed that Kliner would fire just slightly above the horizontal to hit me with the top of the spray and that the bottom of the spray would decapitate Roscoe and Charlie. It told me my bullet would take a hair over seven hundredths of a second to cover the length of the warehouse and that I should aim high up on his right side to rotate the shotgun away from the women.

After that, my brain just shut down. Handed me all that information and sat back to mock my attempt to haul my arm up faster than Kliner could haul the Ithaca's barrel up. It was a race in agonizing slow motion. I was leaning half off the balcony slowly bringing my arm up as if I was lifting an enormous weight. A hundred feet away Kliner was slowly raising the shotgun barrel as if it was mired in molasses. They came up together, slowly, inch by inch, degree by degree. Up and up. It took for ever. It took the whole of my lifetime. Flames were bursting and exploding at the bottom of the mountain. They were spreading upward and outward through the money. Kliner's yellow teeth were parting in a wolfish smile. Charlie was screaming. Roscoe was slowly floating down toward the concrete floor like gossamer. My arm and Kliner's shotgun were travelling slowly upward together, inch by ghastly inch.

My arm got there first. I fired and hit Kliner in the right upper chest and the huge .44 slug hurled him off his feet. The Ithaca barrel whipped sideways as he pulled the trigger. The shotgun boomed and fired point-blank into the enormous mountain of money. The air was instantly thick with tiny scraps of paper. Shreds and fragments of dollar bills were blasted all over the place. They swirled like a thick blizzard and burst into flames as they settled into the fire.

Then time restarted and I was racing down the stairs to the warehouse floor. Flames were ripping through the greasy mountain faster than a man could run. I fought through the smoke and caught Roscoe under one arm and Charlie under the other. Spun them off their feet and carried them back towards the staircase. I could feel a gale of oxygen sucking in under the roller door to feed the fire. The whole huge shed was bursting into flame. The enormous dune of money was exploding. I was running flat out for the stairs, dragging the two women with me.

I ran straight into Picard. He reared up off the floor in front of me and the impact sent me sprawling. He stood there like a wounded giant bellowing in fury. His right shoulder was shattered and pumping blood. His shirt was soaked an appalling crimson. I staggered up off the floor and he hit me with his left hand. It was a shuddering impact and it rocked me back. He followed it up with another swinging left that hit me on the arm and sent the Desert

357

Eagle clattering over the concrete. The fire was billowing around us and my lungs were burning and I could hear Charlie Hubble screaming hysterically.

Picard had lost his revolver. He stood unsteadily in front of me, rocking back and forth, swinging his massive left arm ready for another blow. I threw myself inside the swing and hit him in the throat with my elbow. I hit him harder than I had ever hit anything before in my life. But he just shook himself and stepped nearer. Swung his enormous left fist and knocked me sideways into the fire.

I was breathing pure smoke as I rolled out. Picard stepped nearer. He was standing in a burning drift of money. He leaned forward and kicked me in the chest. Like being hit by a truck. My jacket caught fire. I tore it off and hurled it at him. But he just swatted it aside and swung his leg back for the kick that was going to kill me. Then his body started jerking like somebody was behind him, hitting him with a hammer. I saw Finlay standing there shooting Picard with the handgun he'd got from the station house. He fired six shots into Picard's back. Picard turned and looked at him. Took a step towards him. Finlay's gun clicked empty.

I scrabbled for my big Israeli automatic. Swept it up off the hot concrete and shot Picard through the back of the head. His skull exploded under the impact of the huge bullet. His legs crumpled and he started falling. I fired my last four shells into him before he hit the floor.

Finlay grabbed Charlie and raced away through the flames. I hauled Roscoe off the floor and hurled myself at the stairs and dragged her up and out through the office. Out and down the fire escape as the flames boiled out through the door after us. We hurled ourselves through the gap in the fence. I hoisted Roscoe high into my arms and ran across the field to the tree.

Behind us the superheated air blew the roof off the shed and flames burst a hundred feet into the night sky. All around us burning fragments of dollar bills were drifting down. The warehouse was blasting like a furnace. I could feel the heat on my back and Roscoe was beating away the flaming paper that was landing on us. We raced for the tree. Didn't stop. Raced on to the road. Two hundred yards. A hundred yards. Behind me I could hear screeching and tearing as the metal shed distorted and burst. Up ahead Hubble was standing next to the Bentley. He flung open the rear doors and raced for the driver's seat.

358

The four of us crammed into the back and Hubble stamped on the gas. The car shot forward and the doors slammed shut. The children were in the front. Both screaming. Charlie was screaming. Roscoe was screaming. I noticed with a kind of detached curiosity that I was screaming, too.

Hubble blasted a mile down the road. Then he jammed to a stop and we untangled ourselves and fell out of the car. Stumbled about. Hugged and kissed and cried, staggering about in the dirt at the side of the old county road. The four Hubbles clung together. Roscoe and Finlay and I clung together. Then Finlay was dancing around, yelling and laughing like a madman. All his old Boston reserve was gone. Roscoe was huddled in my arms. I was watching the fire, a mile away. It was getting worse. It was getting higher. It was spreading to the farmers' sheds next in line. Bags of nitrogen fertilizer and drums of tractor oil were exploding like bombs.

We all turned to watch the inferno and the explosions. Seven of us, in a ragged line on the road. From a mile away, we watched the firestorm. Great spouts of flame were leaping a thousand feet. Exploding oil drums were blowing up like mortar shells. The night sky was full of burning banknotes like a million orange stars. It looked like hell on earth.

'Christ,' Finlay said. 'Did we do that?'

'You did that, Finlay,' I said. 'You dropped the match.'

We laughed and hugged. We danced and laughed and slapped each other's backs. We swung the children up in the air and hugged them and kissed them. Hubble hugged me and pounded me on the back. Charlie hugged me and kissed me. I lifted Roscoe off her feet and kissed her long and hard. On and on. She wrapped her legs around my waist and locked her arms behind my head. We kissed like we would die if we stopped.

Then I drove slowly and quietly back to town. Finlay and Roscoe squeezed together with me in the front. The four Hubbles squeezed into the back. Soon as we lost the glow of the fire behind us, we picked up the glow of the station house burning in front of us. I slowed as we drove past. Burning fiercely. It was going to burn to the ground. Hundreds of people were milling about in a ragged circle, watching it. Nobody was doing anything about it.

I picked up speed again and we rolled through the silent town. Made the right up Beckman opposite the statue of old Caspar Teale. Jinked around the silent white church. Drove the mile up to the familiar white mailbox at number twenty-five. I turned in and wound my way up the driveway. Stopped at the door just long enough for the Hubbles to spill out. Hauled the old car around and back down the driveway. Rolled down Beckman again and stopped at the bottom.

'Out, Finlay,' I said.

He grinned and got out. Walked off into the night. I drove across the bottom of Main Street and coasted down to Roscoe's place. Stopped on her drive. We stumbled into the house. Dragged a chest of drawers down the hallway and shoved it up against the splintered door. Sealed ourselves off from the world.

THIRTY-FOUR

IT DIDN'T WORK OUT FOR ROSCOE AND ME. IT NEVER REALLY stood a chance. There were too many problems. It lasted a hair over twenty-four hours, and then it was over. I was back on the road.

It was five o'clock Sunday morning when we hauled that chest of drawers over and shoved it up against the broken door. We were both exhausted. But the adrenalin was still boiling through us. So we couldn't sleep. Instead, we talked. And the more we talked, the worse it got.

Roscoe had been a prisoner the best part of sixty-four hours. She hadn't been mistreated. She told me they hadn't touched her. She'd been terrified, but they'd just worked her like a slave. Thursday, Picard had driven her off in his car. I had watched them go. I'd waved them off. She'd updated him with our progress. A mile up the county road, he'd pulled his gun on her. Disarmed her, handcuffed her, driven her up to the warehouse. He'd driven right in through the roller door and she'd been put straight to work with Charlie Hubble. The two of them had been in there working the whole time I'd been sitting under the highway, watching the place. Roscoe herself had unloaded the red truck the Kliner kid had brought in. Then I'd followed it out to that truck stop near Memphis and wondered why the hell it was empty.

Charlie Hubble had been in there working five and a half days. Since Monday evening. Kliner had already started panicking by

361

then. The Coast Guard retreat was coming too soon for him. He knew he had to work fast to clear the stockpile. So Picard had brought the Hubbles straight to the warehouse. Kliner had made the hostages work. They'd slept just a few hours a night, lying down on the dune of dollars, handcuffed to the bottom of the office stairs.

Saturday morning, when his son and the two gatemen hadn't come back, Kliner had gone crazy. Now he had no staff at all. So he worked the hostages around the clock. They didn't sleep at all Saturday night. Just ploughed on with the hopeless task of trying to box up the huge pile. They were falling further and further behind. Every time an incoming truck spilled a new load out on the warehouse floor, Kliner had become more and more frantic.

So Roscoe had been a slave the best part of three days. In fear for her life, in danger, exhausted and humiliated for three long days. And it was my fault. I told her that. The more I told her, the more she said she didn't blame me. It was my fault, I was saying. It wasn't your fault, she was saying. I'm sorry, I was saying. Don't be, she was telling me.

We listened to each other. We accepted what was being said. But I still thought it was my fault. Wasn't a 100 per cent sure she didn't think so, too. Despite what she was saying. We didn't fall out about it. But it was the first faint sign of a problem between us.

We showered together in her tiny stall. Stayed in there the best part of an hour. We were soaping off the stink of the money and the sweat and the fire. And we were still talking. I was telling her about Friday night. The ambush in the storm up at Hubble's place. I told her all about it. I told her about the bags with the knives and the hammer and the nails. I told her what I'd done to the five of them. I thought she'd be happy about it.

And that was the second problem. Not a big deal as we stood there with the hot water beating down on us. But I heard something in her voice. Just a tiny tremor. Not shock or disapproval. Just a hint of a question. That maybe I had gone too far. I could hear it in her voice.

I felt somehow I'd done it all for her and Joe. I hadn't done it because I had wanted to do it. It was Joe's business and it was her town and these were her people. I'd done it because I'd seen her trying to melt into her kitchen wall, crying like her heart was breaking. I'd done it for Joe and Molly. At the same time as feeling I needed no justification at all, I had been justifying it to myself

362

like that.

It didn't feel like a problem at the time. The shower loosened us up. Steamed some glow back into us. We went to bed. Left the drapes open. It was a glorious day. The sun was up in a bright blue sky and the air looked fresh and clean. It looked like it should look. Like a new day.

We made love with great tenderness, great energy, great joy. If somebody had told me then that I'd be back on the road the next morning, I'd have thought they were crazy. I told myself there were no problems. I was imagining them. And if there were problems, there were good reasons for them. Maybe the after-effects of the stress and the adrenalin. Maybe the deep fatigue. Maybe because Roscoe had been a hostage. Maybe she was reacting like a lot of hostages do. They feel some kind of a faint jealousy against anybody who hadn't been a hostage with them. Some kind of a faint resentment. Maybe that was feeding the guilt I was carrying for letting her get captured in the first place. Maybe a lot of things. I fell asleep certain we'd wake up happy and I'd stay there for ever.

We did wake up happy. We slept through until late afternoon. Then we spent a gorgeous couple of hours with the afternoon sun streaming in the window, dozing and stretching, kissing and laughing. We made love again. We were fuelled up with the joy of being safe and alive and alone together. It was the best love-making we ever had. It was also the last. But we didn't know that at the time.

Roscoe took the Bentley up to Eno's for some food. She was gone an hour and came back with news. She'd seen Finlay. She was talking about what was going to happen next. That was the big problem. It made the other tiny problems look like nothing at all.

'You should see the station house,' she said. 'Nothing left more than a foot high.'

She put the food on a tray and we ate it sitting on the bed. Fried chicken.

'All four warehouses burned down,' she said. 'There was debris exploding all over the highway. The state police got involved. They had to get fire trucks all the way from Atlanta and Macon.'

'State police are involved?' I said.

She laughed.

363

'Everybody's involved,' she said. 'It sort of snowballed. The Atlanta fire chief called in the bomb squad because of the explosions, because he didn't know for sure what they were. The bomb squad can't go anywhere without notifying the FBI, in case it's terrorism, so the Bureau is interested. Then the National Guard got involved this morning.'

'The National Guard?' I said. 'Why?'

'This is the best part,' she said. 'Finlay says when the roof blew off the warehouse last night, the sudden updraft of air blew the money all over the place. Remember those burning pieces that kept landing on us? There are millions of dollar bills all over the place. Miles around. The wind blew them everywhere, in the fields, all over the highway. Most of them are partially burned, of course, but some of them aren't. Soon as the sun came up, thousands of people came out of nowhere, swarming around all over the place, picking all the money up. So the National Guard was ordered in to disperse the crowds.'

I ate some food. Thought about it.

'Governor calls in the Guard, right?' I asked her.

She nodded. Mouth full of chicken wing.

'The governor's involved,' she said. 'He's in town right now. And Finlay called the Treasury Department, because of Joe. They're sending a team down here. I told you, it sort of snowballed.'

'What the hell else?' I said.

'Big problems here, of course,' she said. 'Rumours are flying around. Everybody seems to know the Foundation is finished. Finlay says half of them are pretending they never knew what was going on, and the other half are mad as hell their thousand dollars a week is going to stop. You should have seen old Eno, when I picked up the food. Looked like he's furious.'

'Finlay worried?' I said.

'He's OK,' she said. 'Busy, of course. We're down to a four-person police department. Finlay, me, Stevenson and the desk man. Finlay says that's half of what we need, because of the crisis, but twice as many as we can afford, because the Foundation subsidy is going to stop. But anyway, there's nothing anybody can do about hiring and firing without the mayor's approval, and we haven't got a mayor any more, have we?'

I sat there on the bed, eating. The problems started bearing down on me. I hadn't really seen them clearly before. But I was seeing them now. A huge question was forming in my mind. It was a question for Roscoe. I wanted to ask it straight away and get her honest, spontaneous response. I didn't want to give her any time to think about her answer.

'Roscoe?' I said.

She looked up at me. Waited.

'What are you going to do?' I asked her.

She looked at me like it was an odd question.

'Work my butt off, I guess,' she said. 'There's going to be a lot to do. We're going to have to rebuild this whole town. Maybe we can make something better out of it, create something worthwhile. And I can play a big part in it. I'll move up the totem pole a couple of notches. I'm really excited. I'm looking forward to it. This is my town and I'm going to be really involved in it. Maybe I'll get on the town board. Maybe I'll even run for mayor. That would be a hell of a thing, wouldn't it? After all these years, a Roscoe for mayor, instead of a Teale?'

I looked at her. It was a great answer, but it was the wrong answer. Wrong for me. I didn't want to try to change her mind. I didn't want to put any kind of pressure on her at all. That's why I had asked her straight out, before I told her what I was going to have to do. I had wanted her honest, natural response. And I had got it. It was right for her. This was her town. If anybody could fix it, she could. If anybody should stick around, working her butt off, she should.

But it was the wrong answer for me. Because I knew by then I had to go. I knew by then that I had to get out fast. The problem was what was going to happen next. The whole thing had got out of hand. Before, it had all been about Joe. It had been private. Now it was public. It was like those half-burnt dollar bills. It was scattered all over the damn place.

Roscoe had mentioned the governor, the Treasury Department, the National Guard, the state police, the FBI, Atlanta fire investigators. A half-dozen competent agencies, all looking at what had gone on in Margrave. And they'd be looking hard. They'd be calling Kliner the counterfeiter of the century. They'd find out the mayor had disappeared. They'd find out that four police officers had been involved. The FBI would be looking for Picard. Interpol would get involved because of the Venezuela connection. The heat would be tremendous. There would be six agencies competing like mad to get a result. They'd tear the place apart.

And one or other of them would snarl me up. I was a stranger in the wrong place at the wrong time. It would take about a minute and a half to realize I was the brother of the dead government investigator who had started the whole thing off. They'd look at my agenda. Somebody would think: revenge. I would be hauled in, and they would go to work on me.

I wouldn't be convicted. There was no risk of that. There was no evidence hanging around. I'd been careful every step of the way. And I knew how to bullshit. They could talk to me until I grew a long white beard and they wouldn't get anything from me. That was for sure. But they'd try. They'd try like crazy. They'd keep me two years in Warburton. Two years up there on the holding floor. Two years of my life. That was the problem. No way could I stand still for that. I'd only just got my life back. I'd had six months of freedom in thirty-six years. Those six months had been the happiest months I'd ever had.

So I was getting out. Before any of them ever knew I'd been there in the first place. My mind was made up. I had to become invisible again. I had to get far away from the Margrave spotlight, where those diligent agencies would never look. It meant my dreams of a future with Roscoe were going to be snuffed out before they were even started. It meant I had to tell Roscoe she wasn't worth gambling two years of my life for. I had to tell her that.

We talked about it all night. We didn't fall out over it. Just talked about it. She knew what I was going to do was right for me. I knew what she was going to do was right for her. She asked me to stay. I thought hard, but said no. I asked her to come with me. She thought hard, but said no. Nothing more to say.

Then we talked about other things. We talked about what I would be doing, and what she would be doing. And I slowly realized that staying there would tear me apart just as much as leaving was going to. Because I didn't want the stuff she was talking about. I didn't want elections and mayors and votes and boards and committees. I didn't want property taxes and maintenance and chambers of commerce and strategies. I didn't want to be sitting there all bored and chafing. Not with the tiny resentments and guilts and disapprovals growing bigger and bigger until they choked us. I wanted what I was talking about. I wanted the open road and a new place every day. I wanted miles to travel and absolutely no idea where I was going. I wanted to ramble. I had rambling on my mind.

We sat around talking, miserable, until dawn. I asked her to do one last thing for me. I asked her to arrange a funeral for Joe. I told her I wanted Finlay to be there, and the Hubbles, and the two old barbers, and her. I told her to ask the old guy's sister to be there and sing a sad song for Joe. I told her to ask the old lady where the meadow was where she'd sung along with Blind Blake's guitar, sixty-two years ago. I asked her to scatter Joe's ashes on the grass there.

Roscoe drove me down to Macon in the Bentley. Seven in the morning. We hadn't slept at all. The trip took us an hour. I sat in the back, behind the new black glass. I didn't want anybody to see me. We drove up the rise from her place and threaded through traffic. The whole town was getting packed. Even before we got up to Main Street, I could see the place was swarming. There were dozens of cars parked up everywhere. There were television trucks from the networks and CNN. I hunched down in the back of the car. People were crowding everywhere, even at seven in the morning. There were ranks of dark blue government sedans all over. We turned at the corner where the coffee shop was. People were lining up on the sidewalk, waiting to get in for breakfast.

We drove through the sunny town. Main Street was parked solid. There were vehicles up on the sidewalks. I saw fire chiefs' cars and state police cruisers. I glanced into the barbershop as we crawled past, but the old guys weren't there. I would miss them. I would miss old Finlay. I would always wonder how things turned out for him. Good luck, Harvard guy, I thought. Good luck, too, to the Hubbles. This morning was the start of a long road for them. They were going to need a lot of luck. Good luck, too, to Roscoe. I sat there, silently wishing her the best of everything. She deserved it. She really did.

She drove me all the way south to Macon. She found the bus depot. Parked up. Handed me a small envelope. Told me not to open it right away. I put it in my pocket. Kissed her goodbye. Got out of the car. Didn't look back. I heard the sound of the big tyres on the pavement and I knew she was gone. I walked into the depot. Bought a ticket. Then I crossed the street to a cheap store and bought new clothes. Changed in their cubicle, left the filthy old fatigues in their garbage can. Then I strolled back and got on a bus for California.

I had tears in my eyes for more than a hundred miles. Then the old bus rattled over the state line. I looked out at the southeast corner of Alabama. Opened Roscoe's envelope. It was the photograph of Joe. She'd taken it from Molly Beth's valise. Taken it out of the frame. Trimmed it with scissors to fit my pocket. On the back she had written her telephone number. But I didn't need that. I had already committed it to memory.

DIE TRYING

If I listed all the ways she helps me, this dedication would be longer than the book itself. So I'll just say: to my wife Jane, with a lot of thanks.

ONE

NATHAN RUBIN DIED BECAUSE HE GOT BRAVE. NOT THE SUSTAINED kind of thing which wins you a medal in a war, but the split-second kind of blurting outrage which gets you killed on the street.

He left home early, as he always did, six days a week, fifty weeks a year. A cautious breakfast, appropriate to a short, round man aiming to stay in shape through his forties. A long walk down the carpeted corridors of a lakeside house, appropriate to a man who earned a thousand dollars on each of those three hundred days he worked. A thumb on the button of the garage door-opener and a twist of the wrist to start the silent engine of his expensive, imported sedan. A CD into the player, a backward sweep into his gravel driveway, a dab on the brake, a snick of the selector, a nudge on the gas, and the last short drive of his life was under way. Six forty-nine in the morning, Monday.

The only light on his route to work was green, which was the proximate cause of his death. It meant that as he pulled into his secluded slot behind his professional building the prelude ahead of Bach's B minor fugue still had thirty-eight seconds left to run. He sat and heard it out until the last organ blast echoed to silence, which meant that as he got out of his car the three men were near enough for him to interpret some kind of intention in their approach. So he glanced at them. They looked away and altered course, three men in step, like dancers or soldiers. He turned toward his building. Started walking. But then he stopped. And looked back. The three men were at his car. Trying the doors.

'Hey!' he called.

It was the short universal sound of surprise, anger, challenge. The sort of instinctive sound an earnest, naive citizen makes when something should not be happening. The sort of instinctive sound which gets an earnest, naive citizen killed. He found himself heading straight back to his car. He was outnumbered three to one but he was in the right, which swelled him up and gave him confidence. He strode back and felt outraged and fit and commanding.

But those were illusory feelings. A soft, suburban guy like him was never going to be in command of a situation like that. His fitness was just health-club tone. It counted for nothing. His tight abdominals ruptured under the first savage blow. His face jerked forward and down and hard knuckles pulped his lips and smashed his teeth. He was caught by rough hands and knotted arms and held upright like he weighed nothing at all. His keys were snatched from his grasp and he was hit a crashing blow on the ear. His mouth filled with blood. He was dropped onto the blacktop and heavy boots smashed into his back. Then his gut. Then his head. He blacked out like a television set in a thunderstorm. The world just disappeared in front of him. It collapsed into a thin hot line and sputtered away to nothing.

So he died, because for a split-second he got brave. But not then. He died much later, after the split-second of bravery had faded into long hours of wretched gasping fear, and after the long hours of fear had exploded into long minutes of insane screaming panic.

Jack Reacher stayed alive, because he got cautious. He got cautious because he heard an echo from his past. He had a lot of past, and the echo was from the worst part of it.

He had served thirteen years in the army, and the only time he was wounded it wasn't with a bullet. It was with a fragment of a Marine sergeant's jawbone. Reacher had been stationed in Beirut, in the US compound out by the airport. The compound was truck-bombed. Reacher was standing at the gate. The Marine sergeant was standing a hundred yards nearer the explosion. The jawbone fragment was the only piece left of the guy. It hit Reacher a hundred yards away and went tumbling through his gut like a bullet. The army surgeon who patched Reacher up told him afterward he was lucky. He told him a real bullet in the gut would have felt much worse. That was the echo Reacher was hearing. And he was paying a whole lot of attention to it, because thirteen years later he was standing there with a handgun pointing straight at his stomach. From a range of about an inch and a half.

The handgun was a nine-millimeter automatic. It was brand new. It was oiled. It was held low, lined up right on his old scar. The guy holding it looked more or less like he knew what he was doing. The safety mechanism was released. There was no visible tremor in the muzzle. No tension. The trigger finger was ready to go to work. Reacher could see that. He was concentrating hard on that trigger finger.

He was standing next to a woman. He was holding her arm. He had never seen her before. She was staring at an identical nine-millimeter pointed at her own gut. Her guy was more tensed up than his. Her guy looked uneasy. He looked worried. His gun was trembling with tension. His fingernails were chewed. A nervous, jumpy guy. The four of them were standing there on the street, three of them still like statues and the fourth hopping slightly from foot to foot.

They were in Chicago. Center of the city, a busy sidewalk, a Monday, last day of June. Broad daylight, bright summer sunshine. The whole situation had materialized in a split second. It had happened in a way which couldn't have been choreographed in a million years. Reacher had been walking down the street, going nowhere, not fast, not slow. He had been about to pass the exit door of a storefront dry-cleaner's. The door had opened up in his face and an old metal walking cane had clattered out on the sidewalk right in front of him. He'd glanced up to see a woman in the doorway. She was about to drop an armful of nine dry-cleaning bags. She was some way short of thirty, expensively dressed, dark, attractive, self-assured. She had some kind of a bad leg. Some kind of an injury. Reacher could see from her awkward posture it was causing her pain. She'd thrown him a would-you-mind look and he'd thrown her a no-problem look and scooped up the metal cane. He'd taken the nine bags from her with one hand and given her the cane with the other. He'd flicked the bags up over his shoulder and felt the nine wire hangers bite into his finger. She had planted the cane on the sidewalk and eased her forearm into the curved-metal clip. He had offered his hand. She had paused. Then she had nodded in an embarrassed fashion and he had taken her arm and waited a beat, feeling helpful but awkward. Then they had turned together to move away. Reacher had figured he would maybe stroll a few steps with her until she was steady on her feet. Then he would let her arm go and hand back her garments. But he'd turned straight into the two guys with the nine-millimeter automatics.

The four of them stood there, face to face in pairs. Like four people eating together in a tight booth in a diner. The two guys with the guns were white, well fed, vaguely military, vaguely alike. Medium height, short brown hair. Big hands, muscular. Big, obvious faces, bland pink features. Tense expressions, hard eyes. The nervous guy was smaller, like he burned up his energy worrying. They both wore checked shirts and poplin windbreakers. They stood there, pressed together. Reacher was a lot taller than the other three. He could see all around them, over their heads. He stood there, surprised, with the woman's dry-cleaning slung over his shoulder. The woman was leaning on her crutch, just staring, silent. The two men were pointing the guns. Close in. Reacher felt they'd all been standing like that for a long time. But he knew that feeling was deceptive. It probably hadn't been more than a second and a half.

The guy opposite Reacher seemed to be the leader. The bigger one. The calmer one. He looked between Reacher and the woman and jerked his automatic's barrel toward the kerb.

'In the car, bitch,' the guy said. 'And you, asshole.'
He spoke urgently, but quietly. With authority. Not much of an accent. Maybe from California, Reacher thought. There was a sedan at the kerb. It had been waiting there for them. A big car, black, expensive. The driver was leaning across behind the front passenger seat. He was stretching over to pop the rear door. The guy opposite Reacher motioned with the gun again. Reacher didn't move. He glanced left and right. He figured he had about another second and a half to make some kind of an assessment. The two guys with the nine-millimeter automatics didn't worry him too much. He was one-handed, because of the dry-cleaning, but he figured the two guys would go down without too much

of a problem. The problems lay beside him and behind him. He stared up into the dry-cleaner's window and used it like a mirror. Twenty yards behind him was a solid mass of hurrying people at a crosswalk. A couple of stray bullets would find a couple of targets. No doubt about that. No doubt at all. That was the problem behind him. The problem beside him was the unknown woman. Her capabilities were an unknown quantity. She had some kind of a bad leg. She would be slow to react. Slow to move. He wasn't prepared to go into combat. Not in that environment, and not with that partner.

The guy with the Californian accent reached up and grabbed Reacher's wrist where it was pinned against his collar by the weight of the nine clean garments hanging down his back. He used it to pull him toward the car. His trigger finger still looked ready to go to work. Reacher was watching it, corner of his eye. He let the woman's arm go. Stepped over to the car. Threw the bags into the rear seat and climbed in after them. The woman was pushed in behind him. Then the jumpy guy crowded in on them and slammed the door. The leader got in front on the right. Slammed the door. The driver nudged the selector and the car moved smoothly and quietly away down the street.

The woman was gasping in pain and Reacher figured she had the jumpy guy's gun jammed in her ribs. The leader was twisted around in the front seat with his gun hand resting against the thick leather headrest. The gun was pointing straight at Reacher's chest. It was a Glock 17. Reacher knew all about that weapon. He had evaluated the prototype for his unit. That had been his assignment during his light-duty convalescence after the Beirut wound. The Glock was a tough little weapon. Seven and a half inches long from firing pin to muzzle tip. Long enough to make it accurate. Reacher had hit thumbtack heads at seventy-five feet with it. And it fired a decent projectile. It delivered quarter-ounce bullets at nearly eight hundred miles an hour. Seventeen rounds to a magazine, hence the name. And it was light. For all its power, it weighed under two pounds. The important parts were steel. The rest of it was plastic. Black polycarbonate, like an expensive camera. A fine piece of craftsmanship.

But he hadn't liked it much. Not for the specialized requirements of his unit. He'd recommended rejection. He'd supported the Beretta 92F instead. The Beretta was also a nine-millimeter, a half-pound heavier, an inch longer, two fewer rounds in the magazine. But it had about 10 per cent more stopping power than the Glock. That was important to him. And it wasn't plastic. The Beretta had been Reacher's choice. His unit commander had agreed. He had circulated Reacher's paper and the army as a whole had backed his recommendation. The same week they promoted him and pinned on his Silver Star and his Purple Heart, they ordered Berettas even though the Beretta was more expensive and NATO was crazy for the Glock and Reacher had been just about a lone voice and was not long out of West Point. Then he had been assigned elsewhere and served all around the world and hadn't really seen a Glock 17 since. Until now. Twelve years later he was getting a pretty damn good second look at one.

He switched his attention away from the gun and took another look at the guy holding it. He had a decent tan which whitened near his hairline. A recent haircut. The driver had a big shiny brow, thinning hair swept back, pink and vivid features, the smirk that pig-ugly guys use when they think they're handsome. Same cheap chainstore shirt, same windbreaker. Same corn-fed bulk. Same in-charge confidence, edged around with a slight breathlessness. Three guys, all of them maybe thirty or thirty-five, one leader, one solid follower, one jumpy follower. All of them tense but rehearsed, racing through some kind of a mission. A puzzle. Reacher glanced past the steady Glock into the leader's eyes. But the guy shook his head.

'No talking, asshole,' he said. 'Start talking, I'll shoot you. That's a damn promise. Keep quiet, you could be OK.'

Reacher believed him. The guy's eyes were hard and his mouth was a tight line. So he said nothing. Then the car slowed and pulled onto a lumpy concrete forecourt. It headed around behind an abandoned industrial building. They had driven south. Reacher figured they were now maybe five miles south of the Loop. The driver eased the big sedan to a stop with the rear door lined up with the back of a small panel truck. The truck was standing alone on the empty lot. It was a Ford Econoline, dirty white, not old, but well used. There had been some kind of writing on the side. It had been painted over with fresh white paint which didn't exactly match the bodywork. Reacher scanned around. The lot was full of trash. He saw a paint can discarded near the truck. A brush. There was nobody in sight. The place was deserted. If he was going to make some kind of a move, this was the right time to make it, and the right location. But the guy in front smiled a thin smile and leaned right over into the back of the car. Caught Reacher's collar with his left hand and ground the tip of the Glock's muzzle into Reacher's ear with his right.

'Sit still, asshole,' the guy said.

The driver got out of the car and skipped around the hood. Pulled a new set of keys from his pocket and opened up the rear doors of the truck. Reacher sat still. Jamming a gun into a person's ear is not necessarily a smart move. If the person suddenly jerks his head around toward it, the gun comes out. It rolls around the person's forehead. Then even a quick trigger-finger won't do much damage. It might blow a hole in the person's ear, just the outside flap, and it's sure to shatter the person's eardrum. But those are not fatal wounds. Reacher spent a second weighing those odds. Then the jumpy guy dragged the woman out of the car and hustled her straight into the back of the truck. She hopped and limped across the short distance. Straight out of one door and in through the other. Reacher watched her, corner of his eye. Her guy took her pocketbook from her and tossed it back into the car. It fell at Reacher's feet. It thumped heavily on the thick carpet. A big pocketbook, expensive leather, something heavy in it. Something metal. Only one metal thing women carry could make a heavy thump like that. He glanced across at her, suddenly interested.

She was sprawled in the back of the truck. Impeded by her leg. Then the leader in the front pulled Reacher along the leather seat and passed him on to the jumpy guy. As soon as one Glock was out of his ear, the other was jammed into his side. He was dragged over the rough ground. Across to the rear of the truck. He was pushed inside with the woman. The jumpy guy covered them both with the trembling Glock while the leader reached into the car and pulled out the woman's metal crutch. He walked over and tossed it into the truck. It clanged and boomed on the metal siding. He left her dry-cleaning in the back of the sedan with her handbag. Then he pulled a set of handcuffs from the pocket of his jacket. He caught the woman's right wrist and cuffed it with half the handcuff. Pulled her roughly sideways and caught Reacher's left wrist. Snapped the other half of the cuff onto it. Shook the cuff to check it was secure. Slammed the truck's left rear door. Reacher saw the driver emptying plastic bottles into the sedan. He caught the pale color and the strong smell of gasoline. One bottle into the back seat, one into the front. Then the leader swung the truck's right rear door shut. Last thing Reacher saw before darkness enveloped him was the driver, pulling a matchbook from his pocket.

TWO

ONE THOUSAND SEVEN HUNDRED AND TWO MILES FROM CHICAGO by road guest quarters were being prepared. They took the form of a single room. The room was following an unconventional design, specified by a thorough man after a great deal of careful thought. The design called for several unusual features.

The quarters were designed for a specific purpose, and for a specific guest. The nature of the purpose and the identity of the guest had dictated the unusual features. The construction was concentrated on the second floor of an existing building. A corner room had been selected. It had a series of large windows on the two outside walls. They faced south and east. The glass had been smashed out and replaced by heavy plywood sheeting nailed to the remaining windowframes. The plywood was painted white on the outside, to match the building's siding. On the inside, the plywood was left unfinished.

The corner room's ceiling was torn out. It was an old building, and the ceiling had been made of heavy plaster. It had been pulled down in a shower of choking dust. The room was now open to the rafters. The interior walling was torn off. The walls had been paneled in old pine, worn smooth with age and polish. That was all gone. The framing of the building and the heavy old tarpaper behind the exterior siding was exposed. The floorboards were pulled up. The dusty ceiling of the room below was visible under the heavy joists. The room was just a shell.

The old plaster from the ceiling and the boards from the walls and the floor, had been thrown out through the windows before they were covered over with the plywood. The two men who had done the demolition work had shoveled all that debris into a large pile, and they had backed their truck up to the pile ready to cart the trash away. They were very anxious to leave the place looking neat and tidy. This was the first time they had worked for this particular employer, and there had been hints of more work to come. And looking around, they could see that there was plenty more needed doing. All in all, an optimistic situation. New contracts were hard to find, and this particular employer, had shown no concern over price. The two men felt that to make a good first impression was very much in their long-term interest. They were hard at work loading their truck with every last plaster fragment when the employer himself stopped by.

'All done?' he asked.

The employer was a huge guy, freakishly bloated, with a high voice and two nickel-sized red spots burning on his pale cheeks. He moved lightly and quietly, like a guy a quarter his size. The overall effect was a guy people looked away from and answered quickly.

'Just clearing up,' the first guy said to him. 'Where do we dump this stuff?'

'I'll show you,' the employer said. 'You'll need to make two trips. Bring those boards separately, right?'

The second guy nodded. The floorboards were eighteen inches wide, from back when lumbermen had the pick of any tree they wanted. No way would they fit into the flatbed with the rest of the junk. They finished loading the plaster and their employer squeezed into their truck with them. He was such a big guy, it made for a tight fit. He pointed beyond the old building.

'Drive north,' he said, 'about a mile.'

The road led them straight out of town and then wound upward through some steep bends. The employer pointed to a place.

'In there,' he said, 'all the way in back, OK?'

He strolled quietly away and the two guys unloaded their truck. Drove it back south and heaved the old pine boards in. Followed the winding bends again and unloaded. They carried the boards inside and stacked them neatly. All the way in back of the dark space. Then the employer stepped out of the shadows. He had been waiting for them. He had something in his hand.

'We're all done,' the first guy said.

The employer nodded.

'You sure are,' he said.

His hand came up. He was holding a gun. A dull black automatic. He shot the first guy in the head. The crash of the bullet was deafening. Blood and bone and brain sprayed everywhere. The second guy froze in terror. Then he ran. He launched himself sideways in a desperate sprint for cover. The employer smiled. He liked it when they ran. He dropped his huge arm to a shallow angle. Fired and put a bullet through the back of the guy's knee. Smiled again. Now it was better. He liked it when they ran, but he liked it better when they were squirming on the floor. He stood and listened to the guy's yelping for a long moment. Then he strolled quietly over and took careful aim. Put a bullet through the other knee. He watched for a while, then he tired of the game. Shrugged and put a final bullet through the guy's head. Then he laid the gun on the ground and rolled the two bodies over and over until they were stacked neatly in line with the old floorboards.

THREE

THEY HAD BEEN ON THE ROAD AN HOUR AND THIRTY-THREE minutes. Some urban crawling, then an acceleration to a steady cruise. Maybe sixty miles covered. But in the noisy darkness inside the panel truck Reacher had no idea which direction those sixty miles were taking him.

He was handcuffed to the young woman with the bad leg and within the first few minutes of their forced acquaintance they had worked out how to get as comfortable as they were ever going to get. They had crabbed around inside the truck until they were sitting sideways on the floor, legs straight out, propped against the big wheel well on the right, braced against the motion. The woman sat against the rear side and Reacher sat on the forward side. Their cuffed wrists lay together on the flat top of the metal bulge like they were lovers idling their time away in a café.

At first they hadn't spoken. They'd just sat for a long time in stunned silence. The immediate problem was the heat. It was the middle of the last day of June in the Midwest. They were shut into an enclosed metal space. There was no ventilation. Reacher figured the rush of air over the outside of the truck's body must be cooling it to an extent, but nowhere near enough.

He just sat there in the gloom and used the hot dead time

thinking and planning like he was trained to do. Staying calm, staying relaxed, staying ready, not burning his energy away with useless speculation. Assessing and evaluating. The three guys had shown a measure of efficiency. No great talent, no real finesse, but no significant mistakes. The jumpy guy with the second Glock was the weakest component of the team, but the leader had covered for him pretty well. An efficient threesome. Not at all the worst he'd ever seen. But, at that point, he wasn't worrying. He'd been in worse situations and survived them. Much worse situations, and more than once. So he wasn't worrying yet.

Then he noticed something. He noticed that the woman wasn't worrying yet either. She was calm too. She was just sitting there, swaying, cuffed to his wrist, thinking and planning like maybe she was trained to do, as well. He glanced across at her in the gloom and saw her looking steadily at him. A quizzical stare, calm, in control, faintly superior, faintly disapproving. The confidence of youth. She met his gaze. Held it for a long moment. Then she stuck out her cuffed right hand, which jarred his left wrist, but it was an encouraging gesture. He reached around and shook her hand and they smiled brief ironic smiles together at their mutual formality.

'Holly Johnson,' she said.

She was assessing him carefully. He could see her eyes traveling around his face. Then they flicked down to his clothing and back up to his face. She smiled again, briefly, like she had decided he merited some kind of courtesy.

'Nice to meet you,' she said.

He looked back at her. Looked at her face. She was a very good-looking woman. Maybe twenty-six, twenty-seven. He looked at her clothes. A line from an old song ran through his head: hundred dollar dresses, that I ain't paid for yet. He waited for the next line, but it didn't come. So he smiled back at her and nodded.

'Jack Reacher,' he said. 'Pleasure's all mine, Holly, believe me.'

It was difficult to speak, because the truck was cruising noisily. The sound of the engine was fighting with the roar from the road. Reacher would have been happy to sit quiet for a while, but Holly wasn't.

'I need to get rid of you,' she said.

A confident woman, well in control of herself. He made no reply.

Just glanced at her and glanced away. The next line was: cold, cold-blooded woman. A dying fall, a sad poignant line. An old Memphis Slim song. But the line was not right for her. Not right at all. This was not a cold-blooded woman. He glanced over again and shrugged at her. She was staring at him. Impatient with his silence.

'You understand exactly what's happening?' she asked him.

He watched her face. Watched her eyes. She was staring straight at him. Astonishment on her face. She thought she was stuck in there with an idiot. She thought he didn't understand exactly what was happening.

'It's pretty clear, right?' he said. 'From the evidence?'

'What evidence?' she said. 'It was all over in a split second.'

'Exactly,' he said. 'That's all the evidence I need, right? Tells me more or less what I need to know.'

He stopped talking and started resting again. Next opportunity to get away would be the next time the truck stopped. Could be some hours away. He felt he could be in for a long day. Felt he should be prepared to conserve his resources.

'So what do you need to know?' the woman said.

Her eyes were steady on his.

'You've been kidnaped,' he said. 'I'm here by accident.'

She was still looking at him. Still confident. Still thinking. Still not sure whether or not she was cuffed to an idiot.

'It's pretty clear, right?' he said again. 'It wasn't me they were after.'

She made no reply. Just arched a fine eyebrow.

'Nobody knew I was going to be there,' he said. 'I didn't even know I was going to be there. Until I got there. But it was a well planned operation. Must have taken time to set up. Based on surveillance, right? Three guys, one in the car, two on the street. The car was parked exactly level. They had no idea where I was going to be. But obviously they knew for sure where you were going to be. So don't be looking at me like I'm the idiot here. You're the one made the big mistake.'

'Mistake?' the woman said.

'You're too regular in your habits,' Reacher said. 'They studied your movements, maybe two or three weeks, and you walked right into their arms. They weren't expecting anybody else to be there. That's clear, right? They only brought one set of handcuffs.'

He raised his wrist, which raised hers too, to make his point. The woman went quiet for a long moment. She was revising her opinion of him. Reacher rocked with the motion of the vehicle and smiled.

'And you should know better,' he said. 'You're a government agent of some sort, right? DEA, CIA, FBI, something like that, maybe a Chicago PD detective? New in the job, still fairly dedicated. And fairly wealthy. So somebody is either looking for a ransom, or you've already become a potential problem to somebody, even though you're new, and either way you should have taken more care of yourself.'

She looked across at him. Nodded, eyes wide in the gloom. Impressed.

'Evidence?' she asked.

He smiled at her again.

'Couple of things,' he said. 'Your dry-cleaning. My guess is every Monday lunchbreak you take last week's clothes in to get them cleaned and you pick up this week's clothes to wear. That means you must have about fifteen or twenty outfits. Looking at that thing you got on, you're not a cheap dresser. Call it four hundred bucks an outfit, you've got maybe eight grand tied up in things to wear. That's what I call moderately wealthy, and that's what I call too regular in your habits.'

She nodded slowly.

'OK,' she said. 'Why am I a government agent?'

'Easy enough,' he said. 'You had a Glock 17 shoved at you, you were bundled into a car, you were thrown in a truck, handcuffed to a complete stranger and you've got no idea where the hell they're taking you, or why. Any normal person would be falling apart over all that, screaming the place down. But not you. You're sitting there quite calmly, which suggests some kind of training, maybe some kind of familiarity with upsetting or dangerous situations. And maybe some kind of sure knowledge there'll be a bunch of people looking to get you back soon as they can.'

He stopped and she nodded for him to continue.

'Also, you had a gun in your bag,' he said. 'Something fairly heavy, maybe a .38, long barrel. If it was a private weapon, a dresser like you would choose something dainty, like a snub .22.

But it was a big revolver, so you were issued with it. So you're some kind of an agent, maybe a cop.'

The woman nodded again, slowly.

'Why am I new in the job?' she asked.

'Your age,' Reacher said. 'What are you? Twenty-six?'

'Twenty-seven,' she said.

'That's young for a detective,' he said. 'College, a few years in uniform? Young for the FBI, DEA, CIA, too. So whatever you are, you're new at it.'

She shrugged.

'OK,' she said. 'Why am I fairly dedicated?'

Reacher pointed, left-handed, rattling their shared handcuff.

'Your injury,' he said. 'You're back to work after some kind of an accident, before you're really recovered. You're still using that crutch for your bad leg. Most people in your position would be staying home and drawing sick pay.'

She smiled.

'I could be handicapped,' she said. 'Could have been born this way.'

Reacher shook his head in the gloom.

'That's a hospital crutch,' he said. 'They loaned it to you, short term, until you're over your injury. If it was a permanent thing, you'd have bought your own crutch. Probably you'd have bought a dozen. Sprayed them all different to match all your expensive outfits.'

She laughed. It was a pleasant sound above the drone and boom of the truck's engine and the roar of the road.

'Pretty good, Jack Reacher,' she said. 'I'm an FBI special agent. Since last fall. I just ripped up my cruciate ligaments playing soccer.'

'You play soccer?' Reacher said. 'Good for you, Holly Johnson. What kind of an FBI agent since last fall?'

She was quiet for a beat.

'Just an agent,' she said. 'One of many at the Chicago office.'

Reacher shook his head.

'Not just an agent,' he said. 'An agent who's doing something to somebody who maybe wants to retaliate. So who are you doing something to?'

She shook her head back at him.

'I can't discuss that,' she said. 'Not with civilians.'

He nodded. He was comfortable with that.

'OK,' he said.

'Any agent makes enemies,' she said.

'Naturally,' he replied.

'Me as much as anybody,' she said.

He glanced across at her. It was a curious remark. Defensive. The remark of a woman trained and eager and ready to go, but chained to a desk since last fall.

'Financial section?' he guessed.

She shook her head.

'I can't discuss it,' she said again.

'But you already made enemies,' he said.

She gave him a half-smile which died fast. Then she went quiet. She looked calm, but Reacher could feel in her wrist that she was worried for the first time. But she was hanging in there. And she was wrong.

'They're not out to kill you,' he said. 'They could have killed you in that waste ground. Why haul you away in this damn truck? And there's your crutch, too.'

'What about my crutch?' she said.

'Doesn't make any sense,' he said. 'Why would they toss your crutch in here if they're going to kill you? You're a hostage, Holly, that's what you are. You sure you don't know these guys? Never saw them before?'

'Never,' she said. 'I don't know who the hell they are, or what the hell they want from me.'

He stared at her. She sounded way too definite. She knew more than she was telling him. They went quiet in the noise. Rocked and bounced with the movement of the truck. Reacher stared into the gloom. He could feel Holly making decisions, next to him. She turned sideways again.

'I need to get you out of here,' she said again.

He glanced at her. Glanced away and grinned.

'Suits me, Holly,' he said. 'Sooner the better.'

'When will somebody miss you?' she asked.

That was a question he would have preferred not to answer. But she was looking hard at him, waiting. So he thought about it, and he told her the truth.

'Never,' he said.

'Why not?' she asked. 'Who are you, Reacher?'

He looked across at her and shrugged.

'Nobody,' he said.

She carried on looking at him, quizzically. Maybe irritated.

'OK, what kind of nobody?' she asked.

He heard Memphis Slim in his head: got me working in a steel mill.

'I'm a doorman,' he said. 'At a club in Chicago.'

'Which club?' she asked.

'A blues place on the South Side,' he said. 'You probably don't know it.'

She looked at him and shook her head.

'A doorman?' she said. 'You're playing this pretty cool for a doorman.'

'Doormen deal with a lot of weird situations,' he said.

She looked like she wasn't convinced and he put his face down near his wristwatch to check the time. Two-thirty in the afternoon.

'And how long before somebody misses you?' he asked.

She looked at her own watch and made a face.

'Quite a while,' she said. 'I've got a case conference starting at five o'clock this afternoon. Nothing before then. Two and a half hours before anybody even knows I'm gone.'

FOUR

RIGHT INSIDE THE SHELL OF THE SECOND-FLOOR ROOM, A SECOND shell was taking shape. It was being built from brand-new softwood two-by-fours, nailed together in the conventional way, looking like a new room growing right there inside the old room. But the new room was going to be about a foot smaller in every dimension than the old room had been. A foot shorter in length, a foot narrower in width, and a foot shorter in height.

The new floor joists were going to be raised a foot off the old joists with twelve-inch lengths of the new softwood. The new lengths looked like a forest of short stilts, ready to hold the new floor up. More short lengths were ready to hold the new framing a foot away from the old framing all the way around the sides and the ends. The new framing had the bright yellowness of new wood. It gleamed against the smoky honey color of the old framing. The old framing looked like an ancient skeleton which was suddenly growing a new skeleton right inside itself.

Three men were building the new shell. They were stepping from joist to joist with practiced skill. They looked like men who had built things before. And they were working fast. Their contract demanded they finish on time. The employer had been explicit about it. Some kind of a rush job. The three carpenters were not complaining about that. The employer had accepted their first bid. It had been an inflated bid, with a large horse-trading margin built in. But the guy had not eaten into that margin. He had not negotiated at all. He had just nodded and told them to start work as soon as the wrecking crew had finished. Work was hard to find, and employers who accepted your first price were even harder to find. So the three men were happy to work hard, work fast, and work late. They were anxious to make a good first impression. Looking around, they could see the potential for a lot more employment.

So they were giving it their best shot. They ran up and down the stairs with tools and fresh lumber. They worked by eye, marking cut-lines in the wood with their thumbnails, using their nail guns and their saws until they ran hot. But they paused frequently to measure the gap between the old framing and the new. The employer had made it clear that dimension was critical. The old framing was six inches deep. The new framing was four. The gap was twelve inches.

'Six and four and twelve,' one guy said. 'Twenty-two inches total.'

'OK?' the second guy asked the crew chief.

'Ideal,' the crew chief said. 'Exactly what he told us.'

FIVE

HOLLY JOHNSON'S FIVE O'CLOCK CASE CONFERENCE WAS ALLOCATED to the Chicago FBI office's third-floor meeting room. This was a large room, better than forty feet by twenty, and it was more or less filled by a long polished table flanked by thirty chairs, fifteen on each side. The chairs were substantial and leather and the table was made of fine hardwood, but any tendency for the place to look like a corporate boardroom was defused by the scruffy government wallcovering and the cheap carpet. There were ninety square yards of carpet on the floor and the whole ninety together had probably cost less than just one of the chairs.

Five o'clock in the summer, the afternoon sun streamed in through the wall of windows and gave the people arriving in the room a choice. If they sat facing the windows, they got the sun in their eyes and squinted through the meeting and ended up with a blinding headache. And the sun overpowered the air conditioning, so if they sat backs to the windows, they got heated up to a point where it got uncomfortable and they started worrying about whether their deodorant was still OK at five o'clock in the afternoon. A tough choice, but the top option was to avoid the headache and take the risk of heating up. So the early attenders took the seats on the window side.

First into the room was the FBI lawyer with special responsibility for financial crime. He stood for a moment and made a judgment about the likely duration of the meeting. Maybe forty-five minutes, he thought, knowing Holly, so he turned and tried to assess which seat might get the benefit of the shade from the slim pillar splitting the wall of windows into two. The bar of shadow was lying to the left of the third chair in the row, and he knew it would inch toward the head of the table as time passed. So he spilled his pile of folders onto the table in front of the second chair and shrugged his jacket off and claimed the place by dropping it onto the chair. Then he turned again and strolled to the credenza at the end of the room for a cup of coffee from the filter machine.

Next in were two agents working on cases that might be tied in to the mess that Holly Johnson was dealing with. They nodded to the lawyer and saw the place he'd claimed. They knew there was no point in choosing between the other fourteen chairs by the window. They were all going to get equally hot. So they just dumped their portfolios at the nearest two places and lined up for coffee.

'She not here yet?' one of them said to the lawyer.

'Haven't seen her all day,' the lawyer said.

'Your loss, right?' the other guy said.

Holly Johnson was a new agent, but talented, and that was making her popular. In the past the Bureau would have taken no pleasure at all in busting the sort of businessmen that Holly was employed to chase down, but times had changed and the Chicago office had gotten quite a taste for it. The businessmen now looked like scumbags, not solid citizens, and the agents were sick and tired of looking at them as they rode the commuter trains home. The agents would be getting off the train miles before the bankers and the stockbrokers were anywhere near their expensive suburbs. They would be thinking about second mortgages and even second jobs, and they'd be thinking about the years of private-detective work they were going to have to put in to boost up the mean government pension. And the executives would be sitting there with smug smiles. So when one or two of them started to take a fall, the Bureau was happy enough about it. When the ones and twos turned into tens and twenties, and then hundreds, it became a blood sport.

The only drawback was that it was hard work. Probably more

difficult to nail than anything else. That was where Holly Johnson's arrival had made things easier. She had the talent. She could look at a balance sheet and just know if anything was wrong with it. It was like she could smell it. She'd sit at her desk and look at the papers, cock her head slightly to one side, and think. Sometimes she'd think for hours, but when she stopped thinking, she'd know what the hell was going on. Then she'd explain it all in the case conference. She'd make it all sound easy and logical, like there was no way anybody could be in any kind of doubt about it. She was a woman who made progress. She was a woman who made her fellow agents feel better on those commuter trains at night. That's what was making her popular.

Fourth person into the third-floor meeting room was the agent assigned to help Holly out with the fetching and carrying until she recovered from her soccer injury. His name was Milosevic. A slight frame, a slight West Coast accent. Less than forty, casually dressed in expensive designer khaki, gold at his neck and on his wrist. He was also a new arrival, recently transferred in to the Chicago office, because that was where the Bureau found it needed its financial people. He joined the line for coffee and looked around the room.

'She's late?' he said.

The lawyer shrugged at him and Milosevic shrugged back. He liked Holly Johnson. He had worked with her five weeks, since the accident on the soccer field, and he had enjoyed every minute of it.

'She's not usually late for anything,' he said.

Fifth person in was Brogan, Holly's section head. Irish, from Boston via California. The young side of middle age. Dark hair, red Irish face. A tough guy, handsomely dressed in an expensive silk jacket, ambitious. He'd come to Chicago the same time as Milosevic, and he was pissed it wasn't New York. He was looking for the advancement he was sure he deserved. There was a theory that Holly's arrival in his section was enhancing his chances of getting it.

'She not here yet?' he said.

The other four shrugged at him.

'I'll kick her ass,' Brogan said.

Holly had been a stock analyst on Wall Street before applying to join the FBI. Nobody was clear why she'd made the change.

She had some kind of exalted connections, and some kind of an illustrious father, and the easy guess was she wanted to impress him somehow. Nobody knew for sure whether the old guy was impressed or not, but the feeling was he damn well ought to be. Holly had been one of ten thousand applicants in her year, and she'd passed right at the top of the four hundred who made it. She'd creamed the recruitment criteria. The Bureau had been looking for college graduates in law or accountancy, or else graduates in flimsier disciplines who'd then worked somewhere for three years at least. Holly had qualified in every way. She had an accountancy degree from Yale, and a Master's from Harvard, and three years on Wall Street on top of all that. She'd blitzed the intelligence tests and the aptitude assessments. She'd charmed the three serving agents who'd grilled her at her main interview.

She'd sailed through the background checks, which was understandable on account of her connections, and she'd been sent to the FBI Academy at Quantico. Then she'd really started to get serious. She was fit and strong, she learned to shoot, she murdered the leadership reaction course, she scored outstanding in the simulated shootouts in Hogan's Alley. But her major success was her attitude. She did two things at once. First she bought into the whole Bureau ethic in the biggest way possible. It was totally clear to everybody that here was a woman who was going to live and die for the FBI. But second, she did it in a way which avoided the slightest trace of bullshit. She tinged her attitude with a gentle mocking humor which saved people from hating her. It made them love her instead. There was no doubt the Bureau had signed a major new asset. They sent her to Chicago and sat back to reap the benefits.

Last into the third-floor conference room was a bunch of men who came in together. Thirteen agents and the agent-in-charge, McGrath. The thirteen agents were clustered around their boss, who was conducting a sort of rolling policy review as he walked. The thirteen agents were hanging onto every word. McGrath had every advantage in the book. He was a man who'd been to the top, and then come back down again into the field. He'd spent three years in the Hoover Building as an assistant director of the FBI, and then he'd applied for a demotion and a pay cut to take him back to a Field Office. The decision had cost him ten thousand dollars a year in income, but it had bought him back his sanity, and it had bought him undying respect and blind affection from the agents he worked with.

An agent-in-charge in a Field Office like Chicago is like the captain on a great warship. Theoretically there are people above him, but they're all a couple of thousand miles away in Washington. They're theoretical. The agent-in-charge is real. He runs his command like the hand of God. That's how the Chicago office looked at McGrath. He did nothing to undermine the feeling. He was remote, but he was approachable. He was private, but he made his people feel he'd do anything at all for them. He was a short, stocky man, burning with energy, the sort of tireless guy who radiates total confidence. The sort of guy who makes a crew better just by leading it. His first name was Paul, but he was called Mack, like the truck.

He let his thirteen agents sit down, ten of them backs to the window and three of them with the sun in their eyes. Then he hauled a chair around and stuck it at the head of the table ready for Holly. He walked down to the other end and hauled another chair around for himself. Sat sideways on to the sun. Started getting worried.

'Where is she?' he said. 'Brogan?'

The section head shrugged, palms up.

'She should be here, far as I know,' he said.

'She leave a message with anybody?' McGrath asked. 'Milosevic?'

Milosevic and the other fifteen agents and the Bureau lawyer all shrugged and shook their heads. McGrath started worrying more. People have a pattern, a rhythm, like a behavioral fingerprint. Holly was only a minute or two late, but that was so far from normal that it was setting the bells ringing. In eight months he had never known her be late. It had never happened. Other people could be five minutes late into the meeting room and it would seem normal. Because of their pattern. But not Holly. At three minutes past five in the afternoon, McGrath stared at her empty chair and knew there was a problem. He stood up again in the quiet room and walked to the credenza on the opposite wall. There was a phone next to the coffee machine. He picked it up and dialed his office.

'Holly Johnson call in?' he asked his secretary.

'No, Mack,' she said.

So he dabbed the cradle and dialed the reception counter, two floors below.

'Any messages from Holly Johnson?' he asked the agent at the door.

'No, chief,' the agent said. 'Haven't seen her.'

He hit the button again and called the main switchboard.

'Holly Johnson call in?' he asked.

'No, sir,' the switchboard operator said.

He held the phone and gestured for pen and paper. Then he spoke to the switchboard again.

'Give me her pager number,' he said. 'And her cellphone, will you?'

The earpiece crackled and he scrawled down the numbers. Cut the switchboard off and dialed Holly's pager. Just got a long low tone telling him the pager was switched off. Then he tried the cellphone number. He got an electronic bleep and a recorded message of a woman telling him the phone he was dialing was unreachable. He hung up and looked around the room. It was ten after five, Monday afternoon.

SIX

SIX-THIRTY ON REACHER'S WATCH, THE MOTION INSIDE THE TRUCK changed. Six hours and four minutes they'd cruised steadily, maybe fifty-five or sixty miles an hour, while the heat peaked and fell away. He'd sat, hot and rocking and bouncing in the dark with the wheel well between him and Holly Johnson, ticking off the distance against a map inside his head. He figured they'd been taken maybe three hundred and ninety miles. But he didn't know which direction they were headed. If they were going east, they would be right through Indiana and just about out of Ohio by now, maybe just entering Pennsylvania or West Virginia. South, they would be out of Illinois, into Missouri or Kentucky, maybe even into Tennessee if he'd underestimated their speed. West, they'd be hauling their way across Iowa. They might have looped around the bottom of the lake and headed north up through Michigan. Or straight out northwest, in which case they could be up near Minneapolis.

But they'd gotten somewhere, because the truck was slowing. Then there was a lurch to the right, like a pull off a highway. There was gear noise and thumping over broken pavement. Cornering forces slammed them around. Holly's crutch slid and rattled side to side across the ridged metal floor. The truck whined up grades and down slopes, paused at invisible road junctions, accelerated, braked hard, turned a tight left, and then drove slowly down a straight lumpy surface for a quarter hour.

'Farming country somewhere,' Reacher said.

'Obviously,' Holly said. 'But where?'

Reacher just shrugged at her in the gloom. The truck slowed almost to a stop and turned a tight right. The road surface got worse. The truck bounced forward maybe a hundred and fifty yards and stopped. There was the sound of the passenger door opening up in front. The engine was still running. The passenger door slammed shut. Reacher heard a big door opening and the truck moved slowly forward. The engine noise boomed against metal walls. Reacher heard the door noise again and the engine noise echoed louder. Then it shut down and died away into stillness.

'We're in some sort of a barn,' Reacher said. 'With the door closed.'

Holly nodded impatiently.

'I know that,' she said. 'A cow barn. I can smell it.'

Reacher could hear muffled conversation outside the truck. Footsteps walking around to the rear doors. A key going into the lock. The handle turning. A blinding flood of light as the door opened. Reacher blinked against the sudden electric brightness and stared out across Holly at three men, two Glocks and a shotgun.

'Out,' the leader said.

They struggled out, handcuffed together. Not easy. They were stiff and sore and cramped from bracing themselves against the wheel well for six solid hours. Holly's knee had gone altogether. Reacher started back for her crutch.

'Leave it there, asshole,' the leader said.

The guy sounded tired and irritable. Reacher gave him a steady look and shrugged. Holly stiffened and tried her weight on her leg. Gasped in pain and gave it up. Glanced impersonally at Reacher like he was some kind of a tree and stretched around with her free left hand to hold on tight around his neck. It was the only way she could stay upright.

'Excuse me, please,' she muttered.

The leader gestured with his Glock over to his left. They were in a large cow barn. No cows, but they hadn't been long absent, judging by the odor. The truck was parked in a wide central aisle. Either side were cow stalls, roomy, made up from galvanized steel-piping

402

efficiently welded together. Reacher twisted and held Holly's waist and the two of them hopped and staggered over to the stall the guy with the Glock was pointing at. Holly seized a railing and held on, embarrassed.

'Excuse me,' she muttered again.

Reacher nodded and waited. The driver with the shotgun covered them and the leader walked away. He heaved the big door open and stepped through. Reacher caught a glimpse of darkening sky. Cloudy. No clue at all to their location.

The leader was gone five minutes. There was silence in the barn. The other two guys stood still, weapons out and ready. The jumpy guy with the Glock was staring at Reacher's face. The driver with the shotgun was staring at Holly's breasts. Smiling a half-smile. Nobody spoke. Then the leader stepped back in. He was carrying a second pair of handcuffs and two lengths of heavy chain.

'You're making a big mistake here,' Holly said to him. 'I'm an FBI agent.'

'I know that, bitch,' the guy said. 'Now be quiet.'

'You're committing a serious crime,' Holly said.

'I know that, bitch,' the guy said again. 'And I told you to be quiet. Another word out of you, I'll shoot this guy in the head. Then you can spend the night with a corpse chained to your wrist, OK?'

He waited until she nodded silently. Then the driver with the shotgun took up position behind them and the leader unlocked their cuff and freed their wrists. He looped one of the chains around the stall railing and locked the ends into the spare half of the cuff dangling from Reacher's left arm. Pulled it and rattled it to check it was secure. Then he dragged Holly two stalls away and used the new cuffs and the second length of chain to lock her to the railing, twenty feet from Reacher. Her knee gave way and she fell heavily with a gasp of pain onto the dirty straw. The leader ignored her. Just walked back to where Reacher was chained up. Stood right in front of him.

'So who the hell are you, asshole?' he said.

Reacher didn't reply. He knew the keys to both cuffs were in this guy's pocket. He knew it would take him about a second and a half to snap his neck with the loop of chain hanging off his wrist. But the other two guys were out of reach. One Glock, one shotgun, too far away to grab before he'd unlocked himself, too near to get a chance to do that. He was dealing with a reasonably efficient set of opponents. So he just shrugged and looked at the straw at his feet. It was clogged with dung.

'I asked you a damn question,' the guy said.

Reacher looked at him. In the corner of his eye he saw the jumpy guy ratchet his Glock upward a degree or two.

'I asked you a question, asshole,' the leader said again, quietly.

The jumpy guy's Glock was jutting forward. Then it was straight out, shoulder-high. Aimed right at Reacher's head. The muzzle was trembling through a small jerky circle, but probably not trembling enough to make the guy miss. Not from that sort of a close distance. Reacher looked from one guy to the other. The guy with the shotgun tore his attention away from Holly's breasts. He raised the weapon to his hip. Pointed it in Reacher's direction. It was an Ithaca 37. Twelve-bore. The five-shot version with the pistol grip and no shoulder stock. The guy racked a round into the chamber. The crunch-crunch of the mechanism was loud in the barn. It echoed off the metal walls. Died into silence. Reacher saw the trigger move through the first eighth-inch of its short travel.

'Name?' the leader asked.

The shotgun trigger tightened another eighth. If it fired on that trajectory, Reacher was going to lose both his legs and most of his stomach.

'Name?' the leader asked for the second time.

It was a twelve-bore, wouldn't kill him outright, but he'd bleed to death in the dirty straw. Femoral artery gone, about a minute, maybe a minute and a half. In those circumstances, no real reason to make a big deal out of giving this guy a name.

'Jack Reacher,' he said.

The leader nodded in satisfaction, like he'd achieved a victory.

'You know this bitch?' he asked.

Reacher glanced across at Holly.

'Better than I know some people,' he said. 'I just spent six hours handcuffed to her.'

'You some kind of a wiseguy, asshole?' the leader asked.

Reacher shook his head.

'Innocent passerby,' he said. 'I never saw her before.'

'You with the Bureau?' the guy asked.

Reacher shook his head again.

'I'm a doorman,' he said. 'Club back in Chicago.'

'You sure, asshole?' the guy said.

Reacher nodded.

'I'm sure,' he said. 'I'm a wise enough guy that I can recall what I do for a living, one day to the next.'

There was silence for a long moment. Tension. Then the jumpy guy with the Glock came out of his shooting stance. The driver with the shotgun swung his weapon down toward the straw on the floor. He turned his head and went back to staring at Holly's breasts. The leader nodded at Reacher.

'OK, asshole,' he said. 'You behave yourself, you stay alive for now. Same for the bitch. Nothing's going to happen to anybody. Not just yet.'

The three men regrouped in the center aisle and walked out of the barn. Before they locked the door, Reacher saw the sky again, briefly. Darker. Still cloudy. No stars. No clues. He tested the chain. It was securely fastened to the handcuff at one end and the railing at the other. Maybe seven feet long. He could hear Holly doing the same experiment. Tightening her chain and scoping out the radius it gave her to move through.

'Would you mind looking away?' she called across.

'Why?' he called back.

There was a short silence. Then a sigh. Part embarrassed, part exasperated.

'Do you really need to ask?' she called. 'We were in that truck six hours, and it didn't have a bathroom, did it?'

'You going in the next stall?' he asked.

'Obviously,' she said.

'OK,' he said. 'You go right and I'll go left. I won't look if you won't.'

The three men came back to the barn within an hour with food. Some kind of a beef stew in a metal mess tin, one for each of them. Mostly rare steak chunks and a lot of hard carrots. Whoever these guys were, cooking was not their major talent. Reacher was clear on that. They handed out an enamel mug of weak coffee, one for each of them. Then they got in the truck. Started it up and backed it out of the barn. Turned the bright lights off. Reacher caught a glimpse of dim emptiness outside. Then they pulled the big door shut and locked it. Left their prisoners in the dark and the quiet.

'Gas station,' Holly called from twenty feet away. 'They're filling up for the rest of the ride. Can't do it with us inside. They figure we'd be banging on the side and shouting out for help.'

Reacher nodded and finished his coffee. Sucked the fork from the stew clean. Bent one of the prongs right out and put a little kink into the end with pressure from his thumbnail. It made a little hook. He used it to pick the lock on his handcuff. Took him eighteen seconds, beginning to end. He dropped the cuff and the chain in the straw and walked over to Holly. Bent down and unlocked her wrist. Twelve seconds. Helped her to her feet.

'Doorman, right?' she said.

'Right,' he said. 'Let's take a look around.'

'I can't walk,' she said. 'My crutch is in the damn truck.'

Reacher nodded. She stayed in her stall, clinging to the railing. He scouted around the big empty barn. It was a sturdy metal structure, built throughout with the same flecked, galvanized metal as the stall railings. The big door was locked from the outside. Probably a steel bar padlocked into place. No problem if he could get at the padlock, but he was inside and the padlock was outside.

The walls met the floor with a right-angle flange bolted firmly into the concrete. The walls themselves were horizontal metal panels maybe thirty feet long, maybe four feet tall. They were joined together with more right-angle flanges bolted together. Each flange gave a lip about six inches deep. Like a giant stepladder with the treads four feet apart.

He climbed the wall, hauling himself quickly upward, flange to flange, four feet at a time. The way out of the barn was right there at the top of the wall, seven sections up, twenty-eight feet off the ground. There was a ventilation slot between the top of the wall and the overhanging slope of the metal roof. About eighteen inches high. A person could roll horizontally through the gap like an old-fashioned highjumper, hang down outside and drop twenty feet to the ground below.

He could do that, but Holly Johnson couldn't. She couldn't even walk over to the wall. She couldn't climb it and she sure as hell couldn't hang down outside and drop twenty feet onto a set of wrecked cruciate ligaments.

'Get going,' she called up to him. 'Get out of here, right now.'

He ignored her and peered out through the slot into the darkness. The overhanging eaves gave him a low horizon. Empty country as far as the eye could see. He climbed down and went up the other three walls in turn. The second side gave out onto country just as empty as the first. The third had a view of a farmhouse. White shingles. Lights in two windows. The fourth side of the barn looked straight up the farm track. About a hundred and fifty yards to a featureless road. Emptiness beyond. In the far distance, a single set of headlight beams. Flicking and bouncing. Widely spaced. Growing larger. Getting nearer. The truck, coming back.

'Can you see where we are?' Holly called up to him.

'No idea,' Reacher called back. 'Farming country somewhere. Could be anywhere. Where do they have cows like this? And fields and stuff?'

'Is it hilly out there?' Holly called. 'Or flat?'

'Can't tell,' Reacher said. 'Too dark. Maybe a little hilly.'

'Could be Pennsylvania,' Holly said. 'They have hills and cows there.'

Reacher climbed down the fourth wall and walked back to her stall.

'Get out of here, for Christ's sake,' she said to him. 'Raise the alarm.'

He shook his head. He heard the diesel slowing to turn into the track.

'That may not be the best option,' he said.

She stared at him.

'Who the hell gave you an option?' she said. 'I'm ordering you. You're a civilian and I'm FBI and I'm ordering you to get yourself to safety right now.'

Reacher just shrugged and stood there.

'I'm ordering you, OK?' Holly said again. 'You going to obey me?'

Reacher shook his head again.

'No,' he said.

She glared at him. Then the truck was back. They heard the roar of the diesel and the groan of the springs on the rough track outside. Reacher locked Holly's cuff and ran back to his stall. They heard the truck door slam and footsteps on the concrete. Reacher chained his wrist to the railing and bent the fork back into shape. When the barn door opened and the light came on, he was sitting quietly on the straw.

SEVEN

THE MATERIAL USED TO PACK THE TWENTY-TWO-INCH CAVITY between the outside of the old walls and the inside of the new walls was hauled over from its storage shed in an open pickup truck. There was a ton of it and it took four trips. Each consignment was carefully unloaded by a team of eight volunteers. They worked together like an old-fashioned bucket-brigade attending a fire. They passed each box along, hand to hand, into the building, up the stairs to the second floor. The boxes were stacked in the hallway outside the modified corner room. The three builders opened each box in turn and carried the material into the room. Then they stacked it carefully into the wide spaces behind the new softwood framing. The unloaders generally paused for a moment and watched them, grateful for a moment of rest.

The process lasted most of the afternoon because of the amount of material and the care they took in moving it. When the last of the four loads was stacked upstairs, the eight volunteers dispersed. Seven of them headed for the mess hall. The eighth stretched in the last of the afternoon sun and strolled off. It was his habit. Four or five times a week, he would take a long walk on his own, especially after a period of heavy work. It was assumed to be his way of relaxing.

He strolled in the forest. There was a beaten path running west through the silence. He followed it for a half-mile. Then he paused and stretched again. He used the weary twisting motion of a tired man easing a sore back to glance around a complete circle. Then he stepped sideways off the path. Stopped strolling. Started an urgent walk. He dodged trees and followed a wide looping course west, then north. He went straight for a particular tree. There was a large flat rock bedded in needles at its base. He stood still and waited. Listened hard. Then he ducked down and heaved the rock to one side. Underneath was a rectangular shape wrapped in oilcloth. He unfolded the cloth and took out a small hand-held radio. Pulled the stubby antenna and hit a button and waited. Then he whispered a long and excited message.

When the old building was quiet again, the employer stopped by with some strange new instructions. The three builders asked no questions. Just listened carefully. The guy was entitled to get what he wanted. The new instructions meant a certain amount of work would have to be redone. In the circumstances, not a problem. Even less of a problem when the employer offered a cash bonus on top of the bid price.

The three builders worked fast and it took them less time than it might have. But it was already evening by the time they finished. The junior man stayed behind to pack tools and coil cables. The crew chief and the other guy drove north in the dark and parked exactly where the employer had told them to. Got out of their truck and waited in the silence.

'In here,' a voice called. The employer. 'All the way in back.'

They went in. The place was dark. The guy was waiting for them, somewhere in the shadows.

'These boards any use to you?' the employer asked.

There was a stack of old pine boards, way in back.

'They're good lumber,' the employer said. 'Maybe you can use them. Like recycling, you know?'

There was something else on the ground beside the stack of boards. Something strange. The two carpenters stared. Strange humped shapes. The two carpenters stared at the strange humped shapes, then they stared at each other. Then they turned around. The employer smiled at them and raised a dull black automatic.

The resident agent at the FBI's remote satellite station was a smart enough guy to realize it was going to be important. He didn't know exactly how or why it was going to be important, but an undercover informant doesn't risk a radio message from a concealed location for no reason. So he copied the details into the FBI computer system. His report flashed across the computer network and lodged in the massive mainframe on the first floor of the FBI's Hoover Building in Washington, DC. The Hoover Building database handles more new reports in a day than there are seconds, so it took a long moment for the FBI software to scan through and pick out the key words. Once it had done so, it lodged the bulletin high in its memory and waited.

At exactly the same time, the system was logging a message from the FBI Field Office in Chicago. The bureau chief up there, Agent-in-Charge McGrath, was reporting that he'd lost one of his people. Special Agent Holly Johnson was missing, last seen twelve o'clock Chicago time, whereabouts currently unknown, contact attempted but not achieved. And because Holly Johnson was a pretty special case, the message carried an eyes-only code which kept it off every terminal in the building except the one all the way upstairs in the director's office.

The director of the FBI got out of a budget review meeting just before seven-thirty in the evening. He walked back to his office suite and checked his messages. His name was Harland Webster and he had been with the Bureau thirty-six years. He had one more year to run on his term as director, and then he'd be gone. So he wasn't looking for trouble, but he found it glowing on the monitor of his desktop terminal. He clicked on the report and read it through twice. He sighed at the screen.

'Shit,' he said. 'Shit, shit, shit.'

The report in from McGrath in Chicago was not the worst news Webster had ever had in thirty-six years, but it came pretty damn close. He buzzed the intercom on his desk and his secretary answered.

'Get me McGrath in Chicago,' he said.

'He's on line one,' his secretary told him. 'He's been waiting for you.'

Webster grunted and hit the button for line one. Put the call on the speakerphone and leaned back in his chair.

'Mack?' he said. 'So what's the story?'

McGrath's voice came in clear from Chicago.

'Hello, chief,' he said. 'There is no story. Not yet. Maybe we're worrying too early, but I got a bad feeling when she didn't show. You know how it is.'

'Sure, Mack,' Webster said. 'You want to confuse me with some facts?'

'We don't have any facts,' McGrath said. 'She didn't show for a five o'clock case conference. That struck me as unusual. There were no messages from her anywhere. Her pager and her cellphone are out of commission. I asked around and the last anybody saw of her was about twelve o'clock.'

'She was in the office this morning?' Webster asked.

'All morning,' McGrath said.

'Any appointments before this five o'clock thing?' Webster said.

'Nothing in her diary,' McGrath said. 'I don't know what she was doing or where she was doing it.'

'Christ, Mack,' Webster said. 'You were supposed to take care of her. You were supposed to keep her off the damn streets, right?'

'It was her lunchbreak,' McGrath said. 'What the hell could I do?'

There was a silence in the director's suite, broken only by the faint hum on the speakerphone. Webster drummed his fingers on his desk.

'What was she working on?' he asked.

'Forget it,' McGrath said. 'We can assume this is not interference by a Bureau suspect, right? Doesn't make any kind of sense in her case.'

Webster nodded to himself.

'In her case, I agree, I guess,' he said. 'So what else are we looking at?'

'She was injured,' McGrath said. 'Tore up her knee playing ball. We figure maybe she fell, made it worse, maybe ended up in the ER. We're checking the hospitals now.'

Webster grunted.

'Or else there's a boyfriend we don't know about,' McGrath said. 'Maybe they're in a motel room somewhere, getting laid.'

'For six hours?' Webster said. 'I should be so lucky.'

There was silence again. Then Webster sat forward.

'OK, Mack,' he said. 'You know what to do. And you know what not to do, case like hers, right? Keep in touch. I've got to go to the Pentagon. I'll be back in an hour. Call me then if you need me.'

Webster broke the connection and buzzed his secretary to call his car. Then he walked out to his private elevator and rode down to the underground parking lot. His driver met him there and they walked together over to the director's bulletproof limousine.

'Pentagon,' Webster said to his driver.

Traffic wasn't bad, seven-thirty on a June Monday evening. Took about eleven minutes to do the two and a half miles. Webster spent the time making urgent calls on his mobile. Calls to various locations within such a tight geographical radius that he could probably have reached them all by shouting. Then the big car came up to the Pentagon River Entrance and the Marine sentry stepped over. Webster clicked off his phone and buzzed his window down for the identification ritual.

'The director of the FBI,' he said. 'To see the chairman of the joint chiefs of staff.'

The sentry snapped a salute and waved the limousine through. Webster buzzed the window back up and waited for the driver to stop. Then he got out and ducked in through the personnel door. Walked through to the chairman's suite. The chairman's secretary was waiting for him.

'Go right through, sir,' she said. 'The general will be along in a moment.'

Webster walked into the chairman's office and stood waiting. He looked out through the window. The view was magnificent, but it had a strange metallic tint. The window was made of one-way, bulletproof Mylar. It was a great view, but the window was on the outside of the building, right next to the River Entrance, so it had to be protected. Webster could see his car, with his driver waiting beside it. Beyond the car was a view of the Capitol, across the Potomac. Webster could see sailboats in the Tidal Basin, with the last of the evening sun glinting low on the water. Not a bad office, Webster thought. Better than mine, he thought.

Meeting with the chairman of the joint chiefs of staff was a problem for the director of the FBI. It was one of those Beltway oddities, a meeting where there was no cast-iron ranking. Who was superior? Both were presidential appointees. Both reported to the president through just one intermediary, the defense secretary or the attorney general. The chairman of the joint chiefs of staff was the highest-ranking military post that the nation had to offer. The director of the FBI was the highest-ranking law-enforcement post. Both men were at the absolute top of their respective greasy poles. But which greasy pole was taller? It was a problem for Webster. In the end, it was a problem for him because the truth was his pole was shorter. He controlled a budget of two billion dollars and about twenty-five thousand people. The chairman oversaw a budget of two hundred billion and about a million people. Two million if you added in the National Guard and the Reserves. The chairman was in the Oval Office about once a week. Webster got there twice a year, if he was lucky. No wonder this guy's office was better.

The chairman himself was impressive too. He was a four-star general whose rise had been spectacular. He had come from nowhere and blitzed upward through the army just about faster than his tailor could sew the ribbons on his uniform. The guy had ended up lopsided with medals. Then he had been hijacked by Washington and moved in and made the place his own, like it was some military objective. Webster heard his arrival in the anteroom and turned to greet him as he came into the office.

'Hello, General,' he said.

The chairman sketched a busy wave and grinned.

'You want to buy some missiles?' he said.

Webster was surprised.

'You're selling them?' he said. 'What missiles?'

The chairman shook his head and smiled.

'Just kidding,' he said. 'Arms limitation. Russians have gotten rid of a bomber base in Siberia, so now we've got to get rid of the missiles we assigned against it. Treaty compliance, right? Got to play fair. The big stuff, we're selling to Israel. But we've still got about a couple hundred little ones, you know, Stingers, shoulder-launch surface-to-air things. All surplus. Sometimes I think we should sell

414

them to the dope dealers. God knows they've got everything else they want. Better weapons than we've got, most of them.'

The chairman talked his way around to his chair and sat down. Webster nodded. He'd seen presidents do a similar thing, tell a joke, tell a light-hearted story, man-to-man, get the ice broken, make the meeting work. The chairman leaned back and smiled.

'So what can I do for you, Director?' he asked.

'We got a report in from Chicago,' Webster said. 'Your daughter is missing.'

EIGHT

B Y MIDNIGHT IN CHICAGO THE THIRD-FLOOR CONFERENCE ROOM WAS
set up as a command center. FBI technicians had swarmed
all evening, running phone lines into the room and installing
computer terminals in a line down the center of the hardwood table.
Now at midnight it was dark and cool and quiet. Shiny blackness
outside the wall of glass. No scramble to decide which side of the
table was better.

Nobody had gone home. There were seventeen agents sprawled
in the leather chairs. Even the Bureau lawyer was still there. No
real reason for that, but the guy was feeling the same triple-layered
response they all were. The Bureau looks after its own. That was
layer number one. The Chicago Field Office looks after Holly
Johnson. That was layer number two. Not just because of her
connections. That had nothing to do with it. Holly was Holly.
And layer number three was what McGrath wanted, McGrath got.
If McGrath was worried about Holly, then they all were worried,
and they all were going to stay worried until she was found, safe
and sound. So they were all still there. Quiet, and worried. Until
McGrath came loudly and cheerfully into the room, making a big
entrance, smoking like his life depended on it.

'Good news, people, listen up, listen up,' he called out.

He dodged his way through to the head of the table. Murmuring died into sudden silence. Eighteen pairs of eyes followed him.

'We found her,' he called out. 'We found her, OK? She's safe and well. Panic's over, folks. We can all relax now.'

Eighteen voices started talking all at once. All asking the same urgent questions. McGrath held his hands up for quiet, like a nominee at a rally.

'She's in the hospital,' he said. 'What happened is her surgeon got a window for this afternoon he wasn't expecting. He called her, she went right over, they took her straight to the OR. She's fine, she's convalescing, and she's embarrassed as all hell for the fuss she's caused.'

The eighteen voices started up again, and McGrath let them rumble on for a moment. Then he held his hands up again.

'So, panic over, right?' he called out again, smiling.

The rumbling got lighter in tone as relief fueled the voices.

'So, people, home to bed,' McGrath said. 'Full working day tomorrow, right? But thanks for being here. From me, and from Holly. Means a lot to her. Brogan and Milosevic, you stay awhile, share out her workload for the rest of the week. The rest of you, goodnight, sleep well, and thanks again, gentlemen.'

Fifteen agents and the lawyer smiled and yawned and stood up. Jostled cheerfully and noisily out of the room. McGrath and Brogan and Milosevic were left scattered in random seats, far from each other. McGrath walked over in the sudden silence to the door. Closed it quietly. Turned back and faced the other two.

'That was all bullshit,' he said. 'As I'm sure you both guessed.'

Brogan and Milosevic just stared at him.

'Webster called me,' McGrath said. 'And I'm sure you can both guess why. Major, major DC involvement. They're going apeshit down there. VIP kidnap, right? Webster's been given personal responsibility. He wants total secrecy and minimum numbers. He wants everybody up here off this case right now except me plus a team of two. My choice. I picked the two of you because you know her best. So it's the three of us. We deal direct with Webster, and we don't talk to anybody else at all, OK?'

Brogan stared at him and nodded. Milosevic nodded in turn. They knew they were the obvious choices for the job. But to be chosen by McGrath for any reason was an honor. They knew it, and they knew McGrath knew they knew it. So they nodded again, more firmly. Then there was silence for a long moment. McGrath's cigarette smoke mingled with the silence up near the ceiling. The clock on the wall ticked around toward half past midnight.

'OK,' Brogan said finally. 'So what now?'

'We work all night, is what,' McGrath said. 'All day, all night, every day, every night, until we find her.'

He glanced at the two of them. Reviewed his choices. An adequate team, he thought. A good mixture. Brogan was older, drier, a pessimist. A compact man with a tidy, ordered approach, laced with enough imagination to make him useful. An untidy private life, with a girlfriend and a couple of ex-wives somewhere, all costing him big bucks and worry, but it never interfered with his work. Milosevic was younger, less intuitive, flashier, but solid. A permanent sidekick, which was not necessarily a fault. A weakness for big expensive four-wheel-drives, but everybody needs some kind of a hobby. Both of them were medium-term Bureau veterans, with mileage on their clocks and scalps on their belts. Both of them were focused and neither of them ever bitched about the work or the hours. Or the salary, which made them just about unique. An adequate team. They were new to Chicago, but this investigation was not going to stay in Chicago. McGrath was just about sure of that.

'Milo, you figure out her movements,' he said. 'Every step, every minute from twelve noon.'

Milosevic nodded vaguely, like he was already lost in doing that.

'Brogan, background checks,' McGrath said. 'We need to find some reason here.'

Brogan nodded dourly, like he knew the reason was going to be the beginning and the end of the whole thing.

'I start with the old guy?' he asked.

'Obviously,' McGrath said. 'That's what I would do.'

'OK, which one?' Brogan asked.

'Whichever one,' McGrath replied. 'Your choice.'

Seventeen hundred and two miles away another executive decision had been taken. A decision about the third carpenter. The employer drove back to the white building in the crew chief's pickup. The third carpenter had finished up stacking the tools and he took a step forward when he saw the vehicle approaching. Then he stopped in puzzlement when he saw the huge figure at the wheel. He stood, uncertain, while the employer pulled up at the curb and heaved himself out.

'OK?' the employer said to him.

'Where are the guys?' the carpenter asked.

'Something came up,' the employer said. 'Something came up.'

'Problem?' the guy asked.

He went quiet, because he was thinking about his share of the price. A minority share, for sure, because he was the junior guy, but a minority share of that price was still more cash than he'd seen in a long time.

'You got a saw there?' the employer asked.

The guy just looked at him.

'Dumb question, right?' the employer said. 'You're a carpenter and I'm asking you if you got a saw? Just show me your best saw.'

The guy stood still for a moment, then he ducked down and pulled a power saw from the stack of tools. A big thing in dull metal, wicked circular blade, fresh sawdust caked all around it.

'Crosscut?' the employer asked. 'Good for ripping through real tough stuff?'

The guy nodded.

'It does the job,' he said, cautiously.

'OK, here's the deal,' the employer said. 'We need a demonstration.'

'Of the saw?' the guy asked.

'Of the room,' the employer said.

'The room?' the guy repeated.

'Supposed to be nobody can get out of it,' the employer said. 'That's the idea behind it, right?'

'You designed it,' the guy said.

'But did you build it right?' the employer said. 'That's what I'm asking here. We need a trial run. A demonstration to prove it serves its purpose.'

'OK, how?' the guy asked.

'You go in there,' the employer said. 'See if you can get out by morning. You built it, right? So you know all the weak spots. If anybody can get out, you can, that's for damn sure, right?'

The guy was quiet for a long moment. Trying to understand.

'And if I can?' he asked.

The employer shrugged.

'Then you don't get paid,' he said. 'Because you didn't build it right.'

The guy went quiet again. Wondering if the employer was joking.

'You spot the flaw in my logic?' the employer asked. 'The way you're figuring it right now, it's in your interest just to sit there on your ass all night, then tomorrow you say to me no sir, I couldn't get out of there, no sir, not at all.'

The carpenter laughed a short nervous laugh.

'That's how I was thinking,' he said.

'So what you need is an incentive,' the employer said. 'Understand? To make sure you try real hard to get out.'

The carpenter glanced up at the blanked-off second-story corner. When he glanced back down, there was a dull black automatic in the employer's hand.

'There's a sack in the truck,' the employer said, 'go get it, OK?'

The carpenter just looked around, astonished. The employer pointed the gun at his head.

'Get the sack,' he said quietly.

There was nothing in the pickup bed. There was a burlap sack on the passenger seat. Wrapped into a package maybe a foot and a half long. It was heavy. Felt like reaching into a freezer at the market and pulling out a side of pig.

'Open it up,' the employer called. 'Take a look.'

The carpenter peeled back the burlap. First thing he saw was a finger. Icy white, because the blood had drained. Yellow workman's calluses standing out, big and obvious.

'I'm going to put you in the room now,' the employer called to him. 'You don't get out by morning, I'm going to do that to you, OK? With your own damn saw, because mine went dull doing those.'

420

NINE

REACHER LAY QUIETLY ON THE DIRTY STRAW IN HIS STALL IN THE cow barn. Not asleep, but his body was shut down to the point where he might as well have been. Every muscle was relaxed and his breathing was slow and even. His eyes were closed because the barn was dark and there was nothing to see. But his mind was wide awake. Not racing, but just powering steadily along with that special nighttime intensity you get in the absence of any other distractions.

He was doing two things at once. First he was keeping track of time. It was nearly two hours since he had last looked at his watch, but he knew what time it was to within about twenty seconds. It was an old skill, born of many long wakeful nights on active service. When you're waiting for something to happen, you close your body down like a beach house in winter and you let your mind lock on to the steady pace of the passing seconds. It's like suspended animation. It saves energy and it lifts the responsibility for your heartbeat away from your unconcious brain and passes it on to some kind of a hidden clock. Makes a huge black space for thinking in. But it keeps you just awake enough to be ready for whatever you need to be ready for. And it means you always know what time it is.

The second simultaneous thing Reacher was doing was playing around with a little mental arithmetic. He was multiplying big numbers in his head. He was thirty-seven years and eight months old, just about to the day. Thirty-seven multiplied by three hundred and sixty-five was thirteen thousand five hundred and five. Plus twelve days for twelve leap years was thirteen thousand five hundred and seventeen. Eight months counting from his birthday in October forward to this date in June was two hundred and forty-three days. Total of thirteen thousand seven hundred and sixty days since he was born. Thirteen thousand seven hundred and sixty days, thirteen thousand seven hundred and sixty nights. He was trying to place this particular night somewhere on that endless scale. In terms of how bad it was.

Truth was, it wasn't the best night he had ever passed, but it was a long way from being the worst. A very long way. The first four or so years of his life, he couldn't remember anything at all, which left about twelve thousand three hundred nights to account for. Probability was, this particular night was up there in the top third. Without even trying hard, he could have reeled off thousands of nights worse than this one. Tonight, he was warm, comfortable, uninjured, not under any immediate threat, and he'd been fed. Not well, but he felt that came from a lack of skill rather than from active malice. So physically he had no complaints.

Mentally it was a different story. He was suspended in a vacuum just as impenetrable as the darkness inside the cow barn. The problem was the total lack of information. He was not a guy who necessarily felt uncomfortable with some lack of information. He was the son of a Marine officer and he had lived the military life literally all the way since birth. Therefore confusion and unpredictability were what he was accustomed to. But tonight there was just too much missing.

He didn't know where he was. Whether by accident or by design, the three kidnapers had given him absolutely no clue at all where they were headed. It made him feel adrift. His particular problem was, living the military life from birth, out of those thirteen thousand seven hundred and sixty days of his life he'd spent probably much less than a fifth of them actually inside the United States. He was as American as the president, but he'd lived and served all over the world most of his life. Outside the

United States. It had left him knowing his own country about as well as the average seven-year-old knows it. So he couldn't decode the subtle rhythms and feel and smells of America as well as he wanted to. It was possible that somebody else could interpret the unseen contours of the invisible landscape or the feel of the air or the temperature of the night and say yes, I'm in this state now or that state now. It was possible people could do that. But Reacher couldn't. It gave him a problem.

Added to that he had no idea who the kidnapers were. Or what their business was. Or what their intentions were. He'd studied them closely, every opportunity he'd had. Conclusions were difficult. The evidence was all contradictory. Three of them, youngish, maybe somewhere between thirty and thirty-five, fit, trained to act together with a measure of efficiency. They were almost military, but not quite. They were organized, but not official. Their appearance shrieked: amateurs.

Because they were so neat. They all had new clothes, plain chainstore cottons and poplins, fresh haircuts. Their weapons were fresh out of the box. The Glocks were brand-new. The shotgun was brand-new, packing grease still visible. Those factors meant they weren't any kind of professionals. Because professionals do this stuff every day. Whoever they are, Special Forces, CIA, FBI, detectives, it's their job. They wear working clothes. They use weapons they signed out last year, the year before, tried and trusted weapons, chipped weapons, scratched weapons, working tools. Put three professionals together on any one day, and you'll see last night's pizza on one guy's shirt, another guy won't have shaved, the third guy will be wearing the awful old pants his buddies make jokes about behind his back. It's possible you'll see a new jacket once in a while, or a fresh gun, or new shoes, but the chances of seeing everything new all at once on three working professionals on the same day are so slim as to be absurd.

And their attitude betrayed them. Competent, but jumpy, uptight, hostile, rude, tense. Trained to some degree, but not practiced. Not experienced. They'd rehearsed the theory, and they were smart enough to avoid any gross errors, but they didn't have the habituation of professionals. Therefore these three were some kind of amateurs. And they had kidnaped a brand-new FBI agent. Why? What the hell could a brand-new FBI agent have done to anybody? Reacher had no idea. And the brand-new FBI agent in question wasn't saying. Just another component he couldn't begin to figure. But not the biggest component. The biggest component he couldn't begin to figure was why the hell he was still there.

He had no problem with how he had gotten grabbed up in the first place. Just a freak of chance had put him alongside Holly Johnson at the exact time the snatch was going down. He was comfortable with that. He understood freak chances. Life was built out of freak chances, however much people would like to pretend otherwise. And he never wasted time speculating about how things might have been different, if this and if that. Obviously if he'd been strolling on that particular Chicago street a minute earlier or a minute later, he'd have been right past that dry-cleaners and never known a damn thing about all this. But he hadn't been strolling a minute earlier or a minute later, and the freak chance had happened, and he wasn't about to waste his time wondering where he'd be now if it hadn't.

But what he did need to pin down was why he was still there, just over fourteen hours later, according to the clock inside his head. He'd had two marginal chances and one cast-iron certainty of getting out. Right away, on the street, he could have made it. Probably. The possibility of collateral damage had stopped him. Then in the abandoned lot, getting into the white truck, he might have made it. Probably. Three against one, both times, but they were three amateurs against Jack Reacher, and he felt comfortable enough about those odds.

The cast-iron certainty was he could have been out of the cow barn, say an hour after the three guys returned from the gas station with the truck. He could have slipped the cuff again, climbed the wall and dropped down into the barnyard and been away. Just jogged over to the road and walked away and disappeared. Why hadn't he done that?

He lay there in the huge inky blackness of relaxation and realized it was Holly that was keeping him there. He hadn't bailed out because he couldn't take the risk. The three guys could have panicked and wasted her and run. Reacher didn't want that to happen. Holly was a smart, spirited woman. Sharp, impatient, confident, tough as hell. Attractive, in a shy, unforced sort of a way. Dark, slim, a lot of intelligence and energy.

Great eyes. Eyes were Reacher's thing. He was lost in a pair of pretty eyes.

But it wasn't her eyes that were doing it to him. Not her looks. Or her intelligence or her personality. It was her knee. That's what was doing it to him. Her guts and her dignity. The sight of a good-looking spirited woman cheerfully fighting an unaccustomed disability seemed like a brave and noble thing to Reacher. It made her his type of person. She was coping with it. She was doing it well. She wasn't complaining. She wasn't asking for his help. And because she wasn't asking for it, she was going to get it.

TEN

FIVE-THIRTY TUESDAY MORNING FBI SPECIAL AGENT BROGAN WAS alone in the third-floor meeting room, using one of the newly installed phone lines for an early call to his girlfriend. Five-thirty in the morning is not the best time to deliver an apology for a broken date from the night before, but Brogan had been very busy, and he anticipated being busier still. So he made the call. He woke her and told her he had been tied up, and probably would be for the rest of the week. She was sleepy and annoyed, and made him repeat it all twice. Then she chose to interpret the message as a cowardly prelude to some kind of a brush-off. Brogan got annoyed in turn. He told her the Bureau had to come first. Surely she understood that? It was not the best point to be making to a sleepy, annoyed woman at five-thirty in the morning. They had a short row and Brogan hung up, depressed.

His partner Milosevic was alone in his own office cubicle. Slumped in his chair, also depressed. His problem was a lack of imagination. It was his biggest weakness. McGrath had told him to trace Holly Johnson's every move from noon yesterday. But he hadn't come up with anything. He had seen her leaving the FBI Building. Stepping out of the door, onto the street, forearm jammed into the curved-metal clip of her hospital cane. He had seen her getting that far. But then

426

the picture just went blank. He'd thought hard all night, and told McGrath nothing.

Five-forty, he went to the bathroom and got more coffee. Still miserable. He walked back to his desk. Sat down, lost in thought for a long time. Then he glanced at the heavy gold watch on his wrist. Checked the time. Smiled. Felt better. Thought some more. Checked his watch again. He nodded to himself. Now he could tell McGrath where Holly Johnson had gone at twelve o'clock yesterday.

Seventeen hundred and two miles away panic had set in. Numb shock had carried the carpenter through the first hours. It had made him weak and aquiescent. He had let the employer hustle him up the stairs and into the room. Then numb shock had made him waste his first hours, just sitting and staring. Then he had started up with a crazy optimism that this whole thing was some kind of a bad Halloween joke. That made him waste his next hours convinced nothing was going to happen. But then, like prisoners everywhere locked up alone in the cold small hours of the night, all his defenses stripped away and left him shaking and desperate with panic.

With half his time gone, he burst into frantic action. But he knew it was hopeless. The irony was crushing him. They had worked hard on this room. They had built it right. Dollar signs had danced in front of their eyes. They had cut no corners. They had left out all their usual shoddy carpenters' tricks. Every single board was straight and tight. Every single nail was punched way down below the grain. There were no windows. The door was solid. It was hopeless. He spent an hour running around the room like a madman. He ran his rough palms over every square inch of every surface. Floor, ceiling, walls. It was the best job they had ever done. He ended up crouched in a corner, staring at his hands, crying.

'The dry-cleaner's,' McGrath said. 'That's where she went.'

He was in the third-floor conference room. Head of the table, seven o'clock, Tuesday morning. Opening a fresh pack of cigarettes.

'She did?' Brogan said. 'The dry-cleaner's?'

McGrath nodded.

'Tell him, Milo,' he said.

Milosevic smiled.

427

'I just remembered,' he said. 'I've worked with her five weeks, right? Since she bust up her knee? Every Monday lunchtime, she takes in her cleaning. Picks up last week's stuff. No reason for it to be any different yesterday.'

'OK,' Brogan said. 'Which cleaners?'

Milosevic shook his head.

'Don't know,' he said. 'She always went on her own. I always offered to do it for her, but she said no, every time, five straight Mondays. OK if I helped her out on Bureau business, but she wasn't about to have me running around after her cleaning. She's a very independent type of a woman.'

'But she walked there, right?' McGrath said.

'Right,' Milosevic said. 'She always walked. With maybe eight or nine things on hangers. So we're safe to conclude the place she used is fairly near here.'

Brogan nodded. Smiled. They had some kind of a lead. He pulled the Yellow Pages over and opened it up to D.

'What sort of a radius are we giving it?' he said.

McGrath shrugged.

'Twenty minutes there, twenty minutes back,' he said. 'That would be about the max, right? With that crutch, I can't see her doing more than a quarter-mile in twenty minutes. Limping like that? Call it a square, a half-mile on a side, this building in the center. What does that give us?'

Brogan used the AAA street map. He made a crude compass with his thumb and forefinger. Adjusted it to a half-mile according to the scale in the margin. Drew a square across the thicket of streets. Then he flipped back and forth between the map and the Yellow Pages. Ticked off names with his pencil. Counted them up.

'Twenty-one establishments,' he said.

McGrath stared at him.

'Twenty-one?' he said. 'Are you sure?'

Brogan nodded. Slid the phone book across the shiny hardwood.

'Twenty-one,' he said. 'Obviously people in this town like to keep their clothes real clean.'

'OK,' McGrath said. 'Twenty-one places. Hit the road, guys.'

Brogan took ten addresses and Milosevic took eleven. McGrath issued them both with large color blow-ups of Holly Johnson's file photograph. Then he nodded them out and waited in his chair at the head of the conference-room table, next to the telephones, slumped, staring into space, smoking, drumming a worried little rhythm with the blunt end of his pencil.

He heard faint sounds much earlier than he thought he should. He had no watch and no windows, but he was certain it was not yet morning. He was certain he had another hour. Maybe two. But he could hear noise. People moving in the street outside. He held his breath and listened. Maybe three or four people. He quartered the room again. Frozen with indecision. He should be pounding and kicking at the new pine boards. He knew that. But he wasn't. Because he knew it was hopeless, and because he felt in his gut he must be silent. He had become sure of that. Convinced. If he was silent, they might leave him alone. They might forget he was in there.

Milosevic found the right place, the seventh of the eleven establishments on his list. It was just opening up for business, seven-forty in the morning. Just a storefront place, but elegant, not really aimed at the typical commuter's cheap worsteds. It advertised all kinds of specialized processes and custom treatments. There was a Korean woman in charge of the store. Milosevic showed her his FBI shield and placed Holly's file picture flat on the counter in front of her.

'You ever see this person?' he asked her.

The Korean woman looked at the picture, politely, with concentration, her hands clasped together behind her back.

'Sure,' she said. 'That's Miss Johnson, comes in every Monday.'

Milosevic stepped closer to the counter. He leaned up close to the woman.

'She come in yesterday?' Milosevic asked her.

The woman thought about it and nodded.

'Sure,' she said. 'Like I told you, she comes in every Monday.'

'What kind of time?' he asked.

'Lunch hour,' the woman said. 'Always lunch hour.'

'About twelve?' he said. 'Twelve-thirty, something like that?'

'Sure,' the woman said. 'Always lunch hour on a Monday.'

'OK, yesterday,' Milosevic said. 'What happened?'

The woman shrugged.

'Nothing happened,' she said. 'She came in, she took her garments, she paid, she left some garments to be cleaned.'

'Anybody with her?' he asked.

'Nobody with her,' the woman said. 'Nobody ever with her.'

'Which direction was she headed?' Milosevic asked.

The woman pointed back towards the Federal Building.

'She came from that direction,' she said.

'I didn't ask you where she came from,' Milosevic said. 'Where did she head when she left?'

The woman paused.

'I didn't see,' she said. 'I took her garments through to the back. I heard the door open, but I couldn't see where she went. I was in back.'

'You just grabbed her stuff?' Milosevic said. 'Rushed through to the back before she was out of here?'

The woman faltered, like she was being accused of an impoliteness.

'Not rushed,' she said. 'Miss Johnson was walking slow. Bad leg, right? I felt I shouldn't stare at her. I felt she was embarrassed. I walked her clothes through to the back so she wouldn't feel I was watching her.'

Milosevic nodded and tilted his head back and sighed up at the ceiling. Saw a video camera mounted high above the counter.

'What's that?' he said.

The Korean woman twisted and followed his gaze.

'Security,' she said. 'Insurance company says we got to have it.'

'Does it work?' he asked.

'Sure it works,' the woman said. 'Insurance company says it's got to.'

'Does it run all the time?' Milosevic asked.

The woman nodded and giggled.

'Sure it does,' she said. 'It's running right now. You'll be on the tape.'

Milosevic checked his watch.

'I need yesterday's tape,' he said. 'Immediately.'

The woman faltered again. Milosevic pulled his shield for the second time.

'This is an FBI investigation,' he said. 'Official federal business. I need that tape, right now, OK?'

The woman nodded and held up her hand to make him wait. Stepped through a door to the rear of the establishment. Came back out after a long moment with a blast of chemical smell and a video cassette in her hand.

'You let me have it back, OK?' she said. 'Insurance company says we got to keep them for a month.'

Milosevic took it straight in and by eight-thirty the Bureau technicians were swarming all over the third-floor conference room again, hooking up a standard VHS player to the bank of monitors piled down the middle of the long table. There was a problem with a fuse, and then the right wire proved too short, so a computer had to be moved to allow the video player to get nearer to the center of the table. Then the head tech handed McGrath the remote and nodded.

'All yours, chief,' he said.

McGrath sent him out of the room and the three agents crowded around the screens, waiting for the picture to roll. The screens faced the wall of windows, so they all three had their backs to the glass. But at that time of day, there was no danger of anybody getting uncomfortable because right then the bright morning sun was blasting the other side of the building.

That same sun rolled on seventeen hundred and two miles from Chicago and made it bright morning outside the white building. He knew it had come. He could hear the quiet ticking as the old wood frame warmed through. He could hear muffled voices outside, below him, down at street level. The sound of people starting a new day.

His fingernails were gone. He had found a gap where two boards were not hard together. He had forced his fingertips down and levered with all his strength. His nails had torn off, one after the other. The board had not moved. He had scuttled backward into a corner and curled up on the floor. He had sucked his bloodied fingers and now his mouth was smeared all around with blood, like a child's with cake.

He heard footsteps on the staircase. A big man, moving lightly. The sound halted outside the door. The lock clicked back. The door opened. The employer looked in at him. Bloated face, two nickel-sized red spots burning high on his cheeks.

'You're still here,' he said.

The carpenter was paralyzed. Couldn't move, couldn't speak.

'You failed,' the employer said.

There was silence in the room. The only sound was the slow ticking of the wood frame as the morning sun slid over the roof.

'So what shall we do now?' the employer asked.

The carpenter just stared blankly at him. Didn't move. Then the employer smiled a relaxed, friendly smile. Like he was suddenly surprised about something.

'You think I meant it?' he said, gently.

The carpenter blinked. Shook his head, slightly, hopefully.

'You hear anything?' the employer asked him.

The carpenter listened hard. He could hear the quiet ticking of the wood, the song of the forest birds, the silent sound of sunny morning air.

'You were just kidding around?' he asked.

His voice was a dry croak. Relief and hope and dread were jamming his tongue into the roof of his mouth.

'Listen,' the employer said.

The carpenter listened. The frame ticked, the birds sang, the warm air sighed. He heard nothing else. Silence. Then he heard a click. Then he heard a whine. It started slow and quiet and stabilized up at a familiar loud pitch. It was a sound he knew. It was the sound of a big power saw being run up to speed.

'Now do you think I meant it?' the employer screamed.

ELEVEN

HOLLY JOHNSON HAD BEEN MILDLY DISAPPOINTED BY REACHER'S assessment of the cash value of her wardrobe. Reacher had said he figured she had maybe fifteen or twenty outfits, four hundred bucks an outfit, maybe eight grand in total. Truth was she had thirty-four business suits in her closet. She'd worked three years on Wall Street. She had eight grand tied up in the shoes alone. Four hundred bucks was what she had spent on a blouse, and that was when she felt driven by native common sense to be a little economical.

She liked Armani. She had thirteen of his spring suits. Spring clothes from Milan were just about right for most of the Chicago summer. Maybe in the really fierce heat of August she'd break out her Moschino shifts, but June and July, September too if she was lucky, her Armanis were the thing. Her favorites were the dark-peach shades she'd bought in her last year in the brokerage house. Some mysterious Italian blend of silks. Cut and tailored by people whose ancestors had been fingering fine materials for hundreds of years. They look at it and consider it and cut it and it just falls into marvelous soft shapes. Then they market it and a Wall Street broker buys it and loves it and is still wearing it two years into the future when she's a new FBI agent and she gets snatched off a Chicago street. She's still wearing it eighteen hours later after a sleepless night on the filthy straw in a cow barn. By that point, the thing is no longer something that Armani would recognize.

The three kidnapers had returned with the truck and backed it into the cow barn's central concrete aisle. Then they had locked the barn door and disappeared. Holly guessed they had spent the night in the farmhouse. Reacher had slept quietly in his stall, chained to the railing, while she tossed and turned in the straw, sleepless, thinking urgently about him.

His safety was her responsibility. He was an innocent passerby, caught up in her business. Whatever else lay ahead for her, she had to take care of him. That was her duty. He was her burden. And he was lying. Holly was absolutely certain he was not a blues club doorman. And she was pretty certain what he was. The Johnson family was a military family. Because of her father, Holly had lived on army bases her whole life, right up to Yale. She knew the army. She knew soldiers. She knew the types and she knew Reacher was one. To her practiced eye, he looked like one. Acted like one. Reacted like one. It was possible a doorman could pick locks and climb walls like an ape, but if a doorman did go ahead and do that, he would do it with an air of unfamiliarity and daring and breathlessness which would be quite distinctive. He wouldn't do it like it came as naturally as blinking. Reacher was a quiet, contained man, relaxed, fit, clearly trained to the point of some kind of superhuman calm. He was probably ten years older than she was, but somewhere less than forty, about six feet five, huge, maybe two-twenty, blue eyes, thinning fair hair. Big enough to be a doorman, and old enough to have been around, that was for sure, but he was a soldier. A soldier, claiming to be a doorman. But why?

Holly had no idea. She just lay there, uncomfortable, listening to his quiet breathing, twenty feet away. Doorman or soldier, ten years older or not, it was her responsibility to get him to safety. She didn't sleep. Too busy thinking, and her knee was too painful. At eight-thirty on her watch, she heard him wake up. Just a subtle change in the rhythm of his breathing.

'Good morning, Reacher,' she called out.

'Morning, Holly,' he said. 'They're coming back.'

It was silent, but after a long moment she heard footsteps outside. Climbs like an ape, hears like a bat, she thought. Some doorman.

'You OK?' Reacher called to her.

She didn't answer. His welfare was her responsibility, not the other way around. She heard a rattle as the barn door was unlocked. It rolled open and daylight flooded in. She caught a glimpse of empty green country. Pennsylvania, maybe, she thought. The three kidnapers walked in and the door was pulled shut.

'Get up, bitch,' the leader said to her.

She didn't move. She was seized by an overpowering desire not to be put back inside the truck. Too dark, too uncomfortable, too tedious. She didn't know if she could take another day in there, swaying, jolting, above all totally unaware of where the hell she was being taken, or why, or by who. Instinctively she grabbed the metal railing and held on, arm tensed, like she was going to put up a struggle. The leader stood still and pulled out his Glock. Looked down at her.

'Two ways of doing this,' he said. 'The easy way, or the hard way.'

She didn't reply. Just sat there in the straw and held on tight to the railing. The ugly driver took three steps nearer and started smiling, staring at her breasts again. She felt naked and revolted under his gaze.

'Your choice, bitch,' the leader said.

She heard Reacher moving in his stall.

'No, it's your choice,' she heard him call to the guy. 'We need to be a little mutual here. Co-operative, right? You want us to get back in your truck, you need to make it worth our while.'

His voice was calm and low. Holly stared across at him. Saw him sitting there, chained up, unarmed, facing a loaded automatic weapon, totally powerless by any reasonable definition of the word, three hostile men staring down at him.

'We need some breakfast,' Reacher said. 'Toast, with grape jelly. And coffee, but make it a lot stronger than last night's crap, OK? Good coffee is very important to me. You need to understand that. Then put a couple of mattresses in the truck. One queen size, one twin. Make us a sofa in there. Then we'll get in.'

There was total silence. Holly glanced between the two men. Reacher was fixing the leader with a calm, level gaze from the floor. His blue eyes never blinked. The leader was staring down at him. Tension visible in the air. The driver had torn his gaze away from her body and was looking at Reacher. Anger in his eyes. Then the leader snapped around and nodded the other two out of the barn with him. Holly heard the door locking behind them.

'You eat toast?' Reacher said to her.

She was too breathless to answer.

'When they bring it, send it back,' he said. 'Make them do it over. Say it's too pale or too burnt or something.'

'What the hell do you think you're doing?' she asked.

'Psychology,' Reacher said. 'We need to start getting some dominance here. Situation like this, it's very important.'

She stared at him.

'Just do it, OK?' he said, calmly.

She did it. The jumpy guy brought the toast. It was just about perfect, but she rejected it. She looked at it with the disdain she'd use on a sloppy balance sheet and said it was too well done. She was standing with all her weight on one foot, looking like a mess, dung all over her peach Armani, but she managed enough haughty contempt to intimidate the guy. He went back to the farmhouse kitchen and made more.

It came with a pot of strong coffee and Holly and Reacher ate their separate breakfasts, chains clanking, twenty feet apart, while the other two guys hauled mattresses into the barn. One queen, one twin. They pulled them up into the back of the truck and laid the queen out on the floor and stood the twin at right angles to it, up against the back of the cab bulkhead. Holly watched them do it and felt a whole lot better about the day. Then she suddenly realized exactly where Reacher's psychology had been aimed. Not just at the three kidnapers. At her too. He didn't want her to get into a fight. Because she'd lose. He'd risked doing what he'd done to defuse a hopeless confrontation. She was amazed. Totally amazed. She thought blankly: for Christ's sake, this guy's got it ass-backward. *He's* trying to take care of *me*.

'You want to tell us your names?' Reacher asked, calmly. 'We're spending some time together, we can be a little civilized about it, right?'

436

Holly saw the leader just looking at him. The guy made no reply.

'We've seen your faces,' Reacher said. 'Telling us your names isn't going to do you any harm. And we might as well try to get along.'

The guy thought about it and nodded.

'Loder,' he said.

The little jumpy guy shifted feet.

'Stevie,' he said.

Reacher nodded. Then the ugly driver realized all four were looking at him. He ducked his head.

'I'm not telling you my name,' he said. 'Hell should I?'

'And let's be real clear,' the guy called Loder said. 'Civilized is not the same thing as friendly, right?'

Holly saw him aim his Glock at Reacher's head and hold it there for a long moment. Nothing in his face. Not the same thing as friendly. Reacher nodded. A small cautious movement. They left their toast plates and their coffee mugs lying on the straw and the guy called Loder unlocked their chains. They met in the central aisle. Two Glocks and a shotgun aimed at them. The ugly driver leering. Reacher looked him in the eye and ducked down and picked Holly up like she weighed nothing at all. Carried her the ten paces to the truck. Put her down gently inside. They crawled forward together to the improvised sofa. Got themselves comfortable.

The truck's rear doors slammed and locked. Holly heard the big barn door open up. The truck's engine turned over and caught. They drove out of the barn and bounced a hundred and fifty yards over the rough track. Turned an invisible right angle and cruised straight and slow down a road for fifteen minutes.

'We aren't in Pennsylvania,' Holly said. 'Roads are too straight. Too flat.'

Reacher just shrugged at her in the dark.

'We aren't in handcuffs anymore, either,' he said. 'Psychology.'

TWELVE

'**H**ELL IS THIS?' AGENT-IN-CHARGE MCGRATH SAID.
He thumbed the remote and rewound the tape. Then he pressed play and watched it again. But what he saw meant nothing at all. The video screens were filled with jerky speeding images and shashy white snow.

'Hell is going on here?' he asked again.

Brogan crowded in and shook his head. Milosevic pushed closer to look. He'd brought the tape in, so he felt personally responsible for it. McGrath hit rewind again and tried once more. Same result. Just a blur of disjointed flashing pictures.

'Get the damn tech guy back in here,' he shouted.

Milosevic used the phone on the credenza next to the coffee pot. Called upstairs to tech services. The head tech was in the room within a minute. The tone of Milosevic's voice had told him to hurry more effectively than any words could have.

'Damn tape won't run properly,' McGrath told him.

The technician took the remote in his hand with that blend of familiarity and unfamiliarity that tech guys use the world over. They're all at home with complex equipment, but each individual piece has its own peculiarities. He peered at the buttons and pressed rewind, firmly, with a chewed thumb. The tape whirred back and he pressed play and watched the disjointed stream of flashing images and video snow.

'Can you fix that?' McGrath asked him.

The tech stopped the tape and hit rewind again. Shook his head.

'It's not broken,' he said. 'That's how it's supposed to be. Typical cheap surveillance video. What it does is record a freeze-frame, probably every ten seconds or so. Just one frame, every ten seconds. Like a sequence of snapshots.'

'Why?' McGrath asked him.

'Cheap and easy,' the guy said. 'You can get a whole day on one tape that way. Low cost, and you don't have to remember to change the cassette every three hours. You just change it in the morning. And assuming a stick-up takes longer than ten seconds to complete, you've got the perp's face right there on tape, at least once.'

'OK,' McGrath said impatiently. 'So how do we use it?'

The tech used two fingers together. Pressed play and freeze at the same time. Up on the screen came a perfect black-and-white still picture of an empty store. In the bottom-left corner was Monday's date and the time, seven thirty-five in the morning. The tech held the remote out to McGrath and pointed to a small button.

'See this?' he said. 'Frame-advance button. Press this and the tape rolls on to the next still. Usually for sports, right? Hockey? You can see the puck go right in the net. Or for porn. You can see whatever you need to see. But on this type of a system, it jumps you ahead ten seconds. Like on to the next snapshot, right?'

McGrath calmed down and nodded.

'Why's it in black-and-white?' he said.

'Cheap camera,' the tech guy said. 'The whole thing is a cheap system. They only put them in because the insurance companies tell them they got to.'

He handed the remote to McGrath and headed back for the door.

'You want anything else, you let me know, OK?' he called.

He got no reply because everybody was staring at the screen as McGrath started inching his way through the tape. Every time he hit the frame-advance button, a broad band of white snow scrolled down the screen and unveiled a new picture, same aspect, same angle, same dim monochrome gray, but the timecode at the bottom jumped ahead ten seconds. The third frame showed a woman behind the counter. Milosevic touched the screen with his finger.

'That's the woman I spoke to,' he said.

McGrath nodded.

'Wide field of view,' he said. 'You can see all the way from behind the counter right out into the street.'

'Wide-angle lens on the camera,' Brogan said. 'Like a fisheye sort of thing. The owner can see everything. He can see the customers coming in and out, and he can see if the help is fiddling the register.'

McGrath nodded again and trawled through Monday morning, ten seconds at a time. Customers jumped in and out of shot. The woman behind the counter jumped from side to side, fetching and carrying and ringing up the payments. Outside, cars flashed in and out of view.

'Fast-forward to twelve o'clock,' Milosevic said. 'This is taking way too long.'

McGrath nodded and fiddled with the remote. The tape whirred forward. He pressed stop and play and freeze and came up with four o'clock in the afternoon.

'Shit,' he said.

He wound back and forward a couple of times and came up with eleven forty-three and fifty seconds.

'Close as we're going to get,' he said.

He kept his finger hard on the frame-advance button and the white snow scrolled continuously down the screen. One hundred and fifty-seven frames later, he stopped.

'There she is,' he said.

Milosevic and Brogan shouldered together for a closer look. The still frame showed Holly Johnson on the far right of the picture. She was outside, on the sidewalk, crutch in one hand, clothes on hangers in the other. She was hauling the door open with a spare finger. The time in the bottom left of the frame was stopped at ten minutes and ten seconds past twelve noon.

'OK,' McGrath said quietly. 'So let's see.'

He hit the button and Holly jumped halfway over to the counter. Even frozen on the misty monochrome screen her awkward posture was plain to see. McGrath hit the button again and the snow rolled over and Holly was at the counter. Ten seconds later the Korean woman was there with her. Ten seconds after that, Holly had folded back a hem on one of her suits and was showing the woman something. Probably the position of a particular stain. The two women stayed like that for a couple of minutes, heads together for twelve frames, jumping slightly from one shot to the next. Then the Korean woman was gone and the clothes were off the counter and Holly was standing alone for five frames. Fifty seconds. Behind her on the left, a car nosed into shot on the second frame and stayed there for the next three, parked at the kerb.

Then the woman was back with an armful of clean clothes in bags. She was frozen in the act of laying them flat on the counter. Ten seconds later she had torn five tags off the hangars. Ten seconds after that, she had another four lined up next to the register.

'Nine outfits,' McGrath said.

'That's about right,' Milosevic said. 'Five for work, Monday to Friday, and I guess four for evening wear, right?'

'What about the weekend?' Brogan said. 'Maybe it's five for work, two for evening wear and two at the weekend?'

'Probably wears jeans at the weekend,' Milosevic said. 'Jeans and a shirt. Just throws them in the machine, maybe.'

'God's sake, does it matter?' McGrath said.

He pressed the button and the Korean woman's fingers were caught dancing over the register keys. The next two stills showed Holly paying in cash and accepting a couple of dollars' change.

'How much is all that costing her?' Brogan asked out loud.

'Nine garments?' Milosevic said. 'Best part of fifty bucks a week, that's for damn sure. I saw the price list in there. Specialized processes and gentle chemicals and all.'

The next frame showed Holly starting toward the exit door on the left of the picture. The top of the Korean woman's head was visible, on her way through to the back of the store. The time was showing at twelve fifteen exactly. McGrath hitched his chair closer and stuck his face a foot from the glowing monochrome screen.

'OK,' he said. 'So where did you go now, Holly?'

She had the nine cleaned garments in her left hand. She was holding them up, awkwardly, so they wouldn't drag on the floor. Her right elbow was jammed into the curved-metal clip of her crutch, but her hand wasn't gripping the handle. The next frame showed it reaching out to push the door open. McGrath hit the button again.

'Christ,' he shouted.

Milosevic gasped out loud and Brogan looked stunned. There was no doubt about what they were seeing. The next frame showed an unknown man attacking Holly Johnson. He was tall and heavy. He was seizing her crutch with one hand and her cleaning with the other. No doubt about it. Both his arms were extended and he was taking her crutch and her cleaning away from her. He was caught in a perfect snapshot through the glass door. The three agents stared at him. There was total silence in the conference room. Then McGrath hit the button again. The timecode jumped ahead ten seconds. There was another gasp as they caught their breath simultaneously.

Holly Johnson was suddenly surrounded by a triangle of three men. The tall guy who had attacked her had been joined by two more. The tall guy had Holly's cleaning slung up over his shoulder and he had seized Holly's arm. He was staring straight up into the store window like he knew a camera was in there. The other two guys were facing Holly head-on.

'They pulled guns on her,' McGrath shouted. 'Son of a bitch, look at that.'

He thumbed the button again until the bar of snow cleared away from the bottom of the frame and the whole picture stabilized into perfect sharpness. The two new guys had their right arms bent at ninety degrees, and there was tension showing in their shoulder muscles.

'The car,' Milosevic said. 'They're going to put her in the car.'

Beyond Holly and the triangle of men was the car which had parked up fourteen frames ago. It was just sitting there at the curb. McGrath hit the button again. The bar of white snow scrolled down. The small knot of people on the screen jumped sideways ten feet. The tall guy who had attacked Holly was leading the way into the back of the car. Holly was being pushed in after him by one of the new guys. The other new guy was opening the front passenger door. Inside the car, a fourth man was plainly visible through the side glass, sitting at the wheel.

McGrath hit the button again. The bar of snow scrolled down. The street was empty. The car was gone. Like it had never been there at all.

THIRTEEN

'**W**E NEED TO TALK,' HOLLY SAID.

'So talk,' Reacher replied.

They were sprawled out on the mattresses in the gloom inside the truck, rocking and bouncing, but not much. It was pretty clear they were heading down a highway. After fifteen minutes of a slow straight road, there had been a deceleration, a momentary stop, and a left turn followed by steady acceleration up a ramp. Then a slight sway as the truck nudged left onto the pavement. Then a steady droning cruise, maybe sixty miles an hour, which had continued ever since and was feeling like it would continue forever.

The temperature inside the dark space had slowly climbed higher. Now it was pretty warm. Reacher had taken his shirt off. But the truck had started cool from the night in the cow barn, and Reacher felt as long as it kept moving through the air, it was going to be tolerable. The problem would come if they stopped for any length of time. Then the truck would heat up like a pizza oven and it would get as bad as it had gotten the day before.

The twin-sized mattress had been standing upright on its long edge, up against the forward bulkhead, and the queen-size had been flat on the floor, jammed up against it, making a crude sofa. But the ninety-degree angle between the seat and the back had made the whole thing uncomfortable. So Reacher had slid the queen-size backward, with Holly riding on it like a sled, and laid the twin flat next to it. Now they had an eight-foot by six-six flat padded area. They were lying down on their backs, heads together so they could talk, bodies apart in a decorous V shape, rocking gently with the motion of the ride.

'You should do what I tell you,' Holly said. 'You should have gotten out.'

He made no reply.

'You're a burden to me,' she said. 'You understand that? I've got enough on my hands here without having to worry about you.'

He didn't reply. They lay rocking in silence. He could smell yesterday morning's shampoo in her hair.

'So you've got to do what I tell you from now on,' she said. 'Are you listening to me? I just can't afford to be worrying about you.'

He turned his head to look at her, close up. She was worrying about him. It came as a big surprise, out of nowhere. A shock. Like being on a train, stopped next to another train in a busy railroad station. Your train begins to move. It picks up speed. And then all of a sudden it's not your train moving. It's the other train. Your train was stationary all the time. Your frame of reference was wrong. He thought his train was moving. She thought hers was.

'I don't need your help,' she said. 'I've already got all the help I need. You know how the Bureau works? You know what the biggest crime in the world is? Not bombing, not terrorism, not racketeering. The biggest crime in the world is messing with Bureau personnel. The Bureau looks after its own.'

Reacher stayed quiet for a spell. Then he smiled.

'So then we're both OK,' he said. 'We just lay back here, and pretty soon a bunch of agents is going to come bursting in to rescue us.'

'I trust my people,' Holly said to him.

There was silence again. The truck droned on for a couple of minutes. Reacher ticked off the distance in his head. About four hundred and fifty miles from Chicago, maybe. East, west, north or south. Holly gasped and used both hands to shift her leg.

'Hurting?' Reacher said.

'When it gets out of line,' she said. 'When it's straight, it's OK.'

444

'Which direction are we headed?' he asked.

'Are you going to do what I tell you?' she asked.

'Is it getting hotter or colder?' he said. 'Or staying the same?'

She shrugged.

'Can't tell,' she said. 'Why?'

'North or south, it should be getting hotter or colder,' he said. 'East or west, it should be staying more or less the same.'

'Feels the same to me,' she said. 'But inside here you can't really tell.'

'Highway feels fairly empty,' Reacher said. 'We're not pulling out to pass people. We're not getting slowed down by anybody. We're just cruising.'

'So?' Holly said.

'Might mean we're not going east,' he said. 'There's a kind of barrier, right? Cleveland to Pittsburgh to Baltimore. Like a frontier. Gets much busier. We'd be hitting more traffic. What is it, Tuesday? About eleven o'clock in the morning? Roads feel too empty for the east.'

Holly nodded.

'So we're going north or west or south,' she said.

'In a stolen truck,' he said. 'Vulnerable.'

'Stolen?' she said. 'How do you know that?'

'Because the car was stolen too,' he said.

'How do you know that?' she repeated.

'Because they burned it,' he said.

Holly rolled her head and looked straight at him.

'Think about it,' he said. 'Think about their plan. They came to Chicago in their own vehicle. Maybe some time ago. Could have taken them a couple of weeks to stake you out. Maybe three.'

'Three weeks?' she said. 'You think they were watching me three weeks?'

'Probably three,' he said. 'You went to the cleaners every Monday, right? Once a week? Must have taken them a while to confirm that pattern. But they couldn't grab you in their own vehicle. Too easy to trace, and it probably had windows and all, not suitable for long-distance transport of a kidnap victim. So I figure they stole this truck, in Chicago, probably yesterday morning. Painted over whatever writing was on the side. You notice the patch of white paint? Fresh, didn't match the rest? They disguised it, maybe

445

changed the plates. But it was still a hot truck, right? And it was their getaway vehicle. So they didn't want to risk it on the street. And people getting into the back of a truck looks weird. A car is better. So they stole the black sedan and used that instead. Switched vehicles on that waste ground, burned the black car, and they're away.'

Holly shrugged. Made a face.

'Doesn't prove they stole anything,' she said.

'Yes it does,' Reacher said. 'Who buys a new car with leather seats, knowing they're going to burn it? They'd have bought some old clunker instead.'

She nodded, reluctantly.

'Who are these people?' she said, more to herself than to Reacher.

'Amateurs,' Reacher said. 'They're making one mistake after another.'

'Like what?' she said.

'Burning is dumb,' he said. 'Attracts attention. They think they've been smart, but they haven't. Probability is they burned their original car, as well. I bet they burned it right near where they stole the black sedan.'

'Sounds smart enough to me,' Holly said.

'Cops notice burning cars,' Reacher said. 'They'll find the black sedan, they'll find out where it was stolen from, they'll go up there and find their original vehicle, probably still smoldering. They're leaving a trail, Holly. They should have parked both cars in the long-term lot at O'Hare. They would have been there a year before anybody noticed. Or just left them both down on the South Side somewhere, doors open, keys in. Two minutes later, two residents down there got themselves a new motor each. Those cars would never have been seen again. That's how to cover your tracks. Burning feels good, feels like it's real final, but it's dumb as hell.'

Holly turned her face back and stared up at the hot metal roof. She was asking herself: just who the hell is this guy?

FOURTEEN

THIS TIME, MCGRATH DID NOT MAKE THE TECH CHIEF COME DOWN to the third floor. He led the charge himself up to his lab on the sixth, with the video cassette in his hand. He burst in through the door and cleared a space on the nearest table. Laid the cassette in the space like it was made of solid gold. The guy hurried over and looked at it.

'I need photographs made,' McGrath told him.

The guy picked up the cassette and took it across to a bank of video machines in the corner. Flicked a couple of switches. Three screens lit up with white snow.

'You tell absolutely nobody what you're seeing, OK?' McGrath said.

'OK,' the guy said. 'What am I looking for?'

'The last five frames,' McGrath said. 'That should just about cover it.'

The tech chief didn't use a remote. He stabbed at buttons on the machine's own control panel. The tape rolled backwards and the story of Holly Johnson's kidnap unfolded in reverse.

'Christ,' he said.

He stopped on the frame showing Holly turning away from the counter. Then he inched the tape forward. He jumped Holly to the

447

door, then face to face with the tall guy, then into the muzzles of the guns, then to the car. He rolled back and did it for a second time. Then a third.

'Christ,' he said again.

'Don't wear the damn tape out,' McGrath said. 'I want big photographs of those five frames. Lots of copies.'

The tech chief nodded slowly.

'I can give you laser prints right now,' he said.

He punched a couple of buttons and flicked a couple of switches. Then he ducked away and booted up a computer on a desk across the room. The monitor came up with Holly leaving the dry-cleaner's counter. He clicked on a couple of menus.

'OK,' he said. 'I'm copying it to the hard disk. As a graphics file.'

He darted back to the video bank and nudged the tape forward one frame. Came back to the desk and the computer captured the image of Holly making to push open the exit door. He repeated the process three more times. Then he printed all five graphics files on the fastest laser he had. McGrath stood and caught each sheet as it flopped into the output bin.

'Not bad,' he said. 'I like paper better than video. Like it really exists.'

The tech chief gave him a look and peered over his shoulder.

'Definition's OK,' he said.

'I want blow-ups,' McGrath told him.

'No problem now it's in the computer,' the tech said. 'That's why the computer is better than paper.'

He sat down and opened the fourth file. The picture of Holly and the three kidnapers in a tight knot on the sidewalk scrolled onto the screen. He clicked the mouse and pulled a tight square round the heads. Clicked again. The monitor redrew into a large blow-up. The tall guy was staring straight out of the screen. The two new guys were caught at an angle, staring at Holly.

The tech hit the print button and then he opened the fifth file. He zoomed in with the mouse and put a tight rectangle round the driver, inside the car. He printed that out, too. McGrath picked up the new sheets of paper.

'Good,' he said. 'Good as we're going to get, anyway. Shame your damn computer can't make them all look right at the camera.'

'It can,' the tech chief said.

'It can?' McGrath said. 'How?'

'In a manner of speaking,' the guy said. He touched the blow-up of Holly's face with his finger. 'Suppose we wanted a face-front picture of her, right? We'd ask her to move around right in front of the camera and look right up at it. But suppose for some reason she can't move at all. What would we do? We could move the camera, right? Suppose you climbed up on the counter and unbolted the camera off the wall and moved it down and around a certain distance until it was right in front of her. Then you'd be seeing a face-front picture, correct?'

'OK,' McGrath said.

'So what we do is we calculate,' the tech said. 'We calculate that if we did hypothetically move that camera right in front of her, we'd have to move it what? Say six feet downward, say ten feet to the left, and turn it through about forty degrees, and then it would be plumb face-on to her. So we get those numbers and we enter them into the program and the computer will do a kind of backward simulation, and draw us a picture, just the same as if we'd really moved the actual camera right around in front of her.'

'You can do that?' McGrath said. 'Does it work?'

'Within its limitations,' the tech chief said. He touched the image of the nearer gunman. 'This guy, for instance, he's pretty much side on. The computer will give us a full-face picture, no problem at all, but it's going to be just guessing what the other side of his face looks like, right? It's programmed to assume the other side looks pretty much like the side it can see, with a little bit of asymmetry built in. But if the guy's got one ear missing or something, or a big scar, it can't tell us that.'

'OK,' McGrath said. 'So what do you need?'

The tech chief picked up the wide shot of the group. Pointed here and there on it with a stubby forefinger.

'Measurements,' he said. 'Make them as exact as possible. I need to know the camera position relative to the doorway and the sidewalk level. I need to know the focal length of the camera lens. I need Holly's file photograph for calibration. We know exactly what she looks like, right? I can use her for a test run. I'll get it set up so she comes out right, then the other guys will come out right as well, assuming they've all got two ears and so on, like I said. And bring me a square of tile off the store's floor and one of those smocks the counter woman was wearing.'

'What for?' McGrath said.

'So I can use them to decode the grays in the video,' the tech said. 'Then I can give you your mugshots in color.'

The commander selected six women from that morning's punishment detail. He used the ones with the most demerits, because the task was going to be hard and unpleasant. He stood them at attention and drew his huge bulk up to its full height in front of them. He waited to see which of them would be the first to glance away from his face. When he was satisfied none of them dared to, he explained their duties. The blood had sprayed all over the room, hurled around by the savage centrifugal force of the blade. Chips of bone had spattered everywhere. He told them to heat water in the cookhouse and carry it over in buckets. He told them to draw scrubbing brushes and rags and disinfectant from the stores. He told them they had two hours to get the room looking pristine again. Any longer than that, they would earn more demerits.

It took two hours to get the data. Milosevic and Brogan went out to the dry-cleaning establishment. They closed the place down and swarmed all over it like surveyors. They drew a plan with measurements accurate to the nearest quarter-inch. They took the camera off the wall and brought it back with them. They tore up the floor and took the tiles. They took two smocks from the woman and two posters off the wall, because they thought they might help with the colorizing process. Back on the sixth floor of the Federal Building, the tech chief took another two hours to input the data. Then he ran the test, using Holly Johnson to calibrate the program.

'What do you think?' he asked McGrath.

McGrath looked hard at the full-face picture of Holly. Then he passed it around. Milosevic got it last and stared at it hardest. Covered some parts with his hand and frowned.

'Makes her look too thin,' he said. 'I think the bottom right quarter is wrong. Not enough width there, somehow.'

'I agree,' McGrath said. 'Makes her jaw look weird.'

The tech chief exited to a menu screen and adjusted a couple of numbers. Ran the test again. The laser printer whirred. The sheet of stiff paper came out.

'That's better,' McGrath said. 'Just about on the nose.'

'Color OK?' the tech asked.

'Should be a darker peach,' Milosevic said. 'On her dress. I know that dress. Some kind of an Italian thing.'

The tech exited to a color palette.

'Show me,' he said.

Milosevic pointed to a particular shade.

'More like that,' he said.

They ran the test again. The hard disk chattered and the laser printer whirred.

'That's better,' Milosevic said. 'Dress is right. Hair color is better as well.'

'OK,' the tech said. He saved all the parameters to disk. 'Let's go to work here.'

The FBI never uses latest-generation equipment. The feeling is better to use stuff that has been proven in the field. So the tech chief's computer was actually a little slower than the computers in the rich kids' bedrooms up and down the North Shore. But not much slower. It gave McGrath five prints within forty minutes. Four mugshots of the four kidnapers, and a close-up side view of the front half of their car. All in glowing color, all with the grain enhanced and smoothed away. McGrath thought they were the best damn pictures he had ever seen.

'Thanks, chief,' he said. 'These are brilliant. Best work anybody has done around here for a long time. But don't say a word. Big secret, right?'

He clapped the tech on the shoulder and left him feeling like the most important guy in the whole building.

The six women worked hard and finished just before their two hours were up. The tiny cracks between the boards were their biggest problem. The cracks were tight, but not tight enough to stop the blood seeping in. But they were too tight to get a brush down in there. They had to sluice them out with water and rag them dry. The boards were turning a wet brown color. The women were praying they wouldn't warp as they dried. Two of them were throwing up. It was adding to their workload. But they finished in

451

time for the commander's inspection. They stood rigidly to attention on the damp floor and waited. He checked everywhere, with the wet boards creaking under his bulk. But he was satisfied with their work and gave them another two hours to clean the smears off the corridor and the staircase, where the body had been dragged away.

The car was easy. It was quickly identified as a Lexus. Four-door. Late model. The pattern of the alloy wheel dated it exactly. Color was either black or dark gray. Impossible to be certain. The computer process was good, but not good enough to be definitive about dark automotive paint standing in bright sunshine.

'Stolen?' Milosevic said.

McGrath nodded.

'Almost certainly,' he said. 'You do the checking, OK?'

Fluctuations in the value of the yen had put the list price of a new Lexus four-door somewhere up there with Milosevic's annual salary, so he knew which jurisdictions were worth checking with and which weren't. He didn't bother with anywhere south of the Loop. He put in calls to the Chicago cops, and then all the departments on the North Shore right up to Lake Forest.

He got a hit just before noon. Not exactly what he was looking for. Not a stolen Lexus. But a missing Lexus. The police department in Wilmette came back to him and said a dentist up there had driven his brand-new Lexus to work, before seven on Monday morning, and parked it in the lot behind his professional building. A chiropractor from the next office suite had seen him turn into the lot. But the dentist had never made it into the building. His nurse had called his home and his wife had called the Wilmette PD. The cops had taken the report and sat on it. It wasn't the first case of a husband disappearing they'd ever heard of. They told Milosevic the guy's name was Rubin and the car was the new shade of black, mica flecks in the paint to make it sparkle, and it had vanity plates reading: ORTHO 1.

Milosevic put the phone down on that call and it rang again straightaway with a report from the Chicago Fire Department. A unit had attended an automobile fire which was putting up a cloud of oily smoke into the land-side flightpath into Meigs Field Airport. The fire truck had arrived in an abandoned industrial lot just before one o'clock Monday and found a black Lexus burning fiercely. They

452

had figured it was burned to the metal anyway, not much more smoke to come, so they had saved their foam and just left it to burn out. Milosevic copied the location and hung up. Ducked into McGrath's office for instructions.

'Check it out,' McGrath told him.

Milosevic nodded. He was always happy with road work. It gave him the chance to drive his own brand-new Ford Explorer, which he liked to use in preference to one of the Bureau's clunky sedans. And the Bureau liked to let him do exactly that, because he never bothered to claim for his personal gas. So he drove the big shiny four-wheel-drive five miles south and found the wreck of the Lexus, no trouble at all. It was parked at an angle on a lumpy concrete area behind an abandoned industrial building. The tires had burned away and it was settled on the rims. The plates were still readable: ORTHO 1. He poked through the drifts of ash inside, still slightly warm, and then he pulled the shaft of the burned key from the ignition and popped the trunk. Then he staggered four steps away and threw up on the concrete. He retched and spat and sweated. He pulled his cellular phone from his pocket and fired it up. Got straight through to McGrath in the Federal Building.

'I found the dentist,' he said.

'Where?' McGrath asked.

'In the damn trunk,' Milosevic said. 'Slow-roasted. Looks like he was alive when the fire started.'

'Christ,' McGrath said. 'Is it connected?'

'No doubt about that,' he said.

'You sure?' McGrath asked him.

'No doubt about it,' Milosevic said again. 'I found other stuff. Burned, but it's all pretty clear. There's a .38 right in the middle of what looks like a metal hinge, could be from a woman's pocketbook, right? Coins, and a lipstick tube, and the metal parts from a mobile phone and a pager. And there are nine wire hangers on the floor. Like you get from a dry-cleaner's?'

'Christ,' McGrath said again. 'Conclusions?'

'They stole the Lexus up in Wilmette,' Milosevic said. 'Maybe the dentist guy disturbed them in the act. So he went for them and they overpowered him and put him in the trunk. Burned him along with the rest of the evidence.'

'Shit,' McGrath said. 'But where's Holly? Conclusions on that?'

'They took her to Meigs Field,' Milosevic said. 'It's about a half-mile away. They put her in a private plane and dumped the car right here. That's what they did, Mack. They flew her out somewhere. Four guys, capable of burning another guy up while he was still alive, they've got her alone somewhere, could be a million miles away from here by now.'

FIFTEEN

THE WHITE TRUCK DRONED ON STEADILY, ANOTHER HOUR, MAYBE sixty more miles. The clock inside Reacher's head ticked around from eleven to twelve noon. The first faint stirrings of worry were building inside him. They had been gone a day. Nearly a full twenty-four hours. Out of the first phase, into the middle phase. No progress. And he was uncomfortable. The air inside the vehicle was about as hot as air could get. They were still lying flat on their backs on the hot mattress, heads together. The horsehair padding was overheating them. Holly's dark hair was damp and spread out. On her left, it was curled against Reacher's bare shoulder.

'Is it because I'm a woman?' she asked. Tense. 'Or because I'm younger than you? Or both?'

'Is what because?' he asked back. Wary.

'You think you've got to take care of me,' she said. 'You're worrying about me, because I'm young and a woman, right? You think I need some older man's help.'

Reacher stirred. He didn't really want to move. He wasn't comfortable, but he guessed he was happy enough where he was. In particular, he was happy with the feel of Holly's hair against his shoulder. His life was like that. Whatever happened there were always some little compensations available.

'Well?' she asked.

'It's not a gender thing, Holly,' he said. 'Or an age thing. But you do need help, right?'

'And I'm a younger woman and you're an older man,' she said. 'Therefore obviously you're the one qualified to give it. Couldn't be any other way around, right?'

Reacher shook his head, lying down.

'It's not a gender thing,' he said again. 'Or an age thing. I'm qualified because I'm qualified, is all. I'm just trying to help you out.'

'You're taking stupid risks,' she said. 'Pushing them and antagonizing them is not the way to do this, for God's sake. You'll get us both killed.'

'Bullshit,' Reacher said. 'They need to see us as people, not cargo.'

'Says who?' Holly snapped. 'Who suddenly made you the big expert?'

He shrugged at her.

'Let me ask you a question,' he said. 'If the boot was on the other foot, would you have left me alone in that barn?'

She thought about it.

'Of course I would have,' she said.

He smiled. She was probably telling the truth. He liked her for it.

'OK,' he said. 'Next time you tell me, I'm gone. No argument.'

She was quiet for a long moment.

'Good,' she said. 'You really want to help me out, you do exactly that.'

He shrugged. Moved a half-inch closer to her.

'Risky for you,' he said. 'I get away, they might figure on just wasting you and disappearing.'

'I'll take the risk,' she said. 'That's what I'm paid for.'

'So who are they?' he asked her. 'And what do they want?'

'No idea,' she said.

She said it too quickly. He knew she knew.

'They want you, right?' he said. 'Either because they want you personally, or because they want any old FBI agent and you were right there on the spot. How many FBI agents are there?'

456

'Bureau has twenty-five thousand employees,' she said. 'Of which ten thousand are agents.'

'OK,' he said. 'So they want you in particular. One out of ten thousand is too big a coincidence. This is not random.'

She looked away. He glanced at her.

'Why, Holly?' he asked.

She shrugged and shook her head.

'I don't know,' she said.

Too quickly. He glanced at her again. She sounded sure, but there was some big defensive edge there in her reply.

'I don't know,' she said again. 'All I can figure is maybe they mistook me for somebody else from the office.'

Reacher laughed and turned his head toward her. His face touched her hair.

'You're joking, Holly Johnson,' he said. 'You're not the type of woman gets confused with somebody else. And they watched you three weeks. Long enough to get familiar.'

She smiled away from him, up at the metal roof, ironically.

'Once seen, never forgotten, right?' she said. 'I wish.'

'You in any doubt about that?' Reacher said. 'You're the best-looking person I saw this week.'

'Thanks, Reacher,' she said. 'It's Tuesday. You first saw me Monday. Big compliment, right?'

'But you get my drift,' he said.

She sat up, straight from the waist like a gymnast, and used both hands to flip her leg sideways. Propped herself on one elbow on the mattress. Hooked her hair behind her ear and looked down at him.

'I don't get anything about you,' she said.

He looked back up at her. Shrugged.

'You got questions, you ask them,' he said. 'I'm all in favor of freedom of information.'

'OK,' she said. 'Here's the first question: who the hell are you?'

He shrugged again and smiled.

'Jack Reacher,' he said. 'No middle name, thirty-seven years and eight months old, unmarried, club doorman in Chicago.'

'Bullshit,' she said.

'Bullshit?' he repeated. 'Which part? My name, my age, my marital status or my occupation?'

457

'Your occupation,' she said. 'You're not a club doorman.'

'I'm not?' he said. 'So what am I?'

'You're a soldier,' she said. 'You're in the army.'

'I am?' he said.

'It's pretty obvious,' she said. 'My dad is army. I've lived on bases all my life. Everybody I ever saw was in the army, right up until I was eighteen years old. I know what soldiers look like. I know how they act. I was pretty sure you were one. Then you took your shirt off, and I knew for definite.'

Reacher grinned.

'Why?' he said. 'Is that a really uncouth, soldierly kind of a thing to do?'

Holly grinned back at him. Shook her head. Her hair came loose. She swept it back behind her ear, one finger bent like a small pale hook.

'That scar on your stomach,' she said. 'Those awful stitches. That's a M.A.S.H. job for sure. Some field hospital somewhere, took them about a minute and a half. Any civilian surgeon did stitches like that, he'd get sued for malpractice so fast he'd get dizzy.'

Reacher ran his finger over the lumpy skin. The stitches looked like a plan of the ties at a busy railroad yard.

'The guy was busy,' he said. 'I thought he did pretty well, considering the circumstances. It was in Beirut. I was a long way down the priority list. I was only bleeding to death slowly.'

'So I'm right?' Holly said. 'You're a soldier?'

Reacher smiled up at her again and shook his head.

'I'm a doorman,' he said. 'Like I told you. Blues joint on the South Side. You should try it. Much better than the tourist places.'

She glanced between his huge scar and his face. Clamped her lips and slowly shook her head. Reacher nodded at her, like he was conceding the point.

'I used to be a soldier,' he said. 'I got out, fourteen months ago.'

'What unit?' she asked.

'Military Police,' he said.

She screwed her face up in a mock grimace.

'The baddest of the bad,' she said. 'Nobody likes you guys.'

'Tell me about it,' Reacher said.

'Explains a lot of things,' she said. 'You guys get a lot of special training. So I guess you really are qualified. You should have told me, damn it. Now I guess I have to apologize for what I said.'

He made no reply to that.

'Where were you stationed?' she asked.

'All over the world,' he said. 'Europe, Far East, Middle East. Got so I didn't know which way was up.'

'Rank?' she asked.

'Major,' he said.

'Medals?' she asked.

He shrugged.

'Dozens of the damn things,' he said. 'You know how it is. Theater medals, of course, plus a Silver Star, two Bronzes, Purple Heart from Beirut, campaign things from Panama and Grenada and Desert Shield and Desert Storm.'

'A Silver Star?' she asked. 'What for?'

'Beirut,' he said. 'Pulled some guys out of the bunker.'

'And you got wounded doing that?' she said. 'That's how you got the scar and the Purple Heart?'

'I was already wounded,' he said. 'Got wounded before I went in. I think that was what impressed them.'

'Hero, right?' she said.

He smiled and shook his head.

'No way,' he said. 'I wasn't feeling anything. Wasn't thinking. Too shocked. I didn't even know I was hit until afterward. If I'd known, I'd have fallen down in a dead faint. My intestine was hanging out. Looked really awful. It was bright pink. Sort of squashy.'

Holly was quiet for a second. The truck droned on. Another twenty miles covered. North or south or west. Probably.

'How long were you in the service?' she asked.

'All my life,' he said. 'My old man was a Marine officer, served all over. He married a Frenchwoman in Korea. I was born in Berlin. Never even saw the States until I was nine years old. Five minutes later we were in the Philippines. Round and round the world we went. Longest I was ever anywhere was four years at West Point. Then I joined up and it started all over again. Round and round the world.'

'Where's your family now?' she asked.

'Dead,' he said. 'The old man died, what? Ten years ago, I guess. My mother died two years later. I buried the Silver Star with her.

459

She won it for me, really. Do what you're supposed to do, she used to tell me. About a million times a day, in a thick French accent.'

'Brothers and sisters?' she said.

'I had a brother,' he said. 'He died last year. I'm the last Reacher on earth, far as I know.'

'When did you muster out?' she said.

'April last year,' he said. 'Fourteen months ago.'

'Why?' she asked.

Reacher shrugged.

'Just lost interest, I guess,' he said. 'The defense cuts were happening. Made the army seem unnecessary, somehow. Like if they didn't need the biggest and the best, they didn't need me. Didn't want to be part of something small and second-rate. So I left. Arrogant, or what?'

She laughed.

'So you became a doorman?' she said. 'From a decorated major to a doorman? Isn't that kind of second-rate?'

'Wasn't like that,' he said. 'I didn't set out to be a doorman, like it was a new career move or anything. It's only temporary. I only got to Chicago on Friday. I was planning to move on, maybe Wednesday. I was thinking about going up to Wisconsin. Supposed to be a nice place, this time of year.'

'Friday to Wednesday?' Holly said. 'You got a problem with commitment or something?'

'I guess,' he said. 'Thirty-six years I was always where somebody else told me to be. Very structured sort of a life. I suppose I'm reacting against it. I love moving around when I feel like it. It's like a drug. Longest I've ever stayed anywhere was ten consecutive days. Last fall, in Georgia. Ten days, out of fourteen months. Apart from that, I've been on the road more or less all the time.'

'Making a living by working the door at clubs?' she asked.

'That was unusual,' he said. 'Mostly I don't work at all, just live off my savings. But I came up to Chicago with a singer, one thing led to another, I got asked to work the door at the club the guy was headed for.'

'So what do you do if you don't work?' she asked.

'I look at things,' he said. 'You got to remember I'm a thirty-seven-year-old American but I've never really been in America much. You been up the Empire State Building?'

'Of course,' she said.

'I hadn't,' he said. 'Not before last year. You been to the Washington museums?'

'Sure,' she said.

'I hadn't,' he said again. 'Not before last year. All that kind of stuff. Boston, New York, Washington, Chicago, New Orleans, Mount Rushmore, the Golden Gate, Niagara. I'm like a tourist. Like I'm catching up, right?'

'I'm the other way around,' Holly said. 'I like to travel overseas.'

Reacher shrugged.

'I've seen overseas,' he said. 'Six continents. I'm going to stay here now.'

'I've seen the States,' she said. 'My dad traveled all the time, but we stayed here, apart from two tours to Germany.'

Reacher nodded. Thought back to the time he'd spent in Germany, man and boy. Many years in total.

'You picked up on the soccer in Europe?' he asked.

'Right,' Holly said. 'Really big deal there. We were stationed one time near Munich, right? I was just a kid, eleven maybe. They gave my father tickets to some big game in Rotterdam, Holland. European Cup, the Bayern Munich team against some English team, Aston Villa, you ever heard of them?'

Reacher nodded.

'From Birmingham, England,' he said. 'I was stationed near a place called Oxford at one point. About an hour away.'

'I hated the Germans,' Holly said. 'So arrogant, so overpowering. They were so sure they were going to cream these Brits. I didn't want to go and watch it happen. But I had to, right? NATO protocol sort of a thing, would have been a big scandal if I'd refused. So we went. And the Brits creamed the Germans. The Germans were so furious. I loved it. And the Aston Villa guys were so cute. I was in love with soccer from that night on. Still am.'

Reacher nodded. He enjoyed watching soccer, to an extent. But you had to be exposed early and gradually. It looked very free-form, but it was a very technical game. Full of hidden attractions. But he could see how a young girl could be seduced by it, long ago in Europe. A frantic night under floodlights in Rotterdam. Resentful and unwilling at first, then hypnotized by the patterns made by the white ball

461

on the green turf. Ending up in love with the game afterward. But something was ringing a warning bell. If the eleven-year-old daughter of an American serviceman had refused to go, it would have caused some kind of an embarrassment within NATO? Was that what she had said?

'Who was your father?' he asked her. 'Sounds like he must have been an important sort of a guy.'

She shrugged. Wouldn't answer. Reacher stared at her. Another warning bell had started ringing.

'Holly, who the hell is your father?' he asked urgently.

The defensive tone that had been in her voice spread to her face. No answer.

'Who, Holly?' Reacher asked again.

She looked away from him. Spoke to the metal siding of the truck. Her voice was almost lost in the road noise. Defensive as hell.

'General Johnson,' she said quietly. 'At that time, he was C-in-C Europe. Do you know him?'

Reacher stared up at her. General Johnson. Holly Johnson. Father and daughter.

'I've met him,' he said. 'But that's not the point, is it?'

She glared at him. Furious.

'Why?' she said. 'What exactly is the damn point?'

'That's the reason,' he said. 'Your father is the most important military man in America, right? That's why you've been kidnaped, Holly, for God's sake. These guys don't want Holly Johnson, FBI agent. The whole FBI thing is incidental. These guys want General Johnson's daughter.'

She looked down at him like he had just slapped her hard in the face.

'Why?' she said. 'Why the hell does everybody assume everything that ever happens to me is because of who my damn father is?'

SIXTEEN

CGRATH BROUGHT BROGAN WITH HIM AND MET MILOSEVIC AT Meigs Field Airport in Chicago. He brought the four computer-aided mugshots and the test picture of Holly Johnson. He came expecting total co-operation from the airport staff. And he got it. Three hyped-up FBI agents in the grip of fear about a colleague are a difficult proposition to handle with anything other than total co-operation.

Meigs Field was a small commercial operation, right out in the lake, water on three sides, just below the 12th Street beach, trying to make a living in the gigantic shadow of O'Hare. Their record-keeping was immaculate and their efficiency was first-class. Not so they could be ready to handle FBI inquiries on the spur of the moment but so they could keep on operating and keep on getting paid right under the nose of the world's toughest competitor. But their records and their efficiency helped McGrath. Helped him realize within about thirty seconds that he was heading up a blind alley.

The Meigs Field staff were certain they had never seen Holly Johnson or any of the four kidnapers at any time. Certainly not on Monday, certainly not around one o'clock. They were adamant about it. They weren't overdoing it. They were just sure about it, with the quiet certainty of people who spend their working days being quietly sure about things, like sending small planes up into the busiest air lanes on the planet.

And there were no suspicious take-offs from Meigs Field, nowhere between noon and, say, three o'clock. That was clear. The paperwork was explicit on the subject. The three agents were out of there as briskly as they had entered. The tower staff nodded to themselves and forgot all about them before they were even back in their cars in the small parking lot.

'OK, square one,' McGrath said. 'You guys go check out this dentist situation up in Wilmette. I've got things to do. And I've got to put in a call to Webster. They must be climbing the walls down there in DC.'

Seventeen hundred and two miles from Meigs Field the young man in the woods wanted instructions. He was a good agent, well trained, but as far as undercover work was concerned he was new and relatively inexperienced. Demand for undercover operators was always increasing. The Bureau was hard put to fill all the slots. So people like him got assigned. Inexperienced people. He figured as long as he always remembered he didn't have all the answers, he'd be OK. He had no ego problem with it. He was always willing to ask for guidance. He was careful. And he was realistic. Realistic enough to know he was now in over his head. Things were turning bad in a way which made him sure they were about to explode into something much worse. How, he didn't know. It was just a feeling. But he trusted his feelings. Trusted them enough to stop and turn around before he reached his special tree. He breathed hard and changed his mind and set off strolling back the way he had come.

Webster had been waiting for McGrath's call. That was clear. McGrath got him straightaway, like he'd been sitting there in his big office suite just waiting for the phone to ring.

'Progress, Mack?' Webster asked.

'Some,' McGrath said. 'We know exactly what happened. We got it all on a security video in a dry-cleaner's store. She went in there at twelve-ten. Came out at twelve-fifteen. There were four guys. Three on the street, one in a car. They grabbed her.'

'Then what?' Webster asked.

'They were in a stolen sedan,' McGrath said. 'Looks like they killed the owner to get it. Drove her five miles south, torched the sedan. Along with the owner in the trunk. They burned him alive. He was a dentist, name of Rubin. What they did with Holly, we don't know yet.'

In Washington, Harland Webster was silent for a long time.

'Is it worth searching the area?' he asked, eventually.

McGrath's turn to be quiet for a second. Unsure of the implications. Did Webster mean search for a hideout, or search for another body?

'My gut says no,' he said. 'They must know we could search the area. My feeling is they moved her somewhere else. Maybe far away.'

There was silence on the line again. McGrath could hear Webster thinking.

'I agree with you, I guess,' Webster said. 'They moved her out. But how, exactly? By road? By air?'

'Not air,' McGrath said. 'We covered commercial flights yesterday. We just hit a private field. Nothing doing.'

'What about a helicopter?' Webster said. 'In and out, secretly?'

'Not in Chicago, chief,' McGrath said. 'Not right next door to O'Hare. More radar here than the air force has got. Any unauthorized choppers in and out of here, we'd know about it.'

'OK,' Webster said. 'But we need to get this under control. Abduction and homicide, Mack, it's not giving me a good feeling. You figure a second stolen vehicle? Rendezvoused with the stolen sedan?'

'Probably,' McGrath said. 'We're checking now.'

'Any ideas who they were?' Webster said.

'No,' McGrath told him. 'We got pretty good pictures off the video. Computer enhancements. We'll download them to you right away. Four guys, white, somewhere between thirty and forty, three of them kind of alike, ordinary, neat, short hair. The fourth guy is real tall, computer says he's maybe six-five. I figure him for the ringleader. He was the one got to her first.'

'You got any feeling for a motive yet?' Webster asked.

'No idea at all,' McGrath said.

There was silence on the line again.

'OK,' Webster said. 'You keeping it real tight up there?'

'Tight as I can,' McGrath said. 'Just three of us.'

465

'Who are you using?' Webster asked.

'Brogan and Milosevic,' McGrath said.

'They any good?' Webster asked.

McGrath grunted. Like he would choose them if they weren't?

'They know Holly pretty well,' he said. 'They're good enough.'

'Moaners and groaners?' Webster asked. 'Or solid, like people used to be?'

'Never heard them complain,' McGrath said. 'About anything. They do the work, they do the hours. They don't even bitch about the pay.'

Webster laughed.

'Can we clone them?' he said.

The levity peaked and died within a couple of seconds. But McGrath appreciated the attempt at morale.

'So how you doing down there?' he asked.

'In what respect, Mack?' Webster said, serious again.

'The old man,' McGrath said. 'He giving you any trouble?'

'Which one, Mack?' Webster asked.

'The general?' McGrath said.

'Not yet,' Webster said. 'He called this morning, but he was polite. That's how it goes. Parents are usually pretty calm, the first day or two. They get worked up later. General Johnson won't be any different. He may be a bigshot, but people are all the same underneath, right?'

'Right,' McGrath said. 'Have him call me, if he wants first-hand reports. Might help his situation.'

'OK, Mack, thanks,' Webster said. 'But I think we should keep this dentist thing away from everybody, just for the moment. Makes the whole deal look worse. Meantime, send me your stuff. I'll get our people working on it. And don't worry. We'll get her back. Bureau looks after its own, right? Never fails.'

The two Bureau chiefs let the lie die into silence and hung up their phones together.

The young man strolled out of the forest and came face to face with the commander. He was smart enough to throw a big salute and look nervous, but he kept it down to the sort of nervousness any grunt showed around the commander. Nothing more, nothing suspicious. He stood and waited to be spoken to.

'Job for you,' the commander said. 'You're young, right? Good with all this technical shit?'

The man nodded cautiously.

'I can usually puzzle stuff out, sir,' he said.

The commander nodded back.

'We got a new toy,' he said. 'Scanner, for radio frequencies. I want a watch kept.'

The young man's blood froze hard.

'Why, sir?' he asked. 'You think somebody's using a radio transmitter?'

'Possibly,' the commander said. 'I trust nobody and I suspect everybody. I can't be too careful. Not right now. Got to look after the details. You know what they say? Genius is in the details, right?'

The young man swallowed and nodded.

'So get it set up,' the commander said. 'Make a duty rota. Two shifts, sixteen hours a day, OK? Constant vigilance is what we need right now.'

The commander turned away. The young man nodded and breathed out. Glanced instinctively back in the direction of his special tree and blessed his feelings.

Milosevic drove Brogan north in his new truck. They detoured via the Wilmette post office so Brogan could mail his twin alimony checks. Then they went looking for the dead dentist's building. There was a local uniform waiting for them in the parking lot in back. He was unapologetic about sitting on the report from the dentist's wife. Milosevic started giving him a hard time about that, like it made the guy personally responsible for Holly Johnson's abduction.

'Lots of husbands disappear,' the guy said. 'Happens all the time. This is Wilmette, right? Men are the same here as anywhere, only here they got the money to make it all happen. What can I say?'

Milosevic was unsympathetic. The cop had made two other errors. First, he had assumed that it was the murder of the dentist that had brought the FBI out into his jurisdiction. Second, he was more uptight about covering his own ass on the issue than he was about four killers snatching Holly Johnson right off the street. Milosevic was out of patience with the guy. But then the guy redeemed himself.

'What is it with people?' he said. 'Burning automobiles? Some asshole burned a car out by the lake. We got to get it moved. Residents are giving us noise.'

'Where exactly?' Milosevic asked him.

The cop shrugged. He was anxious to be very precise.

'That turn-out on the shore,' he said. 'On Sheridan Road, just this side of Washington Park. Never saw such a thing before, not in Wilmette.'

Milosevic and Brogan went to check it out. They followed the cop in his shiny cruiser. He led them to the place. It wasn't a car. It was a pickup, a ten-year-old Dodge. No license plates. Doused with gasoline and pretty much totally burned out.

'Happened yesterday,' the cop said. 'Spotted about seven-thirty in the morning. Commuters were calling it in, on their way to work, one after the other.'

He circled round and looked over the wreck, carefully.

'Not local,' he said. 'That's my guess.'

'Why not?' Milosevic asked him.

'This is ten years old, right?' the guy said. 'Around here, there are a few pickups, but they're toys, you know? Big V8s, lots of chrome? An old thing like this, nobody would give it room on their driveway.'

'What about gardeners?' Brogan asked. 'Pool boys, something like that?'

'Why would they burn it?' the cop said. 'They needed to change it, they'd chop it in against a new one, right? Nobody burns a business asset, right?'

Milosevic thought about it and nodded.

'OK,' he said. 'This is ours. Federal investigation. We'll send a flatbed for it soon as we can. Meanwhile, you guard it, OK? And do it properly, for God's sake. Don't let anybody near it.'

'Why?' the cop asked.

Milosevic looked at him like he was a moron.

'This is their truck,' he said. 'They dumped it here and stole the Lexus for the actual heist.'

The Wilmette cop looked at Milosevic's agitated face and then he looked across at the burned truck. He wondered for a moment how four guys could fit across the Dodge's bench seat. But he didn't say anything. He didn't want to risk more ridicule. He just nodded.

468

SEVENTEEN

HOLLY WAS SITTING UP ON THE MATTRESS, ONE KNEE UNDER HER chin, the injured leg straight out. Reacher was sitting up beside her, hunched forward, worried, one hand fighting the bounce of the truck and the other hand plunged into his hair.

'What about your mother?' he asked.

'Was your father famous?' Holly asked him back.

Reacher shook his head.

'Hardly,' he said. 'Guys in his unit knew who he was, I guess.'

'So you don't know what it's like,' she said. 'Every damn thing you do, it happens because of your father. I got straight As in school, I went to Yale and Harvard, went to Wall Street, but it wasn't me doing it, it was this weird other person called General Johnson's daughter doing it. It's been just the same with the Bureau. Everybody assumes I made it because of my father, and ever since I got there half the people are still treating me especially nice, and the other half are still treating me especially tough just to prove how much they're not impressed.'

Reacher nodded. Thought about it. He was a guy who had done better than his father. Forged ahead, in the traditional way. Left the old man behind. But he'd known guys with famous parents. The sons of great soldiers. Even the grandsons.

However bright they burned, their light was always lost in the glow.

'OK, so it's tough,' he said. 'And the rest of your life you can try to ignore it, but right now it needs dealing with. It opens up a whole new can of worms.'

She nodded. Blew an exasperated sigh. Reacher glanced at her in the gloom.

'How long ago did you figure it out?' he asked.

She shrugged.

'Immediately, I guess,' she said. 'Like I told you, it's a habit. Everybody assumes everything happens because of my father. Me too.'

'Well, thanks for telling me so soon,' Reacher said.

She didn't reply to that. They lapsed into silence. The air was stifling and the heat was somehow mixing with the relentless drone of the noise. The dark and the temperature and the sound were like a thick soup inside the truck. Reacher felt like he was drowning in it. But it was the uncertainty that was doing it to him. Many times he'd traveled thirty hours at a stretch in transport planes, worse conditions than these. It was the huge new dimension of uncertainty that was unsettling him.

'So what about your mother?' he asked her again.

She shook her head.

'She died,' she said. 'I was twenty, in school. Some weird cancer.'

'I'm sorry,' he said. Paused, nervously. 'Brothers and sisters?'

She shook her head again.

'Just me,' she said.

He nodded, reluctantly.

'I was afraid of that,' he said. 'I was kind of hoping this could be about something else, you know, maybe your mother was a judge or you had a brother or a sister who was a congressman or something.'

'Forget it,' she said. 'There's just me. Me and Dad. This is about Dad.'

'But what about him?' he said. 'What the hell is this supposed to achieve? Ransom? Forget about it. Your old man's a big deal, but he's just a soldier, been clawing his way up the army pay-scales all his life. Faster than most guys, I agree, but I know those pay-scales.

I was on those scales thirteen years. Didn't make me rich and they won't have made him rich. Not rich enough for anybody to be thinking about a ransom. Somebody wanted a ransom out of kidnaping somebody's daughter, there are a million people ahead of you in Chicago alone.'

Holly nodded.

'This is about influence,' she said. 'He's responsible for two million people and two hundred billion dollars a year. Scope for influence there, right?'

Reacher shook his head.

'No,' he said. 'That's the problem. I can't see what this is liable to achieve.'

He got to his knees and crawled forward along the mattresses.

'Hell are you doing?' Holly asked him.

'We got to talk to them,' he said. 'Before we get where we're going.'

He lifted his big fist and started pounding on the bulkhead. Hard as he could. Right behind where he figured the driver's head must be. He kept on pounding until he got what he wanted. Took a while. Several minutes. His fist got sore. But the truck lurched off the highway and started slowing. He felt the front wheels washing into gravel. The brakes bit in. He was pressed up against the bulkhead by the momentum. Holly rolled a couple of feet along the mattress. Gasped in pain as her knee twisted against the motion.

'Pulled off the highway,' Reacher said. 'Middle of nowhere.'

'This is a big mistake, Reacher,' Holly said.

He shrugged and took her hand and helped her into a sitting position, back against the bulkhead. Then he slid forward and put himself between her and the rear doors. He heard the three guys getting out of the cab. Doors slammed. He heard their footsteps crunching over the gravel. Two coming down the right flank, one down the left. He heard the key sliding into the lock. The handle turned.

The left-hand rear door opened two inches. First thing into the truck was the muzzle of the shotgun. Beyond it, Reacher saw a meaningless sliver of sky. Bright blue, small white clouds. Could have been anywhere in the hemisphere. Second thing into the truck was a Glock 17. Then a wrist. The cuff of a cotton shirt. The Glock was rock-steady. Loder.

'This better be good, bitch,' he called.

Hostile. A lot of tension in the voice.

'We need to talk,' Reacher called back.

The second Glock appeared in the narrow gap. Shaking slightly.

'Talk about what, asshole?' Loder called.

Reacher listened to the stress in the guy's voice and watched the second Glock trembling through its random zigzags.

'This isn't going to work, guys,' he said. 'Whoever told you to do this, he isn't thinking straight. Maybe it felt like some kind of a smart move, but it's all wrong. It isn't going to achieve anything. It's just going to get you guys in a shitload of trouble.'

There was silence at the rear of the truck. Just for a second. But long enough to tell Reacher that Holly was right. Long enough to know he'd made a bad mistake. The steady Glock snapped back out of sight. The shotgun jerked, like it had just changed ownership. Reacher flung himself forward and smashed Holly down flat on the mattress. The shotgun barrel tipped upward. Reacher heard the small click of the trigger a tiny fraction before an enormous explosion. The shotgun fired into the roof. A huge blast. A hundred tiny holes appeared in the metal. A hundred tiny points of blue light. Spent shot rattled and bounced down and ricocheted around the truck like hail. Then the sound of the gun faded into the hum of temporary deafness.

Reacher felt the slam of the door. The sliver of daylight cut off. He felt the rock of the vehicle as the three men climbed back into the cab. He felt the shake as the rough diesel caught. Then a forward lurch and a yaw to the left as the truck pulled back onto the highway.

First thing Reacher heard as his hearing came back was a quiet keening as the air whistled out through the hundred pellet holes in the roof. It grew louder as the miles rolled by. A hundred high-pitched whistles, all grouped together a couple of semitones apart, fighting and warbling like some kind of demented birdsong.

'Insane, right?' Holly said.

'Me or them?' he said.

He nodded an apology. She nodded back and struggled up to a sitting position. Used both hands to straighten her knee. The holes in the roof were letting light through. Enough light that Reacher could see her face clearly. He could interpret her expression. He could see the flicker of pain. Like a blind coming down in her eyes, then snapping back up. He knelt and swept the spent pellets off the mattress. They rattled across the metal floor.

'Now you've got to get out,' she said. 'You'll get yourself killed soon.'

The highlights in her hair flashed under the random bright illumination.

'I mean it,' she said. 'Qualified or not, I can't let you stay.'

'I know you can't,' he said.

He used his discarded shirt to sweep the pellets into a pile near the doors. Then he straightened the mattresses and lay back down. Rocked gently with the motion. Stared at the holes in the sheet metal above him. They were like a map of some distant galaxy.

'My father will do what it takes to get me back,' Holly said.

Talking was harder than it had been before. The drone of the motor and the rumble of the road were complicated by the high-pitched whistle from the roof. A full spectrum of noise. Holly lay down next to Reacher. She put her head next to his. Her hair fanned out and brushed his cheek and fell to his neck. She squirmed her hips and straightened her leg. There was still space between their bodies. The decorous V shape was still there. But the angle was a little tighter than it had been before.

'But what can he do?' Reacher said. 'Talk me through it.'

'They're going to make some kind of demand,' she said. 'You know, do this or do that, or we hurt your girl.'

She spoke slowly and there was a tremor in her voice. Reacher let his hand drop into the space between them and found hers. He took it and squeezed gently.

'Doesn't make any sense,' he said. 'Think about it. What does your father do? He implements long-term policy, and he's responsible for short-term readiness. Congress and the president and the defense secretary thrash out the long-term policy, right? So if the joint chairman tried to stand in their way, they'd just replace him. Especially if they know he's under this kind of pressure, right?'

'What about short-term readiness?' she said.

'Same sort of a thing,' Reacher said. 'He's only chairman of a committee. There's the individual chiefs of staff in there too. Army, navy, air force, Marines. If they're all singing a different song from what your father is reporting upwards, that's not going to stay a secret for long, is it? They'll just replace him. Take him out of the equation altogether.'

Holly turned her head. Looked straight at him.

'Are you sure?' she said. 'Suppose these guys are working for Iraq or something? Suppose Saddam wants Kuwait again. But he doesn't want another Desert Storm. So he has me kidnaped, and my father says sorry, can't be done, for all kinds of invented reasons?'

Reacher shrugged.

'The answer's right there in the words you used,' he said. 'The reasons would be invented. Fact is, we could do Desert Storm again, if we had to. No problem. Everybody knows that. So if your father started denying it, everybody would know he was bullshitting, and everybody would know why. They'd just sideline him. The military is a tough place, Holly, no room for sentiment. If that's the strategy these guys are pursuing, they're wasting their time. It can't work.'

She was quiet for a long moment.

'Then maybe this is about revenge,' she said slowly. 'Maybe somebody is punishing him for something in the past. Maybe I'm going to Iraq. Maybe they want to make him apologize for Desert Storm. Or Panama, or Grenada, or lots of things.'

Reacher lay on his back and rocked with the motion. He could feel slight breaths of air stirring, because of the holes in the roof. He realized the truck was now a lot cooler, because of the new ventilation. Or because of his new mood.

'Too arcane,' he said. 'You'd have to be a pretty acute analyst to blame the joint chairman for all that stuff. There's a string of more obvious targets. Higher-profile people, right? The president, the defense secretary, foreign service people, field generals. If Baghdad was looking for a public humiliation they'd pick somebody their people could identify, not some paper-shuffler from the Pentagon.'

'So what the hell is this about?' Holly said.

Reacher shrugged again.

'Ultimately, nothing,' he said. 'They haven't thought it through properly. That's what makes them so dangerous. They're competent, but they're stupid.'

*   *   *

474

The truck droned on another six hours. Another three hundred and fifty miles, according to Reacher's guess. The inside temperature had cooled, but Reacher wasn't trying to estimate their direction by the temperature anymore. The pellet holes in the roof had upset that calculation. He was relying on dead reckoning instead. A total of eight hundred miles from Chicago he figured, and not in an easterly direction. That left a big spread of possibilities. He trawled clockwise round the map in his head. Could be in Georgia, Alabama, Mississippi, Louisiana. Could be in Texas, Oklahoma, the southwest corner of Kansas. Probably no further west than that. Reacher's mental map had brown shading there, showing the eastern slopes of the mountains, and the truck wasn't laboring up any grades. Could be in Nebraska or South Dakota. Maybe he was going to pass right by Mount Rushmore, second time in his life. Could have kept on past Minneapolis, into North Dakota. Eight hundred miles from Chicago, anywhere along a giant arc drawn across the continent.

The light coming in through the pellet holes had been gone for hours when the truck slowed and steered right. Up a ramp. Holly stirred and turned her head. Looked straight at Reacher. Questions in her eyes. Reacher shrugged back and waited. The truck paused and swung a right. Cruised down a straight road, then hung a left, a right, and carried on straight, slower. Reacher sat up and found his shirt. Shrugged himself into it. Holly sat up.

'Another hideout,' she said. 'This is a well planned operation, Reacher.'

This time it was a horse farm. The truck bumped down a long track and turned. Backed up. Reacher heard one of the guys getting out. His door slammed. The truck lurched backward into another building. Reacher heard the exhaust noise beat against the walls. Holly smelled horse smell. The engine died. The other two guys got out. Reacher heard the three of them grouping at the rear of the truck. Their key slid into the lock. The door cracked open. The shotgun poked in through the gap. This time, not pointing upward. Pointing level.

'Out,' Loder called. 'The bitch first. On its own.'

Holly froze. Then she shrugged at Reacher and slid across the mattresses. The door snapped wide open and two pairs of hands seized her and dragged her out. The driver moved into view, aiming the shotgun straight in at Reacher. His finger was tight on the trigger.

'Do something, asshole,' he said. 'Please, just give me a damn excuse.'

Reacher stared at him. Waited five long minutes. Then the shotgun jabbed forward. A Glock appeared next to it. Loder gestured. Reacher moved slowly forward toward the two muzzles. Loder leaned in and snapped a handcuff onto his wrist. Looped the chain into the free half and locked it. Used the chain to drag him out of the truck by the arm. They were in a horse barn. It was a wooden structure. Much smaller than the cow barn at their previous location. Much older. It came from a different generation of agriculture. There were two rows of stalls flanking an aisle. The floor was some kind of cobbled stone. Green with moss.

The central aisle was wide enough for horses, but not wide enough for the truck. It was backed just inside the door. Reacher saw a frame of sky around the rear of the vehicle. A big, dark sky. Could have been anywhere. He was led like a horse down the cobbled aisle. Loder was holding the chain. Stevie was walking sideways next to Reacher. His Glock was jammed high up against Reacher's temple. The driver was following, with the shotgun pressed hard into Reacher's kidney. It bumped with every step. They stopped at the end stall, farthest from the door. Holly was chained up in the space opposite. She was wearing a handcuff, right wrist, chain looped through the spare half into an iron ring bolted into the back wall of the stall.

The two guys with the guns fanned out in a loose arc and Loder shoved Reacher into his stall. Opened the cuff with the key. Looped the chain through the iron ring bolted into the timber on the back wall, looped it again, twice, and relocked it into the cuff. He pulled at it and shook it to confirm it was secure.

'Mattresses,' Reacher said. 'Bring us the mattresses out of the truck.'

Loder shook his head, but the driver smiled and nodded.

'OK,' he said. 'Good idea, asshole.'

He stepped up inside and dragged the queen-size out. Struggled with it all the way down the aisle and flopped it into Holly's stall. Kicked it straight.

476

'The bitch gets one,' he said. 'You don't.'

He started laughing and the other two joined in. They strolled away down the aisle. The driver pulled the truck forward out of the barn and the heavy doors creaked shut behind it. Reacher heard a heavy crossbeam slamming down into its retaining brackets on the outside and the rattle of another chain and a padlock. He glanced across at Holly. Then he looked down at the damp stone floor.

Reacher was squatted down, jammed into the far angle of the stall's wooden walls. He was waiting for the three guys to come back with dinner. They arrived after an hour. With one Glock and the shotgun. And one metal mess tin. Stevie walked in with it. The driver took it from him and handed it to Holly. He stood there leering at her for a second and then turned to face Reacher. Pointed the shotgun at him.

'Bitch eats,' he said. 'You don't.'

Reacher didn't get up. He just shrugged through the gloom.

'That's a loss I can just about survive,' he said.

Nobody replied to that. They just strolled back out. Pushed the heavy wooden doors shut. Dropped the crossbeam into place and chained it up. Reacher listened to their footsteps fade away and turned to Holly.

'What is it?' he asked.

She shrugged across the distance at him.

'Some sort of a thin stew,' she said. 'Or a thick soup, I guess. One or the other. You want some?'

'They give you a fork?' he asked.

'No, a spoon,' she said.

'Shit,' he said. 'Can't do anything with a damn spoon.'

'You want some?' she asked again.

'Can you reach?' he said.

She spent some time eating, then she stretched out. One arm tight against the chain, the other pushing the mess tin across the floor. Then she swiveled and used her good foot to slide the tin farther across the stone. Reacher slid forward, feet first, as far as his chain would let him go. He figured if he could stretch far enough, he could hook his foot around the tin and drag it in toward him. But it was hopeless. He was six-five, and his arms were about the longest the army tailors had ever seen, but even so he came up four feet short.

He and Holly were stretched out in a perfect straight line, as near together as their chains would let them get, but the mess tin was still way out of his reach.

'Forget it,' he said. 'Get it back while you can.'

She hooked her own foot around the tin and pulled it back.

'Sorry,' she said. 'You're going to be hungry.'

'I'll survive,' he said. 'Probably awful, anyway.'

'Right,' she said. 'It's shit. Tastes like dog food.'

Reacher stared through the dark at her. He was suddenly worried.

Holly lay down apologetically on her mattress and calmly went to sleep, but Reacher stayed awake. Not because of the stone floor. It was cold and damp, and hard. The cobblestones were wickedly lumpy. But that was not the reason. He was waiting for something. He was ticking off the minutes in his head, and he was waiting. His guess was it would be about three hours, maybe four. Way into the small hours, when resistance is low and patience runs out.

A long wait. The thirteen thousand seven hundred and sixty-first night of his life, way down there in the bottom third of the scale, lying awake and waiting for something to happen. Something bad. Something he maybe had no chance of preventing. It was coming. He was certain of that. He'd seen the signs. He lay and waited for it, ticking off the minutes. Three hours, maybe four.

It happened after three hours and thirty-four minutes. The nameless driver came back into the barn. Wide awake and alone. Reacher heard his soft footsteps on the track outside. He heard the rattle of the padlock and the chain. He heard him lift the heavy crossbar out of its brackets. The barn door opened. A bar of bright moonlight fell across the floor. The driver stepped through it. Reacher saw a flash of his pink pig's face. The guy hurried down the aisle. No weapon in his hand.

'I'm watching you,' Reacher said, quietly. 'You back off, or you're a dead man.'

The guy stopped opposite. He wasn't a complete moron. He stayed well out of range. His bright eyes traveled up from the handcuff on Reacher's wrist, along the chain, and rested on the iron ring in the wall. Then he smiled.

'You watch if you want to,' he said. 'I don't mind an audience. And you might learn something.'

Holly stirred and woke up. Raised her head and glanced around, blinking in the dark.

'What's going on?' she said.

The driver turned to her. Reacher couldn't see his face. It was turned away. But he could see Holly's.

'We're going to have us a little fun, bitch,' the driver said. 'Just you and me, with your asshole friend here watching and learning.'

He put his hands down to his waist and unbuckled his belt. Holly stared at him. Started to sit up.

'Got to be joking,' she said. 'You come near me, I'll kill you.'

'You wouldn't do that,' the driver said. 'Now would you? After I gave you a mattress and all? Just so we could be comfortable while we're doing it?'

Reacher stood up in his stall. His chain clanked loudly in the silent night.

'I'll kill you,' he called. 'You touch her, you're a dead man.'

He said it once, and then he said it again. But it was like the guy wasn't hearing him. Like he was deaf. Reacher was hit with a clang of fear. If the guy wasn't going to listen to him, there was nothing he could do. He shook his chain. It rattled loudly through the silence of the night. It had no effect. The guy was just ignoring him.

'You come near me, I'll kill you,' Holly said again.

Her leg was slowing her down. She was trapped in an awkward struggle to stand up. The driver darted into her stall. Raised his foot and stamped it down on her knee. She screamed in agony and collapsed and curled into a ball.

'You do what I tell you, bitch,' the driver said. 'Exactly what I tell you, or you'll never walk again.'

Holly's scream died into a sob. The driver pulled his foot back and carefully kicked her knee like he was aiming for a field goal right at the end of the last quarter. She screamed again.

'You're a dead man,' Reacher yelled.

The driver turned round and faced him. Smiled a wide smile.

'You keep your mouth tight shut,' he said. 'One more squeak out of you, it'll be harder on the bitch, OK?'

The ends of his belt were hanging down. He balled his fists and propped them on his hips. His big vivid face was glowing. His hair was bushed up like he'd just washed it and combed it back. He turned his head and spoke to Holly over his shoulder.

'You wearing anything under that suit?' he asked her.

Holly didn't speak. Silence in the barn. The guy turned to face her. Reacher saw her tracking his movements.

'I asked you a question, bitch,' he said. 'You want another kick?'

She didn't reply. She was breathing hard. Fighting the pain. The driver unzipped his pants. The sound of the zip was loud. It fought with the rasping of three people breathing hard.

'You see this?' he asked. 'You know what this is?'

'Sort of,' Holly muttered. 'It looks a little like a penis, only smaller.'

He stared at her, blankly. Then he bellowed in rage and rushed into her stall, swinging his foot. Holly dodged away. His short wide leg swung and connected with nothing. He staggered off-balance. Holly's eyes narrowed in a gleam of triumph. She dodged back and smashed her elbow into his stomach. She did it right. Used his own momentum against him, used all her weight like she wanted to punch his spine right out through his back. Caught him with a solid blow. The guy gasped and spun away.

Reacher whooped in admiration. And relief. He thought: couldn't have done it better myself, kid. The guy was heaving. Reacher saw his face, crumpled in pain. Holly was snarling in triumph. She scrambled on one knee after him. Going for his groin. Reacher willed her on. She launched herself at him. The guy turned and took it on the thigh. Holly had planned for that. It left his throat open to her elbow. Reacher saw it. Holly saw it. She lined it up. The killing blow. A vicious arcing curve. It was going to rip his head off. She swung it in. Then her chain snapped tight and stopped her short. It clanked hard against the iron ring and jerked her backward.

Reacher's grin froze on his face. The guy staggered out of range. Stooped and panted and caught his breath. Then he straightened up and hitched his belt higher. Holly faced him, one-handed. Her chain was tight against the wall, vibrating with the tension she had on it.

'I like a fighter,' the guy gasped. 'Makes it more interesting for me. But make sure you save yourself some energy for later. I don't want you just lying there.'

480

Holly glared at him, breathing hard. Crackling with aggression. But she was one-handed. The guy stepped in again and she swung a stinging punch. Fast and low. He crowded left and blocked it. She couldn't deliver the follow-up. Her other arm was pinned back. He raised his foot and kicked for her stomach. She arched around it. He kicked out again and stumbled straight into an elbow, hard against his ear. It was the wrong elbow, with no force behind it because of her impossible position. A poor blow. It left her off-balance. The driver stepped close and kicked her in the gut. She went down. He kicked out again and caught her knee. Reacher heard it crunch. She screamed in agony. Collapsed on the mattress. The driver breathed fast and stood there.

'I asked you a damn question,' he said.

Holly was deathly white and trembling. She was writhing around on the mattress, one arm pinned behind her, gasping with the pain. Reacher saw her face, flashing through the bar of bright moonlight.

'I'm waiting, bitch,' the guy said.

Reacher saw her face again. Saw she was beaten. The fight was out of her.

'Want another kicking?' the driver said.

There was silence in the barn again.

'I'm waiting for an answer,' the guy said.

Reacher stared over, waiting. There was still silence. Just the rasping of three people breathing hard in the quiet. Then Holly spoke.

'What was the question?' she said, quietly.

The guy smiled down at her.

'You wearing anything under that suit?' he said.

Holly nodded. Didn't speak.

'OK, what?' the guy said to her.

'Underwear,' she said, quietly.

The guy cupped a hand behind his ear.

'Can't hear you, bitch,' he said.

'I'm wearing underwear, you bastard,' she said, louder.

The guy shook his head.

'Bad name,' he said. 'I'm going to need an apology for that.'

'Screw you,' Holly said.

'I'll kick you again,' the guy said. 'In the knee. I do that, you'll never walk without a stick, the whole rest of your life, you bitch.'

Holly looked away.

'Your choice, bitch,' the guy said.

He raised his foot. Holly stared down at her mattress.

'OK, I apologize,' she said. 'I'm sorry.'

The guy nodded, happily.

'Describe your underwear to me,' he said. 'Lots of detail.'

She shrugged. Turned her face away and spoke to the wooden wall.

'Bra and pants,' she said. 'Victoria's Secret. Dark peach.'

'Skimpy?' the driver asked.

She shrugged again, miserably, like she knew for sure what the next question was going to be.

'I guess,' she said.

'Want to show it to me?' the guy said.

'No,' she said.

The driver took a step closer.

'So you do want another kicking?' he said.

She didn't speak. The guy cupped his hand behind his ear again.

'Can't hear you, bitch,' he said.

'What was the question?' Holly muttered.

'You want another kicking?' the guy said.

Holly shook her head.

'No,' she said again.

'OK,' he said. 'Show me your underwear and you won't get one.'

He raised his foot. Holly raised her hand. It went to the top button on her suit. Reacher watched her. There were five buttons down the front of her suit. Reacher willed her to undo each of them slowly and rhythmically. He needed her to do that. It was vital. Slowly and rhythmically, Holly, he pleaded silently. He gripped his chain with both hands. Four feet from where it looped into the iron ring on the back wall. He tightened his hands around it.

She undid the top button. Reacher counted: one. The driver leered down. Her hand slid to the next button. Reacher tightened his grip again. She undid the second button. Reacher counted: two. Her hand slid down to the third button. Reacher turned square-on to

482

face the rear wall of his stall and took a deep breath. Turned his head and watched over his shoulder. Holly undid the third button. Her breasts swelled out. Dark-peach brassiere. Skimpy and lacy. The driver shuffled from foot to foot. Reacher counted: three. He exhaled right from the bottom of his lungs. Holly's hand slid down to the fourth button. Reacher took a deep breath, the deepest breath of his whole life. He tightened his hold on the chain until his knuckles shone white. Holly undid the fourth button. Reacher counted: four. Her hand slid down. Paused a beat. Waited. Undid the fifth button. Her suit fell open. The driver leered down and made a small sound. Reacher jerked back and smashed his foot into the wall. Right under the iron ring. He smashed his weight backward against the chain, two hundred and twenty pounds of coiled fury exploding against the force of his kick. Splinters of damp wood burst out of the wall. The old planks shattered. The bolts tore right out of the timber. Reacher was hurled backward. He swarmed up to his feet, his chain whipping and flailing angrily behind him.

'Five!' he screamed.

He seized the driver by the arm and hurled him into his stall. Threw him against the back wall. The guy smashed into it and hung like a broken doll. He staggered forward and Reacher kicked him in the stomach. The guy jackknifed in the air, feet right off the ground, and smashed flat on his face on the cobblestones. Reacher doubled his chain and swung it through the air. Aimed the lethal length at the guy's head like a giant metal whip. The iron ring centrifuged out like an old medieval weapon. But at the last second Reacher changed his mind. Wrenched the chain out of its trajectory and let it smash and spark into the stones on the floor. He grabbed the driver, one hand on his collar and one hand in his hair. Lifted him bodily across the aisle to Holly's mattress. Jammed his ugly face down into the softness and leaned on him until he suffocated. The guy bucked and thrashed, but Reacher just planted a giant hand flat on the back of his skull and waited patiently until he died.

Holly was staring at the corpse and Reacher was sitting next to her, panting. He was spent and limp from the explosive force of tearing the iron ring out of the wall. It felt like a lifetime of physical effort had gone into one split second. A lifetime supply of adrenalin was boiling through him. The clock inside his head had exploded and stopped. He had no idea how long they had been sitting there. He shook himself and staggered to his feet. Dragged the body away and left it in the aisle, up near the open door. Then he wandered back and squatted next to Holly. His fingers were bruised from his desperate grip on the chain, but he forced them to be delicate. He did up all her buttons, one by one, right to the top. She was taking quick short breaths. Then she flung her arms round his neck and held on tight. Her breathing sucked and blew against his shirt.

They held each other for a long moment. He felt the fury drain out of her. They let each other go and sat side by side on the mattress, staring into the gloom. She turned to him and put her small hand lightly on top of his.

'Now I guess I owe you,' she said.

'My pleasure,' Reacher said. 'Hey, believe me.'

'I needed help,' she said quietly. 'I've been fooling myself.'

He flipped his hand over and closed it around hers.

'Bullshit, Holly,' he said, gently. 'Time to time, we all need help. Don't feel bad about it. If you were fit, you'd have slaughtered him. I could see that. One arm and one leg, you were nearly there. It's just your knee. Pain like that, you've got no chance. Believe me, I know what it's like. After the Beirut thing, I couldn't have taken candy from a baby, best part of a year.'

She smiled a slight smile and squeezed his hand. The clock inside his head started up again. Getting close to dawn.

EIGHTEEN

S EVEN-TWENTY WEDNESDAY MORNING EAST COAST TIME, GENERAL
Johnson left the Pentagon. He was out of uniform, dressed in a
lightweight business suit, and he walked. It was his preferred
method of getting around. It was a hot morning in Washington, and
already humid, but he stepped out at a steady speed, arms swinging
loosely through a small arc, head up, breathing hard.

He walked north through the dust on the shoulder of George
Washington Boulevard, along the edge of the great cemetery
on his left, through Lady Bird Johnson Park, and across the
Arlington Memorial Bridge. Then he walked clockwise around
the Lincoln Memorial, past the Vietnam Wall, and turned right
along Constitution Avenue, the Reflecting Pool on his right, the
Washington Monument up ahead. He walked past the National
Museum of American History, past the National Museum of
Natural History, and turned left onto 9th Street. Exactly three
and a half miles, on a glorious morning, an hour's brisk walk
through one of the world's great capital cities, past landmarks
the world's tourists flock to photograph, and he saw absolutely
nothing at all except the dull mist of worry hanging just in front
of his eyes.

He crossed Pennsylvania Avenue and entered the Hoover Building through the main doors. Laid his hands palms-down on the reception counter.

'The chairman of the joint chiefs of staff,' he said. 'To see the director.'

His hands left two palm-shaped patches of dampness on the laminate. The agent who came down to show him upstairs noticed them. Johnson was silent in the elevator. Harland Webster was waiting for him at the door to his private suite. Johnson nodded to him. Didn't speak. Webster stood aside and gestured him into the inner office. It was dark. There was a lot of mahogany paneling, and the blinds were closed. Johnson sat down in a leather chair and Webster walked around him to his desk.

'I don't want to get in your way,' Johnson said.

He looked at Webster. Webster worked for a moment, decoding that sentence. Then he nodded, cautiously.

'You spoke with the president?' he asked.

Johnson nodded.

'You understand it's appropriate for me to do so?' he asked.

'Naturally,' Webster said. 'Situation like this, nobody should worry about protocol. You call him or go see him?'

'I went to see him,' Johnson said. 'Several times. I had several long conversations with him.'

Webster thought: face to face. Several long conversations. Worse than I thought, but understandable.

'And?' he asked.

Johnson shrugged.

'He told me he'd placed you in personal command,' he said.

Webster nodded.

'Kidnaping,' he said. 'It's Bureau territory, whoever the victim is.'

Johnson nodded, slowly.

'I accept that,' he said. 'For now.'

'But you're anxious,' Webster said. 'Believe me, General, we're all anxious.'

Johnson nodded again. And then he asked the question he'd walked three and a half miles to ask.

'Any progress?' he said.

Webster shrugged.

'We're into the second full day,' he said. 'I don't like that at all.'

486

He lapsed into silence. The second full day of a kidnaping is a kind of threshold. Any early chance of a resolution is gone. The situation starts to harden up. It starts to become a long, intractable set-piece. The danger to the victim increases. The best time to clear up a kidnaping is the first day. The second day, the process gets tougher. The chances get smaller.

'Any progress?' Johnson asked again.

Webster looked away. The second day is when the kidnapers start to communicate. That had always been the Bureau's experience. The second day, sick and frustrated about missing your first and best chance, you sit around, hoping desperately the guys will call. If they don't call on the second day, chances are they aren't going to call at all.

'Anything I can do?' Johnson asked.

Webster nodded.

'You can give me a reason,' he said. 'Who would threaten you like this?'

Johnson shook his head. He'd been asking himself the same question since Monday night.

'Nobody,' he said.

'You should tell me,' Webster said. 'Anything secret, anything hidden, better you tell me right now. It's important, for Holly's sake.'

'I know that,' Johnson said. 'But there's nothing. Nothing at all.'

Webster nodded. He believed him, because he knew it was true. He had reviewed the whole of Johnson's Bureau file. It was a weighty document. It started on page one with brief biographies of his maternal great-grandparents. They had come from a small European principality which no longer existed.

'Will Holly be OK?' Johnson asked quietly.

The recent file pages recounted the death of Johnson's wife. A surprise, a vicious cancer, no more than six weeks, beginning to end. Covert psychiatric opinion commissioned by the Bureau had predicted the old guy would hold up because of his daughter. It had proven to be a correct diagnosis. But if he lost her too, you didn't need to be a psychiatrist to know he wouldn't handle it well. Webster nodded again and put some conviction into his voice.

'She'll be fine,' he said.

'So what have we got so far?' Johnson asked.

'Four guys,' Webster said. 'We've got their pickup truck. They abandoned it prior to the snatch. Burned it and left it. We found it north of Chicago. It's being airlifted down here to Quantico, right now. Our people will go over it.'

'For clues?' Johnson said. 'Even though it burned?'

Webster shrugged.

'Burning is pretty dumb,' he said. 'It doesn't really obscure much. Not from our people, anyway. We'll use that pickup to find them.'

'And then what?' Johnson asked.

Webster shrugged again.

'Then we'll go get your daughter back,' he said. 'Our hostage rescue team is standing by. Fifty guys, the best in the world at this kind of thing. Waiting right by their choppers. We'll go get her, and we'll tidy up the guys who grabbed her.'

There was a short silence in the dark quiet room.

'Tidy them up?' Johnson said. 'What does that mean?'

Webster glanced around his own office and lowered his voice. Thirty-six years of habit.

'Policy,' he said. 'A major DC case like this? No publicity. No media access. We can't allow it. This sort of thing gets on TV, every nut in the country is going to be trying it. So we go in quietly. Some weapons will get discharged. Inevitable in a situation like this. A little collateral damage here and there.'

Johnson nodded slowly.

'You're going to execute them?' he asked, vaguely.

Webster just looked at him, neutrally. Bureau psychiatrists had suggested to him the anticipation of deadly revenge could help sustain self-control, especially with people accustomed to direct action, like other agents, or soldiers.

'Policy,' he said again. 'My policy. And like the man says, I've got personal command.'

The charred pickup was lifted onto an aluminum platform and secured with nylon ropes. An air force Chinook hammered over from the military compound at O'Hare and hovered above it, its downdraft whipping the lake into a frenzy. It winched its chain down and eased the pickup into the air. Swung round over the lake and dipped its nose and roared back west to O'Hare. Set its load down right in front of the open nose of a Galaxy transport. Air force ground crew winched the platform inside. The cargo door closed on it and four minutes later the Galaxy was taxiing. Four minutes later again it was in the air, groaning east towards Washington. Four hours after that, it was roaring over the capital, heading for Andrews Air Force Base. As it landed, another borrowed Chinook took off and waited in mid air. The Galaxy taxied to its apron and the pickup was winched out. The Chinook swooped down and swung it into the air. Flew it south, following I–95 into Virginia, forty miles, all the way to Quantico.

The Chinook set it down gently on the tarmac right outside the vehicle lab. Bureau techs ran out, white coats flapping in the fierce downdraft, and dragged the platform in through the roller door. They winched the wreck off the platform and pulled it into the center of the large shed. They rolled arc lights into a rough circle around it and lit them up. Then they stood there for a second, looking exactly like a team of pathologists getting ready to go to work on a corpse.

General Johnson retraced his steps exactly. He made it down 9th Street, past Natural History, past American History, his mouth forced into a tense rigid oval, breathing hard. He walked the length of the reflecting pool with his throat clamping and gagging. He swung left into Constitution Avenue and made it as far as the Vietnam Wall. Then he stopped. There was a fair crowd, stunned and quiet, as always. He looked at them. He looked at himself in the black granite. He didn't stand out. He was in a lightweight gray suit. It was OK. So he let his vision blur with his tears and he moved forward and turned and sat against the base of the wall, sobbing and crying with his back pressed against the golden names of boys who had died thirty years ago.

NINETEEN

REACHER BALLED HIS LOOSE CHAIN INTO HIS HAND AND SLIPPED OUT of the barn into the pre-dawn twilight. He walked twenty paces and stopped. Freedom. The night air was soft and infinite around him. He was unconfined. But he had no idea where he was. The barn stood alone, isolated fifty yards from a clutch of farm buildings of similar old vintage. There was a house, and a couple of small sheds, and an open structure with a new pickup parked in it. Next to the pickup was a tractor. Next to the tractor, ghostly white in the moonlight, was the truck. Reacher walked over the rocky track toward it. The front doors were locked. The rear doors were locked. He ran back to the horse barn and searched through the dead driver's pockets. Nothing except the padlock key from the barn door. No keys to the truck.

He ran back, squeezing the mass of chain to keep it from making a sound, past the tractor barn, and looked at the house. Walked right around it. The front door was locked tight. The back door was locked tight. And there was a dog behind it. Reacher heard it move in its sleep. He heard a low, sleepy growl. He walked away.

He stood on the track, halfway back to the horse barn, and looked around. He trained his eyes on the indistinct horizon and turned a full circle in the dark. Some kind of a huge, empty landscape.

Flat, endless, no discernible features. The damp night smell of a million acres of something growing. A pale streak of dawn in the east. He shrugged and ducked back inside. Holly raised herself on one elbow and looked a question at him.

'Problems,' he said. 'The handcuff keys are in the house. So are the truck keys. I can't go in for them because there's a dog in there. It's going to bark and wake everybody up. There's more than the two others in there. This is some kind of a working farm. There's a pickup and a tractor. Could be four or five armed men in there. When that damn dog barks, I've had it. And it's nearly daylight.'

'Problems,' Holly said.

'Right,' he said. 'We can't get at a vehicle, and we can't just walk away because you're chained up and you can't walk and we're about a million miles from anywhere, anyway.'

'Where are we?' she asked.

He shrugged.

'No idea,' he said.

'I want to see,' she said. 'I want to see outside. I'm sick of being closed in. Can't you get this chain off?'

Reacher ducked behind her and looked at the iron ring in her wall. The timber looked a little better than his had been. Closer grained. He shook the ring and he knew it was hopeless. She nodded, reluctantly.

'We wait,' she said. 'We wait for a better chance.'

He hurried back to the middle stalls and checked the walls, low down, where it was dampest and the siding was made from the longest boards. He tapped and kicked at them. Chose one particular place and pressed hard with his foot. The board gave slightly and opened a gap against its rusty nail. He worked the gap and sprung the next board, and the next, until he had a flap which would open tall enough to crawl through. Then he ducked back into the center aisle and piled the loose end of his chain onto the dead driver's stomach. Fished in the trouser pocket and pulled out the padlock key. Held it in his teeth. Bent down and picked up the body and the chain together. Carried them out through the open door.

He carried them about twenty-five yards. Away from the house. Then he rested the body on its feet, supporting it by the shoulders, like he was dancing with a drunken partner. Ducked forward and jacked it up onto his shoulder. Caught the chain with one hand and walked away down the track.

He walked fast for twenty minutes. More than a mile. Along the track to a road. Turned left down the road and out into the empty countryside. It was horse country. Railed paddocks ran left and right beside the road. Endless flat grassland, cool and damp in the last of the night. Occasional trees looming through the dark. A narrow, straight, lumpy road surface.

He walked down the center of the road. Then he ducked onto the grassy shoulder and found a ditch. It ran along the base of the paddock rail. He turned a complete circle, with the dead driver windmilling on his shoulder. He could see nothing. He was more than a mile from the farm and he could have been more than a hundred miles from the next one. He bent over and dropped the body into the ditch. It flopped down through the long grass and landed face-down in mud. Reacher turned and ran the mile back to the farm. The streak of dawn was lightening the sky.

He turned into the rough track. There were lights in the windows of the farmhouse. He sprinted for the barn. Pushed the heavy wooden doors closed from the outside. Lifted the crossbeam into its supports and locked it in place with the padlock key. Ran back to the track and hurled the key far into the field. Wednesday was flaming up over the horizon. He sprinted for the far side of the barn and found the gap he'd sprung in the siding. Pushed his chain in ahead of him. Squeezed his shoulders through and forced his way back inside. Pulled the boards back flush with the old timbers, best as he could. Then he came back into the aisle and stood bent over, breathing hard.

'All done,' he said. 'They'll never find him.'

He scooped up the metal mess tin with the cold remains of the soup in it. Scratched around in his stall for the fallen bolts. He gathered as many wood splinters as he could find. Slopped them around in the cold soup and forced them back into the ragged bolt holes. He walked over to Holly's stall and put the tin back on the ground. Kept the spoon. He assembled the bolts through the holes in the base of the iron ring, hanging there off his length of chain. Forced them home among the sticky splinters. Used the back of the spoon to press them firmly in. He ran the chain through the loop until it was hanging straight down and resting on the stone floor. Minimum stress on the fragile assembly.

He tossed the spoon back to Holly. She caught it one-handed and put it back in the tin. Then he ducked down and listened through the boards. The dog was outside. He could hear it snuffling. Then he heard people. Footsteps on the track. They ran to the doors of the barn. They shook and rattled the crossbeam. Retreated. There was shouting. They were calling a name, over and over again. The crack around the barn door was lighting up with morning. The timbers of the barn were creaking as the sun flooded over the horizon and warmed them through.

The footsteps ran back to the barn. The padlock rattled and the chain came off. The crossbeam thumped to the ground. The door groaned open. Loder stepped inside. He had the Glock in his hand and strain showing in his face. He stood just inside the door. His eyes were flicking back and forward between Reacher and Holly. The strain in his face was edged by anger. Some kind of a cold light in his eyes. Then the jumpy guy stepped in behind him. Stevie. He was carrying the driver's shotgun. And smiling. He crowded past Loder and ran down the central cobbled aisle. Raised the shotgun and pointed it straight at Reacher. Loder started after him. Stevie crunched a round into the chamber. Reacher shifted a foot to his left, so the iron ring was hidden from view behind him.

'What's the problem?' he asked.

'You are, asshole,' Loder said. 'Situation has changed. We're a man short. So you just became one person too many.'

Reacher was on his way to the floor as Stevie pulled the trigger. He landed flat on the hard cobbles and hurled himself forward as the shotgun boomed and the stall blew apart. The air was instantly thick with splinters of damp wood and the stink of gunpowder. The plank holding the iron ring fell out of the shattered wall and the chain clattered to the floor. Reacher rolled over and glanced up. Stevie lifted the shotgun vertical and crunched another round into the chamber. Swung the barrel down and aimed again.

'Wait!' Holly screamed.

Stevie glanced at her. Impossible not to.

'Don't be a damn fool,' she yelled. 'Hell are you doing? You don't have the time for this.'

Loder turned to face her.

'He's run, right?' she said. 'Your driver? Is that what happened? He bailed out and ran for it, right? So you need to get going. You don't have time for this.'

Loder stared at her.

'Right now you're ahead of the game,' Holly said urgently. 'But you shoot this guy, you got the local cops a half-hour behind you. You need to get going.'

Reacher gasped up at her from the floor. She was magnificent. She was sucking all their attention her way. She was saving his life.

'Two of you, two of us,' she said urgently. 'You can handle it, right?'

There was silence. Dust and powder drifted in the air. Then Loder stepped back, covering them both with his automatic. Reacher watched the disappointment on Stevie's face. He stood slowly and pulled the chain clear of the wreckage. The iron ring fell out of the smashed wood and clanked on the stones.

'Bitch is right,' Loder said. 'We can handle it.'

He nodded to Stevie. Stevie ran for the door and Loder turned and pulled his key and unlocked Holly's wrist. Dropped her cuff on her mattress. The weight of the chain pulled it back toward the wall. It pulled off the edge of the mattress and slid onto the cobblestones with a loud metallic sound.

'OK, asshole, real quick,' Loder said. 'Before I change my mind.'

Reacher looped his chain into his hand. Ducked down and picked Holly up, under her knees and shoulders. They heard the truck start up. It slewed backward into the entrance. Jammed to a stop. Reacher ran Holly to the truck. Laid her down inside. Climbed in after her. Loder slammed the doors and shut them into darkness.

'Now I guess I owe you,' Reacher said quietly.

Holly just waved it away. An embarrassed little gesture. Reacher stared at her. He liked her. Liked her face. He gazed at it. Recalled it white and disgusted as the driver taunted her. Saw the smooth swell of her breasts under his filthy drooling gaze. Then the picture changed to Stevie smiling and shooting at him, chained to the wall. Then he heard Loder say: the situation has changed.

Everything had changed. He had changed. He lay and felt the old anger inside him grinding like gears. Cold, implacable anger.

Uncontrollable. They had made a mistake. They had changed him from a spectator into an enemy. A bad mistake to make. They had pushed open the forbidden door, not knowing what would come bursting back out at them. He lay there and felt like a ticking bomb they were carrying deep into the heart of their territory. He felt the flood of anger, and thrilled with it, and savored it, and stored it up.

Now there was only one mattress inside the truck. It was only three feet wide. And Stevie was a very erratic driver. Reacher and Holly were lying down, pressed tight together. Reacher's left wrist still had the cuff and the chain locked onto it. His right arm was around Holly's shoulders. He was holding her tight. Tighter than he really needed to.

'How much farther?' she asked.

'We'll be there before nightfall,' he said, quietly. 'They didn't bring your chain. No more overnight stops.'

She was silent for a moment.

'I don't know if I'm glad or not,' she said. 'I hate this truck, but I don't know if I want to actually arrive anywhere.'

Reacher nodded.

'It reduces our chances,' he said. 'Rule of thumb is escape while you're on the move. It gets much harder after that.'

The motion of the truck indicated they were on a highway. But either the terrain was different, or Stevie couldn't handle the truck, or both, because they were swaying violently. The guy was swinging late into turns and jamming the vehicle from side to side, like he was having a struggle staying between the lane markers. Holly was getting thrown against Reacher's side. He pulled her closer and held her tighter. She snuggled in close, instinctively. He felt her hesitate, like she realized she'd acted without thinking, then he felt her decide not to pull away again.

'You feel OK?' she asked him. 'You killed a man.'

He was quiet for a long moment.

'He wasn't the first,' he said. 'And I just decided he won't be the last.'

She turned her head to speak at the same time he did. The truck swayed violently to the left. Their lips were an inch apart. The truck swayed again. They kissed. At first it was light and

495

tentative. Reacher felt the new soft lips on his, and the unfamiliar new taste and smell and feel. Then they kissed harder. Then the truck started hammering through a series of sharp curves, and they forgot all about kissing and just held on tight, trying not to be thrown right off the mattress onto the ridged metal floor.

TWENTY

BROGAN WAS THE GUY WHO MADE THE BREAKTHROUGH IN CHICAGO. He was the third guy that morning to walk past the can of white paint out there on the abandoned industrial lot, but he was the first to realize its significance.

'The truck they stole was white,' Brogan said. 'Some kind of ID on the side. They painted over it. Got to be that way. The can was right there, with a brush, about ten feet from the Lexus. Stands to reason they would park the Lexus right next to the truck, right? Therefore the paint can was next to where the truck had been.'

'What sort of paint?' McGrath asked.

'Ordinary household paint,' Brogan said. 'A quart can. Two-inch brush. Price tag still on it, from a hardware store. And there are fingerprints in the splashes on the handle.'

McGrath nodded and smiled.

'OK,' he said. 'Go to work.'

Brogan took the computer-aided mugshots with him to the hardware store named on the paintbrush handle. It was a cramped, family-owned place, two hundred yards from the abandoned lot. The counter was attended by a stout old woman with a mind like a steel trap. Straightaway she identified the picture of the guy who the video had caught at the wheel of the Lexus. She said the paint and the brush had been purchased by him about ten o'clock Monday morning. To prove it, she rattled open an ancient drawer and pulled out Monday's register roll. Seven ninety-eight for the paint, five ninety-eight for the brush, plus tax, right there on the roll.

'He paid cash,' she said.

'You got a video system in here?' Brogan asked her.

'No,' she said.

'Doesn't your insurance company say you got to?' he asked.

The stout old woman just smiled.

'We're not insured,' she said.

Then she leaned under the counter and came up with a shotgun.

'Not by no insurance company, anyway,' she said.

Brogan looked at the weapon. He was pretty sure the barrel was way too short for the piece to be legal. But he wasn't about to start worrying over such a thing. Not right then.

'OK,' he said. 'You take care now.'

More than seven million people in the Chicago area, something like ten million road vehicles, but only one white truck had been reported stolen in the twenty-four-hour period between Sunday and Monday. It was a white Ford Econoline. Owned and operated by a South Side electrician. His insurance company made him empty the truck at night, and store his stock and tools inside his shop. Anything left inside the truck was not covered. That was the rule. It was an irksome rule, but on Monday morning when the guy came out to load up and the truck was gone, it started to look like a rule which made a whole lot of sense. He had reported the theft to the insurance broker and the police, and he was not expecting to hear much more about it. So he was duly impressed when two FBI agents turned up, forty-eight hours later, asking all kinds of urgent questions.

'OK,' McGrath said. 'We know what we're looking for. White Econoline, new paint on the sides. We've got the plates. Now we need to know where to look. Ideas?'

'Coming up on forty-eight hours,' Brogan said. 'Assume an average speed of fifty-five? That would make the max range somewhere more than twenty-six hundred miles. That's effectively anywhere on the North American continent, for God's sake.'

'Too pessimistic,' Milosevic said. 'They probably stopped nights. Call it six hours' driving time on Monday, maybe ten on Tuesday, maybe four so far today, total of twenty hours, that's a maximum range of eleven hundred miles.'

'Needle in a haystack,' Brogan said.

McGrath shrugged.

'So let's find the haystack,' he said. 'Then we'll go look for the needle. Call it fifteen hundred maximum. What does that look like?'

Brogan pulled a road atlas from the stack of reference material on the table. He opened it up to the early section where the whole country was shown all at once, all the states splattered over one page in a colorful mosaic. He checked the scale and traced his fingernail in a circle.

'That's anywhere shy of California,' he said. 'Half of Washington State, half of Oregon, none of California and absolutely all of everywhere else. Somewhere around a zillion square miles.'

There was a depressed silence in the room.

'Mountains between here and Washington State, right?' McGrath said. 'So let's assume they're not in Washington State yet. Or Oregon. Or California. Or Alaska or Hawaii. So we've cut it down already. Only forty-five states to call, right? Let's go to work.'

'They might have gone to Canada,' Brogan said. 'Or Mexico, or a boat or a plane.'

Milosevic shrugged and took the atlas from him.

'You're too pessimistic,' he said again.

'Needle in a damn haystack,' Brogan said back.

Three floors above them the Bureau fingerprint technicians were looking at the paintbrush Brogan had brought in. It had been used once only, by a fairly clumsy guy. The paint was matted up in the bristles, and had run onto the mild steel ferrule which bound the bristles into the wooden handle. The guy had used an action which had put his thumb on the back of the ferrule, and his first two fingers on the front. It was suggestive of a medium-height guy reaching up and brushing paint onto a flat surface, level with his head, maybe a little higher, the paintbrush handle pointing downward. A Ford

Econoline was just a fraction less than eighty-one inches tall. Any signwriting would be about seventy inches off the ground. The computer could not calculate this guy's height, because it had only seen him sitting down inside the Lexus, but the way the brush had been used, he must have been five-eight, five-nine, reaching up and brushing just a little above his eye-level. Brushing hard, with some lateral force. There wasn't going to be a lot of finesse in the finished job.

Wet paint is a pretty good medium for trapping fingerprints, and the techs knew they weren't going to have a lot of trouble. But for the sake of completeness, they ran every process they had, from fluoroscopy down to the traditional gray powder. They ended up with three and a half good prints, clearly the thumb and the first two fingers of the right hand, with the extra bonus of a lateral half of the little finger. They enhanced the focus in the computer and sent the prints down the digital line to the Hoover Building in Washington. They added a code instructing the big database down there to search with maximum speed.

In the labs at Quantico the hunters were divided into two packs. The burned pickup had been torn apart and half the staff were examining the minute physical traces unique to that particular vehicle. The other half were chasing through the fragmented records held by the manufacturers, listening out for the faint echoes of its construction and subsequent sales history.

It was a Dodge, ten years old, built in Detroit. The chassis number and the code stamped into the iron of the engine block were both original. The numbers enabled the manufacturer to identify the original shipment. The pickup had rolled out of the factory gate one April and had been loaded onto a railroad wagon and hauled to California. Then it had been driven to a dealership in Mojave. The dealer had paid the invoice in May and, beyond that, the manufacturer had no further knowledge of the vehicle.

The dealership in Mojave had gone belly-up two years later. New owners had bought the franchise. Current records were in their computer. Ancient history from before the change in ownership was all in storage. Not every day that a small automotive dealership on the edge of the desert gets a call from the FBI Academy at Quantico, so there was a promise of rapid action.

The sales manager himself undertook to get the information and call right back.

The vehicle itself was pretty much burned out. All the soft clues were gone. There were no plates. There was nothing significant in the interior. There were no bridge tokens, no tunnel tokens. The windshield stickers were gone. All that was left was the mud. The vehicle technicians had cut away both of the rear wheel wells, the full hoop of sheet metal right above the driven tires, and carried them carefully across to the Materials Analysis Unit. Any vehicle writes its own itinerary in the layers of mud it throws up underneath. Bureau geologists were peeling back the layers and looking at where the pickup had been, and where it had come from.

The mud was baked solid by the burning tires. Some of the softer crystals had vitrified into glass. But the layers were clear. The outer layers were thin. The geologists concluded they had been deposited during a long journey across the country. Then there was a couple of years' worth of mixed rock particles. The particular mixture was interesting. There was such a combination of sands there that identifying their exact origin should be easy enough. Under that mixture was a thick base layer of desert dust. Straightaway the geologists agreed that the truck had started its life out near the Mojave desert.

Every single law-enforcement agency in forty-five states had the description and the plate number of the stolen white Econoline. Every single officer on duty in the whole nation had been briefed to look for it, parked or mobile, burned or hidden or abandoned. For a short time that Wednesday, that white Econoline was the most hunted vehicle on the planet.

McGrath was sitting at the head of the table in the quiet conference room, smoking, waiting. He was not optimistic. If the truck was parked and hidden, it would most likely never be found. The task was too huge. Any closed garage or building or barn could hide it for ever. If it was still somewhere on the road, the chances were better. So the biggest gamble of his life was: after forty-eight hours, had they gotten where they were going, or were they still on their way?

Two hours after starting the patient search, the fingerprint database

501

brought back a name: Peter Wayne Bell. There was a perfect match, right hand, thumb and first two fingers. The computer rated the match on the partial from the little finger as very probable.

'Thirty-one years old,' Brogan said. 'From Mojave, California. Two convictions for sex offences. Charged with a double rape, three years ago, didn't go down. Victims were three months in the hospital. This guy Bell had an alibi from three of his friends. Victims couldn't make the ID, too shaken up by the beatings.'

'Nice guy,' McGrath said.

Milosevic nodded.

'And he's got Holly,' he said. 'Right there in the back of his truck.'

McGrath said nothing in reply to that. Then the phone rang. He picked it up. Listened to a short barked sentence. He sat there and Brogan and Milosevic saw his face light up like a guy who sees his teams all win the pennant on the same day, baseball, football, basketball and hockey, all on the same day that his son graduates summa cum laude from Harvard and his gold stocks go through the roof.

'Arizona,' he shouted. 'It's in Arizona, heading north on US60.'

An old hand in an Arizona State Police cruiser had spotted a white panel truck making bad lane changes round the sharp curves on US60, as it winds away from the town of Globe seventy miles east of Phoenix. He had pulled closer and read the plate. He saw the blue oval and the Econoline script on the back. He had thumbed his mike and called it in. Then the world had gone crazy. He was told to stick with the truck, no matter what. He was told that helicopters would be coming in from Phoenix and Flagstaff, and from Albuquerque way over in New Mexico. Every available mobile unit would be coming in behind him from the south. Up ahead the National Guard would be assembling a roadblock. Within twenty minutes, he was told, you'll have more back-up than you've ever dreamed of. Until then, he was told, you're the most important lawman in America.

The sales manager from the Dodge dealership in Mojave, California, called Quantico back within an hour. He'd been over to the storage room and dug out the records for the sales made ten years ago by the previous franchise owners. The pickup in question had been sold to a citrus farmer down in Kendall, fifty miles south of Mojave, in May of that year. The guy had been back for servicing and emissions testing for the first four years, and after that they'd never seen him again. He had bought on a four-year time payment plan and his name was Dutch Borken.

A half-hour later the stolen white Econoline was twenty-eight miles further north on US60 in Arizona, and it was the tip of a long teardrop-shape of fifty vehicles cruising behind it. Above it, five helicopters were hammering through the air. In front of it, ten miles to the north, the highway was closed and another forty vehicles were stationary on the pavement, parked up in a neat arrowhead formation. The whole operation was being co-ordinated by the agent-in-charge from the FBI's Phoenix office. He was in the lead helicopter, staring down through the clear desert air at the roof of the truck. He was wearing a headset with a throat mike, and he was talking continuously.

'OK, people,' he said. 'Let's go for it, right now. Go go go!'

His lead chopper swooped upward out of the way and two others arrowed down. They hovered just in front of the truck, low down, one on each side, keeping pace. The police cars behind fanned out across the whole width of the highway and they all hit their lights and sirens together. A third chopper swung down and flew backward, right in front of the truck, eight feet off the ground, strobes flashing, rotors beating the air. The co-pilot started a sequence of clear gestures, hands wide, palms out, like he was personally slowing the truck. Then the sirens all stopped and the enormous bullhorn on the front of the helicopter fired up. The co-pilot's voice boomed out, amplified grotesquely beyond the point of distortion, clearly audible even over the thrashing and hammering of the rotor blades.

'Federal Agents,' his voice screamed. 'You are commanded to stop at once. I repeat, you are commanded to stop your vehicle at once.'

The truck kept on going. The helicopter right in front of it swung and wobbled in the air. Then it settled again, even closer to the windshield, flying backward, not more than ten feet away.

'You are surrounded,' the co-pilot shouted through the huge bullhorn. 'There are a hundred police officers behind you. The road is closed ahead. You have no option. You must slow your vehicle and come to a complete stop. You must do that right now.'

The cruisers all lit up their sirens again and two of them pulled alongside. The truck was locked into a solid raft of hostile traffic. It sped on for a long moment, then it slowed. Behind it, the frantic convoy braked and swerved. The helicopters rose up and kept pace. The truck slowed more. Police cruisers pulled alongside, two deep, door to door, bumper to bumper. The truck coasted to a halt. The helicopters held station overhead. The lead cars swerved around in front and jammed to a stop, inches from the truck's hood. All around, officers jumped out. The highway was thick with police. Even over the beating of the helicopter rotors, the crunching of shotgun mechanisms and the clicking of a hundred revolver hammers were clearly audible.

In Chicago, McGrath did not hear the shotguns and the revolvers, but he could hear the Phoenix agent-in-charge shouting over the radio. The output from the throat mike in his helicopter was patched through Washington and was crackling out through a speaker on the long hardwood table. The guy was talking continuously, excited, half in a stream of instructions to his team, half as a running commentary on the sight he was seeing on the road below. McGrath was sitting there, hands cold and wet, staring at the noisy speaker like if he stared at it hard enough it would change into a crystal ball and let him see what was going down.

'He's stopping, he's stopping,' the guy in the helicopter was saying. 'He's stationary now, he's stopped on the road, he's surrounded. Hold your fire, wait for my word, they're not coming out, open the doors, open the damn doors and drag them out, OK, we got two guys in the front, two guys, one driver, one passenger, they're coming out, they're out, secure them, put them in a car, get the keys, open up the back, but watch out, there are two more in there with her. OK, we're going to the back, we're going around to the rear, the doors are locked back there, we're trying the key. You know what? There's still writing on the side of this truck. The writing is still there. It says Bright Spark Electrics. I thought it was supposed to be blanked out, right? Painted over or something?'

In Chicago, a deathly hush fell over the third-floor conference

504

room. McGrath went white. Milosevic looked at him. Brogan stared calmly out of the window.

'And why is it heading north?' McGrath asked. 'Back toward Chicago?'

The crackling from the speaker was still there. They turned back toward it. Listened hard. They could hear the thump of the rotor blades behind the urgent voice.

'The rear doors are open,' the voice said. 'The doors are open, they're open, we're going in, people are coming out, here they come, what the hell is this? There are dozens of people in there. There are maybe twenty people in there. They're all coming out. They're still coming out. There are twenty or thirty people in there. What the hell is going on here?'

The guy broke off. Evidently he was listening to a report radioed up from the ground. McGrath and Brogan and Milosevic stared at the hissing speaker. It stayed quiet for a long time. Nothing coming through at all except the guy's loud breathing and the hammering of the blades and the waterfall of static. Then the voice came back.

'Shit,' it said. 'Shit, Washington, you there? You listening to this? You know what we just did? You know what you sent us to do? We just busted a load of wetbacks. About thirty illegals from Mexico. Just got picked up from the border. They're on their way up to Chicago. They say they all got jobs promised up there.'

TWENTY-ONE

THE WHITE ECONOLINE DRONED ON. IT WAS MOVING FASTER THAN it had been before. But it was out of the curves. It had lurched around the last of the tight bends, and it had settled to a fast, straight cruise. Noisier than before, because of the extra speed and the whine of the slipstream through the hundred random holes in the roof.

Reacher and Holly were tight together on the three-foot mattress. They were lying on their backs, staring up at the holes. Each hole was a bright point of light. Not blue, just a point of light so bright it had no color at all. Just a bright point in the dark. Like a mathematical proposition. Total light against the total dark of the surrounding sheet metal. Light, the opposite of dark. Dark, the absence of light. Positive and negative. Both propositions were contrasted vividly up there on the metal roof.

'I want to see the sky,' Holly said.

It was warm in the truck. Not hot, like it had been the first day and a half. The whistling slipstream had solved that problem. The rush of air was keeping it comfortable. But it was warm enough that Reacher had taken his shirt off. He had balled it up and crammed it under his head.

'I want to see the whole sky,' Holly said. 'Not just little bits of it.'

Reacher said nothing in reply. He was counting the holes.

'What time is it?' Holly asked him.

'Hundred and thirteen,' Reacher said.

Holly turned her head to him.

'What?' she said.

'Hundred and thirteen holes in the roof,' he said.

'Great,' she said. 'What time is it?'

'Three-thirty, Central,' he said.

She snuggled closer. She moved her weight onto her side. Her head was resting on his right shoulder. Her leg was resting on his. His thigh was jammed between hers.

'Wednesday, right?' she said.

'Wednesday,' he said.

She was physically closer to him than many women had allowed themselves to get. She felt lithe and athletic. Firm, but soft. Young. Scented. He was drifting away and enjoying the sensation. He was slightly breathless. But he wasn't kidding himself about her motivation. She was relaxed about it, but she was doing it to rest her painful knee, and to keep herself from rolling off the mattress onto the floor.

'Fifty-one hours,' she said. 'Fifty-one hours, and I haven't seen the sky.'

One hundred and thirteen was a prime number. You couldn't make it by multiplying any other numbers together. Hundred and twelve, you could make by multiplying fifty-six by two, or twenty-eight by four, or fourteen by eight. Hundred and fourteen, you could make by multiplying fifty-seven by two, or nineteen by six, or thirty-eight by three. But one hundred and thirteen was prime. No factors. The only way to make a hundred and thirteen was by multiplying a hundred and thirteen by one. Or by firing a shotgun into a truck in a rage.

'Reacher, I'm getting worried,' Holly said.

Fifty-one hours. Fifty-one was not a prime number. You could make fifty-one by multiplying seventeen by three. Three tens are thirty, three sevens are twenty-one, thirty and twenty-one make fifty-one. Not a prime number. Fifty-one had factors. He dragged the weight of the chain up with his left wrist and held her tight, both arms around her.

507

'You'll be OK,' he said to her. 'They're not going to hurt you. They want to trade you for something. They'll keep you fit and well.'

He felt her shake her head against his shoulder. Just one small shake, but it was very definite.

'I'm not worried about me,' she said. 'I'm worried about you. Who the hell's going to trade something for you?'

He said nothing. Nothing he could say to that. She snuggled closer. He could feel the scratch of her eyelashes against the skin on the side of his chest as she blinked. The truck roared on, faster than it wanted to go. He could feel the driver pushing it against its natural cruising speed.

'So I'm getting a little worried,' she said.

'You look out for me,' he said. 'And I'll look out for you.'

'I'm not asking you to do that,' she said.

'I know you're not,' he said.

'Well, I can't let you do that,' she said.

'You can't stop me,' he said. 'This is about me now, too. They made it that way. They were going to shoot me down. I've got a rule, Holly: people mess with me at their own risk. I try to be patient about it. I had a teacher once, grade school somewhere. Philippines, I think, because she always wore a big white hat. So it was somewhere hot. I was always twice the size of the other kids, and she used to say to me: count to ten before you get mad, Reacher. And I've counted way past ten on this one. Way past. So you may as well face it, win or lose, now we do it together.'

They went quiet. The truck roared on.

'Reacher?' Holly said.

'What?' he said.

'Hold me,' she said.

'I am holding you,' he said.

He squeezed her gently, both arms, to make his point. She pressed closer.

'Reacher?' she said again.

'Yes?' he said.

'You want to kiss me again?' she said. 'Makes me feel better.'

He turned his head and smiled at her in the dark.

'Doesn't do me a whole lot of harm, either,' he said.

Eight hours at maybe sixty-five or seventy miles an hour.

Somewhere between five hundred and five hundred and fifty miles. That's what they'd done. That was Reacher's estimation. And it was beginning to give him a clue about where they were.

'We're somewhere where they abolished the speed limit,' he said.

Holly stirred and yawned.

'What?' she said.

'We've been going fast,' he said. 'Up to seventy miles an hour, probably, for hours. Loder is pretty thorough. He wouldn't let Stevie drive this fast if there was any danger of getting pulled over for it. So we're somewhere where they raised the limit, or abolished it altogether. Which states did that?'

She shrugged.

'I'm not sure,' she said. 'Mainly the western states, I think.'

Reacher nodded. Traced an arc on the map in his head.

'We didn't go east,' he said. 'We figured that already. So I figure we're in Texas, New Mexico, Colorado, Wyoming, or Montana. Maybe as far as Idaho, Utah, Nevada or Arizona. Not in California yet.'

The truck slowed slightly, and they heard the engine note harden up. Then they heard the crunch as the driver came down out of fifth gear into fourth.

'Mountains,' Holly said.

It was more than a hill. More than an up-grade. It was a smooth, relentless climb. A highway through the mountains. Clearly engineered to help out the laboring traffic, but they were adding hundreds of feet, every mile they drove. Reacher felt the lurch as the truck pulled out to pass slower vehicles. Not many, but a few. It stayed in fourth gear, the guy's foot hard down, hammering uphill, then relaxing, changing up to fifth, then down again, charging upwards.

'We could run out of gas,' Holly said.

'It's diesel, not gas,' Reacher said. 'We used these things in the army. Thirty-five gallon tank. Diesel will do maybe twenty-five to the gallon, highway mileage. Best part of nine hundred miles, before they run out.'

'That could get us all the way out of the States,' she said.

They cruised on. The truck roared through the mountains for hours, then it left the highway. Night had fallen. The bright holes in the roof had dimmed. Then they had disappeared. They had turned darker than the roof itself. Positive and negative. They felt the lurch as the truck pulled to the right, off the highway, and they felt the tires grabbing at the pavement as the truck hauled around a tight right. Then there was a confusing blur of turns and stops and starts. Bumpy downhill bends and tight uphill turns with the truck grinding in a low gear. Periods of cruising down gently winding roads, bad surfaces, good surfaces, gradients, gravel under the wheels, potholes in the road. Reacher could imagine the headlight beams flicking left and right and bouncing up and down.

The truck slowed almost to a stop. Turned a tight right. Pattered over some kind of a wooden bridge. Then it yawed and bumped its way along a rutted track. It was moving slowly, shuddering from side to side. It felt like they were driving up a dry riverbed. Some kind of a stony, narrow track. It felt like this was the very last leg of the journey. It felt like they were very close to their destination. The urgency had gone out of the guy's driving. It felt like the truck was nearly home.

But the final leg took a long time. The speed was low and the road was bad. Stones and small rocks were popping under the tires. The tires were squirming sideways across the loose surface. The truck ground on for forty minutes. Fifty minutes. Reacher got cold. He sat up and shook out his shirt. Put it on. An hour on the bumpy track. At this speed, maybe fifteen miles, maybe twenty.

Then they were there. The truck lurched up over a final heave and leveled out. Rolled forward another few yards and stopped. The engine noise died. It was replaced by an awesome silence. Reacher could hear nothing at all except a vast emptiness and the ticking of the muffler as it cooled. He could hear the two guys in front, sitting quiet and exhausted. Then they got out. He heard their doors open and their seat springs bounce. He heard their feet on gravel. Their doors slammed, enormously loud metallic clangs in the stillness. He heard them crunch around to the rear. He could hear the sound of the keys swinging gently in the driver's hand.

The key slid into the lock. The lock clicked back. The handle turned. The door swung open. Loder propped it back with the metal stay. Then he opened the other door. Propped it back. Gestured them out with the Glock. Reacher helped Holly along the ridged floor. He stepped down. The chain on his wrist clattered to the earth. He lifted Holly down beside him. They stood together, leaning back against the edge of the truck's ridged metal floor. Looking out and around.

Holly had wanted to see the sky. She was standing there under the vastest sky Reacher had ever seen. It was a dark inky-blue, almost black, and it was huge. It stretched up to an infinite height. It was as big as a planet. It was peppered with a hundred billion bright stars. They were far away, but they were unnaturally vivid. They dusted back to the far cold reaches of the universe. It was a gigantic night sky and it stretched on forever.

They were in a forest clearing. Reacher could smell a heavy scent of pines. It was a strong smell. Clean and fresh. There was a black mass of trees all around. They covered the jagged slopes of mountains. They were in a forest clearing, surrounded by mountainous wooded slopes. It was a big clearing, infinitely dark, silent. Reacher could see the faint black outlines of buildings off to his right. They were long, low huts. Some kind of wooden structures, crouching in the dark.

There were people on the edge of the clearing. Standing among the nearest trees. Reacher could see their vague shapes. Maybe fifty or sixty people. Just standing there, silent. They were in dark clothing. They had darkened faces. Their faces were smudged with night camouflage. He could see their eyes, white against the black trees. They were holding weapons. He could see rifles and machine guns. Slung casually over the shoulders of the silent, staring people. They had dogs. Several big dogs, on thick leather leashes.

There were children among the people. Reacher could make them out. Children, standing together in groups, silent, staring, big sleepy eyes. They were clustered behind the adults, still, their shoulders facing diagonally away in fear and perplexity. Sleepy children, woken up in the middle of the night to witness something.

Loder turned himself around in a slow circle and waved the silent staring people nearer. He moved his arm in a wide inclusive gesture, like a ringmaster in a circus.

'We got her,' he yelled into the silence. 'The federal bitch is here.'

His voice boomed back off the distant mountains.

'Where the hell are we?' Holly asked him.

511

Loder turned back and smiled at her.

'Our place, bitch,' he said quietly. 'A place where your federal buddies can't come get you.'

'Why not?' Holly asked him. 'Where the hell are we?'

'That could be hard for you to understand,' Loder said.

'Why?' Holly said. 'We're somewhere, right? Somewhere in the States?'

Loder shook his head.

'No,' he said.

Holly looked blank.

'Canada?' she said.

The guy shook his head again.

'Not Canada, bitch,' he said.

Holly glanced around at the trees and the mountains. Glanced up at the vast night sky. Shuddered in the sudden chill.

'Well, this isn't Mexico,' she said.

The guy raised both arms in a descriptive little gesture.

'This is a brand-new country,' he said.

TWENTY-TWO

THE ATMOSPHERE IN THE CHICAGO FIELD OFFICE WEDNESDAY evening was like a funeral, and in a way it was a funeral, because any realistic hope of getting Holly back had died. McGrath knew his best chance had been an early chance. The early chance was gone. If Holly was still alive, she was a prisoner somewhere on the North American continent, and he would not get even the chance to find out where until her kidnapers chose to call. And, so far, approaching sixty hours after the snatch, they had not called.

He was at the head of the long table in the third-floor conference room. Smoking. The room was quiet. Milosevic was sitting to one side, back to the windows. The afternoon sun had inched its way around to evening and fallen away into darkness. The temperature in the room had risen and fallen with it, down to a balmy summer dusk. But the two men in there were chilled with anticlimax. They barely looked up as Brogan came in to join them. He was holding a sheaf of computer printouts. He wasn't smiling, but he looked reasonably close to it.

'You got something?' McGrath asked him.

Brogan nodded purposefully and sat down. Sorted the printouts into four separate handfuls and held them up, each one in turn.

'Quantico,' he said. 'They've got something. And the crime database in DC. They've got three somethings. And I had an idea.'

He spread his papers out and looked up.

'Listen to this,' he said. 'Graphic granite, interlocking crystals, cherts, gneisses, schists, shale, foliated metamorphics, quartzites, quartz crystals, red-bed sandstones, Triassic red sand, acidic volcanics, pink feldspar, green chlorite, ironstone, grit, sand and silt. You know what all that stuff is?'

McGrath and Milosevic shrugged and shook their heads.

'Geology,' Brogan said. 'The people down in Quantico looked at the pickup. Geologists, from the Materials Analysis Unit. They looked at the shit thrown up under the wheel arches. They figured out what the stuff is, and they figured out where that pickup has been. Little tiny pieces of rock and sediment stuck to the metal. Like a sort of a geological fingerprint.'

'OK, so where has it been?' McGrath asked.

'Started out in California,' Brogan said. 'Citrus grower called Dutch Borken bought it, ten years ago, in Mojave. The manufacturer traced that for us. That part is nothing to do with geology. Then the scientists say it was in Montana for a couple of years. Then they drove it over here, northern route, through North Dakota, Minnesota and Wisconsin.'

'They sure about this?' McGrath said.

'Like a trucker's logbook,' Brogan said. 'Except written with shit on the underneath, not with a pen on paper.'

'So who is this Dutch Borken?' McGrath asked. 'Is he involved?' Brogan shook his head.

'No,' he said. 'Dutch Borken is dead.'

'When?' McGrath asked.

'Couple of years ago,' Brogan said. 'He borrowed money, farming went all to hell, the bank foreclosed, he stuck a twelve-bore in his mouth and blew the top of his head all over California.'

'So?' McGrath said.

'His son stole the pickup,' Brogan said. 'Technically, it was the bank's property, right? The son took off in it, never been seen again. The bank reported it, and the local cops looked for it, couldn't find it. It's not licensed. DMV knows nothing about it. Cops gave up on it, because who cares about a ratty old pickup? But my guess is this

Borken boy stole it and moved to Montana. The pickup was definitely in Montana two years, scientists are dead sure about that.'

'We got anything on this Borken boy?' McGrath asked him.

Brogan nodded. Held up another sheaf of paper.

'We got a shitload on him,' he said. 'He's all over our database like ants at a picnic. His name is Beau Borken. Thirty-five years old, six feet in height and four hundred pounds in weight. Big guy, right? Extreme right-winger, paranoid tendencies. Now a militia leader. Balls-out fanatic. Links to other militias all over the damn place. Prime suspect in a robbery up in the north of California. Armored car carrying twenty million in bearer bonds was hit. The driver was killed. They figured militia involvement, because the bad guys were wearing bits and pieces of military uniforms. Borken's outfit looked good for it. But they couldn't make it stick. Files are unclear as to why not. And also, what's good for us is before all that, Beau Borken was one of the alibis Peter Wayne Bell used to get off the rape bust. So he's a documented associate of somebody we can place on the scene.'

Milosevic looked up.

'And he's based in Montana?' he said.

Brogan nodded.

'We can pinpoint the exact region, more or less,' he said. 'The scientific guys at Quantico are pretty hot for a couple of particular valleys, northwest corner of Montana.'

'They can be that specific?' Milosevic said.

Brogan nodded again.

'I called them,' he said. 'They said this sediment in the wheel arches was local to a particular type of a place. Something to do with very old rock getting scraped up by glaciers about a million years ago, lying there nearer the surface than it should be, all mixed up with the regular rock which is still pretty old, but newer than the old rock, you know what I mean? A particular type of a mixture? I asked them, how can you be so sure? They said they just recognize it, like I would recognize my mother fifty feet away on the sidewalk. They said it was from one of a couple of north–south glacial valleys, northwest corner of Montana, where the big old glaciers were rolling down from Canada. And there was some sort of crushed sandstone in there, very different, but it's what the Forest Service use on the forest tracks up there.'

'OK,' McGrath said. 'So our guys were in Montana for a couple of years. But have they necessarily gone back there?'

Brogan held up the third of his four piles of paper. Unfolded a map. And smiled for the first time since Monday.

'You bet your ass they have,' he said. 'Look at the map. Direct route between Chicago and the far corner of Montana takes you through North Dakota, right? Some farmer up there was walking around this morning. And guess what he found in a ditch?'

'What?' McGrath asked.

'A dead guy,' Brogan said. 'In a ditch, horse country, miles from anywhere. So naturally the farmer calls the cops, the cops print the corpse, the computer comes back with a name.'

'What name?' McGrath asked.

'Peter Wayne Bell,' Brogan said. 'The guy who drove away with Holly.'

'He's dead?' McGrath said. 'How?'

'Don't know how,' Brogan said. 'Maybe some kind of a falling out? This guy Bell kept his brains in his jockey shorts. We know that, right? Maybe he went after Holly, maybe Holly aced him. But put a ruler on the map and take a look. They were all on their way back to Montana. That's for damn sure. Has to be that way.'

'In what?' McGrath said. 'Not in a white truck.'

'Yes in a white truck,' Brogan said.

'That Econoline was the only truck missing,' McGrath said.

Brogan shook his head. He held up the fourth set of papers.

'My new idea,' he said. 'I checked if Rubin rented a truck.'

'Who?' McGrath said.

'Rubin is the dead dentist,' Brogan said. 'I checked if he rented a truck.'

McGrath looked at him.

'Why should the damn dentist rent a truck?' he said.

'He didn't,' Brogan said. 'I figured maybe the guys rented the truck, with the dentist's credit cards, after they captured him. It made a lot of sense. Why risk stealing a vehicle if you can rent one with a stolen wallet full of credit cards and driver's licenses and stuff? So I called around. Sure enough, Chicago-You-Drive, some South Side outfit, they rented an Econoline to a Dr Rubin, Monday morning, nine o'clock. I ask them, did the photo on the license match the guy? They say they never look. As long as the credit card goes through the machine, they don't care. I ask them, what color was the Econoline? They say, all our trucks are white. I ask them, writing on the side? They say sure, Chicago-You-Drive, green letters, head height.'

McGrath nodded.

'I'm going to call Harland Webster,' he said. 'I want to get sent to Montana.'

'Go to North Dakota first,' Webster said.

'Why?' McGrath asked him.

There was a pause on the line.

'One step at a time,' Webster said. 'We need to check out this Peter Wayne Bell situation. So stop off in North Dakota first, OK?'

'You sure, chief?' McGrath said.

'Patient grunt work,' Webster said. 'That's what's going to do it for us. Work the clues, right? It's worked so far. Your boy Brogan did some good work. I like the sound of him.'

'So let's go with it, chief,' McGrath said. 'All the way to Montana, right?'

'No good rushing around until we know something,' Webster said back. 'Like who and where and why. That's what we need to know, Mack.'

'We know who and where,' he said. 'This Beau Borken guy. In Montana. It's clear enough, right?'

There was another pause on the line.

'Maybe,' Webster said. 'But what about why?'

McGrath jammed the phone into his shoulder and lit up his next cigarette.

'No idea,' he said, reluctantly.

'We looked at the mugshots,' Webster said. 'I sent them over to the Behavioral Science Unit. Shrinks looked them over.'

'And?' McGrath asked.

'I don't know,' Webster said. 'They're a pretty smart bunch of people down there, but how much can you get from gazing at a damn photograph?'

'Any conclusions at all?' McGrath asked.

'Some,' Webster said. 'They felt three of the guys belonged together, and the big guy was kind of separate. The three looked the same. Did you notice that? Same kind of background, same looks, same genes maybe. They could all three be related. This guy Bell was from California. Mojave, right? Beau Borken, too. The feeling is the three of them are probably all from the same area. All West Coast types. But the big guy is different. Different clothes, different stance, different physically. The anthropologists down there in Quantico think he could be foreign, at least partly, or maybe second-generation. Fair hair and blue eyes, but there's something in his face. They say maybe he's European. And he's big. Not pumped up at the gym, just big, like naturally.'

'So?' McGrath asked. 'What were their conclusions?'

'Maybe he is European,' Webster said. 'A big tough guy, maybe from Europe, they're worried he's some kind of a terrorist. Maybe a mercenary. They're checking overseas.'

'A terrorist?' McGrath said. 'A mercenary? But why?'

'That's the point,' Webster said. 'The why part is what we need to nail down. If this guy really is a terrorist, what's his purpose? Who recruited who? Who is the motivating force here? Did Borken's militia hire him to help them out, or is it the other way around? Is this his call? Did he hire Borken's militia for local color inside the States?'

'What the hell is going on?' McGrath asked.

'I'm flying up to O'Hare,' Webster said. 'I'll take over day-to-day from here, Mack. Case this damn big, I've got to, right? The old guy will expect it.'

'Which old guy?' McGrath asked sourly.

'Whichever, both,' Webster said.

Brogan drove out to O'Hare, middle of the evening, six hours after the debacle with the Mexicans in the truck in Arizona. McGrath sat beside him in the front seat, Milosevic in the back. Nobody spoke. Brogan parked the Bureau Ford on the military compound tarmac, inside the wire fence. They sat in the car, waiting for the FBI Lear from Andrews. It landed after twenty minutes. They saw it taxi quickly over toward them. Saw it come to a halt, caught in the glare of the airport floodlights, engines screaming. The door opened and the steps dropped down. Harland Webster appeared in the opening and looked around. He caught sight of them and gestured them over. A sharp, urgent gesture. Repeated twice.

They climbed inside the small plane. The steps folded in and the

518

door sucked shut behind them. Webster led them forward to a group of seats. Two facing two across a small table. They sat, McGrath and Brogan facing Webster, Milosevic next to him. They buckled their belts and the Lear began to taxi again. The plane lurched through its turn onto the runway and waited. It quivered and vibrated and then rolled forward, accelerating down the long concrete strip before suddenly jumping into the air. It tilted northwest and throttled back to a loud cruise.

'OK, try this,' Webster said. 'The joint chairman's daughter's been snatched by some terrorist group, some foreign involvement. They're going to make demands on him. Demands with some kind of a military dimension.'

McGrath shook his head.

'That's crap,' he said. 'How could that possibly work? They'd just replace him. Old soldiers willing to sit on their fat asses in the Pentagon aren't exactly thin on the ground.'

Brogan nodded cautiously.

'I agree, chief,' he said. 'That's a non-viable proposition.'

Webster nodded back.

'Exactly,' he said. 'So what does that leave us with?'

Nobody answered that. Nobody wanted to say the words.

The Lear chased the glow of the setting sun west and landed at Fargo in North Dakota. An agent from the Minneapolis Field Office was up there to meet them with a car. He wasn't impressed by Brogan or Milosevic, and he was too proud to show he was impressed by the Chicago agent-in-charge. But he was fairly tense about meeting with Harland Webster. Tense, and determined to show him he meant business.

'We found their hideout, sir,' the guy said. 'They used it last night and moved on. It's pretty clear. About a mile from where the body was found.'

He drove them northwest, two hours of tense, darkening silence as the car crawled like an insect through endless gigantic spreads of barley and wheat and beans and oats. Then he swung a right and his headlights opened up a vista of endless grasslands and dark gray sky. The sun was gone in the west. The local guy threaded through the turns and pulled up next to a ranch fence. The fence disappeared onward into the dark, but the headlights caught police tape strung between a couple of trees and a police cruiser, and a coroner's wagon waiting twenty yards away.

'This is where the body was found,' the local guy said.

He had a flashlight. There wasn't much to see. Just a ditch between the blacktop and the fence, overgrown with grass, trampled down over a ten-yard stretch. The body was gone, but the medical examiner had waited with the details.

'Pretty weird,' the doctor said. 'The guy was suffocated. That's for sure. He was smothered, pushed face down into something soft. There are petechiae all over the face, and in the eyes. Small pinpoint hemorrhages, which you get with asphyxia.'

McGrath shrugged.

'What's weird about that?' he said. 'I'd have suffocated the scumbag myself, given half a chance.'

'Before and after,' the doctor said. 'Extreme violence before. Looks to me like the guy was smashed against a wall, maybe the side of a truck. The back of his skull was cracked, and he broke three bones in his back. Then he was kicked in the gut. His insides are a mess. Just slopping around in there. Extreme violence, awesome force. Whoever did that, I wouldn't want him to get mad at me, that's for damn sure.'

'What about after?' McGrath said.

'The body was moved,' the doctor said. 'Hypostasis pattern is all screwed up. Like somebody beat on the guy, suffocated him, left him for an hour, then thought better of it and moved the body out here and dumped it.'

Webster and McGrath and Brogan all nodded. Milosevic stared down into the ditch. They regrouped on the shoulder and stood looking at the vast dark landscape for a long moment and then turned together back to the car.

'Thank you, doc,' Webster said vaguely. 'Good work.'

The doctor nodded. The car doors slammed. The local agent started up and continued on down the road, west, toward where the sun had set.

'The big guy is calling the shots,' Webster said. 'It's clear, right? He hired the three guys to do a job of work for him. Peter Wayne Bell stepped out of line. He started to mess with Holly. A helpless, disabled woman, young and pretty, too much of a temptation for an animal like that, right?'

'Right,' Brogan said. 'But the big guy is a professional. A mercenary or a terrorist or something. Messing with the prisoner was not in his game plan. So he got mad and offed Bell. Enforcing some kind of discipline on the troops.'

Webster nodded.

'Had to be that way,' he said. 'Only the big guy could do that. Partly because he's the boss, therefore he's got the authority, and partly because he's physically powerful enough to do that kind of serious damage.'

'He was protecting her?' McGrath said.

'Protecting his investment,' Webster said back, sourly.

'So maybe she's still OK,' McGrath said.

Nobody replied to that. The car turned a tight left after a mile and bounced down a track. The headlight beams jumped over a small cluster of wooden buildings.

'This was their stopping place,' the local guy said. 'It's an old horse farm.'

'Inhabited?' McGrath asked.

'It was until yesterday,' the guy said. 'No sign of anybody today.'

He pulled up in front of the barn. The five men got out into the dark. The barn door stood open. The local guy waited with the car and Webster and McGrath and Brogan and Milosevic stepped inside. Searched with their flashlights. It was dark and damp. Cobbled floor, green with moss. Horse stalls down both sides. They walked in. Down the aisle to the end. The stall on the right had been peppered with a shotgun blast. The back wall had just about disintegrated. Planks had fallen out. Wood splinters lay all around, crumbling with decay.

The end stall on the left had a mattress in it. Laid at an angle on the mossy cobbles. There was a chain looped through an iron ring on the back wall. The ring had been put there a hundred years ago to hold a horse by a rope. But last night it had held a woman, by a chain attached to her wrist. Webster ducked down and came up with the bright chrome handcuff, locked into the ends of the loop of chain. Brogan knelt and picked long dark hairs off the mattress. Then he rejoined Milosevic and searched through the other stalls in turn. McGrath stared at them. Then he walked out of the barn. He turned to face west and stared at the point where the sun had fallen over the horizon. He stood and stared into the infinite dark in that direction like if he stared long enough and hard enough he could focus his eyes five hundred miles away and see Holly.

TWENTY-THREE

NOBODY COULD SEE HOLLY BECAUSE SHE WAS ON HER OWN, LOCKED in the prison room that had been built for her. She had been taken from the forest clearing by four silent women dressed in dull green fatigues, night camouflage smearing their faces, automatic weapons slung at their shoulders, ammunition pouches chinking and rattling on their belts. They had pulled her away from Reacher and dragged her in the dark across the clearing, into the trees, through a gauntlet of hissing, spitting, jeering people. Then a painful mile down a stony path, out of the forest again and over to the large white building. They had not spoken to her. Just marched her in and pushed her up the stairs to the second floor. They had pulled open the stout new door and pushed her up the step into the room. The step was more than a foot high, because the floor inside the room was built up higher than the floor in the hallway outside. She crawled up and in and heard the door slamming and the key turning loudly behind her.

There were no windows. A bulb in the ceiling behind a wire grille lit the room with a vivid, hot yellow light. All four walls, the floor and the ceiling were made from new pine boards, unfinished, smelling strongly of fresh lumber. At the far end of the room was a bed. It had a simple iron frame and a thin crushed mattress. Like

523

an army bed, or a prison cot. On the bed were two sets of clothing. Two pairs of fatigue pants and two shirts. Dull green, like the four silent women had been wearing. She limped over to the bed and touched them. Old and worn, but clean. Pressed. The creases in the pants were like razors.

She turned back and inspected the room closely. It was not small. Maybe sixteen feet square. But she sensed it was smaller than it should have been. The proportions were odd. She had noticed the raised floor. It was more than a foot higher than it should have been. She guessed the walls and the ceiling were the same. She limped to the wall and tapped the new boarding. There was a dull sound. A cavity behind. Somebody had built this simple timber shell right inside a bigger room. And they had built it well. The new boards were tight and straight. But there was damp in the tiny cracks between them. She stared at the damp and sniffed the air. She shivered. The room smelled of fear.

One corner was walled off. There was a door set in a simple diagonal partition. She limped over to it and pulled it open. A bathroom. A john, a sink. A trashcan, with a new plastic liner. And a shower over a tub. Cheap white ceramic, but brand new. Carefully installed. Neat tiling. Soap and shampoo on a shelf. She leaned on the doorjamb and stared at the shower. She stared at it for a long time. Then she shrugged off her filthy Armani suit. She balled it up and threw it in the trashcan. She started the shower running and stepped under the torrent of water. She washed her hair three times. She scrubbed her aching body all over. She stood in the shower for the best part of an hour.

Then she limped back to the bed and selected a set of the old fatigues. They fitted her just about perfectly. She lay down on the bed and stared at the pine ceiling and listened to the silence. For the first time in more than sixty hours she was alone.

Reacher was not alone. He was still in the forest clearing. He was twenty feet from the white Econoline, chained to a tree, guarded by six silent men with machine guns. Dogs were padding free through the clearing. Reacher was leaning back on the rough bark, waiting, watching his guards. He was cold. He could feel pine resin sticking to his thin shirt. The guards were cautious. They were standing in a line, six feet away from him, weapons pointed at him, eyes gleaming white out of darkened faces. They were dressed in olive fatigues. There were some kind of semicircular flashes on their shoulders. It was too dark for Reacher to read them.

The six men were all maybe forty years old. They were lean and bearded. Comfortable with their weapons. Alert. Silent. Accustomed to night duty. Reacher could see that. They looked like the survivors of a small infantry platoon. Like they had stepped into the forest on night patrol twenty years ago as young recruits and had never come back out again.

They snapped to attention at the sound of footsteps approaching behind them. The sounds were grotesquely loud in the still night. Boots smashed into shale and gun stocks slapped into palms. Reacher glanced into the clearing and saw a seventh man approaching. Younger, maybe thirty-five. A tall man, clean-shaven, no camouflage on his face, crisp fatigues, shiny boots. Same semicircular flashes at the shoulder. Some kind of an officer.

The six forty-year-old grunts stood back and saluted and the new guy crunched up face to face with Reacher. He took a cigarette pack from his pocket and a cigarette from the pack. Lit it and kept the lighter burning to illuminate Reacher's face. Stared over the wavering flame with an expressionless gaze. Reacher stared back at him. The guy had a small head on wide shoulders, a thin hard face starved into premature lines and crevices. In the harsh shadow of the flame, it looked like he had no lips. Just a slit where his mouth should be. Cold eyes, burning under the thin skin stretched over his brow. A military buzz-cut, maybe a week old, just growing out. He stared at Reacher and let the flame die. Ran a hand across his scalp. Reacher heard the loud rasp of the stubble passing under his palm in the still night air.

'I'm Dell Fowler,' the guy said. 'I'm chief-of-staff here.'

A quiet voice. West Coast. Reacher looked back at him and nodded, slowly.

'You want to tell me what staff you're chief of?' he said.

'Loder didn't explain?' the guy called Fowler asked.

'Loder didn't explain anything,' Reacher said. 'He had his hands full just getting us here.'

Fowler nodded and smiled a chilly smile.

'Loder's an idiot,' he said. 'He made five major mistakes. You're one of them. He's in all kinds of deep shit now. And so are you.'

525

He gestured to one of the guards. The guard stepped forward and handed him a key from his pocket. The guard stood with his weapon ready and Fowler unlocked Reacher's chain. It clattered down the tree trunk to the ground. Metal on wood, a loud sound in the forest night. A dog padded near and sniffed. People moved in the trees. Reacher pushed away from the trunk and squeezed some circulation back into his forearm. All six guards took a pace forward. Weapons slapped back to the ready position. Reacher watched the muzzles and Fowler caught his arm and turned him. Cuffed his hands together again, behind his back. Nodded. Two guards melted away into the trees. A third jabbed the muzzle of his gun into Reacher's back. A fourth took up position to the rear. Two walked point out in front. Fowler fell in beside Reacher and caught his elbow. Walked him across toward a small wooden hut on the opposite edge of the clearing. Clear of the trees, the moonlight was brighter. Reacher could make out the writing on Fowler's shoulder flash. It read: Montana Militia.

'This is Montana?' he said. 'Loder called it a brand-new country.'

Fowler shrugged as he walked.

'He was premature,' he said. 'Right now, this is still Montana.'

They reached the hut. The point men opened the door. Yellow light spilled out into the darkness. The guard with the weapon in Reacher's back used it to push him inside. Loder was standing against the far wall. His hands were cuffed behind him. He was guarded by another lean, bearded man with a machine gun. This guy was a little younger than the other grunts, neater beard. A livid scar running laterally across his forehead.

Fowler walked around and sat behind a plain desk. Pointed to a chair. Reacher sat down, handcuffed, six soldiers behind him. Fowler watched him sit and then transferred his attention across to Loder. Reacher followed his gaze. First time he'd seen Loder on Monday, he'd seen a degree of calm competence, hard eyes, composure. That was all gone. The guy was shaking with fear. His cuffs were rattling behind him. Reacher watched him and thought: this guy is terrified of his leaders.

'So, five mistakes,' Fowler said.

His voice was still quiet. And it was confident. Relaxed. The quiet confident voice of a person very secure about his power.

Reacher heard the voice die into silence and listened to the creak of boots on wood behind him.

'I did my best,' Loder said. 'She's here, right?'

His voice was supplicant and miserable. The voice of a man who knows he's in deep shit without really understanding exactly why.

'She's here, right?' he said again.

'By a miracle,' Fowler replied. 'You caused a lot of stress elsewhere. People had their work cut out covering for your incompetence.'

'What did I do wrong?' Loder asked.

He pushed forward off the wall, hands cuffed behind him, and moved into Reacher's view. Glanced desperately at him, like he was asking for a testimonial.

'Five mistakes,' Fowler said again. 'One, you burned the pickup, and two, you burned the car. Way too visible. Why didn't you just put an ad in the damn paper?'

Loder made no reply. His mouth was working, but no sound was coming out.

'Three, you snarled this guy up,' Fowler said.

Loder glanced at Reacher again and shook his head vigorously.

'This guy's a nobody,' he said. 'No heat coming after him.'

'You should still have waited,' Fowler said. 'And four, you lost Peter. What exactly happened to him?'

Loder shrugged again.

'I don't know,' he said.

'He got scared,' Fowler said. 'You were making so many mistakes, he got scared and he ran. That's what happened. You got any other explanation?'

Loder was just staring blankly.

'And five, you killed the damn dentist,' Fowler said. 'They're not going to overlook that, are they? This was supposed to be a military operation, right? Political? You added an extra factor there.'

'What dentist?' Reacher asked.

Fowler glanced at him and smiled a lipless smile, indulgent, like Reacher was an audience he could use to humiliate Loder a little more.

'They stole the car from a dentist,' he said. 'The guy caught them at it. They should have waited until he was clear.'

527

'He got in the way,' Loder said. 'We couldn't bring him with us, could we?'

'You brought me,' Reacher said to him.

Loder stared at him like he was a moron.

'The guy was a Jew,' he said. 'This place isn't for Jews.'

Reacher glanced around the room. Looked at the shoulder flashes. Montana Militia, Montana Militia, Montana Militia. He nodded slowly. A brand-new country.

'Where have you taken Holly?' he asked Fowler.

Fowler ignored him. He was still dealing with Loder.

'You'll stand trial tomorrow,' he told him. 'Special tribunal. The commander presiding. The charge is endangering the mission. I'm prosecuting.'

'Where's Holly?' Reacher asked him again.

Fowler shrugged. A cool gaze.

'Close by,' he said. 'Don't you worry about her.'

Then he glanced up over Reacher's head and spoke to the guards.

'Put Loder on the floor,' he said.

Loder offered no resistance at all. Just let the younger guy with the scar hold him upright. The nearest guard reversed his rifle and smashed the butt into Loder's stomach. Reacher heard the air punch out of him. The younger guy dropped him and stepped neatly over him. Walked out of the hut, alone, duty done. The door slammed noisily behind him. Then Fowler turned back to Reacher.

'Now let's talk about you,' he said.

His voice was still quiet. Quiet, and confident. Secure. But it was not difficult to be secure holed up in the middle of nowhere with six armed subordinates surrounding a handcuffed man on a chair. A handcuffed man who has just witnessed a naked display of power and brutality. Reacher shrugged at him.

'What about me?' he said. 'You know my name. I told Loder. No doubt he told you. He probably got that right. There isn't much more to say on the subject.'

There was silence. Fowler thought about it. Nodded.

'This is a decision for the commander,' he said.

It was the shower which convinced her. She based her conclusions on it. Some good news, some bad. A brand-new bathroom, cheaply but carefully fitted out in the way a pathetic houseproud woman down on her luck in a trailer park would choose. That bathroom communicated a lot to Holly.

It meant she was a hostage, to be held long term, but to be held with a certain measure of respect. Because of her value in some kind of a trade. There were to be no doubts about her day-to-day comfort or safety. Those factors were to be removed from the negotiation. Those factors were to be taken for granted. She was to be a high-status prisoner. Because of her value. Because of who she was.

But not because of who she was. Because of who her father was. Because of the connections she had. She was supposed to sit in this crushing, fear-filled room and be somebody's daughter. Sit and wait while people weighed her value, one way and the other. While people reacted to her plight, feeling a little reassured by the fact that she had a shower all to herself.

She eased herself off the bed. To hell with that, she thought. She was not going to sit there and be negotiated over. The anger rose up inside her. It rose up and she turned it into a steely determination. She limped to the door and tried the handle for the twentieth time. Then she heard footsteps on the stairs. They clattered down the corridor. Stopped at her door. A key turned the lock. The handle moved against her grip. She stepped back and the door opened.

Reacher was pushed up into the room. A blur of camouflaged figures behind him. They shoved him up through the door and slammed it shut. She heard it locking and the footsteps tramping away. Reacher was left standing there, gazing around.

'Looks like we have to share,' he said.

She looked at him.

'They were only expecting one guest,' he added.

She made no reply to that. She just watched his eyes examining the room. They flicked around the walls, the floor, the ceiling. He twisted and glanced into the bathroom. Nodded to himself. Turned back to face her, waiting for her comment. She was pausing, thinking hard about what to say and how to say it.

'It's only a single bed,' she said at last.

She tried to make the words count for more. She tried to make them like a long speech. Like a closely reasoned argument. She tried to make them say: OK, in the truck, we were close. OK, we kissed. Twice. The first time, it just happened. The second time, I asked you to, because I was looking for comfort and reassurance. But now we've been apart for an hour or two. Long enough for me to get to feeling a little silly about what we did. She tried to make those five words say all that, while she watched his eyes for his reaction.

'There's somebody else, right?' he said.

She saw that he said it as a joke, as a throwaway line to show her he agreed with her, that he understood, as a way to let them both off the hook without getting all heavy about it. But she didn't smile at him. Instead, she found herself nodding.

'Yes, there is somebody,' she said. 'What can I say? If there wasn't, maybe I would want to share.'

She thought: he looks disappointed.

'In fact, I probably would want to,' she added. 'But there is somebody and I'm sorry. It wouldn't be a good idea.'

It showed in his face and she felt she had to say more.

'I'm sorry,' she said again. 'It's not that I wouldn't want to.'

She watched him. He just shrugged at her. She saw he was thinking: it's not the end of the world. And then he was thinking: it just feels like it. She blushed. She was absurdly gratified. But ready to change the subject.

'What's going on here?' she asked. 'They tell you anything?'

'Who's the lucky guy?' Reacher asked.

'Just somebody,' she said. 'What's going on here?'

His eyes were clouded. He looked straight at her.

'Lucky somebody,' he said.

'He doesn't even know,' she said.

'That you're gone?' he asked.

She shook her head.

'That I feel this way,' she said.

He stared at her. Didn't reply. There was a long silence in the room. Then she heard footsteps again. Hurrying, outside the building. Clattering inside. Coming up the stairs. They stopped outside the door. The key slid in. The door opened. Six guards clattered inside. Six machine guns. She took a painful step backward. They ignored her completely.

'The commander is ready for you, Reacher,' the point man said.

He signaled him to turn around. He clicked handcuffs on, behind his back. Tightened them hard. Pushed him to the door with the barrel of his gun and out into the corridor. The door slammed and locked behind the gaggle of men.

Fowler pulled the headphones off and stopped the tape recorder.

'Anything?' the commander asked him.

'No,' Fowler said. 'She said it's only a single bed, and he sounded pissed, like he wants to get in her pants. So she said she's got another boyfriend.'

'I didn't know that,' the commander said. 'Did she say who?'

Fowler shook his head.

'But it works OK?' the commander asked him.

'Clear as a bell,' Fowler said.

Reacher was pushed down the stairs and back out into the night. Back the way he had come, a mile up a stony path. The point man gripped his elbow and hustled him along. They were hurrying. Almost running. They were using their gun muzzles like cattle prods. They covered the distance in fifteen minutes. They crunched across the clearing to the small wooden hut. Reacher was pushed roughly inside.

Loder was still on the floor. But there was somebody new sitting at the plain wooden desk. The commander. Reacher was clear on that. He was an extraordinary figure. Maybe six feet tall, probably four hundred pounds. Maybe thirty-five years old, thick hair, so blond it was nearly white, cut short at the sides and brushed long across the top like a German schoolboy's. A smooth pink face, bloated tight by his bulk, bright red nickel-sized spots burning high up on the cheeks. Tiny colorless eyes forced into slits between the cheeks and the white eyebrows. Wet red lips pursed above a chin strong enough to hold its shape in the blubber.

He was wearing an enormous black uniform. An immaculate black shirt, military cut, no insignia except a pair of the same shoulder flashes everybody else was wearing. A wide leather belt, gleaming like a mirror. Crisp black riding pants, flared wide at the top, tucked into high black boots which matched the belt for shine.

'Come in and sit down,' he said, quietly.

Reacher was pushed over to the chair he had occupied before.

He sat, with his hands crushed behind him. The guards stood to rigid attention all around him, not daring to breathe, just staring blankly into space.

'I'm Beau Borken,' the big man said. 'I'm the commander here.'

His voice was high. Reacher stared at the guy and felt some kind of an aura radiating out of him like a glow. The glow of total authority.

'I have to take a decision,' Borken said. 'I need you to help me with it.'

Reacher realized he was looking away from the guy. Like the glow was overpowering him. He forced himself to turn his head slowly and stare directly into the big white face.

'What decision?' he asked.

'Whether you should live,' Borken said. 'Or whether you should die.'

Holly pulled the side panel off the bath. She had known plumbers leave trash under the tub, out of sight behind the panel. Offcuts of pipe, scraps of wood, even tools. Used blades, lost wrenches. Stuff that could prove useful. Some apartments she'd had, she'd found all kinds of things. But there was nothing. She lay down and felt right into the back recesses and came up with nothing at all.

And the floor was solid all the way under the fixtures. The plumbing ran down through tight holes. It was an expert job. It was possible she could force a lever down alongside the big pipe running down out of the john. If she had a pry-bar she might get a board loose. But there was no pry-bar in the room. Nor any substitute. The towel bar was plastic. It would bend and break. There was nothing else. She sat on the floor and felt the disappointment wash over her. Then she heard more footsteps outside her door.

This time they were quiet. They were muffled, not clattering. Somebody approaching quietly and cautiously. Somebody with no official business. She stood up slowly. Stepped out of the bathroom and pulled the door to hide the dismantled tub. Limped back toward the bed as the lock clicked and the door opened.

A man came into the room. He was a youngish man, dressed in camouflage fatigues, black smears on his face. A vivid red scar running laterally across his forehead. A machine gun slung at his shoulder. He turned and closed the door, quietly. Turned back with his fingers to his lips.

She stared at him. Felt her anger rising. This time, she wasn't chained up. This time, the guy was going to die. She smiled a crazy smile at the logic of it. The bathroom was going to save her. She was a high-status prisoner. Supposed to be held with dignity and respect. Somebody came in to abuse her, and she killed him, they couldn't argue with that, could they?

But the guy with the scar just held his fingers to his lips and nodded toward the bathroom. He crept quietly over and pushed the door. Gestured for her to follow. She limped after him. He glanced down at the side panel on the floor and shook his head. Reached in and started the shower. Set it running hard against the empty tub.

'They've got microphones,' the guy said. 'They're listening for me.'

'Who the hell are you?' she asked.

He squatted down and put the panel back on the bath.

'No good,' he said. 'There's no way out.'

'Got to be,' she said.

The guy shook his head.

'They had a trial run,' he said. 'The commander put one of the guys who built this place in here. Told him if he didn't get out, he'd cut his arms off. So I assume he tried real hard.'

'And what happened?' she asked.

The guy shrugged.

'The commander cut his arms off,' he said.

'Who the hell are you?' she asked again.

'FBI,' the guy said. 'Counter-terrorism. Undercover. I guess I'm going to have to get you out.'

'How?' she asked.

'Tomorrow,' he said. 'I can get a jeep. We'll have to make a run for it. I can't call in for assistance because they're scanning for my transmitter. We'll just get the jeep and head south and hope for the best.'

'What about Reacher?' she asked. 'Where have they taken him?'

'Forget him,' the guy said. 'He'll be dead by morning.'

Holly shook her head.

'I'm not going without him,' she said.

'Loder displeased me,' Beau Borken said.

Reacher shrugged and glanced downward. Loder had squirmed up into a sideways sitting position, crammed into the angle between the floor and the wall.

'Did he displease you?' Borken asked.

Reacher made no reply.

'Would you like to kick him?' Borken asked.

Reacher kept quiet. He could see where this game was going. If he said yes, he'd be expected to hurt the guy badly. Which he had no objection to in principle, but he'd prefer to do it on his own terms. If he said no, Borken would call him a coward with no sense of natural justice and no self-respect. An obvious game, with no way to win. So he kept quiet, which was a tactic he'd used a thousand times before: when in doubt, just keep your mouth shut.

'In the face?' Borken asked. 'In the balls, maybe?'

Loder was staring up at Reacher. Something in his face. Reacher saw what it was. His eyes widened in surprise. Loder was pleading with him to give him a kicking, so that Borken wouldn't.

'Loder, lie down again,' Borken said.

Loder squirmed his hips away from the wall and dropped his shoulders to the floor. Wriggled and pushed until he was lying flat on his back. Borken nodded to the nearest guard.

'In the face,' he said.

The guard stepped over and used the sole of his boot to force Loder's head sideways, so his face was presented to the room. Then he stepped back and kicked out. A heavy blow from a heavy boot. Loder's head snapped backward and thumped into the wall. Blood welled from his nose. Borken watched him bleed for a long moment, mildly interested. Then he turned back to Reacher.

'Loder's one of my oldest friends,' he said.

Reacher said nothing.

'Begs two questions, doesn't it?' Borken said. 'Question one: why am I enforcing such strict discipline, even against my old friends? And question two: if that's how I treat my friends, how the hell do I treat my enemies?'

Reacher said nothing. When in doubt, just keep your mouth shut.

'I treat my enemies a hell of a lot worse than that,' Borken said. 'So much worse, you really don't want to think about it. You really don't, believe me. And why am I being so strict? Because we're two days away from a unique moment in history. Things are going to happen which will change the world. Plans are made and operations are underway. Therefore I have to bring my natural caution to a new pitch. My old friend Loder has fallen victim to a historical force. So, I'm afraid, have you.'

Reacher said nothing. He dropped his gaze and watched Loder. He was unconscious. Breathing raggedly through clotting blood in his nose.

'You got any value to me as a hostage?' Borken asked.

Reacher thought about it. Made no reply. Borken watched his face and smiled. His red lips parted over small white teeth.

'I thought not,' he said. 'So what should I do with a person who's got no value to me as a hostage? During a moment of great historical tension?'

Reacher stayed silent. Just watching. Easing his weight forward, ready.

'You think you're going to get a kicking?' Borken asked.

Reacher tensed his legs, ready to spring.

'Relax,' Borken said. 'No kicking for you. When the time comes, it'll be a bullet through the head. From behind. I'm not stupid, you know. I've got eyes, and a brain. What are you, six five? About two twenty? Clearly fit and strong. And look at you, tension in your thighs, getting ready to jump up. Clearly trained in some way. But you're not a boxer. Because your nose has never been broken. A heavyweight like you with an unbroken nose would need to be a phenomenal talent, and we'd have seen your picture in the newspapers. So you're just a brawler, probably been in the service, right? So I'll be cautious with you. No kicking, just a bullet.'

The guards took their cue. Six rifles came down out of the slope and six fingers hooked around six triggers.

'You got felony convictions?' Borken asked.

Reacher shrugged and spoke for the first time.

'No,' he said.

'Upstanding citizen?' Borken asked.

Reacher shrugged again.

'I guess,' he said.

535

Borken nodded.

'So I'll think about it,' he said. 'Live or die, I'll let you know, first thing in the morning, OK?'

He lifted his bulky arm and snapped his fingers. Five of the six guards moved. Two went to the door and opened it. A third went out between them. The other two waited. Borken stood up with surprising grace for a man of his size and walked out from behind the desk. The wooden floor creaked under his bulk. The four waiting guards fell in behind him and he walked straight out into the night without a backward glance.

He walked across the clearing and into another hut. Fowler was waiting for him, the headphones in his hand.

'I think somebody went in there,' he said.

'You think?' Borken said.

'The shower was running,' Fowler said. 'Somebody went in there who knows about the microphones. She wouldn't need another shower. She just had one, right? Somebody went in there and ran the shower to mask the talking.'

'Who?' Borken asked.

Fowler shook his head.

'I don't know who,' he said. 'But I can try to find out.'

Borken nodded.

'Yes, you can do that,' he said. 'You can try to find out.'

In the accommodation huts, men and women were working in the gloom, cleaning their rifles. The word about Loder had traveled quickly. They all knew about the tribunal. They all knew the likely outcome. Any six of them could be selected for the firing squad. If there was going to be a firing squad. Most people figured there probably was. An officer like Loder, the commander might limit it to a firing squad. Probably nothing worse. So they cleaned their rifles, and left them locked and loaded next to their beds.

Those of them with enough demerits to be on tomorrow's punishment detail were trying to get some sleep. If he didn't limit it to a firing squad, they could be in for a lot of work. Messy, unpleasant work. And even if Loder got away with it, there was always the other guy. The big guy who had come in with the federal bitch. There wasn't much chance of him surviving past breakfast time. They couldn't remember the last time any stray stranger had lasted longer than that.

Holly Johnson had a rule. It was a rule bred into her, like a family motto. It had been reinforced by her long training at Quantico. It was a rule distilled from thousands of years of military history and hundreds of years of law-enforcement experience. The rule said: hope for the best, but plan for the worst.

She had no reason to believe she would not be speeding south in a jeep just as soon as her new ally could arrange it. He was Bureau-trained, the same as she was. She knew that if the tables were turned, she would get him out, no problem at all. So she knew she could just sit tight and wait. But she wasn't doing that. She was hoping for the best, but she was planning for the worst.

She had given up on the bathroom. No way out there. Now she was going over the room itself, inch by inch. The new pine boarding was nailed tight to the frame, all six surfaces. It was driving her crazy. Inch-thick pine board, the oldest possible technology, used for ten thousand years, and there was no way through it. For a lone woman without any tools, it might as well have been the side of a battleship.

So she concentrated on finding tools. It was like she was personally speeding through Darwin's evolutionary process. Apes came down from the trees and they made tools. She was concentrating on the bed. The mattress was useless. It was a thin, crushed thing, no wire springs inside. But the bed frame was more promising. It was bolted together from iron tubes and flanges. If she could take it apart, she could put one of the little right-angle flanges in the end of the longest tube and make a pry-bar seven feet long. But the bolts were all painted over. She had strong hands, but she couldn't begin to move them. Her fingers just bruised and slipped on her sweat.

Loder had been dragged away and Reacher was locked up alone with the last remaining guard from the evening detail. The guard sat behind the plain desk and propped his weapon on the wooden surface with the muzzle pointing directly at him sitting on his chair. His hands were still cuffed behind him. He had decisions to make. First was no way could he sit all night like that. He glanced calmly at the guard and eased himself up and slid his hands underneath.

Pressed his chest down onto his thighs and looped his hands out under his feet. Then he sat up and leaned back and forced a smile, hands together in his lap.

'Long arms,' he said. 'Useful.'

The guard nodded slowly. He had small piercing eyes, set back in a narrow face. They gleamed out above the big beard, through the camouflage smudges, but the gleam looked innocent enough.

'What's your name?' Reacher asked him.

The guy hesitated. Shuffled in his seat. Reacher could see some kind of natural courtesy was prompting a reply. But there were obvious tactical considerations for the guy. Reacher kept on forcing the smile.

'I'm Reacher,' he said. 'You know my name. You got a name? We're here all night, we may as well be a little civilized about it, right?'

The guy nodded again, slowly. Then he shrugged.

'Ray,' he said.

'Ray?' Reacher said. 'That your first name or your last?'

'Last,' the guy said. 'Joseph Ray.'

Reacher nodded.

'OK, Mr Ray,' he said. 'Pleased to meet you.'

'Call me Joe,' Joseph Ray said.

Reacher forced the smile again. The ice was broken. Like conducting an interrogation. Reacher had done it a thousand times. But never from this side of the desk. Never when he was the one wearing the cuffs.

'Joe, you're going to have to help me out a little,' he said. 'I need some background here. I don't know where I am, or why, or who all you guys are. Can you fill me in on some basic information?'

Ray was looking at him like he was maybe having difficulty knowing where to start. Then he was glancing around the room like maybe he was wondering whether he was allowed to start at all.

'Where exactly are we?' Reacher asked him. 'You can tell me that, right?'

'Montana,' Ray said.

Reacher nodded.

'OK,' he said. 'Where in Montana?'

'Near a town called Yorke,' Ray said. 'An old mining town, just about abandoned.'

Reacher nodded again.

'OK,' he said. 'What are you guys doing here?'

'We're building a bastion,' Ray said. 'A place of our own.'

'What for?' Reacher asked him.

Ray shrugged. An inarticulate guy. At first, he said nothing. Then he sat forward and launched into what seemed to Reacher like a mantra, like something the guy had rehearsed many times. Or like something the guy had been told many times.

'We came up here to escape the tyranny of America,' he said. 'We have to draw up our borders and say, it's going to be different inside here.'

'Different how?' Reacher asked him.

'We have to take America back, piece by piece,' Ray said. 'We have to build a place where the white man can live free, unmolested, in peace, with proper freedoms and proper laws.'

'You think you can do that?' Reacher said.

'It happened before,' Ray said. 'It happened in 1776. People said enough is enough. They said we want a better country than this. Now we're saying it again. We're saying we want our country back. And we're going to get it back. Because now we're acting together. There were a dozen militias up here. They all wanted the same things. But they were all acting alone. Beau's mission was to put people together. Now we're unified and we're going to take our country back. We're starting here. We're starting now.'

Reacher nodded. Glanced to his right and down at the dark stain where Loder's nose had bled onto the floor.

'Like this?' he said. 'What about voting and democracy? All that kind of stuff? You should vote people out and vote new people in, right?'

Ray smiled sadly and shook his head.

'We've been voting for two hundred and twenty years,' he said. 'Gets worse all the time. Government's not interested in how we vote. They've taken all the power away from us. Given our country away. You know where the government of this country really is?'

Reacher shrugged.

'DC, right?' he said.

'Wrong,' Ray said. 'It's in New York. The United Nations building. Ever asked yourself why the UN is so near Wall Street? Because that's the government. The United Nations and the banks. They run the world. America's just a small part of it. The president is just one voice on a damn committee. That's why voting is no damn good. You think the United Nations and the world banks care what we vote?'

'You sure about all this?' Reacher asked.

Ray nodded, vigorously.

'Sure I'm sure,' he said. 'I've seen it at work. Why do you think we send billions of dollars to the Russians when we got poverty here in America? You think that's the free choice of an American government? We send it because the world government tells us to send it. You know we got camps here? Hundreds of camps all over the country? Most of them are for United Nations troops. Foreign troops, waiting to move in when we start any trouble. But forty-three of them are concentration camps. That's where they're going to put us when we start speaking out.'

'You sure?' Reacher said again.

'Sure I'm sure,' Ray said again. 'Beau's got the documents. We've got the proof. There are things going on you wouldn't believe. You know it's a secret federal law that all babies born in the hospital get a microchip implanted just under their skin? When they take them away, they're not weighing them and cleaning them up. They're implanting a microchip. Pretty soon the whole population is going to be visible to secret satellites. You think the space shuttle gets used for science experiments? You think the world government would authorize expenditure for stuff like that? You got to be kidding. The space shuttle is there to launch surveillance satellites.'

'You're joking, right?' Reacher said.

Ray shook his head.

'No way,' he said. 'Beau's got the documents. There's another secret law, guy in Detroit sent Beau the stuff. Every car built in America since 1985 has a secret radio transmitter box in it, so the satellites can see where it's going. You buy a car, the radar screens in the UN Building know where you are, every minute of the day and night. They've got foreign forces training in America, right now, ready for the official takeover. You know why we send so much money to Israel? Not because we care what happens to the Israelis. Why should we care? We send the money because that's where the UN is training the secret world army. It's like an experimental place. Why do you think the UN never stops the Israelis from invading people? Because the UN has told them what to do in the first place. Training them for the world takeover. There are three thousand helicopters right now, at airbases round the US, all ready for them to use. Helicopters, painted flat black, no markings.'

'You sure?' Reacher said again. He was keeping his voice somewhere between worried and skeptical. 'I never heard about any of this stuff.'

'That proves it, right?' Ray said.

'Why?' Reacher asked.

'Obvious, right?' Ray said. 'You think the world government is going to allow media access to that stuff? World government controls the media, right? They own it. So it's logical that whatever doesn't appear in the media is what is really happening, right? They tell you the safe stuff, and they keep the secrets away from you. It's all true, believe me. I told you, Beau's got the documents. Did you know every US highway sign has a secret mark on the back? You drive out and take a look. A secret sign, to direct the world troops around the country. They're getting ready to take over. That's why we need a place of our own.'

'You think they're going to attack you?' Reacher asked.

'No doubt about it,' Ray said. 'They're going to come right after us.'

'And you figure you can defend yourselves?' Reacher said. 'A few guys in some little town in Montana?'

Joe Ray shook his head.

'Not a few guys,' he said. 'There are a hundred of us.'

'A hundred guys?' Reacher said. 'Against the world government?'

Ray shook his head again.

'We can defend ourselves,' he said. 'Beau's a smart leader. This territory is good. We're in a valley here. Sixty miles north to south, sixty miles east to west. Canadian border along the northern edge.'

He swept his hand through the air, above eye level, left to right like a karate chop, to demonstrate the geography. Reacher nodded. He was familiar with the Canadian border. Ray used his other hand, up and down the left edge of his invisible map.

541

'Rapid River,' he said. 'That's our western border. It's a big river, completely wild. No way to cross it.'

He moved the Canadian border hand across and rubbed a small circle in the air, like he was cleaning a pane of glass.

'National forest,' he said. 'You seen it? Fifty miles, east to west. Thick virgin forest, no way through. You want an eastern border, that forest is as good as you're going to get.'

'What about the south?' Reacher asked.

Ray chopped his hand sideways at chest level.

'Ravine,' he said. 'Natural-born tank trap. Believe me, I know tanks. No way through, except one road and one track. Wooden bridge takes the track over the ravine.'

Reacher nodded. He remembered the white truck pattering over a wooden structure.

'That bridge gets blown,' Ray said. 'No way through.'

'What about the road?' Reacher asked.

'Same thing,' Ray said. 'We blow the bridge and we're safe. Charges are set right now.'

Reacher nodded slowly. He was thinking about air attack, artillery, missiles, smart bombs, infiltration of special forces, airborne troops, parachutes. He was thinking about navy SEALs bridging the river or Marines bridging the ravine. He was thinking about NATO units rumbling straight down from Canada.

'What about Holly?' he asked. 'What do you want with her?'

Ray smiled. His beard parted and his teeth shone out as bright as his eyes.

'Beau's secret weapon,' he said. 'Think about it. The world government is going to use her old man to lead the attack. That's why they appointed him. You think the president appoints those guys? You got to be joking. Old man Johnson's a world government guy, just waiting for the secret command to move. But when he gets here, what's he going to find?'

'What?' Reacher asked.

'He comes up from the south, right?' Ray said. 'First building he sees is that old courthouse, southeast corner of town. You were just there. She's up on the second floor, right? You notice the new construction? Special room, double walls, twenty-two inches apart. The space is packed with dynamite and blasting caps from the old

542

mine stores. The first stray shell will blow old man Johnson's little girl to kingdom come.'

Reacher nodded again, slowly. Ray looked at him.

'We're not asking much,' he said. 'Sixty miles by sixty miles, what is that? Thirty-six hundred square miles of territory.'

'But why now?' Reacher asked. 'What's the big hurry?'

'What's the date?' Ray asked back.

Reacher shrugged.

'July something?' he said.

'July second,' Ray said. 'Two days to go.'

'To what?' Reacher said.

'Independence Day,' Ray said. 'July fourth.'

'So?' Reacher asked.

'We're declaring independence,' Ray said. 'Day after tomorrow. The birth of a brand-new nation. That's when they'll come for us, right? Freedom for the little guys? That's not in their plan.'

TWENTY-FOUR

THE BUREAU LEAR REFUELED AT FARGO IN AND FLEW STRAIGHT
southwest to California. McGrath had argued again in
favor of heading straight for Montana, but Webster had
overruled him. One step at a time was Webster's patient way,
so they were going to check out the Beau Borken story in
California and then they were going to Peterson Air Force Base
in Colorado to meet with General Johnson. McGrath was about
the only Bureau guy alive capable of shouting at Webster, and
he had, but arguing is not the same thing as winning, so they
were all in the air heading first for Mojave, McGrath and Webster
and Brogan and Milosevic, all overtired, overanxious and morose
in the hot noisy cabin.

'I need all the background I can get,' Webster said. 'They put
me in personal charge and these are not the type of guys I can be
vague with, right?'

McGrath glared at him and thought: don't play your stupid
Beltway games with Holly's life, Webster. But he said nothing.
Just sat tight until the tiny plane started arrowing down toward
the airfield on the edge of the desert.

They were on the ground just after two o'clock in the morning,
West Coast time. The Mojave agent-in-charge met them on the

deserted tarmac in his own car. Drove them south through the sleeping town.

'The Borkens were a Kendall family,' he said. 'Small town, fifty miles from here. Farming place, mostly citrus. One-man police department. The sheriff is waiting for us down there.'

'He know anything?' McGrath asked.

The guy at the wheel shrugged.

'Maybe,' he said. 'Small town, right?'

Fifty miles through the desert night at eighty-five took them just thirty-six minutes. Kendall was a small knot of buildings adrift in a sea of groves. There was a gas station, a general store, a grower's operation and a low cement building with whip antennas spearing upward from the roof. A smart black-and-white was parked up on the apron outside. It was marked: Kendall County Sheriff. There was a single light in the office window behind the car.

The five agents stretched and yawned in the dry night air and trooped single file into the cement building. The Kendall County sheriff was a guy about sixty, solid, gray. He looked reliable. Webster waved him back into his seat and McGrath laid the four glossy mugshots on his desk in front of him.

'You know these guys?' he asked.

The sheriff slid the photographs nearer and looked at each of them in turn. He picked them up and shuffled them into a new order. Laid them back down on the desk like he was dealing a hand of giant playing cards. Then he nodded and reached down to his desk pedestal. Rolled open a drawer. Lifted out three buff files. He placed the files underneath three of the photographs. Laid a stubby finger on the first face.

'Peter Wayne Bell,' he said. 'Mojave kid, but he was down here a lot. Not a very nice boy, as I believe you know.'

He nodded across to his monitor screen on a computer cart at the end of the desk. A page from the National Crime Center Database was glowing green. It was the report from the North Dakota cops about the identity of the body they had found in a ditch. The identity, and the history.

The sheriff moved his wrist and laid a finger on the next photograph. It was the gunman who had pushed Holly Johnson into the back of the Lexus.

'Steven Stewart,' he said. 'Called Stevie, or Little Stevie. Farm

545

boy, a couple of bushels short of a wagonload, know what I mean? Jumpy, jittery sort of a boy.'

'What's in his file?' Webster asked.

The sheriff shrugged.

'Nothing too serious,' he said. 'The boy was just too plain dumb for his own good. Group of kids would go out and mess around, and guess who'd be the one still stood there when I roll up? Little Stevie, that's who. I locked him up a dozen times, I guess, but he never did much of what you would want to call serious shit.'

McGrath nodded and pointed to the photograph of the gunman who had gotten into the front seat of the Lexus.

'This guy?' he asked.

The sheriff moved his finger and laid it on the guy's glossy throat.

'Tony Loder,' he said. 'This is a fairly bad guy. Smarter than Stevie, dumber than you or me. I'll give you the file. Maybe it won't keep you Bureau guys awake nights, but it sure won't help you sleep any better than you were going to anyhow.'

'What about the big guy?' Webster asked.

The sheriff jumped his finger along the row and shook his grizzled head.

'Never saw this guy before,' he said. 'That's for damn sure. I'd remember him if I had.'

'We think maybe he's a foreigner,' Webster said. 'Maybe European. Maybe had an accent. That ring any bells with you?'

The sheriff just kept on shaking his head.

'Never saw him before,' he said again. 'I'd remember.'

'OK,' McGrath said. 'Bell, Little Stevie Stewart, Tony Loder and the mystery man. Where do these Borken guys fit in?'

The sheriff shrugged.

'Old Dutch Borken never fit in nowhere,' he said. 'That was his problem. He was in Nam, infantry grunt, moved out here when he got out of the service. Brought a pretty wife and a little fat ten-year-old boy with him, started growing citrus, did pretty well for a long while. He was a strange guy, a loner, never saw much of him. But he was happy enough, I guess. Then the wife took sick and died, and the boy started acting weird, the market took a couple of hits, profits were down, the growers all started getting into the banks for loans, interest went up, land went down, the collateral was disappearing, irrigation water got expensive, they all started going belly-up one after the other. Borken took it bad and swallowed his shotgun.'

Webster nodded.

'The little fat ten-year-old was Beau Borken?' he asked.

The sheriff nodded.

'Beau Borken,' he said. 'Very strange boy. Very smart. But obsessed.'

'With what?' McGrath asked.

'Mexicans started coming up,' the sheriff said. 'Cheap labor. Young Beau was dead set against it. He started hollering about keeping Kendall white. Joined the John Birch types.'

'So he was a racist?' McGrath said.

'At first,' the sheriff said. 'Then he got into all that conspiracy stuff. Talking about the Jews running the government. Or the United Nations, or both, or some damn thing. The government was all communists, taking over the world, secret plans for everything. Big conspiracy against everybody, especially him. Banks controlled the government, or was it the government controlled the banks? So the banks were all communists and they were out to destroy America. He figured the exact reason the bank loaned his father the money was so it could default him later and give the farm to the Mexicans or the blacks or some damn thing. He was raving about it, all the time.'

'So what happened?' Webster said.

'Well, of course, the bank did end up defaulting him,' the sheriff said. 'The guy wasn't paying the loan, was he? But they didn't give his land to the Mexicans. They sold it on to the same big corporation owns everything else around here, which is owned by the pension funds, which probably means it's owned by you and me, not communists or Mexicans or anybody else, right?'

'But the boy blamed the conspiracy for his father's death?' Brogan asked.

'He sure did,' the sheriff said. 'But the truth is it was Beau himself who did for the old man. I figure old Dutch could have faced just about anything, except his only boy had turned out to be a complete lunatic. A cruel, selfish, weird boy. That's why he swallowed the damn shotgun, if you want to know the truth.'

'So where did Beau go?' Webster asked.

'Montana,' the sheriff said. 'That's what I heard. He was into all those right-wing groups, you know, the militias. Built himself up to leader. Said the white man was going to have to stand and fight.'

'And those other guys went with him?' Brogan asked.

'The three of them for sure,' the sheriff said. 'This big guy, I never saw before. But Little Stevie and Loder and Peter Bell, they were all in awe of Beau, like little robots. They all went up there together. They had a little cash, and they stripped the Borken place of anything they could carry, and they headed north. Figured to buy some cheap land up there and defend themselves, you know, although against who I can't say, because the way I hear it there ain't nobody up there, and if there is they're all white people anyway.'

'What's in his file?' Webster asked.

The sheriff shook his head.

'Just about nothing,' he said. 'Beau's way too smart to get caught doing anything bad.'

'But?' McGrath said. 'He's doing stuff without getting caught?'

The sheriff nodded.

'That armored car robbery?' he said. 'North of the state some-where? I heard about that. Didn't stick to him, did it? I told you, way too smart.'

'Anything else we should know?' Webster asked.

The sheriff thought for a while and nodded again.

'There was a fifth guy,' he said. 'Name of Odell Fowler. He'll turn up alongside of Beau, for sure. You can bet on that. Loder and Stevie and Bell get sent out doing mischief, you can be damn sure Borken and Fowler are sitting there in the shadows pulling their strings.'

'Anything else?' Webster said again.

'Originally there was a sixth guy,' the sheriff said. 'Guy named Packer. Six of them, all thick as thieves. But Packer took up with a Mexican girl. Couldn't help himself, I guess, just plain fell in love with her. Beau told him to stop seeing her. They fell out about it, a lot of tension going on. One day Packer's not around any more, and Beau is all smiling and relaxed. We found Packer out in the scrub, nailed to a big wooden cross. Crucified. Dead for a couple of days.'

'And you figure Borken did it?' Brogan asked.

'Couldn't prove it,' the sheriff replied. 'But I'm sure of it. And

I'm sure he talked the others into helping him do it. He's a born leader. He can talk anybody into doing anything, I can promise you that.'

Kendall back to Mojave was fifty miles by car. Mojave to Peterson Air Force Base in Colorado was another eight hundred and thirty miles by Lear. Three hours of travel, door to door, which put them down at Peterson through the gorgeous mountain dawn. It was the kind of sight people pay money to see, but the four FBI men took no notice at all. Thursday July third, the fourth day of the crisis, and no proper rest and no proper nutrition had left them ragged and focused on nothing except the job in hand.

General Johnson himself was not available to meet them. He was elsewhere on the giant base, on duty glad-handing the returning night patrols. His aide saluted Webster, shook hands with the other three, and walked them all over to a crew room reserved for their use. There was a huge photograph on the table, black-and-white, crisply focused. Some kind of a landscape. It looked like the surface of the moon.

'That's Anadyr, in Siberia,' the aide said. 'Satellite photograph. Last week, there was a big air base there. A nuclear bomber base. The runway was aimed straight at our missile silos in Utah. Arms reduction treaty required it to be blown up. The Russians complied last week.'

The four agents bent for another look. There was no trace of any man-made structure in the picture. Just savage craters.

'Complied?' McGrath said. 'Looks like they did an enthusiastic job of work.'

'So?' Webster said.

The aide pulled a map from the portfolio. Unfolded it and stepped around so that the agents could share his view. It was a slice of the world, eastern Asia and the western United States, with the mass of Alaska right in the center and the North Pole right at the top. The aide stretched his thumb and finger apart and spanned the distance from Siberia southeast down to Utah.

'Anadyr was here,' he said. 'Utah is here. Naturally we knew all about the bomber base, and we had countermeasures in place, which included big missile bases in Alaska, here, and then a chain of four small surface-to-air facilities strung out north to south all

549

the way underneath Anadyr's flightpath into Utah, which are here, here, here and here, straddling the line between Montana and the Idaho panhandle.'

The agents ignored the red dots in Idaho. But they looked closely at the locations in Montana.

'What sort of bases are these?' Webster asked.

The aide shrugged.

'They were kind of temporary,' he said. 'Thrown together in the sixties, just sort of survived ever since. Frankly, we didn't expect to have to use them. The Alaska missiles were more than adequate. Nothing would have gotten past them. But you know how it was, right? Couldn't be too ready.'

'What sort of weapons?' McGrath asked.

'There was a Patriot battery at each facility,' the aide said. 'We pulled those out a while back. Sold them to Israel. All that's left is Stingers, you know, shoulder-launch infantry systems.'

Webster looked at the guy.

'Stingers?' he said. 'You were going to shoot Soviet bombers down with infantry systems?'

The aide nodded. Looked definite about it.

'Why not?' he said. 'Don't forget, those bases were basically window-dressing. Nothing was supposed to get past Alaska. But the Stingers would have worked. We supplied thousands of them to Afghanistan. They knocked down hundreds of Soviet planes. Mostly helicopters, I guess, but the principle is good. A heat-seeker is a heat-seeker, right? Makes no difference if it gets launched off a truck or off a GI's shoulder.'

'So what happens now?' Webster asked him.

'We're closing the bases down,' the guy said. 'That's why the general is here, gentlemen. We're pulling the equipment and the personnel back here to Peterson, and there's going to be some ceremonies, you know, end-of-an-era stuff.'

'Where are these bases?' McGrath asked. 'The Montana ones? Exactly?'

The aide pulled the map closer and checked the references.

'Southernmost one is hidden on some farmland near Missoula,' he said. 'Northern one is hidden in a valley, about forty miles south of Canada, near a little place called Yorke. Why? Is there a problem?'

McGrath shrugged.

'We don't know yet,' he said.

The aide showed them where to get breakfast and left them to wait for the general. Johnson arrived after the eggs but before the toast, so they left the toast uneaten and walked back together to the crew room. Johnson looked a lot different from the glossy guy Webster had met with Monday evening. The early hour and three days' strain made him look twenty pounds thinner and twenty years older. His face was pale and his eyes were red. He looked like a man on the verge of defeat.

'So what do we know?' he asked.

'We think we know most of it,' Webster answered. 'Right now our operational assumption is your daughter's been kidnaped by a militia group from Montana. We know their location, more or less. Somewhere in the northwestern valleys.'

Johnson nodded slowly.

'Any communication?' he asked.

Webster shook his head.

'Not yet,' he said.

'So what's the reason?' Johnson asked. 'What do they want?'

Webster shook his head again.

'We don't know that yet,' he said.

Johnson nodded again, vaguely.

'Who are they?' he asked.

McGrath opened the envelope he was carrying.

'We've got four names,' he said. 'Three of the snatch squad, and there's pretty firm evidence about who the militia leader is. A guy named Beau Borken. That name mean anything to you?'

'Borken?' Johnson said. He shook his head. 'That name means nothing.'

'OK,' McGrath said. 'What about this guy? His name's Peter Bell.'

McGrath passed Johnson the computer print of Bell at the wheel in the Lexus. Johnson took a long look at it and shook his head.

'He's dead,' McGrath said. 'Didn't make it back to Montana.'

'Good,' Johnson said.

McGrath passed him another picture.

'Steven Stewart?' he said.

Johnson paid the print some attention, but ended up shaking his head.

'Never saw this guy before,' he said.

'Tony Loder?' McGrath asked.

Johnson stared at Loder's face and shook his head.

'No,' he said.

'Those three and Borken are all from California,' McGrath said. 'There may be another guy called Odell Fowler. You heard that name?'

Johnson shook his head.

'And there's this guy,' McGrath said. 'We don't know who he is.'

He passed over the photograph of the big guy. Johnson glanced at it, then glanced away. But then his gaze drifted back.

'You know this one?' McGrath asked him.

Johnson shrugged.

'He's vaguely familiar,' he said. 'Maybe somebody I once saw?'

'Recently?' McGrath asked.

Johnson shook his head.

'Not recently,' he said. 'Probably a long time ago.'

'Military?' Webster asked.

'Probably,' Johnson said again. 'Most of the people I see are military.'

His aide crowded his shoulder for a look.

'Means nothing to me,' he said. 'But we should fax this to the Pentagon. If this guy is military maybe there'll be somebody somewhere who served with him.'

Johnson shook his head.

'Fax it to the military police,' he said. 'This guy's a criminal, right? Chances are he was in trouble before, in the service. Somebody there will remember him.'

TWENTY-FIVE

THEY CAME FOR HIM AN HOUR AFTER DAWN. HE WAS DOZING ON his hard chair, hands cuffed in his lap, Joseph Ray awake and alert opposite him. He had spent most of the night thinking about dynamite. Old dynamite, left over from abandoned mining operations. He imagined hefting a stick in his hand. Feeling the weight. Figuring the volume of the cavity behind Holly's walls. Picturing it packed with old dynamite. Old dynamite, rotting, the nitroglycerin sweating out, going unstable. Maybe a ton of unstable old dynamite packed in all around her, still not so far gone it would explode with random movement, but gone bad enough it would explode under the impact of a stray artillery shell. Or a stray bullet. Or even a sharp blow with a hammer.

Then there was a rattle of feet on shale as a detachment of men halted outside the hut. The door was flung open and Reacher turned his head and saw six guards. The point man clattered inside and hauled him up by the arm. He was dragged outside into the bright morning sun to face five men, line abreast, automatic rifles at the slope. Camouflage fatigues, beards. He stood and squinted in the light. The rifle muzzles jerked him into rough formation and the six men marched him across the diameter of the clearing to a narrow path running away from the sun into the forest.

Fifty yards in there was another clearing. A rough scrubby rectangle, small in area. Two plywood and cedar structures. Neither had any windows. The guards halted him and the point man used his rifle barrel to indicate the left-hand building.

'Command hut,' he said.

Then he pointed to the right.

'Punishment hut,' he said. 'We try to avoid that one.'

The six men laughed with the secure confidence of an elite detachment and the point man knocked on the command hut door. Paused a beat and opened it. Reacher was shoved inside with a rifle muzzle in the small of his back.

The hut was blazing with light. Electric bulbs added to green daylight from mossy skylights set into the roof. There was a plain oak desk and matching chairs, big old round things like Reacher had seen in old movies about newspaper offices or country banks. There was no decor except flags and banners nailed to the walls. There was a huge red swastika behind the desk, and several similar black-and-white motifs on the other walls. There was a detailed map of Montana pinned to a board on the back wall. A tiny portion of the northwest corner of the state was outlined in black. There were bundles of pamphlets and manuals stacked on the bare floor. One was titled: Dry It, You'll Like It. It claimed to show how food could be preserved to withstand a siege. Another claimed to show how guerillas could derail passenger trains. There was a polished mahogany bookcase, incongruously fine, packed with books. The bar of daylight from the door fell across them and illuminated their cloth spines and gold-blocked titles. They were standard histories of the art of war, translations from German and Japanese. There was a whole shelf with texts about Pearl Harbor. Texts that Reacher himself had studied, elsewhere and a long time ago.

He stood still. Borken was behind the desk. His hair gleamed white in the light. The black uniform showed up gray. Borken was just staring silently at him. Then he waved him to a chair. Motioned the guards to wait outside.

Reacher sat heavily. Fatigue was gnawing at him and adrenalin was burning his stomach. The guards tramped across the floor and stepped outside. They closed the door quietly. Borken moved his arm and rolled open a drawer. Took out an ancient handgun. Laid it on the desktop with a loud clatter.

'I made my decision,' he said. 'About whether you live or die.'

Then he pointed at the old revolver lying on the desk.

'You know what this is?' he asked.

Reacher glanced at it through the glare and nodded.

'It's a Marshal Colt,' he said.

Borken nodded.

'You bet your ass it is,' he said. 'It's an original 1873 Marshal Colt, just like the US cavalry were given. It's my personal weapon.'

He picked it up, right-handed, and hefted it.

'You know what it fires?' he said.

Reacher nodded again.

'Forty-fives,' he said. 'Six shots.'

'Right first time,' Borken said. 'Six forty-fives, nine hundred feet per second out of a seven and a half inch barrel. You know what those bullets could do to you?'

Reacher shrugged.

'Depends if they hit me or not,' he said.

Borken looked blank. Then he grinned. His wet mouth curled upward and his tight cheeks nearly forced his eyes shut.

'They'd hit you,' he said. 'If I'm firing, they'd hit you.'

Reacher shrugged again.

'From there, maybe,' he said.

'From anywhere,' Borken said. 'From here, from fifty feet, from fifty yards, if I'm firing, they'd hit you.'

'Hold up your right hand,' Reacher said.

Borken looked blank again. Then he put the gun down and held up his huge white hand like he was waving to a vague acquaintance or taking an oath.

'Bullshit,' Reacher said.

'Bullshit?' Borken repeated.

'For sure,' Reacher said. 'That gun's reasonably accurate, but it's not the best weapon in the world. To hit a man at fifty yards with it, you'd need to practice like crazy. And you haven't been.'

'I haven't?' Borken said.

'No, you haven't,' Reacher said. 'Look at the damn thing. It was designed in the 1870s, right? You seen old photographs? People were much smaller. Scrappy little guys, just immigrated from Europe, been starving for generations. Small people, small hands. Look at the stock on that thing. Tight curve, way too small for you. You grab that thing, your hand looks like a bunch of bananas around it. And that stock is hundred-and-twenty-year-old walnut. Hard as a rock. The back of the stock and the end of the frame below the hammer would be pounding you with the recoil. You used that gun a lot, you'd have a pad of callus between your thumb and forefinger I could see from here. But you haven't, so don't tell me you've been practicing with it, and don't tell me you can be a marksman without practicing with it.'

Borken looked hard at him. Then he smiled again. His wet lips parted and his eyes closed into slits. He rolled open the opposite drawer and lifted out another handgun. It was a Sig-Sauer 9mm. Maybe five years old. Well used, but well maintained. A big boxy grip for a big hand.

'I lied,' he said. 'This is my personal weapon. And now I know something. I know my decision was the right one.'

He paused so Reacher could ask him about his decision. Reacher stayed silent. Clamped his lips. He wasn't about to ask him about anything, not even if it would be the last sentence he would ever live to say.

'We're serious here, you know,' Borken said to him. 'Totally serious. We're not playing games. And we're correct about what's going on.'

He paused again, so Reacher could ask him what was going on. Reacher said nothing. Just sat and stared into space.

'America has got a despotic government,' Borken said. 'A dictatorship, controlled from abroad by our enemies. Our current president is a member of a world government which controls our lives in secret. His federal system is a smokescreen for total control. They're planning to disarm us and enslave us. It's started already. Let's be totally clear about that.'

He paused. Picked up the old revolver again. Reacher saw him checking the fit of the stock in his hand. Felt the charisma radiating out of him. Felt compelled to listen to the soft, hypnotic voice.

'Two main methods,' Borken said. 'The first is the attempt to disarm the civilian population. The second amendment guarantees our right to bear arms, but they're going to abolish that. The gun laws, all this beefing about crime, homicides, drug wars, it's all aimed at disarming people like us. And when we're disarmed, they can do what they like with us, right? That's why it was in the Constitution in the first place. Those old guys were smart. They knew the only thing that could control a government was the people's willingness and ability to shoot them down.'

Borken paused again. Reacher stared up at the swastika behind his head.

'Second method is the squeeze on small business,' Borken said. 'This is a personal theory of mine. You don't hear it much around the Movement. But I spotted it. It puts me way ahead of the others in my understanding.'

Borken waited, but Reacher still stayed silent. Looking away.

'It's obvious, right?' Borken said to him. 'World government is basically a communistic type of government. They don't want a strong small-business sector. But that's what America had. Millions of people, all working hard for themselves and making a living. Too many just to murder out of hand, when the time comes. So the numbers have to be reduced in advance. So the federal government was instructed to squeeze the small businessman. They put on all kinds of regulations, all kinds of laws and taxes, they rig the markets, they bring the small guy to his knees, then they order the banks to come sniffing round with attractive loans, and as soon as the ink is dry on the loan papers they jack up the interest, and rig the market some more, until the poor guy defaults. Then they take away his business, and so that's one less for the gas ovens when the time comes.'

Reacher glanced at him. Said nothing.

'Believe it,' Borken said. 'It's like they're solving a corpse-disposal problem in advance. Get rid of the middle class now, they don't need so many concentration camps later.'

Reacher was just staring at Borken's eyes. Like looking at a bright light. The fat red lips were smiling an indulgent smile.

'I told you, we're way ahead of the others,' he said. 'We've seen it coming. What else is the Federal Reserve for? That's the key to this whole thing. America was basically a nation founded on business, right? Control business, you control everything. How do you control business? You control the banks. How do you control the banks? You set up a bullshit Federal Reserve system. You tell the banks what to do. That's the key. The world government controls everything, through the Fed. I've seen it happen.'

His eyes were open wide. Shining with no color.

'I saw them do it to my own father,' he screamed. 'May his poor soul rest in peace. The Fed bankrupted him.'

Reacher tore his gaze away. Shrugged at the corner of the room. Said nothing. He started trying to recall the sequence of titles in Borken's fine mahogany bookcase. Warfare from ancient China through Renaissance Italy through Pearl Harbor. He concentrated on naming the titles to himself, left to right, trying to resist the glare of Borken's attention.

'We're serious here,' Borken was saying again. 'You may look at me and think I'm some kind of a despot, or a cult leader, or whatever the world would want to label me. But I'm not. I'm a good leader, I won't deny that. Even an inspired leader. Call me intelligent and perceptive, I won't argue with you. But I don't need to be. My people don't need any encouraging. They don't need much leading. They need guidance, and they need discipline, but don't let that fool you. I'm not coercing anybody. Don't make the mistake of underestimating their will. Don't ignore their desire for a change for the better.'

Reacher was silent. He was still concentrating on the books, skimming in his mind through the events of December 1941, as seen from the Japanese point of view.

'We're not criminals here, you know,' Borken was saying. 'When a government turns bad, it's the very best people who stand up against it. Or do you think we should all just act like sheep?'

Reacher risked another glance at him. Risked speaking.

'You're pretty selective,' he said. 'About who's here and who's not.'

Borken shrugged.

'Like unto like,' he said. 'That's nature's way, isn't it? Black people have got the whole of Africa. White people have got this place.'

'What about Jewish dentists?' Reacher asked. 'What place have they got?'

Borken shrugged again.

'That was an operational error,' he said. 'Loder should have waited until he was clear. But mistakes happen.'

'Should have waited until I was clear, too,' Reacher said.

Borken nodded.

'I agree with you,' he said. 'It would have been better for you that way. But they didn't, and so here you are among us.'

558

'Just because I'm white?' Reacher said.

'Don't knock it,' Borken replied. 'White people got precious few rights left.'

Reacher stared at him. Stared around the bright, hate-filled room. Shuddered.

'I've made a study of tyranny,' Borken said. 'And how to combat it. The first rule is you make a firm decision, to live free or die, and you mean it. Live free or die. The second rule is you don't act like a sheep. You stand up and you resist them. You study their system and you learn to hate it. And then you act. But how do you act? The brave man fights back. He retaliates, right?'

Reacher shrugged. Said nothing.

'The brave man retaliates,' Borken repeated. 'But the man who is both brave and clever acts differently. He retaliates first. In advance. He strikes the first blows. He gives them what they don't expect, when and where they don't expect it. That's what we're doing here. We're retaliating first. It's their war, but we're going to strike the first blows. We're going to give them what they don't expect. We're going to upset their plans.'

Reacher glanced back at the bookcase. Five thousand classic pages, all saying the same thing: don't do what they expect you to do.

'Go look at the map,' Borken said.

Reacher thrust his cuffed hands forward and lifted himself awkwardly out of the chair. Walked over to the map of Montana on the wall. He found Yorke in the top left-hand corner. Well inside the small black outline. He checked the scale and looked at the contour shading and the colors. The river Joseph Ray had talked about lay thirty miles to the west, on the other side of high mountains. It was a thick blue slash running down the map. There were enormous brown heights shown to the north, all the way up to Canada. The only road ran north through Yorke and terminated at some abandoned mine workings. A few haphazard tracks ran through solid forest to the east. To the south, contour lines merged together to show a tremendous east–west ravine.

'Look at that terrain, Reacher,' Borken said quietly. 'What does it tell you?'

Reacher looked at it. It told him he couldn't get out. Not on foot, not with Holly. There were weeks of rough walking east and north. Natural barriers west and south. The terrain made a better prison than wire fences or minefields could have. He had once been in Siberia, after glasnost, following up on ancient stories about Korean MIAs. The gulags had been completely open. No wire, no barriers. He had asked his hosts: but where are the fences? The Russians had pointed out over the miles of snow and said: there are the fences. Nowhere to run. He looked up at the map again. The terrain was the barrier. To get out was going to require a vehicle. And a lot of luck.

'They can't get in,' Borken said. 'We're impregnable. We can't be stopped. And we mustn't be stopped. That would be a disaster of truly historic proportions. Suppose the Redcoats had stopped the American Revolution in 1776?'

Reacher glanced around the tiny wooden room and shuddered.

'This isn't the American Revolution,' he said.

'Isn't it?' Borken asked. 'How is it different? They wanted freedom from a tyrannical government. So do we.'

'You're murderers,' Reacher said.

'So were they in 1776,' Borken said. 'They killed people. The established system called that murder, too.'

'You're racists,' Reacher said.

'Same in 1776,' Borken said. 'Jefferson and his slaves? They knew black people were inferior. Back then, they were exactly the same as we are now. But then they became the new redcoats. Slowly, over the years. It's fallen to us to get back to how it should have stayed. Live free or die, Reacher. It's a noble aim. Always has been, don't you think?'

He was leaning forward with his great bulk pressing tight against the desk. His hands were in the air. His colorless eyes were shining.

'But there were mistakes made in 1776,' he said. 'I've studied the history. War could have been avoided if both sides had acted sensibly. And war should always be avoided, don't you think?'

Reacher shrugged.

'Not necessarily,' he said.

'Well, you're going to help us avoid it,' Borken said. 'That's my decision. You're going to be my emissary.'

'Your what?' Reacher said.

'You're independent,' Borken said. 'Not one of us. No ax to grind. An American like them, an upstanding citizen, no felony

560

convictions. A clever, perceptive man. You notice things. They'll listen to you.'

'What?' Reacher said again.

'We're organized here,' Borken said. 'We're ready for nationhood. You need to understand that. We have an army, we have a treasury, we have financial reserves, we have a legal system, we have democracy. I'm going to show all that to you today. I'm going to show you a society ready for independence, ready to live free or die, and just a day away from doing so. Then I'm going to send you south to America. You're going to tell them our position is strong and their position is hopeless.'

Reacher just stared at him.

'And you can tell them about Holly,' Borken said quietly. 'In her special little room. You can tell them about my secret weapon. My insurance policy.'

'You're crazy,' Reacher said.

The hut went silent. Quieter than silent.

'Why?' Borken whispered. 'Why am I crazy? Exactly?'

'You're not thinking straight,' Reacher said. 'Don't you realize that Holly counts for nothing? The president will replace Johnson faster than you can blink an eye. They'll crush you like a bug and Holly will be just another casualty. You should send her back out with me.'

Borken was shaking his bloated head, happily, confidently.

'No,' he said. 'That won't happen. There's more to Holly than who her father is. Hasn't she told you that?'

Reacher stared at him and Borken checked his watch.

'Time to go,' he said. 'Time for you to see our legal system at work.'

Holly heard the quiet footsteps outside her door and eased off the bed. The lock clicked back and the young soldier with the scarred forehead stepped up into the room. He had his finger to his lips and Holly nodded. She limped to the bathroom and set the shower running noisily into the empty tub. The young soldier followed her in and closed the door.

'We can only do this once a day,' Holly whispered. 'They'll get suspicious if they hear the shower too often.'

The young guy nodded.

'We'll get out tonight,' he said. 'Can't do it this morning. We're all on duty at Loder's trial. I'll come by just after dusk, with a jeep. We'll make a run for it in the dark. Head south. Risky, but we'll make it.'

'Not without Reacher,' Holly said.

The young guy shook his head.

'Can't promise that,' he said. 'He's in with Borken now. God knows what's going to happen to him.'

'I go, he goes,' Holly said.

The young guy looked at her, nervously.

'OK,' he said. 'I'll try.'

He opened the bathroom door and crept out. Holly watched him go and turned the shower off. Stared after him.

He looped north and west and took a long route back through the woods, same way as he had come. The sentry Fowler had hidden in the trees fifteen feet off the main path never saw him. But the one he had hidden in the backwoods did. He caught a glimpse of a camouflage uniform hustling through the undergrowth. Spun around fast, but was too late to make the face. He shrugged and thought hard. Figured he'd keep it to himself. Better to ignore it than report he'd failed to make the actual ID.

So the young man with the scar hurried all the way and was back in his hut two minutes before he was due to escort his commander down to the tribunal hearing.

In the daylight, the courthouse on the southeast corner of the abandoned town of Yorke looked pretty much the same as a hundred others Reacher had seen all over rural America. Built early in the century. Big, white, pillared, ornate. Enough square solidity to communicate its serious purpose, but enough lightness in its details to make it a handsome structure. He saw a fine cupola floating off the top of the building, with a fine clock in it, probably paid for by a public subscription held long ago among a long-forgotten generation. More or less the same as a hundred others, but the roof was steeper-pitched than some, and heavier built. He guessed it had to be that way in the north of Montana. That roof could be carrying a hundred tons of snow all winter long.

But this was the third morning of July, and there was no snow on the roof. Reacher was warm after walking a mile in the pale northern sun. Borken had gone ahead separately and Reacher had been marched down through the forest by the same six elite guards. Still in handcuffs. They marched him straight up the front steps and inside. The first-floor interior was one large space, interrupted by pillars holding up the second floor, paneled in broad smooth planks sawed from huge pines. The wood was dark from age and polish, and the panels were stern and simple in their design.

Every seat was taken. Every bench was full. The room was a sea of camouflage green. Men and women. Sitting rigidly upright, rifles exactly vertical between their knees. Waiting expectantly. Some children, silent and confused. Reacher was led in front of the crowd, over to a table in the well of the court. Fowler was waiting there. Stevie next to him. He nodded to a chair. Reacher sat. The guards stood behind him. A minute later, the double doors opened and Beau Borken walked over to the judge's bench. The old floor creaked beneath his bulk. Every person in the room except Reacher stood up. Stood to attention and saluted, as if they were hearing an inaudible cue. Borken was still in his black uniform, with belt and boots. He had added a large holster to hold his Sig-Sauer. He held a slim leather-bound book. He came in with six armed men in a loose formation. They took up station in front of the bench and stood at rigid attention, gazing forward, looking blank.

The people sat down again. Reacher glanced up at the ceiling and quartered it with his eyes. Worked out which was the southeast corner. The doors opened again and the crowd drew breath. Loder was pushed into the room. He was surrounded by six guards. They pushed him to the table opposite Fowler's. The accused's table. The guards stood behind him and forced him into the chair with their hands on both his shoulders. His face was white with fear and crusted with blood. His nose was broken and his lips were split. Borken stared across at him. Sat down heavily in the judge's chair and placed his big hands, palms down, on the bench. Looked around the quiet room and spoke.

'We all know why we're here,' he said.

Holly could sense there was a big crowd in the room below her. She could feel the faint rumble of a body of people holding themselves still and quiet. But she didn't stop working. No reason to believe her Bureau contact would fail, but she was still going to spend the day preparing. Just in case.

Her search for a tool had led her to the one she had brought in with her. Her metal crutch. It was a one-inch aluminum tube, with an elbow clip and a handle. The tube was too wide and the metal was too soft to act as a pry-bar. But she realized that maybe if she pulled the rubber foot off, the open end of the tube could be molded into a makeshift wrench. She could maybe crush the tube around the shape of the bolts holding the bed together. Then she could bend the tube at a right angle, and maybe use the whole thing like a flimsy tire iron.

But first she had to scrape away the thick paint on the bolts. It was smooth and slick, and it welded the bolts to the frame. She used the edge of the elbow clip to flake the top layers. Then she scraped at the seams until she saw bright metal. Now her idea was to limp back and forth from the bathroom with a towel soaked in hot water. She would press the towel hard on the bolts and let the heat from the water expand the metal and crack its grip. Then the soft aluminum of the crutch might just prove strong enough to do the job.

'Reckless endangerment of the mission,' Beau Borken said.

His voice was low and hypnotic. The room was quiet. The guards in front of the judge's bench stared forward. The guard at the end was staring at Reacher. He was the younger guy with the trimmed beard and the scar on his forehead Reacher had seen guarding Loder the previous night. He was staring at Reacher with curiosity.

Borken held up the slim leather-bound volume and swung it slowly, left to right, like it was a searchlight and he wanted to bathe the whole of the room with its bright beam.

'The Constitution of the United States,' he said. 'Sadly abused, but the greatest political tract ever devised by man. The model for our own constitution.'

He turned the pages of the book. The rustle of stiff paper was loud in the quiet room. He started reading.

'The Bill of Rights,' he said. 'The fifth amendment specifies no person shall be held to answer for a capital crime without a grand jury indictment except in cases arising in the militia in times of public danger. It says no person shall be deprived of life or liberty without due process of law. The sixth amendment specifies the accused shall have the right to a speedy public trial in front of a local jury. It says the accused has the right to assistance of counsel.'

Borken stopped again. Looked around the room. Held up the book.

'This book tells us what to do,' he said. 'So we need a jury. Doesn't say how many. I figure three men will do. Volunteers?'

There was a flurry of hands. Borken pointed randomly here and there and three men walked across the pine floor. They stacked their rifles and filed into the jury box. Borken turned in his seat and spoke to them.

'Gentlemen,' he said. 'This is a militia matter and this is a time of public danger. Are we agreed on that?'

The new jurymen all nodded and Borken turned and looked down from the bench toward Loder, alone at his table.

'You had counsel?' he said.

'You offering me a lawyer now?' Loder asked.

His voice was thick and nasal. Borken shook his head.

'There are no lawyers here,' he said. 'Lawyers are what went wrong with the rest of America. We're not going to have lawyers here. We don't want them. The Bill of Rights doesn't say anything about lawyers. It says counsel. Counsel means advice. That's what my dictionary says. You had advice? You want any?'

'You got any?' Loder said.

Borken nodded and smiled a cold smile.

'Plead guilty,' he said.

Loder just shook his head and dropped his eyes.

'OK,' Borken said. 'You've had counsel, but you're pleading not guilty?'

Loder nodded. Borken looked down at his book again. Turned back to the beginning.

'The Declaration of Independence,' he said. ' "It is the right of the people to alter or to abolish the old government and to institute new government in such form as to them shall seem most likely to effect their safety and happiness." '

He stopped and scanned the crowd.

'You all understand what that means?' he said. 'The old laws are gone. Now we have new laws. New ways of doing things. We're putting right two hundred years of mistakes. We're going back to

565

where we should have been all along. This is the first trial under a brand-new system. A better system. A system with a far stronger claim to legitimacy. We have the right to do it, and what we are doing is right.'

There was a slight murmur from the crowd. Reacher detected no disapproval in the sound. They were all hypnotized. Basking in Borken's bright glow like reptiles in a hot noontime sun. Borken nodded to Fowler. Fowler stood up next to Reacher and turned to the jury box.

'The facts are these,' Fowler said. 'The commander sent Loder out on a mission of great importance for all our futures. Loder performed badly. He was gone for just five days, but he made five serious mistakes. Mistakes which could have wrecked the whole venture. Specifically, he left a trail by burning two vehicles. Then he mistimed two operations and thereby snarled up two civilians. And finally he allowed Peter Bell to desert. Five serious mistakes.'

Fowler stood there. Reacher stared at him, urgently.

'I'm calling a witness,' Fowler said. 'Stevie Stewart.'

Little Stevie stood up fast and Fowler nodded him across to the old witness box, alongside and below the judge's bench. Borken leaned down and handed him a black book. Reacher couldn't see what book it was, but it wasn't a Bible. Not unless they had started making Bibles with swastikas on the cover.

'You swear to tell the truth here?' Borken asked.

Stevie nodded.

'I do, sir,' he said.

He put the book down and turned to Fowler, ready for the first question.

'The five mistakes I mentioned?' Fowler said. 'You see Loder make them?'

Stevie nodded again.

'He made them,' he said.

'He take responsibility for them?' Fowler asked.

'Sure did,' Stevie said. 'He played the big boss the whole time we were away.'

Fowler nodded Stevie back to the table. The courtroom was silent. Borken smiled knowingly at the jurymen and glanced down at Loder.

'Anything to say in your defence?' he asked quietly.

The way he said it he made it sound absurd that anybody could possibly dream up any kind of defense to those kinds of charges. The courtroom stayed silent. Still. Borken was watching the crowd. Every pair of eyes was locked onto the back of Loder's head.

'Anything to say?' Borken asked him again.

Loder stared forward. Made no reply. Borken turned toward the jury box and looked at the three men sitting on the old worn benches. Looked a question at them. The three men huddled for a second and whispered. Then the guy on the left stood up.

'Guilty, sir,' he said. 'Definitely guilty.'

Borken nodded in satisfaction.

'Thank you, gentlemen,' he said.

The crowd set up a buzz. He turned to quell it with a look.

'I am required to pass sentence,' he said. 'As many of you know, Loder is an old acquaintance of mine. We go back a long way. We were childhood friends. And friendship means a great deal to me.'

He paused and looked down at Loder.

'But other things mean more,' he said. 'Performance of my duties means more. My responsibility to this emerging nation means more. Sometimes, statesmanship must be put above every other value a man holds dear.'

The crowd was silent. Holding its breath. Borken sat for a long moment. Then he glanced over Loder's head at the guards behind him and made a small delicate motion with his head. The guards grabbed Loder's elbows and hauled him to his feet. They formed up and hustled him out of the room. Borken stood and looked at the crowd. Then he turned and walked to the doors and was gone. The people in the public benches shuffled to their feet and hurried out after him.

Reacher saw the guards walking Loder to a flagpole on the patch of lawn outside the courthouse. Borken was striding after them. The guards reached the flagpole and shoved Loder hard up against it, facing it. They held his wrists and pulled, so he was pressed up against the pole, hugging it, face tight against the dull white paint. Borken came up behind him. Pulled the Sig-Sauer from its holster. Clicked the safety catch. Cocked a round into the chamber. Jammed the muzzle into the back of Loder's neck and fired. There was an explosion of pink blood and the roar of the shot cannoned off the mountains.

TWENTY-SIX

'HIS NAME IS JACK REACHER,' WEBSTER SAID.
'Good call, General,' McGrath said. 'I guess they remembered him.'

Johnson nodded.

'Military police keeps good records,' he said.

They were still in the commandeered crew room inside Peterson Air Force Base. Ten o'clock in the morning, Thursday July third. The fax machine was rolling out a long reply to their inquiry. The face in the photograph had been identified immediately. The subject's service record had been pulled straight off the Pentagon computer and faxed along with the name.

'You recall this guy now?' Brogan asked.

'Reacher?' Johnson repeated vaguely. 'I don't know. What did he do?'

Webster and the general's aide were crowding the machine, reading the report as the paper spooled out. They twisted it right side up and walked slowly away to keep it up off the floor.

'What did he do?' McGrath asked them urgently.

'Nothing,' Webster said.

'Nothing?' McGrath repeated. 'Why would they have a record on him if he didn't do anything?'

568

'He was one of them,' Webster said. 'Major Jack Reacher, military police.'

The aide was racing through the length of paper.

'Silver Star,' he said. 'Two Bronzes, Purple Heart. This is a hell of a record, sir. This guy was a hero, for God's sake.'

McGrath opened up his envelope and pulled out the original video pictures of the kidnap, black-and-white, unenlarged, grainy. He selected the first picture of Reacher's involvement. The one catching him in the act of seizing Holly's crutch and pulling the dry-cleaning from her grasp. He slid the photograph across the table.

'Big hero,' he said.

Johnson bent to study the picture. McGrath slid over the next. The one showing Reacher gripping Holly's arm, keeping her inside the tight crush of attackers. Johnson picked it up and stared at it. McGrath wasn't sure whether he was staring at Reacher or at his daughter.

'He's thirty-seven,' the general's aide read aloud. 'Mustered out fourteen months ago. West Point, thirteen years' service, big heroics in Beirut right at the start. Sir, you pinned a Bronze on him, ten years ago. This is an absolutely outstanding record throughout. He's the only non-Marine in history to win the Wimbledon.'

Webster looked up.

'Tennis?' he said.

The aide smiled briefly.

'Not Wimbledon,' he said. 'The Wimbledon. Marine Sniper School runs a competition, the Wimbledon Cup. For snipers. Open to anybody, but a Marine always wins it, except one year Reacher won it.'

'So why didn't he serve as a sniper?' McGrath asked.

The aide shrugged.

'Beats me,' he said. 'Lots of puzzles in this record. Like why did he leave the service at all? Guy like this should have made it all the way to the top.'

Johnson had a picture in each hand and he was staring closely at them.

'So why did he leave?' Brogan asked. 'Any trouble?'

The aide shook his head. Scanned the paper.

'Nothing in the record,' he said. 'No reason given. We were shedding numbers at the time, but the idea was to cull the no-hopers. A guy like this shouldn't have been shaken out.'

Johnson swapped the photographs into the opposite hands, like he was looking for a fresh perspective.

'Anybody know him real well?' Milosevic asked. 'Anybody we can talk to?'

'We can dig up his old commander, I guess,' the aide said. 'Might take us a day to get hold of him.'

'Do it,' Webster said. 'We need information. Anything at all will help.'

Johnson put the photographs down and slid them back to McGrath.

'He must have turned bad,' he said. 'Sometimes happens. Good men can turn bad. I've seen it myself, time to time. It can be a hell of a problem.'

McGrath reversed the photographs on the shiny table and stared at them.

'You're not kidding,' he said.

Johnson looked back at him.

'Can I keep that picture?' he said. 'The first one?'

McGrath shook his head.

'No,' he said. 'You want a picture, I'll take one myself. You and your daughter standing together in front of a headstone, this asshole's name on it.'

TWENTY-SEVEN

FOUR MEN WERE DRAGGING LODER'S BODY AWAY AND THE CROWD was dispersing quietly. Reacher was left standing on the courthouse steps with his six guards and Fowler. Fowler had finally unlocked the handcuffs. Reacher was rolling his shoulders and stretching. He had been cuffed all night and all morning and he was stiff and sore. His wrists were marked with red weals where the hard metal had bitten down.

'Cigarette?' Fowler asked.

He was holding his pack out. A friendly gesture. Reacher shook his head.

'I want to see Holly,' he said.

Fowler was about to refuse, but then he thought some more and nodded.

'OK,' he said. 'Good idea. Take her out for some exercise. Talk to her. Ask her how we're treating her. That's something you're sure to be asked later. It'll be very important to them. We don't want you giving them any false impressions.'

Reacher waited at the bottom of the steps. The sun had gone pale and watery. Wisps of mist were gathering in the north. But some of the sky was still blue and clear. After five minutes Fowler brought Holly down. She was walking slowy, with a little staccato rhythm as her good leg alternated with the thump of her crutch. She walked through the door and stood at the top of the steps.

'Question for you, Reacher,' Fowler called down. 'How far can you run in a half-hour with a hundred and twenty pounds on your back?'

Reacher shrugged.

'Not far enough, I guess,' he said.

Fowler nodded.

'Right,' he said. 'Not far enough. If she's not standing right here in thirty minutes, we'll come looking for you. We'll give it a two-mile radius.'

Reacher thought about it and nodded. A half-hour with a hundred and twenty pounds on his back might get him more than two miles. Two miles was probably pessimistic. But he thought back to the map on Borken's wall. Thought about the savage terrain. Where the hell would he run? He made a show of checking his watch. Fowler walked away, up behind the ruined office building. The guards slung their weapons over their shoulders and stood easy. Holly smoothed her hair back. Stood face up to the pale sun.

'Can you walk for a while?' Reacher asked her.

'Slowly,' she said.

She set off north along the middle of the deserted street. Reacher strolled beside her. They waited until they were out of sight. They glanced at each other. Then they turned and flung themselves together. Her crutch toppled to the ground and he lifted her a foot in the air. She wrapped her arms around him and buried her face in his neck.

'I'm going crazy in there,' she said.

'I've got bad news,' he said.

'What?' she said.

'They had a helper in Chicago,' he said.

She stared up at him.

'They were only gone five days,' he said. 'That's what Fowler said at the trial. He said Loder had been gone just five days.'

'So?' she said.

'So they didn't have time for surveillance,' he said. 'They hadn't been watching you. Somebody told them where you were going to be, and when. They had help, Holly.'

The color in her face drained away. It was replaced by shock.

'Five days?' she said. 'You sure?'

Reacher nodded. Holly went quiet. She was thinking hard.

'So who knew?' he asked her. 'Who knew where you'd be, twelve o'clock Monday? A roommate? A friend?'

Her eyes were darting left and right. She was racing through the possibilities.

'Nobody knew,' she said.

'Were you ever tailed?' he asked.

She shrugged helplessly. Reacher could see she desperately wanted to say yes, I was tailed. Because he knew to say no was too awful for her to contemplate.

'Were you?' he asked again.

'No,' she said quietly. 'By a bozo like one of these? Forget it. I'd have spotted them. And they'd have had to hang around all day outside the Federal Building, just waiting. We'd have picked them up in a heartbeat.'

'So?' he asked.

'My lunchbreak was flexible,' she said. 'It varied, sometimes by a couple of hours either way. It was never regular.'

'So?' he asked again.

She stared at him.

'So it was inside help,' she said. 'Inside the Bureau. Had to be. Think about it, no other possibility. Somebody in the office saw me leave and dropped a dime.'

He said nothing. Just watched the dismay on her face.

'A mole inside Chicago,' she said. A statement, not a question. 'Inside the Bureau. No other possibility. Shit, I don't believe it.'

Then she smiled. A brief, bitter smile.

'And we've got a mole inside here,' she said. 'Ironic, right? He identified himself to me. Young guy, big scar on his forehead. He's undercover for the Bureau. He says we've got people in a lot of these groups. Deep undercover, in case of emergency. He called it in when they put the dynamite in my walls.'

He stared back at her.

'You know about the dynamite?' he said.

She grimaced and nodded.

'No wonder you're going crazy in there,' he said.

Then he stared at her in a new panic.

'Who does this undercover guy call in to?' he asked urgently.

573

'Our office in Butte,' Holly said. 'It's just a satellite office. One resident agent. He communicates by radio. He's got a transmitter hidden out in the woods. But he's not using it now. He says they're scanning the frequencies.'

He shuddered.

'So how long before the Chicago mole blows his cover?' he said.

Holly went paler.

'Soon, I guess,' she said. 'Soon as somebody figures we were headed out in this direction. Chicago will be dialing up the computers and trawling for any reports coming out of Montana. His stuff will be top of the damn pile. Christ, Reacher, you've got to get to him first. You've got to warn him. His name is Jackson.'

They turned back. Started hurrying south through the ghost town.

'He says he can break me out,' Holly said. 'Tonight, by jeep.'

Reacher nodded grimly.

'Go with him,' he said.

'Not without you,' she said.

'They're sending me anyway,' he said. 'I'm supposed to be an emissary. I'm supposed to tell your people it's hopeless.'

'Are you going to go?' she asked.

He shook his head.

'Not if I can help it,' he said. 'Not without you.'

'You should go,' she said. 'Don't worry about me.'

He shook his head again.

'I am worrying about you,' he said.

'Just go,' she said. 'Forget me and get out.'

He shrugged. Said nothing.

'Get out if you get the chance, Reacher,' she said. 'I mean it.'

She looked like she meant it. She was glaring at him.

'Only if you're gone first,' he said finally. 'I'm sticking around until you're out of here. I'm definitely not leaving you with these maniacs.'

'But you can't stick around,' she said. 'If I'm gone, they'll go apeshit. It'll change everything.'

He looked at her. Heard Borken say: she's more than his daughter.

574

'Why, Holly?' he said. 'Why will it change everything? Who the hell are you?'

She didn't answer. Glanced away. Fowler strolled into view, coming north, smoking. He walked up to them. Stopped right in front of them. Pulled his pack.

'Cigarette?' he asked.

Holly looked at the ground. Reacher shook his head.

'She tell you?' Fowler asked. 'All the comforts of home?'

The guards were standing to attention. They were in a sort of honor guard on the courthouse steps. Fowler walked Holly to them. A guard took her inside. At the door, she glanced back at Reacher. He nodded to her. Tried to make it say: see you later, OK? Then she was gone.

'Now for the grand tour,' Fowler said. 'You stick close to me. Beau's orders. But you can ask any questions you want, OK?'

Reacher glanced vaguely at him and nodded. Glanced at the six guards behind him. He walked down the steps and paused. Looked over at the flagpole. It was set dead center in the remains of a fine square of lawn in front of the building. He walked across to it and stood in Loder's blood and looked around.

The town of Yorke was pretty much dead. Looked like it had died some time ago. And it looked like it had never been much of a place to begin with. The road came through north to south, and there had been four developed blocks flanking it, two on the east side and two on the west. The courthouse took up the whole of the southeastern block and it faced what might have been some kind of a county office on the southwestern block. The western side of the street was higher. The ground sloped way up. The foundation of the county office building was about level with the second floor of the courthouse. It had started out the same type of structure, but it had fallen into ruin, maybe thirty years before. The paint was peeled and the siding showed through iron-gray. There was no glass in any window. The sloping knoll surrounding it had returned to mountain scrub. There had been an ornamental tree dead center. It had died a long time ago, and it was now just a stump, maybe seven feet high, like an execution post.

The northern blocks were rows of faded, boarded-up stores. There had once been tall ornate frontages concealing simple square buildings, but the decay of the years had left the frontages the same dull brown as the boxy wooden structures behind. The signs above the doors had faded to nothing. There were no people on the sidewalks. No vehicle noise, no activity, no nothing. The place was a ghost. It looked like an abandoned cowboy town from the Old West.

'This was a mining town,' Fowler said. 'Lead, mostly, but some copper, and a couple of seams of good silver for a while. There was a lot of money made here, that's for damn sure.'

'So what happened?' Reacher asked.

Fowler shrugged.

'What happens to any mining place?' he said. 'It gets worked out, is what. Fifty years ago, people were registering claims in that old county office like there was no tomorrow, and they were disputing them in that old courthouse, and there were saloons and banks and stores up and down the street. Then they started coming up with dirt instead of metal and they moved on, and this is what got left behind.'

Fowler was looking around at the dismal view and Reacher was following his gaze. Then he transferred his eyes upward a couple of degrees and took in the giant mountains rearing on the horizon. They were massive and indifferent, still streaked with snow on the third of July. Mist hung in the passes and floated through the dense conifers. Fowler moved and Reacher followed him up a track launching steeply northwest behind the ruined county office. The guards followed in single file behind. He realized this was the track he'd stumbled along twice in the dark the night before. After a hundred yards they were in the trees. The track wound uphill through the forest. Progress was easier in the filtered green daylight. After a mile of walking they had made maybe a half-mile of straight-line progress and they came out in the clearing the white truck had driven into the previous night. There was a small sentry squad, armed and immaculate, standing at attention in the center of the space. But there was no sign of the white truck. It had been driven away.

'We call this the Bastion,' Fowler said. 'These were the very first acres we bought.'

In the clear daylight, the place looked different. The Bastion was a big, tidy clearing in the brush, nestled in a mountain bowl three hundred feet above the town itself. There was no man-made perimeter. The perimeter had been supplied a million years ago by the great glaciers grinding down from the pole. The north and the west sides were mountainous, rearing straight up to the high peaks. Reacher saw snow again, packed by the wind into the high north-facing gullies. If it was there in July it must be there twelve months of the year.

To the southeast the town was just visible below them through the gaps in the trees where the track had been carved out. Reacher could see the ruined county building and the white courthouse set below it like models. Directly south the mountain slopes fell away into the thick forest. Where there were no trees there were savage ravines. Reacher gazed at them quietly. Fowler pointed.

'Hundred feet deep, some of those,' he said. 'Full of elk and bighorn sheep. And we got black bears roaming. A few of the folk have seen mountain lions on the prowl. You can hear them in the night, when it gets real quiet.'

Reacher nodded and listened to the stunning silence. Tried to figure out how much quieter the nights could be. Fowler turned and pointed here and there.

'This is what we built,' he said. 'So far.'

Reacher nodded again. The clearing held ten buildings. They were all large utilitarian wooden structures, built from plywood sheet and cedar, resting on solid concrete piles. There was an electricity supply into each building from a loop of heavy cable running between them.

'Power comes up from the town,' Fowler said. 'A mile of cable. Running water, too, piped down from a pure mountain lake through plastic tubing, installed by militia labor.'

Reacher saw the hut he'd been locked into most of the night. It was smaller than the others.

'Administration hut,' Fowler said.

One of the huts had a whip antenna on the roof, maybe sixty feet high. Short-wave radio. And Reacher could see a thinner cable, strapped to the heavy power line. It snaked into the same hut, and didn't come out again.

'You guys are on the phone?' he asked. 'Unlisted, right?'

He pointed and Fowler followed his gaze.

'The phone line?' he said. 'Runs up from Yorke with the power cable. But there's no telephone. World government would tap our calls.'

He gestured Reacher to follow him over to the hut with the antenna, where the line terminated. They pushed in together through the narrow door. Fowler spread his hands in a proud little gesture.

'The communications hut,' he said.

The hut was dark and maybe twenty feet by twelve. Two men inside, one crouched over a tape recorder, listening to something on headphones, the other slowly turning the dial of a radio scanner. Both the long sides of the hut had crude wooden desks built into the walls. Reacher glanced up at the gable and saw the telephone wire running in through a hole drilled into the wall. It coiled down and fed a modem. The modem was wired into a pair of glowing desktop computers.

'The National Militia Internet,' Fowler said.

A second wire bypassed the desktops and fed a fax machine. It was whirring away to itself and slowly rolling a curl of paper out.

'The Patriotic Fax Network,' Fowler said.

Reacher nodded and walked closer. The fax machine sat on the counter next to another computer and a large short-wave radio.

'This is the shadow media,' Fowler said. 'We depend on all this equipment for the truth about what's going on in America. You can't get the truth any other way.'

Reacher took a last look around and shrugged.

'I'm hungry,' he said. 'That's the truth about me. No dinner and no breakfast. You got some place with coffee?'

Fowler looked at him and grinned.

'Sure,' he said. 'Mess hall serves all day. What do you think we are? A bunch of savages?'

He dismissed the six guards and gestured again for Reacher to follow him. The mess hall was next to the communications hut. It was about four times the size, twice as long and twice as wide. Outside it had a sturdy chimney on the roof, fabricated from bright galvanized metal. Inside it was full of rough trestle tables in neat lines, simple benches pushed carefully underneath. It smelled of old food and the dusty smell that large communal spaces always have.

There were three women working in there. They were cleaning the tables. They were dressed in olive fatigues, and they all had

578

long, clean hair and plain, unadorned faces, red hands and no
jewelry. They paused when Fowler and Reacher walked in. They
stopped working and stood together, watching. Reacher recognized
one of them from the courtroom. She gave him a cautious nod of
greeting. Fowler stepped forward.

'Our guest missed breakfast,' he said.

The cautious woman nodded again.

'Sure,' she said. 'What can I get you?'

'Anything,' Reacher said. 'As long as it's got coffee with it.'

'Five minutes,' the woman said.

She led the other two away through a door where the kitchen
was bumped out in back. Fowler sat down at a table and Reacher
took the bench opposite.

'Three times a day, this place gets used for meals,' Fowler said.
'The rest of the time, afternoons and evenings mainly, it gets used
as the central meeting place for the community. Beau gets up on
the table and tells the folk what needs doing.'

'Where is Beau right now?' Reacher asked.

'You'll see him before you go,' Fowler said. 'Count on it.'

Reacher nodded slowly and focused through the small window
toward the mountains. The new angle gave him a glimpse of a
farther range, maybe fifty miles distant, hanging there in the
clear air between the earth and the sky. The silence was still
awesome.

'Where is everybody?' he asked.

'Working,' Fowler said. 'Working, and training.'

'Working?' Reacher said. 'Working at what?'

'Building up the southern perimeter,' Fowler said. 'The ravines
are shallow in a couple of places. Tanks could get through. You
know what an abatis is?'

Reacher looked blank. He knew what an abatis was. Any
conscientious West Pointer who could read knew what an abatis
was. But he wasn't about to let Fowler know exactly how much
he knew about anything. So he just looked blank.

'You fell some trees,' Fowler said. 'Every fifth or sixth tree, you
chop it down. You drop it facing away from the enemy. The trees
round here, they're mostly wild pines, the branches face upward,
right? So when they're felled, the branches are facing away from
the enemy. Tank runs into the chopped end of the tree, tries to

push it along. But the branches snag against the trees you left standing. Pretty soon that tank is trying to push two or three trees over. Then four or five. Can't be done. Even a big tank like an Abrams can't do it. Fifteen-hundred horsepower gas turbine on it, sixty-three tons, it's going to stall when it's trying to push all those trees over. Even if they ship the big Russian tanks in against us, it can't be done. That's an abatis, Reacher. Use the power of nature against them. They can't get through those damn trees, that's for sure. Soviets used it against Hitler, Kursk, the Second World War. An old commie trick. Now we're turning it around against them.'

'What about infantry?' Reacher said. 'Tanks won't come alone. They'll have infantry right there with them. They'll just skip ahead and dynamite the trees.'

Fowler grinned.

'They'll try,' he said. 'Then they'll stop trying. We've got machine gun positions fifty yards north of the abatises. We'll cut them to pieces.'

The cautious woman came back out of the kitchen carrying a tray. She put it down on the table in front of Reacher. Eggs, bacon, fried potatoes, beans, all on an enamel plate. A metal pint mug of steaming coffee. Cheap flatware.

'Enjoy,' she said.

'Thank you,' Reacher said.

'I don't get coffee?' Fowler said.

The cautious woman pointed to the back.

'Help yourself,' she said.

Fowler tried a man-to-man look at Reacher and got up. Reacher kept on looking blank. Fowler walked back to the kitchen and ducked in the door. The woman watched him go and laid a hand on Reacher's arm.

'I need to talk to you,' she whispered. 'Find me after lights-out, tonight. I'll meet you outside the kitchen door, OK?'

'Talk to me now,' Reacher whispered back. 'I could be gone by then.'

'You've got to help us,' the woman whispered.

Then Fowler came back out into the hall and the woman's eyes clouded with terror. She straightened up and hurried away.

There were six bolts through each of the long tubes in the bed frame. Two of them secured the mesh panel which held up the mattress. Then there were two at each end, fixing the long tube to the right-angle flanges attached to the legs. She had studied the construction for a long time, and she had spotted an improvement. She could leave one flange bolted to one end. It would stand out like a rigid right-angled hook. Better than separating the flange and then jamming it into the open end. More strength.

But it still left her with six bolts. She would have to take the flange off the leg. An improvement, but not a shortcut. She worked fast. No reason to believe Jackson would fail, but his odds had just worsened. Worsened dramatically.

Next to the mess hall were the dormitories. There were four large buildings, all of them immaculate and deserted. Two of them were designated as barracks for single men and single women. The other two were subdivided by plywood partitions. Families lived there, the adults in pairs in small cubicles behind the partitions, the children in an open dormitory area. Their beds were three-quarter size iron cots, lined up in neat rows. There were half-size footlockers at the ends of the cots. No drawings on the walls, no toys. The only decor was a tourist poster from Washington DC. It was an aerial photograph taken from the north on a sunny spring day, with the White House in the right foreground, the Mall in the middle and the Capitol end-on to the left. It was framed in plastic and the tourist message had been covered over with paper and a new title had been hand-lettered in its place. The new title read: This Is Your Enemy.

'Where are all the kids right now?' Reacher asked.

'In school,' Fowler said. 'Winter, they use the mess hall. Summer, they're out in the woods.'

'What do they learn?' Reacher asked.

Fowler shrugged.

'Stuff they need to know,' he said.

'Who decides what they need to know?' Reacher asked.

'Beau,' Fowler said. 'He decides everything.'

'So what has he decided they need to know?' Reacher asked.

'He studied it pretty carefully,' Fowler said. 'Comes down to the Bible, the Constitution, history, physical training, woodsmanship, hunting, weapons.'

'Who teaches them all that stuff?' Reacher asked.

'The women,' Fowler replied.

'The kids happy here?' Reacher asked.

Fowler shrugged again.

'They're not here to be happy,' he said. 'They're here to survive.'

The next hut was empty, apart from another computer terminal, standing alone on a desk in a corner. Reacher could see a big keyboard lock fastened to it.

'I guess this is our treasury department,' Fowler said. 'All our funds are in the Caymans. We need some, we use that computer to send it anywhere we want.'

'How much you got?' Reacher asked.

Fowler smiled, like a conspirator.

'Shitloads,' he said. 'Twenty million in bearer bonds. Less what we've spent already. But we got plenty left. Don't you worry about us getting short.'

'Stolen?' Reacher asked.

Fowler shook his head and grinned.

'Captured,' he said. 'From the enemy. Twenty million.'

The final two buildings were storehouses. One stood in line with the last dormitory. The other was set some distance away. Fowler led Reacher into the nearer shed. It was crammed with supplies. One wall was lined with huge plastic drums filled with water.

'Beans, bullets and bandages,' Fowler said. 'That's Beau's motto. Sooner or later we're going to face a siege. That's for damn sure. And it's pretty obvious the first thing the government is going to do, right? They're going to fire artillery shells armed with plague germs into the lake which feeds our water system. So we've stockpiled drinking water. Twenty-four thousand gallons. That was the first priority. Then we got canned food, enough for two years. Not enough if we get a lot of people coming in to join us, but it's a good start.'

The storage shed was crammed. One floor-to-ceiling bay was packed with clothing. Familiar olive fatigues, camouflage jackets, boots. All washed and pressed in some army laundry, packed up and sold off by the bale.

'You want some?' Fowler asked.

Reacher was about to move on, but then he glanced down at

what he was wearing. He had been wearing it continuously since Monday morning. Three days solid. It hadn't been the best gear to start with, and it hadn't improved with age.

'OK,' he said.

The biggest sizes were at the bottom of the pile. Fowler heaved and shoved and dragged out a pair of pants, a shirt, a jacket. Reacher ignored the shiny boots. He liked his own shoes better. He stripped and dressed hopping from foot to foot on the bare wooden floor. He did up the shirt buttons and shrugged into the jacket. The fit felt good enough. He didn't look for a mirror. He knew what he looked like in fatigues. He'd spent enough years wearing them.

Next to the door, there were medical supplies ranged on shelves. Trauma kits, plasma, antibiotics, bandages. All efficiently laid out for easy access. Neat piles, with plenty of space between. Borken had clearly rehearsed his people in rushing around and grabbing equipment and administering emergency treatment.

'Beans and bandages,' Reacher said. 'What about the bullets?'

Fowler nodded toward the distant shed.

'That's the armory,' he said. 'I'll show you.'

The armory was bigger than the other storage shed. Huge lock on the door. It held more weaponry than Reacher could remember seeing in a long time. Hundreds of rifles and machine guns in neat rows. The stink of fresh gun oil everywhere. Floor-to-ceiling stacks of ammo boxes. Familiar wooden crates of grenades. Shelves full of handguns. Nothing heavier than an infantryman could carry, but it was still a hell of an impressive sight.

The two bolts securing the mesh base were the easiest. They were smaller than the others. The big bolts holding the frame together took all the strain. The mesh base just rested in there. The bolts holding it down were not structural. They could have been left out altogether and the bed would have worked just the same.

She flaked and scraped the paint back to the bare metal. Heated the bolt heads with the towel. Then she pulled the rubber tip off her crutch and bent the end of the aluminum tube into an oval. She used the strength in her fingers to crush the oval tight over the head of the bolt. Used the handle to turn the whole of the crutch like a giant socket wrench. It slipped off the bolt. She cursed quietly and used one hand to crush it

583

tighter. Turned her hand and the crutch together as a unit. The bolt moved.

There was a beaten earth path leading out north from the ring of wooden buildings. Fowler walked Reacher down it. It led to a shooting range. The range was a long, flat alley painstakingly cleared of trees and brush. It was silent and unoccupied. It was only twenty yards wide, but over a half-mile long. There was matting laid at one end for the shooters to lie on and far in the distance Reacher could see the targets. He set off on a slow stroll toward them. They looked like standard military-issue plywood cutouts of running, crouching soldiers. The design dated right back to the Second World War. The crude screenprinting depicted a German infantryman, with a coal-scuttle helmet and a savage snarl. But as he got closer Reacher could see these particular targets had crude painted additions of their own. They had new badges daubed on the chests in yellow paint. Each new badge had three letters. Four targets had: FBI. Four had: ATF. The targets were staggered backwards over distances ranging from three hundred yards right back to the full eight hundred. The nearer targets were peppered with bullet holes.

'Everybody has to hit the three-hundred-yard targets,' Fowler said. 'It's a requirement of citizenship here.'

Reacher shrugged. Wasn't impressed. Three hundred yards was no kind of a big deal. He kept on strolling down the half-mile. The four-hundred-yard targets were damaged, the five-hundred-yard boards less so. Reacher counted eighteen hits at six hundred yards, seven at seven hundred, and just two at the full eight hundred.

'How old are these boards?' he asked.

Fowler shrugged.

'A month,' he said. 'Maybe two. We're working on it.'

'You better,' Reacher said.

'We don't figure to be shooting at distance,' Fowler replied. 'Beau's guess is the UN forces will come at night. When they think we're resting up. He figures they might succeed in penetrating our perimeter to some degree. Maybe by a half-mile or so. I don't think they will, but Beau's a cautious guy. And he's the one with all the responsibility. So our tactics are going to be nighttime outflanking maneuvers. Encircle the UN penetration in the forest and mow it down with crossfire. Up close and personal, right? That training's going pretty well. We can move fast and quiet in the dark, no lights, no sound, no problem at all.'

Reacher looked at the forest and thought about the wall of ammunition he'd seen. Thought about Borken's boast: impregnable. Thought about the problems an army faces fighting committed guerrillas in difficult terrain. Nothing is ever really impregnable, but the casualties in taking this place were going to be spectacular.

'This morning,' Fowler said. 'I hope you weren't upset.'

Reacher just looked at him.

'About Loder, I mean,' Fowler said.

Reacher shrugged. Thought to himself: it saved me a job of work.

'We need tough discipline,' Fowler said. 'All new nations go through a phase like this. Harsh rules, tough discipline. Beau's made a study of it. Right now, it's very important. But it can be upsetting, I guess.'

'It's you should be upset,' Reacher said. 'You heard of Joseph Stalin?'

Fowler nodded.

'Soviet dictator,' he said.

'Right,' Reacher said. 'He used to do that.'

'Do what?' Fowler asked.

'Eliminate potential rivals,' Reacher said. 'On trumped-up charges.'

Fowler shook his head.

'The charges were fair,' he said. 'Loder made mistakes.'

Reacher shrugged.

'Not really,' he said. 'He did a reasonable job.'

Fowler looked away.

'You'll be next,' Reacher said. 'You should watch your back. Sooner or later, you'll find you've made some kind of a mistake.'

'We go back a long way,' Fowler said. 'Beau and me.'

'So did Beau and Loder, right?' Reacher said. 'Stevie will be OK. He's no threat. Too dumb. But you should think about it. You'll be next.'

Fowler made no reply. Just looked away again. They walked together back down the grassy half-mile. Took another beaten track north. They stepped off the path to allow a long column of children to file past. They were marching in pairs, boys and girls together, with a woman in fatigues at the head of the line and another at the tail. The children were dressed in cut-down military surplus gear and they were carrying tall staffs in their right hands. Their faces were blank and acquiescent. The girls had untrimmed straight hair, and the boys had rough haircuts done with bowls and blunt shears. Reacher stood and watched them pass. They stared straight ahead as they walked. None of them risked a sideways glance at him.

The new path ran uphill through a thin belt of trees and came out on a flat area fifty yards long and fifty yards wide. It had been leveled by hand. Discarded fieldstone had been painted white and laid at intervals around the edge. It was quiet and deserted.

'Our parade ground,' Fowler said sourly.

Reacher nodded and scanned around. To the north and west, the high mountains. To the east, thick virgin forest. South, he could see over the distant town, across belts of trees, to the fractured ravines beyond. A cold wind lifted his new jacket and grabbed at his shirt, and he shivered.

The bigger bolts were much harder. Much more contact area, metal to metal. Much more paint to scrape. Much more force required to turn them. The more force she used, the more the crushed end of the crutch was liable to slip off. She took off her shoe and used it to hammer the end into shape. She bent and folded the soft aluminum around the head of the bolt. Then she clamped it tight with her fingers. Clamped until the slim tendons in her arm stood out like ropes and sweat ran down her face. Then she turned the crutch, holding her breath, waiting to see which would give first, the grip of her fingers or the grip of the bolt.

The wind grabbing at Reacher's shirt also carried some faint sounds to him. He glanced at Fowler and turned to face the western edge of the parade ground. He could hear men moving in the trees. A line of men, bursting out of the forest.

They crashed out of the trees, six men line abreast, automatic rifles at the slope. Camouflage fatigues, beards. The same six guards who had stood in front of the judge's bench that morning. Borken's personal detail. Reacher scanned across the line of faces. The younger guy with the scar was at the left-hand end of the line.

Jackson, the FBI plant. They paused and reset their course. Rushed across the leveled ground toward Reacher. As they approached, Fowler stood back, leaving Reacher looking like an isolated target. Five of the men fanned out into a loose arc. Five rifles aimed at Reacher's chest. The sixth man stepped up in front of Fowler. No salute, but there was a deference in his stance which was more or less the same thing.

'Beau wants this guy back,' the soldier said. 'Something real urgent.'

Fowler nodded.

'Take him,' he said. 'He's beginning to piss me off.'

The rifle muzzles jerked Reacher into a rough formation and the six men hustled him south through the thin belt of trees, moving fast. They passed through the shooting range and followed the beaten earth path back to the Bastion. They turned west and walked past the armory and on into the forest toward the command hut. Reacher lengthened his stride and sped up. Pulled ahead. Let his foot hit a root and went down heavily on the stones. First guy to him was Jackson. Reacher saw the scarred forehead. He grabbed Reacher's arm.

'Mole in Chicago,' Reacher breathed.

'On your feet, asshole,' Jackson shouted back.

'Hide out and run for it tonight,' Reacher whispered. 'Maximum care, OK?'

Jackson glanced at him and replied with a squeeze of his arm. Then he pulled him up and shoved him ahead down the path into the smaller clearing. Beau Borken was framed in his command hut doorway. He was dressed in huge baggy camouflage fatigues, dirty and disheveled. Like he had been working hard. He stared at Reacher as he approached.

'I see we gave you new clothes,' he said.

Reacher nodded.

'So let me apologize for my own appearance,' Borken said. 'Busy day.'

'Fowler told me,' Reacher said. 'You've been building abatises.'

'Abatises?' Borken said. 'Right.'

Then he went quiet. Reacher saw his big white hands, opening and closing.

'Your mission is canceled,' Borken said quietly.

'It is?' Reacher said. 'Why?'

Borken eased his bulk down out of the doorway and stepped close. Reacher's gaze was fixed on his blazing eyes and he never saw the blow coming. Borken hit him in the stomach, a big hard fist on the end of four hundred pounds of bodyweight. Reacher went down like a tree and Borken smashed a foot into his back.

TWENTY-EIGHT

'HIS NAME IS JACKSON,' WEBSTER SAID.
'How long has he been in there?' Milosevic asked.
'Nearly a year,' Webster said.

Eleven o'clock in the morning, Thursday July third, inside Peterson. The section head at Quantico was faxing material over from Andrews down the air force's own secure fax network as fast as the machines could handle it. Milosevic and Brogan were pulling it off the machines and passing it to Webster and McGrath for analysis. On the other side of the table General Johnson and his aide were scanning a map of the northwest corner of Montana.

'You got people undercover in all these groups?' Johnson asked.

Webster shook his head and smiled.

'Not all of them,' he said. 'Too many groups, not enough people. I think we just got lucky.'

'I didn't know we had people in this one,' Brogan said.

Webster was still smiling.

'Lots of things lots of people don't know,' he said. 'Safer that way, right?'

'So what is this Jackson guy saying?' Brogan asked.

'Does he mention Holly?' Johnson asked.

'Does he mention what the hell this is all about?' Milosevic asked.

Webster blew out his cheeks and waved his hand at the stack of curling fax paper. McGrath was busy sifting through it. He was separating the paper into two piles. One pile for routine stuff, the other pile for important intelligence. The routine pile was bigger. The important intelligence was sketchy.

'Analysis, Mack?' Webster said.

McGrath shrugged.

'Up to a point, pretty much normal,' he said.

Johnson stared at him.

'Normal?' he said.

Webster nodded.

'This is normal,' he said. 'We got these militia groups all over the country, which is why we can't cover them all. Too damn many. Our last count was way over four hundred groups, all fifty states. Most of them are just amateur wackos, but some of them we consider pretty serious antigovernment terrorists.'

'This bunch?' Johnson asked.

McGrath looked at him.

'This bunch is totally serious,' he said. 'One hundred people, hidden out in the forest. Very well armed, very well organized, very self-contained. Very well funded, too. Jackson has reported mail fraud, phony bank drafts, a little low-grade counterfeiting. Probably armed robbery as well. The feeling is they stole twenty million bucks in bearer bonds, armored car heist up in the north of California. And, of course, they're selling videos and books and manuals to the rest of the wackos, mail-order. Big boom industry right now. And naturally they decline to pay income tax or license their vehicles or anything else that might cost them anything.'

'Effectively, they control Yorke County,' Webster said.

'How is that possible?' Johnson asked.

'Because nobody else does,' Webster said. 'You ever been up there? I haven't. Jackson says the whole place is abandoned. Everything pulled out, a long time ago. He says there's just a couple dozen citizens still around, spread out over miles of empty territory, bankrupt ranchers, leftover miners, old folk. No effective county government. Borken just eased his way in and took it over.'

590

'He's calling it an experiment,' McGrath said. 'A prototype for a brand-new nation.'

Johnson nodded, blankly.

'But what about Holly?' he said.

Webster stacked the paper and laid his hand on it.

'He doesn't mention her,' he said. 'His last call was Monday, the day she was grabbed up. They were building a prison. We have to assume it was for her.'

'This guy calls in?' Brogan said. 'By radio?'

Webster nodded.

'He's got a transmitter concealed in the forest,' he said. 'He wanders off when he can, calls in. That's why it's all so erratic. He's been averaging one call a week. He's pretty inexperienced and he's been told to be cautious. We assume he's under surveillance. Brave new world up there, that's for damn sure.'

'Can we call him?' Milosevic asked.

'You're kidding,' Webster said. 'We just sit and wait.'

'Who does he report to?' Brogan asked.

'Resident agent at Butte, Montana,' Webster said.

'So what do we do?' Johnson asked.

Webster shrugged. The room went quiet.

'Right now, nothing,' he said. 'We need a position.'

The room stayed quiet and Webster just looked hard at Johnson. It was a look between one government man and another and it said: you know how it is. Johnson stared back for a long time, expressionless. Then his head moved through a fractional nod. Just enough to say: for the moment, I know how it is.

Johnson's aide coughed into the silence.

'We've got missiles north of Yorke,' he said. 'They're moving south right now, on their way back here. Twenty grunts, a hundred Stingers, five trucks. They'll be heading straight through Yorke, any time now. Can we use them?'

Brogan shook his head.

'Against the law,' he said. 'Military can't participate in law enforcement.'

Webster ignored him and glanced at Johnson and waited. They were his men, and Holly was his daughter. The answer was better coming straight from him. There was a silence, and then Johnson shook his head.

'No,' he said. 'We need time to plan.'

The aide spread his hands wide.

'We can plan,' he said. 'We've got radio contact, ground-to-ground. We should go for it, General.'

'Against the law,' Brogan said again.

Johnson made no reply. He was thinking hard. McGrath riffed through the pile of paper and pulled the sheet about the dynamite packing Holly's prison walls. He held it face down on the shiny table. But Johnson shook his head again.

'No,' he said again. 'Twenty men against a hundred? They're not frontline troops. They're not infantry. And their Stingers won't help us. I assume these terrorists don't have an air force, right? No, we wait. Bring the missile unit right back here, fastest. No engagement.'

The aide shrugged and McGrath slipped the dynamite report back into the pile. Webster looked around and slapped both palms lightly on the tabletop.

'I'm going back to DC,' he said. 'Got to get a position.'

Johnson shrugged his shoulders. He knew nothing could start without a trip back to DC to get a position. Webster turned to McGrath.

'You three move up to Butte,' he said. 'Get settled in the office there. If this guy Jackson calls, put him on maximum alert.'

'We can chopper you up there,' the aide said.

'And we need surveillance,' Webster said. 'Can you get the air force to put some camera planes over Yorke?'

Johnson nodded.

'They'll be there,' he said. 'Twenty-four hours a day. We'll give you a live video feed into Butte. A rat farts, you'll see it.'

'No intervention,' Webster said. 'Not yet.'

TWENTY-NINE

S HE HEARD FOOTSTEPS IN THE CORRIDOR AT THE EXACT MOMENT the sixth bolt came free. A light tread. Not Jackson. Not a man treading carefully. A woman, walking normally. The steps halted outside her door. There was a pause. She rested the long tube back on the frame. A key went into the lock. She pulled the mattress back into place. Dragged the blanket over it. Another pause. The door opened.

A woman came into the room. She looked like all of them looked, white, lean, long straight hair, strong plain face, no make-up, no adornment, red hands. She was carrying a tray, with a white cloth mounded up over it. No weapon.

'Lunch,' she said.

Holly nodded. Her heart was pounding. The woman was standing there, the tray in her hands, looking around the room, staring hard at the new pine walls.

'Where do you want this?' she asked. 'On the bed?'

Holly shook her head.

'On the floor,' she said.

The woman bent and placed the tray on the floor.

'Guess you could use a table,' she said. 'And a chair.'

Holly glanced down at the flatware and thought: tools.

'You want me to get them to bring you a chair?' the woman asked.

'No,' Holly said.

'Well, I could use one,' the woman said. 'I've got to wait and watch you eat. Make sure you don't steal the silverware.'

Holly nodded vaguely and circled around the woman. Glanced at the open door. The woman followed her gaze and grinned.

'Nowhere to run,' she said. 'We're a long way from anywhere, and there's some difficult terrain in the way. North, you'd reach Canada in a couple of weeks, if you found enough roots and berries and bugs to eat. West, you'd have to swim the river. East, you'd get lost in the forest or eaten by a bear, and even if you didn't, you're still a month away from Montana. South, we'd shoot you. The border is crawling with guards. You wouldn't stand a chance.'

'The road is blocked?' Holly asked.

The woman smiled.

'We blew the bridge,' she said. 'There is no road, not anymore.'

'When?' Holly asked her. 'We drove in.'

'Just now,' the woman said. 'You didn't hear it? I guess you wouldn't, not with these walls.'

'So how does Reacher get sent out?' Holly asked. 'He's supposed to be carrying some sort of a message.'

The woman smiled again.

'That plan has changed,' she said. 'Mission canceled. He's not going.'

'Why not?' Holly asked.

The woman looked straight at her.

'We found out what happened to Peter Bell,' she said.

Holly went quiet.

'Reacher killed him,' the woman said. 'Suffocated him. In North Dakota. We were just informed. But I expect you know all about it, right?'

Holly stared at her. She thought: Reacher's in big trouble. She saw him, handcuffed and alone somewhere.

'How did you find out?' she asked quietly.

The woman shrugged.

'We have a lot of friends,' she said.

Holly kept on staring at her. She thought: the mole. They know we were in North Dakota. Takes a map and a ruler to figure out

594

where we are now. She saw computer keyboards clicking and Jackson's name scrolling up on a dozen screens.

'What's going to happen to Reacher?' she asked.

'A life for a life,' the woman said. 'That's the rule here. Same for your friend Reacher as for anybody else.'

'But what's going to happen to him?' Holly asked again.

The woman laughed.

'Doesn't take much imagination,' she said. 'Or maybe it does. I don't expect it's going to be anything real simple.'

Holly shook her head.

'It was self-defense,' she said. 'The guy was trying to rape me.'

The woman looked at her, scornfully.

'So how is that self-defense?' she said. 'Wasn't trying to rape him, was he? And you were probably asking for it, anyhow.'

'What?' Holly said.

'Shaking your tail at him?' the woman said. 'We know all about smart little city bitches like you. Poor old Peter never stood a chance.'

Holly just stared at her. Then she glanced at the door.

'Where is Reacher now?' she asked.

'No idea,' the woman said. 'Chained to a tree somewhere, I guess.'

Then she grinned.

'But I know where he's going,' she said. 'The parade ground. That's where they usually do that sort of stuff. We're all ordered up there to watch the fun.'

Holly stared at her. Then she swallowed. Then she nodded.

'Will you help me with this bed?' she asked. 'Something wrong with it.'

The woman paused. Then she followed her over.

'What's wrong with it?' she asked.

Holly pulled the blanket back and heaved the mattress onto the floor.

'The bolts seem a little loose,' she said.

'Where?' the woman said.

'Here,' Holly said.

She used both hands on the long tube. Whipped it upward and spun and smashed it like a blunt spear into the side of the woman's head. The flange hit her like a metal fist. Skin tore and a neat rectangle of bone punched deep into her brain and she bounced off the mattress and was dead before she hit the floor. Holly stepped carefully over the tray of lunch and limped calmly toward the open door.

THIRTY

HARLAND WEBSTER GOT BACK TO THE HOOVER BUILDING FROM Colorado at three o'clock Thursday afternoon, East Coast time. He went straight to his office suite and checked his messages. Then he buzzed his secretary.

'Car,' he said.

He went down in his private elevator to the garage and met his driver. They walked over to the limousine and got in.

'White House,' Webster said.

'You seeing the president, sir?' the driver asked, surprised.

Webster scowled forward at the back of the guy's head. He wasn't seeing the president. He didn't see the president very often. He didn't need reminding of that, especially not by a damn driver sounding all surprised that there even was such a possibility.

'Attorney general,' he said. 'White House is where she is right now.'

His driver nodded silently. Cursed himself for opening his big mouth. Drove on smoothly and unobtrusively. The distance between the Hoover Building and the White House was exactly sixteen hundred yards. Less than a mile. Not even far enough to click over the little number in the speedometer on the limousine's dash. It would have been quicker to walk. And cheaper. Firing up the cold V8 and hauling all that bulletproof plating sixteen hundred yards really ate up the gas. But the director couldn't walk anywhere. Theory was he'd get assassinated. Fact was there were probably about eight people in the city who would recognize him. Just another DC guy in a gray suit and a quiet tie. Anonymous. Another reason old Webster was never in the best of tempers, his driver thought.

Webster knew the attorney general pretty well. She was his boss but his familiarity with her did not come from their face-to-face meetings. It came instead from the background checks the Bureau had run prior to her confirmation. Webster probably knew more about her than anybody else on earth did. Her parents and friends and ex-colleagues all knew their own separate perspectives. Webster had put all of those together and he knew the whole picture. Her Bureau file took up as much disk space as a short novel. Nothing at all in the file made him dislike her. She had been a lawyer, faintly radical at the start of her career, built up a decent practice, grabbed a judgeship, never annoyed the law-enforcement community, without ever becoming a rabid foaming-at-the-mouth pain in the ass. An ideal appointment, sailed through her confirmation with no problem at all. Since then she had proved to be a good boss and a great ally. Her name was Ruth Rosen and the only problem Webster had with her was that she was twelve years younger than him, very good looking, and a whole lot more famous than he was.

His appointment was for four o'clock. He found Rosen alone in a small room, two floors and eight Secret Service agents away from the Oval Office. She greeted him with a strained smile and an urgent inclination of her elegant head.

'Holly?' she asked.

He nodded. He gave her the spread, top to bottom. She listened hard and ended up pale, with her lips clamped tight.

'We totally sure this is where she is?' she asked.

He nodded again.

'Sure as we can be,' he said.

'OK,' she said. 'Wait there, will you?'

She left the small room. Webster waited. Ten minutes, then twenty, then a half-hour. He paced. He gazed out of the window. He opened the door and glanced out into the corridor. A secret serviceman glanced back at him. Took a pace forward. Webster shook his head in answer to the question the guy hadn't asked and closed the door again. Just sat down and waited.

Ruth Rosen was gone an hour. She came back in and closed the door. Then she just stood there, a yard inside the small room, pale, breathing hard, some kind of shock on her face. She said nothing. Just let it dawn on him that there was some kind of a big problem happening.

'What?' he asked.

'I'm out of the loop on this,' she said.

'What?' he asked again.

'They took me out of the loop,' she said. 'My reactions were wrong. Dexter is handling it from here.'

'Dexter?' he repeated. Dexter was the president's White House chief of staff. A political fixer from the old school. As hard as a nail, and half as sentimental. But he was the main reason the president was sitting there in the Oval Office with a big majority of the popular vote.

'I'm very sorry, Harland,' Ruth Rosen said. 'He'll be here in a minute.'

He nodded sourly and she went back out the door and left him to wait again.

The relationship between the rest of the FBI and the Field Office in Butte, Montana, is similar to the relationship between Moscow and Siberia, proverbially speaking. It's a standard Bureau joke. Screw up, the joke goes, and you'll be working out of Butte tomorrow. Like some kind of an internal exile. Like KGB foul-ups were supposedly sent out to write parking tickets in Siberia.

But on that Thursday July third, the Field Office in Butte felt like the center of the universe for McGrath and Milosevic and Brogan. It felt like the most desirable posting in the world. None of the three had ever been there before. Not on business, not on vacation. None of them would have ever considered going there. But now they were peering out of the air force helicopter like kids on their way to the Magic Kingdom. They were looking at the landscape below and swiveling their gaze northwest toward where they knew Yorke County was hiding under the distant hazy mist.

The resident agent at Butte was a competent Bureau veteran still reeling after a personal call from Harland Webster direct from the Hoover Building. His instructions were to drive the three Chicago agents to his office, brief them on the way, get them installed, rent them a couple of jeeps, and then get the hell out and stay the hell out until further notice. So he was waiting at the Silver Bow County Airport when the dirty black air force chopper clattered in. He piled the agents into his government Buick and blasted back north to town.

'Distances are big around here,' he said to McGrath. 'Don't ever forget that. We're still two hundred forty miles shy of Yorke. On our roads, that's four hours, absolute minimum. Me, I'd get some mobile units and move up a lot closer. Basing yourselves down here won't help you much, not if things start to turn bad up there.'

McGrath nodded.

'You hear from Jackson again?' he asked.

'Not since Monday,' the resident agent said. 'The dynamite thing.'

'Next time he calls, he speaks to me, OK?' McGrath said.

The Butte guy nodded. Fished one-handed in his pocket while he drove. Pulled out a small radio receiver. McGrath took it from him. Put it into his own pocket.

'Be my guest,' the Butte guy said. 'I'm on vacation. Webster's orders. But don't hold your breath. Jackson doesn't call often. He's very cautious.'

The Field Office was just a single room, second floor of a two-floor municipal building. A desk, two chairs, a computer, a big map of Montana on the wall, a lot of filing space, and a ringing telephone. McGrath answered it. He listened and grunted. Hung up and waited for the resident agent to take the hint.

'OK, I'm gone,' the old guy said. 'Silver Bow Jeep will bring you a couple of vehicles over. Anything else you guys need?'

'Privacy,' Brogan said.

The old guy nodded and glanced around his office. Then he was gone.

'Air force has put a couple of spy planes up there,' McGrath said. 'Satellite gear is coming in by road. The general and his aide are coming here. Looks like they're going to be our guests for the duration. Can't really argue with that, right?'

Milosevic was studying the map on the wall.

600

'Wouldn't want to argue with that,' he said. 'We're going to need some favors. You guys ever seen a worse-looking place?'

McGrath and Brogan joined him in front of the map. Milosevic's finger was planted on Yorke. Ferocious green and brown terrain boiled all around it.

'Four thousand square miles,' Milosevic said. 'One road and one track.'

'They chose a good spot,' Brogan said.

'I spoke with the president,' Dexter said.

He sat back and paused. Webster stared at him. What the hell else would he have been doing? Pruning the Rose Garden? Dexter was staring back. He was a small guy, burned up, dark, twisted, the way a person gets to look after spending every minute of every day figuring every possible angle.

'And?' Webster said.

'There are sixty-six million gun-owners in this country,' Dexter said.

'So?' Webster asked.

'Our analysts think they all share certain basic sympathies,' Dexter said.

'What analysts?' Webster said. 'What sympathies?'

'There was a poll,' Dexter said. 'Did we send you a copy? One adult in five would be willing to take up arms against the government, if strictly necessary.'

'So?' Webster asked again.

'There was another poll,' Dexter said. 'A simple question, to be answered intuitively, from the gut. Who's in the right, the government or the militias?'

'And?' Webster said.

'Twelve million Americans sided with the militias,' Dexter said.

Webster stared at him. Waited for the message.

'So,' Dexter said. 'Somewhere between twelve and sixty-six million voters.'

'What about them?' Webster asked.

'And where are they?' Dexter asked back. 'You won't find many of them in DC or New York or Boston or LA. It's a skewed sample. Some places they're a tiny minority. They look like weirdos. But

601

other places they're a majority. Other places they're absolutely normal, Harland.'

'So?' he said.

'Some places they control counties,' Dexter said. 'Even states.'

Webster stared at him.

'God's sake, Dexter, this isn't politics,' he said. 'This is Holly.'

Dexter paused and glanced around the small White House room. It was painted a subtle off-white. It had been painted and repainted that same subtle color every few years, while presidents came and went. He smiled a connoisseur's smile.

'Unfortunately, everything's politics,' he said.

'This is Holly,' Webster said again.

Dexter shook his head. Just a slight movement.

'This is emotion,' he said. 'Think about innocent little emotional words, like patriot, resistance, crush, underground, struggle, oppression, individual, distrust, rebel, revolt, revolution, rights. There's a certain majesty to those words, don't you think? In an American context?'

Webster shook his head doggedly.

'Nothing majestic about kidnaping women,' he said. 'Nothing majestic about illegal weapons, illegal armies, stolen dynamite. This isn't politics.'

Dexter shook his head again. The same slight movement.

'Things have a way of becoming politics,' he said. 'Think about Ruby Ridge. Think about Waco, Harland. That wasn't politics, right? But it became politics pretty damn soon. We hurt ourselves with maybe sixty-six million voters there. And we were real dumb about it. Big reactions are what these people want. They figure that harsh reprisals will upset people, bring more people into their fold. And we gave them big reactions. We fueled their fire. We made it look like big government was just about itching to crush the little guy.'

The room went silent.

'The polls say we need a better approach,' Dexter said. 'And we're trying to find one. We're trying real hard. So how would it look if the White House stopped trying just because it happens to be Holly who's involved? And right now? The fourth of July weekend? Don't you understand anything? Think about it, Harland. Think about the reaction. Think about words like vindictive, self-interested, revenge, personal, words like that,

Harland. Think about what words like those are going to do to our poll numbers.'

Webster stared at him. The off-white walls crushed in on him.

'This is about Holly, for God's sake,' he said. 'This is not about poll numbers. And what about the general? Has the president said all this to him?'

Dexter shook his head.

'I've said it all to him,' he said. 'Personally. A dozen times. He's been calling every hour, on the hour.'

Webster thought: now the president won't even take Johnson's calls anymore. Dexter has really fixed him.

'And?' he asked.

Dexter shrugged.

'I think he understands the principle,' he said. 'But, naturally, his judgment is kind of colored right now. He's not a happy man.'

Webster lapsed into silence. Started thinking hard. He was a smart enough bureaucrat to know if you can't beat them, you join them. You force yourself to think like they think.

'But busting her out could do you good,' he said. 'A lot of good. It would look tough, decisive, loyal, no-nonsense. Could be advantageous. In the polls.'

Dexter nodded.

'I totally agree with you,' he said. 'But it's a gamble, right? A real big gamble. A quick victory is good, a foul-up is a disaster. A big gamble, with big poll numbers at stake. And right now, I'm doubting if you can get the quick victory. Right now, you're half-cocked. So right now my money would be on the foul-up.'

Webster stared at him.

'Hey, no offense, Harland,' Dexter said. 'I'm paid to think like this, right?'

'So what the hell are you saying here?' Webster asked him. 'I need to move the hostage rescue team into place right now.'

'No,' Dexter said.

'No?' Webster repeated incredulously.

Dexter shook his head.

'Permission denied,' he said. 'For the time being.'

Webster just stared at him.

'I need a position,' he said.

603

The room stayed silent. Then Dexter spoke to a spot on the off-white wall, a yard to the left of Webster's chair.

'You remain in personal command of the situation,' he said. 'Holiday weekend starts tomorrow. Come talk to me Monday. If there's still a problem.'

'There's a problem now,' Webster said. 'And I'm talking to you now.'

Dexter shook his head again.

'No, you're not,' he said. 'We didn't meet today and I didn't speak with the president today. We didn't know anything about it today. Tell us all about it on Monday, Harland, if there's still a problem.'

Webster just sat there. He was a smart enough guy, but right then he couldn't figure if he was being handed the deal of a lifetime or a suicide pill.

Johnson and his aide arrived in Butte an hour later. They came in the same way, air force helicopter from Peterson up to the Silver Bow County Airport. Milosevic took an air-to-ground call as they were on approach and went out to meet them in a two-year-old Grand Cherokee supplied by the local dealership. Nobody spoke on the short ride back to town. Milosevic just drove and the two military men bent over charts and maps from a large leather case the aide was carrying. They passed them back and forth and nodded, as if further comment was unnecessary.

The upstairs room in the municipal building was suddenly crowded. Five men, two chairs. The only window faced southeast over the street. The wrong direction. The five men were instinctively glancing at the blank wall opposite. Through that wall was Holly, two hundred and forty miles away.

'We're going to have to move up there,' General Johnson said.

His aide nodded.

'No good staying here,' he said.

McGrath had made a decision. He had promised himself he wouldn't fight turf wars with these guys. His agent was Johnson's daughter. He understood the old guy's feelings. He wasn't going to squander time and energy proving who was boss. And he needed the old guy's help.

'We need to share facilities,' he said. 'Just for the time being.'

There was a short silence. The general nodded slowly. He knew enough about Washington to decode those five words with a fair degree of accuracy.

'I don't have many facilities available,' he said in turn. 'It's the holiday weekend. Exactly seventy-five per cent of the US army is on leave.'

Silence. McGrath's turn to do the decoding and the slow nodding.

'No authorization to cancel leave?' he asked.

The general shook his head.

'I just spoke with Dexter,' he said. 'And Dexter just spoke with the president. Feeling was this thing is on hold until Monday.'

The crowded room went silent. The guy's daughter was in trouble, and the White House fixer was playing politics.

'Webster got the same story,' McGrath said. 'Can't even bring the hostage rescue team up here yet. Time being, we're on our own, the three of us.'

The general nodded to McGrath. It was a personal gesture, individual to individual, and it said: we've leveled with each other, and we both know what humiliation that cost us, and we both know we appreciate it.

'But there's no harm in being prepared,' the general said. 'Like the little guy suspects, the military is comfortable with secret maneuvers. I'm calling in a few private favors that Mr Dexter need never know about.'

The silence in the room eased. McGrath looked a question at him.

'There's a mobile command post already on its way,' the general said.

He took a large chart from his aide and spread it out on the desk.

'We're going to rendezvous right here,' he said.

He had his finger on a spot northwest of the last habitation in Montana short of Yorke. It was a wide curve on the road leading into the county, about six miles shy of the bridge over the ravine.

'The satellite trucks are heading straight there,' he said. 'I figure we move in, set up the command post, and seal off the road behind us.'

McGrath stood still, looking down at the map. He knew that

605

to agree was to hand over total control to the military. He knew that to disagree was to play petty games with his agent and this man's daughter. Then he saw that the general's finger was resting a half-inch south of a much better location. A little farther north, the road narrowed dramatically. It straightened to give a clear view north and south. The terrain tightened. A better site for a roadblock. A better site for a command post. He was amazed that the general hadn't spotted it. Then he was flooded with gratitude. The general had spotted it. But he was leaving room for McGrath to point it out. He was leaving room for give-and-take. He didn't want total control.

'I would prefer this place,' McGrath said.

He tapped the northerly location with a pencil. The general pretended to study it. His aide pretended to be impressed.

'Good thinking,' the general said. 'We'll revise the rendezvous.'

McGrath smiled. He knew damn well the trucks were already heading for that exact spot. Probably already there. The general grinned back. The ritual dance was completed.

'What can the spy planes show us?' Brogan asked.

'Everything,' the general's aide said. 'Wait until you see the pictures. The cameras on those babies are unbelievable.'

'I don't like it,' McGrath said. 'It's going to make them nervous.'

The aide shook his head.

'They won't even know they're there,' he said. 'We're using two of them, flying straight lines, east to west and west to east. They're thirty-seven thousand feet up. Nobody on the ground is even going to be aware of them.'

'That's seven miles up,' Brogan said. 'How can they see anything from that sort of height?'

'Good cameras,' the aide said. 'Seven miles is nothing. They'll show you a cigarette pack lying on the sidewalk from seven miles. The whole thing is automatic. The guys up there hit a button and the camera tracks whatever it's supposed to track. Just keeps pointing at the spot on the ground you chose, transmitting high-quality video by satellite, then you turn around and come back, and the camera swivels around and does it all again.'

'Undetectable?' McGrath asked.

'They look like airliners,' the aide said. 'You look up and you see a tiny little vapor trail and you think it's TWA on the way somewhere. You don't think it's the air force checking whether you polished your shoes this morning, right?'

'Seven miles, you'll see the hairs on their heads,' Johnson said. 'What do you think we spent all those defense dollars on? Crop dusters?'

McGrath nodded. He felt naked. Time being, he had nothing to offer except a couple of rental jeeps, two years old, waiting at the sidewalk.

'We're getting a profile on this Borken guy,' he said. 'Shrinks at Quantico are working it up now.'

'We found Jack Reacher's old CO,' Johnson said. 'He's doing desk duty in the Pentagon. He'll join us, give us the spread.'

McGrath nodded.

'Forewarned is forearmed,' he said.

The telephone rang. Johnson's aide picked it up. He was the nearest.

'When are we leaving?' Brogan asked.

McGrath noticed he had asked Johnson direct.

'Right now, I guess,' Johnson said. 'The air force will fly us up there. Saves six hours on the road, right?'

The aide hung up the phone. He looked like he'd been kicked in the gut.

'The missile unit,' he said. 'We lost radio contact, north of Yorke.'

THIRTY-ONE

HOLLY PAUSED IN THE CORRIDOR. SMILED. THE WOMAN HAD LEFT her weapon propped against the wall outside the door. That had been the delay. She had used the key, put the tray on the floor, unslung her weapon, propped it against the wall and picked up the tray again before nudging open the door.

She swapped the iron tube for the gun. Not a weapon she had used before. Not one she wanted to use now. It was a tiny submachine gun. An Ingram MAC 10. Obsolete military issue. Obsolete for a reason. Holly's class at Quantico had laughed about it. They called it the phone booth gun. It was so inaccurate you had to be in a phone booth with your guy to be sure of hitting him. A grim joke. And it fired way too quickly. A thousand rounds per minute. One touch on the trigger and the magazine was empty.

But it was a better weapon than part of an old iron bed frame. She checked the magazine. It was full, thirty shells. The chamber was clean. She clicked the trigger and watched the mechanism move. The gun worked as well as it was ever going to. She smacked the magazine back into position. Straightened the canvas strap and slung it tight over her shoulder. Clicked the cocking handle to the fire position and closed her hand around the grip. Took a firm hold on her crutch and eased to the top of the stairs.

She smelled the first sentry before she saw him. He was moving upwind toward her, smoking. The odor of the cigarette and the unwashed uniform drifted down to her and she pulled silently to her right. She looped a wide circle around him and waited. He walked on down the hill and was gone.

The second sentry heard her. She sensed it. Sensed him stopping and listening. She stood still. Thought hard. She didn't want to use the Ingram. It was too inaccurate. She was certain to miss with it. And the noise would be fatal. So she bent down and scratched up two small stones. An old jungle trick she had been told about as a child. She tossed the first stone twenty feet to her left. Waited. Tossed the second thirty feet. She heard the sentry figure something was moving slowly away to the left. Heard him drift in that direction. She drifted right. A wide circle, and onward, up the endless hill.

Fowler shouldered through the small semicircle of onlookers. Stepped up face to face with him. Stared hard at him. Then six guards were coming through the crowd. Five of them had rifles leveled and the sixth had a length of chain in his hand. Fowler stood aside and the five rifles jammed hard into Reacher's gut. He glanced down at them. The safety catches were off and they were all set to automatic fire.

'Time to go,' Fowler said.

He vanished behind the sturdy trunk and Reacher felt the cuffs come off. He leaned forward off the tree and the muzzles tracked back, following the motion. Then the cuffs went back on, with the chain looped into them. Fowler gripped the chain and Reacher was dragged through the Bastion, facing the five guards. They were all walking backward, their rifles leveled a foot from his head. People were lined into a tight cordon. He was dragged between them. The people hissed and muttered at him as he passed. Then they broke ranks and ran ahead of him, up toward the parade ground.

The third sentry caught her. Her knee let her down. She had to scale a high rocky crag, and because of her leg, she had to do it backwards. She sat on the rock like it was a chair and used her good leg and the crutch to push herself upward, a foot at a time. She reached the top and rolled over on her back on the ground, gasping from the effort, and then she squirmed upright and stood, face-to-face with the sentry.

For a split second she was blank with surprise and shock. He wasn't. He had stood at the top of the bluff and watched every inch of her agonizing progress. So he wasn't surprised. But he was slow. An opponent like Holly, he should have been quick. He should have been ready. Her reaction clicked in before he could get started. Basic training took over. It came without thinking. She balled her fist and threw a fast, low uppercut. Caught him square in the groin. He folded forward and down and she wrapped her left arm around his throat and crunched him in the back of his neck with her right forearm. She felt his vertebrae smash and his body go slack. Then she clamped her palms over his ears and twisted his head around savagely, one way and then the other. His spinal cord severed and she turned him and dropped him over the crag. He thumped and crashed his way down over the rocks, dead limbs flailing. Then she cursed and swore bitterly. Because she should have taken his rifle. It was worth a dozen Ingrams. But there was no way she was going to climb all the way down to get it. Climbing back up again would delay her too long.

The parade ground was full of people. All standing in neat ranks. Reacher guessed there were maybe a hundred people there. Men and women. All in uniform. All armed. Their weapons formed a formidable array of firepower. Each person had either a fully automatic rifle or a machine gun slung over their left shoulder. Each person had an automatic pistol on their belt. They all had ammunition pouches and grenades hung regulation style from loops on their webbing. Many of them had smeared night-camouflage on their faces.

Their uniforms were adapted from US army surplus. Camouflage jackets, camouflage pants, jungle boots, forage caps. Same stuff as Reacher had seen piled up in the storehouse. But each uniform had additions. Each jacket had an immaculate shoulder flash, woven in maroon silk, spelling out Montana Militia in an elegant curve. Each jacket had the wearer's name stenciled onto olive tape and sewn above the breast pocket. Some of the men had single chromium stars punched through the fabric on the breast pocket. Some kind of rank.

Beau Borken was standing on an upturned wooden crate, west edge of the leveled area, his back to the forest, his massive bulk looming over his troops. He saw Fowler and Reacher and the guards arriving through the trees.

'Attention!' he called.

There was a shuffling as the hundred militia members snapped into position. Reacher caught a smell of canvas on the breeze. The smell of a hundred army-surplus uniforms. Borken waved a bloated arm and Fowler used the chain to drag Reacher up toward the front of the gathering. The guards seized his arms and shoulders and he was turned and maneuvered so he was left standing next to the box, suddenly isolated, facing the crowd.

'We all know why we're here,' Borken called out to them.

She had no idea how far she had come. It felt like miles. Hundreds of feet uphill. But she was still deep in the woods. The main track was still forty yards south on her left. She felt the minutes ticking away and her panic rising. She gripped the crutch and moved on northwest again, as fast as she dared.

Then she saw a building ahead of her. A wooden hut, visible through the trees. The undergrowth petered out into stony shale. She crept to the edge of the wood and stopped. Listened hard over the roar of her breathing. Heard nothing. She gripped the crutch and raised the Ingram tight against the strap. Limped across the shale to the corner of the hut. Looked out and around.

It was the clearing where they had arrived the night before. A wide circular space. Stony. Ringed with huts. Deserted. Quiet. The absolute silence of a recently abandoned place. She came out from behind the hut and limped to the center of the clearing, pirouetting on her crutch, jabbing the Ingram in a wide circle, covering the trees on the perimeter. Nothing. Nobody there.

She saw two paths, one running west, a wider track running north. She swung north and headed back into the cover of the trees. She forgot all about trying to stay quiet and raced north as fast as she could move.

'We all know why we're here,' Borken called out again.

The orderly crowd shuffled, and a wave of whispering rose to the trees. Reacher scanned the faces. He saw Stevie in the front rank. A chromium star through his breast pocket. Little Stevie was an officer. Next to Stevie he saw Joseph Ray. Then he realized Jackson was not there. No scarred forehead. He double-checked. Scanned everywhere. No sign of him anywhere on the parade ground. He clamped his teeth to stop a smile. Jackson was hiding out. Holly might still make it.

She saw him. She stared out of the forest over a hundred heads and saw him standing next to Borken. His arms were cuffed behind him. He was scanning the crowd. Nothing in his face. She heard Borken say: we all know why we're here. She thought: yes, I know why I'm here. I know exactly why I'm here. She looked left and right. A hundred people, rifles, machine guns, pistols, grenades. Borken on the box with his arms raised. Reacher, helpless beside him. She stood in the trees, heart thumping, staring. Then she took a deep breath. Set the Ingram to the single-shot position and fired into the air. Burst out of the trees. Fired again. And again. Three shots into the air. Three bullets gone, twenty-seven left in the magazine. She clicked the Ingram back to full auto and moved into the crowd, parting it in front of her with slow menacing sweeps of her gun hand.

She was one woman moving slowly through a crowd of a hundred people. They parted warily around her then, as she passed them by, they unslung their weapons and cocked them and leveled them at her back. A wave of loud mechanical noises trailed behind her like a slow tide. By the time she reached the front rank, she had a hundred loaded weapons trained on her from behind.

'Don't shoot her!' Borken screamed. 'That's an order! Nobody fire!'

He jumped down off the box. Panic in his face. He raised his arms out wide and danced desperately around her, shielding her body with his huge bulk. Nobody fired. She limped away from him and turned to face the crowd.

'Hell are you doing?' Borken screamed at her. 'You think you can shoot a hundred people with that little popgun?'

Holly shook her head.

'No,' she said quietly.

Then she reversed the Ingram and held it to her chest.

'But I can shoot myself,' she said.

THIRTY-TWO

THE CROWD WAS SILENT. THEIR BREATHING WAS SWALLOWED UP by the awesome mountain silence. Everybody was staring at Holly. She was holding the Ingram reversed, the muzzle jammed into a spot above her heart. Thumb backward on the trigger, tensed. Borken's bloated face was greased with panic. His huge frame was shaking and trembling. He was hopping around next to his upturned box, staring wide-eyed at her. She was looking back at him, calmly.

'I'm a hostage, right?' she said to him. 'Important to them, important to you, because of who I am. All kinds of importance to all kinds of people. You expect them to do stuff to keep me alive. So now it's your turn. Let's talk about what stuff you're prepared to do to keep me alive.'

Borken saw her glance at Reacher.

'You don't understand,' he screamed at her. Wild urgency in his voice. 'I'm not going to kill this guy. This guy stays alive. The situation has changed.'

'Changed how?' she asked, calmly.

'I'm commuting his sentence,' Borken said. Still panic in his voice. 'That's why we're here. I was just going to announce it. We know who he is. We just found out. We were just informed.

He was in the army. Major Jack Reacher. He's a hero. He won the Silver Star.'

'So?' Holly asked.

'He saved a bunch of Marines,' Borken said urgently. 'In Beirut. Ordinary fighting men. He pulled them out of a burning bunker. Marines will never attack us while he's here. Never. So I'm going to use him as another hostage. He's good insurance, against the damn Marines. I need him.'

She stared at him. Reacher stared at him.

'His sentence is commuted,' Borken said again. 'Five years on punishment detail. That's all. Nothing else. No question about it. I need him alive.'

He stared at her with a salesman's beam like the problem was solved. She stared back and forth between him and Reacher. Reacher was watching the crowd. The crowd was angry. The circus had left town before the performance. Reacher felt like they had all taken a step toward him. They were testing Borken's power over them. Holly glanced at him, fear in her eyes. Nodded to him. An imperceptible movement of her head. She would be safe, she was saying, whatever happened. Her identity protected her like an invisible magic cloak. Reacher nodded back. Without turning around, he judged the distance to the trees behind him. Maybe twenty feet. Shove Fowler at the front rank, drag the chain, sprint like hell, he might be in the trees before anybody could aim a weapon. Twenty feet, standing start, using the momentum of shouldering Fowler away to help him, maybe four or five strides, maybe three seconds, maybe four. In the trees, he would stand a chance against the bullets. He imagined them smacking into the trunks either side of him as he ran and dodged. A forest is a fugitive's best friend. It takes a lot of luck to hit a guy running through trees. He shifted his weight and felt his hamstrings tighten. Felt the flood of adrenalin. Fight or flight. But then Borken flung his arms wide again. Held them out like an angel's wings and used the awesome power of his eyes on his people.

'I have made my decision,' he called. 'Do you understand?'

There was a long pause. It went on for seconds. Then a hundred heads snapped back.

'Yes, sir!' a hundred voices yelled.

'Do you understand?' he called again.

A hundred heads snapped back again.

'Yes, sir!' a hundred voices yelled.

'Five years on punishment detail,' Borken called. 'But only if he can prove who he is. We are informed this man is the only non-Marine in history to win the Marine Sniper competition. We are told this man can put six bullets through a silver dollar a thousand yards away. So I'm going to shoot against him. Eight hundred yards. If he wins, he lives. If he loses, he dies. Do you understand?'

A hundred heads snapped back.

'Yes, sir!' a hundred voices yelled.

The rumble from the crowd started up again. This time they sounded interested. Reacher smiled inwardly. Smart move, he thought. They wanted a spectacle, Borken was giving them one. Fowler breathed out and pulled a key from his pocket. Ducked around and unlocked the handcuffs. The chain fell to the floor. Reacher breathed out and rubbed his wrists.

Then Fowler stepped over to Holly in the press of people. Stepped right in front of her. She paused for a long moment and glanced at Borken. He nodded.

'You have my word,' he said, with as much dignity as he could recover.

She glanced at Reacher. He shrugged and nodded. She nodded back and looked down at the Ingram. Clicked the safety on and looped the strap off her shoulder. Grinned and dropped the gun to the floor. Fowler bent at her feet and scooped it up. Borken raised his arms for quiet.

'To the rifle range,' he called out. 'Orderly fashion. Dismiss.'

Holly limped over and walked next to Reacher.

'You won the Wimbledon?' she asked, quietly.

He nodded.

'So can you win this?' she asked.

He nodded again.

'With my head in a bag,' he said.

'Is that such a good idea?' she asked quietly. 'Guy like this, he's not going to be happy to get beat.'

Reacher shrugged.

'He wants a big performance, he's going to get one,' he said. 'He's

617

all shaken up. You started it. I want to keep it going. Long run, it'll do us good.'

'Well, take care,' she said.

'Watch me,' Reacher said.

Two brand-new targets were placed side by side at the extreme end of the range. Borken's was on the left with ATF daubed across its chest. Reacher's was on the right with FBI over its heart. The rough matting was pulled back to give maximum distance. Reacher figured he was looking at about eight hundred and thirty yards. Fifty yards shy of a full half-mile. A hell of a long way.

The swarm of people had settled into a rough semicircle, behind and beside the matting. The nearer targets were flung into the undergrowth to clear their view. Several people had field glasses. They peered up the range and then their noise faded as one after the other they settled into quiet anticipation.

Fowler made the trip to the armory in the clearing below. He walked back with a rifle in each hand. One for Borken, one for Reacher. Identical guns. The price of a small family car in each hand. They were .50-inch Barrett Model 90s. Nearly four feet long, over twenty-two pounds in weight. Bolt-action repeaters, fired a bullet a full half-inch across. More like an artillery shell than a rifle bullet.

'One magazine each,' Borken said. 'Six shots.'

Reacher took his weapon and laid it on the ground at his feet. Little Stevie marshaled the crowd backwards to clear the matting. Borken checked his rifle and flicked the bipod legs out. Smacked the magazine into place. He set the weapon down gently on the matting.

'I shoot first,' he said.

He dropped to his knees and forced his bulk down behind the rifle. Pulled the stock to him and snuggled it in close. Dragged the bipod legs an inch to the left and swung the butt a fraction to the right. He smacked the bolt in and out and pressed himself close to the ground. Eased his cheek against the stock and put his eye to the scope. Joseph Ray stepped from the edge of the crowd and offered Reacher his field glasses. Reacher nodded silently and took them. Held them ready. Borken's finger tightened against the trigger. He fired the first shot.

The Barrett's huge muzzle brake blasted gas sideways and downward. Dust blasted back up off the matting. The rifle kicked and boomed. The sound crashed through the trees and came back off the mountains, seconds later. A hundred pairs of eyes flicked from Borken to the target. Reacher raised the field glasses and focused eight hundred and thirty yards up the range.

It was a miss. The target was undamaged. Borken peered through the scope and grimaced. He hunkered down again and waited for the dust to clear. Reacher watched him. Borken was just waiting. Steady breathing. Relaxed. Then his finger tightened again. He fired the second shot. The rifle kicked and crashed and the dust blasted upward. Reacher raised the field glasses again. A hit. There was a splintered hole on the target's right shoulder.

There was a murmur from the crowd. Field glasses were passed from hand to hand. The whispers rose and fell. The dust settled. Borken fired again. Too quickly. He was still wriggling. Reacher watched him making the mistake. He didn't bother with the field glasses. He knew that half-inch shell would end up in Idaho.

The crowd whispered. Borken glared through the scope. Reacher watched him do it all wrong. His relaxation was disappearing. His shoulders were tensed. He fired the fourth. Reacher handed the field glasses back to Joseph Ray on the edge of the crowd. He didn't need to look. He knew Borken was going to miss with the rest. In that state he'd have missed at four hundred yards. He'd have missed at two hundred. He'd have missed across a crowded room.

Borken fired the fifth and then the sixth and stood up slowly. He lifted the big rifle and used the scope to check what everybody already knew.

'One hit,' he said.

He lowered the rifle and looked across at Reacher.

'Your shot,' he said. 'Life or death.'

Reacher nodded. Fowler handed him his magazine. Reacher used his thumb to test the spring. He pressed down on the first bullet and felt the smooth return. The bullets were shiny. Polished by hand. Sniper's bullets. He bent and lifted the heavy rifle. Held it vertical and clicked the magazine into place. He didn't smack at it like Borken had done. He pressed it home gently with his palm.

He opened the bipod legs, one at a time. Clicked them against their detents. Glanced up the range and laid the rifle on the matting.

619

Squatted next to it and lay down, all in one fluid motion. He lay like a dead man, arms flung upward around the gun. He wanted to lie like that for a long time. He was tired. Deathly tired. But he stirred and laid his cheek gently against the stock. Snuggled his right shoulder close to the butt. Clamped his left hand over the barrel, fingers under the scope. Eased his right hand toward the trigger. Moved his right eye to the scope. Breathed out.

Firing a sniper rifle over a long distance is a confluence of many things. It starts with chemistry. It depends on mechanical engineering. It involves optics and geophysics and meteorology. Governing everything is human biology.

The chemistry is about explosions. The powder behind the bullet in the shell case has to explode perfectly, predictably, powerfully, instantly. It has to smash the projectile down the barrel at maximum speed. The half-inch bullet in the Barrett chamber weighs a hair over two ounces. One minute it's stationary. A thousandth of a second later it's doing nearly nineteen hundred miles an hour, leaving the barrel behind on its way to the target. That powder has to explode fast, explode completely, and explode hard. Difficult chemistry. Weight for weight, that explosion has got to be the best explosion on the planet.

Then mechanical engineering takes over for a spell. The bullet itself has to be a perfect little artifact. It's got to be as good as any manufactured article has ever been. It has got to be cast better than any jewelry. It must be totally uniform in size and weight. Perfectly round, perfectly streamlined. It has to accept ferocious rotation from the rifling grooves inside the barrel. It has to spin and hiss through the air with absolutely no wobble, no bias.

The barrel has to be tight and straight. No good at all if a previous shot has heated and altered the barrel shape. The barrel has to be a mass of perfect metal, heavy enough to remain inert. Heavy enough to kill the tiny vibrations of the bolt and the trigger and the firing pin. That's why the Barrett Reacher was holding cost as much as a cheap sedan. That's why Reacher's left hand was loosely clamped over the top of the gun. He was damping any residual shock with it.

Optics play a big part. Reacher's right eye was an inch behind a Leupold & Stevens scope. A fine instrument. The target was showing small, behind the fine data lines etched into the glass.

Reacher stared hard at it. Then he eased the stock down and saw the target disappear and the sky swim into view. He breathed out again and stared at the air.

Because geophysics are crucial. Light travels in a straight line. But it's the only thing that does. Bullets don't. Bullets are physical things which obey the laws of nature, like any other physical things. They follow the curvature of the earth. Eight hundred and thirty yards is a significant piece of curvature. The bullet comes out of the barrel and rises above the line of sight, then it passes through it, then it falls below it. In a perfect curve, like the earth.

Except it's not a perfect curve, because the very first millisecond the bullet is gone, gravity is plucking at it like a small insistent hand. The bullet can't ignore it. It's a two-ounce copper-jacketed lead projectile traveling at nearly nineteen hundred miles an hour, but gravity has its way. Not very successfully, at first, but its best ally soon chips in. Friction. From the very first millisecond of its travel, air friction is slowing the bullet down and handing gravity a larger and larger say in its destiny. Friction and gravity work together to haul that bullet down.

So you aim way high. You aim maybe ten feet directly above the target and eight hundred and thirty yards later the curvature of the earth and the pull of its gravity bring that bullet home to where you want it.

Except you don't aim directly above the target. Because that would be to ignore meteorology. Bullets travel through air, and air moves. It's a rare day when the air is still. The air moves one way or another. Left or right, up or down, or any combination. Reacher was watching the leaves on the trees and he could see a slow steady breeze coming out of the north. Dry air, moving slowly right to left across his line of sight. So he was aiming about eight feet to the right and ten feet above where he wanted to put the bullet. He was going to launch that projectile and let nature curve it left and down.

Human biology was all that stood in the way. Snipers are people. People are quivering, shuddering masses of flesh and muscle. The heart is beating away like a giant pump and the lungs are squeezing huge volumes of air in and out. Every nerve and every muscle is trembling with microscopic energy. Nobody is ever still. Even the calmest person is vibrating like crazy. Say there's a yard between the rifle's firing pin and the muzzle. If the muzzle moves a tiny fraction, then eight hundred and thirty yards later the bullet is going to miss by eight hundred and thirty tiny fractions. A multiplying effect. If the shooter's vibration disturbs the muzzle by even a hundredth of an inch, the bullet will be eight-point-three inches off target. About the width of a man's head.

So Reacher's technique was to wait. Just to gaze through the sight until his breathing was regular and his heartbeat was slow. Then to tighten the trigger, finger slowly and wait some more. Then to count the heartbeats. One-and-two-and-three-and-four. Keep on waiting until the rhythm was slow. Then to fire between beats. Right when the vibration was as small as a human being could get it.

He waited. He breathed out, long and slow. His heart beat once. It beat again. He fired. The stock jumped against his shoulder and his view was obliterated by the blast of dust from the matting under the muzzle. The heavy thump of the shot crashed off the mountainsides and came back to him with a wave of whispering from the crowd. He had missed. The running, crouching screenprint with FBI daubed on its chest was undamaged.

He let the dust settle and checked the trees. The wind was steady. He breathed out and let his heartrate drop. He fired again. The big rifle kicked and crashed. The dust flew. The crowd stared and whispered. Another miss.

Two misses. He breathed steadily and fired again. A miss. And again. Another miss. He paused for a long time. Picked up his rhythm again and fired the fifth. He missed the fifth. The crowd was restless. Borken lumbered nearer.

'All on the last shot,' he grinned.

Reacher made no reply. No way could he afford the physical disturbance involved in speaking. The disruption to his breathing, the muscular contraction of his lungs and throat, would be fatal. He waited. His heart beat. And again. He fired the sixth. He missed. He dropped the sight and stared at the plywood target. Undamaged.

Borken was staring at him. Questions in his eyes. Reacher got to his knees and lifted the rifle. Snapped the empty magazine out. Pushed the bolt home. Traced a finger along the neat engraving on the side of the stock. Folded the bipod legs. Laid the warm gun neatly on the matting. He stood up and shrugged. Borken stared at him. Glanced at Fowler. Fowler glanced back, puzzled. They had watched a man shooting for his life, and they had watched him miss every shot.

'You knew the rules,' Borken said quietly.

Reacher stood still. Ignored him. Gazed up at the blue sky. A pair of vapor trails were crawling across it, like tiny chalk lines far overhead in the stratosphere.

'Wait, sir,' Joseph Ray called loudly.

He came forward out of the crowd. Bristling with urgency. Self-important. Things to say. He was one of the few men in the Bastion with any actual military service behind him and he prided himself on seeing things that other people missed. He thought it gave him an edge. Made him useful in special ways.

He looked hard at the matting and lay himself down exactly where Reacher had lain. Glanced down the range to the targets. Closed one eye and stared through half his field glasses like a telescope. Focused on the screenprint of the running man. Moved his line of sight a fraction and focused just beyond the hunch of the target's shoulder. Stared into the distance and nodded to himself.

'Come on,' he said.

He got to his feet and started jogging down the range. Fowler went with him. Eight hundred and thirty yards later Ray passed the target without a second glance. Carried on jogging. Fowler followed. Fifty yards. A hundred. Ray dropped to his knees and stared backward. Aligned himself with the target and the matting, way back in the far distance. Turned and pointed forward, using his whole arm and finger like a rifle barrel. Stood up again and walked fifty more yards to a particular tree.

It was an orphan silver birch. A straggly wild survivor, forcing its way up alongside the tall pines. Its trunk was contorted as it fought for light and air, one way and then the next. It was narrow, not more than seven or eight inches across. Six feet from the ground, it had six bullet holes in it. Big fresh half-inch holes. Three of them were in a perfect straight vertical line maybe seven inches high. The other three were curled in a loose curve to the right, running from the top hole out and back to the middle hole and out and back again to the bottom hole. Joseph Ray stared hard at them. Then he realized what they were. He grinned. The six holes made a perfect capital B, right there on the white bark. The letter covered an area of maybe seven inches by five. About the dimensions of a fat man's face.

Fowler shouldered past Ray and turned and leaned on the trunk. Stood and pressed the back of his head against the ragged holes. Raised his field glasses and looked back down the range toward the matting. He figured he was more than a hundred and fifty yards behind the target. The target had been more than eight hundred yards from the matting. He did the math in his head.

'A thousand yards,' he breathed.

Fowler and Joseph Ray paced it out together on the way back to Borken. Ray kept his stride long, just about exactly a yard. Fowler counted. Nine hundred and ninety strides, nine hundred and ninety yards. Borken knelt on the matting and used Ray's field glasses. He closed one eye and stared across the distance. He could barely even see the white tree. Reacher watched him try to keep the surprise out of his face. Thought to himself: you wanted a big performance, you got one. You like it, fat boy?

'OK,' Borken said. 'So let's see how damn smart you're going to act now.'

The five guards that had been six when Jackson was with them formed up in a line. They moved forward and took up position around Reacher and Holly. The crowd started filing away, quietly. Their feet crunched and slid on the stony ground. Then that sound was gone and the rifle range was quiet.

Fowler stooped and picked up the guns. He hefted one in each hand and walked away through the trees. The five guards unslung their weapons with the loud sound of palms slapping on wood and metal.

'OK,' Borken said again. 'Punishment detail.'

He turned to Holly.

'You too,' he said. 'You're not too damn valuable for that. You can help him. He's got a task to perform for me.'

The guards stepped forward and marched Reacher and Holly behind Borken, slowly down through the trees to the Bastion and on along the beaten-earth track to the command-hut clearing. They halted there. Two of the guards peeled off and walked to the stores. They were back within five minutes with their weapons shouldered. The first guard was carrying a long-handled shovel in his left hand and a crowbar in his right. The second was carrying two olive fatigue shirts. Borken took them from him and turned to face Reacher and Holly.

'Take your shirts off,' he said. 'Put these on.'

Holly stared at him.

'Why?' she said.

Borken smiled.

'All part of the game,' he said. 'You're not back by nightfall, we turn the dogs loose. They need your old shirts for the scent.'

Holly shook her head.

'I'm not undressing,' she said.

Borken looked at her and nodded.

'We'll turn our backs,' he said. 'But you only get one chance. You don't do it, these boys will do it for you, OK?'

He gave the command and the five guards fanned out in a loose arc, facing the trees. Borken waited for Reacher to turn away and then swiveled on his heels and stared up in the air.

'OK,' he said. 'Get on with it.'

The men heard unbuttoning sounds and the rasp of cotton. They heard the old shirt fall to the ground and the new one slipping on. They heard fingernails clicking against buttons.

'Done,' Holly muttered.

Reacher took off his jacket and his shirt and shivered in the mountain breeze. He took the new shirt from Borken and shrugged it on. Slung the jacket over his shoulder. Borken nodded and the guard handed Reacher the shovel and the crowbar. Borken pointed into the forest.

'Walk due west a hundred yards,' he said. 'Then north another hundred. You'll know what to do when you get there.'

Holly looked at Reacher. He looked back and nodded. They strolled together into the trees, heading west.

Thirty yards into the woods, as soon as they were out of sight, Holly stopped. She planted her crutch and waited for Reacher to turn and rejoin her.

'Borken,' she said. 'I know who he is. I've seen his name in our files. They tagged him for a robbery, northern California somewhere. Twenty million dollars in bearer bonds. Armored car driver was killed. Sacramento office investigated, but they couldn't make it stick.'

Reacher nodded.

'He did it,' he said. 'That's for damn sure. Fowler admitted it. Says they've got twenty million in the Caymans. Captured from the enemy.'

Holly grimaced.

'It explains the mole in Chicago,' she said. 'Borken can afford a pretty handsome bribe with twenty million bucks in the bank, right?'

Reacher nodded again, slowly.

'Anybody you know would take a bribe?' he asked.

She shrugged.

'They all bitch about the salary,' she said.

He shook his head.

'No,' he said. 'Think of somebody who doesn't bitch about it. Whoever's got Borken's bearer bonds behind him isn't worried about money anymore.'

She shrugged again.

'Some of them don't grumble,' she said. 'Some of them just put up with it. Like me, for instance. But I guess I'm different.'

He looked at her. Walked on.

'You're different,' he repeated. 'That's for damn sure.'

He said it vaguely, thinking about it. They walked on for ten yards. He was walking slower than his normal pace and she was limping at his side. He was lost in thought. He was hearing Borken's high voice claiming: she's more than his daughter. He was hearing her own exasperated voice asking: why the hell does everybody assume everything that ever happens to me is because of who my damn father is? Then he stopped walking again and looked straight at her.

'Who are you, Holly?' he asked.

'You know who I am,' she said.

He shook his head again.

'No, I don't,' he said. 'At first I thought you were just some woman. Then you were some woman called Holly Johnson. Then you were an FBI agent. Then you were General Johnson's daughter. Then Borken told me you're even more than that. She's more than his daughter, he said. That stunt you pulled, he was shitting himself. You're some kind of a triple-A gold-plated hostage, Holly. So who the hell else are you?'

She looked at him. Sighed.

'Long story,' she said. 'Started twenty-eight years ago. My father was made a White House Fellow. Seconded to Washington. They used to do that, with the fast-track guys. He got friendly with another guy. Political analyst, aiming to be a Congressman. My mother was pregnant with me, his wife was pregnant, he asked my parents to be godparents, my father asked them to be godparents. So this other guy stood up at my christening.'

'And?' Reacher said.

'The guy got into a career,' Holly said. 'He's still in Washington. You probably voted for him. He's the president.'

Reacher walked on in a daze. Kept glancing at Holly, gamely matching him stride for stride. A hundred yards west of the punishment hut, there was an outcrop of rock, bare of trees. Reacher and Holly turned there and walked north, into the breeze.

'Where are we going?' Holly said. Her voice had an edge of worry.

Reacher stopped suddenly. He knew where they were going. The answer was on the breeze. He went cold. His skin crawled. He stared down at the implements in his hands like he'd never seen such things before.

'You stay here,' he said.

She shook her head.

'No,' she said. 'I'm coming with you, wherever it is.'

'Please, Holly,' he said. 'Stay here, will you?'

She looked surprised by his voice, but she carried on shaking her head.

'I'm coming with you,' she said again.

He gave her a bleak look and they walked on north. He forced himself onward, toward it. Fifty yards. Each step required a conscious effort of will. Sixty yards. He wanted to turn and run. Just run and never stop. Hurl himself across the wild river and get the hell out. Seventy yards. He stopped.

'Stay here, Holly,' he said again. 'Please.'

'Why?' she asked.

'You don't need to see this,' he said, miserably.

She shook her head again and walked on. He caught her up. They smelled it long before they saw it. Faint, sweet, unforgettable. One of

627

the most common and one of the most terrible smells in mankind's long and awful history. The smell of fresh human blood. Twenty paces after they smelled it, they heard it. The insane buzzing of a million flies.

Jackson was crucified between two young pines. His hands had been dragged apart and nailed to the trees through the palms and wrists. He had been forced up onto his toes and his feet had been nailed flat against the base of the trunks. He was naked and he had been mutilated. He had taken several minutes to die. Reacher was clear on that.

He was immobile, staring at the crawling mass of blue shiny flies. Holly had dropped her crutch and her face was white. Ghastly staring white. She fell to her knees and retched. Spun herself away from the dreadful sight and fell forward on her face. Her hands clawed blindly in the forest dirt. She bucked and screamed into the buzzing forest silence. Screamed and cried.

Reacher watched the flies. His eyes were expressionless. His face was impassive. Just a tiny muscle jumping at the corner of his jaw gave anything away. He stood still for several minutes. Holly went silent, on the forest floor beside him. He dropped the crowbar. Slung his jacket over a low branch. Stepped over directly in front of the body and started digging.

He dug with a quiet fury. He smashed the shovel into the earth as hard as he could. He chopped through tree roots with single savage blows. When he hit rocks, he heaved them out and hurled them into a pile. Holly sat up and watched him. She watched the blazing eyes in his impassive face and the bulging muscles in his arms. She followed the relentless rhythm of the shovel. She said nothing.

The work was making him hot. The flies were checking him out. They left Jackson's body and buzzed around his head. He ignored them. Just strained and gasped his way six feet down into the earth. Then he propped the shovel against a tree. Wiped his face on his sleeve. Didn't speak. Took the crowbar and stepped close to the corpse. Batted away the flies. Levered the nails out of the left hand. Jackson's body flopped sideways. The left arm pointed grotesquely down into the pit. The flies rose in an angry cloud. Reacher walked around to the right hand. Pried the nails out. The body flopped forward into the hole. He extracted the nails from the feet. The body tumbled free into the grave. The air was dark with flies and loud with their sound. Reacher slid down into the hole and straightened the corpse out. Crossed the arms over the chest.

He climbed back out. Without pausing he picked up the shovel and started filling the hole. He worked relentlessly. The flies disappeared. He worked on. There was too much dirt. It mounded up high when he had finished, like graves always do. He pounded the mound into a neat shape and dropped the shovel. Bent and picked up the rocks he'd cleared. Used them to shore up the sides of the mound. Placed the biggest one on top, like some kind of a headstone.

Then he stood there, panting like a wild man, streaked with dirt and sweat. Holly watched him. Then she spoke for the first time in an hour.

'Should we say a prayer?' she asked.

Reacher shook his head.

'Way too late for that,' he said quietly.

'You OK?' she asked.

'Who's the mole?' he asked in turn.

'I don't know,' she said.

'Well, think about it, will you?' he said, angrily.

She glared up at him.

'Don't you think I have been?' she said. 'What the hell else do you think I was doing for the last hour?'

'So who the hell is it?' he asked. Still angry.

She paused. Went quiet again.

'Could be anybody,' she said. 'There are a hundred agents in Chicago.'

She was sitting on the forest floor, small, miserable, defeated. She had trusted her people. She had told him that. She had been full of naive confidence. I trust my people, she had said. He felt a wave of tenderness for her. It crashed over him. Not pity, not concern, just an agonizing tenderness for a good person whose bright new world was suddenly dirty and falling apart. He stared at her, hoping she would see it. She stared back, eyes full of tears. He held out his hands. She took them. He lifted her to her feet and held her. He lifted her off the ground and crushed her close. Her breasts were against his pounding chest. Her tears were against his neck.

Then her hands were behind his head, pulling him close. She

629

squirmed her face up and kissed him. She kissed him angrily and hungrily on the mouth. Her arms were locking around his neck. He felt her wild breathing. He knelt and laid her gently on the soft earth. Her hands burrowed at his shirt buttons. His at hers.

They made love naked on the forest floor, urgently, passionately, greedily, as if they were defying death itself. Then they lay panting and spent in each other's arms, gazing up at the sunlight spearing down through the leaves.

He stroked her hair and felt her breathing slow down. He held her silently for a long time, watching the dust motes dancing in the sunbeams over her head.

'Who knew your movements on Monday?' he asked softly.

She thought about it. Made no reply.

'And which of them didn't know about Jackson then?' he asked.

No reply.

'And which of them isn't short of money?' he asked.

No reply.

'And which of them is recent?' he asked. 'Which of them could have come close enough to Beau Borken somewhere to get bought off? Sometime in the past? Maybe investigating the robbery thing in California?'

She shuddered in his arms.

'Four questions, Holly,' he said. 'Who fits?'

She ran through all the possibilities. Like a process of elimination. An algorithm. She boiled the hundred names down. The first question eliminated most of them. The second question eliminated a few more. The third question eliminated a handful. It was the fourth question which proved decisive. She shuddered again.

'Only two possibilities,' she said.

THIRTY-THREE

MILOSEVIC AND BROGAN WERE STRAPPED SIDE BY SIDE IN THE rear of the air force chopper. McGrath and Johnson and the general's aide were crushed into the middle row of seats. The aircrew were shoulder to shoulder in the front. They lifted off from Silver Bow and clattered away northwest over the town of Butte, nose down, low altitude, looking for maximum airspeed. The helicopter was an old Bell, rebuilt with a new engine, and it was pushing a hundred and twenty miles an hour, which made for a lot of noise inside. Consequently McGrath and Johnson were screaming into their radio mikes to make themselves understood.

McGrath was patched through to the Hoover Building. He was trying to talk to Harland Webster. He had one hand cupped over the mike and the other was clamping the earphone to his head. He was talking about the missile unit. He didn't know if Webster was hearing him. He just repeated his message over and over, as loud as he could. Then he flicked the switch and tore off the headset. Tossed it forward to the co-pilot.

Johnson was talking to Peterson. Radio contact had not been restored. He limited himself to requesting an update by secure landline direct to the mobile command post in two hours' time. He failed to decipher the reply. He pulled off his headset and looked a question at McGrath. McGrath shrugged back at him. The helicopter clattered onward.

Harland Webster heard the shrieking din cut off. He hung up his phone in the sudden silence of his office. Leaned forward and buzzed through to his secretary.

'Car,' he said.

He walked through to the elevator and rode down to the garage. Walked over to his limousine. His driver was holding the door for him.

'White House,' he said.

This time, the driver said nothing. Just fired it up and eased out of the garage. Bumped up and out into the afternoon rush. Crawled the sixteen hundred yards west in silence. Webster was directed to the same off-white room. He waited there a quarter-hour. Dexter came in. Clearly not pleased to see him back so soon.

'They've stolen some missiles,' Webster said.

'What missiles?' Dexter asked.

He described everything as well as he could. Dexter listened. Didn't nod. Didn't ask any questions. Didn't react. Just told him to wait in the room.

The air force Bell put down on a gravel turnout two hundred yards south of where the road into Yorke narrowed and straightened into the hills. The pilot kept the engine turning and the five passengers ducked out and ran bent over until they were out of the fierce downdraft. There were vehicles on the road ahead. A random pattern of military vehicles slewed across the blacktop. One of them was turning slowly in the road. It turned in the narrow space between the rocky walls and straightened as it approached. It slowed and halted fifty yards away. General Johnson stepped out into view. The car moved forward and stopped in front of him. It was a new Chevrolet, sprayed a dull olive green. There were white stenciled letters and figures on the hood and along the sides. An officer slid out. He saluted the general and skipped around to open all the doors. The five men squeezed in and the car turned again and rolled the two hundred yards north to the mess of vehicles.

'The command post is on its way, sir,' the officer said. 'Should be here inside forty minutes. The satellite trucks are an hour behind it. I suggest you wait in the car. It's getting cold outside.'

'Word from the missile unit?' Johnson asked.

The officer shook his head in the gloom.

'No word, sir,' he said.

Webster waited most of an hour. Then the door of the small off-white room cracked open. A secret service agent stood there. Blue suit, curly wire running up out of his collar to his earpiece.

'Please come with me, sir,' the agent said.

Webster stood up and the guy raised his hand and spoke into his cuff. Webster followed him along a quiet corridor and into an elevator. The elevator was small and slow. It took them down to the first floor. They walked along another quiet corridor and paused in front of a white door. The agent knocked once and opened it.

The president was sitting in his chair behind his desk. The chair was rotated away and he had his back to the room. He was staring out through the bulletproof windows at the darkness settling over the garden. Dexter was in an armchair. Neither asked him to sit down. The president didn't turn around. As soon as he heard the door click shut, he started speaking.

'Suppose I was a judge,' he said. 'And suppose you were some cop and you came to me for a warrant?'

Webster could see the president's face reflected in the thick glass. It was just a pink smudge.

'OK, sir, suppose I was?' he said.

'What have you got?' the president asked him. 'And what haven't you got? You don't even know for sure Holly's there at all. You've got an undercover asset in place and he hasn't confirmed it to you. You're guessing, is all. And these missiles? The army has lost radio contact. Could be temporary. Could be any number of reasons for that. Your undercover guy hasn't mentioned them.'

'He could be experiencing difficulties, sir,' Webster said. 'And he's been told to be cautious. He doesn't call in with a running commentary. He's undercover, right? He can't just disappear into the forest any old time he wants to.'

The president nodded. The pink smudge in the glass moved up and down. There was a measure of sympathy there.

'We understand that, Harland,' he said. 'We really do. But we

633

have to assume that with matters of this magnitude, he's going to make a big effort, right? But you've heard nothing. So you're giving us nothing but speculation.'

Webster spread his hands. Spoke directly to the back of the guy's head.

'Sir, this is a big deal,' he said. 'They're arming themselves, they've taken a hostage, they're talking about secession from the Union.'

The president nodded.

'Don't you understand, that's the problem?' he said. 'If this were about three weirdos in a hut in the woods with a bomb, we'd send you in there right away. But it isn't. This could lead to the biggest constitutional crisis since 1860.'

'So you agree with me,' Webster said. 'You're taking them seriously.'

The president shook his head. Sadly, like he was upset but not surprised Webster didn't get the point.

'No,' he said. 'We're not taking them seriously. That's what makes this whole thing so damn difficult. They're a bunch of deluded idiots, seeing plots everywhere, conspiracies, muttering about independence for their scrubby little patch of worthless real estate. But the question is: how should a mature democratic nation react to that? Should it massacre them all, Harland? Is that how a mature nation reacts? Should it unleash deadly force against a few deluded idiot citizens? We spent a generation condemning the Soviets for doing that. Are we going to do the same thing?'

'They're criminals, sir,' Webster said.

'Yes, they are,' the president agreed, patiently. 'They're counterfeiters, they own illegal weapons, they don't pay federal taxes, they foment racial hatred, maybe they even robbed an armored car. But those are details, Harland. The broad picture is they're disgruntled citizens. And how do we respond to that? We encourage disgruntled citizens in Eastern Europe to stand up and declare their nationhood, right? So how do we deal with our own disgruntled citizens, Harland? Declare war on them?'

Webster clamped his jaw. He felt adrift. Like the thick carpets and the quiet paint and the unfamiliar scented air inside the Oval Office were choking him.

'They're criminals,' he said again. It was all he could think of to say.

The president nodded. Still a measure of sympathy.

'Yes, they are,' he agreed again. 'But look at the broad picture, Harland. Look at their main offense. Their main offense is they hate their government. If we deal with them harshly for that, we could face a crisis. Like we said, there are maybe sixty million Americans ready to be tipped over the edge. This administration is very aware of that, Harland. This administration is going to tread very carefully.'

'But what about Holly?' he asked. 'You can't just sacrifice her.'

There was a long silence. The president kept his chair turned away.

'I can't react because of her, either,' he said quietly. 'I can't allow myself to make this personal. Don't you see that? A personal, emotional, angry response would be wrong. It would be a bad mistake. I have to wait and think. I've talked it over with the general. We've talked for hours. Frankly, Harland, he's pissed at me, and, again frankly, I don't blame him. He's just about my oldest friend and he's pissed at me. So don't talk to me about sacrifice, Harland. Because sacrifice is what this office is all about. You put the greater good in front of friendship, in front of all your own interests. You do it all the time. It's what being president means.'

There was another long silence.

'So what are you saying to me, Mr President?' Webster asked.

Another long silence.

'I'm not saying anything to you,' the president said. 'I'm saying you're in personal command of the situation. I'm saying come see Mr Dexter Monday morning, if there's still a problem.'

Nobody waited in the car. Too restless for that. They got out into the chill mountain air and milled aimlessly around. Johnson and his aide strolled north with the driver and looked at the proposed location for the command post. McGrath and Brogan and Milosevic kept themselves apart as a threesome. McGrath smoked, lost in thought. Time to time, he would duck back into the army Chevrolet and use the carphone. He called the Montana State Police, the power company, the phone company, the Forest Service.

Brogan and Milosevic strolled north. They found an armored vehicle. Not a tank, some kind of a personnel carrier. There were the officer who had met them with the car and maybe eight soldiers near it. Big, silent men, pitching tents on the shoulder in the lee of the rocks. Brogan and Milosevic nodded a greeting to them and strolled back south. They rejoined McGrath and waited.

Within forty minutes they all heard the faint roar of heavy diesels far to the south. The noise built and then burst around the curve. There was a small convoy of trucks. Big, boxy vehicles, mounted high on exaggerated drivetrains, big wheels, huge tires, axles grinding around. They roared nearer, moving slow in low gear. The officer from the car ran to meet them. Pointed them up to where he wanted them. They roared slowly past and stopped two abreast in the road where it straightened into the rock cutting.

There were four vehicles. Black and green camouflage, rolls of netting on the flanks, stenciled numbers and big single stars in white. The front two trucks bristled with antennas and small dishes. The rear two were accommodations. Each vehicle had hydraulic jacks at each corner. The drivers lowered the jacks and the weight came up off the tires. The jacks pushed against the camber of the road and leveled the floors. Then the engines cut off and the loud diesel roaring died into the mountain silence.

The four drivers vaulted down. They ran to the rear of their trucks and opened the doors. Reached in and folded down short aluminum ladders. Went up inside and flicked switches. The four interiors lit up with green light. The drivers came back out. Regrouped and saluted the officer.

'All yours, sir,' the point man said.

The officer nodded. Pointed to the Chevy.

'Drive back in that,' he said. 'And forget you were ever here.'

The point man saluted again.

'Understood, sir,' he said.

The four drivers walked to the Chevy. Their boots were loud in the silence. They got in the car and fired it up. Turned in the road and disappeared south.

Back in his office, Webster found the Borken profile on his desk and a visitor waiting for him. Green uniform under a khaki trenchcoat, maybe sixty, sixty-five, iron-gray stubble on part of his head, battered brown leather briefcase under his arm, battered canvas suit carrier on the floor at his feet.

'I understand you need to talk to me,' the guy said. 'I'm General Garber. I was Jack Reacher's CO for a number of years.'

Webster nodded.

'I'm going to Montana,' he said. 'You can talk to me there.'

'We anticipated that,' Garber said. 'If the Bureau can fly us out to Kalispell, the air force will take us on the rest of the way by helicopter.'

Webster nodded again. Buzzed through to his secretary. She was off-duty.

'Shit,' Webster said.

'My driver is waiting,' Garber said. 'He'll take us out to Andrews.'

Webster called ahead from the car and the Bureau Lear was waiting ready. Twenty minutes after leaving the White House Webster was in the air heading west over the center of the city. He wondered if the president could hear the scream of his engines through his thick bulletproof glass.

The air force technicians arrived with the satellite trucks an hour after the command post had been installed. There were two vehicles in their convoy. The first was similar to the command post itself; big, high, boxy, hydraulic jacks at each corner, a short aluminum ladder for access. The second was a long flatbed truck with a big satellite dish mounted high on an articulated mechanism. As soon as it was parked and level, the mechanism kicked in and swung the dish up to find the planes, seven miles up in the darkening sky. It locked on and the delicate electronics settled down to tracking the moving signals. There was a continuous motor sound as the dish moved through a subtle arc, too slowly for the eye to detect. The techs hauled out a cable the thickness of a sapling's trunk from the flatbed and locked it into a port on the side of the closed truck. Then they swarmed up inside and fired up the monitors and the recorders.

McGrath hitched a ride with the soldiers in the armored carrier. They rumbled a mile south and met a waiting Montana State Police cruiser on the road. The State guy conferred with McGrath and opened his trunk. Pulled out a box of red danger flares and an array of temporary road signs. The soldiers jogged south and put a pair of flares either side of a sign reading: Danger, Road Out. They came back north and set up a trio of flares in the center of the blacktop with a sign reading: Bridge Out Ahead. Fifty yards farther north, they blocked the whole width of the road with more flares. They strung Road Closed signs across behind them. When the State guy had slalomed his way back south and disappeared, the soldiers took axes from their vehicle and started felling trees. The armored carrier nudged them over and pushed them across the road, engine roaring, tires squealing. It lined them up in a rough zigzag. A vehicle could get through, but only if it slowed to a dead crawl and threaded its way past. Two soldiers were posted as sentries on the shoulders. The other six rode back north with McGrath.

Johnson was in the command vehicle. He was in radio contact with Peterson. The news was bad. The missile unit had been out of radio contact for more than eight hours. Johnson had a rule of thumb. He had learned it by bitter experience in the jungles of Vietnam. The rule of thumb said: when you've lost radio contact with a unit for more than eight hours, you mark that unit down as a total loss.

Webster and Garber did not talk during the plane ride. That was Webster's choice. He was experienced enough as a bureaucrat to know that whatever he heard from Garber, he'd only have to hear all over again when the full team was finally assembled. So he sat quietly in the noisy jet whine and read the Borken profile from Quantico. Garber was looking questions at him, but he ignored them. Explain it to Garber now, and he'd only have to do it all over again for McGrath and Johnson.

The evening air at Kalispell was cold and gray for the short noisy walk across the apron to the air force Bell. Garber identified himself to the co-pilot, who dropped a short ladder to the tarmac. Garber and Webster scrambled up inside and sat where they were told. The co-pilot signaled with both hands that they should fasten their harnesses and that the ride would take about twenty-five minutes. Webster nodded and listened to the beat of the rotor as it lifted them all into the air.

General Johnson had just finished another long call to the White House when he heard the Bell clattering in. He stood framed in the command-post doorway and watched it put down on the same gravel turnout, two hundred yards south. He saw two figures spill out and crouch away. He saw the chopper lift and yaw and turn south.

He walked down and met them halfway. Nodded to Garber and pulled Webster to one side.

'Anything?' he asked.

Webster shook his head.

'No change,' he said. 'White House is playing safe. You?'

'Nothing,' Johnson said.

Webster nodded. Nothing more to say.

'What we got here?' he asked.

'Far as the White House knows, nothing,' Johnson said. 'We've got two camera planes in the air. Officially, they're on exercises. We've got eight Marines and an armored car. They're on exercises too. Their COs know where they are, but they don't know exactly why, and they're not asking.'

'You sealed the road?' Webster asked.

Johnson nodded.

'We're all on our own up here,' he said.

THIRTY-FOUR

REACHER AND HOLLY SAT ALONE IN THE FOREST, BACKS TO TWO adjacent pines, staring at the mound above Jackson's grave. They sat like that until the afternoon light faded and died. They didn't speak. The forest grew cold. The time for the decision arrived.

'We're going back,' Holly said.

It was a statement, not a question. A lot of resignation in her voice. He made no reply. He was breathing low, staring into space, lost in thought. Reliving in his mind her taste and smell. Her hair and her eyes. Her lips. The feel of her, strong and lithe and urgent underneath him.

'Nightfall,' she said.

'Not just yet,' he said.

'We have to,' she said. 'They'll send the dogs after us.'

He didn't speak again. Just sat there, eyes locked into the distance.

'There's nowhere else to go,' she said.

He nodded slowly and stood up. Stretched and caught his breath as his tired muscles cramped. Helped Holly up and took his jacket down off the tree and shrugged it on. Left the crowbar lying in the dirt next to the shovel.

'We leave tonight,' he said. 'Shit's going to hit the fan tomorrow. Independence Day.'

'Sure, but how?' she asked.

'I don't know yet,' he said.

'Don't take risks on my account,' she said.

'You'd be worth it,' he said.

'Because of who I am?' she asked.

He nodded.

'Because of who you are,' he said. 'Not because of who your father is. Or your damn godfather. And no, I didn't vote for him.'

She stretched up and kissed him on the mouth.

'Take care, Reacher,' she said.

'Just be ready,' he said. 'Maybe midnight.'

She nodded. They walked the hundred yards south to the rocky outcrop. Turned and walked the hundred yards east to the clearing. Came out of the woods straight into a semicircle of five guards waiting for them. Four rifles. Center man was Joseph Ray. He was in charge of the detail, with a Glock 17 in his hand.

'She goes back to her room,' Ray said. 'You go in the punishment hut.'

The guards formed up. Two of them stepped either side of Holly. Her eyes were blazing and they didn't try to take her elbows. Just walked slowly beside her. She turned and glanced back at Reacher.

'See you later, Holly,' Reacher called.

'Don't you bet on that, Ms Johnson,' Joseph Ray said, and laughed.

He escorted Reacher to the door of the punishment hut. Took out a key and unlocked the door. Swung it open. Pushed Reacher through, gun out and ready. Then he pulled the door closed again and relocked it.

The punishment hut was the same size and shape as Borken's command hut. But it was completely empty. Bare walls, no windows, lights meshed with heavy wire. On the floor near one end was a perfect square of yellow paint, maybe twelve inches by twelve. Apart from that the hut was featureless.

'You stand on that square,' Ray said.

Reacher nodded. He was familiar with that procedure. Being forced to stand at attention, hour after hour, never moving, was

641

an effective punishment. He had heard about it, time to time. Once, he'd seen the results. After the first few hours, the pain starts. The back goes, then the agony spreads upward from the shins. By the second or third day, the ankles swell and burst and the thigh bones strike upward and the neck collapses.

'So stand on it,' Ray said.

Reacher stepped to the corner of the hut and bent to the floor. Made a big show of brushing the dust away with his hand. Turned and lowered himself gently so he was sitting comfortably in the angle of the walls. Stretched his legs out and folded his hands behind his head. Crossed his ankles and smiled.

'You got to stand on the square,' Ray said.

Reacher looked at him. He had said: believe me, I know tanks. So he had been a soldier. A grunt, in a motorized unit. Probably a loader, maybe a driver.

'Stand up,' Ray said.

Give a grunt a task, and what's the thing he's most afraid of? Getting chewed out by an officer for failing to do it, that's what.

'Stand up, damn it,' Ray said.

So either he doesn't fail, or if he does, he conceals it. No grunt in the history of the world has ever just gone to his officer and said: I couldn't do it, sir.

'I'm telling you to stand up, Reacher,' Ray said quietly.

If he fails, he keeps it a big secret. Much better that way.

'You want me to stand up?' Reacher asked.

'Yeah, stand up,' Ray said.

Reacher shook his head.

'You're going to have to make me, Joe,' he said.

Ray was thinking about it. It was a reasonably slow thought process. Its progress was visible in his body language. First the Glock came up. Then it went back down. Shooting at the prisoner was its own admission of failure. It was the same thing as saying: I couldn't make him do it, sir. Then he glanced at his hands. Glanced across at Reacher. Glanced away. Unarmed combat was rejected. He stood there in a fog of indecision.

'Where did you serve?' Reacher asked him.

Ray shrugged.

'Here and there,' he said.

'Like where and where?' Reacher asked.

'I was in Germany twice,' Ray said. 'And I was in Desert Storm.'

'Driver?' Reacher asked.

'Loader,' Ray answered.

Reacher nodded.

'You boys did a good job,' he said. 'I was in Desert Storm. I saw what you boys did.'

Ray nodded. He took the opening, like Reacher knew he would. If you can't let them beat you, you let them join you. Ray moved casually to his left and sat down on the floor, back against the door, Glock resting against his thigh. He nodded again.

'We whupped them,' he said.

'You sure did,' Reacher said. 'You whupped them real good. So, Germany and the desert. You liked it there?'

'Not much,' Ray said.

'You liked their systems?' Reacher asked.

'What systems?' Ray asked back.

'Their governments,' Reacher said. 'Their laws, their liberties, all that stuff.'

Ray looked mystified.

'Never noticed,' he said. 'Never paid any attention.'

'So how do you know they're better than ours?' Reacher asked.

'Who says they're better?' Ray said.

'You do,' Reacher said. 'Last night you were telling me how bad it is here in America. Got to be better everywhere else, right?'

Ray shook his head.

'I never told you that,' he said.

'So is it or isn't it?' Reacher asked.

'I don't know,' Ray said. 'Probably. Lot of things wrong with America.'

Reacher nodded.

'Lot of things,' he said. 'I agree with you. But I'll tell you something. It's better in America than everyplace else. I know because I've been everyplace else. Everyplace else is worse. A lot worse. Lot of things wrong in America, but plenty more things wrong everyplace else. You guys should think about that.'

Ray looked across through the gloom.

'You think we're wrong?' he asked.

Reacher nodded.

'I know you're wrong,' he said. 'For certain. All that stuff you were telling me is bullshit. All of it. It's not happening.'

'It is happening,' Ray said. 'Beau says so.'

'Think about it, Joe,' Reacher said. 'You were in the service. You saw how it all operated. You think those guys could organize all that stuff and keep it a secret? They ever even give you a pair of boots the right size?'

Ray laughed.

'Not hardly,' he said.

'Right,' Reacher said. 'So if they can't organize your damn boots, how can they organize all this other stuff Beau is talking about? What about these transmitters hidden in all the new cars? You think Detroit can do all that stuff? They'd be recalling them all because they didn't work right. You a gambling man, Joe?'

'Why?' he asked.

'What are the odds?' Reacher said. 'Against they could organize a huge massive conspiracy like that and keep it all a secret for years and years?'

A slow smile spread across Ray's face and Reacher saw that he was losing. Like talking to the wall. Like teaching a chimpanzee to read.

'But they haven't kept it a secret,' Ray said triumphantly. 'We found out about it. I told you, Beau's got the proof. He's got the documents. It's not a secret at all. That's why we're here. Beau's right, no doubt about it. He's a smart guy.'

Reacher closed his eyes and sighed.

'You better hope so,' he said. 'He's going to need to be.'

'He's a smart guy,' Ray said again. 'And he's got staying power. He's putting us all together. There were a dozen groups up here. Their leaders quit and left. All their people came and joined Beau because they trust him. He's a smart guy, Reacher, and he's our only hope left. You won't change anybody's mind about him. You can forget about that. Far as we're concerned we love him, and we trust him to do right.'

'What about Jackson?' Reacher asked. 'You think he did right about that?'

Ray shrugged.

'Jackson was a spy,' he said. 'Shit like that happens. Beau's studied the history. It happened in 1776, right? Redcoats had spies all over.

We hanged them then, just the same. Plenty of old ladies back east got old oak trees in their front yards, famous for being where they strung up the redcoat spies. Some of them charge you a buck and a half just to take a look at them. I know, I went there once.'

'What time is lights-out here?' Reacher asked.

'Ten o'clock,' Ray said. 'Why?'

Reacher paused. Stared at him. Thought back over their conversation. Gazed at his lean, mobile face. Looked into his crazy eyes, burning deep under his brow.

'I got to be someplace else after lights-out,' Reacher said.

Ray laughed again.

'And you think I'm going to let you?' he said.

Reacher nodded.

'If you want to live,' he said.

Ray lifted the pistol off his thigh and pointed it one-handed at Reacher's head.

'I'm the one got the gun here,' he said.

'You wouldn't live to pull the trigger,' Reacher said.

'Trigger's right here,' Ray said. 'You're all the way over there.'

Reacher waved him a listen-up gesture. Leaned forward and spoke quietly.

'I'm not really supposed to tell you this,' he said. 'But we were warned we'd meet a few guys smarter than the average, and we're authorized to explain a couple of things to them, if the operational circumstances make it advisable.'

'What circumstances?' Ray asked. 'What things?'

'You were right,' Reacher said. 'Most of the things you've said are correct. A couple of inaccuracies, but we spread a little disinformation here and there.'

'What are you talking about?' Ray asked.

Reacher lowered his voice to a whisper.

'I'm World Army,' he said. 'Commander of the advance party. I've got five thousand UN troops in the forest. Russians mostly, a few Chinese. We've been watching you on the satellite surveillance. Right now, we've got an X-ray camera on this hut. There's a laser beam pointed at your head. Part of the SDI technology.'

'You're kidding,' Ray said.

Reacher shook his head. Deadly serious.

'You were right about the microchips,' he said. 'Look at this.'

645

He stood up slowly and pulled his shirt up to his chest. Turned slightly so Ray could see the huge scar on his stomach.

'Bigger than the modern ones,' he said. 'The latest ones go in with no mess at all. The ones we put in the babies. But these old ones work just the same. The satellites know where I am at all times, like you said. You start to pull that trigger, the laser blows your head off.'

Ray's eyes were burning. He looked away from Reacher's scar and glanced nervously up at the roof.

'*Suis pas américain,*' Reacher said. '*Suis un soldat français, agent du gouvernement mondial depuis plusieurs années, parti en mission clandestine il y a deux mois. Il faut évaluer l'élément de risque que votre bande représent par ici.*'

He spoke as fast as he could and ended up sounding exactly like an educated Parisian woman. Exactly like he recalled his dead mother sounding. Ray nodded slowly.

'You foreign?' he asked.

'French,' Reacher said. 'We operate international brigades. I said I'm here to check out the degree of risk you people represent to us.'

'I saw you shooting,' Ray said. 'I spotted it. A thousand yards.'

'Guided by satellite,' Reacher said. 'I told you, SDI technology, through the microchip. We can all shoot two miles, perfect score every time.'

'Christ,' Ray said.

'I need to be out in the open at ten o'clock,' Reacher said. 'It's a safety procedure. You got a wife here?'

Ray nodded.

'What about kids?' Reacher asked. 'Any of these kids yours?'

Ray nodded again.

'Sure,' he said. 'Two boys.'

'If I'm not out by ten, they all die,' Reacher said. 'If I get taken prisoner, the whole place gets incinerated. Can't afford for my microchip to get captured. I told them you guys wouldn't understand how it works but my chief said some of you could be smarter than I thought. Looks like my chief was right.'

Ray nodded proudly and Reacher checked his watch.

'It's seven-thirty, right?' he said. 'I'm going to sleep two and a half hours. The satellite will wake me at ten exactly. You wait and see.'

He lay back down on the floor and curled his arm under his head. Set the alarm in his head for two minutes to ten. Said to himself: don't let it fail me tonight.

THIRTY-FIVE

'I REFUSE TO BELIEVE IT,' GENERAL GARBER SAID.

'He's involved,' Webster said in reply. 'That's for damn sure. We got the pictures, clear as day.'

Garber shook his head.

'I was promoted lieutenant forty years ago,' he said. 'Now I'm a three-star general. I've commanded thousands of men. Tens of thousands. Got to know most of them well. And out of all of them, Jack Reacher is the single least likely man to be involved in a thing like this.'

Garber was sitting ramrod-straight at the table in the mobile command post. He had shed his khaki raincoat to reveal an old creased uniform jacket. It was a jacket which bore the accumulated prizes of a lifetime of service. It was studded with badges and ribbons. It was the jacket of a man who had served forty years without ever making a single mistake.

Johnson was watching him carefully. Garber's grizzled old head was still. His eyes were calm. His hands were laid comfortably on the table. His voice was firm, but quiet. Definite, like he was being asked to defend the proposition that the sky was blue and the grass was green.

'Show the general the pictures, Mack,' Webster said.

McGrath nodded and opened his envelope. Slid the four stills over the table to Garber. Garber held each one up in turn, tilted to catch the green light from the overhead. Johnson was watching his eyes. He was waiting for the flicker of doubt, then the flicker of resignation. He saw neither.

'These are open to interpretation,' Garber said.

His voice was still calm. Johnson heard an officer loyally defending a favored subordinate. Webster and McGrath heard a policeman of sorts expressing a doubt. They figured forty years' service had bought the guy the right to be heard.

'Interpretation how?' Webster asked.

'Four isolated moments out of a sequence,' Garber said. 'They could be telling us the wrong story.'

Webster leaned over and pointed at the first still.

'He's grabbing her stuff,' he said. 'Plain as day, General.'

Garber shook his head. There was silence. Just electronic hum throughout the vehicle. Johnson saw a flicker of doubt. But it was in McGrath's eyes, not Garber's. Then Brogan rattled his way up the ladder. Ducked his head into the truck.

'Surveillance tapes, chief,' he said. 'We've been reviewing the stuff the planes got earlier. You should come see it.'

He ducked out again and the four men glanced at each other and got up. Walked the short distance through the cold evening to the satellite truck and up the ladder. Milosevic was in shirt sleeves, bathed in the blue light from a bank of video screens. He shuttled a tape back and pressed play. Four screens lit up with a perfect clear overhead view of a tiny town. The quality of the picture was magnificent. Like a perfect movie picture, except filmed vertically downward, not horizontal.

'Yorke,' Milosevic said. 'The old courthouse, bottom right. Now watch.'

He hit fast wind and watched the counter. Slowed the tape and hit play again.

'This is a mile and a quarter away,' he said. 'The camera tracked northwest. There's a parade ground, and this rifle range.'

The camera had zoomed out for a wide view of the area. There were two clearings with huts to the south and a flat parade ground to the north. In between was a long narrow scar in the undergrowth, maybe a half-mile long and twenty yards wide.

The camera zoomed right out for a moment, to establish the scale, then it tightened in on a crowd at the eastern end of the range. Then it tightened farther to a small knot of people standing on some brown matting. There were four men clearly visible. And one woman. General Johnson gasped and stared at his daughter.

'When was this?' he asked.

'Few hours ago,' Milosevic said. 'She's alive and well.'

He froze the picture and tapped his fingernail four times on the glass.

'Reacher,' he said. 'Stevie Stewart. We figure this one is Odell Fowler. And the fat guy is Beau Borken. Matches his file photo from California.'

Then he hit play again. The camera held steady on the matting, from seven miles up in the sky. Borken pressed his bulk to the floor and lay motionless. Then a silent puff of dust was seen under the muzzle of his rifle.

'They're shooting a little over eight hundred yards,' Milosevic said. 'Some kind of a competition, I guess.'

They watched Borken's five final shots, and then Reacher picked up his rifle.

'That's a Barrett,' Garber said.

Reacher lay motionless and then fired six silent shots, well spaced. The crowd milled around, and eventually Reacher was lost to sight in the trees to the south.

'OK,' Webster said. 'How do you want to interpret that, General Garber?'

Garber shrugged. A dogged expression on his face.

'He's one of them, no doubt about it,' Webster said. 'Did you see his clothes? He was in uniform. Showing off on the range? Would they give him a uniform and a rifle to play with if he wasn't one of their own?'

Johnson spooled the tape back and froze it. Looked at Holly for a long moment. Then he walked out of the trailer. Called over his shoulder to Webster.

'Director, we need to go to work,' he said. 'I want to make a contingency plan well ahead of time. No reason for us not to be ready for this.'

Webster followed him out. Brogan and Milosevic stayed at the video console. McGrath was watching Garber. Garber was staring at the blank screen.

'I still don't believe it,' he said.

He turned and saw McGrath looking at him. Nodded him out of the trailer. The two men walked together into the silence of the night.

'I can't prove it to you,' Garber said. 'But Reacher is on our side. I'll absolutely guarantee that, personally.'

'Doesn't look that way,' McGrath said. 'He's the classic type. Fits our standard profile perfectly. Unemployed ex-military, malcontent, dislocated childhood, probably full of all kinds of grievances.'

Garber shook his head.

'He's none of those things,' he said. 'Except unemployed ex-military. He was a fine officer. Best I ever had. You're making a big mistake.'

McGrath saw the look on Garber's face.

'So you'd trust him?' he asked. 'Personally?'

Garber nodded grimly.

'With my life,' he said. 'I don't know why he's there, but I promise you he's clean, and he's going to do what needs doing, or he's going to die trying.'

Exactly six miles north, Holly was trusting to the same instinct. They had taken her disassembled bed away, and she was lying on the thin mattress on the floorboards. They had taken the soap and the shampoo and the towel from the bathroom as a punishment. They had left the small pool of blood from the dead woman's head untouched. It was there on the floor, a yard from her makeshift bed. She guessed they thought it would upset her. They were wrong. It made her happy. She was happy to watch it dry and blacken. She was thinking about Jackson and staring at the stain like it was a Rorschach blot telling her: you're coming out of the shadow now, Holly.

Webster and Johnson came up with a fairly simple contingency plan. It depended on geography. The exact same geography they assumed had tempted Borken to choose Yorke as the location for his bastion. Like all plans based on geography, it was put together using a map. Like all plans put together using a map, it was only as good as the map was accurate. And like most maps theirs was way out of date.

They were using a large-scale map of Montana. Most of its information was reliable. The main features were correct. The western obstacle was plain to see.

'We assume the river is impassable, right?' Webster said.

'Right,' Johnson agreed. 'The spring melts are going to be in full flow. Nothing we can do there before Monday. When we get some equipment.'

The roads were shown in red like a man had placed his right hand palm-down on the paper. The small towns of Kalispell and Whitefish nestled under the palm. Roads fanned out like the four fingers and the thumb. The index finger ran up through a place called Eureka to the Canadian border. The thumb ran out northwest through Yorke and stopped at the old mines. That thumb was now amputated at the first knuckle.

'They assume you'll come up the road,' Johnson said. 'So you won't. You'll loop east to Eureka and come in through the forest.'

He ran his pencil down the thumb and across the back of the hand. Back up the index finger and stopped it at Eureka. Fifty miles of forest lay between Eureka and Yorke. The forest was represented on the map by a large green stain. Deep and wide. They knew what that green stain meant. They could see what it meant by looking around them. The area was covered in virgin forest. It ran rampant up and down the mountainsides. Most places the vegetation was so dense a man could barely squeeze between the tree trunks. But the green stain to the east of Yorke was a national forest. Owned and operated by the Forest Service. The green stain showed a web of threads running through it. Those threads were Forest Service tracks.

'I can get my people here in four hours,' Webster said. 'The hostage rescue team. On my own initiative, if it comes to it.'

Johnson nodded.

'They can walk right through the woods,' he said. 'Probably drive right through.'

Webster nodded.

'We called the Forest guys,' he said. 'They're bringing us a detailed plan.'

'Perfect,' Johnson said. 'If things turn bad, you call your team in, send them direct to Eureka, we'll all make a little noise on the southern flank, and they muscle in straight through from the east.'

Webster nodded again. The contingency plan was made. Until the National Forests guy came up the short aluminum ladder into the command post. McGrath brought him inside with Milosevic and Brogan. Webster made the introductions and Johnson asked the questions. Straight away the Forest guy started shaking his head.

'Those tracks don't exist,' he said. 'At least, most of them don't.'

Johnson pointed to the map.

'They're right here,' he said.

The Forest guy shrugged. He had a thick book of topographical plans under his arm. He opened it up to the correct page. Laid it over the map. The scale was much larger, but it was obvious the web of threads was a different shape.

'Mapmakers know there are tracks,' the guy said. 'So they just show them any old place.'

'OK,' Johnson said. 'We'll use your maps.'

The Forest guy shook his head.

'These are wrong, too,' he said. 'They might have been right at some stage, but they're wrong now. We spent years closing off most of these tracks. Had to stop the bear hunters getting in. Environmentalists made us do it. We bulldozed tons of dirt into the openings of most of the through tracks. Ripped up a lot of the others. They'll be totally overgrown by now.'

'OK, so which tracks are closed?' Webster asked. He had turned the plan and was studying it.

'We don't know,' the guy said. 'We didn't keep very accurate records. Just sent the bulldozers out. We caught a lot of guys closing the wrong tracks, because they were nearer, or not closing them at all, because that was easier. The whole thing was a mess.'

'So is there any way through?' Johnson asked.

The Forest guy shrugged.

'Maybe,' he said. 'Maybe not. No way of knowing, except to try it. Could take a couple of months. If you do get through, keep a record and let us know, OK?'

Johnson stared at him.

'Let me get this straight,' he said. 'You're the damn Forest Service and you want us to tell you where your own tracks are?'

The guy nodded.

'That's about the size of it,' he said. 'Like I told you, our records are lousy. The way we figured it, who the hell would ever care?'

The general's aide walked him back to the roadblock. There was silence in the command vehicle. McGrath and Brogan and Milosevic studied the map.

'We can't get through, they can't get through,' McGrath said. 'We've got them bottled up. We need to start exploiting that.'

'How?' Webster said.

'Control them,' McGrath said. 'We already control their road. We can control their power and their telephone line, too. The lines more or less follow the road. Separate spurs up out of Kalispell. We should cut the phone line so it terminates right here, in this vehicle. Then they can't communicate with anybody except us. Then we tell them we control their power. Threaten to cut it off if they don't negotiate.'

'You want a negotiation?' Johnson asked.

'I want a stalling tactic,' McGrath said. 'Until the White House loosens up.'

Webster nodded.

'OK, do it,' he said. 'Call the phone company and get the line run in here.'

'I already did,' McGrath said. 'They'll do it first thing in the morning.'

Webster yawned. Checked his watch. Gestured to Milosevic and Brogan.

'We should get a sleeping rota going,' he said. 'You two turn in first. We'll sleep two shifts, call it four hours at a time.'

Milosevic and Brogan nodded. Looked happy enough about it.

'See you later,' McGrath said. 'Sleep tight.'

They left the trailer and closed the door quietly. Johnson was still fiddling with the map. Twisting it and turning it on the table.

'Can't they do the phone thing faster?' he asked. 'Like tonight?'

Webster thought about it and nodded. He knew fifty per cent of any battle is keeping the command structure harmonious.

'Call them again, Mack,' he said. 'Tell them we need it now.'

McGrath called them again. He used the phone at his elbow. Had a short conversation which ended with a chuckle.

'They're sending the emergency linemen,' he said. 'Should be done in a couple of hours. But we'll get an invoice for it. I told them to send it to the Hoover Building. The guy asked me where that was.'

He got up and waited in the doorway. Johnson and Webster stayed at the table. They huddled together over their map. They looked at the southern ravine. It had been formed a million years ago when the earth shattered under the weight of a billion tons of ice. They assumed it was accurately represented on paper.

THIRTY-SIX

REACHER WOKE UP EXACTLY TWO MINUTES BEFORE TEN O'CLOCK. He did it in his normal way, which was to come round quickly, motionless, no change in his breathing. He felt his arm curled under his head and opened his eyes the smallest fraction possible. The other side of the punishment hut, Joseph Ray was still sitting against the door. The Glock was on the floor beside him. He was checking his watch.

Reacher counted off ninety seconds in his head. Ray was glancing between the roof of the hut and his watch. Then he looked across at Reacher. Reacher snapped upright in one fluid movement. Pressed his palm against his ear like he was listening to a secret communication. Ray's eyes were wide. Reacher nodded and stood up.

'OK,' he said. 'Open the door, Joe.'

Ray took out the key from his pocket. Unlocked the door. It swung open.

'You want to take the Glock?' Ray asked.

He held the gun out, butt first. Anxiety in his eyes. Reacher smiled. He had expected nothing less. Ray was dumb, but not that dumb. He had been given two and a half hours to scope it out. This was a final test. If he took the gun, he was bullshitting. He was certain it was unloaded and the clip was in Ray's pocket.

'Don't need it,' Reacher said. 'We've got the whole place covered. I got weapons at my disposal more powerful than a nine-millimeter, believe me, Joe.'

Ray nodded and straightened up.

'Don't forget the laser beams,' Reacher said. 'You step out of this hut, you're a dead man. Nothing I can do about that right now. *Vous comprenez, mon ami?*'

Ray nodded again. Reacher slipped out into the night. Ray swung the door closed. Reacher backtracked silently and waited around the corner of the hut. Knelt down and found a small rock. Hefted it in his hand and waited for Ray to follow him.

He didn't come. Reacher waited eight minutes. Long experience had taught him: if they don't come after six minutes, they aren't coming at all. People think in five-minute segments, because of the way clocks are laid out. They say: I'll wait five minutes. Then, because they're cautious, they add another minute. They think it's smart. Reacher waited the first five, then the extra one, then added two more for the sake of safety. But Ray didn't come. He wasn't going to.

Reacher avoided the clearing. He kept to the trees. He skirted the area in the forest. Ignored the beaten earth paths. He wasn't worried about the dogs. They weren't out. Fowler had talked about mountain lions roaming. Nobody leaves dogs out at night where there are mountain lions on the prowl. That's a sure way of having no dogs left in the morning.

He made a complete circuit of the Bastion, hidden in the trees. The lights were all out and the whole place was still and silent. He waited in the trees behind the mess hall. The kitchen was a square hut, awkwardly connected to the back of the main structure. There were no lights on, but the door was open, and the woman who had served him breakfast was waiting in the shadows. He watched her from the trees. He waited five minutes. Then six. No other movement anywhere. He tossed his small rock onto the path to her left. She jumped at the sound. He called softly. She came out of the shadows. Alone. She walked over to the trees. He took her elbow and pulled her back into the darkness.

'How did you get out of there?' she whispered to him.

657

It was impossible to tell how old she was. Maybe twenty-five, maybe forty-five. She was a handsome woman, lean, long straight hair, but careworn and worried. A flicker of spirit and resilience underneath. She would have been comfortable a hundred years ago, stumbling down the Oregon trail.

'How did you get out?' she whispered again.

'I walked out the door,' Reacher whispered back.

The woman just looked at him blankly.

'You've got to help us,' she whispered.

Then she stopped and wrung her hands and twisted her head left and right, peering into the dark, terrified.

'Help how?' he asked. 'Why?'

'They're all crazy,' the woman said. 'You've got to help us.'

'How?' he asked again.

She just grimaced, arms held wide, like it was obvious, or like she didn't know where to start, or how.

'From the beginning,' he said.

She nodded, twice, swallowing, collecting herself.

'People have disappeared,' she said.

'What people?' he asked. 'How did they disappear?'

'They just disappeared,' she said. 'It's Borken. He's taken over everything. It's a long story. Most of us were up here with other groups, just surviving on our own, with our families, you know? I was with the Northwestern Freemen. Then Borken started coming around, talking about unity. He fought and argued. The other leaders disagreed with his views. Then they just started disappearing. They just left. Borken said they couldn't stand the pace. They just disappeared. So he said we had to join with him. Said we had no choice. Some of us are more or less prisoners here.'

Reacher nodded.

'And now things are happening up at the mines,' she said.

'What things?' he asked her.

'I don't know,' she said. 'Bad things, I guess. We're not allowed to go up there. They're only a mile up the road, but they're off limits. Something was going on there today. They said they were all working in the south, on the border, but when they came back for lunch, they came from the north. I saw them from the kitchen window. They were smiling and laughing.'

'Who?' Reacher asked.

'Borken and the ones he trusts,' she said. 'He's crazy. He says they'll attack us when we declare independence and we have to fight back. Starting tomorrow. We're all scared. We got families, you know? But there's nothing we can do. You oppose him, and you either get banished, or he raves at you until you agree with him. Nobody can stand up to him. He controls us, totally.'

Reacher nodded again. The woman sagged against him. Tears were on her cheeks.

'And we can't win, can we?' she said. 'Not if they attack us. There's only a hundred of us, trained up. We can't beat an army with a hundred people, can we? We're all going to die.'

Her eyes were wide and white and desperate. Reacher shrugged. Shook his head and tried to make his voice sound calm and reassuring.

'It'll be a siege,' he said. 'That's all. A stand-off. They'll negotiate. It's happened before. And it'll be the FBI, not the army. The FBI know how to do this kind of a thing. You'll all be OK. They won't kill you. They won't come here looking to kill anybody. That's just Borken's propaganda.'

'Live free or die,' she said. 'That's what he keeps saying.'

'The FBI will handle it,' he said again. 'Nobody's looking to kill you.'

The woman clamped her lips and screwed her wet eyes shut and shook her head wildly.

'No, Borken will kill us,' she said. 'He'll do it, not them. Live free or die, don't you understand? If they come, he'll kill us all. Or else he'll make us all kill ourselves. Like a mass suicide thing. He'll make us do it, I know he will.'

Reacher just stared at her.

'I heard them talking,' she said. 'Whispering about it all the time, making secret plans. They said women and children would die. They said it was justifiable. They said it was historic and important. They said the circumstances demanded it.'

'You heard them?' Reacher asked. 'When?'

'All the time,' she whispered again. 'They're always making plans. Borken and the ones he trusts. Women and children have to die, they said. They're going to make us kill ourselves. Mass suicide. Our families. Our children. At the mines.

659

I think they're going to make us go in the mines and kill ourselves.'

He stayed in the woods until he was well north of the parade ground. Then he tracked east until he saw the road, running up out of Yorke. It was potholed and rough, gleaming gray in the moonlight. He stayed in the shadow of the trees and followed it north.

The road wound up a mountainside in tight hairpin bends. A sure sign it led to something worthwhile, otherwise the labor consumed in its construction would have been meaningless. After a mile of winding and a thousand feet of elevation, the final curve gave out onto a bowl the size of a deserted stadium. It was part natural, part blasted, hanging there in the belly of the giant peaks. The back walls of the bowl were sheer rock faces. There were semicircular holes blasted into them at intervals. They looked like giant mouseholes. Some of them had been built out with waste rock, to provide sheltered entrances. Two of the entrances had been enlarged into giant stone sheds, roofed with timber.

The bowl was floored with loose shale. There were piles of earth and spoil everywhere. Ragged weeds and saplings were forcing their way through. Reacher could see the rusted remains of rail tracks, starting nowhere and running a few yards. He squatted against a tree, well back in the woods, and watched.

There was nothing happening. The whole place was deserted and silent. Quieter than silent. It had that total absence of sound that gets left behind when a busy place is abandoned. The natural sounds were long gone. The swaying trees cleared, the rushing streams diverted, the rustling vegetation burned off, replaced by clattering machines and shouting men. Then when the men and the machines leave, there is nothing left behind to replace their noise. Reacher strained his ears but heard nothing at all. Silent as the moon.

He stayed in the woods. To approach from the south meant to approach uphill. He skirted around to the west and gained an extra hundred feet of height. Paused and looked down into the bowl from a new perspective.

Still nothing. But there had been something. Some recent activity. The moonlight was showing vehicle tracks in the shale. There was a mess of ruts in and out of one of the stone sheds. A couple of years' worth. The motor pool. There were newer ruts into the other stone shed. The bigger shed. Bigger ruts. Somebody had driven some large vehicles into that shed. Recently.

He scrambled down out of the woods and onto the shale. His shoes on the small flat stones sounded like rifle shots in the silent night. The crunch of his steps came back off the sheer walls like thunder. He felt tiny and exposed, like a man in a bad dream walking naked across a football field. He felt like the surrounding mountains were a huge crowd in the bleachers, staring silently at him. He stopped behind a pile of rock and squatted and listened. The echo of his footsteps crashed and died into silence. He heard nothing. Just a total absence of sound.

He crept noisily to the doors of the smaller shed. Up close, it was a big structure. Probably built to shelter giant machines and pumping engines. The doors were twelve feet high. They were built out of peeled logs, strapped together with iron. They were like the sides of a log house, hinged into a mountainside.

There was no lock. It was hard to imagine how there could have been. No lock Reacher had ever seen could have matched the scale of those doors. He put his back against the right-hand door and levered the left-hand one open a foot. The iron hinge moved easily on a thick film of grease. He slid sideways through the gap and stepped inside.

It was pitch dark. He could see nothing. He stood and waited for his night vision to build. But it never came. Your eyes can open wider and wider, wide as they can get, but if there's no light at all, you won't see anything. He could smell a strong smell of damp and decay. He could hear the silence vanishing backward into the mountain, like there was a long chamber or tunnel in front of him. He moved inward, hands held out in front of him like a blind man.

He found a vehicle. His shin hit the front fender before his hands hit the hood. It was high. A truck or a pickup. Civilian. Smooth gloss automotive spray. Not matt military paint. He trailed his fingers round the edge of the hood. Down the side. A pickup. He felt his way around the back and up the other side. Felt for the driver's door. Unlocked. He opened it. The courtesy light blazed like a million-candlepower searchlight. Bizarre shadows were thrown all around. He was in a giant cavern. It had no back. It opened right into the hillside. The rock roof sloped down and became a narrow excavated seam, running far out of sight.

He reached into the pickup cab and switched the headlights on. The beams were reflected off the rock. There were a dozen vehicles parked in neat lines. Old sedans and pickups. Surplus jeeps with crude camouflage. And the white Ford Econoline with the holes in the roof. It looked sad and abandoned after its epic journey from Chicago. Worn out and low on its springs. There were workbenches with old tools hanging above them. Cans of paint and drums of oil. Bald tires in piles and rusted tanks of welding gas.

He searched the nearest vehicles. Keys in all of them. A flashlight in the glove box of the third sedan he checked. He took it. Stepped back to the pickup and killed its headlights. Walked back to the big wooden doors and out into the night.

He waited and listened. Nothing. He swung the motor-pool door closed and set off for the larger shed. A hundred yards across the noisy shale. The larger shed had the same type of log doors. Even bigger. And they were locked. The lock was the crudest thing he had ever seen. It was an old warped log laid across two iron brackets and chained into place. The chains were fastened with two big padlocks. Reacher ignored them. No need to fiddle with the padlocks. He could see that the warp in the old log would let him in.

He forced the doors apart where they met at the bottom. The curve in the log in the brackets let them gap by about a foot. He put his arms inside, then his head, then his shoulders. He scrabbled with his feet and pushed his way through. Stood up inside and flicked the flashlight on.

It was another giant cavern. Same darkness. Same strong smell of damp and decay. Same sloping roof running backward to a low seam. The same hush, like all the sound was sucking back deep into the mountain. The same purpose. A vehicle store. But these vehicles were all identical. Five of them. Five current-issue US army trucks. Marked with the white stencils of the army air artillery. Not new trucks, but well-maintained. Neat canvas siding at the rear.

Reacher walked around to the back of the first truck. Stepped up onto the tow-hitch and looked over the tailgate. Empty. It had slatted wooden benches running forward along each side. A troop carrier. Reacher couldn't begin to count the miles he'd traveled on benches like those, swaying, staring at the steel floor, waiting to get where he was going.

The steel floor was stained. At odds with the clean exterior. There were black stains on the floor. Some kind of a thick liquid, dried into pools. Reacher stared at them. Couldn't begin to count the number of stains like that he'd seen. He jumped down and ran to the second vehicle. Stepped up and leaned in with the flashlight.

There were no benches in the rear of the second vehicle. Instead, there were racks bolted to both sides. Precisely constructed racks, welded up out of angle-iron and fitted with steel clips and thick rubber pads to hold their delicate cargo. The left hand rack held five missile launchers. Slim steel tubes, six feet long, dull black metal, with a large box of electronics and an open sight and a pistol grip bolted to the forward end. Five of them, precisely parallel, neatly aligned.

The right hand rack held twenty-five Stinger missiles. Inches apart, side by side in their rubber mountings, control surfaces folded back, ready to load. Dull alloy, with batch numbers stenciled on, and a broad band of garish orange paint wrapping the fuel section.

He ran to the other three trucks. Each was the same. Five launchers, twenty-five missiles. A total of twenty launchers and one hundred missiles. The entire ordnance requirement of a whole air artillery mobile unit. A unit which deployed twenty men. He walked back to the first truck and stared in at the blood on the floor. Then he heard the rats. At first he thought it was footsteps outside on the shale. He snapped the flashlight off. Then he realized the sounds were nearer, and behind him. There were rats scuffling at the rear of the cavern. He lit the flashlight up again and jogged into the cave and found the twenty men.

They were heaped into a large pile of corpses just before the roof got too low for a man to stand. Twenty dead soldiers. A hell of a mess. They had all been shot in the back. Reacher could see that. They had been standing together in a group somewhere, and they had been mown down with heavy machine gun fire from the rear. He bent and grunted and turned a couple of them over. Not the toughest guys he'd ever seen. Docile, reservist types, deployed to a lonely base deep inside friendly territory. Ambushed and murdered for their weapons.

But how? He knew how. An old ground-to-air unit, nearing obsolescence, stationed in the far north of Montana. A leftover from Cold War paranoia. Certainly due for decommissioning. Probably already in the process of decommissioning. Probably on its way south to Peterson in Colorado. Final orders probably transmitted in clear by radio. He remembered the radio scanner back in the communications hut. The operator beside it, patiently turning the dial. He imagined the recall order being accidentally intercepted, the operator running to Borken, Borken's bloated face lighting up with an opportunistic smile. Then some hasty planning and a brutal ambush somewhere in the hills. Twenty men shot down, thrown into their own truck, piled into this cavern. He stood and gazed at the appalling sight. Then he snapped the flashlight off again.

Because he had been right about the noise. It was the noise of footsteps on the shale outside. He heard them again. They were getting closer. They were building to a deafening crunching sound in the night. They were heading straight for the shed. On the shale, no way of telling how many people there were.

He heard them stop outside the massive doors. Heard the jingle of keys. Heard the padlocks rattle. The chains were pulled off and the log lifted aside. The doors sagged open. He dropped to the ground. Lay face down and pressed himself up against the pile of cold and oozing bodies.

Four feet. Two voices. Voices he knew well. Fowler and Borken. Talking quietly, walking confidently. Reacher let his body sag against the pile. A rat ran over his hand.

'Did he say when?' Fowler was asking.

His voice was suddenly loud against the rock.

'First thing tomorrow morning,' Borken was saying. 'Phone company starts its linemen when? About eight o'clock? Maybe seven-thirty?'

'Let's be cautious,' Fowler said. 'Let's call it seven-thirty. First thing they do is cut the line.'

They had flashlights. The beams flicked and swung as they walked.

'No problem,' Borken said. 'Seven o'clock here is nine o'clock on the East Coast. Perfect timing. We'll do it at seven. DC first, then New York, then Atlanta. Should be all done by ten past. Ten minutes that shook the world, right? Twenty minutes to spare.'

They stopped at the second truck. Unbolted the tailboard. It came down with a loud metallic clang.

'Then what?' Fowler asked.

'Then we wait and see,' Borken replied. 'Right now, they've only

664

got eight Marines up here. They don't know what to do. They're not sure about the forest. White House is pussyfooting, like we thought. Give them twelve hours for a decision, they can't try anything before dark tomorrow, earliest. And by then this place will be way down their list of priorities.'

They were leaning into the truck. Their voices were muffled by the thick canvas siding.

'Does he need the missile as well?' Fowler asked.

'Just the launcher,' Borken answered. 'It's in the electronic part.'

Reacher lay among the scuffling rats and heard the sound of the clips being undone. Then the squeak of the rubber as a launcher came out of its mountings. Then the rattle of the tailgate bolts ramming home. The footsteps receded. The flashlight beams flicked back toward the doors.

The hinges creaked and the bulky timber doors thumped shut. Reacher heard the launcher being laid gently on the shale and the gasps as the two men lifted the old log back into the brackets. The rattle of the chain and the click of the padlocks. The crunch of the footsteps crossing the shale.

He rolled away from the corpses and hit out at a rat. Caught it with an angry backhand and sent it squealing off into the dark. He sat up and waited. Walked slowly to the door. Listened hard. Waited six minutes. Put his hands into the gap at the bottom of the doors and pulled them apart.

They wouldn't move more than an inch. He laid his palms flat on the smooth timbers and bunched up his shoulders and heaved. They were rock solid. Like trying to push over a tree. He tried for a minute. He was straining like a weightlifter. The doors were jammed. Then he suddenly realized why. They had put the warped old log back in the brackets the other way around. The curve pointing in toward him, not out away from him. Clamping the doors with extra efficiency, instead of allowing the foot of loose movement it had allowed before.

He pictured the log as he had seen it. More than a foot thick, warped, but dried like iron. Curving away, it was no problem. Curving in, it would be immovable. He glanced at the army trucks. Gave it up. There was no space to hit the doors with any kind of momentum. The truck would be pressing on them with all the torque of a big diesel engine, but it wouldn't be enough. He couldn't imagine how much force it would take to shatter that old log.

He thought about using a missile. Gave it up. Too noisy and it wouldn't work anyway. They didn't arm themselves until they were thirty feet into the air. And they only carried six and a half pounds of explosive. Enough to smash a jet engine in flight, but six and a half pounds of explosive against those old timbers would be like scratching at them with a nailfile. He was trapped inside, and Holly was waiting.

It was not in his nature to panic. Never had been. He was a calm man, and his long training had made him calmer. He had been taught to assess and evaluate, and to use pure force of will to prevail. You're Jack Reacher, he had been told. You can do anything. First his mother had told him, then his father, then the quiet deadly men in the training schools. And he had believed them.

But, at the same time, he hadn't believed them. Part of his mind always said: you've just been lucky. Always lucky. And, in the quiet times, he would sit and wait for his luck to run out. He sat on the stony ground with his back against the timbers of the door and asked himself: has it run out now?

He flicked the flashlight beam around the cavern. The rats were staying away from him. They were interested in the darkness in back. They're deserting me, he thought. Deserting the sinking ship. Then his mind clicked in again. No, they're interested in the tunnels, he thought. Because tunnels lead places. He remembered the giant mouseholes blasted into the rock face, north wall of the bowl. Maybe all interconnected by these narrow seams in back.

He ran back into the depth of the cavern, past the trucks, past the grotesque heap of corpses. Back to where he could no longer stand. A rat disappeared into the seam to his left. He dropped to his stomach and flicked the flashlight on. Crawled after it.

He crawled into a skeleton. He scrabbled with his feet and came face to face with a grinning skull. And another. There were four or five skeletons jammed into the excavated seam. Jumbled bones in a pile. He gasped in shock and backed off a foot. Looked carefully. Used the flashlight close up.

All males. He could see that from the five pelvises. The skulls showed gunshot wounds. All in the temples. Neat entry wounds, neat exit holes. Jacketed high-velocity handgun bullets. Fairly recent, certainly within a year. The flesh hadn't decayed. It had been eaten off. He could see the parallel scrape marks on the bones from rodent teeth.

The bones were all disturbed. The rats had hauled them away to eat. There were scraps of clothing material here and there. Some of the ribcages were still covered. Rats don't disturb clothing much. Not on the torso. Why should they? They eat their way in through the inside. The soft parts first. They come to the ribs from the back.

The clothing material was khaki and olive green. Some black and gray camouflage. Reacher saw a colored thread. Traced it back to a shoulder flash hidden under a gnawed shoulder blade. It was a curved felt badge embroidered in silk. It said: Northwestern Freemen. He pulled at the skeleton's jacket. The ribcage collapsed. The breast pocket had three chromium stars punched through.

Reacher made a thorough search, lying on his stomach, up to his armpits in bones. He pieced together five separate uniforms. He found two more badges. One said: White Christian Identity. The other said: Montana Constitutional Militia. He lined up the five splintered skulls. Checked the teeth. He was looking at five men, middle-aged, maybe between forty and fifty. Five leaders. The leaders who had disappeared. The leaders who could not stand the pace. The leaders who had abandoned their members to Beau Borken.

The roof was too low for Reacher to climb over the bones. He had to push them aside and crawl through them. The rats showed no interest. These bones were picked clean. Their new feast lay back inside the cavern. They swarmed back in that direction. He held the flashlight out in front of him and pushed on into the mountain against the squealing tide.

He lost his sense of direction. He hoped he was going roughly west, but he couldn't tell. The roof came down to a couple of feet. He was crawling through an old geological seam, excavated long ago for its ore. The roof came down even more. Down to a foot and a half. It was cold. The seam narrowed. His arms were out in front of him. The seam became too narrow to pull them back. He was crawling down a slim rock tube, a billion tons of mountain above him, no idea where he was going. And the flashlight was failing. The battery was spent. Its light was fading to a dull orange glow.

He was breathing hard. And shaking. Not from exertion. From

dread. From terror. This was not what he had expected. He had visualized a stroll down a spacious abandoned gallery. Not this narrow crack in the rock. He was pushing himself head-first into his worst childhood nightmare. He was a guy who had survived most things, and he was a guy who was rarely afraid. But he had known since his early boyhood that he was terrified of being trapped in the dark in a space too small to turn his giant frame. All his damp childhood nightmares had been about being closed into tight spaces. He lay on his stomach and screwed his eyes shut. Lay and panted and gagged. Forced the air in and out through his clamping throat. Then he inched himself slowly onward into the nightmare.

The glow from the flashlight finally died a hundred yards into the tunnel. The darkness was total. The seam was narrowing. It was pushing his shoulders down. He was forcing himself into a space that was way too small for him. His face was forced sideways. He fought to stay calm. He remembered what he had said to Borken: people were smaller then. Scrappy little guys, migrating west, seeking their fortune in the bowels of the mountain. People half the size of Reacher, squirming along, maybe on their backs, chipping the bright veins out of the rock roof.

He was using the dead flashlight like a blind man uses a white cane. It smashed on solid rock two feet ahead of his face. He heard the tinkle of glass over the rasping of his breath. He struggled ahead and felt with his hands. A solid wall. The tunnel went no farther. He tried to move backward. He couldn't move at all. To push himself backward with his hands, he had to raise his chest to get leverage. But the roof was too low to let him do that. His shoulders were jammed up hard against it. He could get no leverage. His feet could push him forward, but they couldn't pull him backward. He went rigid with panic. His throat clamped solid. His head hit the roof and his cheek hit the grit floor. He fought a scream by breathing fast.

He had to go back. He hooked his toes into the grit. Turned his hands inward and planted his thumbs on the floor. Pulled with his toes and pushed with his thumbs. He moved backward a fraction and then the rock clamped hard against his sides. To slide his weight backward, his shoulder muscles were bunching and jamming against the rock. He breathed out and let his arms go limp. Pulled with his toes. They scrabbled uselessly in the grit. He helped them with his thumbs. His shoulders bunched and jammed again. He jerked his hips from side to side. He had a couple of inches spare. He smashed his hands into the shale and heaved backward. His body jammed solid, like a wedge in a door. He tilted sideways and banged his cheek on the roof. Jerked back down and caught his other cheek on the floor. The rock was crushing in on his ribs. This time, he couldn't fight the scream. He had to let it go. He opened his mouth and wailed in terror. The air in his lungs crushed his chest against the floor and his back against the roof.

He couldn't tell if his eyes were open or shut. He pushed forward with his feet and regained the inch he'd moved back. He stretched with his arms. Felt up ahead again. His shoulders were jammed so tight he couldn't move his hands through much of an angle. He spread his fingers and scrabbled them left and right, up and down. Solid rock ahead. No way to go forward. No way to move backward.

He was going to die trapped inside the mountain. He knew it. The rats knew it. They were sniffing up behind him. Coming closer. He felt them at his feet. He kicked out and sent them squealing away. But they came back. He felt their weight on his legs. They were swarming over him. They burrowed up around his shoulders. Slid under his armpits. He felt cold oily fur on his face as they forced their way past. The flick of their tails as they ran ahead.

To where? He let them run over his arm, to estimate their direction. They were moving ahead of him, into the blind darkness. He felt with his hands. Felt them flowing left. Their passage was stirring the air. The air was cool. He felt it move, a faint breeze, on the sweat on the left side of his face. He jammed himself hard against the right hand wall and moved his left arm sideways, ahead of him. Felt for the left hand wall. It wasn't there. He was stuck at a junction in the tunnels. A new seam ran at a right angle away from the end of the seam he was in. A tight, narrow right angle. Ninety degrees. He forced himself backward as far as his thumbs would push him. He scraped his face on the end wall and jammed his side into the rock. Folded himself arms first around the corner and dragged his legs behind him.

The new seam was no better. It was no wider. The roof was no higher. He hauled himself along, gasping and sweating and shaking. He propelled himself with his toes, an inch at a time. The rats forced their way past him. The rock tore at his sides and his back. But there was still a slight breeze on his face. The tunnel was heading somewhere. He was gasping and panting. He crawled on. Then the new seam widened. Still very low. A flat, low crack in the rock. He crawled on through it, exhausted. Fifty yards. A hundred. Then he felt the roof soar away above him. He pushed on with his toes and suddenly he felt the air change and he was lying halfway into the motor-pool cavern. He realized his eyes were wide open and the white Econoline was right there in front of him in the dark.

He rolled onto his back and lay gasping on the grit. Gasping and shaking. Staggered to his feet and looked back. The seam was invisible. Hidden in the shadow. He made it as far as the white truck and collapsed against its side. The luminous figures on his watch showed he'd been in the tunnels nearly three hours. Most of the time jammed there sweating in panic. A three-hour screaming nightmare come to life. His pants and his jacket were shredded. Every muscle in his body was on fire. His face and hands and elbows and knees were bleeding. But it was the fear that had done it to him. The fear of not getting through. He could still feel the rock pressing down on his back and pressing up on his chest. He could feel it clamping inward on his ribs. He got up again and limped to the doors. Pushed them open and stood in the moonlight, arms out, eyes crazy, mouth open, breathing in lungfuls of the sweet night air.

He was halfway across the bowl before he started thinking straight. So he ran back and ducked into the motor pool once more. Found what he wanted. He found it on one of the jeep's towhook assemblies. Some heavy stiff wire, ready to feed a trailer's electric circuits. He wrenched it out and stripped the insulation with his teeth. Ran back to the moonlight.

He kept close to the road, all the way back to Yorke. Two miles, twenty minutes at a slow agonizing jog through the trees. He looped around behind the ruined northeastern block and approached the courthouse from the rear. Circled it silently in the shadows. Waited and listened.

He tried to think like Borken. Complacent. Happy with his perimeter. Constant information from inside the FBI. Reacher locked into the punishment hut, Holly locked into her prison room. Would he post a sentry? Not tonight. Not when he was expecting heavy action tomorrow and beyond. He would want his people fresh. Reacher nodded and gambled he was right.

He arrived at the courthouse steps. Deserted. He tried the door. Locked. He smiled. Nobody posts a sentry behind a locked door. He bent the wire into a shallow hook and felt for the mechanism. An old two-lever. Eight seconds. He stepped inside. Waited and listened. Nothing. He went up the stairs.

The lock on Holly's door was new. But cheap. He worked quietly which delayed him. Took him more than thirty seconds before the last tumbler clicked back. He pulled the door open slowly and stepped onto the built-up floor. Glanced apprehensively at the walls. She was on a mattress on the floor. Fully dressed and ready. Awake and watching him. Huge eyes bright in the gloom. He gestured her outside. Turned and climbed down and waited in the corridor for her. She picked up her crutch and limped to the door. Climbed carefully down the step and stood next to him.

'Hello, Reacher,' she whispered. 'How are you doing?'

'I've felt better,' he whispered back. 'Time to time.'

She turned and glanced back into her room. He followed her gaze and saw the dark stain on the floor.

'Woman who brought me lunch,' she whispered.

He nodded.

'What with?' he whispered back.

'Part of the bed frame,' she said.

He saw the satisfaction on her face and smiled.

'That should do it,' he said, quietly. 'Bed frames are good for that.'

She took a last look at the room and gently closed the door. Followed him through the dark and slowly down the stairs. Across the lobby and through the double doors and out into the bright silent moonlight.

'Christ,' she said, urgently. 'What happened to you?'

He glanced down and checked himself over in the light of the moon. He was gray from head to foot with dust and grit. His clothing was shredded. He was streaked with sweat and blood. Still shaky.

'Long story,' he said. 'You got somebody in Chicago you can trust?'

'McGrath,' she said immediately. 'He's my agent-in-charge. Why?'

They crossed the wide street arm-in-arm, looking left and right. Skirted the mound in front of the ruined office building. Found the path running northwest.

'You need to send him a fax,' he said. 'They've got missiles. You need to warn him. Tonight, because their line is going to be cut first thing in the morning.'

'The mole tell them that?' she asked.

He nodded.

'How?' she asked. 'How is he communicating?'

'Short-wave radio,' Reacher said. 'Has to be. Anything else is traceable.'

He swayed and leaned on a tree. Gave her the spread, everything, beginning to end.

'Shit,' she said. 'Ground-to-air missiles? Mass suicide? A nightmare.'

'Not our nightmare,' he said. 'We're out of here.'

'We should stay and help them,' she said. 'The families.'

He shook his head.

'Best help is for us to get out,' he said. 'Maybe losing you will change their plan. And we can tell them about the layout around here.'

'I don't know,' she said.

'I do,' he said. 'First rule is stick to priorities. That's you. We're out of here.'

She shrugged and nodded.

'Now?' she asked.

'Right now,' he said.

'How?' she asked.

'Jeep through the forest,' he said. 'I found their motor pool. We get up there, steal a jeep, by then it should be light enough to find our way through. I saw a map in Borken's office. There are plenty of tracks running east through the forest.'

She nodded and he pushed off the tree. They hustled up the winding path to the Bastion. A mile, in the dark. They stumbled on the stones and saved their breath for walking. The clearing was dark and silent. They worked their way around beyond the mess hall to the back of the communications hut. They came out

672

of the trees and Reacher stepped close and pressed his ear to the plywood siding. There was no sound inside.

He used the wire again and they were inside within ten seconds. Holly found paper and pen. Wrote her message. Dialed the Chicago fax number and fed the sheet into the machine. It whirred obediently and pulled the paper through. Fed it back out into her waiting hand. She hit the button for the confirmation. Didn't want to leave any trace behind. Another sheet fed out. It showed the destination number correct. Timed the message at ten minutes to five, Friday morning, the fourth of July. She shredded both papers small and buried the pieces in the bottom of a trashcan.

Reacher rooted around on the long counter and found a paperclip. Followed Holly back out into the moonlight and relocked the door. Dodged around and found the cable leading down from the short-wave whip into the side of the hut. Took the paperclip and worried at it until it broke. Forced the broken end through the cable like a pin. Pushed it through until it was even, a fraction showing at each side. The metal would short-circuit the antenna by connecting the wire inside to the foil screen. The signal would come down out of the ether, down the wire, leak into the foil and run away to ground without ever reaching the short-wave unit itself. The best way to disable a radio. Smash one up, it gets repaired. This way, the fault is untraceable, until an exhausted technician finally thinks to check.

'We need weapons,' Holly whispered to him.

He nodded. They crept together to the armory door. He looked at the lock. Gave it up. It was a huge thing. Unpickable.

'I'll take the Glock from the guy guarding me,' he whispered.

She nodded. They ducked back into the trees and walked through to the next clearing. Reacher tried to think of a story to explain his appearance to Joseph Ray. Figured he might say something about being beamed over to the UN. Talk about how high-speed beaming can rip you up a little. They crept around behind the punishment hut and listened. All quiet. They skirted the corner and Reacher pulled the door. Walked straight into a nine-millimeter. This time, it wasn't a Glock. It was a Sig-Sauer. Not Joseph Ray's. It was Beau Borken's. He was standing just inside the door with Little Stevie at his side, grinning.

THIRTY-SEVEN

FOUR-THIRTY IN THE MORNING, WEBSTER WAS MORE THAN READY for the watch change. Johnson and Garber and the general's aide were dozing in their chairs. McGrath was outside with the telephone linemen. They were just finishing up. The job had taken much longer than they had anticipated. Some kind of interface problem. They had physically cut the phone line coming out of Yorke, and bent the stiff copper down to a temporary terminal box they had placed at the base of a pole. Then they had spooled cable from the terminal box down the road to the mobile command vehicle. Connected it into one of the communications ports.

But it didn't work. Not right away. The linemen had fussed with multimeters and muttered about impedances and capacitances. They had worked for three solid hours. They were ready to blame the army truck for the incompatibility when they thought to go back and check their own temporary terminal box. The fault lay there. A failed component. They wired in a spare and the whole circuit worked perfectly. Four thirty-five in the morning, McGrath was shaking their hands and swearing them to silence when Webster came out of the trailer. The two men stood and watched them drive away. The noise of their truck died around the curve. Webster and McGrath stayed standing in the bright moonlight. They stood there for five minutes while McGrath smoked. They didn't speak. Just gazed north into the distance and wondered.

'Go wake your boys up,' Webster said. 'We'll stand down for a spell.'

McGrath nodded and walked down to the accommodation trailers. Roused Milosevic and Brogan. They were fully dressed on their bunks. They got up and yawned. Came down the ladder and found Webster standing there with Johnson and his aide. Garber standing behind them.

'The telephone line is done,' Webster said.

'Already?' Brogan said. 'I thought it was being done in the morning.'

'We figured sooner was better than later,' Webster said. He inclined his head toward General Johnson. It was a gesture which said: he's worried, right?

'OK,' Milosevic said. 'We'll look after it.'

'Wake us at eight,' Webster said. 'Or earlier if necessary, OK?'

Brogan nodded and walked north to the command vehicle. Milosevic followed. They paused together for a look at the mountains in the moonlight. As they paused, the fax machine inside the empty command trailer started whirring. It fed its first communication face upward into the message tray. It was ten to five in the morning, Friday the fourth of July.

Brogan woke General Johnson an hour and ten minutes later, six o'clock exactly. He knocked loudly on the accommodation trailer door and got no response, so he went in and shook the old guy by the shoulder.

'Peterson Air Force Base, sir,' Brogan said. 'They need to talk to you.'

Johnson staggered up to the command vehicle in his shirt and pants. Milosevic joined Brogan outside in the pre-dawn glow to give him some privacy. Johnson was back out in five minutes.

'We need a conference,' he called.

He ducked back into the trailer. Milosevic walked down and roused the others. They came forward, Webster and the general's aide yawning and stretching, Garber ramrod-straight. McGrath was dressed and smoking. Maybe hadn't tried to sleep at all. They filed up the ladder and took their places around the table, bleak red eyes, hair fuzzed on the back from the pillows.

'Peterson called,' Johnson told them. 'They're sending a helicopter search-and-rescue out, first light, looking for the missile unit.'

His aide nodded.

'That would be standard procedure,' he said.

'Based on an assumption,' Johnson said. 'They think the unit has suffered some kind of mechanical and electrical malfunction.'

'Which is not uncommon,' his aide said. 'If their radio fails, their procedure would be to repair it. If a truck also broke down at the same time, their procedure would be to wait as a group for assistance.'

'Circle the wagons?' McGrath asked.

The aide nodded again.

'Exactly so,' he said. 'They would pull off the road and wait for a chopper.'

'So do we tell them?' McGrath asked.

The aide sat forward.

'That's the question,' he said. 'Tell them what exactly? We don't even know for sure that these maniacs have got them at all. It's still possible it's just a radio problem and a truck problem together.'

'Dream on,' Johnson said.

Webster shrugged. He knew how to deal with such issues.

'What's the upside?' he said.

'There is no upside,' Johnson said. 'We tell Peterson the missiles have been captured, the cat's out of the bag, we lose control of the situation, we're seen to have disobeyed Washington by making an issue out of it before Monday.'

'OK, so what's the downside?' Webster asked.

'Theoretical,' Johnson said. 'We have to assume they've been captured, so we also have to assume they've been well hidden. In which case the air force will never find them. They'll just fly around for a while and then go home and wait.'

Webster nodded.

'OK,' he said. 'No upside, no downside, no problem.'

There was a short silence.

'So we sit tight,' Johnson said. 'We let the chopper fly.'

McGrath shook his head. Incredulous.

'Suppose they use them to shoot the chopper down?' he asked.

The general's aide smiled an indulgent smile.

'Can't be done,' he said. 'The IFF wouldn't allow it.'

'IFF?' McGrath repeated.

'Identify Friend or Foe,' the aide said. 'It's an electronic system. The chopper will be beaming a signal. The missile reads it as friendly, refuses to launch.'

'Guaranteed?' McGrath asked.

The aide nodded.

'Foolproof,' he said.

Garber glowered at him. But he said nothing. Not his field of expertise.

'OK,' Webster said. 'Back to bed. Wake us again at eight, Brogan.'

On the tarmac at Peterson, a Boeing CH-47D Chinook was warming its engines and sipping the first of its eight hundred fifty-eight gallons of fuel. A Chinook is a giant aircraft, whose twin rotors thump through an oval of air a hundred feet long and sixty wide. It weighs more than ten tons empty, and it can lift another eleven. It's a giant flying box, the engines and the fuel tanks strapped to the top and the sides, the crew perched high at the front. Any helicopter can search, but when heavy equipment is at stake, only a Chinook can rescue.

Because of the holiday weekend, the Peterson dispatcher assigned a skeleton crew of two. No separate spotter. He figured he didn't need one. How difficult could it be to find five army trucks on some shoulder in Montana?

'You should have stayed here,' Borken said. 'Right, Joe?'

Reacher glanced into the gloom inside the punishment hut. Joseph Ray was standing to attention on the yellow square. He was staring straight ahead. He was naked. Bleeding from the mouth and nose.

'Right, Joe?' Borken said again.

Ray made no reply. Borken walked over and crashed his fist into his face. Ray stumbled and fell backward. Staggered against the back wall and scrambled to regain his position on the square.

'I asked you a question,' Borken said.

Ray nodded. The blood poured off his chin.

677

'Reacher should have stayed here,' he said.

Borken hit him again. A hard straight right to the face. Ray's head snapped back. Blood spurted. Borken smiled.

'No talking when you're on the square, Joe,' he said. 'You know the rules.'

Borken stepped back and placed the muzzle of the Sig-Sauer in Reacher's ear. Used it to propel him out into the clearing. Gestured Stevie to follow.

'You stay on the square, Joe,' he called over his shoulder.

Stevie slammed the door shut. Borken reversed his direction and used the Sig-Sauer to shove Reacher toward him.

'Tell Fowler to get rid of this guy,' he told him. 'He's outlived his usefulness, such as it ever was. Put the bitch back in her room. Put a ring of sentries right around the building. We got things to do, right? No time for this shit. Parade ground at six-thirty. Everybody there. I'm going to read them the proclamation, before we fax it.'

McGrath couldn't sleep. He walked back to the accommodations trailer with the others and got back on his bunk, but he gave it up after ten minutes. Quarter to seven in the morning, he was back in the command vehicle with Brogan and Milosevic.

'You guys take a break if you want,' he said. 'I'll look after things here.'

'We could go organize some breakfast,' Brogan said. 'Diners in Kalispell should be open by now.'

McGrath nodded vaguely. Started into his jacket for his wallet.

'Don't worry about it,' Brogan said. 'I'll pay. My treat.'

'OK, thanks,' McGrath said. 'Get coffee. Lots of it.'

Brogan and Milosevic stood up and left. McGrath stood in the doorway and watched them drive an army sedan south. The sound of the car faded and he was left with the silent humming of the equipment behind him. He turned to sit down. The clock ticked around to seven. The fax machine started whirring.

Holly smoothed her hands over the old mattress like Reacher was there on it. Like it was really his body under her, scarred and battered, hot and hard and muscular, not a worn striped cotton cover stuffed with ancient horsehair. She blinked the tears out of her eyes. Blew a deep sigh and focused on the next decision. No

678

Reacher, no Jackson, no weapon, no tools, six sentries in the street outside. She glanced around the room for the thousandth time and started scoping it out all over again.

McGrath woke the others by thumping on the sides of the accommodations trailer with both fists. Then he ran back to the command post and found a third copy of the message spooling out of the machine. He already had two. Now he had three.

Webster was the first into the trailer. Then Johnson, a minute behind. Then Garber, and finally the general's aide. They rattled up the ladder one by one and hurried over to the table. McGrath was absorbed in reading.

'What, Mack?' Webster asked him.

'They're declaring independence,' McGrath said. 'Listen to this.'

He glanced around the four faces. Started reading out loud.

'"Governments are instituted among men."' he read '"Deriving their just powers from the consent of the governed. It is the right of the people to alter or abolish them after a long train of abuses and usurpations."'

'They're quoting from the original,' Webster said.

'Paraphrasing,' Garber said.

McGrath nodded.

'Listen to this,' he said again. '"The history of the present government of the United States is a history of repeated injuries and usurpations all designed to establish an absolute tyranny over the people."'

'What the hell is this?' Webster said. '1776 all over again?'

'It gets worse,' McGrath said. '"We therefore are the representatives of the Free States of America, located initially in what was formerly Yorke County in what was formerly Montana, and we solemnly publish and declare that this territory is now a free and independent state, which is absolved of allegiance to the United States, with all political connection totally dissolved, and that as a free and independent state has full power to levy war, conclude peace, defend its land borders and its airspace, contract alliances, establish commerce, and to do all other things as all independent states may do."'

He looked up. Shuffled the three copies into a neat stack and laid them on the table in silence.

'Why three copies?' Garber asked.

'Three destinations,' McGrath said. 'If we hadn't intercepted them, they'd be all over the place by now.'

'Where?' Webster asked.

'First one is a DC number,' McGrath said. 'I'm guessing it's the White House.'

Johnson's aide scooted his chair to the computer terminal. McGrath read him the number. He tapped it in, and the screen scrolled down. He nodded.

'The White House,' he said. 'Next?'

'New York somewhere,' McGrath said. Read out the number from the second sheet.

'United Nations,' the aide said. 'They want witnesses.'

'Third one, I don't know,' McGrath said. 'Area code is 404.'

'Atlanta, Georgia,' Garber said.

'What's in Atlanta, Georgia?' Webster asked.

The aide was busy at the keyboard.

'CNN,' he said. 'They want publicity.'

Johnson nodded.

'Smart moves,' he said. 'They want it all on live TV. Christ, can you imagine? The United Nations as umpires and round-the-clock coverage on the cable news? The whole world watching?'

'So what do we do?' Webster asked.

There was a long silence.

'Why did they say airspace?' Garber asked out loud.

'They were paraphrasing,' Webster said. '1776, there wasn't any airspace.'

'The missiles,' Garber said. 'Is it possible they've disabled the IFF?'

There was another long silence. They heard a car pull up. Doors slammed. Brogan and Milosevic rattled up the ladder and stepped into the hush. They carried brown bags and Styrofoam cups with plastic lids.

The giant search-and-rescue Chinook made it north from Peterson in Colorado to Malmstrom Air Force Base outside of Great Falls in Montana without incident. It touched down there and fuel bowsers came out to meet it. The crew walked to the mess for coffee. Walked back twenty minutes later. Took off again and swung gently in the morning air before lumbering away northwest.

THIRTY-EIGHT

'**W**E'RE GETTING NO REACTION,' FOWLER SAID. 'MAKES US wonder why.'

Reacher shrugged at him. They were in the command hut. Stevie had dragged him through the trees to the Bastion, and then Fowler had dragged him back again with two armed guards. The punishment hut was unavailable. Still occupied by Joseph Ray. They used the command hut instead. They sat Reacher down and Fowler locked his left wrist to the arm of the chair with a handcuff. The guards took up position on either side, rifles sloped, watchful. Then Fowler walked up to join Borken and Stevie for the ceremony on the parade ground. Reacher heard faint shouting and cheering in the distance as the proclamation was read out. Then he heard nothing. Ninety minutes later, Fowler came back to the hut alone. He sat down behind Borken's desk and lit a cigarette, and the armed guards remained standing.

'We faxed it an hour ago,' Fowler said. 'No reaction.'

Reacher smelled his smoke and gazed at the banners on the walls. Dark reds and dull whites, vivid crooked symbols in black.

'Do you know why we're getting no reaction?' Fowler asked.

Reacher just shook his head.

'You know what I think?' Fowler said. 'They cut the line. Phone

681

company is colluding with the federal agents. We were told it would happen at seven-thirty. It obviously happened earlier.'

Reacher shrugged again. Made no reply.

'We would expect to be informed about a thing like that,' Fowler said.

He picked up his Glock and propped it in front of him, butt on the desktop, swiveling it like naval artillery left and right.

'And we haven't been,' he said.

'Maybe your pal from Chicago has given you up,' Reacher said.

Fowler shook his head. His Glock came to rest aimed at Reacher's chest.

'We've been getting a stream of intelligence,' he said. 'We know where they are, how many of them there are, what their intentions are. But now, when we still need information, we aren't getting it. Communication has been interrupted.'

Reacher said nothing.

'We're investigating,' Fowler said. 'We're checking the radio right now.'

Reacher said nothing.

'Anything you want to tell us about the radio?' Fowler asked.

'What radio?' Reacher said.

'It worked OK yesterday,' Fowler said. 'Now it doesn't work at all, and you were wandering around all night.'

He ducked down and rolled open the drawer where Borken kept the Colt Marshal. But he didn't come out with a revolver. He came out with a small black radio transmitter.

'This was Jackson's,' he said. 'He was most anxious to show us where it was hidden. In fact he was begging to show us. He screamed and cried and begged. Just about tore his fingernails off digging it up, he was so anxious.'

He smiled and put the unit carefully in his pocket.

'We figure we just switch it on,' he said. 'That should put us straight through to the federal scum, person-to-person. This stage of the process, we need to talk direct. See if we can persuade them to restore our fax line.'

'Terrific plan,' Reacher said.

'The fax line is important, you see,' Fowler said. 'Vital. The world must be allowed to know what we're doing here. The world must be allowed to watch and witness. History is being made here. You understand that, right?'

Reacher stared at the wall.

'They've got cameras, you know,' Fowler said. 'Surveillance planes are up there right now. Now it's daylight again, they can see what we're doing. So how can we exploit that fact?'

Reacher shook his head.

'You can leave me out of it,' he said.

Fowler smiled.

'Of course we'll leave you out of it,' he said. 'Why would they care about seeing you nailed to a tree? You're nothing but a piece of shit, to us and to them. But Holly Johnson, there's a different story. Maybe we'll call them up on their own little transmitter and tell them to watch us do it with their own spy cameras. That might make them think about it. They might trade a fax line for her left breast.'

He ground out his cigarette. Leaned forward. Spoke quietly.

'We're serious here, Reacher,' he said. 'You saw what we did to Jackson. We could do that to her. We could do that to you. We need to be able to communicate with the world. We need that fax line. So we need the short-wave to confirm what the hell they've done with it. We need those things very badly. You understand that, right? So if you want to avoid a lot of unnecessary pain, for you and for her, you better tell me what you did to the radio.'

Reacher was twisted around, looking at the bookcase. Trying to recall the details of the inexpert translations of the Japanese Pearl Harbor texts he'd read.

'Tell me now,' Fowler said softly. 'I can keep them away from you and from her. No pain for either of you. Otherwise, nothing I can do about it.'

He laid his Glock on the desk.

'You want a cigarette?' he asked.

He held out the pack. Smiled. The good cop. The friend. The ally. The protector. The oldest routine in the book. Requiring the oldest response. Reacher glanced around. Two guards, one on each side of him, the right-hand guard nearer, the left-hand guard back almost against the side wall. Rifles held easy in the crook of their arms. Fowler behind the desk, holding out the pack. Reacher shrugged and nodded. Took a cigarette with his free right hand. He hadn't smoked in ten years, but when somebody offers you a lethal weapon you take it.

'So tell me,' Fowler said. 'And be quick.'

He thumbed his lighter and held it out. Reacher bent forward and lit his cigarette from the flame. Took a deep draw and leaned back. The smoke felt good. Ten years, and he still enjoyed it. He inhaled deeply and took another lungful.

'How did you disable our radio?' Fowler asked.

Reacher took a third pull. Trickled the smoke out of his nose and held the cigarette like a sentry does, between the thumb and forefinger, palm hooded around it. Take quick deep pulls, and the coal on the end of a cigarette heats up to a couple of thousand degrees. Lengthens to a point. He rotated his palm, like he was studying the glowing tip while he thought about something, until the cigarette was pointing straight forward like an arrow.

'How did you disable our radio?' Fowler asked again.

'You'll hurt Holly if I don't tell you?' Reacher asked back.

Fowler nodded. Smiled his lipless smile.

'That's a promise,' he said. 'I'll hurt her so bad she'll be begging to die.'

Reacher shrugged unhappily. Sketched a listen-up gesture. Fowler nodded and shuffled on his chair and leaned close. Reacher snapped forward and jammed the cigarette into his eye. Fowler screamed and Reacher was on his feet, the chair cuffed to his wrist clattering after him. He windmilled right and the chair swung through a wide arc and smashed against the nearer guard's head. It splintered and jerked away as Reacher danced to his left. He caught the farther guard with a forearm smash to the throat as his rifle came up. Snapped back and hit Fowler with the wreckage of the chair. Used the follow-through momentum to swing back to the first guard. Finished him with an elbow to the head. The guy went down. Reacher grabbed his rifle by the barrel and swung straight back at the other guard. Felt skull bones explode under the butt. He dropped the rifle and spun and smashed the chair to pieces against Fowler's shoulders. Grabbed him by the ears and smashed his face into the desktop, once, twice, three times. Took a leg from the broken chair and jammed it crossways under his throat. Folded his elbows around each exposed end and locked his hands together. Tested his grip and bunched his shoulders. Jerked hard, once, and broke Fowler's neck against the chair leg with a single loud crunch.

He took both rifles and the Glock and the handcuff key. Out of the door and around to the back of the hut. Straight into the trees. He put the Glock in his pocket. Took the handcuff off his wrist. Put a rifle in each hand. Breathing hard. He was in pain. Swinging the heavy wooden chair had opened the red weal on his wrist into a wound. He raised it to his mouth and sucked at it and buttoned the cuff of his shirt over it.

Then he heard a helicopter. The faint bass thumping of a heavy twin-rotor machine, a Boeing, a Sea Knight or a Chinook, far to the southeast. He thought: last night Borken talked about eight Marines. They've only got eight Marines, he said. The Marines use Sea Knights. He thought: they're going for a frontal assault. Holly's paneled walls flashed into his mind and he set off racing through the trees.

He got as far as the Bastion. The thumping from the air built louder. He risked stepping out onto the stony path. It was a Chinook. Not a Sea Knight. Search-and-rescue markings, not Marine Corps. It was following the road up from the southeast, a mile away, a hundred feet up, using its vicious downdraft to part the surrounding foliage and aid its search. It looked slow and ponderous, hanging nose-down in the air, yawing slightly from side to side as it approached. Reacher guessed it must be pretty close to the town of Yorke itself.

Then he glanced into the clearing and saw a guy, fifty yards away. A grunt, camouflage fatigues. A Stinger on his shoulder. Turning and aiming through the crude open sight. He saw him acquire the target. The guy steadied himself and stood with his feet apart. His hand fumbled for the activator. The missile's infrared sensor turned on. Reacher waited for the IFF to shut it down. It didn't happen. The missile started squealing its high-pitched tone. It was locked on the heat from the Chinook's engines. The guy's finger tightened on the trigger.

Reacher dropped the rifle in his left hand. Swung the other one up and clicked the safety off with his thumb as he did so. Stepped to his left and leaned his shoulder on a tree. Aimed at the guy's head and fired.

But the guy fired first. A fraction of a second before Reacher's bullet killed him, he pulled the Stinger's trigger. Two things happened. The Stinger's rocket motor lit up. It exploded along its launch tube. Then the guy was hit in the head. The impact knocked him sideways. The launcher caught the rear of the missile and flipped it. It came out and stalled tail-down in the air like a javelin, cushioned on the thrust of its launch, virtually motionless.

Then it corrected itself. Reacher watched in horror as it did exactly what it was designed to do. Its eight little wings popped out. It hung almost vertical until it acquired the helicopter again. Then its second-stage rocket lit up and it blasted into the sky. Before the guy's body hit the ground it was homing in on the Chinook at a thousand miles an hour.

The Chinook was lumbering steadily northwest. A mile away. Following the road. The road ran straight up through the town. Between the abandoned buildings. On the southeast corner the first building it passed was the courthouse. The Chinook was closing on it at eighty miles an hour. The Stinger was heading in to meet it at a thousand miles an hour.

One mile at a thousand miles an hour. One thousandth of an hour. A fraction over three and a half seconds. It felt like a lifetime to Reacher. He watched the missile all the way. A wonderful, brutal weapon. A simple, unshakable purpose. Designed to recognize the exact heat-signature of aircraft exhaust, designed to follow it until it either got there or ran out of fuel. A simple three-and-a-half-second mission.

The Chinook pilot saw it early. He wasted the first second of its flight, frozen. Not in horror, not in fear, just in simple disbelief that a heat-seeking missile had been fired at him from a small wooded clearing in Montana. Then his instinct and training took over. Evade and avoid. Evade the missile, avoid crashing on settlements below. Reacher saw him throw the nose down and the tail up. The big Chinook wheeled away and spewed a wide fan of exhaust into the atmosphere. Then the tail flipped the other way, engines screaming, superheated fumes spraying another random arc. The missile patiently followed the first curve. Tightened its radius. The Chinook dropped slowly and then rose violently in the air. Spiraled upward and away from the town. The missile turned and followed the second arc. Arrived at where the heat had been a split-second before. Couldn't find it. It turned a full lazy circle right underneath the helicopter. Caught an echo of the new maneuver and set about climbing a relentless new spiral.

The pilot won an extra second, but that was all. The Stinger caught him right at the top of his desperate climb. It followed the trail of heat all the way into the starboard engine itself. Exploded hard against the exhaust nacelle.

Six and a half pounds of high explosive against ten tons of aircraft, but the explosive always wins. Reacher saw the starboard engine disintegrate, then the rear rotor housing blow off. Shattered fragments of the drivetrain exploded outward like shrapnel and the rotor detached and spun away in terrible slow motion. The Chinook stalled in the air and fell, tail-down, checked only by the screaming forward rotor, and slowly spun to the earth, like a holed ship slips slowly below the sea.

Holly heard the helicopter. She heard the low-frequency beat pulsing faintly through her walls. She heard it grow louder. Then she heard the explosion and the shriek of the forward rotor grabbing the air. Then she heard nothing.

She jammed her elbow into her crutch and limped across to the diagonal partition. The prison room was completely empty except for the mattress. So her search was going to have to start again in the bathroom.

'Only one question,' Webster said. 'How long can we keep the lid on this?'

General Johnson said nothing in reply. Neither did his aide. Webster moved his gaze across to Garber. Garber was looking grim.

'Not too damn long,' he said.

'But how long?' Webster asked. 'A day? An hour?'

'Six hours,' Garber said.

'Why?' McGrath asked.

'Standard procedure,' Garber said. 'They'll investigate the crash, obviously. Normally they'd send another chopper out. But not if there's a suspicion of ground fire. So they'll come by road from Malmstrom. Six hours.'

Webster nodded. Turned to Johnson.

'Can you delay them, General?' he asked.

Johnson shook his head.

'Not really,' he said. His voice was low and resigned. 'They just lost a Chinook. Crew of two. I can't call them and say, do me a favor, don't investigate that. I could try, I guess, and they might agree at first, but it would leak, and then we'd be back where we started. Might gain us an hour.'

Webster nodded.

'Seven hours, six hours, what's the difference?' he said.

Nobody replied.

'We've got to move now,' McGrath said. 'Forget the White House. We can't wait any longer. We need to do something right now, people. Six hours from now, the whole situation blows right out of control. We'll lose her.'

Six hours is three hundred and sixty minutes. They wasted the first two sitting in silence. Johnson stared into space. Webster drummed his fingers on the table. Garber stared at McGrath, a wry expression on his face. McGrath was staring at the map. Milosevic and Brogan were standing in the silence, holding the brown bags of breakfast and the Styrofoam cups.

'Coffee here, anybody wants it,' Brogan said.

Garber waved him over.

'Eat and plan,' he said.

'Map,' Johnson said.

McGrath slid the map across the table. They all sat forward. Back in motion. Three hundred and fifty eight minutes to go.

'Ravine's about four miles north of us,' the aide said. 'All we got is eight Marines in a LAV-25.'

'That tank thing?' McGrath asked.

The aide shook his head.

'Light Armored Vehicle,' he said. 'LAV. Eight wheels, no tracks.'

'Bulletproof?' Webster asked.

'For sure,' the aide said. 'They can drive it all the way to Yorke.'

'If it gets through the ravine,' Garber said.

Johnson nodded.

'That's the big question,' he said. 'We need to go take a look.'

The Light Armored Vehicle looked just like a tank to McGrath's hasty civilian glance, except there were eight wheels on it instead of tracks. The hull was welded up out of brutal sloping armor plates and there was a turret with a gun. The driver sat forward, and the commander sat in the turret. In the rear, two rows of three Marines sat back to back, facing weapon ports. Each port had its own periscope. McGrath could visualize the vehicle rumbling into battle, invulnerable, weapons bristling out of those ports. Down into the ravine, up the other side, along the road to Yorke to the courthouse. He pulled Webster to one side and spoke urgently.

'We never told them,' he said. 'About the dynamite in the walls.'

'And we're not going to,' Webster said quietly. 'The old guy would freak out. He's close to falling apart right now. I'm going to tell the Marines direct. They're going in there. They'll have to deal with it. Makes no difference if Johnson knows in advance or not.'

McGrath intercepted Johnson and Webster ran over to the armored vehicle. McGrath saw the Marine commander leaning down from the turret. Saw him nodding and grimacing as Webster spoke. Then the general's aide fired up the army Chevrolet. Johnson and Garber crammed into the front with him. McGrath jumped in back. Brogan and Milosevic crushed in alongside him.

Webster finished up and raced back to the Chevy. Squeezed in next to Milosevic. The LAV fired up its big diesel with a blast of black smoke. Then it crunched into gear and lumbered off north. The Chevy accelerated in its wake.

Four miles north they crested a slight rise and entered a curve. Slowed and jammed to a stop in the lee of a craggy outcrop. The Marine commander vaulted down from the turret and ran north on the road. Webster and Johnson and McGrath got out and hurried after him. They paused together in the lee of the rockface and crept around the curve. Stared out and down into the ravine. It was an intimidating sight.

It ran left to right in front of them, more or less straight. And it was not just a trench. It was a trench and a step. The whole crust of the earth had fractured, and the southern plate had fallen below the level of the northern plate. Like adjacent sections of an old concrete highway where a car thumps up an inch at the seam. Expanded to geological size, that inch was a fifty-foot disparity.

Where the earth had fractured and fallen, the edges had broken up into giant boulders. The scouring of the glaciers had tumbled those boulders south. The ice and the heave and the weather over a million years had raked out the fracture and turned it into a trench. It had cut back the rock plates to where they became solid again. Some places, it had carved a hundred-yard width. Other places, tougher seams of rock had kept the gap down to twenty yards.

Then the roots of a thousand generations of trees and the frozen water of the winters had eroded the edges until there was a steep ragged descent to the bottom and a steep ragged rise back up the northern side to the top, fifty feet higher than the starting point. There were stunted trees and tangled undergrowth and rock slides. The road itself was lifted progressively on concrete trestles and rose gently across a bridge. Then more concrete trestles set it down on the level ground to the north and it snaked away through the forest into the mountains.

But the bridge was blown. Charges had been exploded against the two center trestles. A twenty-foot section of the center span had fallen a hundred feet into the trench. The four men in the lee of the outcrop could see fragments of the road lying shattered in the bottom of the ravine.

'What do you think?' Johnson asked urgently.

The Marine commander was giving it a fast sweep through his field glasses. Left and right, up and down, examining the exact terrain.

'I think it's shit, sir,' he said.

'Can you get through?' Johnson asked him.

The guy lowered his field glasses and shook his head.

'Not a hope in hell,' he said.

He stepped across, shoulder-to-shoulder with the general, so Johnson could share the same line of sight. Started talking rapidly and pointing as he did so.

'We could get down to the bottom,' he said. 'We could go in right there, where the rock slide gives us a reasonable descent. But getting up the other side is the problem, sir. The LAV can't climb much more than forty-five degrees. Most of the north face looks a lot steeper than that. Some places, it's near enough vertical. Any gentle slopes are overgrown. And they've felled trees. See there, sir?'

He pointed to a wooded area on the slope opposite. Trees had been felled and left lying with their chopped ends facing south.

'Abatises,' the Marine said. 'The vehicle is going to stall against them. No doubt about that. Coming uphill, slowly, those things would stop a tank. We go in there, we'll be trapped in the ditch, no doubt at all.'

'So what the hell do we do?' Johnson said.

The Marine officer shrugged.

'Bring me some engineers,' he said. 'The gap they blew is only about twenty feet wide. We can bridge that.'

'How long will that take?' Webster asked.

The Marine shrugged again.

'All the way up here?' he said. 'Six hours? Maybe eight?'

'Way too long,' Webster said.

Then the radio receiver in McGrath's pocket started crackling.

THIRTY-NINE

R EACHER WAS HIDING OUT IN THE WOODS, WORRIED ABOUT THE dogs. They were the only thing he wasn't certain about. People, he could handle. Dogs, he had very little experience.

He was in the trees, north of the Bastion, south of the rifle range. He had heard the Chinook hit the ground from a mile away. It hit tail first, smashing and tearing into the wooded slope. It looked to have slipped sideways in the air and missed the courthouse by two hundred yards. No explosions. Not from the courthouse or from the chopper itself. No sound of fuel tanks going up. Reacher was reasonably optimistic for the crew. He figured the trees and the collapse of the big boxy body might have cushioned the impact for them. He had known chopper crews survive worse.

He had an M-16 rifle in his hand and a Glock in his pocket. The Glock was fully loaded. Seventeen shells. The M-16 had the short clip. Twenty shells, less the one that had killed the guy with the missile. The second M-16 had the long clip. A full load of thirty. But it was hidden in the trees. Because Reacher had a rule: choose the weapon you know for sure is in working order.

He felt instinctively that the focus of attention would be in the southeast direction. That was where Holly was being held, and that was where the Chinook had come down. That was where the opposition forces would be massing. He felt people would be turning to face southeast, apprehensively, staring down into the rest of the United States, waiting. So he turned his back and headed northwest.

He moved cautiously. The bulk of the enemy was elsewhere, but he knew there were squads out looking for him. He knew they had already discovered Fowler's body. He had seen two separate patrols searching the woods. Six men in each, heavily armed, crashing through the undergrowth, searching. Not difficult to avoid. But the dogs would be difficult to avoid. That was why he was worried. That was why he was moving cautiously.

He stayed in the trees and skirted the western end of the rifle range. Tracked back east around the parade ground. Fifty yards north, he turned again and paralleled the road up to the mines. He stayed in the trees and moved at a fast jog. Used the time to start laying out some priorities. And a timescale. He figured he had maybe three hours. Bringing down the Chinook was going to provoke some kind of a violent reaction. No doubt about that. But in all his years in the service, he had never known anything happen faster than three hours. So he had three hours, and a lot of ground to cover.

He slowed to a fast walk when the rocky ground started rising under his feet. Followed a wide uphill circle west and cut straight in to the edge of the bowl where the mine entrances were. He heard diesel engines idling. He bent double and crept across to the cover of a rock. Looked out and down.

He was just above halfway up the slope surrounding the bowl. Looking more or less due east across its diameter. The log doors of the farther shed were standing open. Four of the missile unit's trucks were standing on the shale. The four with the weapon racks in back. The troop carrier was still inside.

There was a handful of men in the bowl. They were set in an approximate circle around the cluster of trucks. Reacher counted eight guys. Fatigues, rifles, tense limbs. What had the kitchen woman said? The mines were off limits. Except to the people Borken trusted. Reacher watched them. Eight trusted lieutenants, acting out a reasonable imitation of sentry duty.

He watched them for a couple of minutes. Slid his rifle to his shoulder. He was less than a hundred yards away. He could hear the rattle of the shale as the sentries moved around. He clicked the selector to the single-shot position. He had nineteen shells in the box, and he needed to fire a minimum of eight. He needed to be cautious with ammunition.

The M-16 is a good rifle. Easy to use, easy to maintain. Easy to aim. The carrying handle has a grooved top which lines up with an identical groove in the front sight. At a hundred yards, you squint down the handle groove and let it merge with the front groove, and what you see is what you hit. Reacher rested his weight on the rock and lined up the first target. Practiced the slight sweep that would take him onto the second. And the third. He rehearsed the full sequence of eight shots. He didn't want his elbow snagging somewhere in the middle.

He returned to the first target. Waited a beat and fired. The sound of the shot crashed through the mountains. The right front tire of the first truck exploded. He swept the sights onto the left front. Fired again. The truck dropped to its rims like a stunned ox falling to its knees.

He kept firing steadily. He had fired five shots and hit five tires before anybody reacted. As he fired the sixth he saw in the corner of his eye the sentries diving for cover. Some were just dropping to the ground. Others were running for the shed. He fired the seventh. Paused before the eighth. The farthest tire was the hardest shot. The angle was oblique. The sidewall was unavailable to him. He was going to have to fire at the treads. Possible that the shell might glance off. He fired. He hit. The tire burst. The front of the last truck dropped.

The nearest sentry was still on his feet. Not heading for the shed. Just standing and staring toward the rock Reacher was behind. Raising his rifle. It was an M-16, same as Reacher's. Long magazine, thirty shells. The guy was standing there, sighting it in on the rock. A brave man, or an idiot. Reacher crouched and waited. The guy fired. His weapon was set on automatic. He loosed off a burst of three. Three shots in a fifth of a second. They smashed into the trees fifteen feet above Reacher's head. Twigs and leaves drifted down and landed near him. The guy ran ten yards closer. Fired again. Three more shells. Way off to Reacher's left. He heard the whine of the bullets and the thunking as they hit the trees before he heard the muzzle blast. Bullets which travel faster than sound

694

do that. You hear it all in reverse order. The bullet gets there before the sound of the shot.

Reacher had decisions to take. How close was he going to let this guy get? And was he going to fire a warning shot? The next burst of three was nearer. Low, but nearer. Not more than six feet away. Reacher decided: not much damn closer, and no warning shot. The guy was all pumped up. No percentage in trying a warning shot. This guy was not going to get calmed down in any kind of a hurry.

He lay on his side. Straightened his legs and came out at the base of the rock. Fired once and hit the guy in the chest. He went down in a heap on the shale. The rifle flew off to his right. Reacher stayed where he was. Watched carefully. The guy was still alive. So Reacher fired again. Hit him through the top of the head. Kinder not to leave him with a sucking chest wound for the last ten minutes of his life.

The echoes of the brief firefight died into the mountain silence and then the air was still. The other seven guys were nowhere. The trucks were all resting nose-down on their front rims. Disabled. Maybe they could be driven out of the bowl, but the first of the mountain hairpins was going to strip the blown tires right off. The trucks were neutralized. No doubt about that.

Reacher crawled backward ten yards and stood up in the trees. Jogged down the slope and headed back toward the Bastion. Seventeen shells in the Glock, nine in the rifle. Progress, at a price.

The dogs found him halfway back. Two big rangy animals. German shepherds. He saw them at the same time as they saw him. They were loping along with that kind of infinite energy big dogs display. Long bounding strides, eager expressions, wet mouths gaping. They stopped short on stiff front legs and switched direction in a single fluid stride. Thirty yards away. Then twenty. Then ten. Acceleration. New energy in their movement. Snarls rising in their throats.

People, Reacher was certain about. Dogs were different. People had freedom of choice. If a man or a woman ran snarling toward him, they did so because they chose to. They were asking for whatever they got. His response was their problem. But dogs were different.

No free will. Easily misled. It raised an ethical problem. Shooting a dog because it had been induced to do something unwise was not the sort of thing Reacher wanted to do.

He left the Glock in his pocket. The rifle was better. It was about two and a half feet longer than the handgun. An extra two and a half feet of separation seemed like a good idea. The dogs stopped short of him. The fur on their shoulders was raised. The fur down their backs was raised, following their spines. They crouched, front feet splayed, heads down, snarling loudly. They had yellow teeth. Lots of them. Their eyes were brown. Reacher could see fine dark eyelashes, like a girl's.

One of them was forward of the other. The leader of the pack. He knew dogs had to have a pecking order. Two dogs, one of them had to be superior to the other. Like people. He didn't know how dogs worked it out for themselves. Posturing, maybe. Maybe smell. Maybe fighting. He stared at the forward dog. Stared into its eyes. Time to time, he had heard people talking about dogs. They said: never show fear. Stare the dog down. Don't let it know you're afraid. Reacher wasn't afraid. He was standing there with an M16 in his hands. The only thing he was worried about was having to use it.

He stared silently at the dog like he used to stare at some service guy gone bad. A hard, silent stare like a physical force, like a cold, crushing pressure. Bleak, cold eyes, unblinking. It had worked a hundred times with people. Now it was working with the lead dog.

The dog was only partially trained. Reacher could see that. It could go through the motions. But it couldn't deliver. It hadn't been trained to ignore its victim's input. It was eye to eye with him, backing off fractionally like his glare was a painful weight on its narrow forehead. Reacher turned up the temperature. Narrowed his eyes and bared his own teeth. Sneered like a tough guy in a bad movie. The dog's head dropped. Its eyes swiveled upward to maintain contact. Its tail dropped down between its legs.

'Sit,' Reacher said. He said it calmly but firmly. Plenty of emphasis on the plosive consonant at the end of the word. The dog moved automatically. Shuffled its hind legs inward and sat. The other dog followed suit, like a shadow. They sat side by side and stared up at him.

'Lie down,' Reacher said.

The dogs didn't move. Just stayed sitting, looking at him, puzzled. Maybe the wrong word. Not the command they were accustomed to.

'Down,' Reacher said.

They slid their front paws forward and dropped their bellies to the forest floor. Looking up at him.

'Stay,' Reacher said.

He gave them a look like he meant it and moved off south. Forced himself to walk slow. Five yards into the trees, he turned. The dogs were still on the ground. Their necks were twisted around, watching him walk away.

'Stay,' he called again.

They stayed. He walked.

He could hear people in the Bastion. The sound of a fair-sized crowd trying to keep quiet. He heard it when he was still north of the parade ground. He skirted the area in the trees and walked around the far end of the rifle range. Came through the trees behind the mess hall. Opposite the kitchen door. He walked a circle deep in the woods behind the buildings until he got an angle. Crept forward to take a look.

There were maybe thirty people in the Bastion. They were standing in a tight group. Edging forward into a cluster. All men, all in camouflage fatigues, all heavily armed. Rifles, machine guns, grenade launchers, pockets bulging with spare magazines. The crowd ebbed and flowed. Shoulders touched and parted. Reacher glimpsed Beau Borken in the center of the mass of people. He was holding a small black radio transmitter. Reacher recognized it. It was Jackson's. Borken had retrieved it from Fowler's pocket. He was holding it up to his ear. Staring into space like he'd just switched it on and was waiting for a reply.

FORTY

MCGRATH SNATCHED THE RADIO FROM HIS POCKET. FLIPPED IT open and stared at it. It was crackling loudly in his hand. Webster stepped forward and took it from him. Ducked back to the cover of the rockface and clicked the button.

'Jackson?' he said. 'This is Harland Webster.'

McGrath and Johnson crowded in on him. The three men crouched against the rock wall. Webster moved the unit an inch from his ear so the other two could listen in. In the cover of the rock, in the silence of the mountains, they could hear it crackling and hissing and the fast breathing of a person on the other end. Then they heard a voice.

'Harland Webster?' the voice said. 'Well, well, the head man himself.'

'Jackson?' Webster said again.

'No,' the voice said. 'This is not Jackson.'

Webster glanced at McGrath.

'So who is it?' he asked.

'Beau Borken,' the voice said. 'And as of today, I guess that's President Borken. President of the Free States of America. But feel free to speak informally.'

'Where's Jackson?' Webster asked.

There was a pause. Nothing to hear except the faint electronic sound of FBI telecommunications technology. Satellites and microwaves.

'Where's Jackson?' Webster asked again.

'He died,' the voice said.

Webster glanced at McGrath again.

'How?' he asked.

'Just died,' Borken said. 'Relatively quickly, really.'

'Was he sick?' Webster asked.

There was another pause. Then there was the sound of laughter. A high, tinny sound. A loud, shrieking laugh which overloaded Webster's earpiece and spilled into distortion and bounced off the rock wall.

'No, he wasn't sick, Webster,' Borken said. 'He was pretty healthy, up until the last ten minutes.'

'What did you do to him?' Webster asked.

'Same as I'm going to do to the general's little girl,' Borken said. 'Listen up, and I'll tell you the exact details. You need to pay attention, because you need to know what you're dealing with here. We're serious here. We mean business, you understand? You listening?'

Johnson pushed in close. White and sweating.

'You crazy bastards,' he yelled.

'Who's that?' Borken asked. 'That the general himself?'

'General Johnson,' Webster said.

There was a chuckle on the radio. Just a short, satisfied sound.

'A full house,' Borken said. 'The director of the FBI and the joint chairman. We're flattered, believe me. But I guess the birth of a new nation deserves nothing less.'

'What do you want?' Webster asked.

'We crucified him,' Borken said. 'We found a couple of trees a yard apart, and we nailed him up. We're going to do that to your daughter, General, if you step out of line. Then we cut his balls off. He was pleading and screaming for us not to, but we did it anyway. We can't do that to your kid, her being a woman and all, but we'll find some equivalent, you know what I mean? Do you think she'll be screaming and pleading, General? You know her better than me. Personally, I'm betting she will be. She likes to think she's a tough cookie, but when she sees those blades coming close, she's going to change her damn tune pretty quick, I'm just about sure of that.'

Johnson turned whiter. All his blood just drained away. He fell back and sat heavily against the rock. His mouth was working soundlessly.

'What the hell do you bastards want?' Webster yelled.

There was another silence. Then the voice came back, quiet and firm.

'I want you to stop yelling,' it said. 'I want you to apologize for yelling at me. I want you to apologize for calling me a rude name. I'm the President of the Free States, and I'm owed some courtesy and deference, wouldn't you say?'

His voice was quiet, but McGrath heard it clearly enough. He looked across at Webster in panic. They were close to losing, before they had even started. First rule was to negotiate. To keep them talking, and gradually gain the upper hand. Establish dominance. Classic siege theory. But to start out by apologizing for yelling was to kiss goodbye to any hope of dominance. That was to lie down and roll over. From that point on, you were their plaything. McGrath shook his head urgently. Webster nodded back. Said nothing. Just held the radio without speaking. He knew how to do this. He had been in this situation before. Several times. He knew the protocol. Now, the first one to speak was the weaker one. And it wasn't going to be him. He and McGrath gazed at the ground and waited.

'You still there?' Borken asked.

Webster carried on staring down. Saying nothing.

'You there?' Borken said again.

'What's on your mind, Beau?' Webster asked, calmly.

There was angry breathing over the air.

'You cut my phone line,' Borken said. 'I want it restored.'

'No, we didn't,' Webster said. 'Doesn't your phone work?'

'My faxes,' Borken said. 'I got no response.'

'What faxes?' Webster said.

'Don't bullshit me,' Borken said. 'I know you cut the line. I want it fixed.'

Webster winked at McGrath.

'OK,' he said. 'We can do that. But you've got to do something for us first.'

'What?' Borken asked.

'Holly,' Webster said. 'Bring her down to the bridge and leave her there.'

700

There was another silence. Then the laughter started up again. High and loud.

'No dice,' Borken said. 'And no deals.'

Webster nodded to himself. Lowered his voice. Sounded like the most reasonable man on earth.

'Listen, Mr Borken,' he said. 'If we can't deal, how can we help each other?'

Another silence. McGrath stared at Webster. The next reply was crucial. Win or lose.

'You listen to me, Webster,' the voice said. 'No deals. You don't do exactly what I say, Holly dies. In a lot of pain. I hold all the cards, and I'm not doing deals. You understand that?'

Webster's shoulders slumped. McGrath looked away.

'Restore the fax line,' the voice said. 'I need communications. The world must know what we're doing here. This is a big moment in history, Webster. I won't be denied by your stupid games. The world must witness the first blows being struck against your tyranny.'

Webster stared at the ground.

'This decision is too big for you alone,' Borken said. 'You need to consult with the White House. There's an interest there too, wouldn't you say?'

Even over the tinny hand-held radio the force of Borken's voice was obvious. Webster was flinching like a physical weight was against his ear. Flinching and gasping, as his heart and lungs fought each other for space inside his chest.

'Make your decision,' Borken said. 'I'll call back in two minutes.'

Then the radio went dead. Webster stared at it like he had never seen such a piece of equipment before. McGrath leaned over and clicked the button off.

'OK,' he said. 'We stall, right? Tell him we're fixing the line. Tell him it will take an hour, maybe two. Tell him we're in contact with the White House, the UN, CNN, whoever. Tell him whatever the hell he wants to hear.'

'Why is he doing this?' Webster asked, vaguely. 'Escalating everything? He's making it so we have to attack him. So we have to, right? Like he wants us to. He's giving us no choice. He's provoking us.'

'He's doing it because he's crazy,' McGrath said.

'He must be,' Webster said. 'He's a maniac. Otherwise I just can't understand why he's trying to attract so much attention. Because like he says, he holds all the cards already.'

'We'll worry about that later, chief,' McGrath said. 'Right now, we just need to stall him.'

Webster nodded. Forced himself back to the problem in hand.

'But we need longer than two hours,' he said. 'Hostage Rescue will take at least four to get over here. Maybe five, maybe six.'

'OK, it's the Fourth of July,' McGrath said. 'Tell him the linemen are all off-duty. Tell him it could take us all day to get them back.'

They stared at each other. Glanced at Johnson. He was right out of it. Just slumped against the rockface, white and inert, barely breathing. Ninety hours of mortal stress and emotion had finally broken him. Then the radio in Webster's hand crackled again.

'Well?' Borken asked, when the static cleared.

'OK, we agree,' Webster said. 'We'll fix the line. But it's going to take some time. Linemen are off-duty for the holidays.'

There was a pause. Then a chuckle.

'Independence Day,' Borken said. 'Maybe I should have chosen another date.'

Webster made no reply.

'I want your Marines where I can see them,' Borken said.

'What Marines?' Webster said.

There was another short laugh. Short and complacent.

'You got eight Marines,' Borken said. 'And an armored car. We got lookouts all over the place. We've been watching you. Like you're watching us with those damn planes. You're lucky Stingers don't shoot that high, or you'd have more than a damn helicopter on the ground by now.'

Webster made no reply. Just scanned the horizon. McGrath was doing the same thing, automatically, looking for the glint of the sun on field glasses.

'I figure you're close to the bridge right now,' Borken said. 'Am I right?'

Webster shrugged. McGrath prompted him with a nod.

'We're close to the bridge,' Webster said.

'I want the Marines on the bridge,' Borken said. 'Sitting on the edge in a neat little row. Their vehicle behind them. I want that to happen now, you understand? Or we go to work on Holly. Your choice, Webster. Or maybe it's the general's choice. His daughter, and his Marines, right?'

Johnson roused himself and glanced up. Five minutes later the Marines were sitting on the fractured edge of the roadway, feet dangling down into the abyss. Their LAV was parked up behind them. Webster was still in the lee of the rockface with McGrath and Johnson. The radio still pressed to his ear. He could hear muffled sounds. Like Borken had pressed his hand over the microphone and was using a walkie-talkie. He could hear his muffled voice alternating with crackly replies. Then he heard the hand come away and the voice come back again, loud and clear in the earpiece.

'OK, Webster, good work,' Borken said to him. 'Our scouts can see all eight of them. So can our riflemen. If they move, they die. Who else have you got there with you?'

Webster paused. McGrath shook his head urgently.

'Can't you see?' Webster asked. 'I thought you were watching us.'

'Not right now,' Borken said. 'I pulled my people back a little. Into our defensive positions.'

'There's nobody else here,' Webster said. 'Just me and the general.'

There was another pause.

'OK, you two can join the Marines,' Borken said. 'On the bridge. On the end of the line.'

Webster waited for a long moment. A blank expression on his face. Then he got up and nodded to Johnson. Johnson got up unsteadily and the two of them walked forward together around the curve. Left McGrath on his own, crouched in the lee of the rock.

McGrath waited there two minutes and crawled back south to the Chevrolet. Garber and Johnson's aide were in front and Milosevic and Brogan were in back. They were all staring at him.

'What the hell happened?' Brogan asked.

'We're in deep, deep shit,' McGrath said.

Two minutes of hurried explanation, and the others agreed with him.

'So what now?' Garber asked.

'We go get Holly,' McGrath said. 'Before he realizes we're bullshitting him.'

'But how?' Brogan asked.

McGrath glanced at him. Glanced at Milosevic.

'The three of us,' he said. 'End of the day, this is a Bureau affair. Call it whatever you want, terrorism, sedition, kidnaping, it's all FBI territory.'

'We're going to do it?' Milosevic said. 'Just the three of us? Right now?'

'You got a better way?' McGrath said. 'You want something done properly, you do it yourself, right?'

Garber was twisted around, scanning along the three faces on the rear seat.

'So go do it,' he said.

McGrath nodded and held up his right hand. The thumb and the first two fingers sticking out.

'I'm the thumb,' he said. 'I go in east of the road. Brogan, you're the first finger. You walk a mile west of the road and go in from there. Milo, you're the second finger. You walk two miles west and go north from there. We infiltrate separately, spaced out a mile between each of us. We meet up back on the road a half-mile shy of the town. Clear?'

Brogan made a face. Then he nodded. Milosevic shrugged. Garber glanced at McGrath and the general's aide started the Chevy and rolled it gently south. He stopped it again after four hundred yards where the road came back out of the rock cover and there was clear access left and right into the countryside. The three FBI men checked their weapons. They each had a government-issue .38 in a shiny brown leather shoulder holster. Full load of six, plus another six in a speedloader in their pockets.

'Try to capture a couple of rifles,' McGrath said. 'Don't worry about taking prisoners. You see somebody, you shoot the bastard down, OK?'

Milosevic had the longest walk, so he was first to go. He ducked across the road and struck out due west across the mountain scrub. He made it to a small stand of trees and disappeared. McGrath lit a cigarette and sent Brogan after him. Garber waited until Brogan was in the trees, then he turned back to McGrath.

'Don't forget what I told you about Reacher,' he said. 'I'm not wrong about that guy. He's on your side, believe me.'

McGrath shrugged and said nothing. Smoked in silence. Opened the Chevy's door and slid out. Ground out the cigarette under his shoe and walked away east, across the grassy shoulder and onto the scrub.

McGrath was not far off fifty, and a heavy smoker, but he was a fit man. He had that type of mongrel constitution that age and smoke could not hurt. He was short at five seven, but sturdy. About one-sixty, made up of that hard slabby muscle which needs no maintenance and never fades into fat. He felt the same as he had as a kid. No better, no worse. His Bureau training had been a long time ago, and fairly rudimentary compared to what people were getting now. But he'd aced it. Physically, he'd been indestructible. Not the fastest guy in his class, but easily the best stamina. The training runs in the early days of Quantico had been crude. Around and around in the Virginia woods, using natural obstacles. McGrath would come in maybe third or fourth every time. But if they were sent around again, he could do the same exact time, just about to the second. The faster guys would be struggling at his side as he pounded relentlessly onward. Then they would fall back. Second time around McGrath would come in first. Third time around, he would be the only guy to finish.

So he was jogging comfortably as he approached the southern edge of the ravine. He had worked about three hundred yards east to a point where the slopes were reasonable and not directly overlooked. He went straight down without pausing. Short, stiff strides against the incline. The footing was loose. He skidded on small avalanches of gravel and used the stunted trees to check his speed. He dodged around the litter of rocks in the bottom of the trench and started up the northern slope.

Going up was harder. He kicked his toes into the gravel for grip and hauled himself upward with handfuls of grass. He zigzagged between the small trees and bushes, looking for leverage. The extra fifty feet on the northern rim was a punishment. He tracked right to where a small landslide had created a straight path at a kinder angle. Slipped and slid upward through the crushed rock to the top.

He waited in the overhang, where the earth had fallen away

beneath the crust of roots. Listened hard. Heard nothing except silence. He lifted himself onto the rim. Stood there with his chest against the earth, head and shoulders exposed, looking north into enemy territory. He saw nothing. Just the gentle initial slopes, then the hills, then the giant mountains glowering in the far distance. Blue sky, a million trees, clean air, total silence. He thought: you're a long way from Chicago, Mack.

Ahead of him was a belt of scrub where the ancient rock was too close to the surface for much to grow. Then a ragged belt of trees, interrupted at first by rocky outcrops, then growing denser into the distance. He could see the curved gap in the treetops where the road must run. Three hundred yards to his left. He rolled up onto the grass and ran for the trees. Worked left toward the road and shadowed it north in the forest.

He jogged along, dodging trees like a slow-motion parody of a wide receiver heading for the end zone. The map was printed in his mind. He figured he had maybe three miles to go. Three miles at a slow jog, not much better than a fast walk, maybe forty-five, fifty minutes. The ground was rising gently under his feet. Every fourth or fifth stride, his feet hit the floor a fraction sooner than they should have as the gradient lifted him into the hills. He tripped a couple of times on roots. Once, he slammed into a pine trunk. But he pounded on, relentlessly.

After forty minutes, he stopped. He figured Brogan and Milosevic were having a similar journey, but they were dealing with extra distance because they had tracked west at the outset. So he expected a delay. With luck they would be about twenty minutes behind him. He walked deeper into the woods and sat down against a trunk. Lit a cigarette. He figured he was maybe a half-mile shy of the rendezvous. The map in his head said the road was about due to arrow up into the town.

He waited fifteen minutes. Two cigarettes. Then he stood up and walked on. He went cautiously. He was getting close. He made two diversions to his left and found the road. Just crept through the trees until he caught the gleam of sun on the gray cement. Then he dodged back and carried on north. He walked until he saw the forest thinning ahead. He saw sunlight on open spaces beyond the last trees. He stopped and stepped left and right to find a view. He saw the road running up to the town. He saw buildings. A gray ruin on a knoll on the left. The courthouse on the right. Better preserved. Gleaming white in the sunshine. He stared through the trees at it for a long moment. Then he turned back. Paced five hundred yards into the woods. Drifted over toward the road until he could just make out the gray gleam through the trees. Leaned on a trunk and waited for Brogan and Milosevic.

This time, he resisted the attraction of another cigarette. He had learned a long time ago that to smoke while in hiding was not a smart thing to do. The smell drifts, and a keen nose can detect it. So he leaned on the tree and stared down in frustration. Stared at his shoes. They were ruined from the scramble up the north face of the ravine. He had jabbed them hard into the rocky slope and they were scratched to pieces. He stared at the ruined toecaps and instantly knew he had been betrayed. Panic rose in his throat. His chest seized hard. It hit him like a prison door swinging gently shut. It swung soundlessly inward on greased hinges and clanged shut right in his face.

What had Borken said on the radio? He had said: like you're watching us with those damn planes. But what had the general's aide told him back in the Butte office? You look up and you see a tiny vapor trail and you think it's TWA. You don't think it's the air force checking if you've shined your shoes this morning. So how did Borken know there were surveillance planes in the sky? Because he had been told. But by who? Who the hell knew?

He glanced around wildly and the first thing he saw was a dog coming at him from dead ahead. Then another. They bounded through the trees at him. He heard a sound from behind him. The crunch of feet and the flick of branches. Then the same sound from his right. The snicking and slapping of a weapon from his left. The dogs were at his feet. He spun in a panic-stricken circle. All around him men were coming at him through the trees. Lean, bearded men, in camouflage gear, carrying rifles and machine guns. Grenades slung from their webbing. Maybe fifteen or twenty men. They stepped forward calmly and purposefully. They were in a complete ring, right around him. He turned one way, then the other. He was surrounded. They were raising their weapons. He had fifteen or twenty automatic weapons pointing straight at him like spokes in a wheel.

They stood silent, weapons ready. McGrath glanced from one to the next, in a complete wild circle. Then one of them stepped forward. Some kind of an officer. His hand went straight in under McGrath's jacket. Jerked the .38 out of his holster. Then the guy's hand went into McGrath's pocket. Closed over the speedloader and pulled it out. The guy slipped both items into his own pocket and smiled. Swung his fist and hit McGrath in the face. McGrath staggered and was prodded back forward with the muzzle of a rifle. Then he heard tires on the road. The grumble of a motor. He glanced left and caught a flash of olive green in the sun. A jeep. Two men in it. The soldiers pressed in and forced him out of the forest. They jostled him through the trees and onto the shoulder. He blinked in the sun. He could feel his nose was bleeding. The jeep rolled forward and stopped alongside him. The driver stared at him with curiosity. Another lean, bearded man in uniform. In the passenger seat was a huge man wearing black. Beau Borken. McGrath recognized him from his Bureau file photograph. He stared at him. Then Borken leaned over and grinned.

'Hello, Mr McGrath,' he said. 'You made good time.'

FORTY-ONE

REACHER WATCHED THE WHOLE THING HAPPEN. HE WAS A HUNDRED and fifty yards away in the trees. Northwest of the ambush, high up the slope on the other side of the road. There was a dead sentry at his feet. The guy was lying in the dirt with his head at right angles to his neck. Reacher had his field glasses raised to his eyes. Watching. Watching what, he wasn't exactly sure.

He had caught the gist of the radio conversation in the Bastion. He had heard Borken's side. He had guessed the replies. He had heard the southern lookouts calling in on the walkie-talkies. He knew about the Marines on the bridge. He knew about Webster and Johnson sitting there alongside them, on the end of the line.

He had wondered who else was down there. Maybe more military, maybe more FBI. The military wouldn't come. Johnson would have ordered them to sit tight. If anybody came, it would be the FBI. He figured they might have substantial numbers standing by. He figured they would be coming in, sooner or later. He needed to exploit them. Needed to use them as a diversion while he got Holly out. So he had moved southeast to wait for their arrival. Now, an hour later, he was gazing down at the short stocky guy getting loaded into the jeep. Dark suit, white shirt, town shoes. FBI, for sure.

But not the hostage rescue team. This guy had no equipment. The HRT came in all loaded down with paramilitary gear. Reacher was familiar with their procedures. He had read some of their manuals. Heard about some of their training. He knew guys who had been in and out of Quantico. He knew how the HRT worked. They were a high-technology operation. They looked like regular soldiers, in blue. They had vehicles. This guy he was watching was on foot in the forest. Dressed like he had just stepped out of a meeting.

It was a puzzle. Eight Marines. No hostage rescue team. An unarmed search-and-rescue Chinook. Then Reacher suddenly thought maybe he understood. Maybe this was a very clandestine operation. Low profile. Invisible. They had tracked Holly all the way west from Chicago, but for some reason they maybe weren't gathering any kind of a big force. They were dealing with it alone. Some tactical reason. Maybe a political reason. Maybe something to do with Holly and the White House. Maybe the policy was to deal with this secretly, deal with it hard, tackle it with a tight little team. So tight the right hand didn't know what the left was doing. Hence the unarmed search-and-rescue chopper. It had come in blind. Hadn't known what it was getting into.

In which case this ambushed guy he was watching was direct from Chicago. Part of the original operation that must have started up back on Monday. He looked like a senior guy. Maybe approaching fifty. Could be Brogan, Holly's section head. Could even be McGrath, the top boy. In either case that made Milosevic the mole. Question was, was he up here as well, or was he still back in Chicago?

The jeep turned slowly in the road. The Bureau guy in the suit was in back, jammed between two armed men. His nose was bleeding and Reacher could see a swelling starting on his face. Borken had twisted his bulk around and was talking at him. The rest of the ambush squad was forming up in the road. The jeep drove past them, north toward town. Passed by thirty yards from where Reacher was standing in the trees. He watched it go. Turned and picked up his rifle. Strolled through the woods, deep in thought.

His problem was priority order. He had a rule: stick to the job in hand. The job in hand was getting Holly away safe. Nothing else. But this Bureau guy was in trouble. He thought about Jackson. The last Bureau guy they'd gotten hold of. Maybe this new guy was heading for the same fate. In which case, he ought to intervene. And he liked the look of the guy. He looked tough. Small, but strong. A lot of energy. Some kind of charisma there. Maybe an ally would be a smart thing to have. Two heads, better than one. Two pairs of hands. Four trigger fingers. Useful. But his rule was: stick to the job in hand. It had worked for him many times over the years. It was a rule which had served him well. Should he bend that rule? Or not? He stopped and stood concealed in the forest while the ambush squad marched by on the road. Listened to the sound of their footsteps die away. Stood there and thought about the guy some more and forced himself toward a tough decision.

General Garber watched the whole thing happen, too. He was a hundred and fifty yards south of the ambush. West side of the road, behind a rocky outcrop, exactly three hundred yards south of where Reacher had been. He had waited three minutes and then followed McGrath in through the ravine. Garber was also a reasonably fit man, but a lot older and it had cost him a lot to keep pace with McGrath. He had arrived at the rocky outcrop and collapsed, out of breath. He figured he had maybe fifteen or twenty minutes to recover before the rendezvous took place. Then his plan was to follow behind the three agents and see what was going to happen. He didn't want anybody making mistakes about Jack Reacher.

But the rendezvous had never happened. He had watched the ambush and realized a lot of mistakes had been made about a lot of things.

'You're going to die,' Borken said.

McGrath was jammed between two soldiers on the back seat of the jeep. He was bouncing around because the road was rough. But he couldn't move his arms, because the seat was not really wide enough for three people. So he put the shrug into his injured face instead.

'We're all going to die,' he said. 'Sooner or later.'

'Sooner or later, right,' Borken said. 'But for you, it's going to be sooner not later.'

Borken was twisted around in the front seat, staring. McGrath looked past him at the vast blue sky. He looked at the small white clouds and thought: who was it? Who knew? Air force operational personnel, he guessed, but that link was ludicrous. Had to be somebody nearer and closer. Somebody more involved. The only possibilities were Johnson or his aide, or Webster himself, or Brogan, or Milosevic. Garber, conceivably. He seemed pretty hot on excusing this Reacher guy. Was this some military police conspiracy to overthrow the joint chiefs?

'Who was it, Borken?' he asked.

'Who was what, dead man?' Borken asked back.

'Who's been talking to you?' McGrath said.

Borken smiled and tapped his finger on his temple.

'Common cause,' he said. 'This sort of issue, there are a lot more people than you think on our side.'

McGrath glanced back to the sky and thought about Dexter, safe in the White House. What had Webster said he'd said? Twelve million people? Or was it sixty-six million?

'You're going to die,' Borken said again.

McGrath shifted his focus back.

'So tell me who it was, before I do,' he said.

Borken grinned at him.

'You'll find out,' he said. 'It's going to be a big surprise.'

The jeep pulled up in front of the courthouse. McGrath twisted and looked up at it. There were six soldiers standing guard outside the building. They were fanned into a rough arc, facing south and east.

'She in there?' he asked.

Borken nodded and smiled.

'Right now she is,' he said. 'I may have to get her out later.'

The walkie-talkie on his belt burst into life. A loud burst of static and a quick distorted message. He pressed the key and bent his head down. Acknowledged the information without unclipping the unit. Then he pulled the radio transmitter from his pocket. Flipped it open and pulled up the short antenna. Pressed the send button.

'Webster?' he said. 'You lied to me. Twice. First, there were three of your agents down there with you. We just rounded them all up.'

He listened to the response. Kept the radio tight against his ear. McGrath could not hear what Webster was saying.

'Doesn't matter anyway,' Borken said. 'They weren't all on your side. Some people in this world will do anything for money.'

He paused for a response. Apparently there was none.

'And you bullshitted me,' Borken said. 'You weren't going to fix the line at all, were you? You were just stringing me along.'

Webster was starting a reply, but Borken cut him off.

'You and Johnson,' he said. 'You can get off the bridge now. The Marines stay there. We're watching. You and Johnson walk back to your trucks. Get yourselves in front of those TVs. Should be some interesting action pretty soon.'

He clicked off the radio and folded it back into his pocket. A big wide smile on his face.

'You're going to die,' he said to McGrath for the third time.

'Which one?' McGrath asked. 'Brogan or Milosevic?'

Borken grinned again.

'Guess,' he said. 'Figure it out for yourself. You're supposed to be the big smart federal investigator. Agent-in-charge, right?'

The driver jumped down and pulled a pistol from his holster. Aimed it two-handed at McGrath's head. The left-hand guard squeezed out and unslung his rifle. Held it ready. The right-hand guy did the same. Then Borken eased his bulk down.

'Out,' he said. 'We walk from here.'

McGrath shrugged and eased himself down into the circle of weapons. Borken stepped behind him and caught his arms. Cuffed his wrists together behind his back. Then he shoved him forward. Pointed beyond the ruined county office.

'Up there, dead man,' he said.

They left the jeep behind them next to the courthouse. The two guards formed up. McGrath stumbled across the street and up onto the lumpy knoll. He was pushed past the dead tree. He was pushed left until he found the path. He followed it around behind the old building. The rough ground bit up through the thin soles of his ruined city shoes. He might as well have been walking barefoot.

'Faster, asshole,' Borken grunted at him.

The guards were behind him, prodding him forward with the muzzles of their rifles. He picked up the pace and stumbled on through the woods. He felt the blood clotting on his lip and nose. After a mile, he came out into the clearing he recognized from the surveillance pictures. It looked bigger. From seven miles overhead, it had looked like a neat hole in the trees, with a tidy circle of buildings. From ground level, it looked as big as a stadium. Rough shale on the floor of the clearing, big wooden huts propped expertly on solid concrete piles.

'Wait here,' Borken said.

He walked away and the two guards took up station either side of McGrath as he gazed around. He saw the communications hut, with the phone wire and the whip antenna. He saw the other buildings. Smelled stale institutional food coming out of the largest. Saw the farthest hut, standing on its own. Must be their armory, he thought.

He glanced up and saw the vapor trails in the sky. The urgency of the situation was written up there, white on blue. The planes had abandoned their innocent east–west trawling. Their trails had tightened into continuous circles, one just inside the other. They were flying around and around, centered seven miles above his head. He stared up at them and mouthed: help! He wondered if their lenses were good enough to pick that out. Wondered if maybe Webster or Johnson or Garber or Johnson's gofer could lipread. His best guess was: yes, and no.

Reacher's problem was a hell of an irony. For the first time in his life, he wished his opponents were better shots. He was concealed in the trees a hundred yards northwest of the courthouse. Looking down at six sentries. They were ranged in a loose arc, to the south and east beyond the big white building. Reacher's rifle was trained on the nearest man. But he wasn't shooting. Because if he did, the six men were going to shoot back. And they were going to miss.

Reacher was happy with an M-16 and a range of a hundred yards. He could pretty much absolutely guarantee to hit what he wanted with that weapon at that range. He would bet his life on it. Many times, he had. And normally, the worse shots his opponents were, the happier he'd be about it. But not in this situation.

He would be shooting from a northwest direction. His opponents would be shooting back from the southeast. They would hear his shots, maybe see some muzzle flash, they would take aim, and they would fire. And they would miss. They would shoot high and wide. The targets on the rifle range were mute evidence for that conclusion. There had been some competent shooting at three and four hundred yards. The damaged targets bore witness to that fact. But Reacher's experience was that guys who could shoot just about competently at three or four hundred yards on a range would be useless in a firefight. Lying still on a mat and sighting in on a target in your own time was one thing. Shooting into a noisy confused hailstorm of bullets was a very different thing. A different thing entirely. The guy defending the missile trucks had proved that. His salvos had been all over the place. And that was the problem. Shooting back from the southeast, these guys' stray rounds were going to be all over the place, too. Up and down, left and right. The down rounds and the left rounds were no problem. They were just going to damage the scrubby vegetation. But the up rounds and the right rounds were going to hit the courthouse.

The M-16 uses bullets designated M855. Common NATO rounds, 5.56 millimeters in caliber, just a fraction under a quarter-inch wide. Fairly heavy for their size, because they are a sandwich of lead and steel inside a copper jacket. Designed for penetration. Those stray rounds which hit the courthouse were going to impact the siding at two thousand miles an hour. They were going to punch through the old wood like it wasn't there at all. They were going to smash through the unstable dynamite like a train wreck. The energy of their impact was going to act like a better blasting cap than anything any mining company had ever possessed. That was what those bullets were designed to do. Some committee had asked for a bullet capable of shooting through the sides of ammunition trucks. And that's what had been delivered.

So Reacher wasn't shooting. Three sentries, he might have risked it. He figured he could get off three aimed shots in maybe three seconds. Too fast for any reaction. But six was too many. They were too spaced out. Too much physical movement was required between rounds. The later targets would have time to react. Not much time. Certainly not enough to be accurate. That was the problem.

Reversing the geometry would be no help, either. He could work himself right around to the south. It would take him maybe twenty minutes to skirt around in the trees and come back at them from the opposite direction. But then what? He would be looking at his targets, uphill. The courthouse would be right behind them. He could hit each of them in the head, no problem at all. But he couldn't ask the bullets just to stop there in midair. He couldn't prevent those high-energy copper-jackets bursting on out of the back of those skulls and heading on their uphill trajectories straight toward the courthouse's second-story walls. He shook his head and lowered his rifle.

McGrath saw Borken conferring with somebody on the edge of the clearing. It was the guy who had led the ambush squad. The guy who had taken his gun and his bullets and punched him in the face. The two of them were glancing at their watches and glancing up at the sky. They were nodding. Borken slapped the guy on the shoulder and turned away. Ducked into the trees and disappeared back toward the town. The ambush leader started in toward McGrath. He was smiling. He was unslinging his rifle.

'Show time,' he called.

He stepped near and reversed the rifle in his hands as he did so. Smashed the butt into McGrath's stomach. McGrath went down on the shale. One guard jammed the muzzle of his rifle into McGrath's throat. The other jammed his into McGrath's stomach, right where the blow had landed.

'Lie still, asshole,' the unit leader said. 'I'll be back in a minute.'

McGrath could not move his head because of the rifle in his throat, but he followed the guy with his eyes. He was going into the next-to-last hut in line. Not the armory, which stood on its own. Some kind of an equipment store. He came out with a mallet and ropes and four metal objects. Dull green, army issue. As he got nearer, McGrath recognized what they were. They were tent pegs. Maybe eighteen inches long, designed for some kind of big mess tent.

The guy dropped his load on the shale. The metal pegs clinked on the stones. The guy nodded to the soldier with the gun in McGrath's belly who straightened up and stepped away. The unit leader took his place. Used his own weapon to keep McGrath pinned down.

The soldier got busy. He seemed to know what he was supposed to do. He used the mallet to drive the first peg into the ground. The ground was stony and the guy had to work hard. He was swinging the mallet in a big arc and using a lot of force. He drove the peg down until it was two-thirds buried. Then he paced off maybe eight feet and started driving the second. McGrath followed him with his eyes. When the second peg was in, the guy paced another eight

716

feet at a right angle and hammered the third peg in. The fourth peg completed an exact square, eight feet on each side. McGrath had a pretty good idea what that square was for.

'We normally do this in the woods,' the unit leader said. 'We normally do it vertically, with trees.'

Then the guy pointed upward at the sky.

'But we need to let them see,' he said. 'They can't see properly in the woods. This time of year, too many leaves in the way, right?'

The guard who had driven the tent pegs into the ground was panting from the exertion. He changed places with his leader again. Jammed his rifle into McGrath's gut and leaned on it, recovering. McGrath gasped and squirmed under the pressure. The leader squatted down and sorted through the ropes. Untangled one and caught McGrath by the ankle. Looped the rope around and tied it off, hard. Used the rope to drag McGrath by the leg into the approximate center of the square. Then he tied the loose end to the fourth peg. Tied it tight and tested it.

The second length of rope went around McGrath's other ankle. It was tied off to the third peg. McGrath's legs were forced apart at a right angle. His hands were still cuffed behind his back, crushed against the rocky ground. The leader used the sole of his boot to roll McGrath's upper body sideways. Ducked down and unlocked the cuff. Caught a wrist and looped a rope around. Tied it tight and hauled the wrist up to the second peg. He pulled on it until McGrath's arm was stretched tight, in a perfect straight line with the opposite leg. Then he tied it tight to the peg and reached down for the other wrist. The soldiers jammed their muzzles in tighter. McGrath stared up at the vapor trails and gasped in pain as his arm was stretched tight and he was tied into a perfect cross.

The two soldiers jerked their rifles away and stepped back. They stood with their leader. Gazing down. McGrath lifted his head and looked wildly around. Pulled on the ropes, and then realized he was only pulling the knots tighter. The three men stepped farther back and glanced up at the sky. McGrath realized they were making sure the cameras got an uninterrupted view.

The cameras were getting an uninterrupted view. Seven miles in the sky, the pilots were flying circles, one on a tight radius of a few miles, the other outside him on a wider path. Their cameras were trained downward, under the relentless control of their computers. The inside plane was focusing tight on the clearing where McGrath was spreadeagled. The outer camera was zoomed wider, taking in the whole of the area from the courthouse in the south to the abandoned mines in the north. Their real-time video signals were bouncing down more or less vertically to the dish vehicle parked behind the mobile command post. The dish was focusing the datastream and feeding it through the thick armored cable into the observation truck. Then the decoding computers were feeding the large color monitors. Their phosphor screens were displaying the appalling truth. General Johnson and his aide and Webster were motionless in front of them. Motionless, silent, staring. Video recorders were whirring away, dispassionately recording every second's activity taking place six miles to the north. The whole vehicle was humming with faint electronic energy. But it was as silent as a tomb.

'Can you zoom in?' Webster asked quietly. 'On McGrath?'

The general's aide twisted a black rubber knob. Stared at the screen. He zoomed in until the individual pixels in the picture began to clump together and distort. Then he backed off a fraction.

'Close as we can get,' he said.

It was close enough. McGrath's spreadeagled figure just about filled the screens. The unit leader could be seen from directly above, stepping over the lengths of rope as he circled. He had a knife in his hand. A black handle, a shiny blade, maybe ten inches long. It looked like a big kitchen knife. The sort of thing a gourmet cook might buy. Useful for slicing a tough cut of steak into strips. The sort of tool that would get set out on the kitchen counter by somebody making a stew or a stroganoff.

They saw the guy lay the knife flat on McGrath's chest. Then he used both hands to fold back the flaps on McGrath's jacket. He loosened McGrath's tie and pulled it sideways, almost up under his ear. Then he grasped the shirt and tore it open. The cotton pulled apart under the knife, leaving the knife where it was, now next to the skin. The guy pulled the tails out of the waistband and tucked the shirt right back to the sides. Carefully, well out of the way, like he was a surgeon faced with a difficult emergency procedure.

They saw the guy pick up the knife again. He was squatted down to McGrath's right, leaning over slightly, holding the knife. He was holding it point-down, close to McGrath's belly. The electronic pink

718

of McGrath's skin was reflected in the faces of the watchers inside the observation vehicle.

They saw the guy raise the knife an inch. They saw his index finger slide along the back of the blade, like he was adjusting his grip for extra precision. They saw the blade move down. The pale sun glinted on the steel. Then their view was disrupted. A silent puff of pink mist obscured the picture. When it cleared, the knife was still in the guy's hand. But the guy had no head. His whole head was a shattered pink wound, and he was toppling slowly sideways.

FORTY-TWO

THE LEFT-HAND GUARD WENT DOWN EASILY ENOUGH, TOO. REACHER put a bullet through the side of his head, just above the ear, and he fell heavily, right on top of the spreadeagled Bureau guy. But the right-hand guard reacted. He spun away and hurdled the taut ropes, racing for the trees. Reacher paused a beat and dropped him ten feet away. The guy sprawled and slid noisily through the shale and put up a slick of dust. Twitched once and died.

Then Reacher waited. The last staccato echo of the three shots came back off the farthest mountains and faded into quiet. Reacher watched the trees, all around the Bastion. Watched for movement. The sunlight was bright. Too bright to be sure. There was a lot of contrast between the brightness of the clearing and the dark of the forest. So he waited.

Then he came out from behind the radio hut at a desperate run. He sprinted straight across the clearing to the mess in the middle. Hauled the bodies out of the way. The guard was sprawled right on top of the Bureau guy. The unit leader was across his legs. He dumped them out of the way and found the knife. Sawed through the four coarse ropes. Dragged the Bureau guy upright and pushed him off back the way he'd come. Then he grabbed the two nearest rifles and sprinted after him. Caught him up halfway. The guy was just tottering along. So Reacher caught him under the arms and bundled him to safety. Threw him well into the trees behind the huts and stood bent over, panting. Then he took the magazines off the new rifles and put one in his pocket and one on his own gun. They were both the elongated thirty-shot versions. He'd been down to six rounds. Now he had sixty. A ten-fold increase. And he had another pair of hands.

'Are you Brogan?' he asked. 'Or McGrath?'

The guy answered stiffly and neutrally. There was fear and panic and confusion in his face.

'McGrath,' he said. 'FBI.'

Reacher nodded. The guy was shaken up, but he was an ally. He took Fowler's Glock out of his pocket and held it out to him, butt first. McGrath was panting quietly and glancing wildly toward the deep cover of the trees. There was aggression in his stance. His hands were balled into fists.

'What?' Reacher asked him, concerned.

McGrath darted forward and snatched the Glock and stepped back. Raised it and went into a shooting stance and pointed it two-handed. At Reacher's head. The cut ends of the ropes trailed down from his wrists. Reacher just stared blankly at him.

'Hell are you doing?' he asked.

'You're one of them,' McGrath said back. 'Drop the rifle, OK?'

'What?' Reacher said again.

'Just do it, OK?' McGrath said.

Reacher stared at him, incredulous. Pointed through the trees at the sprawled bodies in the Bastion.

'What about that?' he asked. 'Doesn't that mean anything to you?'

The Glock did not waver. It was rock-steady, pointed straight at his head, at the apex of a perfect braced position. McGrath looked like a picture in a training manual, except for the ropes hanging like streamers from his wrists and ankles.

'Doesn't that count for something?' Reacher asked again, pointing.

'Not necessarily,' McGrath growled back. 'You killed Peter Bell, too. We know that. Just because you don't allow your troops to rape and torture your hostages doesn't necessarily put you on the side of the angels.'

Reacher looked at him for a long moment, astonished. Thought hard. Then he nodded cautiously and dropped the rifle exactly halfway between the two of them. Drop it right at his own feet, McGrath would just tell him to kick it over toward him. Drop it too near McGrath's feet, and it wouldn't work. This guy was an experienced agent. From the look of his shooting stance, Reacher was expecting at least a basic level of competence from him.

McGrath glanced down. Hesitated. He clearly didn't want Reacher near him. He didn't want him stepping nearer to nudge the rifle on toward him. So he slid his own foot forward to drag the weapon back close. He was maybe ten inches shorter than Reacher, all told. Aiming the Glock at Reacher's head from six feet away, he was aiming it upward at a fairly steep angle. As he slid his foot forward, he decreased his effective height by maybe an inch, which automatically increased the upward slope of his arms by a proportionate degree. And as he slid his foot forward, it brought him slightly closer to Reacher, which increased the upward angle yet more. By the time his toe was scrabbling for the weapon, his upper arms were near his face, interfering with his vision. Reacher waited for him to glance down again.

He glanced down. Reacher let his knees go and fell vertically. Lashed back upward with his forearm and batted the Glock away. Swiped a wide arc with his other arm behind McGrath's knees and dumped him flat on his back in the dirt. Closed his hand over McGrath's wrist and squeezed gently until the Glock shook free. He picked it up by the barrel and held it the wrong way around.

'Look at this,' he said.

He shook his cuff back and exposed the crusted weal on his left wrist.

'I'm not one of them,' he said. 'They had me handcuffed most of the time.'

Then he held the Glock out, butt first, offering it again. McGrath stared at it, and then stared back into the clearing. He ducked his head left and right to take in the bodies. Glanced back at Reacher, still confused.

'We had you down as a bad guy,' he said.

Reacher nodded.

'Evidently,' he said. 'But why?'

'Video in the dry cleaners,' McGrath said. 'Looked just like you were snatching her up.'

Reacher shook his head.

'Innocent passerby,' he said.

McGrath kept on looking hard at him. Quizzically, thinking. Reacher saw him arrive at a decision. He nodded in turn and accepted the Glock and laid it on the forest floor, exactly between them, like its positioning was a symbol, a treaty. He started fumbling at his shirt buttons. Cut ends of rope flailed at his wrists and ankles.

'OK, can we start over?' he said, embarrassed.

Reacher nodded and stuck out his hand.

'Sure,' he said. 'I'm Reacher, you're McGrath. Holly's agent-in-charge. Pleased to meet you.'

McGrath smiled ruefully and shook hands limply. Then he started fumbling at the knots on his wrist, one-handed.

'You know a guy called Garber?' McGrath asked.

Reacher nodded.

'Used to work for him,' he said.

'Garber told us you were clean,' McGrath said. 'We didn't believe him.'

'Naturally,' Reacher said. 'Garber always tells the truth. So nobody ever believes him.'

'So I apologize,' McGrath said. 'I'm sorry, OK? But just try and see it my way. You've been public enemy number one for five days.'

Reacher waved the apology away and stood up and helped McGrath to his feet. Bent back down to the dirt and picked up the Glock and handed it to him.

'Your nose OK?' he asked.

McGrath slipped the gun into his jacket pocket. Touched his nose gently and grimaced.

'Bastard hit me,' he said. 'I think it's broken. Just turned and hit me, like they couldn't wait.'

There was a noise in the woods, off to the left. Reacher caught McGrath's arm and pulled him deeper into the forest. Pushed through the brush and got facing east. He stood silently and listened for movement. McGrath was taking the ropes off his ankles and winding himself up to ask a question.

'So is Holly OK?' he said.

Reacher nodded. But grimly.

'So far,' he said. 'But it's going to be a hell of a problem getting her out.'

'I know about the dynamite,' McGrath said. 'That was the last thing Jackson called in. Monday night.'

'It's a problem,' Reacher said again. 'One stray round, and she's had it. And there are a hundred trigger-happy people up here. Whatever we do, we need to do it carefully. Have you got reinforcements coming in? Hostage rescue?'

McGrath shook his head.

'Not yet,' he said. 'Politics.'

'Maybe that's good,' Reacher said. 'They're talking about mass suicide if they look like getting beat. Live free or die, you know?'

'Whichever,' McGrath said. 'Their choice. I don't care what happens to them. I just care about Holly.'

They fell silent and crept together through the trees. Stopped deep in the woods, about level with the back of the mess hall. Now Reacher was winding himself up to ask a question. But he waited, frozen, a finger to his lips. There was noise to his left. A patrol, sweeping the fringe of the forest. McGrath made to move, but Reacher caught his arm and stopped him. Better to stand stock still than to risk making noise of their own. The patrol came nearer. Reacher raised his rifle and switched it to rapid fire. Smothered the sound of the click with his palm. McGrath held his breath. The patrol was visible, ten feet away through the trees. Six men, six rifles. They were glancing rhythmically as they walked, left and right, left and right, between the edge of the sunny clearing and the dark green depths of the woods. Reacher breathed out, silently. Amateurs, with poor training and bad tactics. The bright sun in their eyes on every second glance was ruining their chances of seeing into the gloom of the forest. They were blind. They passed by without stopping. Reacher followed the sound of their progress and turned back to McGrath.

'Where are Brogan and Milosevic?' he whispered.

McGrath nodded, morosely.

'I know,' he said, quietly. 'One of them is bent. I finally figured that out about half a second before they grabbed me up.'

'Where are they?' Reacher asked again.

'Up here somewhere,' McGrath said. 'We came in through the ravine together, a mile apart.'

'Which one is it?' Reacher asked.

McGrath shrugged.

'I don't know,' he said. 'Can't figure it out. I've been going over and over it. They both did good work. Milosevic found the dry cleaner. He brought the video in. Brogan did a lot of work tracing it all back here to Montana. He traced the truck. He liaised with Quantico. My gut says neither one is bent.'

'When was I ID'd?' Reacher asked.

'Thursday morning,' McGrath said. 'We had your complete history.'

Reacher nodded.

'He called it in right away,' he said. 'These people suddenly knew who I was, Thursday morning.'

McGrath shrugged again.

'They were both there at the time,' he said. 'We were all down at Peterson.'

'Did you get Holly's fax?' Reacher asked.

'What fax?' McGrath said. 'When?'

'This morning,' Reacher said. 'Early, maybe ten to five? She faxed you a warning.'

'We're intercepting their line,' McGrath said. 'In a truck, down the road here. But ten to five, I was in bed.'

'So who was minding the store?' Reacher asked.

McGrath nodded.

'Milosevic and Brogan,' he said, sourly. 'The two of them. Ten to five this morning, they'd just gone on duty. Whichever one of them it is must have gotten the fax and concealed it. But which one, I just don't know.'

Reacher nodded back.

'We could figure it out,' he said. 'Or we could just wait and see. One of them will be walking around best of friends and the other will be in handcuffs, or dead. We'll be able to tell the difference.'

McGrath nodded, sourly.

'I can't wait,' he said.

Then Reacher stiffened and pulled him ten yards farther into the woods. He had heard the patrol coming back through the trees.

Inside the courtroom, Borken had heard the three shots. He was sitting in the judge's chair and he heard them clearly. They went:

725

crack crack ... crack and repeated a dozen times as each of the distant slopes cannoned the echo back toward him. He sent a runner back to the Bastion. A mile there, a mile back on the winding path through the woods. Twenty minutes wasted, then the runner got back panting with the news. Three corpses, four cut ropes.

'Reacher,' Borken said. 'I should have wasted him at the beginning.'

Milosevic nodded in agreement.

'I want him kept away from me,' he said. 'I heard the autopsy report on your friend Peter Bell. I just want my money and safe passage out of here, OK?'

Borken nodded. Then he laughed. A sharp, nervous laugh that was part excitement, part tension. He stood up and walked out from behind the bench. Laughed and grinned and slapped Milosevic on the shoulder.

Holly Johnson knew no more than most people do about dynamite. She couldn't remember its exact chemical composition. She knew ammonium nitrate and nitrocellulose were in there somewhere. She wondered about nitroglycerin. Was that mixed in too? Or was that some other kind of explosive? Either way, she figured dynamite was some kind of a sticky fluid, soaked into a porous material and molded into sticks. Heavy sticks, quite dense. If her walls were packed with heavy dense sticks they would absorb a lot of sound. Like a soundproofing layer in a city apartment. Which meant the shots she'd heard had been reasonably close.

She'd heard: crack crack ... crack. But she didn't know who was shooting at who, or why. They weren't handgun shots. She knew the flat bark of a handgun from her time at Quantico. These were shots from a long gun. Not the heavy thump of the big Barratts from the rifle range. A lighter weapon than that. Somebody firing a medium-caliber rifle three times. Or three people firing once, in a ragged volley. But whichever it was, something was happening. And she had to be ready.

Garber heard the shots, too. Crack crack ... crack, maybe a thousand yards northwest of him, maybe twelve hundred. Then a dozen spaced echoes coming back from the mountainsides. He was in no doubt about what they represented. An M-16, firing singles, the first pair in a tight group of two which the military called a double tap. The sound of a competent shooter. The idea was to get the second round off before the first shell case hit the ground. Then a third target, or maybe an insurance shot into the second. An unmistakable rhythm. Like a signature. The audible signature of somebody with hundreds of hours of weapons training behind him. Garber nodded to himself and moved forward through the trees.

'It must be Brogan,' Reacher whispered.

McGrath looked surprised.

'Why Brogan?' he asked.

They were squatted down, backs to adjacent trunks, thirty yards into the woods, invisible. The search patrol had tracked back and missed them again. McGrath had given Reacher the whole story. He had rattled through the important parts of the investigation, one professional to another, in a sort of insider's shorthand. Reacher had asked sharp questions and McGrath had given short answers.

'Time and distance,' Reacher said. 'That was crucial. Think about it from their point of view. They put us in the truck and they raced off straight to Montana. What's that? Maybe seventeen hundred miles? Eighteen hundred?'

'Probably,' McGrath allowed.

'And Brogan's a smart guy,' Reacher said. 'And he knows you're a smart guy. He knows you're smart enough to know that he's smart enough. So he can't dead-end the whole thing. But what he can do is keep you all far enough behind the action to stop you being a problem. And that's what he did. He managed the flow of information. The communication had to be two-way, right? So Monday, he knew they'd rented a truck. But right through Wednesday, he was still focusing you on stolen trucks, right? He wasted a lot of time with that Arizona thing. Then he finally makes the big breakthrough with the rental firm and the stuff with the mud, and he looks like the big hero, but in reality what he's done is keep you way behind the chase. He's given them all the time they need to get us here.'

'But he still got us here, right?' McGrath said. 'A ways behind them, OK, but he brought us right here all the same.'

'No loss to him,' Reacher said. 'Borken was just itching to tell you where she was, soon as she was safely here, right? The destination was never going to be a secret, was it? That was the whole point.

She was a deterrent to stop you attacking. No point in that, without telling you exactly where she was.'

McGrath grunted. Thinking about it. Unconvinced.

'They bribed him,' Reacher said. 'You better believe it. They've got a big war chest, McGrath. Twenty million dollars, stolen bearer bonds.'

'The armored car robbery?' McGrath asked. 'Northern California somewhere? They did that?'

'They're boasting about it,' Reacher said.

McGrath ran it through his head. Went pale. Reacher saw it and nodded.

'Right,' he said. 'Let me make a guess: Brogan was never short of money, was he? Never groused about the salary, did he?'

'Shit,' McGrath said. 'Two alimony checks every month, girlfriend, silk jackets, and I never even thought twice about it. I was just so grateful he wasn't one of the moaners.'

'He's collecting his next payment right now,' Reacher said. 'And Milosevic is dead or locked up somewhere.'

McGrath nodded slowly.

'And Brogan worked out of California,' he said. 'Before he came to me. Shit, I never thought twice. A buck gets ten he was the exact agent who went after Borken. He said Sacramento couldn't make it stick. Said the files were unclear as to why not. Why not is because Borken was handing him bucketfuls of dollars to make sure it didn't stick. And the bastard was taking them.'

Reacher nodded. Said nothing.

'Shit,' McGrath said again. 'Shit, shit, shit. My fault.'

Still Reacher said nothing. More tactful just to keep quiet. He understood McGrath's feelings. Understood his position. He had been in the same position himself, time to time in the past. He had felt the knife slip in, right between the shoulder blades.

'I'll deal with Brogan later,' McGrath said finally. 'After we go get Holly. She mention me at all? She realize I'd come get her? She mention that?'

Reacher nodded.

'She told me she trusted her people,' he said.

FORTY-THREE

FOR THE FIRST TIME IN TWENTY YEARS GENERAL GARBER HAD killed a man. He hadn't meant to. He had meant to lay the man out and take his weapon. That was all. The man was part of an inner screen of sentries. They were posted at haphazard intervals in a line a hundred yards south of the courthouse. Garber had trawled back and forth in the woods and scoped them out. A ragged line of sentries, maybe forty or fifty yards between each one, two on the shoulders of the road and the rest in the forest.

Garber had selected the one nearest to a straight line between himself and the big white building. The man was going to have to move. Garber needed direct access. And he needed a weapon. So he had selected the man and worked nearer to him. He had scraped up a fist-sized rock from the damp forest floor. He had worked around behind him.

Their lack of training made the whole thing easy. A sentry screen should be mobile. They should be moving side-to-side along the length of the perimeter they are told to defend. That way, they cover every inch of the territory, and they find out if the next man in line has been ambushed and dumped on the floor. But these men were static. Just standing there. Watching and listening. Bad tactic.

The selected man was wearing a forage cap. It was camouflaged with the wrong camouflage. It was a black-and-gray interrupted pattern. Carefully designed to be very effective in an urban environment. Useless in a sun-dappled forest. Garber had come up behind the man and swung the rock. Hit him neatly on the back of the head.

Hit him too hard. Problem was, people are different. There's no set amount of impact that will do it. Not like playing pool. You want to roll the ball into the corner pocket, you know just about exactly how hard you need to cue. But skulls are different. Some are hard. This man's wasn't. It cracked like an eggshell and the spinal cord severed right up at the top and the man was dead before he hit the ground.

'Shit,' Garber breathed.

He wasn't worried about the ethics of the situation. Not worried about that at all. Forty years of dealing with hard men gone bad had defined a whole lot of points for him, ethically. He was worried about buzzards. Unconscious men don't attract them. Dead men do. Buzzards circling overhead spread information. They tell the other sentries: one of your number is dead.

So Garber changed his plan slightly. He took the dead man's M-16 and moved forward farther than he really wanted to. He moved up to within twenty yards of where the trees petered out. He worked left and right until he saw a rock outcrop, ten yards beyond the edge of the woods. That would be the site of his next cautious penetration. He slipped behind a tree and squatted down. Stripped the rifle and checked its condition. Reassembled it, and waited.

Harland Webster rolled back the videotape for the fourth time and watched the action again. The puff of pink mist, the guard going down, the second guard taking off, the camera's sudden jerked zoom out to cover the whole of the clearing, the second guard silently sprawling. Then a long pause. Then Reacher's crazy sprint. Reacher tossing bodies out of the way, slashing at the ropes, bundling McGrath to safety.

'We made a mistake about that guy,' Webster said.

General Johnson nodded.

'I wish Garber was still here,' he said. 'I owe him an apology.'

'Planes are low on fuel,' the aide said into the silence.

Johnson nodded again.

'Send one back,' he said. 'We don't need both of them up there anymore. Let them spell each other.'

The aide called Peterson and within half a minute three of the six screens in the vehicle went blank as the outer plane peeled off and headed south. The inner plane relaxed its radius and zoomed its camera out to cover the whole area. The close-up of the clearing fell away to the size of a quarter and the big white courthouse swam into view, bottom right-hand corner of the screens. Three identical views on three glowing screens, one for each of them. They hunched forward in their chairs and stared. The radio in Webster's pocket started crackling.

'Webster?' Borken's voice said. 'You there?'

'I'm here,' Webster replied.

'What's with the plane?' Borken said. 'You losing interest or something?'

For a second, Webster wondered how he knew. Then he remembered the vapor trails. They were like a diagram, up there in the sky.

'Who was it?' he asked. 'Brogan or Milosevic?'

'What's with the plane?' Borken asked again.

'Low fuel,' Webster said. 'It'll be back.'

There was a pause. Then Borken's voice came back.

'OK,' he said.

'So who was it?' Webster asked again. 'Brogan or Milosevic?'

But the radio just went dead on him. He clicked the button off and caught Johnson looking at him. Johnson's face was saying: the military man turned out good and the Bureau guy turned out bad. Webster shrugged. Tried to make it rueful. Tried to make it mean: we both made mistakes. But Johnson's face said: you should have known.

'Could be a problem, right?' the aide said. 'Brogan and Milosevic? Whichever one is the good guy, he still thinks Reacher's his enemy. And whichever one is the bad guy, he knows Reacher's his enemy.'

Webster looked away. Turned back to the bank of screens.

Borken put the radio back in the pocket of his black uniform. Drummed his fingers on the judge's desk. Looked at the people looking back at him.

'One camera is enough,' he said.

'Sure,' Milosevic said. 'One is as good as two.'

'We don't need interference right now,' Borken said. 'So we should nail Reacher before we do anything else.'

Milosevic glanced around, nervously.

'Don't look at me,' he said. 'I'm staying in here. I just want my money.'

Borken looked at him. Still thinking.

'You know how to catch a tiger?' he asked. 'Or a leopard or something? Out in the jungle?'

'What?' Milosevic asked.

'You tether a goat to a stake,' Borken said. 'And lie in wait.'

'What?' Milosevic asked again.

'Reacher was willing to rescue McGrath, right?' Borken said. 'So maybe he's willing to rescue your pal Brogan, too.'

General Garber heard the commotion and risked moving up a few yards. He made it to where the trees thinned out and he crouched. Shuffled sideways to his left to get a better view. The courthouse was dead ahead up the rise. The south wall was face-on to him, but he had a narrow angle down the front. He could see the main entrance. He could see the steps up to the door. He saw a gaggle of men come out. Six men. There were two flanking point men, alert, scanning around, rifles poised. The other four were carrying somebody, spreadeagled, face-down. The person had been seized by the wrists and the ankles. It was a man. Garber could tell by the voice. He was bucking and thrashing and screaming. It was Brogan.

Garber went cold. He knew what had happened to Jackson. McGrath had told him. He raised his rifle. Sighted in on the nearer point man. Tracked him smoothly as he moved right to left. Then his peripheral vision swept the other five. Then he thought about the sentry screen behind him. He grimaced and lowered the rifle. Impossible odds. He had a rule: stick to the job in hand. He'd preached it like a gospel for forty years. And the job in hand was to get Holly Johnson out alive. He crept backward into the forest and shrugged at the two men beside him.

The Chinook crew had clambered out of their wrecked craft and stumbled away into the forest. They had thought they were heading south, but in their disorientation they had moved due north. They had passed straight through the sentry screen without knowing anything about it and come upon a three-star general sitting at the base of a pine. The general had hauled them down and told them to hide. They thought they were in a dream, and they were hoping to wake up. They said nothing and listened as the screaming faded behind the ruined county offices.

Reacher and McGrath heard it minutes later. Faintly, at first, deep in the forest to their left. Then it built louder. They moved together level with a gap between huts where they could see across the Bastion to the mouth of the track. They were ten feet into the forest, far enough back to be well concealed, far enough forward to observe.

They saw the two point men burst out into the sunlight. Then four more men, walking in step, rifles slung, leaning outward, arms counterbalancing something heavy they were carrying. Something that was bucking and thrashing and screaming.

'Christ,' McGrath whispered. 'That's Brogan.'

Reacher stared for a long time. Silent. Then he nodded.

'I was wrong,' he said. 'Milosevic is the bad guy.'

McGrath clicked the Glock's trigger to release the safety device.

'Wait,' Reacher whispered.

He moved right and signaled McGrath to follow. They stayed deep in the trees and paralleled the six men and Brogan across the clearing. The men were moving slow across the shale, and Brogan's screaming was getting louder. They looped past the bodies and the tent pegs and the cut ropes and walked on.

'They're going to the punishment hut,' Reacher whispered.

They lost sight of them as the trees closed around the path to the next clearing. But they could still hear the screaming. Sounded like Brogan knew exactly what was going to happen to him. McGrath remembered recounting Borken's end of the conversation on the radio. Reacher remembered burying Jackson's mangled body.

They risked getting a little closer to the next clearing. Saw the six men head for the windowless hut and stop at the door. The point men turned and covered the area with their rifles. The guy gripping Brogan's right wrist fumbled the key out of his pocket with his spare hand. Brogan yelled for help. He yelled for mercy. The guy unlocked the door. Swung it open. Stopped in surprise on the threshold and shouted.

Joseph Ray came out. Still naked, his clothes balled in his arms. Dried blood all over the bottom of his face like a mask. He danced and stumbled over the shale in his bare feet. The six men watched him go.

'Who the hell's that?' McGrath whispered.

'Just some asshole,' Reacher whispered back.

Brogan was dropped onto the ground. Then he was hauled upright by the collar. He was staring wildly around and screaming. Reacher saw his face, white and terrified, mouth open. The six men threw him into the hut. They stepped in after him. The door slammed. McGrath and Reacher moved closer. They heard screams and the thump of a body hitting the walls. Those sounds went on for several minutes. Then it went quiet. The door opened. The six men filed out, smiling and dusting their hands. The last man darted back for a final kick. Reacher heard the blow land and Brogan scream. Then the guy locked the door and hustled after the others. They crunched over the stones and were gone. The clearing fell silent.

Holly limped across the raised floor to the door. Pressed her ear onto it and listened. All quiet. No sound. She limped back to her mattress and picked up the spare pair of fatigue trousers. Used her teeth to pick the seams. Tore the material apart until she had separated the front panel of one of the legs. It gave her a piece of canvas cloth maybe thirty inches long and six wide. She took it into the bathroom and ran the sink full of hot water. Soaked the strip of cloth in it. Then she took off her trousers. Squeezed the soaking canvas out and bound it as tight as she could around her knee. Tied it off and put her trousers back on. Her idea was the hot wet cloth might shrink slightly as it dried. It might tighten more. It was as near as she was going to get to solving her problem. Keeping the joint rigid was the only way to kill the pain.

Then she did what she'd been rehearsing. She pulled the rubber foot off the bottom of her crutch. Smashed the metal end into the tile in the shower. The tile shattered. She reversed the crutch and used the end of the curved elbow clip to prise the shards off the wall. She selected two. Each was a rough triangle, narrow at the base and pointed. She used the edge of the elbow clip to scrape away the clay at the leading point. Left the vitrified white surface layer intact, like the blade of a knife.

She put her weapons in two separate pockets. Pulled the shower curtain to conceal the damage. Put the rubber foot back on the crutch. Limped back to her mattress and sat down to wait.

The problem with using just one camera was that it had to be set to a fairly wide shot. That was the only way to cover the whole area. So any particular thing was small on the screen. The group of men carrying something had shown up like a large insect crawling across the glass.

'Was that Brogan?' Webster asked out loud.

The aide ran the video back and watched again.

'He's face down,' he said. 'Hard to tell.'

He froze the action and used the digital manipulator to enlarge the picture. Adjusted the joystick to put the spreadeagled man in the center of the screen. Zoomed right in until the image blurred.

'Hard to tell,' he said again. 'It's one of them, that's for sure.'

'I think it was Brogan,' Webster said.

Johnson looked hard. Used his finger and thumb against the screen to estimate the guy's height, head to toes.

'How tall is he?' he asked.

'How tall is he?' Reacher asked suddenly.

'What?' McGrath said.

Reacher was behind McGrath in the trees, staring out at the punishment hut. He was staring at the front wall. The wall was maybe twelve feet long, eight feet high. Right to left there was a two-foot panel, then the door, thirty inches wide, hinged on the right, handle on the left. Then a panel probably seven and a half feet wide running down to the end of the building.

'How tall is he?' Reacher asked again.

'Christ, does it matter?' McGrath said.

'I think it does,' Reacher said.

McGrath turned and stared at him.

'Five nine, maybe five ten,' he said. 'Not an especially big guy.'

The cladding was made up of horizontal eight-by-fours nailed over the frame. There was a seam halfway up. The floor was probably three-quarters board laid over two-by-fours. Therefore the floor started nearly five inches above the bottom of the outside cladding. About an inch and a half below the bottom of the doorway.

'Skinny, right?' Reacher said.

McGrath was still staring at him.

'Thirty-eight regular, best guess,' he said.

Reacher nodded. The walls would be two-by-fours clad inside and out with the plywood. Total thickness five and a half inches, maybe less if the inside cladding was thinner. Call it the inside face of the end wall was five inches in from the corner, and the floor was five inches up from the bottom.

'Right-handed or left-handed?' Reacher asked.

'Speak to me,' McGrath hissed.

'Which?' Reacher said.

'Right-handed,' McGrath said. 'I'm pretty sure.'

The two-by-fours would be on sixteen-inch centers. That was the standard dimension. But from the corner of the hut to the right-hand edge of the door, the distance was only two feet. Two feet less five inches, for the thickness of the end wall, was nineteen inches. There was probably a two-by-four set right in the middle of that span. Unless they skimped it, which was no problem. The wall would be stuffed with fiberglass wadding, for insulation.

'Stand back,' Reacher whispered.

'Why?' McGrath said.

'Just do it,' Reacher replied.

McGrath moved out of the way. Reacher put his eyes on a spot ten inches in from the end of the hut and just shy of five feet up from the bottom. Swayed left and rested his shoulder on a tree. Raised his M-16 and sighted it in.

'Hell are you doing?' McGrath hissed.

Reacher made no reply. Just waited for his heart to beat and fired. The rifle cracked and the bullet punched through the siding a hundred yards away. Ten inches from the corner, five feet from the ground.

'Hell are you doing?' McGrath hissed again.

Reacher just grabbed his arm and pulled him into the woods. Dragged him north and waited. Two things happened. The six men burst back into the clearing. And the door of the punishment hut opened. Brogan was framed in the doorway. His right arm was hanging limp. His right shoulder was shattered and pumping blood. In his right hand, he was holding his Bureau .38. The hammer was back. His finger was tight on the trigger.

Reacher snicked the M-16 to burst fire. Stitched five bursts of three shells into the ground, halfway across the clearing. The six men skidded away, like they were suddenly facing an invisible barrier or a drop off a tall cliff. They ran for the woods. Brogan stepped out of the hut. Stood in a bar of sunshine and tried to lift his revolver. His arm wouldn't work. It hung uselessly.

'Decoy,' Reacher said. 'They thought I'd go in after him. He was waiting behind the door with his gun. I knew he was the bad guy. But they had me fooled for a moment.'

McGrath nodded slowly. Stared at the government-issue .38 in Brogan's hand. Remembered his own being confiscated. He raised the Glock and wedged his wrist against a tree. Sighted down the barrel.

'Forget it,' Reacher said.

McGrath kept his eyes on Brogan and shook his head.

'I'm not going to forget it,' he said quietly. 'Bastard sold Holly out.'

'I meant forget the Glock,' Reacher said. 'That's a hundred yards. Glock won't get near. You'd be lucky to hit the damn hut from here.'

McGrath lowered the Glock and Reacher handed him the M-16. Watched with interest as McGrath sighted it in.

'Where?' Reacher asked.

'Chest,' McGrath said.

Reacher nodded.

'Chest is good,' he said.

McGrath steadied himself and fired. He was good, but not really good. The rifle was still set to burst fire, and it loosed three rounds. The first hit Brogan in the upper left of his forehead, and the other two stitched upward and blasted fragments off the door frame. Good, but not very. But good enough to do the job. Brogan went down like a marionette with the strings cut. He just telescoped into the ground, right in front of the doorway. Reacher took the M-16 back and sprayed the trees on the edge of the clearing until the magazine clicked empty. Reloaded and handed the Glock back to McGrath. Nodded him east through the forest. They turned together and walked straight into Joseph Ray. He was unarmed and half dressed. Blood dried on his face like brown paint. He was fumbling with his shirt buttons. They were done up into the wrong holes.

'Women and children are going to die,' he said.

'You all got an hour, Joe,' Reacher said back to him. 'Spread the word. Anybody wants to stay alive, better head for the hills.'

The guy just shook his head.

'No,' he said. 'We've got to assemble on the parade ground. Those are our instructions. We've got to wait for Beau there.'

'Beau won't be coming,' Reacher said.

Ray shook his head again.

'He will be,' he said. 'You won't beat Beau, whoever you are. Can't be done. We got to wait for him. He's going to tell us what to do.'

'Run for it, Joe,' Reacher said. 'For Christ's sake, get your kids out of here.'

'Beau says they have to stay here,' Ray said. 'Either to enjoy the fruits of victory, or to suffer the consequences of defeat.'

Reacher just stared at him. Ray's bright eyes shone out. His teeth flashed in a brief defiant smile. He ducked his head and ran away.

'Women and children are going to die?' McGrath repeated.

'Borken's propaganda,' Reacher said. 'He's got them all convinced compulsory suicide is the penalty for getting beat around here.'

'And they're standing still for it?' McGrath asked.

'He controls them,' Reacher said. 'Worse than you can imagine.'

'I'm not interested in beating them,' McGrath said. 'Right now, I just want to get Holly out.'

'Same thing,' Reacher said.

They walked on in silence, through the trees in the direction of the Bastion.

'How did you know?' McGrath asked. 'About Brogan?'

Reacher shrugged.

'I just felt it,' he said. 'His face, I guess. They like hitting people in the face. They did it to you. But Brogan was unmarked. I saw his face, no damage, no blood. I figured that was wrong. The excitement of an ambush, the tension, they'd have worked it off by roughing him up a little. Like they did with you. But he was theirs, so he just walked in, handshakes all around.'

McGrath nodded. Put his hand up and felt his nose.

'But what if you were wrong?' he said.

'Wouldn't have mattered,' Reacher said. 'If I was wrong, he wouldn't have been standing behind the door. He'd have been down on the floor with a bunch of broken ribs because all that thumping around would have been for real.'

McGrath nodded again.

'And all that shouting,' Reacher said. 'They paraded along, real slow, with the guy shouting his head off. They were trying to attract my attention.'

'They're good at that,' McGrath said. 'Webster's worried about it. He doesn't understand why Borken seems so set on getting attention, escalating this whole thing way bigger than he needs to.'

They were in the woods. Halfway between the small clearing and the Bastion. Reacher stopped. Like the breath had been knocked out of him. His hands went up to his mouth. He stood breathless, like all the air had been sucked off the planet.

'Christ, I know why,' he said. 'It's a decoy.'

'What?' McGrath asked.

'I'm getting a bad feeling,' Reacher said.

'About what?' McGrath asked him, urgently.

'Borken,' Reacher said. 'Something doesn't add up. His intentions. Strike the first blow. But where's Stevie? You know what? I think there are two first blows, McGrath. This stuff up here and something else, somewhere else. A surprise attack. Like Pearl Harbor, like his damn war books. That's why he's set on escalating everything. Holly, the suicide thing. He wants all the attention up here.'

FORTY-FOUR

HOLLY WAS STANDING UPRIGHT AND FACING HER DOOR WHEN THEY came for her. The tight wrap on her knee was drying stiff. So she had to stand, because her leg would no longer bend. And she wanted to stand, because that was the best way to do it.

She heard the footsteps in the lobby. Heard them clatter up the stairs. Two men, she estimated. She heard them halt outside her door. Heard the key slide in and the lock click back. She blinked once and took a breath. The door opened. Two men crowded in. Two rifles. She stood upright and faced them. One stepped forward.

'Outside, bitch,' he said.

She gripped her crutch. Leaned on it heavily and limped across the floor. Slowly. She wanted to be outside before anybody realized she could move better than they thought. Before anybody realized she was armed and dangerous.

'Strike the first blow,' Reacher said. 'I interpreted that all wrong.'

'Why?' McGrath asked urgently.

'Because I haven't seen Stevie,' Reacher said. 'Not since early this morning. Stevie's not here anymore. Stevie's gone somewhere else.'

'Reacher, you're not making any sense,' McGrath said.

Reacher shook his head like he was clearing it and snapped back into focus. Set off racing east through the trees. Talking quietly, but urgently.

'I was wrong,' he said. 'Borken said they were going to strike the first blow. Against the system. I thought he meant the declaration of independence. I thought that was the first blow. The declaration, and the battle to secure this territory. I thought that was it. On its own. But they're doing something else as well. Somewhere else. They're doing two things at once. Simultaneous.'

'What are you saying?' McGrath asked.

'Attention,' Reacher said. 'The declaration of independence is focusing attention up here in Montana, right?'

'Sure,' McGrath said. 'They planned to have CNN and the United Nations up here watching it happen. That's a lot of attention.'

'But they'd have been in the wrong place,' Reacher said. 'Borken had a bookcase full of theory telling him not to do what they expect. A whole shelf all about Pearl Harbor. And I overheard him talking in the mine. When he was fetching the missile launcher. Fowler was with him. Borken told Fowler by tonight this place will be way down the list of priorities. So they're doing something else someplace else as well. Something different, maybe something bigger. Twin blows against the system.'

'But what?' McGrath asked. 'And where? Near here?'

'No,' Reacher said. 'Probably far away. Like Pearl Harbor was. They're reaching out, trying to land a killer blow somewhere. Because there's a time factor here. It's all co-ordinated.'

McGrath stared at him.

'They planned it well,' Reacher said. 'Getting everybody's attention fixed up here. Independence. That stuff they were going to do with you. They were going to kill you slowly, with the cameras watching. Then the threats of mass suicide, women and children dying. A high-stakes siege. So nobody would be looking anywhere else. Borken's cleverer than I thought. Twin blows, each one covering for the other. Everybody's looking up here, then something big happens someplace else, everybody's looking down there, and he consolidates his new nation back up here.'

'But where is it happening, for God's sake?' McGrath asked. 'And what the hell is it?'

Reacher stopped and shook his head.

'I just don't know,' he said.

Then he froze. There was a crashing noise up ahead and a patrol of six men burst around a tight thicket of pines and stopped dead in front of them. They had M-16s in their hands, grenades on their belts, and surprise and delight on their faces.

Borken had deployed every man he had to the search for Reacher, except for the two he had retained to deal with Holly. He heard them start down the courthouse stairs. He pulled the radio from his pocket and flipped it open. Extended the stubby antenna and pressed the button.

'Webster?' he said. 'Get focused in, OK? We'll talk again in a minute.'

He didn't wait for any reply. Just snapped the radio off and turned his head as he tracked the sound of the footsteps on their way outside.

From seventy-five yards south, Garber saw them come out of the door and down the steps. He had moved out of the woods. He had moved forward and crouched behind the outcrop of rock. He figured that was safe enough, now he had back-up of a sort. The Chinook crewmen were thirty yards behind him, well separated, well hidden, instructed to yell if anybody approached from the rear. So Garber was resting easy, staring up the slope at the big white building.

He saw two armed men, bearded, starting down the steps. They were dragging a smaller figure with a crutch. A halo of dark hair, neat green fatigues. Holly Johnson. He had never seen her before. Only in the photographs the Bureau men had showed him. The photographs had not done her justice. Even from seventy-five yards, he could feel the glow of her character. Some kind of radiant energy. He felt it, and pulled his rifle closer.

The M-16 in Reacher's hands was a 1987 product manufactured by the Colt Firearms Company in Hartford, Connecticut. It was the A2 version. Its principal new feature was the replacement of automatic fire with burst fire. For the sake of economy, the trigger relocked after each burst of three shells. The idea was to waste less ammunition.

Six targets, three shells each from the fresh magazine, a total of eighteen shells and six trigger pulls. Each burst of three shells took a fifth of a second, so the firing sequence itself amounted to just one and a fifth seconds. It was pulling the trigger over and over again which wasted the time. It wasted so much time for Reacher that he ran into trouble after the fourth guy was down. He wasn't aiming. He was just tracking a casual left-to-right arc, close range into the bodies in front of him. The opposing rifles were coming up as a unit. The first four never got there. But the fifth and the sixth were already raised horizontal by the time the fourth went back down, two-and-a-quarter seconds into the sequence.

So Reacher gambled. It was the sort of instinctive gamble you take so fast that to call it a split-second decision is to understate the speed by an absurd factor. He skipped his M-16 straight to the sixth guy, totally sure that McGrath would take the fifth guy with the Glock. The sort of instinctive gamble you take based on absolutely nothing at all except a feeling, which is itself based on absolutely nothing at all except the look of the guy and how he compares with the look of other people worth trusting in the past.

The flat crack of the Glock was lost under the rattle of the M-16 but the fifth guy went down simultaneous with the sixth. Reacher and McGrath crashed sideways together into the brush and flattened into the ground. Stared through the sudden dead silence at the cordite smoke rising gently through the shafts of sunlight. No movement. No survivors. McGrath blew a big sigh and stuck out his hand, from flat on the ground. Reacher twisted around and shook it.

'You're pretty quick for an old guy,' he said.

'That's how I got to be an old guy,' McGrath said back.

They stood up slowly and ducked back farther into the trees. Then they could hear more people moving toward them in the forest. A stream of people was moving northwest out of the Bastion. McGrath raised the Glock again and Reacher snicked the M-16 back to singles. He had twelve shells left. Too few to waste, even with the A2's economy measure. Then they saw women through the trees. Women and children. Some men with them. Family groups. They were marching in columns of two. Reacher saw Joseph Ray, a woman at his side, two boys marching blankly in front of him. He saw the woman from the mess kitchen, marching side by side with a man. Three children walking stolidly in front of them.

'Where are they going?' McGrath whispered.

'The parade ground,' Reacher said. 'Borken ordered it, right?'

'Why don't they just run for it?' McGrath said.

Reacher shrugged and said nothing. He had no explanation. He stood concealed and watched the blank faces pass through the dappled woods. Then he touched McGrath's arm and they sprinted on through the trees and came out behind the mess hall. Reacher glanced cautiously around. Stretched up and grabbed at the roof overhang. Put a foot up on the windowledge and hauled himself up onto the shingles. Crawled up the slope of the roof and steadied himself against the bright metal chimney. Raised the stolen field glasses and trained them southeast, down toward the town, thinking: OK, but what the hell else is happening? And where?

General Johnson's aide had the most aptitude with the computer controls, either from familiarity with such things, or from being younger. He used the rubber knobs and the joystick to focus on the area in front of the courthouse steps. Then he zoomed out a touch to frame the view. He had the western face of the courthouse on the right of the screen and the eastern face of the ruined county office on the left. In between were the two lawns, one abandoned and scrubby, the other still reasonably flat. The road ran vertically up the center of the picture, like a map. The jeep which had brought McGrath in was still there where they had dumped it. The aide used it to check his focus. It came in crisp and clear. It was a military surplus vehicle. Smudged white stencils. They could see the windshield folded down, and a canvas mapcase, and a jerrycan for fuel and a short-handled shovel clipped on the rear.

They all saw the two men bring Holly out. From above, they were in a perfect straight diagonal line, with Holly alone in the middle, like the shape you see when a die rolls a three. They brought her out and waited. Then they saw a huge figure lumbering down the courthouse steps behind them. Borken. He stepped into the road and looked up. Right into the camera, invisible seven miles above him. He stared and waved. Raised his right hand high. There was a black gun in it. Then he looked down and fiddled with something in his left hand. Raised it to his ear. The radio on the desk in front of Webster crackled. Webster picked it up and flipped it open.

'Yes?' he said.

They saw Borken waving up at the camera again.

'See me?' he said.

'We see you,' Webster said quietly.

'See this?' Borken asked.

He raised the gun again. The general's aide zoomed in tight. Borken's huge bulk filled the screen. Upturned pink face, black pistol held high.

'We see it,' Webster said.

The aide zoomed back out. Borken resumed his proper perspective.

'Sig-Sauer P226,' Borken said. 'You familiar with that weapon?'

Webster paused. Glanced around.

'Yes,' he said.

'Nine-millimeter,' Borken said. 'Fifteen shots to a clip.'

'So?' Webster asked.

Borken laughed. A loud sound in Webster's ear.

'Time for some target practice,' Borken said. 'And guess what the target is?'

They saw the two men move toward Holly. Then they saw Holly's crutch come up. She held it level with both hands. She smashed it hard into the first man's gut. She whipped it back and swung it. Spun and hit the second man in the head. But it was light aluminum. No weight behind it. She dropped it and her hands went to her pockets. Came out with something in each palm. Things that glinted and caught the sun. She skipped forward and slashed desperately at the face in front of her. Danced and whirled and swung the glinting weapons.

The aide jerked the zoom control. The first man was down, clutching at his throat and face. Blood on his hands. Holly was spinning fast circles, slashing at the air like a panther in a cage turning on a stiff leg, the other foot dancing in and out as she darted left and right. Webster could hear distorted breathing and gasping through the earpiece. He could hear shouting and screaming. He stared at the screen and pleaded silently: go left, Holly, go for the jeep.

She went right. Swung her left hand high and held her right hand low, like a boxer. Darted for the second man. He raised his rifle, but crossways, in a sheer panic move to ward off the slashing blow. He punched the rifle up to meet her arm and her wrist cracked against the barrel. Her weapon flew off into the air. She kicked hard under the rifle and caught him in the groin. He wheeled away and collapsed. She darted for Borken. Her glittering hand swung a vicious arc. Webster heard a shriek in his ear. The camera showed Borken ducking away, Holly swarming after him.

But the first man was up again, behind her. Hesitating. Then he was swinging his rifle like a bat. He caught her with the stock flat on the back of her head. She went limp. Her leg stayed stiff. She collapsed over it like she was falling over a gate and sprawled on the road at Borken's feet.

Two down. One of them was Holly. Reacher adjusted the field glasses and stared at her. Two still standing. A grunt with a rifle, and Borken with a handgun and the radio. All in a tight knot, visible through the trees twelve hundred yards southeast and three hundred feet below. Reacher stared at Holly, inert on the ground. He wanted her. He loved her for her courage. Two armed men and Borken, and she'd gone for it. Hopeless but she'd gone for it. He lowered the field glasses and hitched his legs around the chimney. Like he was riding a metal horse. The chimney was warm. His upper body was flat on the slope of the roof. His head and shoulders were barely above the ridge. He raised the field glasses again, and held his breath, and waited.

They saw Borken's agitated gestures and then the injured man was getting up and moving in with the other who had hit her. They saw them pinning her arms behind her and dragging her to her feet. Her head was hanging down. One leg was bent, and the other was stiff. They propped her on it and paused. Borken signaled them to move. They dragged her away across the road. Then Borken's voice came back in Webster's ear, loud and breathy.

'OK, fun's over,' he said. 'Put her old man on.'

Webster handed the radio to Johnson. He stared at it. Raised it to his ear.

'Anything you want,' he said. 'Anything at all. Just don't hurt her.'

Borken laughed. A loud, relieved chuckle.

'That's the kind of attitude I like,' he said. 'Now watch this.'

The two men dragged Holly up the knoll in front of the ruined office building. Dragged her over to the stump of the dead tree. They turned her and walked her until her back thumped against the wood. They wrapped her arms around the stump behind her. Her head came up. She shook it, in a daze. One man held both wrists while the other fumbled with something. Handcuffs. He locked her wrists behind the tree. The two men stepped away, back toward Borken. Holly fell and slid down the stump. Then she pushed back and stood up. Shook her head again and gazed around.

'Target practice,' Borken said into the radio.

Johnson's aide fiddled with the zoom and made the picture bigger. Borken was walking away. He walked twenty yards south and turned, the Sig-Sauer pointing at the ground, the radio up at his face.

'Here goes,' he said.

He turned side-on and raised his arm. Held it out absolutely straight, shoulders turned like a duelist in an old movie. Squinted down the barrel and fired. The pistol kicked silently and there was a puff of dust in the ground, three feet from where Holly was standing still.

Borken laughed again.

'Bad shot,' he said. 'I need the practice. Might take me a while to get close. But I've got fourteen more shells, right?'

He fired again. A puff of dust from the earth. Three feet the other side of the stump.

'Thirteen left,' Borken said. 'I guess CNN is your best bet, right? Call them and tell them the whole story. Make it an official statement. Get Webster to back you up. Then patch them through on this radio. You won't give me my fax line, I'm going to have to communicate direct.'

'You're crazy,' Johnson said.

'You're the one who's crazy,' Borken said. 'I'm a force of history. I can't be stopped. I'm shooting at your daughter. The president's godchild. You don't understand, Johnson. The world is changing. I'm changing it. The world must be my witness.'

Johnson was silent. Stunned.

'OK,' Borken said. 'I'm going to hang up now. You make that call. Thirteen bullets left. I don't hear from CNN, the last one kills her.'

Johnson heard the line go dead and looked up at the screens

and saw Borken drop the radio on the ground. Saw him raise the Sig-Sauer two-handed. Saw him sight it in. Saw him put a round right between his daughter's feet.

Reacher rested against the warm chimney and lowered the glasses. Ran a desperate calculation through his head. A calculation involving time and distance. He was twelve hundred yards away to the northwest. He couldn't get there in time. And he couldn't get there silently. He lay chest down on the roof of the mess hall and called down to McGrath. His voice was already quiet and relaxed. Like he was ordering in a restaurant.

'McGrath?' he said. 'Go break into the armory. It's the hut on the end, apart from the others.'

'OK,' McGrath called. 'What do you want?'

'You know what a Barrett looks like?' Reacher called. 'Big black thing, scope, big muzzle brake on it. Find a full magazine. Probably be next to them.'

'OK,' McGrath said again.

'And hurry,' Reacher said.

Garber's view up from the south cleared when the two soldiers came back around and stood behind Beau Borken. They hung back, like they didn't want to put him off his aim. Borken was maybe sixty feet from Holly, shooting up the rise of the knoll. Garber was seventy yards away down the steep slope. Holly was just left of straight ahead. Borken was just to the right. His black bulk was perfectly outlined against the whiteness of the south wall of the courthouse. Garber saw that somebody had blanked the upper-story windows with new white wood. Borken's head was framed dead center against one of the new rectangles. Garber smiled. It would be like shooting for a small pink bullseye on a sheet of white paper. He snicked the M-16 to burst fire and checked it visually. Then he raised it to his shoulder.

McGrath stretched up on his toes and passed the Barrett up toward Reacher. Reacher stretched his hand down and pulled it up. Glanced at it and passed it back down.

'Not this one,' he said. 'Find one with the serial number ending in five-zero-two-four, OK?'

'Why?' McGrath called.

'Because I know for sure it shoots straight,' Reacher said. 'I used it before.'

'Christ,' McGrath said. He set off again at a dead run. Reacher lay back on the roof, trying to keep his heartbeat under control.

Borken's tenth shot was still wide, but not by much. Holly jumped as far as her cuffs would allow. Borken took to pacing back and forth in delight. He was pacing and laughing and stopping to shoot. Garber was tracking his huge bulk left and right against the whiteness of the building. Just waiting for him to stop moving. Because Garber had a rule: make the first shot count.

McGrath found the rifle Reacher had used before and passed it up to the roof. Reacher took it and checked the number. Nodded. McGrath ran like crazy for the mouth of the stony track. Disappeared down it at a sprint. Reacher watched him go. Thumbed the big bullets in the magazine and checked the spring. Pressed the magazine home gently with his palm. Raised the Barrett to his shoulder and balanced it carefully on the ridgeline. Pulled the stock in and ducked his eye to the scope. Used his left thumb to ease the focus out to twelve hundred yards. It racked the lens right out to the stop. He laid his left palm over the barrel. Operated the silky mechanism and put a round in the breech. Stared down at the scene below.

The telescope on the rifle bunched it all up, but the geometry was fine. Holly was up on the knoll, slightly to the right of dead ahead. Handcuffed to the dead tree. He stared at her face for a long moment. Then he nudged the scope. Borken was below her, maybe sixty feet farther on, firing up the rise at her, slightly to the left. He was walking short arcs, back and forth. But anywhere he chose to stop, there was a hundred miles of empty country behind his head. The courthouse walls were well away from Reacher's trajectory. Safe enough. Safe, but not easy. Twelve hundred yards was a hell of a distance. He breathed out and waited for Borken to stop pacing.

Then he froze. In the corner of his eye, he caught the gleam of sun on dull metal. Maybe seventy yards farther on down the slope. A rock. A man behind the rock. A rifle. A familiar head, grizzled hair on some of it. General Garber. Garber, with an M-16, behind a rock, moving the muzzle side to side as he tracked his target, who was walking short arcs seventy yards directly in front of him.

Reacher breathed out and smiled. He felt a warm flood of gratitude. Garber. He had back up. Garber, shooting from just seventy yards. In that split-second he knew Holly was safe. The warm flood of gratitude coursed through him.

Then it changed to an icy blast of panic. His brain kicked in. The compressed geometry below him exploded into a dreadful diagram. Like something on a page, like a textbook explanation of a disaster. From Garber's angle, the courthouse was directly behind Borken. When Borken stopped moving, Garber was going to fire at him. He might hit or he might miss. Either way, his bullet was going to hit the courthouse wall. Probably right up there in the southeastern corner, second floor. The ton of old dynamite would go up in a percussive fireball a quarter mile wide. It would vaporize Holly and shred Garber himself. The shockwave would probably knock Reacher right off the mess hall roof, twelve hundred yards away. How the hell could Garber not know?

Borken stopped pacing. Stood sideways on and steadied himself. Reacher blew out a lungful of air. He moved the Barrett. He put the crosshairs dead center on Holly Johnson's temple, right where the soft dark hair billowed down toward her eyes. He kept his lungs empty and waited for the next thump of his heart. Then he squeezed the trigger.

Garber watched Borken's arm come up. Waited until he had steadied. Squinted down the M-16's sighting grooves and put the pink and white head dead center. It sat there, big and obvious against the blur of sunny white wall behind it. He waited like he'd been taught to a lifetime ago. Waited until his breath was out and his heart was between beats. Then he pulled the trigger.

General Johnson had closed his eyes. His aide was staring at the screen. Webster was watching through a lattice of fingers, mouth open, like a child with a new babysitter watching a horror movie on television, way after his bedtime.

First thing out of the barrel of Reacher's Barrett was a blast of hot gas. The powder in the cartridge exploded in a fraction of a

750

millionth of a second and expanded to a superheated bubble. That bubble of gas hurled the bullet down the barrel and forced ahead of it and around it to explode out into the atmosphere. Most of it was smashed sideways by the muzzle brake in a perfectly balanced radial pattern, like a donut, so that the recoil moved the barrel straight back against Reacher's shoulder without deflecting it either sideways or up or down. Meanwhile, behind it, the bullet was starting to spin inside the barrel as the rifling grooves grabbed at it.

Then the gas ahead of the bullet was heating the oxygen in the air to the point where the air caught fire. There was a brief flash of flame and the bullet burst out through the exact center of it, spearing through the burned air at nineteen hundred miles an hour. A thousandth of a second later, it was a yard away, followed by a cone of gunpowder particles and a puff of soot. Another thousandth of a second later, it was six feet away, and its sound was bravely chasing after it, three times slower.

The bullet took five-hundredths of a second to cross the Bastion, by which time the sound of its shot had just passed Reacher's ears and cleared the ridge of the roof. The bullet had a hand-polished copper jacket, and it was flying straight and true, but by the time it passed soundlessly over McGrath's head it had slowed a little. The friction of the air had heated it and slowed it. And the air was moving it. It was moving it right-to-left as the gentle mountain breeze tugged imperceptibly at it. Half a second into its travel, the bullet had covered thirteen hundred feet and it had moved seven inches to the left.

And it had dropped seven inches. Gravity had pulled it in. The more gravity pulled, the more the bullet slowed. The more it slowed, the more gravity deflected it. It speared onward in a perfect graceful curve. A whole second after leaving the barrel, it was nine hundred yards into its journey. Way past McGrath's running figure, but still over the trees. Still three hundred yards short of its target. Another sixth of a second later, it was clear of the trees and alongside the ruined office building. Now it was a slow bullet. It had pulled four feet left, and five feet down. It passed well clear of Holly and was twenty feet beyond her before she heard the hiss in the air. The sound of its shot was still to come. It had just about caught up with McGrath, running through the trees.

Then there was a second bullet in the air. And a third, and a fourth. Garber fired a second-and-a-quarter later than Reacher. His rifle was set to auto. It fired a burst of three. Three shells in a fifth of a second. His bullets were smaller and lighter. Because they were lighter, they were faster. They came in at well over two thousand miles an hour. He was nearer the target. Because his bullets were faster and lighter and he was nearer, friction and gravity never really chipped in. His three bullets stayed pretty straight.

Reacher's bullet hit Borken in the head a full second-and-a-third after he fired it. It entered the front of his forehead and was out of the back of his skull three ten-thousandths of a second later. In and out without really slowing much more at all, because Borken's skull and brains were nothing to a two-ounce lead projectile with a needle point and a polished copper jacket. The bullet was well on over the endless forest beyond before the pressure wave built up in Borken's skull and exploded it.

The effect is mathematical and concerns kinetic energy. The way it had been explained to Reacher, long ago, it was all about equivalents. The bullet weighed only two ounces, but it was fast. Equivalent to something heavy, but slow. Two ounces moving at a thousand miles an hour was maybe similar to something weighing ten pounds moving at three miles an hour. Maybe something like a sledgehammer swinging hard in a man's hand. That was pretty much the effect. Reacher was watching it through the scope. Heart in his mouth. A full second-and-a-third is a long time to wait. He watched Borken's skull explode like it had been burst from the inside with a sledgehammer. It came apart like a diagram. Reacher saw curved shards of bone bursting outward and red mist blooming.

But what he couldn't see were Garber's three bullets, hurtling through the mess unimpeded, and flying straight on toward the courthouse wall.

FORTY-FIVE

THE CLASSIC MISTAKE IN FIRING AN AUTOMATIC WEAPON IS TO let the recoil from the first bullet jerk the barrel upward, so that the second bullet goes high, and the third higher still. But Garber did not make that mistake. He had enough hours on the range to be reliable from seventy yards. He had been through enough edgy situations to know how to stay cool and concentrated. He put all three bullets right through the exact center of the pink cloud that had been Borken's head.

They spent two ten-thousandths of a second traveling through it and flew on uninterrupted. They smashed through the new plywood sheeting in the windowframe. The leading bullet was distorted slightly by the impact and jerked left, tearing through the inner pine siding twenty-two inches later. It crossed Holly's room and re-entered the wall to the left of the doorway. Smashed right through and buried itself in the far wall of the corridor.

The second bullet came in through the first bullet's hole and therefore traversed the twenty-two-inch gap in a straight line. It came out through the inner siding and was thrown to the right. Crossed the room and smashed on through the bathroom partition and shattered the cheap, white ceramic toilet.

The third shell was rising just a fraction. It hit a nail in the outer wall and turned a right angle. Drilled itself sideways and down through eight of the new two-by-fours like a demented termite before its energy was expended. It ended up looking like a random blob of lead pressed into the back of the new pine boarding.

Reacher saw Garber's muzzle flash through his scope. Knew he must be firing triples. Knew he must have hit the courthouse wall. He stared down from twelve hundred yards away and gripped the ridge of the roof and shut his eyes. Waited for the explosion.

Garber knew his shots hadn't killed Borken. There hadn't been time. Even dealing with tiny fractions of a second, there's a rhythm. Fire . . . hit. Borken had been hit before his bullets could possibly have gotten there. So somebody else was up and shooting. There was a team in action. Garber smiled. Fired again. Pumped his trigger finger nine more times and stitched Borken's two soldiers all over the courthouse wall with his remaining twenty-seven shells.

Milosevic came out of the courthouse lobby and down the steps at a run. He had his Bureau .38 held high in his right hand and his gold shield in his left.

'FBI agent!' he screamed. 'Everybody freeze!'

He glanced to his right at Holly and then at Garber on his way up to meet him and at McGrath racing around from behind the office building. McGrath went straight for Holly. He hugged her tight against the dead tree. She was laughing. She couldn't hug back, because her arms were still cuffed behind the post. McGrath let her go and ran down the slope. Smacked a high five with Milosevic.

'Who's got the keys?' McGrath yelled.

Garber pointed over toward the two dead soldiers. McGrath ran to them and searched through the oozing pockets. Came out with a key and ran back up to the knoll. Ducked around to the back of the stump and unlocked Holly's wrists. She staggered away and McGrath darted forward and grabbed her arm. Milosevic found her crutch on the road and tossed it over. McGrath caught it and handed it to her. She got steady and came down the rise, arm in arm with McGrath. They made it to level ground and stood there together, gazing around in the sudden deafening quiet.

'Who do I thank?' Holly asked.

She was holding McGrath's arm, staring at the remains of Borken, lying sixty feet away. The corpse was flat on its back, high and wide. It had no head.

'This is General Garber,' McGrath said. 'Top boy in the military police.'

Garber shook his head.

'Wasn't me,' he said. 'Somebody beat me to it.'

'Wasn't me,' Milosevic said.

Then Garber nodded behind them.

'Probably this guy,' he said.

Reacher was on his way down the knoll. Out of breath. A frame six five high and two hundred twenty pounds in weight is good for a lot of things, but not for sprinting a mile.

'Reacher,' Holly said.

He ignored her. Ignored everybody. Just ran on south and turned to stare up at the white wall. He saw bullet holes. A lot of bullet holes. Probably thirty holes, most of them scattered over the second floor in the southeastern corner. He stared at them for a second and ran for the jeep parked at the curb. Snatched the shovel from its clips under the spare fuel can. Sprinted for the steps. Crashed through the door and up the stairs to Holly's room. Ran for the front wall.

He could see at least a dozen exit holes punched through the wood. Ragged splintered holes. He smashed the blade of the shovel into one of them. Split the pine board lengthways and used the shovel to wrench it off. Smashed the shovel behind the next and tore it away from the nails securing it. By the time McGrath was in the room, he had exposed four feet of studding. By the time Holly joined them, they were staring into an empty cavity.

'No dynamite,' she said, quietly.

Reacher ducked away to the adjacent wall. Tore enough boards off to be sure.

'There never was any,' Holly said. 'Shit, I can't believe it.'

'There was some,' McGrath said. 'Jackson called it in. Described the whole thing. I saw his report. He unloaded the truck with seven other guys. He carried it up here. He saw it going into the walls, for God's sake. A ton of dynamite. Kind of a hard thing to be confused about.'

'So they put it in,' Reacher said. 'And then they took it out. They

755

let people see it going in, then they took it out again secretly. They used it somewhere else.'

'Took it out again?' Holly repeated.

'Women and children have to die,' Reacher said, slowly.

'What?' Holly asked. 'What are you saying?'

'But not here,' he said. 'Not these women and children.'

'What?' Holly said again.

'Not mass suicide,' Reacher said. 'Mass murder.'

Then he just went blank. He was silent. But in his head he was hearing something. He was hearing the same terrible blast he had heard thirteen years before. The sound of Beirut. The sound of the Marine compound, out near the airport. He was hearing it all over again, and it was deafening him.

'Now we know what it is,' he muttered through the shattering roar.

'What is it?' McGrath asked.

'Low on its springs,' Reacher said. 'But we don't know where it's gone.'

'What?' Holly said again.

'Women and children have to die,' Reacher repeated. 'Borken said so. He said the historical circumstances justified it. But he didn't mean these women and these children up here.'

'What the hell are you talking about?' McGrath said.

Reacher glanced at him, and then at Holly, surprised, like he was seeing them both for the first time.

'I was in the motor pool,' he said. 'I saw the truck. Our truck? It was parked up, low on its springs, like it had a heavy weight inside.'

'What?' Holly said again.

'They've made themselves a truck bomb,' Reacher said. 'Stevie's delivering it somewhere, some public place. That's the other attack. They're going to explode it in a crowd. There's a whole ton of dynamite in it. And he's six hours ahead of us.'

McGrath was first down the stairs.

'Into the jeep,' he yelled.

Garber ran for the jeep. But Milosevic was much nearer. He vaulted in and fired it up. Then McGrath was helping Holly into the front seat. Reacher was on the sidewalk, staring south, lost in thought. Milosevic was drawing his revolver. He was thumbing the hammer back. Garber stopped. Raised his rifle and aimed. Milosevic leaned across in front of Holly. McGrath jumped away. Milosevic stamped on the gas and roared away one-handed with the muzzle jammed into Holly's side. One-handed over the rough road, the jeep was all over the place. No chance of hitting Milosevic. Garber could see that. He lowered his rifle and watched them go.

'Both of them?' Webster said to himself. 'Please, God, no.'

'We could use another chopper right now,' the aide said. 'I don't think we have to worry about the missiles anymore.'

He panned the camera north and west and zoomed in on the mountain bowl in front of the mine entrances. The four missile trucks were sitting inert. The sprawled body of the dead sentry was nearby.

'OK, call in a chopper,' Johnson said.

'Better coming direct from you, sir,' the aide said.

Johnson turned sideways to use the phone. Then he spun back to watch as the jeep drove into shot. It bounced up out of the last hairpin into the bowl and raced across the shale. Swerved around the dead trucks and slewed to a stop in front of the left-hand shed. Milosevic jumped out and danced around the hood. Revolver steady on Holly as he approached. He pulled her out by the arm and dragged her to the big wooden doors. Levered one open with his foot and pushed her inside. He followed her in and the huge door swung shut. Webster glanced away from the screen.

'Call the chopper, sir,' the aide said.

'Make it a fast one,' Webster added.

Quickest way to the mines was a shortcut through the Bastion. It was deserted and quiet. They ran through it and headed north across the rifle range toward the parade ground. Stopped short in the woods. The whole remaining militia population was standing silently in neat ranks, quiet fearful faces turned to the front, where Borken's upturned box still awaited his arrival.

Reacher ignored them and led the others around in the trees. Then in a straight line to the road. Straight north along it. Reacher was carrying the big Barrett. He had retrieved it from the mess hall roof, because he liked it. Garber was hurrying at his side. McGrath was pushing ahead as fast as he could, desperate to get to Holly.

They ducked back into the woods before the last hairpin and

Reacher scouted ahead. He holed up behind the rock he'd used before and covered every inch of the bowl with the Barrett's scope. Then he waved the other two up to join him.

'They're in the motor pool,' he said. 'Left-hand shed.'

He pointed with the fat barrel of the sniper rifle and the others saw the abandoned jeep and nodded. He ran over the shale and crouched behind the hood of the first missile truck. Garber sent McGrath next. Then he ran over. They crouched together behind the truck and stared at the log doors.

'What now?' Garber asked. 'Frontal assault?'

'He's got a gun to her head,' McGrath said. 'I don't want her hurt, Reacher. She's precious to me, OK?'

'Any other way in?' Garber asked.

Reacher stared at the doors and the roaring of the Beirut bomb receded and was replaced by the quiet whimpering of an earlier nightmare. He spent a minute trawling desperately for an alternative. He thought about the rifles and the missiles and the trucks. Then he gave it up.

'Keep him occupied,' he said. 'Talk to him, anything.'

He left the Barrett and took the Glock back from McGrath. Dodged to the next truck, and the next, all the way level with the entrance to the other cavern. The charnel house, full of bodies and skeletons and rats. He heard McGrath calling to Milosevic in a faint faraway voice and he ran to the big log doors. Ducked in through the gap and moved back into the dark.

He had no flashlight. He felt his way around the troop carrier and eased on into the mountain. He held his hand above his head and felt the roof come down. Felt for the bodies in the pile and skirted them. Crouched and headed left for the skeletons. The rats were hearing him and smelling him and squealing angry warnings all the way back to their nests. He dropped to his knees and then lay down and swam through the pile of damp bones. Felt the roof of the tunnel lower and the sides press in. Took a deep breath and felt the fear come back.

The fastest helicopter available on that day was a Marine Corps Night Hawk stationed at Malmstrom. It was a long, fat, humped machine, but it was quick. Within minutes of Johnson's call, it was spinning up and receiving orders to head west and north to a gravel turnout on the last road in Montana. Then it was in the air. The Marine pilot found the road and followed it north, fast and low, until he spotted a cluster of army command vehicles parked tight into a rock cutting. He swung back and put down on the turnout and waited. Saw three men racing south toward him. One was a civilian and two were army. One was a colonel and the other was the chairman of the joint chiefs of staff. The pilot shrugged at his crewman who pointed upward through the plexiglass canopy. There was a lone vapor trail maybe thirty-six thousand feet up. Some big jet was unwinding a tight spiral and streaking south. The pilot shrugged again and figured whatever was happening, it was happening to the south. So he made a provisional course calculation and was surprised when the brass clambered aboard and ordered him to head north into the mountains.

Reacher was laughing. He was hauling himself along through the tunnel and laughing out loud. Shaking and crying with laughter. He was no longer afraid. The tight clamp of the rock on his body was like a caress. He had done this once, and survived it. It was possible. He was going to get through.

The fear had disappeared as suddenly as it had come. He had pushed through the pile of bones in the dark and stretched out and felt the rock clamp down against his back. His chest had seized and his throat had gagged tight. He had felt the hot damp flush of panic and pressed himself into the ground. He had felt his strength drain away. Then he had focused. The job in hand. Holly. Milosevic's revolver pushed against the dark billow of her hair, her fabulous eyes dull with despair. He had seen her in his mind at the end of the tunnel. Holly. Then the tunnel seemed to straighten and become a warm smooth tube. An exact fit for his bulky shoulders. Like it was tailored for him, and him alone. A simple horizontal journey. He had learned a long time ago that some things were worth being afraid of. And some things were not. Things that he had done before and survived did not justify fear. To be afraid of a survivable thing was irrational. And whatever else he was, Reacher knew he was a rational man. In that split second the fear disappeared and he felt himself relax. He was a fighter. An avenger. And Holly was waiting for him. He thrust his arms forward like a swimmer diving for the water and swarmed through the mountain toward her.

759

He charged along with a tidy rhythm. Like marching out on the open road, but doing it lying down in the dark. Small deft movements of hands and feet. Head lowered. Laughing with relief. He felt the tunnel get smaller and hug him. He slid on through. He felt the blank wall ahead and folded himself neatly around the corner. Breathed easily and stopped laughing. Told himself it was time for quiet. He crawled on as fast as he could. Slowed up when he sensed the roof soaring away above him. Crept forward until the smell of the air told him he was nearly through.

Then he heard the helicopter. He heard the faint thumping of the rotors in the distance. He heard feet scuffling forty yards in front of him. The inarticulate sound of surprise and panic. He heard Milosevic's voice. High-pitched. West Coast accent.

'Keep that chopper away from here,' Milosevic screamed through the door.

The noise was getting nearer. Growing louder.

'Keep it away, you hear?' Milosevic screamed. 'I'll kill her, McGrath. That's a promise, you hear?'

It was totally dark. There were vehicles between Reacher and the cracks of light around the door. But not the white truck. That was gone. He rolled up into the space where it had been and pulled the Glock from his pocket. The thumping of the rotor blades was very close. It was battering the doors and filling the cavern.

'I'll trade her with you,' Milosevic screamed through the door. 'I get out of here unharmed, you get her back, OK? McGrath? You hear me?'

If there was a reply, Reacher didn't hear it.

'I'm not with these guys,' Milosevic screamed. 'This whole thing is nothing to do with me. Brogan got me into it. He made me do it.'

The noise was shattering. The heavy doors were shaking.

'I did it for the money, that's all,' Milosevic screamed. 'Brogan was giving me money. Hundreds of thousands of dollars, McGrath. You'd have done the exact same thing. Brogan was making me rich. He bought me a Ford Explorer. The Limited Edition. Thirty-five grand. How the hell else was I ever going to get one?'

Reacher listened to the screaming voice in the darkness. He didn't want to shoot him. For one crazy moment, he felt absurdly grateful to him, because he had banished his childhood nightmare. He had forced him to confront it and defeat it. He had made him a better man. He wanted to run up to him and shake him by the hand. He could picture himself doing it. But then the picture changed. He needed to run up to him and shake him by the throat and ask him if he knew where Stevie had taken the white truck. That was what he needed to do. That was why he didn't want to shoot him. He crept forward in the deafening noise and skirted around the vehicles.

He was operating in a one-dimensional world. He could see nothing because of the darkness. He could hear nothing, because of the helicopter. He sensed movement near the doors. Came out from behind a pickup and saw a shape framed against the cracks of light. A shape that should have been two shapes. Wide at the top, four legs. Milosevic with his arm around Holly's throat, his gun at her head. He waited for his vision to build. Their faces faded in from black to gray. Holly in front of Milosevic. Reacher raised the Glock. Circled left to get an angle. His shin caught a fender. He staggered and backed into a pile of paint cans. They crashed silently to the rock floor, inaudible in the crushing noise from outside. He sprinted closer to the light.

Milosevic sensed it and turned. Reacher saw his mouth open in a silent shout. Saw him twist and push Holly out in front of him like a shield. Saw him stall with indecision, his revolver up in the air. Reacher dodged right, then danced back left. He saw Milosevic track him both ways. Saw Holly use the sway to tear herself out of his grip. The rotor noise was shattering. He saw Milosevic glancing left and right. Saw him making his decision. Reacher was armed, Holly was not. Milosevic lunged forward. The .38 flashed silently in the noise. The brief white flame was blinding in the dark. Reacher lost his sense of where Holly was. He cursed and held his fire. He saw Milosevic aim again. Beyond him, he saw Holly's arm come up and stretch around his head from behind. He saw her hand touch his face with gentle precision. He saw him stumble. Then the door heaved open and Holly staggered away from the shattering flood of noise and sunlight and crashed straight into his arms.

The sunlight fell in a bright bar across Milosevic. He was lying on his back. His .38 was in his hand. The hammer was back. There was a shard of bathroom tile sticking out of his head where his left eye should have been. It was maybe three inches in and three inches out. A small worm of blood was running away from the point of entry.

Then the open door was crowded with people. Reacher saw McGrath and Garber standing in a blast of dust. A Night Hawk was landing behind them. Three men were spilling out and running over. A civilian and a colonel. And General Johnson. Holly twisted and saw them and buried her face back in Reacher's chest.

Garber was the first to them. He pulled them out into the light and the noise. They stumbled awkwardly, four-legged. The downdraft tore at them. McGrath stepped near and Holly pulled herself from Reacher's grip and threw herself at him and hugged him hard. Then General Johnson was moving in on her through the crowd.

'Holly,' he mouthed through the din.

She straightened in the light. Grinned at him. Hooked her hair back behind her ears. Pulled away from McGrath and hugged her father close.

'Still stuff for me to do, Dad,' she screamed over the engines. 'I'll tell you everything later, OK?'

FORTY-SIX

REACHER MADE A TWIRLING SIGNAL WITH HIS HAND TO TELL THE helicopter pilot to keep the engines spinning and ran through the noise and the eddying dust to take the Barrett back from Garber. He waved the others toward the machine. Hustled them up the ladder and followed them in through the sliding door. Laid the Barrett on the metal floor and dumped himself into a canvas chair. Pulled his headset on. Thumbed the button and called through to the pilot.

'Stand by, OK?' he said. 'I'll give you a course as soon as I've got one.'

The pilot nodded and ran the engines up out of idle. The rotor thumped faster and the noise built louder. The weight of the aircraft came up off the tires.

'Where the hell are we going?' Webster shouted.

'We're chasing Stevie, chief,' McGrath shouted back. 'He's driving the truck. The truck is full of dynamite. He's going to explode it somewhere. Remember what the Kendall sheriff said? Stevie always got sent out to do the dirty work? You want me to draw you a damn picture?'

'But he can't have gotten out of here,' Webster yelled. 'The bridge is blown. And there are no tracks through the forest. They closed them all.'

'Forest Service guy didn't say that,' McGrath yelled back. 'They closed some of them. He wasn't sure which ones, was all. What he said was maybe there's a way through, maybe there isn't.'

'They had two years to spy it out,' Reacher shouted. 'You said the pickup had spent time on Forest Service tracks, right? Crushed sandstone all over the underside? They had two whole years to find a way through the maze.'

Webster glanced to his left, east, over to where the forest lay beyond the giant mountain. He nodded urgently, eyes wide.

'OK, so we got to stop him,' he yelled. 'But where has he gone?'

'He's six hours ahead of us,' Reacher shouted. 'We can assume the forest was pretty slow. Call it two hours? Then four hours on the open road. Maybe two hundred miles? Diesel Econoline, hauling a ton, can't be averaging more than about fifty.'

'But which damn direction?' Webster yelled through the noise.

Holly glanced at Reacher. That was a question they had asked each other a number of times, in relation to that exact same truck. Reacher opened up the map in his head and trawled around it all over again, clockwise.

'Could have gone east,' he shouted. 'He'd still be in Montana, past Great Falls. Could be down in Idaho. Could be in Oregon. Could be halfway to Seattle.'

'No,' Garber yelled. 'Think about it the other way around. That's the key to this thing. Where has he been ordered to go? What would the target be?'

Reacher nodded slowly. Garber was making sense. The target.

'What does Borken want to attack?' Johnson yelled.

Borken had said: you study the system and you learn to hate it. Reacher thought hard and nodded again and thumbed his mike and called through to the pilot.

'OK, let's go,' he said. 'Straight on south of here should do it.'

The noise increased louder and the Night Hawk lifted heavily off the ground. It swung in the air and rose clear of the cliffs. Slipped south and banked around. Dropped its nose and accelerated hard. The noise moved up out of the cabin and settled to a deep roar inside the engines. The ground tilted and flashed past below. Reacher saw the mountain hairpins unwinding and the parade ground sliding past. The knot of tiny people was breaking up.

They were drifting away into the trees and being swallowed up under the green canopy. Then the narrow slash of the rifle range was under them, then the broad stony circle of the Bastion. Then the aircraft rose sharply as the ground fell away so that the big white courthouse slipped by underneath as small as a doll house. Then they were over the ravine, over the broken bridge, and away into the vast forested spaces to the south.

Reacher tapped the pilot on the shoulder and spoke through the intercom.

'What speed are we doing?' he asked.

'Hundred and sixty,' the pilot said.

'Course?' Reacher asked.

'Dead on south,' the pilot said.

Reacher nodded. Closed his eyes and started to calculate. It was like being back in grade school. He's two hundred miles ahead, doing fifty miles an hour. You're chasing him at a hundred and sixty. How long before you catch him? Grade-school math had been OK for Reacher. So had fighting in the yard. The fighting part had stayed with him better than the math. He was sure there must be some kind of a formula for it. Something with x and y all over the damn page. Something equaling something else. But if there was a formula, he had long ago forgotten it. So he had to do it by trial and error. Another hour, Stevie would be two hundred and fifty miles from home. The Night Hawk would have done one hundred and sixty. Way behind. An hour after that, Stevie would be three hundred miles out, and the Night Hawk would be three hundred and twenty. Overshot. Therefore they were going to catch him somewhere near the top of the second hour. If they were headed in the right direction.

Flathead Lake came into view, far ahead and far below. Reacher could see the roads snaking across the rugged terrain. He thumbed the button on his mike.

'Still south?' he asked.

'Dead on,' the pilot said.

'Still one-sixty?' Reacher asked.

'Dead on,' the pilot said again.

'OK, stick with it,' Reacher said. 'Hour and fifty minutes, maybe.'

'So where is he going?' Webster asked.

'San Francisco,' Reacher said.

'Why?' McGrath asked.

'Or Minneapolis,' Reacher said. 'But I'm gambling on San Francisco.'

'Why?' McGrath asked again.

'San Francisco or Minneapolis,' Reacher said. 'Think about it. Other possibilities would be Boston, New York, Philly, Cleveland, Richmond in Virginia, Atlanta, Chicago, St Louis and Kansas City in Missouri, or Dallas in Texas.'

McGrath just shrugged blankly. Webster looked puzzled. Johnson glanced at his aide. Garber was motionless. But Holly was smiling. She smiled and winked at Reacher. He winked back and the Night Hawk thumped on south over Missoula at a hundred and sixty miles an hour.

'Christ, it's the Fourth of July,' Webster said suddenly.

'Tell me about it,' Reacher said. 'Lots of people gathered in public places. Families, kids and all.'

Webster nodded grimly.

'OK, where exactly in San Francisco?' he asked.

'I'm not sure,' Reacher said.

'North end of Market,' Holly said. 'Right near Embarcadero Plaza. That's where, chief. I've been there on the Fourth. Big parade in the afternoon, fireworks over the water at night. Huge crowds all day long.'

'Huge crowds everywhere on the Fourth,' Webster said. 'You better be guessing right, people.'

McGrath looked up. A slow smile was spreading over his bruised face.

'We are guessing right,' he said. 'It's San Francisco for sure. Not Minneapolis or anyplace else.'

Reacher smiled back and winked. McGrath had gotten it.

'You want to tell me why?' Webster asked him.

McGrath was still smiling.

'Go figure,' he said. 'You're the damn director.'

'Because it's the nearest?' Webster asked.

McGrath nodded.

'In both senses,' he said, and smiled again.

'What both senses?' Webster asked. 'What are we talking about?'

Nobody answered him. The military men were quiet. Holly and McGrath were staring out through the windows at the ground, two thousand feet below. Reacher was craning up, looking ahead through the pilot's plexiglass canopy.

'Where are we?' he asked him.

The pilot pointed down at a concrete ribbon below.

'That's US 93,' he said. 'Just about to leave Montana and enter Idaho. Still heading due south.'

Reacher nodded.

'Great,' he said. 'Follow 93. It's the only road goes south, right? We'll catch him somewhere between here and Nevada.'

He started worrying near the top of the second hour. Started worrying badly. Started desperate revisions to his grade-school calculations. Maybe Stevie was driving faster than fifty. He was a fast driver. Faster than Bell had been. Maybe he was doing nearer sixty. Where did that put him? Three hundred and sixty miles out. In which case they wouldn't catch him until two hours fifteen minutes had elapsed. What if he was doing seventy? Could that Econoline sustain seventy, hour after hour, with a ton in back? Maybe. Probably. In which case he was four hundred and twenty miles out. A total of two hours forty minutes before they overhauled him. That was the envelope. Somewhere between one hour fifty minutes and two hours forty minutes, somewhere between Montana and Nevada. A whole fifty minutes of rising panic. More than a hundred miles of concrete ribbon to watch before he could know for sure he was wrong and they had to peel off hopelessly northeast toward Minnesota.

The helicopter was flying nose-down, top speed, straight along US 93. The seven passengers were craned forward, staring down at the road. They were over a town called Salmon. The pilot was calling out information like a tour guide. The giant peak of Mount McGuire, ten thousand feet, way off to the right. Twin Peaks, ten and a half thousand feet, up ahead to the right. Borah Peak, highest of all, twelve and a half thousand feet, way ahead to the left. The aircraft rose and fell a thousand feet above the terrain. Hurtled along lower than the surrounding peaks, nose-down to the highway like a bloodhound.

Time ticked away. Twenty minutes. Thirty. The road was pretty much empty. It connected Missoula in the north to Twin Falls in Idaho, three hundred miles to the south. Neither was a booming metropolis and this was a holiday. Everybody had already gotten where they were going. There was an occasional automobile and an occasional trucker working overtime. No white Econoline. There had been two white vehicles, but they were both pickups. There had been one panel truck, but it was dark green. That was all. Nothing else. No white truck. Sometimes the road was empty all the way to the horizon in front of them. The time was ticking away. Like a bomb. Forty minutes. Fifty.

'I'm going to call Minneapolis,' Webster said. 'We blew it.'

McGrath waited, hoping. He shook his head.

'Not yet,' he said. 'That's a desperation move. Mass panic. Can you imagine the crowds? The evacuation? People are going to get trampled.'

Webster peered out and down. Stared at the road for a full minute. Fifty-four minutes into the fifty-minute envelope.

'Get worse than trampled if that damn truck's already up there,' he said. 'You want to imagine that?'

Time ticked away. Fifty-eight minutes. An hour. The road stayed empty.

'There's still time,' Garber said. 'San Francisco or Minneapolis, either one, he's still got to be a long way short.'

He glanced at Reacher. Doubt and trust visible in his eyes, in approximately equal measures. More time ticked away. An hour and five minutes. The road still stayed empty, all the way to the distant horizon. The speeding helicopter reeled it in, only to reveal a new horizon, still empty.

'He could be anywhere,' Webster said. 'San Francisco's wrong, maybe Minneapolis is wrong, too. He could be in Seattle already. Or anywhere.'

'Not Seattle,' Reacher said.

He stared forward. Stared on and on. Fear and panic had him by the throat. He checked his watch again and again. An hour and ten minutes. Eleven. Twelve. Thirteen. Fourteen. An hour and fifteen minutes. He stared at the watch and the empty ribbon below. Then he sat back and went quiet. Chilled with terror. He had hung on as long as he could, but they had reached the point where the math went absurd. To be this far

768

south without passing him, Stevie would need to be driving at a hundred miles an hour. Or a hundred and twenty. Or a hundred and fifty. He glanced at the others and spoke in a voice which didn't sound like his own.

'I blew it,' he said. 'It must have been Minneapolis.'

Then the thump of the engines faded and for the second time that day the huge bass roar of the bomb came back. He kept his eyes wide open so he wouldn't have to see it, but he saw it anyway. Not Marines this time, not hard men camped out in the heat to do a job, but soft people, women and children, small and smaller, camped out in a city park to watch fireworks, vaporizing and bursting into a hazy pink dew like his friends had done thirteen years before. The bone fragments coming out of children and hissing away through the burning air and hitting other children a hundred yards farther on. Hitting them and tearing through their soft guts like shrapnel and putting the luckiest ones in the hospital for a whole agonizing year.

They were all staring at him. He realized tears were rolling down his cheeks and splashing onto his shirt.

'I'm sorry,' he said.

They looked away.

'I got calls to make,' Webster said. 'Why is it Minneapolis now? Why was it ever San Francisco?'

'Federal Reserve branches,' Reacher said quietly. 'There are twelve of them. The nearest two to Montana are San Francisco and Minneapolis. Borken hated the Fed. He thought it was the main instrument of the world government. He thought it was a big conspiracy to eliminate the middle classes. It was his special theory. He said it put him ahead in his understanding. And he believed the Fed ordered his father's bank to finagle the old guy into taking a loan so they could deliberately default him later.'

'So Borken's attacking the Fed?' Johnson asked urgently.

Reacher nodded.

'Twin blows,' he said. 'In the war against the world government. Attack the old system with a surprise move, like Pearl Harbor. At the same time as setting up a brand-new system for converts to flock to. One bird with two stones.'

He stopped talking. Too tired to continue. Too dispirited. Garber was staring at him. Real pain in his face. The beating of the engines was so loud it sounded like total silence.

'The Declaration of Independence was only half of it,' McGrath said. 'Double decoy. We were supposed to be focused up there, worried about Holly, worried about a suicide pact, going crazy, while they bombed the Fed behind our backs. I figured San Francisco because of Kendall, remember? I figured Borken would target the nearest branch to where his old man's farm was.'

Webster nodded.

'Hell of a plan,' he said. 'Holiday weekend, agents on leave, big strategic decisions to make, everybody looking in the wrong place. Then the whole world looking at the bombing while Borken secures his territory back up there.'

'Where is the Fed in Minneapolis?' Johnson asked urgently.

Webster shrugged vaguely.

'No idea,' he said. 'I've never been to Minneapolis. I imagine it's a big public building, probably in a nice spot, parks all around, maybe on the river or something. There's a river in Minneapolis, right?'

Holly nodded.

'It's called the Mississippi,' she said.

'No,' Reacher said.

'It damn well is,' Holly said. 'Everybody knows that.'

'No,' Reacher said again. 'It's not Minneapolis. It's San Francisco.'

'Mississippi goes nowhere near San Francisco,' Holly said.

Then she saw a giant smile spreading across Reacher's face. A final gleam of triumph in his tired eyes.

'What?' she said.

'San Francisco was right,' he said.

Webster grunted in irritation.

'We'd have passed him already,' he said. 'Miles back.'

Reacher thumbed his mike. Shouted up to the pilot.

'Turn back,' he said. 'A big wide loop.'

Then he smiled again. Smiled and closed his eyes.

'We did pass him,' he said. 'Miles back. Right over his damn head. They painted the truck green.'

The Night Hawk swung away into a high banked loop. The passengers swung their gaze from window to window as the landscape rotated below.

'There was paint in the motor pool,' Reacher said. 'I tripped over the cans. Probably camouflage basecoat. They slapped it on this morning. Damn stuff is probably still wet.'

They saw a Kenworth they had passed minutes ago. It was snuffling along a thousand feet below. Then a long stretch of empty pavement. Then a white pickup. More empty road. Then a dark-green panel truck, speeding south.

'Down, down,' Reacher was calling through.

'Is that it?' McGrath asked.

The gap between the panel truck and the pickup in front was lengthening. The truck was falling back. There was nothing behind it, all the way to the horizon. The Night Hawk was losing height. It was dropping toward the truck the way an eagle heads for a baby rabbit.

'Is that it?' McGrath asked again.

'That's it,' Reacher said.

'It sure is,' Holly whooped.

'You positive?' McGrath asked.

'Look at the roof,' Holly told him.

McGrath looked. The roof was streaked with dark-green paint, but he could see it was peppered with tiny holes. Like somebody had fired a shotgun right through it.

'We stared at those damn holes for two whole days,' Holly said. 'I'll remember them the rest of my life.'

'There are a hundred and thirteen of them,' Reacher said. 'I counted. It's a prime number.'

Holly laughed and leaned over. Smacked a joyous high five with him.

'That's our truck,' she said. 'No doubt about it.'

'Can you see the driver?' McGrath asked.

The pilot tilted down and rocked sideways for a close look.

'It's Stevie,' Holly shouted back. 'For sure. We've got him.'

'This thing got weapons?' Webster asked.

'Two big machine guns,' the pilot called through. 'But I'm not going to use them. That I can't do. Military can't get involved in law enforcement.'

'Can you fly this thing straight and level?' Reacher asked him. 'Fifty miles an hour? Maybe sixty? Without asking too many questions?'

The pilot laughed. It came through the headsets tinny and distorted.

'I can fly this thing any old way you want me to,' he said. 'With the general's permission, of course.'

Johnson nodded cautiously. Reacher leaned down and picked the Barrett up off the floor. Unfastened his harness and stood up into a crouch. Waved to Holly to change seats with him. She crawled across in front of McGrath and Reacher eased into her place. He could feel the Night Hawk slowing and dropping in the air. He put some length into Holly's harness and fastened it loosely around his waist. Stretched back for the door release. Tugged at the handle and the door slid back on its runners.

Then there was a gale of air coming in as the slipstream howled through the opening and the aircraft was turning half-sideways, sliding through the air like a car skids through snow. The green truck was below and behind, maybe two hundred feet down. The pilot was stabilizing his speed until he matched the truck's progress and tilting the aircraft so that Reacher's eyeline was pointing straight down at the road.

'How's this?' the pilot asked.

Reacher thumbed his mike button.

'Dead on,' he said. 'Anything up ahead?'

'One vehicle coming north,' the co-pilot said. 'When that's through, you got nothing at all for ten miles.'

'Anything behind?' Reacher asked. He saw the northbound vehicle streak by below.

McGrath stuck his head out into the gale. Ducked back in and nodded.

'Clear behind,' he said.

Reacher raised the Barrett to his shoulder. Put a round in the breech. Shooting at a moving vehicle from another moving vehicle is not a great recipe for accuracy, but he was looking at a distance of less than seventy yards and a target about twenty feet long and seven feet wide, so he wasn't worrying about it. He put the crosshairs on a point two-thirds of the way down the length of the roof. He figured the forward movement of the truck and the backward movement of the air might put the bullet dead center through the load compartment. He wondered vaguely whether the three-foot mattress was still in there.

'Wait,' Webster shouted. 'What if you're wrong? What if it's empty? You're only guessing, right? This whole thing is guesswork. We need proof, Reacher. We need some kind of corroboration here.'

Reacher didn't glance back. Kept his eye on the scope.

'Bullshit,' he said, quietly, concentrating. 'This is going to be all the corroboration we need.'

Webster grabbed his arm.

'You can't do this,' he said. 'You could be killing an innocent man.'

'Bullshit,' Reacher said again. 'If he's an innocent man, I won't be killing him, will I?'

He shook Webster's hand off his arm. Turned to face him.

'Think about it, Webster,' he said. 'Relax. Be logical. The proof comes after I shoot, right? If he's hauling a bomb, we'll know all about it. If he's hauling fresh air, nothing bad will happen to him. He'll just get another hole in his damn truck. Number one hundred and fourteen.'

He turned back to the door. Raised the rifle again. Acquired the target. Out of sheer habit, he waited for his breath to be out and his heart to be between beats. Then he pulled the trigger. It took a thousandth of a second for the sound of the shot to hit his ear, and seventy times as long as that for the big heavy bullet to hit the truck. Nothing happened for a second. Then the truck ceased to exist. It was suddenly a blinding fireball rolling down the highway like a hot white tumbleweed. A gigantic concussion ring blasted outward. The helicopter was hit by a violent shockwave and tossed sideways and five hundred feet higher in the air. The pilot caught it at the top and slewed back. Steadied it in the air and swung around. Dropped the nose. There was nothing to see on the highway except a roiling cloud of thin smoke slowing into a teardrop shape three hundred yards long. No debris, no metal, no hurtling wheels, no clattering wreckage. Nothing at all except microscopic invisible particles of vapor accelerating into the atmosphere way faster than the speed of sound.

The pilot stuck around at a hover for a long moment and then drifted east. Put his craft gently down on the scrub, a hundred yards from the shoulder. Shut the engines down. Reacher sat in the deafening silence and unclipped his belt. Laid the Barrett on the floor and vaulted out through the open door. Walked slowly toward the highway.

A ton of dynamite. A whole ton. A hell of a bang. There was nothing left at all. He guessed there were flattened grasses for a half-mile all around but that was it. The terrible energy of the explosion had blasted outward and met absolutely nothing at all in its path. Nothing soft, nothing vulnerable. It had blasted outward and then weakened and slowed and died to a puff of breeze miles away and it had hurt nothing. Nothing at all. He stood in the silence and closed his eyes.

Then he heard footsteps behind him. It was Holly. He heard her good leg alternating with her bad leg. A long stride, then a shuffle. He opened his eyes and looked at the road. She walked around in front of him and stopped. Laid her head on his chest and put her arms around him. Squeezed him tight and held on. He raised his hand to her head and smoothed her hair behind her ear, like he had seen her do.

'All done,' she said.

'Get a problem, solve a problem,' he said. 'That's my rule.'

She was quiet for a long time.

'I wish it was always that easy,' she said.

The way she said it, after the delay, it was like a long speech. Like a closely reasoned argument. He pretended not to know which problem she was talking about.

'Your father?' he said. 'You're way, way out of his shadow now.'

She shook her head against his chest.

'I don't know,' she said.

'Believe it,' he said. 'That thing you did for me on the parade ground was the smartest, coolest, bravest thing I ever saw anybody do, man or woman, young or old. Better than anything I ever did. Better than anything your old man ever did. He'd give his front-teeth for guts like that. So would I. You're way out of anybody's shadow now, Holly. Believe it.'

'I thought I was,' she said. 'I felt like it. I really did. For a while. But then when I saw him again, I felt just the same as I always did. I called him Dad.'

'He is your dad,' Reacher said.

774

'I know,' she replied. 'That's the problem.'

He was quiet for a long moment.

'So change your name,' he said. 'That might do it.'

He could feel her holding her breath.

'Is that a proposal?' she asked.

'It's a suggestion,' he said.

'You think Holly Reacher sounds good?' she asked.

His turn to stay quiet for a long time. His turn to catch his breath. And, finally, his turn to talk about the real problem.

'It sounds wonderful,' he said. 'But I guess Holly McGrath sounds better.'

She made no reply.

'He's the lucky guy, right?' he said.

She nodded. A small motion of her head against his chest.

'So tell him,' he said.

She shrugged in his arms.

'I can't,' she said. 'I'm nervous.'

'Don't be,' he said. 'He might have something similar to tell you.'

She looked up. He squinted down at her.

'You think so?' she asked.

'You're nervous, he's nervous,' Reacher said. 'Somebody should say something. I'm not about to do it for either of you.'

She squeezed him harder. Then she stretched up and kissed him. Hard and long on the mouth.

'Thank you,' she said.

'For what?' he asked.

'For understanding,' she said.

He shrugged. It wasn't the end of the world. Just felt like it.

'Coming?' she asked.

He shook his head.

'No,' he said.

She left him on the shoulder of US 93, right there in Idaho. He watched her all the way back to the Night Hawk. Watched her climb the short ladder. She paused and turned. Looked back at him. Then she ducked up and in. The door closed. The rotor thumped. He knew he would never see her again. His clothes tore at him and the dust swirled all around him as the helicopter took off. He waved it away. Watched it until it was lost to sight. Then he took a deep breath and looked left and right along the empty highway. Friday, the Fourth of July. Independence Day.

Saturday the fifth and Sunday the sixth, Yorke County was sealed off and secret army units were moving in and out around the clock. Air artillery squads recovered the missile unit. They took it south in four Chinooks. Quartermasters went in and recovered all the ordnance they could find. They collected enough for a small war.

Medical corpsmen removed the bodies. They found the twenty men from the missile unit in the cave. They found the skeletons Reacher had crawled through. They found five mutilated bodies in another cave. Dressed like workmen. Like builders or carpenters. They took Fowler out of the command hut and Borken from the road in front of the courthouse. They brought Milosevic down from the mountain bowl and Brogan out of the small clearing west of the Bastion. They found Jackson's rough grave in the forest and dug him up. They laid eighteen dead militiamen and one dead woman side by side on the rifle range and helicoptered them away.

One of Garber's military investigators flew in alone and took the hard disk out of the financial computer and put it on a chopper for transport to Chicago. Engineers moved in and dynamited the mine entrances. Sappers moved into the Bastion and disabled the water supply and tore down the power lines. They set fire to the huts and watched as they burned. Late Sunday night, when the last of the smoke was rising, they marched back to their choppers and lifted away south.

Early Monday morning, Harland Webster was back in the off-white parlor inside the White House. Ruth Rosen was smiling at him and asking how his holiday weekend had been. He was smiling back at her and saying nothing. An hour later, the morning sun was rolling west to Chicago and three agents were arresting Brogan's girlfriend. They grilled her for thirty minutes and advised her to get out of town, leaving behind anything he had ever bought her. Then the same agents took Milosevic's brand new Ford Explorer out of the Federal Building's parking lot and drove it five miles south. They left it on a quiet street, doors unlocked, keys in. By the time it had been stolen, Holly Johnson was arriving at the knee clinic for an early appointment. An hour after that, she was back at her desk. Before lunch, the missing money from the bearer-bond robbery was following a route of her own choosing out of the Caymans. Six o'clock Monday evening she was home and packing. She threw her bags into her car and drove north. Moved into McGrath's house up in Evanston.

Tuesday morning, there were three separate stories on the National Militia Internet. Refugees from an isolated valley in Montana had drifted south and west to new settlements with reports of a recent world government maneuver. Foreign troops had wiped out a band of militia heroes. The foreign battalion had been led by a French mercenary. He had succeeded only because he had used classified SDI technology, including satellites and lasers and microchips. Journalists picked up on the story and called the Hoover Building. Late Tuesday evening, in a prepared statement, an FBI spokesperson denied all knowledge of any such events.

Early Wednesday morning, after five hitched rides and four buses through seven states, Reacher was finally in Wisconsin. It was where he had aimed to be exactly a week before. He liked it there. It struck him as a fine place to be in July. He stayed until Friday afternoon.